For my mother and best friend, Bertha (Betty) Isachsen, whose humor remains undiminished.

ISABELLA

THE LEGEND OF THE
LITTLE GENERAL

RICKARD ISACHSEN

First published in Australia in 2014

by Rickard Isachsen

www.rickardisachsen.com

Copyright © Rickard Isachsen 2014

Print Book ISBN 978-0-9925666-0-9

Also available as an ebook:
Kindle ISBN 978-0-9925666-2-3 | Epub ISBN 978-0-9925666-1-6

National Library of Australia Cataloguing-in-Publication entry (pbk)

Creator: Isachsen, Rickard, author.

Title: Isabella / Rickard Isachsen.

ISBN: 9780992566609 (paperback)

Series: Isachsen, Rickard. Legend of the little general ; bk 1.

Subjects: Speculative fiction | Historical fiction.

Dewey Number: A823.4

Cover Illustration by: Alia_Design at www.99designs.com.au

ISABELLA

PROLOGUE

One midsummer morning the slender young girl sat quietly on her horse, bareback, high on the ridge overlooking her nation's heavily outnumbered army. They faced the most powerful force ever assembled: massive numbers supported by cavalry and a huge arsenal of the latest weapon of mass destruction.

The pungent smell from thousands of edgy horses drifted up the hills. Only the smell of raw fear from the men was more overwhelming. The soldiers on both sides of the conflict knew that thousands were about to die, and each man could only hope that he would not be among them.

The girl was all too aware that she was about to witness the deaths of every one of her nation's 20,000 soldiers, including her closest family and friends, when the hundreds of cannons designed to obliterate them opened fire. To make matters worse, she also knew that her past actions made her personally responsible for every death on the battlefield.

What she did not know was that fate was about to unleash a set of circumstances beyond her control that would hurl her into the narrow space separating the two front lines. Alone, and in a desperate fight for her life, she would end up facing the long line of cannons just as they opened fire.

The events that led up to this moment of terror had begun not so long before, one midwinter morning ...

PART I - ISABELLA

CHAPTER 1

A midwinter morning in Europe's Northern Region

14th Century

Emperor Aloise Kuiper reclined comfortably on an ornate lounge, its heavily carved wooden back, sides and legs encrusted with pure gold. Gold in its purest form featured prominently throughout the room, and throughout every other room in the City Palace. While Kuiper's station in life had provided him with the richness of foods that allowed his sixty-year-old figure to deteriorate, his intelligence and ruthlessness had not diminished in any way.

Kuiper's rise to power had come about more from that ruthlessness than from his effectiveness as a former senior general. Immediately after the death of King Harald VI in an ambush during the crusade against Spain, he had swiftly eliminated all military opposition, and disenfranchised the *entire* Royal lineage to seize control of both his nation and the Northern Region – the northern half of the European continent.

General Maurice Von Franckel stood before him at attention, in full military regalia. He was tall and handsome with intelligent blue eyes that now stared straight ahead at a point on the wall just above the head of the seated Kuiper. His mustache, in the short bristle style currently popular with army officers, revealed just a few strands of grey. The general wore a smartly tailored uniform, the insignia indicating that he was the nation's most senior army officer. He looked splendid indeed.

Von Franckel finally lowered his eyes and looked at the emperor with distaste as he remembered the fine figure of his former commanding officer in the heady days of the crusade. Now, Kuiper's beautifully embroidered silk shirt strained to its limit to cover his girth. A silk cloak was attached to his shoulders, one side of the magnificent garment hanging over the edge of the couch to almost touch the floor. The emperor appeared relaxed and very much in control.

'At ease, at ease, Maurice.' Kuiper waved a hand at the general, but not towards the gold-encrusted chairs that surrounded the exquisitely carved table. The general would not be permitted to sit.

The surface of the ornately inlaid, six-foot-long table was covered with a variety of foods. Kuiper surveyed the table with interest while he waited for his general to speak.

As General Von Franckel relaxed his posture, the rattle of his sword and various brass attachments to his uniform echoed around the vast, marble-floored room, adding to the crackle from the fireplace that eased the mid-winter chill. However, Von Franckel was far from relaxed; the secondary purpose of his visit would shock the emperor, and he was well aware that those who caused the emperor displeasure often left the palace in a canvas bag.

'Thank you, sir. As you know, I'm here to give you a report regarding the current public unrest. I've spent the past week speaking to my officers, both in the city as well as the provinces.'

'*Unrest*, General? Now there is a good word for rioting, setting fires to government property – and murder.' The emperor's intelligent dark eyes scanned the table as he spoke. Finally, he reached out and selected a pastry, glossy and golden like the furniture. 'So, what's happening, and what are you doing about it?'

'If anything, sir, it's getting worse. The consensus of my officers is that it won't take much for an incident to flare out of control and turn into a full-scale riot, or even a general uprising. The bitter cold is keeping most people off the streets, but when the weather heats up, so will the agitation. My men are handling each incident as best they can.'

'Tell your officers that a few pokes here and there with their swords might send them back to their wives and supper tables.' Kuiper pointed to his own throat as he spoke.

'We're now well into the fourteenth century, and in this modern day and age, we simply can't get away with what we have in the past. No disrespect, sir, but my officers must show restraint. If they don't, and instead resort to brute force, it could be they themselves who trigger a revolt. History has shown that such situations tend to feed upon themselves and rarely end well. I don't *recommend* a heavy hand, sir.' Von Franckel had rehearsed the conversation in his mind for several days, and now waited for the emperor to pick up the baited word that hung in the air.

'Uh huh.' Kuiper indicated the table with a sweep of his hand. 'General – Maurice, help yourself to something.'

'Thank you, sir, but I ate just before I arrived.' He hadn't, but his right hand automatically dropped to his own stomach; it was flat and hard, the wash-board muscles obvious against his palm despite his 44 years.

'So you don't *recommend* a heavy hand. As my most senior officer, Maurice, what exactly *do* you recommend?'

The bait had been taken. General Von Franckel felt cold sweat break out on his forehead. It was time to recommend his plan of action.

'The public is protesting about shortages of food and regular work, sir. Trade with our neighbors is almost non-existent; works to bring roads and water services to outlying districts have ceased; distribution of heating materials and other services has declined. To make matters worse, taxes have increased several times this year alone.' He paused and took a slow, deep breath.

'Maurice, you're telling me what I already *know*. We simply don't have the funds to do those things.' Kuiper stretched both hands towards Von Franckel, palms up, fingers wriggling back and forth. 'I'm waiting for your *recommendation.*'

'We need a diversion, sir.'

'A *diversion*. What kind of diversion?'

'A diversion that will unite the people rather than divide them, which is what is happening right now.'

'Go on.'

'We need a diversion that will create jobs, promote prosperity, and build national pride. We need a diversion that will bring wealth to the nation and also bring you personal riches. And, most importantly, one that will keep the public from objecting to the additional taxes.'

Kuiper's earlier expression of boredom quickly changed to one of interest. *Won't object to taxes. Personal riches?* He sat up and raised his eyebrows. 'And that diversion is?'

'A war, sir!'

The same morning in Europe's Southern Region

The azure ocean shimmered and sparkled in the mid-morning sunlight. It was pleasantly mild for a mid-winter day. A gentle offshore breeze caressed the small table set outside, as two plates of thinly sliced smoked meat, draped delicately over poached eggs, were placed in front of King Ramesses and his guest. A ceramic bowl contained a variety of breads and was placed precisely at the center of the table.

The king looked up at his servant and nodded his thanks. Alphonso bowed and moved well out of hearing range, but within the king's peripheral view, so that he could be summoned by a mere glance in his direction.

Shadecloth had been strung above the table to protect the two men from the glare of the morning sun. The table faced the ocean and was twenty paces from massive granite rocks that led down to the water. Behind it, a series of glass-paneled doors opened on to the slated terrace that ran the full width of the two-story Summer Palace. Well-tended pathways and garden beds, with masses of plants in full flower, completed a stunning vista. The Summer Palace was the king's preferred residence, even in winter.

'Please,' the king said, as he smiled at his visitor and pointed to the plates. To further indicate it was time to start their breakfast, he picked up his utensils and gently stabbed into one of the eggs on his plate. His guest did the same and they ate in silence.

In the distance, the remnants of morning mist rose like drifting smoke to slowly reveal the horizon. Rock formations could be clearly seen below the surface of the crystal-clear water in the bay. The sight was spectacular.

When he had finished the last of his breakfast, the king put down his cutlery and adjusted his tall, lean frame comfortably in the plain wooden chair. He stroked his neatly trimmed grey goatee and smiled at his guest. Both men were dressed informally for their meeting. 'It was good of you to come, Dmitri. An excellent breakfast, a magnificent view, and the company of a good friend. What more can a man wish for?'

Dmitri Talavares, the king's most trusted adviser and lifelong friend, smiled back as he responded, 'Thank you, your Majesty. It's always a pleasure to be here. We have much to discuss and' – he leaned forward, his smile broadening – 'I'm glad to report that it's all good news!'

The king wagged his finger sternly at Dmitri, but his smile clearly showed it was a friendly rebuke that was forthcoming. 'You know the rule, Dmitri.' He waved his hand around to indicate that they were alone except for Alphonso, who stood quietly at a distance. 'When we're alone, it's *Ramesses.*'

'Of course, Ramesses. The habit of holding our discussions in the company of others makes it easy to forget.'

Ramesses glanced towards Alphonso, and then towards the plates. The servant moved at once to the table, discreetly picked up the plates and hastened to the palace doors. Within a minute he was back in the exact spot where he had stood quietly for the last half-hour.

'I hear things are going well in the mines in the Eastern Province, Dmitri,' Ramesses said. He had been given the name *Ramesses* to honor some long-forgotten Egyptian family connection a thousand years earlier.

'Yes indeed, Ramesses. There has been a significant increase in the production of silver, less so from the gold mines in the north, but still an increase there as well. The most exciting news, however, is the production from the diamond mines.'

'I've always had reservations about the diamond mines. It seems like a lot of effort and cost for a modest return, even though you did inform me that a few large diamonds had been extracted.'

'Things have changed. There has been a modest increase in the small and average-size diamonds extracted but, best of all, is the new dig to the east. A substantial number of large gemstones have been recovered since our last meeting. These particular diamonds are rare and highly prized.'

'That's excellent news,'

'Only the mine operator and rotating teams of hand-picked workers are aware of the discoveries at the new dig. The workers fully understand that they will be well rewarded for their silence. They also know that loose tongues will be removed with malice. A few key members of parliament also know, of course.'

'*Members of Parliament*, Dmitri! You want loose tongues? Look no further than your politicians! How will you remove *their* loose tongues?'

Dmitri rolled his eyes and then smiled. 'Starting at the neck, perhaps? But seriously, Ramesses, it can't be helped; some of them have to know. There are also gemstone merchants and jewelers involved, of course. With such valuable merchandise to bring to market, it can't be kept completely secret, but it is kept low key.'

'How are they marketed?'

'The majority of the large gems are exported to the Chinese market. The emperors and warlords of the various regions throughout China – and there are scores, if not hundreds of them – seem to compete to be the wealthiest. And to make an impression, what is the thing they desire most? Diamonds! They also buy our gold, of course, but the large diamonds are now at the top of their shopping lists.'

'Why China? Is it only China? There must be other buyers, surely.'

'Yes, there are others, but mostly for the smaller stones. We do sell a few larger gemstones to other nations, but we deliberately let them think that they are not available in large numbers?'

The king raised his eyebrows in a silent *why?*

Dmitri leaned forward and lowered his voice despite there being no-one within hearing. 'You know our history better than anyone, Ramesses: we've regularly battled many of our neighbor nations over the centuries. We've been invaded and lorded over and then later we've kicked them out. For many years now we've been our own masters and we don't want any of our neighbors getting over-excited about what we've found. We don't want them to start thinking about how much they would like to have it – for nothing. So, softly, softly, keeping it quiet.'

The king turned slightly and studied the ocean for several moments. The mist had fully lifted and the sky was a brilliant blue. He turned back and smiled contently at his visitor.

Dmitri sat back in his chair and returned the smile. 'The prosperity that we've enjoyed in recent years has enabled the government to keep the districts throughout the provinces reasonably content. Every citizen has benefitted in some way from the increase in new infrastructure throughout the nation.'

Ramesses picked up his glass and raised it, obliging Dmitri to do the same. 'You're right. We've had a long period of peace and prosperity, and we must keep it that way.' The glasses clinked. 'This is a wonderful time in our history, Dmitri. Here's to prosperity, and a peace that will last forever!'

CHAPTER 2

Yolanda Valley

A distant clash of metal against metal floated across the valley, quickly becoming louder, sharper and more brutal. It came from the direction of a huge white-washed mud-brick house standing on a large flat-topped plateau on the far side of the valley.

The large and well-maintained home overlooked the valley and faced the general direction of the sea. Views were spectacular even though the ocean itself was not visible, but in summer it did capture the sea breeze.

The house backed onto almost one hundred acres of mostly grassed land, perfectly flat and divided by stone fences into several areas for different uses. A few cottages, barns, and stables were scattered among small groves of fruit and olive trees. One field, obviously designed for training and racing horses, could be seen in the distance; another field was designed for team sport and exercises. Closer to the house was a huge oval, also grassed except for a quartile that was covered with a mix of fine gravel and sand. It was a working arena.

Six muscular young men, bare-chested and sweating heavily, sat in various places on rows of sandstone built in a semi-circle on four levels, designed to resemble a miniature amphitheater. A timber roof covered the theatre to provide shelter from rain and the sun.

Two young men, also bare-chested and perspiring, slashed swords as a team and tried their best to strike a third, considerably older, man. The older man's upper body was covered with a double-layer of thick cowhide, his right arm bound with several layers of leather strips that extended from wrist to shoulder. Oddly, apart from a light sheen on his face, he did not appear to sweat, despite the thick covering. Up close, the sound of the swords was deafening.

A young girl circled the outer perimeter of the oval at a brisk jog. She looked to be about 11 or 12 years old, was pretty, and had short blond hair poking out from beneath a straw hat that protected her face from the morning sun. A long-sleeved blouse, worn outside shorts, billowed behind her as her legs pounded the grass at a steady pace.

The girl's pace was deceptive. Her thin legs did not appear to move particularly fast, but they were unusually long and she was actually moving at an astonishing speed, seemingly effortlessly. In a couple of minutes, she had twice circled the perimeter.

Ten minutes later the older man stepped back and raised his left hand, the open palm facing his two opponents. He then turned and bowed to one of the men, then to the other. The two men lowered their swords instantly and bowed formally in return, handing him their swords. The only other movement was the girls'. She had increased her pace substantially.

In fact, she had continued to run throughout the contest, not once having glanced towards the combatants. As her run approached the amphitheater she gradually slowed, emitting a short ear-splitting whistle at the older man. He stopped and turned towards her.

Suddenly she raised one arm up high, hand open. The older man grinned and, with a careful sweep of his arm, tossed her one of the swords. She caught it easily, walked to the center of the graveled arena, turned, and took up the challenge position. The older man joined her in the center, where he faced her and took up the mirror position. He nodded. *En garde!*

The girl's sword flashed so quickly the man had to jump back and block the strike at the same time. By the time he had blocked it, he had to again jump back because the girl had already struck at his other side. As he blocked, her upper body tilted almost horizontal to the ground, and her right leg struck him high on his left shoulder, knocking him off balance. She moved back, waited for him to regain balance, then stepped forward again; it was an aggressive move against a substantially larger opponent.

This time he was ready for her and thrust at her waist. But the girl was too quick, parried easily, and immediately attacked. Her blade flashed like lightning, first across his body, then backhand; then again and again, relentlessly. With each backhand she briefly gripped her right wrist with her left hand for added power. The man had no choice; he could not cope with such speed and was forced to constantly step back. As his sword was forced up past his shoulder from another blow, the girl's upper body again tilted over, while her leg flashed up in a blur of speed to give his wrist a solid kick. The sword flew high in the air, leaving the man defenseless.

Neither gave the fight another thought – they both dived away from the sword as it spun in the air, the girl shrieking with laughter while the man groaned from over-exertion. She helped him to his feet, picked up the fallen sword and wrapped her arms around him in a big hug.

'Defeated again,' he said with a rueful grin. 'By my extraordinary granddaughter.'

CHAPTER 3

'A war?' Kuiper repeated, incredulous.

'Yes, sir.'

'A war, a war, a war,' Kuiper murmured, wanting to get used to the word. 'I think I like the idea. So, Maurice, my friend, who do you propose should be on the receiving end of this war?'

'Sir, as you're prepared to take it a step further, I'll prepare a detailed report for your consideration at our next meeting. Let's say, three weeks?'

Kuiper nodded in agreement. 'Let's keep the matter between ourselves. Not even Margarethe will know anything about it.'

Although Emperor Aloise Kuiper had a number of mistresses ensconced in the south wing of the palace, he loved only his wife, Empress Margarethe. Now he headed towards the north wing, where he knew she would be enjoying a hot bath.

It was three weeks later when Aloise leaned over the long table in the Library Room and examined the huge map. Each end had been weighted down with a heavy leather-bound volume of never-read literature. Bookshelves covering three walls were filled with books in pristine condition.

Aloise glanced up at the general. 'Show me the target.'

'Here, sir,' the general answered. He stabbed his finger several times at a point on the map. 'This is the place of interest.'

Kuiper nodded, but remained silent.

Von Franckel shivered as he secured another button on his heavy coat. It was still winter and the library had no fireplace to ease the chill. He took a deep breath. *All right, Maurice, it's time to secure your place in history.*

He leaned forward and quickly traced the thick line that separated the target nation from its neighbors. 'Here are their main areas of mineral resources. Coal, tin, and, surprisingly, fine sand from which they produce exquisite glass products. Here are their gold and silver mines. Of particular interest, however, is their new diamond mine located over here, where they have extracted extraordinary gemstones.' He deliberately let the words hang in the air while he took his time to secure another button on his coat.

'Diamonds?' The emperor leaned forward with renewed interest.

'Yes, sir.' The general relaxed – the emperor had again grabbed the baited hook. 'It's common knowledge that they have been mining average-size diamonds for years, and that they export to the Russians and the Chinese in particular.'

Aloise moved a chair closer so that he could sit. His weight caused intense pain in his feet from standing on the cold stone-slab floor. The heavy coat he was wearing for protection against the chill added to the weight.

'What is not common knowledge,' Von Franckel continued, 'is what's happening at their new diamond mine, which is producing substantial quantities of large, high quality gemstones, each worth a fortune. They are keeping this mine a closely guarded secret for fear of unnecessarily piquing the interest of their southern neighbors.'

'If it's such a closely guarded secret, then how do we know about it?'

'We recently sold large quantities of arms to four warlords in China. Two of them were short of cash and gold to pay for their weapons, but they did have substantial valuables appropriated after battles with other warlords. Those valuables included several large diamonds. In fact, they were the most magnificent diamonds that our arms-negotiators had ever seen. When negotiators asked where the diamonds originally came from, the warlords knew and told them. Those lords would sell their mothers for a trinket and could not care less about anyone else's secrets.'

'So, in summary?'

'Alone, the gold and silver reserves would be more than enough to replace the cost of a campaign. Ongoing profits from their silver, gold and established diamond mines would underpin our future domestic funding requirements for a hundred years.'

He paused for a moment before he moved in for the kill.

'The new diamond mine will, of course, be vested directly in you and your family,' he said casually. 'You will then personally pick and choose from the entire production as to which diamonds you will sell and which you will retain for yourself.' Von Franckel deliberately kept his carefully rehearsed words in the present tense, designed to make Kuiper feel that he would be giving up something already his, and of great personal value, should he decide against waging war.

Kuiper nodded, deep in thought. He suspected Margarethe would be as interested in diamonds as he was. 'All right, Maurice,' he said, 'let's do it! You will be in charge, of course. I know I can rely on you for a successful outcome.'

Despite his rehearsals and optimistic expectations, Von Franckel felt a surge of excitement spread throughout his body.

'Do we just issue them with a threatening communication, or do we actually need to conduct a *real* war?'

'Not a communication, sir. It's going to take more than that.' Von Franckel decided to immediately shift to the present tense; hostilities were to be taken as an actual fact. 'We will move with stealth and in complete secret. With a few exceptions, even our own forces won't know who we are going to strike until we are in place. That's when we send them a *letter* – actually a declaration of war. We will then be in position to strike at once if they don't submit immediately.'

'Casualties?' Aloise asked.

'Casualties? Whose casualties, sir? Theirs or ours?'

'Ours, of course, Maurice, ours. I couldn't care less about theirs!' He felt invigorated, his ruthlessness rekindled after a long absence.

'I would be surprised if we suffer *any* casualties at all, sir. At worst, I can guarantee our casualties will be minimal. Our citizens will expect a few casualties, but these will certainly be well within acceptable limits.'

Kuiper looked up at Von Franckel. 'Excellent! So, you'll send our navy? I imagine that would be the quickest way.'

'That would not be the correct course of action, sir.' He had decided to be blunt and frame his response as a correction, knowing that Kuiper would not wish to be corrected a second time. 'They have a formidable navy, not as big as ours, but they do have strong local advantage. Could we do it? Probably. I have given the matter much thought and *probably* is simply not good enough.'

Von Franckel pressed home that he and he alone would be the strategist for the campaign. 'Our casualties would be horrendous. Our remaining forces – even if our initial attack were successful – would be insufficient to take and maintain occupation. It would be unacceptable to the public. Without question, our government would fall; it would be the end of everything as we know it.'

Kuiper fell silent, furious that he had been corrected and put in his place, but he had sufficient presence of mind to know that Von Franckel was correct.

He forced a smile. 'Quite, quite, Maurice.' He thought quietly for several moments before he leaned back in his chair and conceded full authority to his commander-in-chief. 'What do you propose? Wait, let's move to the Study Room; it's more comfortable there and it has a fireplace!' He rose, removed his coat and tossed it over the back of the chair before heading for the doorway.

'Better take the map with you so no-one will know what we're discussing,' he threw over his shoulder. 'The palace is infested with beady-eyed snoops! I've already made *appointments* for a few of them to visit *the block*, but it hasn't stopped the rest.'

Von Franckel shuddered at the thought as he moved the volumes holding down the map and carefully rolled it up. He tried to imagine what might go through the minds of the poor souls, as they knelt over *the block* and waited for the hooded executioner to perform his grisly task. He put the thought out of his mind as he headed toward the Study Room.

The fireplace crackled and, as usual, the low table was generously supplied with a variety of food and wine, and two silver goblets. Aloise signaled with his hand for Von Franckel to help himself.

'Sir, my first priority will be to fix your problems with the riots and discontent throughout the districts. I'll fix them immediately, and everything else will flow from that.'

Aloise raised his glass to Von Franckel and nodded for him to continue.

'I propose that the financial reserves be accessed and be allowed to run down; they will be replenished soon enough.' The general intended to bring up a matter of the *secret* reserves at another time. 'That will allow large-scale employment to commence with the construction of many of the infrastructure programs. Next, we conscript young unemployed men and women into the army. That will get more unemployed off the streets, especially the young men; it's they who are the worst agitators because they have nothing better to do.'

The general leaned forward to pick up a slice of bread and draped two slices of lean smoked pork over it. Kuiper, he noted with interest, had not touched any food. Von Franckel leaned back and took a small bite before continuing

'Next, we increase the manufacture of weapons. That will create more employment and give the economy a substantial boost. We will therefore have a four-pronged attack on unemployment.' The general counted each on his fingers: 'Infrastructure, army, weapons manufacture, and more goods and services on the fringes. That immediately fixes all the problems with the general public.'

Kuiper nodded. So far he was impressed with what he had heard.

'At the same time, we'll increase the size of the army, and its firepower.'

'So you're advocating a land-based invasion?'

'Yes, I am.'

'When do we actually declare war, General?' The emperor reverted to the formal address now that they were talking business.

'It will take a year or more to get the army up to speed and size. It will take another year or so to mobilize, travel and get into position. So, not until we're on their doorstep, sir, when we'll take them by complete surprise.'

'General, I've had confidence in you for a long time. That's why you're my most senior officer, but on this occasion you've excelled. Outstanding! That's enough for one meeting. Come back in a few days and tell me in more detail what you need for the army.'

The general smiled and nodded as he rose to leave.

CHAPTER 4

Von Franckel arrived two weeks later at the palace for his update report, and to present a broad-brush budget estimate for the coming campaign.

'So what have you got for me, General?'

Von Franckel placed a small sheaf of papers on the desk. 'This will give you an overview, sir. Recruitment is underway and weapons design is being upgraded across the board, including the cannons I told you about.'

Aloise sighed heavily. He hated details. They were for others to worry about.

'There is also the matter of necessary materiel to support the campaign. Every cannon needs a cart and every cart requires many oxen or horses to pull it. Every animal needs ...'

'*General!*'

'Sir?'

'Enough! I have no need to know how many sacks of grain you intend to take with you, or how you intend to carry them. That's a job for you and those you delegate to.' He leaned forward. 'All I need to know is how much is this going to cost me, and when do we start?'

'I'm still working on the budget estimate,' the general lied smoothly. The estimate had been completed but he had no intention to present it when the emperor was in such a mood. 'I'll have the estimate to you as soon as I can, sir.'

'It must be *affordable*! Remember that. If it's not affordable, forget it!'

'Yes sir. But keep in mind that guaranteeing domestic security is going to be expensive, so please be prepared for some hard numbers.' The general paused for a moment before he dropped his prepared bomb in the emperor's lap. Aloise Kuiper was not going to be permitted to opt out. 'However, if you think it's going to be too expensive, I shall make the necessary arrangements to cancel everything immediately and let nature take its course.'

'No, no, no, no. It will be fine. Just … keep going and let me have the estimate when you can.'

At the following meeting, Aloise Kuiper was furious. 'Two hundred thousand men! Why not send two million so that we can invade everyone else on the way!'

Von Franckel stayed calm, knowing that his veiled threat at the previous meeting to cancel the campaign and dismantle local security had the emperor cornered. Kuiper was committed and there was no turning back. So he pressed on with confidence.

'Two hundred thousand is actually the ideal number. When our foes see that number, supported by the biggest armory ever assembled, they will submit immediately. If we send fewer troops, they might just think they're in with a chance and put up some resistance. On the other hand, by sending *more* than two hundred thousand, we create a potentially serious problem.'

'Such as?'

'If we leave the home front undermanned, there is a risk that some of the agitators could incite an uprising and overthrow your regime. To further build up our domestic army and weaponry to offset that threat would simply be cost prohibitive.' The general knew that would strike the right chord.

Aloise nodded at the obvious. 'Agreed. Let me see the budget estimate.'

Von Franckel handed him two sheets of paper and waited for the explosion. He was no longer concerned about the consequences.

'I already told you that if it wasn't *affordable*, you were to forget it!' Aloise hissed.

'It seems quite affordable to me.'

'How do you expect this to be funded?'

'From *reserves*, sir.'

'From reserves? Half of our reserves are committed to infrastructure and other economic projects. If we put the remainder toward the campaign, there will be nothing left.'

'Yes, that would be the case if we were speaking only of the *general* reserves. But I wasn't referring exclusively to *general* reserves.'

'What are you talking about, man? If you're not talking about *general* reserves, what reserves are you talk –?' The emperor froze, leaned forward and stared at Von Franckel with unconcealed hatred.

Von Franckel stared back without expression.

'You had this planned all along, didn't you?' It was spring, but the emperor's icy whisper brought winter back into the room.

'No, not at all,' Von Franckel lied. 'As the numbers grew, I came to realize our general reserves would not be enough, but by then it was too late to opt out. You know yourself that if we don't proceed, we will most likely be sent to meet our maker within the year. The only way, therefore, is to move forward and use the *private* reserves.' He smiled inwardly as he thought of the thief in front of him now forced to plunder his own stolen treasure.

Von Franckel had indeed planned it from the beginning. He needed the treasure to later consolidate his own position after the campaign, but only the emperor and a small group of cut-throat loyalists knew in which nations it was hidden, and how to access it. It was impossible to steal it. The answer was as simple as it was elegant: *he would make the emperor bring it to him.* 'Any usage will of course be replenished a thousandfold after the campaign,' he offered as consolation.

'Just get on with it then, General.' Aloise flicked his head in dismissal.

After Aloise calmed down, he studied the figures a little more closely and soon realized that he had been tricked. Most of the base numbers were not only accurate but so easily estimated that they would have been known even before the general first came to him with his proposal. At no time could Von Franckel have considered that the general reserves would be sufficient to fund the campaign.

You lied to me, General, and every lie has its price.

CHAPTER 5

Spring, six weeks later, King's Summer Palace.

'What? A war? What are you *saying?*'
Ramesses' normally tanned face was ashen. He was shouting, furious, disbelieving. His whole life had been turned upside down in an instant. He shook uncontrollably.

Dmitri was flanked by seven senators, the government's most senior members. He had brought them as an additional show of strength to demonstrate the seriousness of his message. The men stood on the back terrace of the Summer Palace, the tension thick in the early spring air.

'It's true, Your Majesty. We have it from the most reliable sources.'

'I don't believe it. I can't believe it. I won't believe it.' The king waved his arms wildly as if the eight men, and the problem they had brought with them, would disappear in a puff of smoke.

Dmitri said nothing. He knew better. He had to allow time for the information to be absorbed. His own reaction had been little different when he was first informed.

The king turned and walked away. Sounds escaped from his mouth, but no words. He stopped after several paces, turned, and glared at Dmitri. 'Just weeks ago, Dmitri, you and I were sitting there. Right there!' He stabbed his finger in the direction of the ocean where the table and chairs were still in their places. 'We drank and toasted to lasting peace and prosperity. You must be mistaken, Dmitri, you must be. Please tell me that there has been a mistake.'

Dmitri forced himself to speak. He was as distressed as Ramesses. 'Your Majesty, a messenger delivered a letter to my office late last night, and I was informed of it this morning, less than two hours ago. As you know, we have a vast intelligence network throughout Europe, and elsewhere. We even keep a quiet eye on those pesky Vikings.' In an attempt at a little humor, he added, 'It only takes ten Vikings and a canoe to make an invasion force!'

The king's face softened at that, and he nodded for Dmitri to continue.

'A few weeks ago our agents in the Northern Region became aware of some exceptionally large diamonds floating around the local market. They made discreet enquiries among the wealthy and discovered that the diamonds had come from China in part payment for supply of arms. Our agents did not know the true significance of that, of course, but passed on the information anyway. I became alarmed and sought more information about what the North knew of the history of those diamonds.'

'The agents now know their origin?' the king asked quietly.

'No, not at all. I found out what I needed more discreetly. I sent a message to all our agents in the North to look and listen for anything unusual. One agent noticed that the Northern army was quietly drafting large numbers of conscripts. That was unusual because the various provinces have been telling their citizens that the government has no money for irrigation or other urgent infrastructure projects. It caused riots in several districts and still nothing was done. Then, all of a sudden, some of those works have commenced.' Dmitri looked about. 'Could we sit down, please, Your Majesty? This will take some time.'

'I'm sorry, gentlemen. I should have realized sooner. Please forgive me. We'll go to the Sun Room.' He turned and walked quickly to the terrace doors and indicated for the others to follow.

Alphonso was never far away and knew what to do. He merely gestured to other servants, who brought enough chairs in a matter of seconds. Others placed plates of snacks on an oval table in the center of the room. Decanters of water and wine, plus nine glasses, were set out on a side table. The king nodded his thanks to Alphonso, who quickly ushered the other servants from the room, allowing the king and his guests to help themselves.

'Now then, Dmitri, please continue.'

'Your Majesty, one particular agent is sharp, one of my best. He realized that no such diamonds could enter their country without the emperor or his advisers being made aware of them. He made contact with his informants within the palace ...'

'Informants? In the palace?' interrupted Ramesses.

'We have quite a few,' Dmitri said and shrugged as if that were quite normal. He chose not to mention that some of his informants disappeared from time to time.

'This agent,' continued Dmitri, 'found out that the Northern Region's top-ranking army officer had been making regular visits to the emperor, and their talks were always behind closed doors. Our agent thought it too much of a coincidence when added to the drafting of new recruits. There had to be a reason. So he followed the general to see who else he was meeting and talking to. He decided not to attempt to get close to the general himself – far too dangerous – but to those the general was talking to: his most senior officers. The agent's spies in the army ...'

'You have spies in their army, too?' asked Ishmael, one of the senators.

'We have more spies in their army than anywhere else on the continent,' Dmitri answered, and chuckled for the first time that morning.

'My agent arranged for his contacts to look and listen carefully to each of those the general spoke to – General Maurice Von Franckel, by the way. After one particular meeting, one of the agents managed to sneak a look at a map that the officers had been studying. The map was huge. Handwritten notations had been made at every point of entry along the borders of one particular nation, including landing points on the coastline.'

Dmitri took a deep breath and sighed. 'I'll finish with a summary of what my chief agent came up with and then we can get down to business.' Everyone in the Sun Room leaned forward, each face a picture of concentration.

'Von Franckel is strutting around like a newly crowned emperor; his officers are noticeably excited; their army is expanding, and even Emperor Kuiper seems excited. The government is spending money they said they didn't have, so they must have a plan to replace it. The officers were studying one map, and it was a map of *our* nation. There is no question, gentlemen, that *they* are going to war, and *we* are the target!'

No-one spoke. One of the senators rose and was soon followed by the others. They took turns to pour wine or water, while some helped themselves to a small snack. The men wandered about the room and occasionally sipped their drinks while they digested Dmitri's information.

Eventually they returned to their chairs, and stared at each other. Each wondered who would speak next.

As befitting, it was the king. 'How will they do it, Dmitri?'

Dmitri shrugged. He really had no idea.

'Naval attack?'

'Yes, quite possibly. They do have a formidable navy, larger than ours from what I hear.'

'A land-based attack, perhaps? Their army is big and getting bigger by the day, from what you tell us.'

'Yes again, quite possibly. We know they're tooling up to manufacture new cannons, so the army must be at least a part of their strategy. One can only speculate. Either way, we have serious problems.'

'So, possibly a naval attack, possibly a land-based attack. What about both at the same time?'

'Yes, again, quite possible, sir. There is no way to tell. We don't have enough information at this point.'

Ramesses thought for a moment. 'If it's a naval attack, we can put up a reasonable defense. For a while at least. If it's land-based, our problems would be greater, don't you think? The North already has a massive army.' He looked around the room. Some nodded slowly, while others glanced away, unable to meet his eyes. 'We are likely to lose, are we not?'

Dmitri nodded. 'Quite likely, sir.'

'So what do we do, gentlemen? Suggestions, please.'

No-one answered.

'We just submit, then? Is that it? Wave our little white flags and march to the slave pits?'

'They would not turn you into a slave, sir.' Trellinis, one of the senators, spoke for the first time. 'They would need the cooperation of the public to make the nation run efficiently. They would not risk a public outrage by turning you and your family into slaves. That would surely be counter-productive.'

'Thank you, Trellinis. I suspect you're right, but it doesn't make me feel much better. I simply could not live while our people are reduced to servitude. I would negotiate free passage somewhere for Sophia and the rest of my family, and then find a suitable spot to fall on my sword.'

There was a shocked silence while they each thought about the consequences for themselves.

It was Dmitri, the consummate thinker and adviser, who spoke next. 'Ultimately, Your Majesty, you will be the one to decide whether to fight or to submit. But that decision does not have to be met just yet. War is coming, but it has not yet been declared. Time is, therefore, on our side – for a while, at least. In the meantime, we need advice.'

Dmitri's comment gave Ramesses some relief. He nodded. 'I agree. That's good counsel, Dmitri. We need advice, and lots of it. Arrange a meeting with General Karamus and Admiral Georgeonous for first light tomorrow.' He looked across at the seven members of parliament. 'You, too, gentlemen. We'll breakfast here. There's not a moment to lose.'

CHAPTER 6

Theo stared across his desk at his son in complete silence and disbelief. His mind was numb, his body paralyzed. He had visions of his financial empire crumbling, collapsing, the rubble cascading over his home, and finally over himself. Everything confiscated or destroyed. He had a sickening vision of himself in rags.

'Any suggestions, Father?' General Vlado Karamus, Commander-in-Chief of the nation's army, spoke after a long silence finally came to an end.

'Submit, of course.' Theo looked at his son with dismay.

'Yes, of course, but how can I make that happen? It's the king who decides those things – and the government, of course.'

'Listen carefully, Vlado. If we don't submit we will be pounded into a mound of rubble. We will lose everything. Do you hear me, Vlado? *Everything!*'

'I hear you, Father. I haven't had a moment to think since Dmitri came to see me at The Barrack just an hour ago.'

'It's all right. We'll think of something. Pour me some wine, will you?' He pointed to a table near the window of the second-story room overlooking the streets of the city.

Vlado did as instructed and also poured a glass for himself.

Theo Karamus was a merchant and banker, well known and much feared, throughout the many provinces and nations that made up the Southern Region – the southern half of Europe. The tentacles of his influence and power reached far beyond those borders and into the Persian Empire, the Balkans, India, China, and the Russian states – even throughout the Northern Region. He had a quick mind, and by the time he reached to take the glass of wine from his son, he already had a plan.

'All right,' he said, 'let's get down to business.'

'Business?'

'War is business, son. When you think about it, everything is business.'

Theo leaned forward, put his elbows on the desk and deliberately focused a penetrating stare on his son. 'When is this meeting with the king?'

'Dmitri said I would receive a sealed message the day before the meeting. He said it would be at the Summer Palace and I was not to discuss this with anyone. I guess the meeting will take place toward the end of the week, to give everyone a chance to pick up a bit more information.'

'Hm. All right, let me think for a bit.' Theo rose, picked up his glass and started to pace the office. He finally stopped at the window and stared out at the constant movement in the streets below: people of all ages, horses, oxen, goats and other animals. After he took a noisy sip, he turned to his son with a broad smile.

'We can make this work. Not only that, we can make it work to our advantage. In fact, if we play this right, we can make what we have now seem like small change. We – that means *you*, Vlado – will offer the North's supreme commander unconditional surrender and a guarantee that we – that means *me* – will run this nation with an iron fist for them. In return, we ask that they simply throw a few concessions our way. As the nation's foremost industrialist and banker I will be the natural person they would want to negotiate with, anyway. And having a son to keep the army in the barracks, it will be an offer too good to refuse.'

Theo Karamus had used his wealth and power to ensure that his son received frequent promotions in the army, culminating in his confirmation by parliament as commander-in-chief.

Vlado Karamus sat quietly and sipped his wine. He had never seriously thought he would face a military conflict and had viewed his appointment as commander-in-chief as little more than a ceremonious one. Dmitri's pronouncement was not welcome news.

'Here's what you'll say at the meeting. And don't worry. I'll send my best man along to back you up. In due course, I'll arrange for my four *Disciplinarians* to dispatch the king and his entire family to meet up with their Egyptian ancestors. Before long, you'll be the second-most powerful man in the nation.'

Theo pulled up a chair and placed it directly in front of the general's. He sat down knee to knee with his son, leaned forward and slowly explained exactly how he was to control the next meeting with the king.

CHAPTER 7

Alphonso had arranged a long table to be set up in the center of the Sun Room. King Ramesses was seated at one end, with his guests five on each side. Food and drinks had been placed buffet-style on the table so they could breakfast without interruption. At both ends of the room the doors were closed, as were the glass-paneled doors leading to the terrace. The King's Guard was placed outside and orders given that no-one was to stand within fifty paces of any door or window.

Ramesses cast his eyes over the visitors as he picked at his food without interest. They were all there: the seven members of government, Dmitri, Admiral Georgeonous and the man he despised more than any other, General Vlado Karamus.

Karamus, he thought bitterly. At just thirty-three, he had been appointed commander-in-chief by parliament, despite Ramesses' best efforts to block it. Vlado Karamus was fully aware of the king's opposition, and resented it. The appointment ensured that Theo Karamus and his wealthy colleagues were first in line for lucrative contracts to provide weapons and supplies to the armed forces. Fear of violence or financial ruin kept everyone in line. Ramesses knew there was nothing he could do about it; he did not have the power to overrule parliament. He wrinkled his nose – corruption had a stench all of its own. He was stuck with General Karamus, and so was his nation.

'Good morning, gentlemen. Thank you for coming.' *As if you had any choice*, he thought. 'It's time to get down to business. Dmitri, would you summarize, please?'

'Yes, sir. As you know, the MPs are already aware of the circumstances facing us. I have fully briefed the admiral and the general.' Dmitri nodded towards each of the two men seated on opposite sides of the table. 'So I suggest we go directly to discussing options and recommendations.'

'Thank you, Dmitri.' Ramesses looked at Trellinis, the most senior member of parliament. 'Parliament excels at debate, so perhaps we should start there. Senator Trellinis?'

'I, ah … ah …' Trellinis looked at his colleagues with dismay at being the first to be put on the spot. He was an experienced debater, however, and quickly saw a way out. 'With respect, sir, the options – and recommendations flowing from those options – are strictly military issues. Our role should be to consider the proposals, not to make them. I suggest that General Karamus …' His voice trailed off.

Ramesses smiled at the response. Theo Karamus had Trellinis in his pocket, so he had expected nothing less. Nevertheless, Trellinis was correct, he thought. He nodded his agreement and turned toward Karamus. 'General?'

For visual effect, Karamus chose to stand. 'Well, it's all quite straight forward, really. First, the options. There are only two. Defend or submit. That's it!'

There were nods of agreement around the table.

'Taking each in turn, let's first consider the *defend* option,' Karamus continued, sufficiently emboldened to pace back and forth along one side of the table. He held up a finger. 'First: the numbers – ours and theirs. In military terms, the only thing that matters is *numbers*. Our navy stands at roughly 15,000.' He raised his eyebrows at Admiral Georgeonous, who nodded his agreement. 'And our army stands at about 26,000.'

The general paced for several moments while he allowed those facts to be absorbed. 'We know that the Northern Region's navy stands at approximately 25,000, which is comparatively small compared to the size of their region, but it's all they need. Their seafaring neighbors are relatively small and therefore not much of a threat. In addition, a navy that size is more than enough to attack any one of them if they wish. However, their navy is not large enough to split it into an attacking force against our nation, as well as a defense force on their own shores.'

Ramesses felt a little better until the general dropped his bombshell.

Karamus placed his hands on the back of his chair and slowly made eye contact with each of the men. He was not going to allow *anyone* to make him face tens of thousands of sword-waving savages, intent on carving him into a thousand pieces – and for nothing.

'Their army is an entirely different story. It's massive. Their weaponry is second to none in Europe and superior to ours in every way. Their army is around fifteen times the size of ours. That is simply an unbeatable number! And we now know they are manufacturing cannons!'

The general sat down, satisfied.

Dmitri turned to the admiral. He would return to Karamus later; he was not satisfied with the commander-in-chief's answer. 'Your views, Admiral?'

'The naval numbers are correct, Dmitri. We would have considerable advance notice if they sent their navy to attack us. It would be impossible for us not to be forewarned of an armada heading our way. Even though they would outnumber us and have better weapons, our home advantage would even things up. I doubt they would launch a naval attack, but if they did, I would give them a fight they would never forget!'

Dmitri smiled, delighted with the admiral's response. Ramesses also nodded his appreciation.

'As for the army situation, however,' Admiral Georgeonous continued, 'I'm sorry to say that I can't disagree with Vlado's summation.'

'Thank you, Admiral.' Dmitri leaned forward in his chair and addressed Karamus. 'General?'

The general raised his eyebrows in a silent *what?*

'You gave us your view on *one* option. You were to give us your view on two options.'

Karamus leaned forward, elbows on the table. 'You mean the *surrender* option?'

Dmitri leaned back. He had no wish to be any closer to Karamus than necessary. 'Yes, you were going to take each in turn. Your view, please, General?'

Karamus glanced at the men seated around the table and feigned bewilderment. 'I'm sorry, Dmitri, I thought the information I provided earlier made the second option redundant.'

'So you're advocating surrender?'

'I didn't say that. That's for His Majesty to decide.'

'But you are saying that we do not have the numbers to defend the Realm?'

'That's only too obvious.'

'And that leaves only the surrender option, yes?'

Karamus was fuming beneath his calm exterior. *You little pipsqueak, Dmitri, you're trying to put words in my mouth. You're trying to pin the* surrender *label on me. We'll, I'm not going to give you the satisfaction of a direct answer.* He instead turned in his chair and addressed the king.

'It's that or suicide, but that is entirely a decision for you, sir.'

The king rose and faced the two military commanders, who scrambled to their feet at the same time. 'I have much thinking to do. Thank you, gentlemen.' The two men took their cue to leave, bowed, mumbled a 'Good day, sir,' and quietly left the room. The king held up a hand towards the others at the table to indicate they should remain.

Dmitri stood, stretched, and moved across the room to stare out the windows overlooking the bay. He folded his arms across his chest and shook his head slowly from side to side. Ramesses smiled and realized he had known his friend so long he could read him like a book.

'You have someone else in mind for advice, don't you, Dmitri?'

'I suspect you know who I have in mind, sir.'

'General Marcus Mondeo. Am I right?'

'Of course you are, sir.'

'You can't be serious, Dmitri!' The outburst came from Senator Trellinis. 'General Mondeo has been retired for almost twenty years. He's in his sixties, an old man, for heaven's sake! General Karamus is the commander of our armed forces. He will be furious if we seek advice from a *former* officer!'

Ramesses was well aware of the close association between Trellinis and the Karamus family, and how it made Trellinis' extravagant lifestyle possible. Ramesses leaned forward and spoke softly. 'I do understand your thinking, Senator, and I don't entirely disagree. However, our nation is now on a precipice and, quite frankly, I could not care less if General Karamus will be furious. I want General Marcus Mondeo.'

'Yes, but ...' Trellinis was lost for words.

'But nothing!' The king locked eyes with Dmitri. 'Dmitri, I want General Mondeo, and I want him now.'

He nodded to his guests and left the room without another word.

CHAPTER 8

'Who told you that, Vlado?' Theo Karamus was furious at not getting the result he had expected.

'Trellinis, Father. He said he tried to dissuade the king, but to no avail. The king wants to speak to General Mondeo before he is prepared to make a final decision.'

'What do you think? Will old Mondeo make any difference to the outcome?'

The general thought it odd that his father should refer to the retired general as *old Mondeo* when his father was, in fact, several years older. 'I can't see how. They all agreed with me, including the admiral and Dmitri. The senators kept right out of it so they're of no concern at all. Don't worry, Father. It's no more than a delaying tactic. Ramesses was simply too weak to make a decision. There is absolutely nothing that General Mondeo can say or do to change anything.'

'When's the next meeting?'

'As soon as the general – the *former* general – comes down from his mountain. No more than a few days at most.'

Theo pursed his lips, deep in thought. 'You're probably right, but take no chances. It won't take much to push Ramesses to a decision, so get in first and make the decision for him. Even he knows he can't dither for long. He's going to need time to plan ahead. He needs to move his family to safety and to plunder the nation's gold and diamonds to buy himself another kingdom somewhere else.'

'You think he'll steal our wealth?'

'I certainly hope so.'

'Why? So that we can then steal it from him?'

'Well, sort of, but not quite. My guess is that he'll probably hide it in one of the Balkan countries. You will form a special squad to track it and keep a close eye on it. At the right time the squad will strike and bring it back here.'

'Then what?'

'We'll make sure that the North's supreme commander is made fully aware of what we've done, and serve it to him on a platter as a token of our goodwill. That will make our offer that much sweeter.'

'So, the North does the work to force our surrender, and we get the reward by running the country for them. That sounds like a good plan, Father!'

'Just make sure you follow my instructions.'

CHAPTER 9

Yolanda Valley - Three Days Later

Two thin clouds of dust rose slowly into the air behind the two riders as they traversed the Yolanda Valley. The clouds hung suspended for a long time in the still morning air, but thinned as they slowly drifted in the direction of the sea. The horses slowed to a walk when they reached the steep slope that led to the top of the plateau, where the huge white-washed house stood. Occasionally, they had to jump and scramble to maintain their grip as they followed the well-worn track up the slope.

In the arena near the house, two young men were sword-fighting with the man whom Colonel Nicholas Manassis and Yannis Christos had come to see. General Marcus Mondeo turned and glared at his visitors. He was tall, well above six feet, had a narrow waist and broad, heavily muscled shoulders. His face was as striking as his piercing blue eyes; he was deeply tanned, the skin weathered. It was a face that had clearly been handsome in his youth and one that continued to command attention.

'Who do you think you are, you fat fool?' he roared at the older rider, 'to arrive here in the middle of a training exercise? I was fighting these men and you distracted me. I could have been injured!'

'Who are you calling *fat*, you old goat?' As he spoke, the colonel swung his right leg over the rump of his horse and slid to the ground, his face red with rage. 'And you have the hide to claim you were fighting *men*! They're *boys*. Is that the best you can do these days – fight little *boys*?'

He walked towards the leather-clad man, put his hands on his hips and leaned forward until their faces almost touched.

'What you need, s-s-*sir*,' he bellowed, 'is a fight with a *man*. A *real* man!'

'And what *you* need is a bit of *discipline! Here!*' The tall man tossed one of the swords to the rider, moved away and raised his own sword.

The rider unbuckled his sword, tossed it aside and raised the sword he had been handed. With his other hand, he felt the flattened tip and the rounded edges of the blade. 'This isn't a sword, it's a *toy*! This wouldn't put a dent in butter on a hot day!'

'It won't draw blood but it will break your bones – and there goes the first one!' The tall man thrust his sword forward at full force without warning. Seemingly without effort or movement of his body, the rider's arm flashed up and parried the thrust. His movement continued in one smooth action as his blade flashed towards his opponent's left knee.

The taller man swayed without stepping back, and his own blade came down at a sharp angle to force the other sword into the gravel. His swaying motion moved smoothly into a crouch as his blade came back in the opposite direction with a powerful blow aimed at the rider's ankles. The rider jumped, both feet off the ground, and the blade just missed contact. At the same time his own blade flashed down towards the leather-clad shoulder of his older opponent.

'*Hah*! Nice try, fat boy!' The leather-clad man moved back and sideways to allow the rider's blade to slide down his own and just miss its target. The *fat boy* – who was not fat at all – grinned savagely at the near miss. The fight continued at a furious pace for several minutes before the leather-clad man suddenly moved away and, as before, raised his left hand, open palm to his opponent, who stopped instantly. Neither had succeeded in making body contact with the other.

This time neither bowed. They stood two paces apart at full attention and gave each other a smart military salute. Then they grinned, shared a warrior's handshake, and embraced.

'You old dog, General!' the rider said. 'Good as ever. I'll have to wait until you're ninety to beat you.'

'No way, Colonel – one hundred, maybe. And you'll have to put on some weight. When you really are a fat boy I might be able to beat *you*. Come, let's have a drink and you can tell me why you're here. I know it's not for the training because you don't need it.' He pointed towards the amphitheater. 'Even through your smile I can see a serious look on your ugly face.'

He led his best friend across the arena towards the table containing water jugs and mugs.

They helped themselves to water and sat on the lowest row of stone seating, the older man finally exhausted. His granddaughter sat in the middle. She took a sip of water, looked around and settled a long gaze on the younger rider for the first time. Colonel Nicholas Manassis also looked towards the other man and raised his hand to beckon him closer.

The young man was still seated comfortably on his horse and had watched the entire scene, bemused. He gently tapped his heels into the side of his mount and moved forward to be within speaking distance.

The short, stocky Colonel Manassis looked up at the rider, then towards his friend. 'It's time for introductions. This,' he said to his friend, 'is Yannis Christos, my right-hand man. The army has at last seen fit to assign me an assistant with a bit of brains. Even a bit is better than none.'

Christos rolled his eyes and nodded once.

'And this, Yannis,' the colonel said, indicating his friend, 'is, of course, General Marcus Mondeo, Chief Trainer of the Armed Forces.'

In one smooth movement Yannis Christos swung his leg over the horse and dropped to the ground with the easy grace of a dancer. He walked forward and put out his hand to the general, who stood and shook it warmly.

'So, you have a *right-hand man*, Nicholas.' The general smiled, sat down and looked at Yannis. 'And what does that role entail, Yannis?'

Yannis Christos appeared serious, troubled. 'Well, General, you'll have to forgive me for being careful with what I say. He's a colonel and my superior officer, and I have a duty to give him respect at all times.'

'Of course, Yannis, I understand.'

Yannis poured himself a glass of water and sat on the edge of the stone seat, turning sideways to face his audience. He looked nervous. 'Um … well, every day is pretty much the same, sir. I arrive at barracks early to prepare his breakfast. Then I spoon-feed him because he can't feed himself.'

'Can't feed himself?' The general was astonished.

'No, sir. I've tried to train him, but every time he tries to feed himself, he dribbles all over his uniform and looks a real mess for parade. I really don't like seeing him like that, especially after I've had to dress him.'

'Dress him?'

'Yes, sir, every morning,' Yannis continued, shaking his head sadly. 'He gets so drunk every night he has no co-ordination in the morning. I make sure I dress him while he's still unconscious. Sometimes I feed him while he's still unconscious.' He leaned forward and glanced around conspiratorially, lowering his voice to a whisper. 'Less mess that way, sir.'

By then the general was roaring with laughter, slapping his thighs.

Colonel Manassis, too, was chuckling delightedly, doubled over, gasping for breath. The other men seated in the amphitheater had joined in. The girl smiled politely.

Yannis waited for the noise to die down and then, straight-faced, continued. 'His eyes can't focus until afternoon, so I have to read all his reports. His daily orders all bear his signature – forged by me, of course. Every afternoon he finds out that he's given the troops the day off with full pay, so he either fires me or breaks my rank down to private. Sometimes both. He is a very ungrateful man, sir. Then, every evening, I help him find his way home to his wife and, every time, his wife begs me to please take him to someone else's wife.' Yannis paused for a heavy sigh. 'Then he promotes me again so that I will pick him up in the morning, and it starts all over again.' He took a sip of water and smirked. 'That about covers it, General.'

Colonel Manassis finally caught his breath. 'It's all true, Marcus, all of it!'

'Ah, so all the rumors are true, then.' The general wiped his eyes with a leather-bound wrist.

The colonel grinned broadly and gave Yannis a friendly pat on the shoulder. His face then turned serious as he stood and leaned towards the general. He spoke softly so that the other young men seated in the amphitheater would not hear. 'I hate to say this, Marcus, but we had better move inside. We have some serious business to discuss.'

The general got up and faced the young soldiers. 'I think you have rested enough, lads. It's time you practiced what you learned this morning. Mary will arrive shortly and prepare some refreshments for you. In the meantime, we will be inside catching up on old times.'

The men smiled, got up and moved towards the rack of modified swords. General Mondeo turned and walked towards the back entry to the house with the others following. Yannis Christos was behind Colonel Manassis and was about to enter when he noticed the girl close behind.

'Colonel?' Yannis spoke softly. Manassis turned and made eye contact with Yannis, who flicked his gaze to indicate the girl behind him. Yannis had understood that the meeting was to be top secret.

Manassis nodded his understanding. 'It's fine, Yannis; it's quite all right.' Yannis shrugged.

They walked through the lounge to the spacious family room, where the general indicated the chairs with a nod of his head. 'Grab a chair, everyone. Let's sit and get down to business.'

In addition to the chairs there was a couch against one wall. Another wall ran almost the full width of the house. Two wide picture-windows were cut into it, designed to take in the magnificent view of the valley. Light flooded in to make the room almost as bright as outside, but cooler in summer. The general gazed out the window while he unwound the leather strapping from his arm.

'A moment, please, Marcus, before we sit. On the way through the doorway, I was reminded of my earlier rudeness.' The colonel shook his head sadly. 'I'm afraid I have been remiss with introductions.' He looked at the girl. 'Please forgive me.'

He introduced Yannis first. 'You of course heard Yannis' name outside. He's my trusted right-hand man and co-conspirator for the destruction of the nation's armed forces.' He chuckled and turned towards the girl. 'And this, Yannis, is the general's granddaughter ...'

The girl held up an open hand, palm towards Manassis, who stopped instantly. He knew her only too well; she would introduce herself, thank you.

The girl took a pace forward and removed her straw hat, holding it against her bony chest with both hands. She cocked her head to one side and gazed intently at Yannis, starting at his feet.

Yannis, she saw, was tall, slender, but not thin. His bare arms were muscular, though not outstandingly so. His nose featured strongly between intelligent dark brown eyes set wide apart. He wore his soft beard trimmed short, revealing full lips surprisingly red for a man. Dark brown hair – almost black – fell in waves over his ears and almost down to his shoulders. High cheekbones and a strong jawline completed a face that women found very attractive.

Yannis looked down as her eyes moved up to meet his and saw ash-blond hair that fell past her ears in soft curls. The hat and perspiration had caused some locks to spike in different directions.

When her gaze reached his, he looked into the most extraordinary eyes he had ever seen. Almond-shaped, slightly angled upwards at the outer edges, they were oversized for her heart-shaped face. The whites were flawless, the irises huge and bluish grey-green like the summer gulf, sparkling as if filled with floating flecks of gold. Then, oddly, the aqua irises suddenly vanished as her pupils dilated before immediately returning to normal. The girl appeared flushed, short of breath, confused, but she regained her composure in an instant. For no reason that he could fathom,

Yannis felt goose-bumps rise at the back of his neck and experienced an odd, uncomfortable sensation, as if his soul had been drawn in through those extraordinary eyes. He felt invaded, guilty somehow. It was as if he had revealed something to her that he did not wish to reveal, yet he had no idea what it was. His eyes moved to her face.

It was a face that displayed a deep, quiet intellect, but most of all it radiated happiness. It was the sweet face of a child who, by day's end, would surprise and shock him, more than anyone else ever would.

Her head remained cocked to one side for another moment while her eyes continued to search his. 'Hm,' she murmured softly. Then she straightened, smiled, took another step forward and put out her hand.

'I am Isabella Mondeo!' she announced.

'Yannis Christos,' he responded, almost mumbling. His throat felt tight as he took her hand. She gave a single firm shake and let go.

Peculiar girl, he thought. Isabella turned and walked towards a wide benchtop screwed into the side wall opposite the couch. She hopped up to perch on top of it, gripped the edge with each hand, and started to swing her legs back and forth in a steady rhythm.

Marcus took to the couch; the other two chose chairs. Yannis turned his chair to face Marcus and sat down, unconsciously pulling at his left ear. The feeling that his mind had been invaded, and his secrets unlocked, remained.

There was a knock on the archway and a smiling, middle-aged woman leaned into the room: Mary, the housekeeper.

'I've prepared some food, General. Would you like me to bring it in now?' She gave Nicholas a broad smile and Yannis a friendly nod.

Marcus nodded distractedly. 'Yes, thank you, Mary.'

The room remained silent while Mary made several trips from the kitchen with plates of food and water jugs. She set the plates on the benchtop after Isabella had wriggled her way to one end.

'Thank you, Mary. That looks wonderful. You have excelled as usual.'

Mary returned the general's compliment with a broad smile and left the room.

Marcus rose and walked to the bench. 'We might as well eat while we talk.' He smiled, picked up a plate and began to fill it with a selection of bread, sliced cold meat and some salad. The others rose and made their own selections.

The general's smile faded as he looked at his friend. 'You have the floor, Nicholas. Please proceed.'

CHAPTER 10

Colonel Manassis took a deep breath and came straight to the point. 'King Ramesses and his closest advisers believe that war is about to be declared against our nation!' He sat back to compose himself.

Yannis had been filled in on the situation during the ride across the valley. His only reaction now was to quietly study his fingernails. Marcus was too astonished to speak. Color drained from his face as he slumped back on the sofa and placed his plate on the ground. His appetite had evaporated instantly. There was no visible reaction from Isabella; her thin legs continued to swing back and forth beneath the benchtop, the rhythm never missing a beat. She stared at the ground, seemingly distracted, as if she were somewhere else.

'Intelligence has it that the internal domestic and political turmoil in the Northern Region has escalated to the point where the emperor's chief military adviser has recommended a military solution. They now plan a military action to stimulate their economy and, ultimately, provide them with new wealth. We are apparently to be on the receiving end of that action!'

'I've heard nothing of this, Nicholas. Not a whisper. Surely there must be some misunderstanding in the intelligence communications.'

'The king has been assured that it's correct. The information we have is that the Northern Region will move by stealth and build up to a surprise attack of such magnitude that we will have no option other than to surrender.'

Isabella froze. Her swinging legs came to a sudden stop. She did not utter a sound as she looked up. Isabella was back in the room.

Marcus took a deep breath and blew out noisily through his mouth. 'Our nation, our people, our children.' He glanced over at Isabella and shook his head sadly. 'Will these wars never stop?'

'As you know, we have much in the way of natural resources. The Northern Region wants them and they intend to take them. They've decided to keep the attack secret until the last moment, so we're going to reciprocate and keep that knowledge secret. The king's advisers suggest this will give us some time.'

'Why are you here? You're wasting your time. There's nothing I can do. I'm long retired and nothing more than a trainer now. I'm given a generous stipend for my services, which are helpful to the army and keep me fit, but this undeclared war – that's well outside my sphere of influence. That will be down to you and your fellow officers.'

'The king wants your advice, Marcus. Dmitri, too. Dmitri is the one who asked me to come. He knows that we're old friends – and family.'

'Dmitri? Dmitri asked you to talk to *me*?'

'Yes. He came to me directly from a meeting with the king. It was the king who insisted that you be consulted before any final decision is made.'

'*Final* decision? That word gives me the impression that a decision of sorts has already been made.'

'That might well be the case. Dmitri did say that several of the most influential senators are very nervous about this. The general opinion seems to be that we could be better off trying to make a deal.'

A snort came from the direction of Isabella, but she did not say a word.

'What does General Karamus advise? He's the man in charge of our armed forces. He's the man to advise what can or can't be done!'

It was Manassis' turn to snort. '*Karamus*! You know yourself why he is where he is. He was dropped into the top job by some of the politicians who owe big favors to rich families and business interests. Even the king was unable to keep him out.' He calmed down. 'The king has already had a meeting with Karamus. The admiral and Dmitri were there too, plus several men from the senate who were sworn to secrecy.'

'And what is his advice – Karamus?'

'First, the admiral. He thinks his navy can give a good account of itself. He says they could win some of the battles, but maybe not the war. As for Karamus, he says he knows the size of the Northern Region's army and thinks we would be quickly overwhelmed. His opinion is that our army is too small – outnumbered almost fifteen to one. In comparison to the North, he considers our army ragtag and lucky to hold out more than a few days. He didn't propose any alternatives. He says the end result is a foregone conclusion.'

'I don't like the sound of what I'm hearing. Tell me I'm wrong in what I'm thinking Karamus is recommending.'

Colonel Manassis looked ill. 'I'm afraid you're reading it correctly, Marcus.'

'Spit it out. What exactly did he advise the king? Give me the bottom line.'

'General Karamus came back the day after the initial meeting with the king. His advice was that as soon as the Northern Region officially declares a state of war, we offer unconditional surrender.'

'*What?*' Isabella hurled herself onto the ground with a thud. She stormed to the center of the room and glared at each of the three men in turn. '*What?*' she hissed again. She was bent forward at the waist, left hand on her hip, the other balled into a tight fist that she waved about in the air. 'How dare he? How dare anyone speak the word *surrender* before anyone has even declared war? I can't believe what I'm hearing!'

'Calm down, Isabella, calm down,' her grandfather said soothingly.

'Calm down?' Isabella was getting louder, both fists waving in the air. 'I'll never be calm again, Grandfather! Get me that weak-kneed General Karamus, give me a sword and I'll put that coward to sword right here and now!'

The three men sat wide-eyed and silent. No one dared speak. Isabella now had the floor.

CHAPTER 11

Isabella lowered her arms and walked quietly to the windows. She stared out over the peaceful valley while she calmed down and collected her thoughts. She then turned her back to the windows and gazed for several seconds at each of the three men seated before her. When she finally spoke, her voice was so soft that the men instinctively leaned forward to hear what she had to say.

'How dare Karamus surrender our nation to someone who has not yet even declared war?'

'*General* Karamus, Isabella,' corrected her grandfather. He spoke as softly as Isabella had spoken for fear of sparking another rage.

'That man might be a soldier, but he is no general. Never was, never will be. Someone should have pinned that rank to his chest with a hammer and a long nail. He will have our people live not only in servitude, but worse, in shame. Give up without a fight? Never! This nation is not his to give! It does not belong to him. This nation is not the king's to give. It does not belong to him. This nation does not belong to you, Grandfather, or to you, Uncle Nicho. It is not yours to give.'

Yannis turned his head to stare at Manassis. *Uncle* Nicho? How did that come about?

Isabella walked over and stood before Yannis, a step away. She was silhouetted against the light that cascaded through the window, so he could not see her eyes clearly, only that they were narrowed and focused on his. 'This nation belongs to *you*, Yannis! And this nation belongs to *me*! The people I have just spoken of, they are *the keepers*. You and I, Yannis, we are *the inheritors*. This nation belongs to *us*!' She looked around the room. 'Do you all understand what I'm saying?'

There was a long silence before Nicholas finally spoke. 'I think you're saying that we are the past and you are the future?'

'That's exactly what I'm saying, Uncle Nicho.'

Manassis groaned theatrically as he put his face in his hands. 'You really know how to make a man feel old, don't you, Isabella?'

Isabella smiled and walked over to him, leaned down and kissed him on the cheek. 'Oh, you poor old dear.' She ruffled his hair playfully before she walked back to stand directly in front of Yannis. This time she chose to stand so close that her knees almost touched his.

Isabella's mind was racing, analyzing. *Uncle Nicho, you have been given the task of getting Grandfather to the Summer Palace to provide unbiased advice. The king's mind is therefore still open to suggestion. Hm-m, that's good; there is still hope. That gives me a chance to do something. I'll give you all something to take back to the king, gentlemen. So ... Yannis Christos, let's take a good look at you for a moment. You're well-muscled, so you're strong; you're slender and you moved like a cat earlier, so you're quick; you're in the army, so you're a natural fighter; your face is unmarked, so you must be a good fighter. Uncle Nicho, Grandfather: you are about to be the targets for my message, and you, Yannis, have just been selected as the ammunition. Please don't hate me for it later.*

Only seconds had passed while she thought, but it was enough. Isabella was ready to attack.

'Yannis Christos!' she barked.

Yannis was so startled he jumped in his seat.

'What ... what?'

'Have you ever been in a fight, Yannis?' Isabella spoke loud, rapid-fire. He was not to be given time to think. She required him to speak only the pure truth. It was Uncle Nicho and Grandfather, the real targets of her attack, who were to hear that truth and then convey her message to the king.

'Yes, of course. It's army tradition.'

'So, one fight or more than one?'

'Many. Why? What are you getting at? Slow down, will you?'

Isabella had no intention of slowing down. 'You'll see soon enough. Your opponents – they were all smaller than you, then? You made sure you couldn't lose, yes?'

'What? No! They were not smaller. They were either a similar size or bigger. In fact, most of them were bigger.' Yannis sounded angry, confused.

Good! Be angry, Yannis, so you will blurt out nothing but truths. 'So, if most of them were bigger than you, why did you not simply run away to save your pretty face? Save yourself from being beaten to a pulp? *Why*, Yannis?'

Yannis was flushed, not quite knowing what to make of the *pretty face* remark. That further unsettled him which, unknown to him, had been Isabella's intention. 'I'm not a coward. Besides, a soldier never runs from a good fight. It's what we do.'

'Let's talk about the men bigger than you. How many of those fights did you lose? All of them? How many did you lose?'

'I didn't lose any of them! For heaven's sake, what's happening here?' He looked towards Marcus and Nicholas in the hope of being rescued from this verbal assault. No help was forthcoming. Isabella had their full attention. They both knew Isabella well enough to know she was headed somewhere. Yannis did not know it, but there was worse to come.

'So, when your opponents were bigger than you, the odds were against you, correct?'

'Yes, I guess.'

'Did you ever think there was a chance you might lose?'

Yannis finally managed to laugh. 'Every time.'

Isabella fell silent. The message was ready for delivery to the two targets. She looked at her grandfather for several seconds. She glanced at Nicholas and then back at Yannis and held his eyes. There was not a sound in the room, the tension palpable. The three men knew something was about to happen.

Isabella moved forward, her knees now gently touching Yannis' knees. It was time for him to feel a connection, however subtle, to her as well as to her words. She looked down at him and felt her heart pounding. *Settle down, Isabella, for heaven's sake,* she told herself. *What's wrong with you?* When she spoke, her speech had returned to a normal pace. Her voice was as soft as when she had started to speak near the windows.

'Yannis, when the odds were against you, was it ever on your mind to give up and run away without a fight?'

'No, never.'

'Let me re-phrase that question: Yannis, when the odds were against you, was it ever in your mind to *surrender* without a fight?'

Yannis slumped back in his seat and stared up at Isabella. He was unable to speak, so he just shook his head.

Marcus and Nicholas looked at each other while they digested what they had just witnessed.

Isabella walked back to the center of the room before she addressed her uncle and grandfather. 'The odds are against us now and the *first* thing that is on Karamus' mind is to surrender without a fight.'

Nicholas spoke. 'Karamus says there are only the two options, Isabella: defend or surrender. And he insisted that surrender is the only practical one.'

'Karamus *would* say there are only two options. He is too much of a coward to put forward the third option.'

'The *third* option?' asked Marcus.

'More on that another time, Grandfather. We must go to the king at once. We cannot allow Karamus to sell us out. Knowing him, he and his family have already figured out a way to profit by it. This is *my* nation and *I* intend to fight for it.' Isabella turned her gaze back to Yannis. 'I can't do much on my own, Yannis, but if you're willing to fight for your nation, give me a sword and I'll fight by your side!'

Yannis looked up at Isabella and found himself nodding without actually intending to.

CHAPTER 12

Marcus seemed to have aged when he rose from the couch. His face looked tired, drawn; his posture was not as straight as it had been just hours earlier. At the same time he felt a stir of excitement deep within after he heard – and understood – Isabella's point of view. Perhaps there were other means at their disposal that could be explored. Perhaps … perhaps … What is your *third option*, Isabella? he wondered. *I got your message. You truly are an extraordinary girl. You never cease to amaze me. So like your mother, rest her soul.*

'Gentlemen, thank you for coming. I will meet you at the Summer Palace in two days. We'll come and see you off. You have a long ride back.' He draped his arm around his granddaughter's shoulder and pulled her tightly against his side. Nicholas and Yannis followed them out through the door leading to the arena.

Nicholas walked over to where the two horses had been tethered by one of the young soldiers, untied them and started to walk back. Isabella had swiftly walked past the other men and then turned so that she directly faced Yannis, and blocked his path. He had no choice but to stop.

She cocked her head to one side as she had done previously and looked up at him. When he met her eyes this time, he was more astonished than when they were first introduced. The eyes gazing into his were emerald green, the golden flecks even more pronounced as they sparkled in the mid-afternoon sun.

'You look very young to be a major, Yannis.' She knew very well that he was not a major. *Poor, unsuspecting Yannis*, she thought. Her second attack was underway.

Yannis was speechless. He could not comprehend what had just happened inside the house, or what was happening in front of him. His world had been turned upside down by a child; her verbal onslaught had kept him constantly off-balance. *Peculiar girl*, he thought again. Peculiar eyes – he must have mistaken the color inside the house. Unable to move towards his horse, he wondered why she was blocking his path.

The general, however, smiled. He had seen similar reactions many times. 'It's all right, Yannis. It's her eyes. They change color depending on the time of day. In the morning sun they are more blue-grey than green; they change to bright green in the afternoon light. As evening comes on, they seem to fade to grey-green. I would hate to think what color they are at midnight. Bright red, most likely!' He chuckled at his own joke, but he had completely misread the scene in front of him.

'I'm not a major, Isabella. I'm a second lieutenant.' Yannis finally found his voice.

'Well, then you look very *old* to be a second lieutenant, Yannis.' Her attack was not to be diverted.

'I'm not *old*, I'm twenty-one!' He sounded furious. 'Well, *almost* twenty-one,' he added sheepishly as he calmed down.

'But that *is* old.'

'Twenty-one isn't old!'

'It's a matter of perspective, isn't it? Grandfather would say you're young, but from *my* perspective you're old.'

'From your perspective? So, what age are you? Seven? Eight?' He seemed pleased with his counter-attack.

'I'm thirteen,' countered Isabella. 'Well, *almost* thirteen,' she smirked, mimicking Yannis' voice in his earlier response. 'Thirteen come summer,' she added.

'Almost old enough to read, then.'

'I mastered the alphabet just last week!' Isabella declared.

'Well, good for you!'

'*And* I can count to ten,' she said. 'Well, *almost* to ten,' she added with another smirk, again mimicking Yannis' voice.

'Wonders never cease,' Yannis mumbled. He glanced briefly at the two men who were watching the exchange with great interest. Yannis shook his head and made a move to reach for the reins of his horse when Isabella cocked her head to one side again and looked him up and down for several moments.

'H-m-m,' she murmured as she pursed her lips. Without warning she moved forward suddenly, leaving Yannis no time to react, and kicked him hard, the blow directed to the outer, fleshy side of his left leg. An expert kick-boxer, Isabella had no wish to break his leg by kicking the inner, bony side. She moved back quickly to observe with great interest the result of her action.

Yannis gasped with shock and pain, his eyes wide in astonishment, mouth open. He hopped on one leg to his horse and leaned against it for support.

The general and Nicholas were as astonished as Yannis. They looked at each other without any comprehension of what they had just witnessed.

Yannis finally found his voice. 'Ahh ..., he gasped. He took a deep breath and exhaled, his cheeks billowing. Turning, he managed to mount his horse but with considerably less grace than when he had dismounted earlier that day.

Isabella stood back, arms folded, and looked thoroughly pleased as she watched the spectacle. Yannis glared at her with a mixture of anger and confusion, but she smiled back sweetly and waved to him and the colonel as they swung their horses towards the track that led to the valley below.

'What was all that about?' Marcus demanded.

Isabella shrugged and hugged her grandfather. Without answering she let go of him, turned and jogged toward the oval. By the time she reached the outer perimeter, she was in full stride, a broad grin on her face.

Instead of following the elliptical line marking on the grass, Isabella peeled off at full pace and headed for one of the outer fields. A waist-high stone fence loomed closer as she ran, with the access gap to the next field slightly to her right. The gate was wide open. Too easy. She ignored the gap and headed straight for the fence. She flexed her thigh muscles, extended the last three strides and allowed her strength to lift her body high into the air. She had timed it perfectly. One foot came down in the natural rhythm to just touch the top of the fence, lifting her even higher. She landed smoothly on the grass on the other side without losing stride or pace. At the same time she gave three short, sharp, ear-splitting whistles as she headed straight for the next stone fence.

A flash, like white lightning, flew out from behind a small grove of olive trees and headed in her direction. *Barca*, her beloved white stallion.

Barca knew exactly what he had to do. He headed towards Isabella at full gallop in a wide sweep on the opposite side of the fence. His bulging eyes were fixed on Isabella, measuring her speed and position as he closed on the fence. Drawing level with it, he slowed to a fast canter for several moments and then moved away from the fence at a slight angle.

Isabella also knew exactly what to do. She and *Barca* had practiced the stunt – and many others – every day for three years. She closed in on the fence at a sharp angle to where a knee-high wooden box had been deliberately placed against it. She extended her stride again: one, two, three. Her right foot struck down on the box; her left foot thrust down on top of the fence for additional lift, and then she seemed to hang, suspended, in the air while *Barca* materialized beneath her. The landing was perfect. She wrapped her legs around *Barca's* shoulders and hung on to the beautifully coiffured mane until the two were in perfect harmony. Isabella worked hours every week on that mane. It was beautiful as well as practical. There was no saddle – too dangerous for stunts. Without prompting, *Barca* immediately went to full gallop and headed for the racetrack.

Isabella's father, Anton, had died six years earlier, killed in a naval shipyard accident. Her mother had suffered from a broken heart that quickly led to depression, followed by a lack of will to live. She died just months later after a short illness. Since then, Isabella had been happy enough to live with her grandfather. She loved him dearly. She loved *Barca* almost as much. Her time was fully taken up with studies, research, training and working her grandfather's property which, she knew, would one day belong to her.

Despite her busy life she had always felt empty inside. When she thought about the future, she could visualize herself in academia, a tutor perhaps. That was all very interesting, but not very exciting for a 12-year-old with a raging fire of ambition in her belly. Isabella felt special, different from the other children she associated with. They seemed to feel it, too, deferring to her, seemingly without conscious thought. Although they were friendly, they kept her at a distance. She had always felt she was destined for something special, but had had no idea what that might be, or when it would present itself.

Now she knew.

Barca was at full gallop when Isabella spread her arms out wide and whooped at the top of her voice. Her hair and blouse trailed behind her in the wind. Only her legs connected her to her horse, yet she felt safe, invincible. She was excited, exhilarated. She whooped again and again. This had easily been the best day of her life. She could not imagine that she would ever have a better one.

You might want to surrender without a fight, Karamus, and destroy my nation's pride for a thousand years. Never! I am going to fight you to the death. I have at last found purpose in my life. I have found my cause.

She had also realized something else that afternoon. Isabella was in love.

Isabella slowed *Barca* to a trot and pointed him towards the water trough. When they reached it she slid down his left side, moved to the front and gave him a hug and some soothing words. *Barca* gently nudged the pocket of her blouse with his nose to remind her that he was owed a treat for the stunt. She laughed and gave him the treat and another hug.

Looking up, she checked the angle of the sun and estimated it was almost time to meet with Zhang Chen, a martial arts grandmaster who had adopted the property, and the Mondeos, for no apparent reason. He had simply turned up one day several years ago, and stayed. Now he lived in a comfortable two-room cottage on the far side of the property, for which he paid no rent. Mary supplied him with all his food needs from the general's stores. In return, Zhang Chen did chores around the property and put her grandfather through a daily fitness regime.

Isabella and Zhang Chen met at exactly the same time every day for an intensive two-hour training session in his craft. She loved every minute of the training, and he loved her for her dedication. He already knew what she did not yet know: when she was older and stronger, she, too, would have the skills of a grandmaster.

Isabella made sure to leave enough grain out to keep *Barca* satisfied until the next day. She tied a blanket over his back for protection against the night chill and gave him another hug. There was no need to tie him to anything as he was free to roam as he pleased. She then headed back to the arena, where she knew Zhang Chen would be waiting for her.

On the way there, her thoughts turned to Yannis. She knew she was crazy; she knew it was inexplicable, impossible. She also knew she was not mistaken. *Suddenly a switch flicked inside me, Yannis, and there it was. My heart exploded. Bang! Just like that, and I'm in love. How on earth am I going to deal with this? You fool, Isabella, you've fallen in love with someone way beyond your reach.*

As she walked across the paddock, she looked down at herself and grimaced. She saw only a bony chest and long thin legs. Shaking her head, she sighed in despair. *Not much of a man-trap, Isabella!* By the time she reached Zhang Chen, she was ready to kick him from one paddock into the next.

CHAPTER 13

'What do you think of Isabella, Yannis? She's something, isn't she?'
They had arrived back at The Barracks building a few minutes earlier. A stableman led their horses away to give them a rub-down, food and water. The two men followed the corridors to Manassis' office at the southern end of the stone building situated in the outer suburbs, overlooking the city. It was a windowless, airless room, but Manassis didn't mind. Only generals were provided rooms with windows and a view.

The colonel sat in a chair, his crossed legs perched on the edge of a small desk. Yannis paced the room slowly to give his left leg a chance to recover.

'What do you mean? What do I think? What am I supposed to think? I don't know how to answer that. She's crazy! She's turned me into a cripple.' Yannis dragged his leg around the room in an exaggerated display of agony.

Nicholas threw his head back and laughed. 'She does schooling, you know.'

'So what? So do many children.'

'She *does* read.'

'So I heard. She's just learned the alphabet. Simply amazing.'

Nicholas ignored the sarcasm. '*And* writes. She researches and writes articles for other students.'

Yannis remained silent.

'*And* she does math, geometry, algebra, astronomy ... The list goes on.' Nicholas brought his feet to the ground and leaned forward, elbows on the table. 'She has difficulty finding tutors to keep up with her. She soaks up everything they know and she then moves on to the next one. She seems to have the answer as soon as the tutor asks the question. Behind that angelic little face is the mind of a future scholar.'

'She'll be a vicious scholar – she'll beat her pupils to a pulp.' Yannis managed a small grin as he leaned down to rub his shin to make his point.

'She spends her spare time with the Royal Scribe, who is recognized as the most knowledgeable scholar in the region. His name's Alexander duPonti, but they call him *the Oracle*. He and the other tutors play a game with her: they impart unusual information to her and then, months later, they try to trick her by asking her about some obscure piece of that information. I hear she surprises them every time. Isabella researches everything she's been told, and by the time her tutors bring up the subject again, she ends up teaching them things even they didn't know.'

'Why are you telling me this? She's still crazy.'

'What she was saying about the alphabet, and counting: she was teasing you, Yannis. She was pulling your leg.'

'You're wrong; she didn't pull my leg; she broke it in ten places!'

'I've never spoken of my private life, Yannis, because it pains me so much when I think about what happened a few years ago. But just so you know: Isabella is my niece, my sister's child, and I've known her from the day she was born. She's an orphan, following a horrible tragedy, and it has taught her to be self-sufficient. I've never known or heard of anyone quite like Isabella.' He took his elbows off the table and leaned back in the chair. 'In answer to your question, Yannis, I'm telling you this because Isabella has a mind superior to anyone you will ever meet; she is an extraordinary human being. You heard her today. She can hold her own debating anyone. There is no doubt that when she's older, she will be a powerful influence throughout the nation as a scholar, or in parliament, perhaps. She really is one of a kind.' He put his elbows back on the table. 'She is also a trickster and clever enough to deliberately slip beneath someone's guard. You will do well not to underestimate her.'

'Well, you're right about one thing: I *did* underestimate her. I have to agree, though, she was very articulate at that meeting,' he admitted grudgingly. 'She had me ready to march at the enemy, sword in hand. I even had a fleeting vision of her, also with sword in hand, and that she was in *front* of me, not by my side as she indicated.'

'Well, there you are. That's what she's capable of. Just think of the influence she'll have when she's in her thirties and forties.'

Yannis remained silent, giving that some thought. 'Tell me, if she's so smart, why did she kick me like that? That really was crazy.'

'You've got me there. That surprised me as much as it did you.'

'No, Nicholas, it did *not* surprise you as much as it did me!'

'Well, *almost* as much.' Nicholas' whole body shook with laughter as he replayed the scene in his mind. He wiped tears away with the back of his hand. After he calmed down, he continued. 'Perhaps you should forget what happened today, Yannis. You got off to a bad start, somehow.'

'Forget it? I'll never forget it!'

Yannis kept staring at his friend with raised eyebrows. He was still waiting for an answer.

The colonel drummed his fingers on the table, deep in thought. Finally he looked up at Yannis and shook his head. 'I really don't know, Yannis. I really don't. Maybe it was something you said.'

'But I didn't say much, especially to her. She was the one doing the talking, not me.'

'True. Well, maybe it was something you *didn't* say.'

'Such as?'

'No idea.'

'She must really hate me.'

'No, that's definitely not the case. If she hated you, she would simply have ignored you. She doesn't have any hate in her anyway. She is much too kind-hearted, full of love, and a joy to be around. No, she's never done anything like that before, so she obviously had a very good reason for kicking you. Think about it, Yannis. She has sent you a *message*, a message only for you, and it's a message of the strongest kind, but it's buried deep. It might take a while, but it is you alone who will have to dig deep enough to find what that message is. I have a feeling that when you do, it will have been worth every minute of your search.'

'Well, next time she sends me a message, I hope it's by note.' He smiled and rubbed his sore leg vigorously. 'And preferably by carrier pigeon!'

CHAPTER 14

The meetings came and went. With each, Aloise Kuiper received a report that called for more expense than the previous. The lists went on and on, and Aloise was getting more depressed by the day. And angrier.

He knew that he would soon be forced to access his private *reserves*. The first portion to be expatriated was hidden in Russia, and it was by far the largest portion. Next would be the Swedish portion, smaller but closer to home. The others would follow soon after, so as to be readily available. He ran through a list in his mind of the order in which he would retrieve the treasure secreted throughout many nations. He remained sure not even Margarethe knew about it.

Aloise was almost as angry at himself as he was with Von Franckel. He thought about the five years of crusades with King Harald VI to accumulate the massive treasure of plundered war booty, but he spared no thought for all the generals he had later murdered to guarantee no opposition to his rise to power. The entire royal lineage was given a simple choice: give up all claims to the throne, keep what they had, shut up, and live, or protest, lose their property and be given an immediate appointment at *the block*. There were no dissenters.

Now General Von Franckel had forced him to dip into his hard-earned funds. Aloise cheered up as he thought about the price he would extract from his general.

It was mid-morning on a beautiful spring day, and a re-focused Kuiper was ensconced on a couch in a sunny corner of the balcony, out of the breeze. As instructed, a low table now contained only a small variety of food.

Empress Margarethe sat in a comfortable cane chair at the end of the table. A slim, beautiful woman in her early forties, she ate sparingly. Although she was very fond of her husband, and they had an affectionate relationship, she didn't love him, and she was more than happy to share him with a number of mistresses who occupied some of his time. Margarethe knew that Aloise was particularly enamored of three young Muslim women, possibly because he knew that he was the only one permitted to see them without their burqa.

Von Franckel was shown onto the balcony by a uniformed guard and headed towards their table. Margarethe immediately stood up to leave and, under the pretext of leaning over to pick up a tiny pastry on her way, hissed at her husband, 'I don't trust that man, Aloise!'

She nodded, but did not speak to or smile at Von Franckel as she passed him on her way back inside the palace. A servant took the opportunity to approach to replenish the table, but the emperor waved him away with a smile.

The bitter cold of winter had receded, and so had Kuiper's depression. He also felt cheered as he scanned Von Franckel's budget estimate update. Perhaps the rot had finally stopped, he thought. He glanced up at the general. 'This is not much changed since last week. Has it been updated?'

'My budget planners had previously come up with absolutely everything they could think of, and then some. I can now actually start examining areas where we can possibly make some savings.'

'Ah, good, good,' Aloise said with a smile. '*Savings* is a term dear to my heart. So, how are things with your officers?'

'For the time being it's strictly on a need-to-know basis and everything is going well. The army itself will be split into three divisions, and I have selected the senior generals for each. They, in turn, will break the divisions down into brigades and companies and select their officers. I will, of course, be in overall command.'

'Of course. Bring me a list as soon as you have one, will you? I mean a list of the generals, as well as their personal choices of officers.' Aloise bit into an apple to disguise his smirk. *When this is over, you are in for a big surprise, my friend.*

The woman slipped unseen from the room and into the passage, where she silently made her way to the palace exit. Without slowing, she nodded to one of the uniformed guardsmen, who immediately followed her to the quiet streets below. Once in the city, the streets were bustling, and noisy, but the crowds parted to give her easy passage as soon as they noticed her, not because of the guardsman two paces behind, but because of her burqa, clearly distinguished by the beautiful gold embroidery and the emperor's crest on the purple veil.

Outside the gold trader's shop, the woman pointed a gloved hand to a spot near the entry before she entered the store. The guardsman nodded once and stood at attention at the designated place. As usual, the turbaned proprietor did not glance her way, but he heard the tinkle of the beaded curtain leading to the private lounge at the rear of the store.

Without pausing, the woman picked up a key and moved to the door leading to a back alley. By the time she slipped into the lane, the purple silk had been fully covered with a plain, black veil. Minutes later, she entered another door, deliberately left unlocked, moved up the stairs and entered a room where a man was waiting for her. She removed the plain veil, followed by the purple veil, which had been pinned to the headscarf.

The man was pouring a glass of wine and half-turned, holding up the bottle with raised eyebrows before he realized his mistake. He grinned sheepishly. 'I should have remembered sooner that Muslims don't touch alcohol. I'm sorry if I offended you.'

She nodded her acceptance of his apology. 'It is of no concern. Being a Muslim woman, my only concern is my man.' She pointed to a chair. 'Now come and sit with your back to me so I can rub your neck and shoulders. While you relax, you can tell me all about your meeting with our esteemed leader.'

When Maurice Von Franckel had finished, she leaned forward, kissed his cheek, and spoke softly into his ear, 'When this is over, he is in for a big surprise, my darling.'

It was less than thirty minutes later when the woman used the key to re-enter the room at the rear of the shop. By the time the shopkeeper heard the beaded screen tinkle for a second time, the purple veil was back in place. Neither acknowledged the other as she moved through the shop and stepped into the bustling street, where she nodded for the guardsman to escort her back to the palace. No-one was permitted to see any part of her, or to hear her voice. She merely had to nod, or point a finger, to get what she wanted.

A gentle tinkle floated across the other noises of the shop as the proprietor entered the private lounge, where he lifted a cushion and removed an envelope left by his visitor.

As always, it was sealed and addressed to the Caliph. Apart from the usual progress report, the two-page letter included a request that the Caliph arrange for a particular number of his men to be conscripted into the Northern army for the coming campaign. The woman wanted someone to maintain a protective eye on the man who gave promise of a more secure future.

The envelope was on its way to the Middle East within the hour.

CHAPTER 15

Mary arrived well before daybreak to prepare an early breakfast. By the time Marcus and Isabella sat down to eat, she had also prepared a basket of food for their journey. She threw in some fruit for good measure, together with a flask of lemon-flavored water.

Marcus attempted some small talk during breakfast but Isabella's responses were little more than single syllables. Deciding not to press the issue, he quickly finished his breakfast and went to inspect their transportation.

He had chosen the lighter of the two carriages, drawn by two horses. Zhang Chen had loaded fodder and water for the horses into the back of the carriage during the previous night. Several lengths of rope secured the provisions, as well as a water canister, for their own use.

Marcus waited for the first sign of light before he eased the horses towards the track leading to the valley. He glanced at Isabella, who sat quietly on the bench to his left, but it was still too dark to read her face.

Isabella had not slept well. The excitement of the previous day had faded, and she worried about following the path of her mother, but for different reasons. To make matters worse, she felt foolish. There had never been a thought about boys other than someone to play or fight with. Then she had looked up to see a young man on a horse, and her life had changed in an instant. She knew only too well that she was still a child and would remain one for several years, but it was not possible to change how she felt.

Nature had intervened much too soon in her emotions, and she allowed observations about physical changes to drift through her mind. Visible changes to young boys were barely noticeable as they became young men: deeper voices and facial hair. Girls, however, were different – drastically different, she realized. She had noticed startling changes to some of her young female friends during regular visits to her tutors and the city's central library. Over a period of just two or three years, everything about them seemed to change. Hair and skin revealed new luster, lips became fuller, eye-lashes longer, figure was reshaped, contracting in some areas, lengthening and expanding in others. Isabella had also noticed that boys seemed to take a sudden interest in the girls as they went through those changes. She started to think about her own appearance and the knowledge that girls began to blossom from approximately her own age. She was recalling an old children's tale about the grub and the rainbow butterfly when her grandfather interrupted her thoughts.

'You're very quiet, Isabella. Is everything all right?'

'I'm fine, Grandfather. I'm just a little tired. There was too much to think about last night to get much sleep.'

'I won't even suggest that you lay down for a nap in the back of the wagon. This road is so bumpy it would curdle water in a can.'

Isabella giggled. 'I'll just lean against you and doze for a bit.' Marcus put his arm around her shoulder as she wrapped her arms around his waist. She needed some quiet time to think, and had no intention of sleeping.

Isabella allowed the events of the previous day and night to replay in her mind. Things would move quickly after the next day, she realized, and there would be little time for further thought. Decisions had to be made before she reached the city, and she promptly reduced them to just two.

Yannis was a man well beyond her reach: should she give him up and follow Mother's path to depression, or should she fight for the impossible? *That's easy, Isabella. I will fight for the impossible. I will never give up.* Decision made. The next decision seemed more difficult. How would she fight? What could she say, or do? For now she would have to remain silent and hide her feelings from Yannis. A smile formed on her lips when she realized that the decision was in fact no more difficult than the first: *it had already been made.* Basic instinct had already moved her to stake her claim without him suspecting. She had kicked him, hard, without provocation, to shock and utterly confuse him. There was no reason he should suspect the real reason: so he would not forget her in a hurry. It would simply be a matter of giving him a reminder from time to time and allowing nature to take its course, for better or worse.

She thought about the long, hard, and possibly heartbreaking road that lay ahead but, with the major decisions made, she did feel happier than she had an hour earlier. Before she drifted off to sleep, her last thought was that perhaps her best hope was for her and Yannis to die side by side on a raging battlefield.

•

They had stayed overnight in a modest home on the outskirts of the city and were about to leave for the Summer Palace. Marcus had told his old friend, Captain Linus Cavarro, a retired and recently widowed naval officer, that he and Isabella were in town to shop for provisions.

Their visit had been unexpected, yet Captain Cavarro had managed to provide a more than adequate meal the evening before. After dinner, the conversation had turned, as usual, to Captain Anton Mondeo, Marcus' son and Isabella's father. Isabella had sat apart as the two men talked, but she drank in every word of their reminiscences. She had loved her father dearly. He had been a big man, strong and comforting, kind and thoughtful, and treated his wife, Anna-Karina, Isabella's mother, like a goddess. His face had started to fade from her memory, so she loved to be reminded of anything about him. It did not matter that she had heard most of it before, because there was always something new. Whenever the conversation drifted toward the accident, the two men seemed to be reminded of her presence and the conversation had turned to earlier, happier times.

Isabella didn't mind. She knew only too well how the accident had happened. Only six years old at the time, she had listened with dismay and rising panic as distraught naval officers, family and friends arrived at their suburban home late one morning to reveal the details of the shipyard tragedy to her mother. Isabella had instinctively embraced her mother to give support, stroked her back, and spoken soft words of comfort. That very moment became a revelation, an awakening for Isabella. It was to shape who she would become and provide her with a strength that would distinguish her from all others. At six years of age she had always been dependent on her parents and others. But as her mother clung fiercely to her, it had dawned on Isabella that their roles had been reversed in an instant.

Isabella now finished the last of the goat's milk and placed the glass back on the table. Marcus smiled at her and pointed wordlessly to the small mustache of milk on her upper lip. She returned his smile with a grin, picked up her napkin and wiped it away. Her face was still slightly flushed from the hot bath she had enjoyed earlier that morning. She had dressed in a smart white cotton dress which she had made herself, contrasted by a vividly colored head-band to keep her hair in place.

Linus Cavarro smiled at Isabella across the breakfast table. 'I hope you were not too bored last night, Isabella. I'm afraid when your grandfather and I get together, we tend to just ramble on about the past.'

'No, it was fine, Uncle Linus, really. I enjoyed it.'

'I'm sorry if we dwelt on your father so much. I hope it didn't upset you.'

'On the contrary, I love to hear about Father.'

Cavarro leaned forward, putting his elbows on the table. 'It's been several months since I last saw you, Isabella. I meant to ask you last night: how have you been? You seem ... different, somehow. A little older, of course, but different.'

'Things have been fine.' Isabella gave him a quizzical look. 'Why, do I look ill?'

'No, no! Just the opposite, in fact. You look radiant, wonderful. I can just start to see a young woman emerging from within.' He made an expansive, sweeping motion with his arms. 'You must be about thirteen now?'

'Yes ... Well, *almost* thirteen.' Isabella could not resist a giggle as she glanced at her grandfather, who rolled his eyes and smiled back.

Cavarro looked towards Marcus. 'I can see a lot of her mother in Isabella, Marcus.' He shook his head sadly. 'The most beautiful woman I ever – oh, I'm sorry! There I go again. I seem to have a gift for upsetting people.'

Isabella leaned forward and put her hand on his wrist. 'It never upsets me to talk about those I love more than anyone else, Uncle Linus.' She glanced over at Marcus. 'Except for you, of course, Grandfather.'

Marcus nodded at them but remained silent. To cover his embarrassment, Cavarro rose and started to clear the table. Marcus also rose and looked meaningfully at Isabella.

'Time to go shopping, Isabella.'

Cavarro looked slightly relieved as he turned back from the kitchen bench and faced them. 'If you need to stay in the city another night, Marcus, just drop in. I have plenty of food and I can really do with the company.' He smiled at Isabella. 'I hope you have a nice day shopping.'

'I'm sure it will prove to be an interesting day,' she offered, glancing at her grandfather.

CHAPTER 16

Marcus and Isabella arrived at the palace mid-morning as arranged. A Royal Guardsman ushered them into a chamber where Dmitri awaited them.

He smiled broadly at Marcus in welcome. They shook hands, and then embraced. Dmitri next turned to Isabella and opened his arms theatrically to indicate he expected a big embrace. He got one. Isabella was tall for her age, while Dmitri was not, so she was able to easily give him a kiss on each cheek without having to stretch.

'I love you, Dmitri. We never see enough of you.'

Dmitri loved that she had always called him by his first name. He felt that it set him apart from all the others whom she called *Uncle*. Isabella was well aware that he loved her familiarity. He was very special to her and she wanted him to know it. Dmitri had been a close family friend from before she was born.

'And I you, Isabella. And by the way ... ah, dare I say it? Something has changed since I last saw you. Your dress, your hair, your face – you look absolutely radiant, Isabella. Stunning.'

Isabella flushed a deep crimson. She suddenly didn't feel as depressed as she had the previous day. She punched his chest with an open fist and exclaimed, 'You're such a comedian, Dmitri. You're not only old now, you poor thing, you're blind as well.'

'You'll find out who the comedian is soon enough. Very soon you will have hordes of boys chasing you around the paddock. You're going to need all of those martial arts skills to keep them under control.'

Isabella grinned and was about to give him another punch when she saw his eyes focus over her shoulder.

'Ah, General Karamus! Good to see you,' he lied as he put out his hand.

'And good to see you, Dmitri.' General Karamus lied just as smoothly as he took the extended hand. He appeared surprisingly confident, sure of himself. 'And Marcus, how are you?'

They shook hands but neither smiled. They did not like each other, and both knew it.

Several male voices could be heard. Within moments Senator Trellinis entered the room, followed by several other senators. Last to enter were Colonel Nicholas Manassis and Second Lieutenant Yannis Christos. There were handshakes all round while Nicholas got a warm hug and a kiss from his niece. Yannis stared at Isabella and nodded politely, but moved several times to maintain a safe distance between them. Isabella looked his way just once, gave him a nod and a brief smile but, to his relief, made no attempt to move closer.

Yannis did not circulate. After he shook hands with Dmitri and Marcus, he moved to stand quietly against the wall, away from the others. The senators were not known to him, nor had he previously met General Karamus, and he did not wish to do so now. He had met Dmitri for the first time when he and Nicholas had given him the report of their meeting with Marcus. Yannis had expected Dmitri to laugh when Colonel Manassis had recounted almost word for word what Isabella had had to say.

To his surprise, Dmitri's face had revealed nothing as he listened. Yannis did not know what to make of the reaction. Perhaps Dmitri had not believed what he was hearing; perhaps he had merely listened politely before moving on to something else.

Yannis was unaware that Dmitri knew Isabella well enough to have expected nothing less from her. He did not know that King Ramesses, who also knew Isabella, had been heartened as Dmitri had repeated what Nicholas had told him. Like Isabella, Ramesses felt that national pride was paramount and should not be readily dismissed.

Without being obvious, Yannis watched Isabella from a distance. The information that Nicholas had related to him at The Barracks on their return from Yolanda Valley had given him an urge to observe her from a different viewpoint. He was intrigued that a young girl could have such an intellect.

When he saw her standing next to Dmitri, he was surprised by how much taller she appeared than he remembered. Perhaps, he thought, that was because she had mostly been standing near her grandfather, who was a giant. Marcus Mondeo towered above everyone in the room, including

Karamus, who was also well over six feet.

Yannis watched Isabella as she moved about the room. A handshake here, a hug there, an animated chat with each of the senators in turn. She did not approach General Karamus, who spoke only to Senator Trellinis. Her posture seemed straighter, her head held higher. She had a poise, a presence that had not been there just days ago.

There was something else, something different. He sensed something, but what? Was it a new focus, perhaps? He had no idea. Her face had more color, a glow, and her skin had a shine that matched her eyes. It was as if she had been charged by a bolt of lightning. He shook his head and wondered what color her eyes were right then.

CHAPTER 17

Just as Admiral Georgeonous quietly slipped into the room, the double doors on the opposite side opened silently. Uniformed royal guardsman flanked the entrance to the conference room. The king could be seen standing at the far end of a large table in the center of the room.

Two other men were present, standing on either side of the king, but several paces behind. The man on his left was short, with a big bush of frizzy white hair and a full, white beard: Alexander duPonti, the Royal Scribe, also known as the Oracle. The man on his right was younger and taller. A hint of grey was just visible in his dark hair and short beard: the scribe's assistant. Next to each was a stool in front of a miniature desk that contained writing material.

Exquisitely carved chairs lined both sides of the conference table, with a more elaborate one at the king's end. The king faced his guests and waited patiently for his presence to be formally announced.

A third guardsman, dressed more ornately than the two standing on each side of the entrance, moved forward to address the visitors.

'Gentlem – oh, I beg your pardon – ladies and gentlemen, His Royal Highness, King Ramesses, welcomes each of you and wishes to thank you for your presence here today. Refreshments have been provided on the main table and at the side table for your comfort during your meeting. A buffet lunch will be served later. You may now enter and make yourselves comfortable.' The guardsman bowed to the visitors, turned to the king and bowed again. 'Ladies and gentlemen, His Majesty, King Ramesses.'

The king was wearing his formal military uniform, distinguished from other senior officers by several medallions and sashes across the shoulders and front. The red jacket contrasted beautifully with his salt-and-pepper mustache, goatee, and thick silver hair brushed straight back. Though almost seventy, his still handsome face was matched by kind, intelligent eyes.

Ramesses smiled and moved forward to greet his guests as they filed into the room. The three guardsmen closed the doors behind them as they left. Instructions had been given that no-one was to enter the room under any circumstance. Lunch was not to be served until the palace staff was summonsed to do so.

The men approached the king to form a short line. Isabella deliberately held back so that she would be last in line. Yannis had no choice other than to move past her to join the line. As he did, he leaned down and hissed softly into her ear, 'It's quite all right, Isabella. Don't worry about it. No, *really*, it's all right. The splintered bone is healing nicely, but thanks for asking.'

Isabella poked him in the small of his back with her index finger as he moved ahead of her with an exaggerated limp, 'Your other leg is looking deliciously inviting today, Yannis,' she whispered. She then poked him again for good measure.

When her turn came, Isabella presented the king, whom she knew well, with a radiant smile and a formal curtsy.

'Enough of that nonsense, Isabella. I hereby give you a royal order to give me a kiss.' Ramesses leaned forward, turned his face to one side and stabbed his cheek several times with his finger.

'You really are a cheeky one, Your Majesty.' Isabella giggled at her little joke and obliged Ramesses with a deliberately loud kiss on his cheek.

Ramesses fondly stroked her cheek before he turned to his visitors. 'Let's get down to business.' Isabella had already located her name card and headed toward her designated chair next to the side-table. She didn't mind not being at the conference table with the other guests. She considered it quite appropriate. On the way to the chair, she paused to give Alexander duPonti, another friend and mentor, a warm embrace.

A few moments later General Vlado Karamus glanced across the room at Isabella, then up the table at Ramesses.

'Your Majesty ...' He had earlier been put off by the very mention of *lunch*. It had been his expectation that the meeting would be over so quickly that he had made arrangements to share a bottle of the nation's finest wine over lunch with his father to celebrate the successful completion of the first stage of their plan. Now he was further irritated by Isabella's presence. She could, of course, do no harm to him or his plans, so she was of no concern personally. However, the meeting was to be attended by the nation's highest-ranked decision-makers only. 'Has there perhaps been some oversight? Should Miss Mondeo not wait outside?'

Ramesses was flooded with a sense of relief. He had planned his opening address to include a specific reference to Isabella to justify her attendance. His concern was real: it was possible that the meeting could proceed in an atmosphere of resistance to her presence. She was, after all, still a child. Such resistance could take considerable time to wear down, if at all.

The question, and particularly because it came from General Karamus, provided Ramesses with the perfect opportunity to open his address with a direct response to start the meeting in a positive vein. He would make his guests intrigued, curious. He rose to give his opening address, the most important speech he would ever give, he thought, as he quickly improvised.

'General, and gentlemen all, rest assured this meeting would, in fact, not be taking place were it not for Isabella. My decision would otherwise more than likely have been made several days ago. Isabella has put forth some ideas – *ideals* is a better description – that were of great interest to me, and I believe we should share and discuss those ideas. I promise you they will astound you.' *There, that will whet your appetites, gentlemen. Thank you so much for your prompt, Karamus.* 'We will also discuss any other matters and opinions that you may have. Please be aware that this is literally a once-in-a-lifetime opportunity to be heard, so please feel free to speak.

'General Marcus Mondeo and Colonel Nicholas Manassis are here at my invitation. You all know General Mondeo. He might be long retired, but he remains the army's chief trainer and adviser. Together with his well-known battle experience, his knowledge of the nation's current military capabilities and its history is second to none.

'A close family friend of Marcus, Colonel Manassis is the ideal partner to assist him in our current crisis. I have assigned the colonel to be the general's liaison to keep him up to date on the minutiae of current events within the army. The colonel's adjutant, Second Lieutenant Yannis Christos, will personally carry out the colonel's orders regarding any matters arising from this and subsequent meetings. Though only a junior officer, it is vital that Yannis has first-hand knowledge and understanding of the rationale behind those orders. I have ordered that from today both will be responsible directly to Marcus, and to no-one else. If any of you should consider that normally accepted protocols have been breached, don't bother to bring them to my attention. There will be no discussion about my orders. All that matters to me is the current crisis facing our nation, and what we are going to do about it.'

The king paused to take a sip of water before continuing.

'At the conclusion of this meeting I will put the matter of the two options to the vote – that is, to defend or to surrender – to see where we stand. Please understand, gentlemen, that I have the power vested in me to overrule the result of that vote. I can rule against your vote even where it is unanimously opposed to my personal wishes.' He paused briefly again for the desired effect. 'However, hear this: it is vitally important to me that you provide me with your honest opinions before you vote. It is most likely therefore that I will agree with the wishes of the majority because I accept that the consensus is likely to reflect the wishes of the people.'

The king indicated the scribes. 'This meeting is of national importance and the royal scribes will therefore take notes of the proceedings. Ladies and gentlemen, the meeting is now open for discussion.'

CHAPTER 18

Ramesses cast his eyes around the table and settled on Admiral Georgeonous. 'Admiral, perhaps you would like to begin with your view, now that you've had some time to think about it.'

The admiral opened his mouth to speak, but that was as far as he got. General Karamus cut him off with a relaxed smile and a firm voice. Karamus had decided to quickly take control of the meeting.

'The Admiral has previously expressed his view, and agrees with my assessment that a naval attack is possible, but unlikely.' Karamus swiveled around to make eye contact with each man at the table. He intended to use the word *my* frequently to emphasize his status and authority. Isabella listened while he recounted military statistics discussed at an earlier meeting. Then he continued, 'My further assessment is that hostilities will be limited to a land-based assault. As commander-in-chief of the army, the defense of the nation rests on my shoulders alone. The odds against us could be as high as fifteen-to-one, so we will be heavily out-manned and out-gunned. Gentlemen, you have now heard that the commanders of the nation's navy and army are of one mind. The end result is a foregone conclusion. My army cannot resist such an overwhelming force for more than a few days.'

Karamus took a sip of water, taking his time to quietly replace the glass on the table. A few moments of silence would allow his audience to absorb his summation. He felt empowered. His father would be proud of him, he thought, as he moved in for his master-stroke.

Ramesses also took a sip of water, mostly to allow his fury to subside. He knew what was coming.

Karamus sat up straight, a confident smile on his face. 'It is therefore obvious that all that remains is to vote on the matter before us. I propose that we now take a vote and that the vote be for the option that is the only viable and practical one: unconditional surrender. Those in favor: I ask that you raise your hand.' Karamus lifted his hand off the table only slightly, and then stopped, the movement cunningly designed to prompt others to follow suit and raise their hands all the way. The general did not want it recorded that his was the first hand to be raised.

The men looked at each other and appeared to be about to vote.

Isabella, who had earlier taken a sip of water and set her glass down quietly so as not to disturb the others, took another sip and slammed the glass back onto the side table with a crash that brought a stunned silence to the room.

'Oh, sorry about that,' she said softly, and smiled innocently. 'By the way, I believe that everyone has forgotten about me.'

Ramesses moved to take back control of the meeting. He slammed his open palm onto the table, the slap almost as loud as Isabella's glass had sounded. 'Indeed we have, Isabella, indeed we have.'

Ramesses rose, turned, and spoke quietly to the two scribes. 'You may disregard the following until I reconvene the meeting.' He then turned to address his guests.

'Perhaps I did not make myself clear earlier. In my opening address I set out the meeting's agenda. So that there will be no further misunderstanding, I will restate that agenda. It is this: we will each voice our thoughts, ideas and suggestions, and no one should feel intimidated. I will then submit to you the ideas put forward by Isabella that we will then discuss. At the conclusion of discussions of *all* ideas and options, we will take a vote. The vote will be the *last* item to take place, not the *first*. Is that clear?'

Without waiting for an answer, Ramesses turned to the scribes and nodded that they could re-commence taking notes. He then looked across and nodded his thanks to Isabella, who sat white-faced with fury. He could see clear signs of the water that had spilled from her glass and down one side of her cotton dress. The king sat down and smiled at the admiral. 'Now then, Admiral, let's start again, shall we? Do you have anything you would like to add to what General Karamus kindly advanced on your behalf?'

'Ah … no, thank you, Your Majesty. I can't disagree from a military point of view, but I would like to hear other opinions before I vote.'

'Thank you, Admiral. Marcus? To save time, you may speak on behalf of Nicholas and Yannis.'

General Mondeo glanced around the table, and then directed his comments to Admiral Georgeonous. 'I agree with you, Admiral, other than a subtle point of difference. I submit that the enemy's certain heavy losses from a naval attack will be unacceptable to them, both militarily and politically, and will therefore not happen.'

Several of those at the table leaned forward and stared at Marcus. He had their full attention. Karamus' face had been dark with fury since Isabella had destroyed his moment within seconds of success. He stared at the table-top without blinking.

'I agree with what you say, Marcus, but tell me about this *subtle difference*,' the admiral asked with a friendly smile.

Marcus nodded and continued. 'The Northern Region has its own domestic problems. They have serious public health issues as we also have. In addition, they have the ongoing threat from England. They will have to retain all of their navy and at least half their army to guarantee security from both England and their own citizens. We can actually consider reassigning some naval personnel to the army. I estimate that we have up to two years to retrain those men. It's therefore likely that the enemy's number will be less than previously estimated, and ours could be greater. The odds remain daunting, but it does mean that we could hold out for weeks rather than days.'

The admiral nodded. 'Could we further increase our number by approaching our allied nations within our own Region, General?'

'Not a bad thought, Admiral, but I believe it would be counterproductive. If we request troops from our allied nations, we would have to disclose the reason for our request. That information is sure to get back to the Northern commanders. Our main strength at the moment is the element of surprise. I believe we're better off to retain that element at the price of being undermanned. Even with additional allied troops we would still be grossly undermanned – perhaps not ten or fifteen to one, but enough to make little difference to the end result. The point is that only the element of surprise gives us an edge. I'm afraid we're on our own.'

Marcus sat back in his seat; there was nothing more to say.

The admiral rubbed his face and ran his fingers through his sparse hair before addressing the head of the table. 'Sir, what Marcus says makes a lot of sense. If the navy can help in any way to defend the nation, let it be recorded that he has my support, and that of every man under my command. My men will be up there in the hills and mountains fighting alongside the army. And so will I, Your Majesty.'

Ramesses rose, walked over to stand next to the admiral and extended his hand. 'It probably won't come to that, Admiral, but let it also be recorded that you have my personal thanks for your courage and loyalty.' They shook hands and Ramesses returned to his seat. He seemed emotional and fidgeted with his glass for a few moments before he looked at Marcus.

'Thank you, Marcus. That does make sense. It was well reasoned and food for thought. Now then, Dmitri, what say you, my friend?'

'I can't disagree with anything that's been said so far. There's not yet enough on the table for me to make a decision, but there is one thing, though. I'm not overly excited about the idea of offering an unconditional surrender as our very first response. We should perhaps commence with providing the enemy with a list of proposals, guarantees of safety, concessions and the like. Would we not be better off to negotiate and come away with *something*? I see an unconditional surrender as a last resort, not a first.'

Oh no, you don't, Karamus thought. *An unconditional surrender is the only way the enemy is going to give me what I want.* 'May I say, Your Majesty,' he began, forcing himself to sound relaxed, friendly, 'that the enemy will accept an unconditional surrender as an act of good faith? Anything less will have them storming through our gates with their swords swinging and their cannons blasting us back to the Stone Age.

'In regard to the admiral's kind offer to bolster my troops: thank you for your generosity, Admiral, but I'm afraid I must decline. Fifteen-to-one or ten-to-one – so what? One week of battle, or ten? It's obvious that the longer a battle lasts, the greater will be our casualties. The end result won't change. I'm sorry, Your Majesty, but I cannot condone or authorize such unnecessary slaughter of my men.'

'It is not for you to authorize, General. That, unfortunately, is my responsibility.' Having cut him off, Ramesses turned his attention to the senators.

'And what does our good government have to say about all of this?'

The senators, some on each side of the long table, leaned toward each other and conferred briefly in low voices, their heads swiveling back and forth before Ishmael looked up the table at Ramesses. 'Your Majesty, as Senator Trellinis noted at a previous meeting, we are of the opinion that the matter is a military one.' He glanced at Karamus with a smirk and undisguised dislike. 'We are also of one mind that it is not appropriate for us to offer opinions in that regard. We will, however, be pleased to contribute by way of debate on any matter other than military, and we will then cast our vote based on all of the facts placed before us.'

'Thank you, Ishmael. That makes sense. We might now –'

'I beg your pardon, Your Majesty, if I might just add something else?'

'Of course, of course, Ishmael. Please feel free to speak your mind.'

Ishmael flicked his eyes briefly at Karamus' darkening face, then back at Ramesses. He looked like a cat with a bowl of warm cream. 'Your Majesty, I must say that in your opening address you piqued our interest. You said that this meeting would not have taken place if not for Isabella. That was a very big statement to make. We know you well enough, sir, to know that you would not have said that if you did not truly believe it to be of vital importance. Quite frankly, Isabella's reputation precedes her and we are anxious to hear what she has to say.'

At last! Ramesses was elated. 'Thank you, Ishmael. I was just about to arrange that. It is indeed appropriate to now turn our attention to what Isabella brings to the table.'

Ramesses rose and smiled at the young girl. 'Speaking of table, Isabella, I will arrange for lunch to be served on it, after which you will take my place at the head of the table. I will find a seat down the other end and listen to you with the others. You will have the floor to yourself.'

It did not seem possible that General Karamus' face could darken further, but it did.

CHAPTER 19

At the exact time King Ramesses and his guests commenced their lunch, General Maurice Von Franckel made his way through the streets in the northern half of Europe to Café Roberto for lunch. Out of uniform, he had to push his way through the crowded streets like everyone else, and lost considerable time in the process. He reached a crossroad, paused, and looked about as if lost. He wasn't. After such a cold night it had turned out to be a surprisingly warm day and he knew it would not look out of place to take his time to remove his jacket and wipe his brow. As he did, his eyes swept over the people hurrying in all directions as far as the eye could see. All clear. He turned east, and continued at a quicker pace.

He had called a meeting of his generals and a select few of the officers to give them their first taste of things to come. He had insisted that the proprietor, Roberto Callandro, a recent Spanish immigrant with a passion for fine food, close the café to other patrons for the entire day. The army was generous in its compensation where generals were concerned, and Roberto promised to provide a lunch and dinner to be remembered.

The streets were a hive of activity as the general fought his way through the thousands of vendors selling everything from the cheapest quality sandals to the finest silks. In his haste to make up lost time, he did not notice the squat middle-aged woman pushing her way along the streets with a basket of squawking chickens on her shoulder. The woman eventually made a quick sale to a heavily bearded man wearing a common head-scarf and robes. The man waited a few seconds before he set off in the same direction as the general. He soon exchanged the chickens for a basket of fruit, and then continued his journey.

Von Franckel reached his destination, stopped and looked around for anything unusual. Satisfied, he entered the café, where an excited Roberto waited to greet him. 'Your guests have been seated and my people are about to bring out the first course, a masterpiece created especially for you, General Von Franckel,' he enthused with a wide smile.

'Thank you, Roberto, you're a good man.' The general could hear the hum of small talk just beyond the entry, and the pleasant smells of garlic and other delicacies wafted his way as he headed towards his men. The dining area went quiet and the men rose as one as soon as he entered the room.

Von Franckel acknowledged them with a nod as he made his way to a chair placed where he could address the room. He remained standing as he motioned for his guests to be seated. 'Gentlemen,' he began as soon as the room quietened, 'enjoy yourselves, and remember: no talk of business until after lunch has been consumed. The staff, including Roberto, will then leave the premises and we will have the place to ourselves. After our meeting I will send for Roberto, who will arrange for dinner to be prepared. You will be allowed a small amount of wine or mead with lunch, but none with dinner. I want no loose tongues after we leave. I assure you all that loose tongues will be an ingredient in Roberto's next masterpiece.'

A subdued chuckle rippled the room. The officers were fully aware that the general's threat, though veiled with humor, would be carried out without hesitation.

Roberto had not exaggerated: each course of the lunch was indeed a masterpiece. By the end, the officers had the feeling of being part of an important, select group and were looking forward to sharing the general's secret.

Chimney-sweeps were a common sight on rooftops throughout the city, particularly at this time of year. As the spring weather warmed, it became time to clean out the winter's thick deposits. There were hundreds of men moving about the rooftops of the linked buildings at any given time, and one more chimney-sweep earlier that day did not raise eyebrows. Narrow bridges joined the roofs where buildings were separated by streets and alleys below. An elderly, stooped man, his clothing black with soot and with a face to match, slowly shuffled his way from rooftop to rooftop. He held his tools in one hand, a slip of paper in the other, wandering in an irregular pattern as if searching for a particular residence. He knew exactly where he was headed, however, but he took his time.

When he reached the target building, he moved quietly past the clothes-drying ropes and headed straight for the hatch that led to a laundry wash-room in the level above Café Roberto's kitchen and dining areas. As soon as he closed the hatch behind him he was no longer stooped, looking considerably younger than just minutes earlier.

He removed his sandals and slowly made his way to a small storeroom next to the washroom, quickly finding what he was looking for. All cafés with large dining areas had at least one. A louvered hatch had been installed to allow the body-heat from the diners to escape. The man removed a length of clean cloth hidden under his clothing, folded it several times, placed it under his head and made himself comfortable. He would not move, eat or drink until sunrise, when he would leave the same way he had arrived, again mingling with the chimney-sweeps doing their morning rounds. Until then he had only one thing to do: *listen and learn.*

CHAPTER 20

Isabella watched closely as the palace staff cleared the table of the lunch remnants, refilled the water jugs and placed a clean glass in front of each guest. She took particular note of the angle of the sun as it cascaded through the bay doors and across the top end of the conference table, and calculated how long she could make use of the sunshine before it moved on across the room. *I need to be at the head of the table within three minutes,* she thought, as she willed the staff out through the double doors. The doors closed thirty seconds later. The men returned to their seats. *Perfect.*

As the men settled into the chairs, Isabella took a few moments to adjust her carefully planned appearance. She quickly removed the colorful hair band and used her fingers to fluff up her hair which she had deliberately washed that morning. It had already taken on a new luster as it fell in soft near-white waves over her ears, framing her face. The cotton dress consisted of a thin, transparent outer layer stitched over a heavy second layer of bleached cotton. Apart from her sandals, she was a picture of pure white from head to toe. She sat quietly waiting for the king to speak. She was ready.

Ramesses pulled up a chair next to Ishmael near the far end of the table and looked across the room to Isabella. 'Gentlemen, now that we are refreshed, we can fully focus on the final phase of our meeting. I think you will find it … m-m-m, most illuminating. Isabella, the floor is yours, my dear.' He sat back and smiled, not realizing just how illuminating it would prove to be.

Isabella stood, turned, and made her way across the room towards the top end of the conference table. On the way she took time to reflect on the two powers she knew she had. She had been aware of both since her earliest memories. Like all girls she had been born with a basic instinct, a built-in perception of the giving and receiving of affection. She had realized from a very young age the power she had over men, particularly older men. She had found that a kiss on the cheek given with genuine affection was returned tenfold. Isabella was aware of being in possession of the most powerful force in the universe: the power of love, which was a thousand times stronger than the power of hate.

She thought about her other power: her eyes. She had always been aware of the reaction in others as they gazed into her oversized and striking eyes. Her eye pigmentation was not unique, but it was the intensity that fascinated people. During the meeting, Isabella had deliberately sat with her back against the bright windows, to throw her face into shadow. Now, as she approached the top of the table, she kept her face low and her eyes downcast.

She had judged the angle of her short walk to arrive two or three paces past the end of the table, just beyond the beam of sunlight that crossed the room. The light had not been foreseen, but she intended to take full advantage of it. In a smooth movement, she turned and stepped forward into the brilliant beam of light. It first penetrated the loose-fitting outer layer of cotton to then settle on the thick inner layer, making it appear she was shimmering and glowing from within. The beam of light made her hair sparkle and glow around her pale face like a silver halo.

Isabella placed her fingertips lightly on the table and slowly raised her face. At the same time she opened her eyes to their fullest extent and deliberately looked briefly at each man at the table. The complete sweep of the table took no more than three or four seconds. To her right sat her grandfather, next Uncle Nicho, Yannis, General Karamus, the king; Ishmael, and some senators. On her immediate left sat Dmitri, and then the admiral, Trellinis and the remaining senators. She felt, as well as saw, the instant effect she had on them. As she opened her mouth to speak, she caught her breath as she felt for the first time a *third* power suddenly surge through her body – the power that had surged out of her mother and into her own young body as her mother clung desperately to her on the day of her father's death. Isabella knew then that she had an inner power when she was *needed*. She had no inkling then just how many times that power would be relied upon by so many in the years ahead. It was the power that was to become her greatest ally.

The king misinterpreted her hesitation. 'It's fine, Isabella,' he said. 'No need to be nervous. Just take your time.'

Isabella smiled warmly at the king as she prepared to speak.

·

King Ramesses had indeed misinterpreted Isabella's momentary hesitation. He had caught his breath when she had moved into the light and swept her enormous green eyes around the table. It was as if a white angel with glowing hair and eyes had materialized out of the sunbeam and was about to address them. Her hesitation brought him back to reality and made him wonder if he had made a mistake in the general strategy for this part of the meeting. Despite the apparition before him, he realized that Isabella was in fact just a child, and he hoped that she had the fortitude to follow through. Perhaps, he thought, it would have been better if he had arranged for Dmitri to inform the meeting of the matters raised by her, and to then put those matters to debate. He knew that option was no longer open to him, and he had to be content with crossing his fingers.

Marcus Mondeo looked at his granddaughter with both pride and disbelief. He could not recognize her as the girl he knew. She glowed like a candle, calm and mature. Her eyes blazed in the sunbeam like emeralds caught in a fire. He knew her well enough to know that she had stage-managed her appearance, and he was close enough to her to feel the energy and confidence that radiated from her. He had no doubt that she knew exactly what she was doing by transforming herself into an image of the angel of mercy.

As he gazed at his niece, Nicholas Manassis could not help thinking of his sister, Anna-Karina, the acknowledged beauty of her time, pursued by every eligible bachelor throughout the Southern Region and beyond. Eventually it had been a handsome young seaman, Anton Mondeo, son of Marcus, who had won her heart. Nicholas had not noticed it before, but now he saw before him two persons: the slight young girl who was his niece, and an angelic young woman desperate to escape the confines of a body no longer adequate for her needs. It was the shimmering image of the emerging young woman that reminded him of his sister, except that this image was, unbelievably, even more striking. His eyes watered as it dawned on him that Isabella was undoubtedly destined to eclipse her mother. Spellbound, he could not wait for her to speak.

General Vlado Karamus, on the other hand, looked at her and saw not just an angel – he saw the angel of death. Every time he had thought he was in control of the meeting, it had been snatched away. Now, control had instead been placed in the hands of this girl. As her eyes moved smoothly from person to person around the table, she made eye contact with him. It was a fleeting moment only, but seemed longer than with the others at the table. A powerful jolt, a charge like lightning, cut through his chest and heart as he felt the icy tentacles of fear spread throughout his body. He wanted nothing more than for this angel of death to go back to where she came from: *hell!*

Yannis Christos was mesmerized. He had seen her in action at her plateau home and knew what she was capable of. He had been on the receiving end of her sharp tongue and her even sharper footwork. Isabella was fearless, he realized. Nicholas had been correct: she was not to be underestimated. He now looked at her pale face and silver halo as her extraordinary eyes swept the table. When her eyes met his for a fleeting moment, powerful feelings swirled and confused his mind: admiration, apprehension and the first hint of fear of her extraordinary power and where it might lead. He was still trying to interpret the nervous tension that had settled in the pit of his stomach when the king interrupted his thoughts.

'It's fine, Isabella,' he said. 'No need to be nervous. Just take your time.'

Isabella smiled warmly at the king as she prepared to speak.

CHAPTER 21

General Von Franckel smiled warmly as he prepared to speak, giving Roberto the pre-arranged signal for him and his staff to vacate the premises. The dining room went deathly quiet. The officers knew they were about to hear something unexpected. They were not disappointed.

The general rose and looked around the room. 'Time for business, gentlemen. I'll get straight to the point. None of this is for discussion with anyone – *ever!* Is that absolutely clear?' He paused momentarily before he continued. 'Consider yourselves to be on a war footing, gentlemen!'

No-one made a sound; their body language said it all. They hunched forward, their eyes shining with excitement. This was what army officers lived for, and what their minions died for. The general continued with his version of the war plan, the approximate timetable, and some of the reason for secrecy. When he finished he slowly paced up and down and looked at his men while they digested the information. As he moved about the room, he touched shoulders here and there to stimulate the feeling of comradeship. 'Questions?' he asked as he continued to pace.

'Why such a high level of secrecy, sir?' one of the first officers asked.

'We don't want the South to get wind of it in case they decide to build up their defenses. The weaker they are, the more likely they will submit without a fight.'

'I rather fancy a bit of a fight, to tell you the truth,' said General Thorsen, rubbing his hands with relish.

'Actually, I'm right with you there, General,' said Von Franckel, 'and I know all of you feel the same.' He smiled as his eyes swept the room; he had won them over by acknowledging their willingness to engage the enemy. He finished pacing and returned to stand behind his chair. 'However,' he said, 'the emperor prefers to secure the target without resorting to battle and risking heavy casualties, if at all possible. Domestic politics, yes?'

'Yes, pity that,' Thorsen said, with an exaggerated sigh. 'Sir, how are we going to keep it quiet? This is shaping up to be one of the biggest military actions of all time. We'll have soldiers swarming over the countryside like ants.'

'Good question, General. It won't be easy, and we might well be found out before we reach the target. By the time we hit the road we will be so powerful, armed and organized, it will be too late for them to do much about it, anyway, so it might not matter. But, obviously, the longer we can keep it secret, the better. Divisions will head off in different directions and at different times. The plan will be to couch it as a series of military exercises. The divisions will meet up nearer the target before they line up for the assault. That's when we present our declaration of war. Their response is pretty much a foregone conclusion.'

'What about other nations where we encroach into their territory during the march?' one of the generals asked.

'Emissaries will travel ahead and explain that we present no threat.'

'They might not believe that, sir.'

Von Franckel chuckled good-naturedly. 'You're right, but when they see a big portion of two hundred thousand soldiers with two thousand cannons march past their front door, and not through it, I guarantee they will choose to believe whatever we tell them.'

That brought a loud cheer from the men, as well as a round of applause.

Von Franckel decided to capitalize on their enthusiasm. He put a serious look on his face. 'Now hear this, and listen carefully.' He paused until he had their full attention. 'The southerners are known to be fearless in battle, and they have thousands of years of experience. There *is* a chance, however, that their total lack of *intelligence* – here he chuckled at the laughter and table-thumping that greeted his remark – 'will lead them to make a tactical mistake by putting up some resistance.' He assumed an exaggeratedly sad look. 'In that event, I guess we will just have to test our new weapons and teach them a lesson – or two. So, just in case, be prepared for battle, gentlemen!'

That brought another cheer, followed by a round of applause and more table-thumping.

The general waited for the din to die down before addressing one of the officers. 'Cicero, Roberto is at the tavern across the street. Let him know we're now ready for his next presentation of culinary magic, would you?'

CHAPTER 22

Isabella smiled warmly at the king and her audience.

'Your Majesty, gentlemen, the military implications of the looming conflict have been discussed in detail among you today, and previously. You have discussed numbers and weaponry of both armies, the possibilities, the probabilities, a three-day conflict or three weeks, potential casualties and final result. The decision you will make today on behalf of our nation will be vital. The effect of that decision will be the most important that our nation will ever face. It is a decision that will be forced upon the people of today, and upon future generations for perhaps a thousand years to come. The military issue is only one *half* of what we should consider. For just a few minutes I ask that you clear your minds of military considerations – disregard them as if they don't matter – so that ...'

A loud sigh of disbelief came from General Karamus, accompanied by a slow shake of his head.

'...so that you can consider without bias the *other* half: the national interest.'

A few of the senators looked at each other, murmured among themselves, and nodded.

'The nation belongs to the people and, rightly or wrongly, I believe our nation belongs to some more than to others. You must consider not just the current and past generations, but also those of the future. How will those future generations view our nation? With national pride? Or will it be with shame and despair?' Isabella paused for a sip of water. The pause was deliberate.

'Something that I said to Grandfather the other day is worth repeating. I told Grandfather – and Uncle Nicho, come to think of it – that our nation does not belong to either of them. With respect, Your Majesty, I believe that this nation does not fully belong to you or most of the others in this room, either, because you could be viewed as the past generation. I believe the nation belongs more to the current generation. Yannis and I belong to the *current* generation. We are the current *and* future generations, as are those yet to be born. As I said to Grandfather, you are *the keepers* and we are *the inheritors*. I am, therefore, the person here today to represent current and future generations. Your decision will affect my generation and all of those to come.'

Isabella thought of some of the methods her tutors had used to teach her, including Alexander duPonti, who now sat just a few paces to her left. The tutors would *throw her a bone* as a challenge, fully aware that she would conduct in-depth research and return with a bone full of meat. Isabella now intended to use the same tactic on those before her. She looked down at the end of the conference table where King Ramesses sat quietly, listening with interest.

'Your Majesty, my readings have taught me that the present is built on lessons from the past, and therefore our future will be built on the lessons of today. Our national pride is built entirely on our history. We have survived countless wars for thousands of years. We are as proud of the wars and battles we have lost as we are of those we have won.' Isabella turned her gaze to the far end of the table, where the senators were listening intently. She realized it was the senators who would ultimately determine the outcome of the meeting.

'Even if it were accepted that eventual defeat is a probability, is it not better for the people to hold their heads high with pride, rather than to hang their heads in shame? To submit, or surrender, without a fight will doom our nation to eternal shame. If we fight, we might be defeated but we will *never* be conquered. Pride will ultimately lead to the redemption and resurrection of our people.'

The bone was on the table. Isabella picked up her glass and waited to see who would pick it up. It was time to begin the debate, and then move in for the kill – *the third option*.

'I'm glad this has been brought up.' Ishmael leaned forward and looked up and down the table. 'I've been agonizing over this very question for weeks, and so have some of my colleagues. Isabella is correct; we celebrate as many battles lost as those won. It is a part of who we are today, our culture. Your Majesty, it is vital that we consider the effect of national interest irrespective of the ultimate outcome of a confrontation.'

'Well, Ishmael, we already know the outcome. That's inevitable,' Karamus said with a smirk.

Isabella placed her glass gently on the table and said softly, 'With respect, General Karamus, I cannot accept the word *inevitable*. I believe nothing is proven *inevitable* until *after* the event.'

'Well, you can believe it this time!'

One of the other senators spoke for the first time. 'If we don't put up at least some resistance, the public might see us as a bunch of cowards, General, both the government as well as the armed forces. We might never be forgiven.'

'You might also not be forgiven for sending ten or twenty thousand soldiers to their deaths. If my troops had to face off against the enemy forces we now speak of, they would take one look at their number and their cannons, throw down their weapons and make a run for it.' The general's voice was rising, frustrated and angry. He felt a knot forming in his stomach, the earlier fear now spreading like fire throughout his limbs. This was not how the meeting was supposed to go.

'I believe you're underestimating your soldiers, General.' It was the king's turn to sound angry.

One of the senators muttered something inaudible to those nearby. Ramesses turned to him immediately. 'What was that, Senator?'

'I'm sorry, Your Majesty. I was just mumbling to myself.'

'Well, let us all hear your mumbling, Vincenzo,' said the king, chuckling. The tension eased immediately.

'It was nothing important, sir. I was just thinking aloud.'

'Think a little louder, please.' A ripple of laughter swept the table.

Isabella remained silent and observed. The bone had been picked up and everyone was having a bite.

'Well, I was thinking about something Isabella said earlier: *we might be defeated but we will never be conquered*. I'm not a soldier but I can imagine soldiers thinking something like that as they face their enemy and almost certain death. Is it not a case that *man might be mortal but pride lives forever?*'

Dmitri nodded his head slowly, as did others. Another senator was emboldened enough to rise to his feet and speak for the first time. 'Yes, well said, Vincenzo. I agree. Without pride we are nothing as a people, are we?' He looked around nervously and sat down.

Karamus was furious. He knew he would make a fool of himself if he spoke, so he chose to remain silent.

'Could we perhaps draw up plans for a defense strategy,' asked Ishmael, 'and consider the implications before making a decision?' He glanced around the table for support.

'I will assist in any way I can in that regard,' the admiral said with enthusiasm.

'What do you think, General Karamus? How long will it take to put something together?' The king looked at Karamus, his eyebrows arched.

Karamus found his voice again and chose to ignore the question. He decided on an emotional approach to the principal decision-maker. 'The matter of your personal safety was raised just recently, Your Majesty. The risk is low if we offer surrender. However, I cannot guarantee your safety or your immediate family's if the enemy is forced to climb over mounds of their own dead to enter our nation.'

Vincenzo spoke again, sounding less nervous than earlier. 'It's not necessarily the enemy who might do you harm, Your Majesty. If you are perceived to be the one who sold your people into servitude without honor, it might be they who put you to the sword.' He looked around at the other senators. 'We might all be put to the sword.'

Ramesses' face drained of color, either from shock or anger, or both. The room was deathly silent while he regained his composure. Eventually he relaxed and looked around at his guests. 'I think that we are all getting a little tired. Perhaps we should adjourn and reconvene the meeting tomorrow?'

That is just not going to happen, Your Majesty. Sorry. Isabella was satisfied that the bone had been chewed to the point of exhaustion and turned toward Colonel Manassis. 'Uncle Nicho?' Nicholas looked up and saw the fire in her eyes blazing brighter than ever. Her voice was a little louder, intense. 'Are you prepared to die for your nation, Uncle Nicho?' The posture of the seated men changed instantly; they sensed a dramatic change in the direction of the meeting.

'Of course, Isabella, without hesitation. It is a soldier's duty.'

Isabella turned to her right and moved slowly along the side of the long table, past her grandfather and uncle, until she reached Yannis, and gently placed her hand on his shoulder. 'You are one of *the inheritors*, Yannis. Come, it's time for you to speak your mind.'

Yannis rose slowly, looking confused, almost panicked. Isabella took him gently by his left arm and guided him to the head of the table, where she gave his arm a gentle squeeze and let go. She moved to his right and remained by his side, almost, but not quite, touching.

Yannis looked down one side of the table, and then up the other. His eyes took in the nation's ruler, King Ramesses, the king's chief adviser, his own commanding officer, the commander-in-chief of the army, the admiral of the navy, the most senior members of parliament – and Isabella. *I'm a junior officer, what am I doing here? Please help me, Isabella.* He leaned forward slightly and placed his knuckles on the edge of the table. After a few moments he straightened, squared his shoulders and clasped his hands behind his back.

Looking at Isabella, he asked, 'What would you like me to say?'

Unseen, Isabella moved her left arm behind Yannis and gently pushed her hand in between his in a firm grip.

'This is not about me wanting you to say anything in particular, Yannis. This is about you and our nation. You have all of the people's representatives before you. It is time to let them know what is in your heart. Speak from your heart, as I did, and you'll find it easy. Tell us what is in your heart right now.'

Yannis' reaction to Isabella's hand between his changed from initial surprise to feeling a transfer of power and strength flow into him. By the time she had finished, he felt relaxed, strong and energized.

He smiled at her. 'Yes, of course. You're quite right, that will be easy.' As he turned to address those at the conference table, he felt the hand between his slide away. He was on his own.

'Your Majesty, ladies and gentlemen, there are indeed a few things I would like to say. Like everyone here I have given thought to the two options of *defend* or *surrender*. Speaking for myself first, I can say that even if I faced an enemy with odds against me of a *thousand* to one, I would choose to die with dignity and pride, rather than to surrender and live in shame. Speaking for my men, I don't have that many under my direct command, but I can confidently say that they also would choose to fight to the death.' Yannis looked towards General Karamus, certain that his career in the army was at an end.

'We have fought, won and lost,' he continued, 'for thousands of years. I do not intend to stand down now. If we are forced to submit to foreign occupation, I will join – or form, if necessary – a resistance force. I pledge my life to be a part of an eventual uprising that will kick the foreigners back to where they came from, just as we have in the past. That comes directly from my heart, and I thank you for listening.'

Karamus was furious. *Just you wait, Second Lieutenant, you'll fly off the cliff right behind Ramesses. You too, Miss Mondeo. You can hold hands with the king as you make your leap to dignity and glory – and sharks.* The vision made him feel considerably better.

Yannis was about to turn away when he felt Isabella's hand return. This time she gripped the outside of his hands. She gave a firm squeeze and then he felt her index finger press sharply twice. After a moment's pause, a third press. This time he understood her message instantly: three! The *three options*. Isabella wanted the matter to be raised as a response to a question. He gave her an almost imperceptible nod and returned to his seat.

'Brilliantly said. Thank you so much, Yannis.' Ramesses beamed. 'You are a true soldier and a citizen to be proud of. This is certainly giving us a different perspective on the two options, yes?'

Yannis took his cue. He leaned forward so he could look down the table and make eye contact with the king. 'There is one more thing on my mind, Your Majesty. You just mentioned *two* options.'

'Yes, of course. What is it?' Ramesses seemed perplexed.

'I must direct my question to Isabella.' He turned his head in the opposite direction, where Isabella was again standing at the head of the table. 'A few days ago you brought up your thoughts regarding the national interest, and you asked the colonel to convey them to His Majesty.'

Isabella nodded.

'You also said that you were dismayed that no one had brought up or discussed the *third option*. I've been intrigued ever since. It must be something you actually prefer over the other two options or you would not have brought it up. You have something else in mind, don't you? What is it exactly that you propose we *really* do?'

Clever boy, Yannis, you're not just a pretty face. Beautifully introduced. I wasn't even sure if you'd get my message. 'Yes, Yannis, there is a third option, but I was beginning to think everyone was getting too tired to hear it.' There was a buzz around the table. Everyone was now fully aware of Isabella's astute mind.

'You must be insane! A *third* option?' Karamus was almost out of his seat. 'There is no such thing as a *third option*. Defend or surrender; surrender or defend. It will add up to *two* any way you say it. Two! Two! Two! The only thing I agree with Miss Mondeo is that we are too tired. I believe we should call it a day, Your Majesty. We should reconvene in a few days and just get down to vote for the only thing that makes sense.'

'On the contrary, General, I'm suddenly not tired at all. Is anyone else tired?' the king asked as he looked up and down the length of the table. All shook their heads, with the exceptions of General Karamus and Senator Trellinis.

Ramesses looked into Isabella's eyes and felt as intimidated by them as everyone else in the room. He expected to detect some nervousness, but she appeared calm, composed, and in full control. He suddenly felt as if he were about to be punched in the stomach. When he finally spoke, his voice was strained.

'So, what is this *third option*? What is it that you propose we should *really* do, my dear?'

It was Isabella's turn to take a pace forward and place her knuckles on the conference table. She looked slowly up and down the table, leaned forward and uttered the one word they least expected.

'*Attack!*'

CHAPTER 23

There were several seconds of shocked silence before pandemonium erupted. A combination of gasps and *what?* moved around the table before Ramesses jumped to his feet, his face ashen.

'Did we hear you correctly? Did you actually say *attack?*'

'Yes, you did hear me correctly, sir.'

'All right, all *right!*' He waved his arms about. 'Everyone calm down, please.' Color returned to his face. He waited a few more moments while the room quietened. Finally he smiled. 'It seems we are all now fully awake, Isabella, and I can confidently say that you have our full attention.'

Karamus' face and body were frozen. *This can't be happening to me. This is going from bad to worse. Next, she'll have me on horseback charging into enemy lines. Father, you should have warned me about this girl. I thought she was a child. She's not a child – she's a monster!*

Marcus and Nicholas sat open-mouthed. They both stared at Isabella, not fully comprehending what they had just heard. Marcus felt his stomach churn; perhaps he had made a mistake to bring her to the meeting. Perhaps she was just an ordinary child after all, a child who did not really comprehend what she was saying. But he knew it was already too late. There was nothing he could do or say. He could only wait to see what was about to unfold.

Yannis looked at Isabella and smiled. She caught his gaze and smiled back. By then, Yannis was as relaxed as Isabella appeared to be. He had quickly recognized an intellect well beyond his own and doubted he would ever again be surprised at what Isabella said or did. He liked what he had just heard.

'Could you please elaborate, Isabella?' Ramesses asked. 'Tell us the logic behind your proposal.'

Isabella got directly to the point. 'It was important that you first considered the implications of at least a limited defensive military action. You have now done so and that idea has not been dismissed. That means we can move on to consider the third option, which is also a military option, but with a considerable difference, and with many advantages.'

Isabella paused briefly for the benefit of the scribes. She took a sip of water before she continued. 'The enemy does not know what we know. That advantage gives us the upper hand once only, and there is not a moment to waste. We therefore have two years, perhaps more, to plan the attack, to train the men, to improve and manufacture weaponry, and to improve the supply chain. Irrespective of the ultimate outcome, the national pride will surge tenfold if we stun the enemy by launching an attack. The ultimate outcome will without question be superior to one of defense.'

'That's true,' interjected Ishmael. 'Two years of advance knowledge is an immense advantage. It could work!' His excitement was infectious. Several heads were nodding in agreement.

Karamus found his voice again. Military strategy was not his strongest point, but it was certainly strong enough to outmaneuver a child. He began to relax. 'If we were to attack hundreds of thousands of enemy troops entrenched on our border, who were armed with an unknown number of cannons, my army would be annihilated, possibly without us inflicting a single casualty upon the enemy. Our casualties would actually be far higher than if we were defending.'

'You are quite correct, General, if we attacked under those circumstances.'

'What other circumstances can there possibly be?'

'We attack *before* they entrench themselves and line up their cannons.'

Karamus groaned in frustration and despair. 'You have forgotten something, just a tiny little something.' His voice rose. 'The enemy will surround us, entrench themselves, line up their cannons and light the fuses *before* – I say again, *before*, Miss Mondeo – they present us with their declaration of war. There is a little thing called timing in military strategy. Why are we having this conversation, Your Majesty?'

Ramesses suspected that *battle* and *attack* were Karamus' two most feared words. The king had no idea where Isabella was headed, but he was starting to enjoy himself at the expense of Karamus' growing fear. He ignored the general's question.

'Please go on, Isabella. You have our interest. Most of us, anyway,' Ramesses added with more of a smirk than a smile.

'If the enemy arrived on our doorstep and presented us with their declaration, it would indeed be folly to attack. You are, of course, quite correct, General Karamus.'

'Well, there you are, then.'

'However, if the circumstances were drastically changed, then so too would the strategy. Wouldn't you agree?' Isabella allowed her eyes to pass over the faces around the table to indicate that the question was not put to Karamus alone. By then, almost all the guests were leaning forward on their elbows, nodding their heads and conferring briefly in soft voices.

Senator Trellinis had been quiet for a long time. He had a resigned expression on his face, the look of one defeated. 'And what circumstance do you propose to change, Miss Mondeo?' Only he and Karamus called her by that name.

'Like so many solutions, Senator Trellinis, it is actually surprisingly simple,' she answered, smiling gently and again leaning forward on her knuckles. '*We* declare war on the Northern Region!' she said quietly.

'We *what?*' We declare war on the Northern Region?' General Karamus was aghast.

'That is correct, sir. And then we immediately attack them!'

CHAPTER 24

'How do you propose we declare war on the Northern Region, Miss Mondeo? Send a rider out to them with a message before they send their rider in to us?'

'Not at all, General. They won't know we are there until the last moment.'

'I'm afraid you have now lost me.'

'I'm sorry, General. I do understand. I'm sure I have lost everyone at this point because I haven't yet explained it.'

'Please explain, Isabella.' Ramesses was fascinated.

'The Northern Region has made a very specific plan of attack. We know they have already commenced that plan. They are recruiting and spending money on the supply chain, weapons and the like. They are fully committed to that plan and will be stuck with it for years. We have studied *that* plan and our responses so far, gentlemen, reflect only *that* plan. Do you all follow me so far?'

Everyone nodded their head, including Karamus and Trellinis, she noted with surprise.

She continued her assault. 'We can now focus on what we are able to do while we have the upper hand. The Northern Region does not know that we know of their plan. They therefore do not know that we can take their plan *and reverse it.*' She heard some breaths being drawn. 'Reversing their plan means they do not come to us – *we* go to them. Reversing their plan means they don't declare war on us – *we* declare war on them. Reversing their plan means they don't attack us on our doorstep – *we* attack them on their doorstep. Well, not quite on their doorstep. That would allow them to draw on their home-based army reserves. We wait for them to travel from home base for a number of weeks, or months, depending on weather conditions. That will disconnect them from their reserves and supply chain.

'We select the site to engage them and prepare that area. At the appropriate time *we* present *them* with a declaration of war and give them the choice of standing down and returning to home base, which they won't do, of course, but convention requires us to give them the opportunity, or to engage in immediate battle on the chosen site. That will be on *our* chosen site and not theirs. Our attack will last for a short time only. We obviously could not sustain an extended assault against their overwhelming number. We then withdraw and issue another challenge to battle at another site. We attack and withdraw, attack and withdraw, all the way back to our border. I assure you they will be thoroughly sore and sorry by the time they arrive here. Their casualties by then might just be so high they could be more concerned about their home politics than they are about us. That is the strategy for the actual war; the strategy for the actual battles is General Karamus' forte, and for him to plan.'

'I love it!' It was Admiral Georgeonous. 'I absolutely love it, Isabella. Brilliant! That is naval strategy at its best, Your Majesty. Strike first, strike unexpectedly and strike hard, and then disappear to strike on another day! We have won battles in the past against far superior ships and numbers doing exactly that! That plan has my full support, sir. Count me in to help in any way I can.'

'I agree,' said Ishmael. He rose to his feet in his excitement. 'Isabella is correct. If it is we who declare war and have the courage to attack the enemy time and again, the nation's pride is assured for a thousand years, no matter the final outcome, as Isabella said. She is absolutely correct, sir.' He resumed his seat and added with a loud theatrical whisper, 'David and Goliath live again!'

Several conversations were underway in subdued tones. Almost all heads were nodding, even Senator Trellinis', who had forced himself to do so. *I must be careful here*, he thought. *I cannot afford to be aligned with Karamus as the only other dissenter. I know only too well why you're against everything, General, and I need to be at least one step removed from you in case things go wrong.*

Ramesses saw Trellinis nod and immediately pinned him with a direct question. 'So, Senator, what do you think? Give us your honest opinion. We would place great value on it.' Ramesses made sure Trellinis was given no room to wriggle.

'I must admit that at first I was shocked when Isabella talked about attacking and declaring war on the Northern Region,' Trellinis said, while stroking his chin. Isabella noticed the change in how he had just referred to her. 'However, when you think about it, if *we* don't declare war, they will. It will lead to a state of war either way. I agree with Isabella that if we decide on her proposal we would have a couple of years to prepare for battle rather than for defense. We can always change our minds later, if circumstances turn against us, and submit at the last moment. In the meantime it does give us a distinct advantage. We potentially, therefore, have much to gain and nothing to lose.'

Ramesses looked at Trellinis in amazement and not without some suspicion at first. He was well aware of Trellinis' allegiance to Karamus but knew that the senator was pragmatic enough to have weighed up his options. Trellinis' opinion, though forced upon him, had to be an honest one.

'Thank you, Senator. That was actually an excellent summation of the position.' He leaned across and squeezed the senator's forearm to show his appreciation, which was genuine.

Isabella had to concede that Trellinis had made valid points. She also noted, without looking directly at him, that Karamus had slumped in his seat. He had just lost his only supporter.

Ramesses turned towards the head of the table. 'Well, Isabella! You are a surprise package, aren't you? What do you have for us next? I have a feeling the meeting is heading towards a close. Should we come back for more talks on another day?'

'Your Majesty, further talk is no more than being *reactive* to what you – we – are facing. Yannis, would you join me again, please?'

Yannis rose at once and came to the head of the table. This time he appeared surprisingly relaxed and full of confidence. Isabella gently squeezed his elbow, let go, and stood at his right, but this time she deliberately did not touch his hands. Her heart had almost burst when her hand was between his earlier.

'Yannis, now that I've answered your question about the *third* option, and now that you have heard everyone discuss the implications of attacking the enemy again and again, do you still stand by what you said earlier? Are you prepared to die on the battlefield in defense of your nation?'

'Yes I am, more than ever,' Yannis answered without hesitation.

'Your Majesty, gentlemen, it's more than just words from Yannis alone. The army is not made up of volunteers. They are in the army because that is their life, and because they are prepared to die for their nation. They are not required to volunteer for the campaign we now speak of; they will do as ordered and do so gladly. For them, there will be glory in victory or defeat.

'However, civilians who might wish to participate – such as Grandfather, for instance – will have to volunteer. Your Majesty, I am not afraid to be a part of what I propose. Let it be recorded that I will now be the first to volunteer. I will be proud to fight on the front line. I will be proud to hold up our standard while staring down the barrels of the enemy's cannons. I will be proud to be the first casualty of war. And I will be proud to fight next to Second Lieutenant Yannis Christos.' Isabella looked up into Yannis' face. 'And to die fighting by his side.'

'Now, now, Isabella, there is no need for you to go to those extremes. You are only a child, after all.' Ramesses sounded almost fatherly.

Isabella placed her hands on her hips and leaned forward, furious, aggressive. Her mouth opened, and then closed. She realized that she was in fact a minor and had no right to argue the point with the king. She straightened, dropped her hands to her sides and relaxed. She met the king's eyes and nodded.

'Isabella, it is most kind of you to concede at least one point for the day.' Ramesses smiled at her and she smiled back.

'I would like it noted for the record, scribe, that Isabella is a child only from the neck down.'

He was rewarded with a smile accompanied by a curtsy. Yannis now seemed comfortable facing the nation's decision-makers and made no move to return to his seat.

'And I would also like it noted for the record, Your Majesty,' said Isabella with a friendly smile, 'that I will remain the first volunteer, and when the campaign begins, I will be there even if I am a stowaway on a wagon-load of horse fodder.'

'So noted,' said Ramesses with a grin. Within seconds the grin faded to a grimace. 'As Isabella has said, the time for talking has ended. The time has come to act!' He moved quickly, decisively. 'It's time for us to count the votes. Isabella, you already know that you cannot vote. Marcus, Nicholas and Yannis – you also cannot vote as you are my independent advisers. So, for the rest of you, those in favor of option three, raise your right hand.'

CHAPTER 25

Ramesses looked up and down the table for the count. There was no need to count for there was only one dissenter: General Karamus. Everyone else grinned with excitement. They felt joined by a common purpose; they were, for once, united in hope. Surprisingly, even Trellinis seemed excited, rejuvenated.

Ashen-faced, Karamus lurched forward, looking as if he were about to present a last-ditch attempt to derail the proceedings. Ramesses felt almost guilty at the perverse pleasure he knew he was about to experience. Not even Karamus would dare interrupt him once he commenced speaking.

Ramesses now turned to the chief scribe. 'Scribe, please note the following carefully: the vote is carried for option *three*, unanimous bar one: General Karamus. Also please note that I concur with that vote, so it is now carried as being authority to issue a declaration of war against the Northern Region at a date to be determined. Please record that I am proud of everyone here for their willingness to openly and honestly discuss all three options without bias, and for their vote on the most vital issue to ever face this nation.

'Please also restate, Scribe, that option three was the proposal put forward by Miss Isabella Mondeo. Isabella, your contribution and your successful debate in support of your proposal will now be recorded in the nation's official history. Whatever the outcome, there is no doubt that one day, when our secrets are revealed, your nation will be as proud of you as all of us are here today.'

Ramesses' eyes watered as he looked up at Isabella, who remained standing next to Yannis. She was finally exhausted and overwhelmed with the result of the vote and its implications, and with the king's words. Her already pale face suddenly turned deathly white and she sagged against Yannis, about to faint. Yannis sensed her predicament and quickly placed his arm around her waist to support her. Her left arm came up and around his back to grab a hold on his shirt.

Isabella's grip relaxed just as suddenly as her composure returned. She gently pushed herself away from Yannis to stand a pace apart, feeling both embarrassed and angry at herself. No more than two seconds had passed. Ramesses was still inhaling to commence his next words, the words that would give him the most pleasure of the day.

'And most of all, I am proud of *you*, General Karamus.' The general looked around, more shocked than earlier, if that were possible. 'I *congratulate* you, General.' In a deliberate move the king rose, beaming, and extended his hand to the general, who had no option other than to rise and take it. Ramesses shook his hand constantly and vigorously while he continued to speak. 'You are not only the nation's most senior commanding officer, you are the man most qualified and capable of leading this campaign on behalf of our great nation. You will have the honor of being at the head of your army as you charge at the enemy in each and every battle to come. You are a hero, General. In time you will be recognized as a hero to your nation and to your proud family. Your place in the nation's history is assured, General, even if you should be killed in one of the many battles that you will lead.' Ramesses felt elated. Isabella had presented him with one of the best moments of his life.

'Thank you, Your Majesty,' Karamus managed to whisper. 'I trust you will forgive me, but I am feeling quite unwell, so I will take my leave. Good evening, sir.' He turned and left the room without another word to anyone, including Trellinis.

Ramesses turned towards Isabella, who looked radiant again, fully recovered. 'Isabella, my dear, do you think I can persuade you away from the side of that handsome young man to come and give an old king a big hug?'

'Thank you for supporting me, Yannis, in more ways than one.' Isabella smiled and reached out to squeeze his arm.

'Does that mean that I'm safe from your savage kicks in future?'

'Oh dear, I'm afraid not. Many more of those to come, actually. Sorry.' She smiled wickedly and headed for the king as Yannis returned to his chair.

The king embraced Isabella for several moments. 'You have today given me one of the best days of my life.' He leaned down to whisper in her ear. 'By the way, you picked an excellent partner to help you present your case. In fact, I believe I might have noticed a little flush and a sparkle of interest in your eyes when you stood back to watch him speak. A splendid young man from all accounts. I believe the young Lieutenant Christos could make the perfect partner of a different kind in a few years, if you know what I mean.' He chuckled as he straightened. Isabella punched him in the chest and hugged him again, but this time it was to hide the flush that had spread over her face for the second time that day. 'By the way, tell your grandfather that I would like the two of you to remain.'

Colonel Manassis approached just as the king and Isabella flicked their eyes toward Yannis; he saw Isabella turn scarlet and punch Ramesses in the chest. Nicholas pursed his lips, changed direction and instead headed for the group of senators.

'Gentlemen,' Ramesses addressed his guests, 'no doubt you are exhausted, so please feel free to take your leave. I will send each of you a sealed message in a couple of days to advise you of our next meeting. We will then discuss how we will make an immediate start.'

The king shook hands with each man as they drifted toward the exit. He had a brief conversation with Dmitri before they shook hands and parted company. Nicholas and Yannis were next to pay their respects and depart.

Yannis had almost reached the corridor when a sixth sense caused him to look back. He was surprised to see Isabella's gaze fixed on him, and their eyes met as she gave him a small wave and a grin. He saw a face with a new maturity that briefly gave a hint of the woman to come, before she suddenly dissolved back into the young girl. Yannis smiled and nodded to her as he turned away, unaware they would not meet again for a long time. He caught up with Nicholas, and they headed back to the city and The Barracks building.

Isabella turned toward the king, who beckoned her over to where he was speaking to the scribes. Marcus was seated close by and listened to their conversation with interest.

'Isabella, the scribes will transcribe their notes to a full account of our meeting as a priority. Two additional copies will be made, one of which will be sealed and secretly delivered to one of our friendly neighbor nations for safe-keeping. That will not only ensure that your contribution is committed to history, no matter what the outcome, but it will also reveal Karamus' cowardice.'

The king turned to Marcus and Isabella as soon as the scribes had departed. 'In private I'm Ramesses to you both. That is a Royal Command. Non-compliance is punishable by ten years as a navy oarsman, a fate worse than death, I assure you. I'll have the guest rooms made up while we have an early dinner and some light conversation. Royalty does have its privileges, for sure, but it is also a lonely life on the personal side. Sophia is absolutely dying to catch up with you both. After that, I suggest an early night as there's no doubt that we are all exhausted. That was surely the most grueling day we will ever experience.'

King Ramesses had no idea just how wrong he was.

CHAPTER 26

'Father, I've just been sentenced to death!'

Theo Karamus was as shocked as his son. He had been furious that Vlado had kept him waiting for hours without having sent word of his delay. Theo had left the café in a rage, and had almost fired the manager as he left, but changed his mind at the last moment. It was his own café and the manager was the best he had had for several weeks. He had spent the remainder of the afternoon pacing his spacious office, occasionally pausing to stare out of the window in a fruitless search for his son's face among the thousands below. By the time Vlado arrived, it was dark, the wicker lights lit. He had finished one bottle of wine and was about to start the second.

His anger rapidly dissipated, replaced with dismay and fear, as he waited for Vlado to compose himself and fill him in on the catastrophic meeting. His son shivered despite the warmth of the upper level room. His face was pale, his eyes unfocused as he contemplated his fate.

Theo rubbed his lumpy nose and waited, determined not to speak first. He had considered every move and counter-move before the meeting. Vlado had merely to present his case and that was that. How could anything go wrong? Trellinis had not yet been in touch, so presumably he had been caught up in the meeting as well. Had Vlado said too much? Had he raised suspicions? Theo's stomach tightened as he thought of the potential consequences if their real plan was revealed.

'Vlado! Pull yourself together!' Theo had not intended to yell, but his rage had returned the moment he opened his mouth. 'What are you talking about? What do you mean: *I have been sentenced to death?*'

Vlado looked as if his father had just slapped his face. He finally found his voice, little more than a whisper. 'It's been decided that we will declare war on the Northern Region, and that I am to lead our army against the North.'

Theo remained silent. This time it was he who was unable to speak. The stunned look on his face was one that Vlado would treasure for the rest of his life. He felt as if, for once, he had his father firmly underfoot. He decided to enjoy the moment and chose to wait for his father to speak first.

'So, tell me about it. What happened?' Theo's voice was flat, defeated.

'*Isabella Mondeo*, that's what happened!'

'Who?'

'Isabella Mondeo. The retired general's granddaughter.'

'Oh yes, her. I've heard of her, but I've never met her. What does the girl have to do with you being sentenced to death?'

'Everything was going to plan. I had everyone in the palm of my hand.'

'Oh, just get on with it.'

'That Mondeo girl was sitting by herself at the side of the room. I can only guess that the old general brought her along for a bit of spectator sport. Just as they were about to vote for my proposal, the king asked her if she would like to say something before the vote. So she said *yes, I would like to say something, thank you very much* – and then she did!'

General Karamus related his own version of what took place. Theo was astute enough to know that he was being given a biased version and would get Trellinis to tell him what really took place. He got up from his seat and walked to the window to disguise his silent laughter as soon as his son started to recount the king's congratulations. He knew only too well how the king must have delighted in his well-chosen words.

Theo finally regained control and turned back from the window to glare at his son. He had always loved him, but had never liked him. Vlado's tall stature and good looks, inherited from his mother and in such contrast to his own short, over-indulged body, were not the only reasons he disliked his son. 'So,' he said, 'the death sentence you speak of is having to charge into the front lines of the enemy to defend your country?'

'That *Miss* Mondeo proposed a series of battles spread from one end of the continent to the other. We could be talking years. With odds of ten or fifteen to one against us, I have no chance of survival. Neither will anyone else, for that matter. Who does she think she is to speak at a meeting of the nation's decision-makers? How could that idiot Ramesses listen to her? How could anyone listen to her? Even that traitor Trellinis voted with her. I've gone down in the records as the only dissenter!'

'Calm down, Vlado, calm down. And keep your voice down. Let me think.' Theo paced the room again and thought hard and fast. *There is always a way, Theo. Success is built on adversity, and every disaster creates opportunities. Think Theo, think. Can't change the circumstances? Then change the plan!* Vlado made to speak after a while, but Theo waved him to silence. Every now and again he snapped his fingers as he paced.

He finally stopped at the window and stared into the night. The streets below were a fairyland of flickering lanterns set up by the thousands of vendors who materialized every evening as soon as the sun started to fade. The aroma of dishes from all corners of the world, together with the sounds of the men and women creating them, floated through the window to caress his senses. Suddenly, in one motion, he spun around, grabbed a chair and sat directly in front of his son. 'We have a new plan,' he said. 'Vlado, pour a couple of glasses of wine, would you?'

Vlado rose and went to the table. 'A new plan? I have to plan battles!' He picked up the bottle and poured a single glass of wine and handed it to his father. 'I feel too ill for wine.'

'Relax. You'll be fine once you hear my new plan.'

'I'm listening.'

'This could work out even better. The key to *any* plan is to make it fit the circumstances. The Northern Region fears casualties – their own, that is. Too political. Their plan is to line up on our border and seize a bloodless victory.' He wagged a finger at his son. 'Miss Mondeo actually has a good point; she has many good points, in fact. Her logic is indisputable. An unexpected attack could cause them thousands of casualties, even if they ultimately win the war. Not good for their campaign leader, not good for their government. No one likes bad news, especially if it's unexpected. Their government will probably hang their commander-in-chief for incompetence.'

'Incompetence?'

'Yes, for not anticipating the attack: bad intelligence, bad battle plan, bad anything, everything. It doesn't matter; they'll blame their commander and stretch his neck simply to be able to point the finger of blame elsewhere.'

Theo rose, glass in hand, and returned to pacing the room. 'If their commander is suddenly faced with a genuine fight on his hands, there is no doubt he will seize a golden opportunity when it presents itself on a silver platter.'

'Why not just get word to them about what is to happen?'

'Absolutely not! That would give us no leverage. And we *must* have leverage.' Theo sat down again. 'Listen carefully, you are to follow *Miss*

Mondeo's plan precisely. It will still lead to surrender, but on *our* terms.' He held up his hand as Vlado was about to protest. 'I said *listen*. The stronger your army when you face the enemy, the better. So prepare your men, the weapons, the training. Make it the most efficient and best-equipped army we have ever had. I will call a meeting of *The Inner Sanctum,* and they will agree to help. The bigger the threat to the enemy, the more their supreme commander will grab at the solution to a potential life-threatening catastrophe. Big, *big* threat and easy solution – that is the very essence of leverage, Vlado. Do you see what I'm getting at?'

'I think so, Father. But what's the solution?'

'Ah! You said you have battles to plan. Well, there you are, then. You only have to plan *one* battle, the first battle, one that will be arranged between you and your opposing commander. That battle will be little more than a skirmish, but arranged in such a way that it will force you to offer surrender. You see? Simple. You will come out of it a war hero. And best of all, my courageous son, you won't even have to draw your sword.'

'I might try some of that wine now, Father.'

CHAPTER 27

Nicholas and Yannis were well known to the duty officer who waved them through the gates at The Barracks with a smile. When they reached the colonel's office, they sat and stared at each other in silence for several moments.

Nicholas spoke first. '*Well*, Yannis!'

'Well, *Nicholas*!'

Nicholas leaned forward and lowered his voice. 'I guess the first thing we need to do is to be careful what we say and where we say it.'

Yannis nodded.

'That was some meeting, Yannis. I expected it to be interesting, but certainly not how it turned out. I'm still in shock, to be honest.'

Yannis put his head all the way back and stared at the ceiling for a moment, and then closed his eyes. 'Instead of planning for early retirement, I'm going to have to sharpen my sword and plan for an early death.'

'The joys of a soldier's life, my friend.'

'The irony is that Karamus' tactic guarantees safety and a long life.'

'That's what makes him the coward that he is.'

'I struggled to keep a straight face when His Majesty congratulated the general. I had an image of him charging the enemy front lines waving a white flag and a stick of celery instead of his sword.'

That brought a chuckle from Nicholas. 'Karamus will send the female camp cooks to the front lines before *he* goes anywhere near it.'

Nicholas put both elbows on the desk and looked directly at Yannis.

'You spoke very well at the meeting. I'm proud of you. I'm proud to have you under my command.'

'I had no intentions of saying anything at that meeting. I was there as an observer. When Isabella got me up, I took one look at the nation's most important people, and I just froze. I had absolutely no idea what to do or say.'

'But what you said was brilliant.'

'I was about to faint when … ah, ah…' Yannis shook his head. He seemed confused.

'When what, Yannis?'

'I honestly don't know what happened, Nicholas. I thought I was going to pass out when suddenly Isabella slipped her hand between mine behind my back. She left her hand there for just a few seconds before she pulled it back out. Next thing I'm off twittering like a bird, so full of confidence I felt like laughing.'

'Hm. Interesting. So tell me, what do you think of Isabella now?'

'You were right that there is no one like her. She really is a one-off, extraordinary. Where I stood paralyzed, she stood and spoke like a seasoned leader. She single-handedly fought off the nation's commander-in-chief to convince a bunch of powerful men to declare war on the Northern Region, and to attack the most powerful army ever to be assembled. There's no doubt she is gifted but, quite frankly, she scares me. That girl would scare the devil himself.'

'Yes, she was amazing today. She is a lioness, that one, she's fearless and with the power to match.'

'I keep reminding myself that she is just a child. If a girl her age can have that much influence, just imagine her influence and power when she's older! Now that's *really* scary.'

'You know, I'm not sure she's been a child since the day her father died. She was only six but I saw a change in her that very day. Her mother, my sister, became ill a few weeks later, and it was Isabella who nursed her and comforted her more than anyone else. At the end it was Isabella who became the mother; the mother became the child. To me, my niece is not a child.'

Yannis nodded, 'I can well believe it. She rescued me today with a simple touch of her hand.'

'If I'm not mistaken, I suspect you were able to return the favor. Everyone was focused on the king when I caught a movement in my side vision and thought I saw Isabella stagger against you. You must have grabbed her, because by the time I looked up the table, she was already pushing away from you. She seemed a bit unsteady at first, but recovered in seconds.'

'I think the stress got to her when she realized it was finally over,' replied Yannis. 'She just tumbled into me and I managed to hold her up before she fell to the floor. She recovered almost instantly, and she was back to normal in a matter of seconds. Amazing!'

'It was lucky that you managed to catch her.'

'I don't think she was all that grateful, to be honest.'

'What on earth makes you say that?'

'She did thank me for it later in a roundabout way. So I asked if she would reward me by not kicking me again.' He shook his head.

'And her response was …?'

'She said *no*. Not only that, she added that there were more kicks to come my way. I'm telling you, she might be smarter than an astronomer, but she's still crazy.'

'So have you figured out the first message yet, Yannis?'

'No, have you?'

'No,' Nicholas lied. He knew that Isabella had many years ahead of her to work on her near-impossible mission of the heart, and he could only hope that it would not end with a broken one. There was no doubt that Yannis could look forward to a sore leg at regular intervals. He had to marvel at Isabella's intelligence and fortitude – she knew she had to maintain her silence at all times, but had devised a method to place her in the forefront of his mind in the years ahead. *Brilliantly conceived, Isabella, and brutally executed.* Yannis was wrong. Isabella was not crazy, and the young man's next query confirmed it.

'Tell me more about Isabella's mother and father.' She had got him thinking about her!

'I'll tell you over dinner. It's time for you to carry the drunken colonel home to his long-suffering wife. Let's go, my friend.'

CHAPTER 28

Zhang Chen was a big man, a man-mountain. He was a physical rarity, a freak in any culture, although there was nothing in his genes to suggest that he should have been. His parents were both of slight build, common for those from the lowest caste in China who never had access to wholesome food. When he had fled his home and his city at age fourteen, he was already a muscular giant of such proportions that no-one, including the toughest of the city's miners, could challenge him.

His deep-rooted shame had led him high into the mountains in northern China, where he had been welcomed into a community of devotees to the martial arts and purity of the mind. His natural strength, speed and dedication had made him the ultimate pupil. By the time he had left the community fifteen years later to search for a wife, Chen had become a new master, the most feared and loved of China's ten Zen Masters.

He had headed west and walked for two years until his search had carried him to the Mondeo property, where he had asked permission to camp the night on their grounds. He had instead been provided with the use of a charming cottage and had received an invitation from General Marcus Mondeo to join the family for dinner.

Arriving at the main house at sunset, he had been greeted at the door by a pair of the most enormous grey-green eyes he had ever seen. After he had got past the eyes, he had noticed the bright smile of a girl aged around seven or eight. Isabella had introduced herself.

Marcus had greeted him in the lounge before they made their way to the dinner table. Mary had then served the meal and Chen had been impressed that Mary then joined them at the table as if a member of the family. Mutual respect – he liked that. As Chen had made to leave, Marcus had invited him to stay on the property longer if he wished. He could do a few chores and in return would receive free rent and food. At the door,

Isabella had reached her arms up for him to lean down. She had given him a brief hug and a kiss on his cheek, said good-night and skipped off to help Mary tidy up.

The show of respect for a complete stranger had given him all the reasons he needed to decide that this was his new family and his new home. Zhang Chen had climbed from the bottom of the ladder to the very top.

Chen now studied his protégé and smiled as they were about to start the next lesson. He had lived on the property for almost five years by this time, and Isabella had become his surrogate daughter. He loved her as much as it was possible for any father to love a daughter. He had told no-one of his status of Zen Master, only that he had some knowledge of the martial arts. As soon as Isabella learned of his skills, she had insisted that he teach her. After her first lesson she had been hooked. They had trained for two hours every day, and Chen loved their time together as much as Isabella did.

He had always pushed her to what he considered the limit for her age, yet she never failed to surprise him. Her thirst for knowledge of the strategy behind each move was insatiable. She was tall for her age, underweight from her intense self-discipline in all forms of sport and training but, above all, she was strong. The previous week she had surprised him with her kicking skills, her speed as well as her strength. Her dedication was second to none, including him. Now he made a decision. It was time to pass on the true secrets of the Zen Master.

'Isabella, before we start today, I say something about who I am, what I am. It time to make changes to your training. Some of new training will be quite interesting; much will be very ... *dangerous.*' Isabella cocked her head to one side and waited with interest for him to continue. She always knew when words were unnecessary.

When Chen had finished his story, Isabella was as wide-eyed as the first time he had seen her. She hugged him and said, 'I always sensed you were holding back on the power within you. I'm ready to learn your secrets, and they will become *my* secrets. I will honor your secrets and I will honor *you*, Zen Master.' She bowed to her Zen Master and immediately took up the challenge position.

By the time she had finished the first of her new lessons, Isabella was hooked for the second time. In his earlier recital, Zhang Chen had taken great care to safeguard some of his secrets. They would remain secret forever.

CHAPTER 29

'Do you want me to come with you, Grandfather?'
It was late morning and Marcus stood in the family room as he read aloud the note just delivered by the king's messenger. The messenger tended to his horse while he waited for the written response he had been instructed to bring back.

'Oh yes, here it is.' He read out loud the next section: '*The king also requests that Miss Isabella Mondeo attend the meeting.*' He looked up at Isabella, who was perched up on the bench, a favorite place where she could swing her legs back and forth, which seemed to assist her thinking process. 'There you are, then. I don't have a choice, I'm afraid. You will have to come with me, no matter what *I* want!'

'Oh you!' Isabella exclaimed with a grin. She jumped off the bench and snatched the letter out of Marcus' hand. 'What else does his Royal Highness have to say about me?' She marched back and forth and mumbled as she read. 'H-m-m, not a lot more,' she said, sounding disappointed. 'Will Uncle Nicho and what's-his-name be there, do you think?'

'No idea. How about you do the note for the messenger while I get Mary to organize a few things for the morning? I'll get Chen to prepare the wagon.'

It was a War Council meeting and lasted three days. Marcus and Isabella stayed at a guest house where they were unknown, after Marcus considered that staying with Captain Cavarro over several days might raise unwanted questions.

People came and went in the conference room. Some stayed minutes, some for hours. Only Marcus and Isabella were in attendance at all times, as were the scribes, who alternated so there would always be one in attendance. King Ramesses personally welcomed each visitor, and Isabella was particularly pleased that the king now treated her as an adult.

Each time there was a knock on the door to the ante-room, Isabella tensed as she swiveled to see the latest arrival before turning away with disinterest. By the end of the first day, she was thoroughly bored after having listened to the admiral, Dmitri, Trellinis and his entourage of senators, all lamenting about the problems they faced. General Karamus was scheduled for the following day. As soon as Isabella realized no further visitors were coming for that day, she wanted nothing more than for the meeting to end.

The king sensed her frustration and kept a hold on her hand as they were about to leave. 'Don't despair. Today's meeting was mainly for listening to all of the problems so that we can later focus only on solutions, what we need to do, and the order in which to do them.' He smiled and let go of her hand.

Isabella felt better. Knowing he was right, she looked up at him and tapped the side of her head. 'I already have a long list of things up here, sir, and the order in which to do them.'

'And the first thing on your list is …?'

'Mobilize the army, sir, starting today, even if it's only twenty men a day. They just need to be organized, told what to take and where to go. The departures can be rotated from the many barracks and camps throughout the various provinces. No-one will notice twenty men a day when they leave from numerous points.'

The king looked thoughtful. 'Interesting. No big groups marching and no huge baggage train for all to see. Perhaps the supply chain can be organized the same way: by stealth. Good point, Isabella. Now off you go! It's been a long day. Please have breakfast before you arrive tomorrow, so we can get straight down to business.' He gave her a brief hug and shook hands with Marcus.

That night, after a surprisingly good dinner prepared by the innkeeper and his wife, Isabella vented her frustration again. 'I have listened all day to the things that are difficult or impossible to do, but not a single suggestion about how to overcome them. I know the king is right, up to a point, but you would have thought someone would have had something positive to offer.'

'Perhaps tomorrow. Don't be too impatient.'

Isabella stifled a yawn. 'By the way, Grandfather, did you hear from Uncle Nicho? Will he be attending the meeting at all?'

Marcus knew she was trying to find out if Yannis would be coming, but he didn't let on. 'There was a list of names attached to the agenda notes, but I didn't look at it, and I forgot to ask. I'm sorry.

'Oh.'

Dmitri's face was grim as he read the report from his local intelligence chief. *Two hundred thousand soldiers! So it was really true.* He broke out in a cold sweat when he read the next section: two thousand cannons of latest design were to be manufactured for the campaign. They were to be more than twice the size of any cannon previously made. Their army was so massive it had to be split into three divisions and deployed in three different directions. Dmitri groaned and rubbed his head in frustration and fear. *That's more than enough to encircle our small nation's entire army!* It was the worst report he had ever read, and he dreaded to be the one to inform the meeting the following day.

Isabella checked the agenda as soon as she entered the conference room and felt a twinge of disappointment when she saw that Colonel Manassis was not scheduled to attend the meeting until the following afternoon.

Dmitri had sent his apologies; he needed to research some matters, he said, and would be a little late. The senators were seated in their usual places, and several senior army officers, sworn to secrecy, had been brought in to discuss administration and logistical matters.

To Isabella it was all boring – until General Karamus arrived. She almost did not recognize him. He entered the room tall and straight, and with a smile on his face. He sat down and smiled at those around the table. He even smiled at Isabella, who was immediately suspicious.

'My battle plans are well advanced,' he reported. He rose and walked over to the large map of Europe that had been hung on the wall. 'I thought we would strike here!' He tapped a spot on the map, far to the north. 'Far enough away from their home base so that they can't get reinforcement. They will be on open ground, which will make them vulnerable. There is a mountain range over here in which we can hide before revealing ourselves and taking them by surprise. It also gives us a natural escape route back into the mountains, where we will have camp sites already set up. I believe this spot to be ideal.' The general turned and looked directly at Isabella. 'What do you think, Isabella?'

Isabella was stunned at what she had just seen and heard and even more surprised that the general had addressed her by her first name. She got up and walked over to study the map. It was perfect. She could not have picked a better spot. She nodded slowly as she returned to her seat.

'It is absolutely perfect, General.'

There were nods of approval around the room. Karamus looked pleased. *I should have realized it sooner, Isabella: keep you happy and I keep everyone happy.*

'Very well, that's the place then.' Ramesses was pleased. 'I think it's time to start discussions about how to achieve our goals. The first item is something Isabella suggested yesterday evening.' The king repeated the idea of mobilizing the troops over a time-frame. He felt certain General Karamus would object to an outsider suggesting a military maneuver. His fears proved unfounded.

'Perfect!' the general said. 'It will actually make it easier for the administrators to handle small and regular numbers gradually, and from different centers. Simpler too, for provisioning them with clothes, boots, soldiers' packs and the like. Good idea, Isabella. I will see to it at once.'

Isabella's warning signals went on full alert. This was not the same man who had left the meeting just two weeks earlier a broken man, filled with fear and hatred. *What happened, General? Why are you suddenly embracing the war? Even accepting me? Have you seen the light and at last put your nation before yourself? Have I misjudged you?*

'In fact,' Karamus mused, 'my fa ... m-m-m ... never mind. I have an idea, but I will have to give it a bit more thought.'

The king nodded. 'Any suggestions? Anyone?'

Admiral Georgeonous leaned forward. 'Sir, I have a suggestion. While the army is being mobilized on a trickle basis, we can make people believe that many are leaving to go into industry, and that we are looking for replacements. I believe several thousand navy personnel would not be an unreasonable estimate of the number who would consider transferring to the army. They are all strong, big as mountains, and well disciplined. Many would relish greater opportunities for battle and glory. Some could go on the campaign, while others remained to boost the number at home.'

'That's a good idea,' Marcus said. 'The navy is spread over large areas of the coast, and some thinning of the ranks would hardly be noticed.'

'Excellent!' the king sounded excited with the progress. At that moment there was a knock on the double doors. 'Come.' The doors opened and Dmitri walked into the room.

Ramesses rose to greet his friend. 'You don't look very happy, Dmitri. What's the matter?'

'I received this report late last night and I had to double-check some of the facts this morning before presenting it to you. It would be better if I read it.' When he finished, Dmitri let the pages fall and glanced at the silent faces. 'Except for the time I first heard of the attack, this is the worst news I have ever received.' He placed his hands over his face and groaned.

'Except for the time I first heard of the attack,' Isabella responded calmly, pointing at the report, 'this is the *best* news I have ever heard.'

'What? I don't understand. Did you say *best* news?' Dmitri stared at Isabella. The others also looked surprised.

'Why yes. The report could not have been better if I'd composed it myself.'

CHAPTER 30

Dmitri picked up the report and quickly glanced through it as if he must have missed something, or misread it. He frowned. 'You see this as good news, Isabella? How so?'

'There are several things of interest in your report. The first is that the Northern Region army will be split into three divisions, with each division taking a geographical course far removed from the others. Correct?'

Dmitri nodded.

'That means that each division cannot reinforce the others until well after our initial attack. Correct?'

Dmitri nodded again, trying without success to second-guess her.

'Then General Karamus will face off against only *one* of those divisions. You should ask the general if he feels that facing off against sixty to seventy thousand soldiers – as bad as that is, I might add – instead of two hundred thousand soldiers is good news or bad news.'

Karamus crashed his huge fist onto the table and roared with laughter. 'She's got you, Dmitri. She's got us both! Isabella is right. You have brought us *good* news, Dmitri.' Karamus was genuinely pleased. *I hate to say it, Isabella, but you are correct. It is indeed good news. I will pose an even greater threat to the enemy and increase my leverage tenfold.*

'What else do you see that we don't, Isabella?'

'The cannons, Dmitri. The two thousand cannons.'

'We're lucky to have twenty, small and not very effective at that.'

'Consider this: to haul the cannons, cannon-balls, powder and associated manpower across icy mountains and raging rivers will take many tens of thousands of horses, oxen and other animals. That's without taking into account the troops, provisions and baggage train. The logistics will be horrendous.'

Dmitri held up his hands in surrender and smiled broadly. 'If you see it as such a negative for them, why would the emperor send so many cannons? The cost of the guns alone will surely test their financial resources.'

Isabella pursed her lips and twisted them slowly from side to side while she thought. No one spoke. Finally she said, 'You have posed a *very* interesting question, Dmitri.' She thought some more and gently drummed her fingers on the table before a smile spread across her youthful face.

'What are you thinking, Isabella?' asked Marcus.

'I can't see that Emperor Kuiper would saddle his army with such a burden, and at the same time sacrifice so much of their financial resources. Our nation makes up only a small part of the Southern Region of Europe. With so many soldiers, they don't really need cannons to make us submit. Or alternatively, with so many cannons, they don't need that many soldiers. I've researched Aloise Kuiper, and he seems to have been little more than a mediocre general who came to power under very suspicious circumstances. No, it's not him. He's being pushed, manipulated. The man in charge of the campaign is their top soldier: General and Commander-in-Chief Maurice Von Franckel.'

Isabella paused for a sip of water to allow the scribe to catch up.

'The cannon has been around for a few years, but it's been found to be very cumbersome. It's not designed to be hauled across fields and mountains. So why send cannons cross-country now? *Prestige and power!* There is tension and jealousy between those two – one who is their greatest soldier and the other a mediocre soldier, but emperor. Even though the hostilities will be directed specifically against our nation,' she paused for effect, 'I believe that Von Franckel's *real* target is not us, but the entire Southern Region!'

There was not a sound in the room.

'Once he's here, our southern European allies will capitulate as soon as he points his finger at them. No-one will dare to resist such firepower. Their campaign will be driven by this arrogant show of power. I have no doubt General Von Franckel is planning to become the next emperor of southern Europe, if not also northern Europe. There will then no longer be two Regions. Von Franckel will simply declare himself emperor of a united Europe. That has already contributed to his greatest mistake. They are shaping an army that can move no faster than their slowest element: the cannon. When the cannons are forced to stop, so will the army. Furthermore, they cannot move very far during winter. There will be insufficient food in the fields for so many soldiers and animals. We can, therefore, plan our attacks accordingly.'

Dmitri sighed. 'Isabella, you do know how to make a man feel better.'

Ramesses rose as he spoke. 'This is without doubt the perfect time to finish up for today. Tomorrow will be a day for discussing logistics and making firm decisions. Ladies and gentlemen, let's get this war up and running!'

CHAPTER 31

Isabella was tired the next day. She had tossed and turned all night thinking about what might happen with the arrival of Uncle Nicho. Everyone was seated in their usual place except General Karamus, who had sent his apologies saying he would be late, due to an urgent meeting. No-one knew that he was actually enjoying a swim in a secluded bay to pass a couple of hours.

Ideas were debated regarding conscription and how to best disperse the army across the European continent. Isabella's heart-rate increased as the morning progressed. A knock on the door at midday made her jump in her seat. She stared at the doors as they opened for General Karamus to enter the room.

He bowed to the king and made his way to his chair. 'Sir, my sincere apologies for being late.' He sat down and leaned forward, his arms resting on the table. 'I have been in intensive discussions with my father, both last night and this morning,' he lied. He had not seen his father for several days. 'The idea I had yesterday might just work. I had to swear him to secrecy and –'

The general was interrupted by another knock on the door. Isabella's heart hammered and she felt faint as the doors swung open to reveal Colonel Manassis. He was alone.

Ramesses walked across the room to greet him and show him to his chair. 'Thank you for coming, Nicholas.' The king glanced briefly at Isabella, and then back to Nicholas. 'And where is the charming Lieutenant Christos? I expected him to accompany you today.'

'He sends his apologies, sir. He felt he could contribute more by focusing on the troop movement plans. He is a superb organizer of manpower. Extraordinary, in fact, sir.'

Isabella was furious. Contribute! Troop movements! Organizer!

Extraordinary, indeed. *I'll give you a kick to remember next time I see you, Second-rate Lieutenant Yannis Christos. An* extraordinary *kick, in fact!*

'Colonel, General Karamus was just about to tell us about discussions he has had with his father. Please continue, General.'

'Um, yes, as I was saying, I had to swear him to secrecy and use all of my persuasive powers to get his agreement. Not that he is not a patriot, or a willing participant, I hasten to add. It's just that my idea is complex in the extreme, and it would involve a number of his closest confidants. I can assure you that what he says, goes, and he has agreed that my proposals be implemented without delay.'

The general went on to explain how troops would be hosted in small numbers in thousands of farms and villages throughout Europe. An invisible army would be created. The growing of grain and breeding of stock for both transport and food would be undertaken by contracted farmers throughout the continent, the Balkans, Russia, and some of the less arid regions of Persia. Storage depots would be disguised in thousands of barns and disused warehouse buildings. There would be no visible uniforms, body armor, army camps or barracks on open display. At the end of his summation, the general received a round of applause.

'Splendid, General, splendid! Thank your father and tell him that the government will secretly fund this enterprise.' The king was ecstatic. He looked at those seated at the table, his eyes shining with excitement. 'How about that, ladies and gentlemen! Three-quarters of our problems have been resolved in thirty minutes!'

Isabella had to admit that Karamus' plan was indeed a coup of major proportions. Most of the obstacles she had foreseen in maintaining secrecy while mobilizing their army were now swept aside, and she could focus on peripheral issues.

'Might I make a suggestion, General Karamus?' Isabella asked.

'Of course, Isabella, please feel free. I have to admit that you have been way ahead of all of us right from the start, so I have no doubt your suggestion will be a good one. I also take the opportunity to publicly apologize to you for my vile behavior toward you at previous meetings. I'm afraid I judged you by your age alone, not for your natural gifts of logic. Everyone values highly what you have to say, and I'm no exception. I am very sorry for the things I said previously.'

Isabella was astounded. 'Ah ... apology accepted, General, thank you,' she stammered, not quite sure what to make of it. *Was he genuine or was he playing a game?* 'There are a couple of things, actually, General, if I may.

Traditionally, battles and crusades take place during the summer months when food and water is more readily available directly off the land. In the current situation, however, we will be going to war on the other side of several snowlines. My suggestion is therefore that provisioning be targeted for stockpiling first on the other side of those lines. Because our retreats must be rapid, we cannot carry them, but without them we will die in the cold of the mountains. The stockpiles closest to home can be completed last.'

'Yes, yes, absolutely. Makes good sense. Consider it done.' Karamus sounded genuinely enthusiastic. 'And the other suggestion?'

'Pigeons.'

'Pigeons?'

'My father and grandfather were both warriors in their time and it is in my blood and in my every breath. Over the years I have studied the rise and eventual disintegration of the Roman Empire, the Crusades and the battles of so many other famed warrior kings and emperors. Remember the Battle of Hastings in 1066, now almost 300 hundred years ago. And the world will never forget the battle of Marathon, where so few overwhelmed so many. Over time, these battles revealed a common thread. In war, the most dangerous enemy is not the enemy itself, but the lack of *communications*. Our most valuable asset is not our weaponry; it is *deception*.'

Isabella paused to allow the men to focus on the two words. 'These two elements, *communications* and *deception,* brought on the downfall of the Carthaginian Barca brothers, sons of Hamilcar the Great, and better known as Hannibal and Hasdrubal. Barca was their family name, a beautiful yet fearsome name that struck terror into the heart of the bravest soldier. It's the name I gave my beautiful stallion and it means *Thunderbolt.* The two brothers were about to merge their separate armies to attack and conquer Rome when a communication between them was intercepted by a consul of one of the Roman armies. Working a deception on the brothers, the consul was able to launch a surprise attack. Hasdrubal was killed and his massive army destroyed. This loss eventually also spelled the end for Hannibal. His army was defeated and he was forced to flee Europe. An almost certain defeat of the Roman Empire by the might of the Carthaginians unravelled due entirely to communications and deception. It changed history as we know it today. Forward planning for good communications and deception can win this war for us.'

'You used the word *win*, Isabella. Was that a slip of the tongue, or do you really think it's possible?'

'As you know, their army will be fragmented, each section bogged down with animals, cannons, other weapons and provisions. We, on the other hand, will be mobile, and can strike in their own territory when they think they are safe and when they least expect it. They won't be given time to set up their order of battle. No, General, the *win* word was not a slip of the tongue.'

'You make it sound easy, Isabella.'

'Not easy, not at all. It's just a glimmer of hope. I do have great concerns, however, about communications in particular.'

'Because our army will be spread all over Europe small in units?'

'Exactly.'

'You don't like my idea?'

'On the contrary, General, I think it is brilliant.'

The general was chuffed. 'Ah ... and so we have your pigeons?'

'I hardly need mention fast horse and messenger stations, and the various signaling systems, including flags and fire beacons. You know those better than I ever will. They won't be of much use to you, though, with the troops spread over thousands of villages and farms throughout the continent.'

'Agreed. That was one of the flaws in my plan,' he lied. He had barely given it a thought. 'It was one of the many matters to sort out later after the master plan had been agreed to.'

'Of course, General. That's the only way to do things.'

'So what do you suggest?'

'Set up a division that will do nothing but breed carrier pigeons. Pigeons are fast and reliable.' She glanced over at King Ramesses. 'Your forefathers, the ancient Egyptians, used carrier pigeons thousands of years ago with great success, sir.' She looked back at General Karamus. 'We would need thousands of eggs to be transported throughout Europe so that birds can be bred and trained. With proper organization, that will allow messages to be sent to and from the troops almost anywhere, advising them where to go next, where to muster and when. Strange as it sounds, pigeons can mean the difference between winning and losing this war. When we have *communications* down to a fine art, we can focus on the second element: *deception*.'

'Consider it done. I'll commission some of my officers to organize special breeding teams and a regular delivery system for the eggs and birds.'

'Wonderful, General.'

Karamus nodded and rubbed his hands together enthusiastically. 'Oh, and by the way, Isabella, twenty soldiers were dispatched for *special duties* in the Balkans this morning, and a similar number will be headed in another direction – Spain, actually – tomorrow. It will be a daily occurrence from now on. Your proposal is already being implemented.'

Isabella grinned with pleasure at the round of applause that followed. She could not resist joining in. It was her proudest moment.

King Ramesses declared the day a resounding success and announced that a late buffet lunch had been prepared on the terrace for everyone's pleasure. Future meetings would be arranged on an *as required* basis.

During the lunch Nicholas came over and put his arm around Isabella's shoulder. 'That went very well, Isabella, so why so forlorn? You are looking very sad and pale.'

Isabella simply shrugged and remained silent. She put her plate down, her appetite suddenly gone.

Nicho gave her a squeeze. 'Yannis sends his regards to you. He said he wanted to come today to witness events, but thought the urgency of his responsibilities should take precedent over his personal wishes.'

Isabella turned her head away so that Uncle Nicho would not see the tears suddenly streaming down her face. Furious at her uncle, she mumbled an excuse and made her way to a bathroom. She closed the door and sank to the floor, sobbing quietly for several minutes. *Do you really think I am so stupid as not to recognize a blatant lie, Uncle Nicho?*

Second Lieutenant Yannis Christos was on his hands and knees as he moved from one map to the next. He had borrowed the huge office of General Zarcas, who was on leave with his family. Maps collected from the military archives were spread out in the approximate shape of the European continent. Unfortunately, the maps used different scales and showed little detail of contours, which made it difficult to visualize the terrain. Towns and rivers were marked in writing so small it had forced him to his knees.

Aching, Yannis got up from the floor to relieve his knees and sat on the edge of the desk. On an impulse he went on a tour of other offices to collect jugs, vases, bowls and other bric-a-brac, including ropes from the stables. The tallest jugs and vases became mountain ranges on his maps, the bowls became lakes, the bric-a-brac became cities, towns and ports. Strung out and joined, the ropes became major rivers. He stared at his final artwork until Europe and the terrain were burned into his brain.

Just weeks ago he would never have thought he would be staring at maps on a floor while planning for an army on the move. Thanks to a slip of a girl who was guiding his nation to war, he was quite likely to become cannon fodder.

An image of Isabella floated into his mind, a ghostly vision of a green-eyed angel framed by a swirling mass of white cotton and glowing in a beam of brilliant white light. As the image faded he saw it change from an angel to a young woman, and then back into a child. *Isabella, you are without doubt the scariest person I have ever met!*

Yannis was well aware of his family's background and was proud of its resilience and perseverance in how it had managed to survive. It was that knowledge that had given him his own strength. Yet, in Isabella's presence he felt weak. In fact, he knew he *was* weak in her presence. As he got up to collect the maps, he had a fleeting thought about what Isabella might be up to, and whether they would ever meet again. *It might be better if we never do.* He had no idea that, at that very moment, Isabella was sitting on the floor of a palace bathroom with her head on her knees, sobbing.

CHAPTER 32

Theo Karamus shook his head in disappointment after he had finished reading the document. It was little more than he had expected. His son had sat on the other side of the desk with a look of confidence as he watched his father review the battle plan that would force his nation to surrender before even engaging the enemy. But his expression faded rapidly when his father shook his head and tossed the report onto the desk.

'What is it, Father? That's a good plan.'

'It's a good plan if you want to deliberately lose a battle.'

'But that's what you said I had to do.'

'The plan is that you be forced to surrender, not beaten to a pulp. With that plan,' Theo declared, pointing at the document on his desk, 'you will simply look like a loser, not a hero. Your opposing general won't even consider your offer of surrender. He will simply chop you and your men into little pieces and move on.'

It was Vlado's turn to shake his head. He was angry. 'I'm lost. I have no idea what you're talking about. How can I surrender if I don't place my army in a losing position? That's the reason generals surrender: when they see no prospect of winning the impending battle!'

Theo leaned forward and stared hard at his son. 'The order of battle must be planned to make it look like you could actually defeat the enemy. You must make the enemy fear you.' He leaned back before adding, 'And then you must engage the enemy in battle.'

'What?'

'I told you weeks ago that you had two years to develop a superbly trained army, a magnificent army. There *must* be a battle. It simply will not do to surrender without a battle of sorts. We need it for leverage and for legitimacy in the surrender.'

'But you said I wouldn't have to draw my sword in battle!'

'That's correct, Vlado. You won't have to draw your sword, but others will. You must make the enemy want to grab your offer of surrender with gratitude and relief, and that will require a different plan.'

'Are you going to give me some hints of where to start?'

'I can do better than that. I will tell you exactly what you need to do.' Theo lowered his voice and quietly outlined his plan.

'What? You can't be serious!' Vlado was on his feet, horrified. 'I will hang! I will never get away with that! How can I possibly make that happen?'

'You don't. I will make it happen. Sit down and I'll tell you how I'll make it happen.' Theo smiled and waited for Vlado to be seated. 'When you leave for the campaign, the king will hand you the declaration of war written by his scribe. It will be undated and will require your counter-signature and date when you present it to your opposing general. You will arrange to deliver the declaration by messenger in a sealed envelope. There are to be no witnesses when you seal that envelope. Is that quite clear, Vlado – no witnesses?'

'Yes, quite clear: *no witnesses.*'

'You will place a *second* message in that envelope, one that I will draft for you. It will outline the means, the method, and the conditions of your offer to surrender. Your opposing general will arrange his battle-order in a way that will signal his acceptance of your conditions. He will then make things happen exactly as I described earlier. Are you with me, so far?'

'Oh, it's just too simple. There will be tens of thousands of soldiers on each side, in full battle readiness, and you're telling me to rely on a letter to make everything happen in a particular way. You play a very dangerous game, Father, and with me sandwiched between the two front lines.'

Theo drummed his fingers on the desk for a few moments. 'Well, there *is* one other option, son.'

'And that is?'

'Just forget about my plan. Simply follow the king's plan and lead the charge into the enemy's front lines on a dozen occasions with your famous war cry.'

The general looked puzzled. 'What famous war cry?'

'I'm sure you'll think of one if you survive the first charge.'

Vlado held up his hands in surrender.

•

Dinner had been served and the remnants cleared away. The meeting of *The Inner Sanctum* was exclusively for the men who controlled all commerce throughout the nation, and beyond. No-one knew of their existence, not even Vlado Karamus, who had not been invited. Theo had arranged for his wife, Nina, to spend the night with her sister, leaving the house secure for the fourteen now seated at the table. Three walls were lined with portraits of the serious-looking faces of Theo's ancestors, observing, it seemed like, the room's occupants with disapproval.

Theo's four *Disciplinarians* stood guard at each exit, and for good reason.

Theo rose and faced these most trusted business associates. He did not smile as he commenced speaking. 'You are about to hear things you are not to speak of to anyone – ever. You will see why soon enough. You will each be required to undertake a number of tasks, all of which must be completed successfully and without exception. At the end of this, I promise you wealth and power beyond your wildest dreams. We are all too enmeshed in each other's affairs for anyone to be given the choice of opting out. To dissenters, I promise one thing only: my men will not allow you to leave here alive.

'Now that we have the formalities out of the way, we can digest the news I have for you.' Theo sat down again and spent the next hour giving his colleagues an overview of the rapidly unfolding events. Some details were left out, including the secret letter Vlado would provide to the commander of the enemy forces. He also left out any reference to Isabella Mondeo. His associates' hostile feelings were to be directed at the king alone. He had very specific plans for King Ramesses and his family when everything was over.

There were few questions at the end of his summation. As chairman, Theo was a master of both clarity and brevity. 'Remember this, gentlemen. This is all about leverage. By following this plan, we will create the most powerful army our nation has ever had, led by my son. That will place *The Inner Sanctum* in a unique position: with the ability to control the guaranteed offer of surrender, *and exclusively on our terms.*'

Theo smiled at his guests. 'That about covers it, gentlemen. Any dissenters?'

As expected, there were none.

CHAPTER 33

The weeks rolled by, then the months. Summer came and went. Meetings were held at the king's Summer Palace every two weeks, disguised as *social events*. Soldiers and supplies left from various cities and towns on a daily basis. Conscription was kept low key to divert suspicion. Applicants from the navy were given first preference and were among the first to be relocated around the Southern Region – the southern half of Europe.

Fall drew to a close as Marcus and Isabella arrived for another meeting at the palace. General Karamus' reports glowed with the successes of the forward planning – so much so that Isabella became suspicious all was not as it should be. She quietly asked Dmitri if he would like to see the shark she had been hand-feeding during breaks in the meetings. Dmitri was astonished, but agreed to accompany her to the nearby grotto.

Marcus and Nicholas were in deep discussions with the king as she and Dmitri left for their stroll. Yannis never accompanied Nicholas, and Isabella no longer asked about him. She had resigned herself to the fact that she was unlikely to ever see him again, and that the ache in her heart was one she would carry for the rest of her life.

Dmitri and Isabella enjoyed some small talk on the way, but as they moved down a slope and out of sight of the palace, Dmitri changed direction and headed to a rocky outcrop. He selected a rock that would provide a small amount of comfort, sat, and beckoned for Isabella to choose another.

He looked around carefully, then at Isabella. 'So, tell me what's really on your mind, Isabella. We both know there's no shark.'

'Am I really that transparent?'

'No, it's just that I know you too well, my dear. If you *really* were friendly with a shark, it would be just you and the shark – two beings, each with amazing power in different worlds. Isabella, you would share your precious shark with no-one.'

Isabella grinned. 'Oh dear, you do know me too well.'

'So tell me what's on your mind.'

'It's General Karamus.'

'Ah.'

'You don't sound surprised.'

'You're suspicious, correct?'

'He's doing all the right things, he's *saying* all the right things, and he's acting like a *real* general. But yes, I can't help being suspicious.'

'Perhaps it's because he's changed from one extreme to the other?'

'And too suddenly.'

'A leopard doesn't change its spots. Is that what you're thinking?'

'Yes, that and more.'

'Such as?'

'At the meeting when he changed his views, he called me *Isabella*.'

'Oh dear, what a *shock!* What a terrible thing to call you! How *could* he!' Dmitri rolled his eyes theatrically.

Isabella's laugh was beautiful and free of pretense. 'If he had continued to call me *Miss Mondeo*, I might actually believe everything he has been saying and doing. But when he first called me *Isabella*, I felt a warning flag go up, and that flag is still up.'

'Tell me more, and think deep, Isabella.'

'When he apologized – which I did appreciate, by the way – it could not have been easy for him. It was not only as if he wanted to please me, but as if he *had* to please me. It's just a feeling deep within. Do you understand what I'm saying?'

Dmitri turned his head and stared silently at the ocean for a long time. He finally turned back to Isabella. 'Yes, unfortunately I do understand, and now I'm worried. I also have been a little suspicious, but I thought I was alone in that regard, so I didn't think too much about it.'

'I don't suppose there's much we can do other than to be on our guard.'

'What I can do is for some of my best agents to move about the continent and see what they can discover. I'll tell them exactly where to go and what to look for, and then report back to me. We'll see if things are happening exactly as the general is telling us.'

'That makes me feel better, much better. In the meantime I have given a lot of thought to a backup plan in case the first part of our plan does not go to plan – pun definitely intended.' Isabella giggled.

Dmitri chuckled. 'Good idea. In intelligence, we call that Plan B.'

'I am actually a further step along the track, Dmitri.' She grinned cheekily at him. 'I don't suppose you also have Plan C?'

'But of course, Isabella!'

CHAPTER 34

'I feel ill.' Vlado Karamus had just finished reading the draft of his surrender letter. The pages detailed the conditions for surrender, and what the enemy commander must do to provide Vlado with the signal that those conditions had been accepted. 'This is high treason, Father. I will be held accountable if something should go wrong.'

'Nothing will go wrong. My opinion is that there's only one person who might be smart enough to suspect anything. We've been very careful, so it's highly unlikely, but at the first sign that she is sticking her pert little nose where it should not be, I will arrange to have it cut off. Let me assure you that it will be a deep cut.'

Vlado was not to be placated so easily. 'But if this letter should fall into the wrong hands ...' He rolled his eyes.

'It won't. Your opposing commander will destroy it as soon as you have surrendered, as stipulated in the letter. As commander-in-chief he has the lawful right to offer any concessions he wishes to secure the surrender of an army, particularly in the case of one as large and dangerous as yours. He will not want it known how the surrender was engineered, or that conditions were demanded. I assure you that he will take full credit for his victory.'

'How do we know he will honor the conditions?'

'He would be foolish to do otherwise. You will give him the opportunity to win not only the battle, but the war, and with few casualties. He then has the guarantee that our nation will be run like clockwork for his emperor, with the cooperation of our nation's wealthiest, most efficient industrialists. Let me assure you, Vlado, the emperor would not hesitate to hang his commander if the agreement were not honored.'

'I guess that makes sense.' He nodded and handed the letter back to his father. 'You'd better put this in a safe place until I need it.' He hesitated before speaking again. 'I'll have many fine officers with me, Father. I consider many of them to be close friends.'

'War is not the time to consider your friends, son.'

With rising alarm, Dmitri read several reports of the illness in the north-eastern part of the Southern Region, as well as in Italy. Days earlier he had received a report from an agent in the Northern Region about this same illness, now severely affecting some of the major cities. His first reaction had been *good riddance to them, serves them right!* But now he was worried. There were reports that the illness had also spread to England. If it could reach across open water, it had no boundaries.

No-one had any idea what caused it or where it came from. Most thought China. At least, the Southern Region was only moderately affected. An idea formed as he thought about what he could do to help. There was still a major problem to be resolved for the coming war. The *camp followers*: the men and women providing the cooking, laundry, nursing and baggage handling needs of the soldiers. No army could survive, or fight, without them. Some 5,000 men and women were needed, and they had to be mobilized, trained and sent in position without being detected before the *invisible* army assembled for their first meal together.

He walked to the door and flung it open. 'Gino, get me a carriage with two horses, would you? I'm in a hurry. And send a rider ahead to the king to let him know I'm on my way and that it's urgent I meet with him.'

An hour later, he arrived at the palace, where he was led without pomp or ceremony into the king's private office. Ramesses moved forward to greet him. 'Dmitri, what is it, my friend? I was told it was very urgent.'

'It is, sir – '

'*Ramesses*, please, Dmitri.' The king indicated the lounge chairs. They sat down and faced each other.

'Ramesses, it is urgent. We have further reports of this illness that's sweeping in from the north and the east, as well as from the western seaboard. I hope it doesn't get worse, but it might. We need to take some measures now in order to keep an eye on things and provide help where we can. At the same time, it might just solve a problem that we've discussed numerous times without solving it.'

'Which problem? We still have so many.'

'The problem of how we mobilize some 5,000 camp followers without raising suspicion. With all the food, equipment and wagons needed, they'll be an army in themselves. It was always going to be difficult to recruit and disperse them without their knowing where they're going, and what they'll be doing.'

'So what are you thinking?'

'Well, just in case this illness turns into an epidemic, it would seem like good policy if we were proactive in setting up government assistance stations, particularly in the far *northern* areas, to provide food and medical supplies if the going gets tough. I suggest some six or seven thousand would be about right, fully equipped, of course.'

'Of course,' the king was smiling.

'That would leave a couple of thousand to spare for that task after we later redirect the 5,000 that we need for our campaign.'

The king nodded.

Dmitri continued, 'We could send our cavalry to escort them.' Dmitri leaned forward and smiled. 'In full uniform, of course. A few thousand soldiers, also in uniform, could be seconded to help them move the food and equipment, and to provide transport. We should let the entire Southern Region know what we're doing; it would be high profile, excellent publicity for both you and the government. No one would suspect that there is anything sinister in something so open. As Isabella has often said: the best place to hide is in plain sight. What do you think?'

Ramesses brought his hands together in a loud clap. 'Sheer genius, Dmitri. We can top up our supply chain anywhere we want, and by how much we want, and we can do it in plain sight. If this illness should turn into something worse – heavens forbid – we will already have people in outlying areas. It's a win-win, Dmitri. Let's do it! I'll make the necessary arrangements for the funding. And let General Karamus know so he can make the necessary military arrangements. Oh, and let Marcus and Isabella know as well, would you?'

Ten minutes later Dmitri was driving his wagon at full speed back to the city.

CHAPTER 35

'*Very clever!* I'm impressed.' They were sitting in the lounge as Isabella handed Dmitri's six-page report back to her grandfather. Marcus had quietly watched Isabella read the document that had been delivered a half-hour earlier. 'It will make many things easier to put into place, and it will be out in the open, as Dmitri says in his report.'

'That's true. I don't like the sound of that illness, though. I've heard from army officers returning from faraway outposts over the last few years about a disease that's been spreading through many of China's regions, and India. It's pretty deadly, from what I hear. No one knows what causes it, and there seems to be no effective treatment. Not even Chinese herbal medicines have any noticeable effect.' Marcus stared out the window with a deep frown. 'The illness sounds like it's very contagious, and bear in mind that people are moving about more than ever these days.'

Marcus folded the letter and put it back in the envelope. He tossed it on the table and stared at it as if it contained the very disease they were talking about.

'There is an idea in the back of my mind that something like this has happened before. I don't remember much of the details other than that it was serious. It could have been about a thousand years ago.'

'I'll see if I can find something about it next time I'm at the library, Grandfather.' Isabella was worried but decided to put the matter to one side for the time being. 'In the meantime we must focus on the war. There are quite a few things I want to research, including some engineering projects. I can stay with Uncle Linus, if that's all right with you.'

'The army has excellent engineers, probably the best in the country.'

'Yes, but first I have to work out what I want them to build.'

It was already early afternoon and she had found nothing about a plague.

Isabella was not sure whether she should be disappointed or relieved. The librarians had not been able to help her. There were no cross-reference records reaching back beyond two hundred years. Any earlier records had been consigned to a number of warehouses scattered about the city. It was time to talk to the Oracle: Alexander duPonti, the Royal Scribe.

Isabella found him an hour later and told him what she had been searching for. His face looked troubled. 'I've been thinking about that since I heard stories about this illness spreading so rapidly. It might have nothing to do with what your grandfather is alluding to, but I guess it wouldn't hurt to have a look. I think I know where those old records are.'

An hour later they were moving slowly down a network of aisles in the basement of an otherwise disused warehouse, checking each side as they went. 'I know what I'm looking for, Isabella. They used a peculiar type of binding back in those days. I'll know them as soon as I see them.'

They were in the second-last aisle when duPonti suddenly exclaimed, 'Aha! Here we are. Now, be very careful. The material will be extremely brittle.' The Oracle got down on his hands and knees to gently poke at the various loosely bound journals. 'This one will do. The journal's marked *Epidemic XII*. It's from the seventh century, so that makes it some seven hundred years old. Let's have a look.' He slowly opened the journal at the middle, and then gently turned the pages toward the beginning, where they both started to read.

'I'm having a have a bit of trouble reading it, Alexander. It's very faded and there are many words I simply don't recognize.'

'Europe was mostly made up of tribal communities back in those days, and their languages were substantially different, even if they were just a few miles apart. I can read most of it if I go slowly. Just point to words you don't understand and I'll translate what I can. The earlier volumes will have a lot of important information, but this volume seems to be right at the peak of the epidemic.'

They had almost reached the center of the volume when Isabella suddenly gasped and clasped her hands to her chest. Her face turned white and she was unable to exhale. She kept drawing breath until she thought her lungs would burst. Her eyes were wide with shock. DuPonti did not look much better. His hand shook as he held the fragile page.

Isabella finally managed to find her voice and pointed to a faint line of text. 'Is that ... is that ... the word for *millions*?' she managed to whisper.

DuPonti simply nodded, unable to speak, and slowly turned the page in the hope of finding better news on the other side. He didn't. It was worse.

'*Oh! Alexander!* Millions. Everywhere. Millions and millions and millions; tens of millions. Dead. Dead. Dead. Everywhere. No nation was spared. No-one was safe. The whole world faced death. It went on and on for generations. About half of Europe's population perished! At its beginning, the signs were just like what's happening right now. I think I'm going to be ill. Oh ... I ...' Isabella stepped away from the table and doubled up with pain. A minute later she straightened up and looked teary-eyed at the scribe. 'I wish I'd never come here, Alexander.'

DuPonti nodded and put the journal back exactly as he had found it. He stared for a long time at the world's worst-ever book of horror. 'I think we've seen enough,' he murmured hoarsely and walked out of the warehouse with his arm around a sobbing Isabella.

'I must have overheard someone talking about it when I was a very young boy,' Marcus said as he sat in the lounge, elbows on knees. 'I vaguely remember the subject, but none of the details.' He had just listened to Isabella's summary of what she and the Oracle had discovered in the archives.

'The present sickness can't have any connection with the past, surely, Grandfather. Not after 700 years.'

'No, absolutely not. Such horror could not happen twice. The starting patterns are similar, though ... But I'm quite sure this illness will fade away just like all the coughing sicknesses that go on every winter in the northern areas. So let's just take advantage of it while we can, as Dmitri suggested.'

Isabella felt better, but not by much. She was still shocked to have discovered how the world had suffered such devastation, almost annihilation. She wondered why information of that epidemic was not more readily available. Perhaps humankind had decided it simply did not wish to ever be reminded of such horror, and had deliberately hidden the details from future generations.

'You're right. If it were going to happen again, it wouldn't wait seven hundred years, would it? It just could not happen again, at least not as bad as that, so, as you say, let's use it to best advantage.'

Marcus nodded, his face serious. Like Isabella, he was not entirely convinced.

CHAPTER 36

Winter was considerably colder than usual, with a layer of snow blanketing the plateau, yet Isabella looked forward to her daily training session in the barn with Chen, followed by a session of sword-fighting techniques with Marcus. She felt warm for hours after each session.

On one cold January day, Chen surprised her by suddenly backing away and putting his hands up. She stopped instantly, bowed, and waited silently for instructions.

'It is near the end of lesson, Isabella, and I am tiring. I notice you now twice as strong as last year and I not getting younger. For future lessons I must wear pads and headgear for protection against your kicks.' He took another step back and stared at her appraisingly. 'No wonder. I just notice. You not only stronger, you getting bigger. Look at yourself!'

Isabella looked down, but two prominent bumps on her chest obscured her view of her lower half. She leaned forward and saw that the bones of her knees had disappeared beneath layers of new muscle and smooth skin. She had been too busy with her other plans to have noticed the changes to her figure.

She flushed but managed to grin at Chen. 'You had better go find an old woman to come and help you out, Zen Master.'

They both doubled up with laughter.

A visit to the city the following week brought news from Dmitri confirming that all was exactly as General Karamus had stated. Isabella responded that she must have made an incorrect and unfair assessment, and would let the matter rest.

King Ramesses had previously sent a message to General Karamus and requested that he ask his father, Theo, to attend the meeting scheduled for the following day. The king wanted to personally thank Theo for his and his associates' excellent efforts in the national interest.

The meeting went well and Karamus Senior beamed at the king's accolades. Strategies and secrets were not discussed in his presence, and he made moves to leave the meeting early so the others could get on with the business at hand.

Isabella had quietly moved to stand near the bay windows so that she would not have to shake hands on his departure. The man repelled her. As she gazed out through the glass panels, she happened to glance into a mirror on the wall slightly to her left, and saw father and son Karamus exchange glances for no more than a fleeting moment. She leaned forward slightly so that her face would not be visible in the mirror if either father or son should glance in her direction. They didn't. Her heart skipped a beat and hammered as she continued to stare out the window. She could scarcely breathe. The look she had seen exchanged between father and son was one of triumphant success, but most of all, of gloating and cunning.

The warning flag shot back up, and now nothing would ever make it go away. Unknown to Isabella, Theo Karamus had noticed that she was standing with her back to the room as he left. There had to be a reason for such discourtesy, and his own warning flag went up.

CHAPTER 37

Only *Barca* noticed the twenty killers as they swarmed up the hill to the plateau and surrounded the house. Although they were almost invisible in the darkness and silent on the thin layer of snow, *Barca* could smell them. *Humans. Intruders.* The gates were closed and it was too dark to jump the fence to investigate the intrusion, so there was nothing he could do other than sniff the air with rising anxiety and fury.

Four hooded figures slowly followed the twenty killers up the hill and headed to the small amphitheater. There they made themselves comfortable to watch the entertainment about to begin.

It was a little after four in the morning, and Marcus was in a deep sleep, blankets pulled over his ears to keep out the cold. A miserable Isabella dozed only occasionally. Most of her night had been spent tossing and turning with mounting frustration as she thought about Yannis and how long it had been since she had seen or heard from him. It would soon be a year.

She lay on her side and stared down the corridor while she tried to turn her mind to things that might help her sleep. There were no internal doors in the house, not even to the bedrooms. Light that came through partially lit other rooms making for reasonable ease of navigation at night. The corridor from Isabella's bedroom led to a private dining area just past the kitchen, then to a guest room and the lounge where they entertained. Other rooms led off the corridor from there, including the master bedroom used by Marcus. All was quiet and dark. Closing her eyes, she rolled over to face the wall in another futile attempt to sleep. Seconds later she sat bolt upright and looked down the corridor again. It was not only dark – it was too dark! When she had gone to bed, the night had been clear, with an almost full moon. Vision should have been more than adequate, but now it barely reached past the private dining area. Her senses told her that something was not as it should be. Fully awake, and with nothing better to do, she slipped out of bed to investigate.

Storm shutters attached to the kitchen window were closed and secured with latches on the outside, as were those in the dining room and the guest bedroom next to it. The lounge windows, however, were clear, as were those in the family room and library. Isabella was puzzled. Why would Grandfather secure some of the windows and not others? Why would he secure any windows at all? Although it was unseasonably cold on the plateau, there had been no expectations of a storm that night.

'Grandfather, wake up! *Grandfather!*' Isabella hissed as she pulled at the blanket covering Marcus' head.

'What? What's happening? What are you doing? What's wrong?' Marcus was still more asleep than awake.

'Grandfather, did you close some of the shutters? Is there a storm coming? Why did you not close all of them?'

'I don't know what you're talking about, darling. I didn't close any shutters. Go back to bed.' Marcus slumped back on the pillow, pulling the blanket back up.

'Well, someone has closed some of the shutters and left some of the windows clear. Who would do that?'

'I don't know. Perhaps Chen saw a storm brewing and was thoughtful enough to close the shutters facing the storm. We'll find out in the morning. Now go back to bed.'

Isabella sighed with resignation. 'Oh, all right. Good night, Grandfather. I'm sorry to wake you, but I worry when something seems out of the ordinary.'

'It's all right, Isabella. Good night.' His reply was muffled under the blanket.

Isabella walked down the short corridor and entered the lounge. Her body went ice cold in an instant. The lounge was dark, no mistake. The shutters had been quietly closed since she had last walked through the room. Chen would not do that. If a storm were coming, he would wake them, so that the entire farm, and the animals, could be secured.

'*Grandfather!* Someone is out there!' This time she did not bother to tug at Marcus' blanket. In a flash it was on the floor, with Isabella already hauling him out of bed. By the time his feet hit the floor, he was fully awake. Battle conditions in the past had conditioned the former general to wake rapidly in an emergency.

'*Tell me what's happening!*' he barked as he pulled on his clothes.

'The lounge window has just been secured, and I saw the library closed on one side, but by the time we look again, it will be fully closed. Come and see! Someone is out there, Grandfather. Someone wants us trapped inside the house!'

The two rushed to the lounge. The library shutters were now fully closed.

'Stay where you are, Grandfather.' Isabella ran to stand with her back against the wall next to one of the family-room windows. She slowly moved her head forward to peer out. It took several moments for the darkness to reveal its secrets. There were shadows where they should not be – shadows that moved when they should not. She did not like what she saw.

Running back to Marcus, she said 'There are people out there. Lots of people. They're just standing there, a few paces apart. We have to assume the house is surrounded. They are quietly closing in to trap us, so they mean to harm us. No, not just harm us; they mean to kill us.'

'What makes you think they want to kill us?'

'We're surrounded, with no chance of escape. To capture us, or hurt us, they will simply demand that we step outside.'

Before Isabella could react, Marcus picked up his sword and lifted his shield from the hook on the wall. 'Well, then, let's do just that. Let's go outside and see who it is and what they want.'

He walked to the door and flung it open just as Isabella managed to scream, 'No, don't! They'll kill you!'

The unmistakable clang of an arrowhead striking the shield gave Marcus his answer before he had even managed to ask the question. He slammed the door shut just as another arrow grazed his upper arm. Dull thuds penetrated the silence as several more arrows struck the door.

Marcus ignored the blood trickling down his arm as he called to those outside. 'What do you want? We are in no condition to fight. I will surrender if you promise no harm will come to Isabella.'

Footsteps crunched in the snow as the attackers neared the door. 'You miserable, stupid old fool!' a deep voice chuckled. 'She's the one we've come for. You're nothing but collateral damage.'

'What can I do to accommodate you? Can we negotiate something? Anything?'

The man laughed as his footsteps moved away. 'Prepare for your journey to the fires of hell.'

Isabella gasped. 'That's why they've trapped us inside. They're going to burn the house with us in it!'

Marcus walked from room to room lighting lamps. 'We need some light while we figure out what to do.'

Isabella nodded. 'I had a bad feeling at the Summer Palace the other day, but I really didn't think it would come to this. Chen is too far away to help us. He won't even know anything is happening. There's not much he could do, anyway. It's too dark and there are too many of them. We're on our own, Grandfather, and we don't have much time.'

Marcus raised his sword and broke a window before knocking a small hole in the storm shutter and peering out. What he saw horrified him. Men with flaming arrows were at the ready, while two men rolled barrels across the snow towards the door.

Isabella peered over his shoulder. 'They are getting ready to burn us. What's in those barrels?'

'Gunpowder.'

'That's what I figured. They want to be really sure, don't they?'

Marcus groaned. 'I'm afraid so.'

One of the four men in the amphitheater rose and moved towards the house. 'Time to have some fun,' he murmured to his three comrades.

'We should have brought some wine to accompany the entertainment,' one of the men added with a satisfied grin.

A series of thuds could be heard from every part of the house as dozens of flaming arrows hit the timber shutters and roof. Isabella threw her arms around Marcus when she heard the unmistakable crackle of fire. 'I love you, Grandfather. I'm so sorry I got you into this.'

Marcus kissed the top of her head. 'I love you too, Isabella, my love. But don't give up. We're not done yet. Our only chance is the cellar.'

'If they find us there, they'll simply roll a barrel down the stairs.'

'That's true, but do you have a better idea?' He coughed as smoke swirled around his face.

'No, I'm out of ideas.'

He grabbed her hand. 'Well, then, let's go!'

'Let's go!' she shouted and they both ran for the kitchen.

Only the kitchen and the adjoining dining room had timber floors. Throughout the remainder of the house the floor consisted of the customary hard-packed soil sealed with a thick cover of a variety of herbs. Not only were herb floors practical and soft; they kept the home smelling fresh. Marcus had deliberately designed the house's position so that the kitchen would cover a fissure in the landscape close to the cliff edge. The fissure opened into a deep, wide cavern, ideal as a larder when the availability of foodstuffs was restricted by distance and hard to come by out of season. The cavern was temperate, always cool in summer and in winter.

For additional stability, Marcus had secured the floor to timber posts driven into the ground in the small private dining area. A trapdoor in one corner of the kitchen, next to several shelving units, revealed a staircase to the rock floor of the cavern four yards below.

'Quickly now! Down you go.' Marcus lifted the trapdoor and moved aside to allow Isabella access to the stairs. 'I'll pull one of the shelves over with my sword-handle as I close the trapdoor. If we're lucky there might just be enough cinders on top to disguise the door. There is the risk it might burn all the way through, though.'

'See if you can get your shield on top of the trapdoor just as you pull the shelf down. A bit of metal there might help a bit.' Marcus took a last look around before he moved to the stairs. Flames could be seen licking the inside of one of the shutters, adding to the light from the lamps. He flicked the shield onto the trapdoor and held it in place with one hand as he hooked the hilt of the sword over the back edge of a shelf unit.

'*Wait!* Grandfather, wait!' Isabella shrieked as she darted up the stairs past Marcus. '*The portraits!* Mummy and Daddy. I can't let them burn! It's all we have left of them.'

'No! There isn't time. That gunpowder could be primed to go off any minute. Better to sacrifice the portraits than our lives.'

'Never!' Isabella ducked past him in an instant and ran to the library to retrieve her most precious possessions. Anton Mondeo smiled at her from his place on the shelf, next to his beautiful wife, both blissfully unaware of the mortal danger now faced by their beloved daughter. She picked up the two small portraits and spun around to flee into the lounge. The main door was directly in front of her on the other side of the room, with the corridor leading to the kitchen and the trapdoor to her left. Isabella froze with shock a second later.

CHAPTER 38

'Get that powder in place now before it's too late, you fool!' the hooded man yelled to one of the killers. 'There are four barrels to place, and I want the blast contained on the inside for maximum power. There must be no evidence left behind to point anyone in our direction.'

'The fire is getting a bit fierce now, boss. It would be safer to do it from the outside.'

'One more comment like that and I swear I will put you to the sword. Is that clear? Now pick up that barrel and follow me.' The hooded man hoisted a barrel onto his shoulder and moved towards the door, his accomplice close behind. 'This is how you do it.' He lifted one leg, kicked down the door that had never been locked, and smashed it against the inside wall.

Isabella froze with shock as the door directly in front of her smashed inwards to reveal two men, each with a large barrel on his shoulder.

'Well, well, well! What have we here? The guest of honor herself, no less.' The hooded man laughed as he entered the room. He indicated where the other man was to place his barrel in the center of the room. 'I'll give you a choice, pretty missy. You can burn as planned, or if you are a really good little girl and stand still for me, I will do you a favor and put you to the sword. Quick and easy. What do you say?'

'Oh, lucky me,' was all she could manage. She kept a tight grip on the wooden frames of the portraits as her gaze flicked towards the corridor leading to the kitchen. It would be impossible to get past the two men.

'Grandfather, stay where you are!' she screamed. 'There's nothing you can do – you will only get in the way. I can handle this!'

The man grinned, revealing a mouthful of rotted teeth. 'Ah, I like that! A sense of humor to the very end.' His revolting grin faded as he put his barrel down and turned to the other man. 'Take care of her while I get the other two barrels in here. I don't know where the old man's hiding, and I don't care. If he tries to run out the door while you finish her off, let him. We'll get him outside. Take no chances. Kill the girl or we'll all die.' He looked around and up at the ceiling. Fire had not yet penetrated the lounge or the ceiling. 'Before you do, loosen the tops of these two barrels, but don't take them off until we leave. As soon as the roof caves in – *boom!*' He roared with laughter as he walked outside, leaving the killer and Isabella alone to get better acquainted.

'I'll just stretch and wring your pretty little neck. That way at least one of us gets to have a little fun.' As he crooked his finger at her, the man grinned, revealing teeth even worse than the hooded man's. Isabella darted towards the corridor and waited for the man to make his counter move before she sprang back to her original position. Her next move was towards the open door, but she darted back as soon as he moved. She had no intention of entering the corridor to reveal where Marcus was, or of trying to escape. Escape was out of the question. The man wanted to play, so she played – played for time. Her timing had to be perfect to have any chance against the two men. Chen had spent nine months teaching her some of the secrets of the Zen Master. He had made a point of stating that some of them were extremely dangerous to those on the receiving end. Isabella briefly wondered whether she had been a competent student.

As soon as she heard the crunch of footsteps in the snow, she gently spun the two portraits across the room to the corridor that led to the kitchen. First one, then the other. A bit of practice for later. Flames had started to lick through the shutters in several places. And the smoke was almost unbearable. She deliberately darted, and then halted in the archway of the family room, knowing full well that the room had no other exit.

'Oh, for heaven's sake, finish her off! Now!' The hooded man was furious as he dumped the barrel on the floor. 'I'll be back in one minute and then we're out of here. I want that girl dead by the time I get back. That's an order. Dump her body on top of the barrels when you're done with her.' He walked out the door to get the last barrel. Isabella allowed herself forty seconds. *Now!*

She widened her eyes in feigned horror as she backed quickly into the family room, forcing the man to follow. His superior had given him a time limit. A little over halfway across the room, she moved to one side and faced the man as he moved to the center, placing himself between Isabella and the couch against the far wall. Having made some rapid calculations, she gave him no time to think as she rushed him. Surprise was as valuable as strength, and the man had no inkling that he was the one to be attacked. Her body spun a full circle and her calloused foot came up to connect with his mouth, forcing his head and body backwards. Rotted teeth sprayed out as she quickly maneuvered her legs and hips against his, at the same time smashing her elbow into his nose that sent him reeling backwards and out of control towards to the couch. Instead of following him, Isabella quickly moved to the far side of the room, reassessed both the distance and the moment when the man would strike the couch, and ran forward at full speed.

Her palms hit the ground at the center of the room, and her body spun before her feet landed, instantly hurling her with maximum force into the air for a full somersault, her body curled into a tight ball, hands around her knees. The man was unable to comprehend what he was seeing as he sprawled on his back on the couch, his legs stretched out on an angle to the ground, leaving his knees exposed. Isabella's body landed shoulders first, like a cannon-ball, directly on the man's knee joints, and instantly smashed them. The breaking sound of bones was louder than the cracking of the fire.

Isabella heard the man scream but did not see him throw up from the pain before passing out. She was already out of the room. Unable to walk, the man was of no further interest to her. The crunching of snow warned her that she had only seconds to get to the corridor to retrieve the portraits. She picked up both and darted to the kitchen, where she held the frame of her father's portrait against the now fierce flames destroying the shutter.

'Get ready, Grandfather,' she hissed at Marcus, who was staring wide-eyed at his granddaughter. 'The shield. The sword. Everything we planned. I'll slip past you and then you do your bit. Pull the trap down as fast as you can and dive for the ground. Our fate will be decided in the next few seconds.'

Another one of the hooded men rose from the amphitheater to move towards the fire. 'It won't be long now. The last barrel is going in and it won't be more than ten minutes before the roof caves in. It's time to get the men to move well back. We probably should move further back ourselves. I don't know what effect the powder will have on the more solid part of the building, and we don't want to be killed by flying debris.' He chuckled as he moved forward to speak to the men surrounding the house.

•

'Where are you? Why is that girl's body not on top of the barrels like I told you, you stupid old woman?' The hooded man dropped the fourth barrel next to the other three, one of which Isabella had deliberately kicked onto its side as she ran for the corridor, spilling some of its contents out from under the loose lid. 'Where are you? We've got to get out of here. Where is that *girl*?'

'Hello-o-o. Here I am, sir.' Isabella moved the picture back and forth against the flames. Two sides of the frame were by then well alight.

The man spun to stare up the corridor at Isabella, who was waving at him with her sweetest smile. His eyes widened when he saw Marcus' face at floor level behind her. 'What do you think you're doing?'

Isabella held up the flaming portrait of her father for the man to see. 'Have you met my father? His name is Anton Mondeo, a wonderful, wonderful man, and he is about to save the life of his precious daughter.' She held the portrait up high enough to enable her to kiss her father's face before she turned the frame on its side. 'Good bye, Father, and thank you for everything.' With a flick of her wrist, the picture was on its way as she had practiced just minutes earlier, spinning towards its target like so many of the fascinating weapons to which she had been introduced by Zhang Chen.

'Now!' she shouted and dived for the trapdoor. There was no time to see if the portrait would land where she had aimed it. If she saw it land, she would die.

As he watched the flaming missile spin its way towards his feet, the hooded man saw Isabella disappear into the floor. He made no attempt to move; there was no point. The fastest man in the world could not outrun the missile or the blast that would follow within a second. He looked down with resigned disinterest at the portrait as it landed on the pile of gunpowder that had spilled from the overturned barrel. A handsome face smiled up at him and seemed to wink just as the powder beneath ignited. He saw nothing else.

The hooded man outside had almost reached the open door. 'It's time to move away, men, all the way to the other side of the arena.' He cupped his hands to his mouth and yelled through the open door. 'Hey, you two, get out of there! Don't worry about the girl and the old man. If the flames don't get them, they'll be done for when the gunpowder – '

He felt nothing as his body vaporized in the blast. The killers still surrounding the building were ground into a paste, before the heat and shockwaves vaporized any remaining trace of them.

Rolling across the plateau like an invisible avalanche, the shockwaves knocked the remaining two hooded men face-first into the sand and gravel of the arena as they were moving away from the house. As soon as they regained their senses, they rose from the sand and ran back to survey the damage and search for their men. Light from the flames was more than adequate to assess the situation. There was no house, no men, no bodies, and no clothes – nothing. They realized at once that they were the only survivors of the twenty-four men who had swarmed up the hill less than an hour earlier.

After watching the fire silently for several minutes, one of them spoke, shock clearly evident in his voice. 'Well, the boss got what he wanted. No witnesses and no evidence left behind. The girl is dead and so is the old man. I think it's time to get out of here, Shaka. Hey, did you see that?'

The other man chuckled, happy to be alive. 'Yeah, just some nosy animal checking to see if a roast is on offer.'

The two surviving *Disciplinarians* watched the fire for another minute before they left as silently as they had arrived.

CHAPTER 39

Zhang Chen was out of bed and in the bedroom archway within an instant of feeling the shockwave. *Earthquake!* In the poorer areas of China where he had spent most of his early life, earthquakes were common and its inhabitants either quickly learned what to do or perished. Thousands perished, anyway, and Chen knew that this could be his time to die.

A moment later the roar of the explosion reached his ears. *No earthquake!* Earthquakes sounded nothing like that. He ripped open the door and ran barefoot onto the snow-covered ground to look around. Smoke and flames soared into the sky at the northern end of the plateau, exactly where the Mondeo home would be. Marcus! *Isabella!*

Within a minute he had dressed in his shaggiest leather gear and headed into the tree-line, where his appearance instantly changed from that of a human to a beast. He dropped to all fours and trotted towards the flames at a steady pace. No-one saw him, but if they had, they would have sworn they had seen a wolf or a bear on the hunt. His heart rate was slow; his mind was fast. The Zen Master's shadow – *the Dark Warrior* – had taken control of his body and his emotions.

On the way he quickly reviewed what he had seen and heard. His chores included keeping inventory of everything in the cottages, barns, main house, and in particular, the cellar. There was nothing at or near the house that could cause an explosion of any kind. Explosives had therefore been brought to the plateau by intruders. Peril – mortal peril – lay ahead.

Moments later he saw the killers: two hooded men staring into the inferno from a distance of a hundred paces. Unable to see their faces clearly, he decided to move across open ground to another clump of trees, closer to the fire. He knew he would be in their direct line of sight, but did not hesitate after untying his ponytail to allow his long hair to cover his face. The bright flames would diffuse the vision of the two men, who would see only what they expected to see: a four-legged animal on the prowl.

He moved closer to where he could clearly see the men's faces, despite the hoods. He did not recognize them and turned his attention to the flames. The mud bricks had vanished, leaving behind nothing but bare earth covered with burning timber. He could guess what had happened: the explosion had destroyed the bricks and internal walls and lifted the timber roof and support beams straight up. They had been smashed into the ground as the pressure wave moved outwards, leaving behind a vacuum. Anything, and anyone in and around the house would have been destroyed, he realized, including Marcus and Isabella.

Surprisingly, there were no signs of anyone else in the vicinity. Two men alone could not have carried the required quantity of gunpowder up the steep hill to the plateau. Others must have left the scene earlier or perished in the explosion. There was an easy way to find out. *The Dark Warrior* moved swiftly down the hill to wait for his prey.

The silence was broken one minute later by the sound of crunching snow and stumbling footsteps on the uneven path. *The Dark Warrior*, on all fours, suddenly appeared from behind rocks and trotted alongside the two men about twenty paces away, just within sight in the dim dawn light. The men saw the shaggy creature and slowed, drawing their swords. The creature slowed to the same pace, moving closer before it emitted a low growl.

Fearful now, the men stopped to stare at the ghostly form closing in on them. They saw its head point at the moon before it let out a blood-curdling howl that turned their blood to ice. Still howling, the beast suddenly rose from the ground like a giant bear and launched itself at the two men.

Petrified with fear of the unknown, the men found that swords were of no use as they were slammed onto their backs. Short, sharp punches to the solar plexus and kidneys left them breathless; pressure to their necks left them paralyzed. They stared up into the face of a man – or was it a beast? – with eyes that seemed to glow red in the lightening sky.

'If you want to get away, you tell me what I want to know,' snarled *the Dark Warrior*. He tapped the throat of one of the men. 'Where girl and general?'

'They're dead. Who are you? What are you?' The man's voice was hoarse.

'Where are others that come with you?'

'What others?'

'Tell me only answers or I kill you. Where are others, and who you work for?'

'If I talk, he will kill me.'

'I kill you and throw you on fire if you do not. Make choice. *Now!*'

'I can't. He won't let me live.'

'Then you no use to me.' *The Dark Warrior's* hands moved like lightning and the man went limp after a loud cracking sound from his neck. Zhang Chen turned his attention to the other man.

'He go into fire now. What about you? Where you want to go?'

'What Shaka said is true. I will be killed if I talk.'

'You can get on horse and ride all the way to Russia. He never find you there. Now tell me, where are others?'

The man hesitated. 'They died in the explosion. It went off before it was supposed to.'

'How many were you?'

'Twenty-four.'

'And everyone die except for two?'

'Everyone. They just vanished.'

'Why did general have to die?'

'It wasn't him. The girl was the target. The general had to die, too, but he was secondary to the target.'

The Dark Warrior was shocked. Isabella was the target of twenty-four killers? What was going on?

'Now for last question and you can go. Who your employer? Give me name.'

'I can go then?'

'Yes, you go then.'

The man groaned. 'His name is Theo Karamus. He did not say why the girl had to die. Karamus just tells us what to do, and we do it.'

'What about son? General Karamus?'

'No, he knows nothing about this. Can I go now?'

'Yes, you go now, but you not go to Russia. Sorry to lie, but you kill my daughter.' Like Shaka, the man did not hear the sound of his neck breaking.

Chen used the men's bodies, one at a time, as shields so he could get close enough to toss them into the inferno. There was nothing else to be done. He walked back to the amphitheater to wait quietly for the fire to burn itself out before he could check on his only hope: the cellar. He curled up and quickly went to sleep in the glow of the heat.

CHAPTER 40

Marcus and Isabella were hurled down the staircase by the blast. Isabella hit the rock floor and gasped for breath as she saw chunks of rock fall away from the sides of the cave. Lovingly built shelving units disintegrated, their contents flying in all directions as the pressure-wave bounced from wall to wall. Marcus was buried beneath rubble and foodstuffs with only one leg visible. The sturdy staircase collapsed and fell at an angle on top of Isabella, injuring her back but providing protection from falling rocks and debris.

Ignoring the pain, she crawled over to Marcus and began to methodically toss debris to one side, starting with his head and chest areas. Coughing and spitting sounds soon let her know he was alive. Fifteen minutes later he was sitting against a wall with his arm around his relieved rescuer.

'How are we going to get out of here? There's no way up now.' Marcus surveyed the damage, including the collapsed staircase. Only one of the four lamps he had lit earlier was still burning.

'I can hear the fire raging up there, so we can't leave anyway,' Isabella said. 'The attackers, minus the two in the house, have most probably already left. There would be little reason for them to wait until daylight after that explosion. They don't know about the cellar, so they would not expect anyone to survive. What we should do right now is move any flammable items away from the trapdoor in case it burns through and collapses on top of us.' She studied their surroundings further. 'Let's get a couple of wine barrels over here as well. We can smash them to flood the area if we need to. Then I think we should get some sleep. Chen knows about the cellar and, on the off-chance that we're here, he'll come and take a look after the fire burns itself out.'

'I hate to say it, Isabella, but we have to be practical and consider all possibilities. There is a chance that the killers have already found Chen and … ah … done something to him.'

Isabella smiled. 'Not a chance. If anyone made contact with him, I pity them.' Marcus did not know about the Zen Master. Conversely, Isabella did not know about *The Dark Warrior*.

Hours later Isabella woke to the sound of water splashing near her, and felt some of it spray on her face. Then everything went quiet. 'Grandfather, wake up! Someone's here.'

'Who is it?'

'I don't know, but we had better be quiet just in case it's the attackers. They could have decided to stay to check things out in daylight.'

Within a minute, another cascade of water poured through the trapdoor. Seconds later a third cascade was followed by the sound of the trapdoor being smashed. It finally gave way and crashed to the floor of the cave in a cloud of soot, together with the bronze shield.

With a mixture of fear and hope, Isabella and Marcus stared up at a clear blue sky. Suddenly a face appeared in the opening – a handsome oriental face that immediately shone with pure joy as his dearest wish was granted.

'Ah! Anyone for cup of tea?'

'There were *twenty-four* sent to kill us?' Isabella asked incredulously as she savored the scalding hot tea in Chen's cottage. 'And they're all dead?'

'To kill *you*, Isabella. You were target. And yes, they all dead. All die in explosion and fire. They ash now.'

'How do you know their number if there is nothing left of them?'

'Two survive explosion. They tell all.'

'But you said they are all dead. How did you … oh, never mind.' She rolled her eyes and looked away.

'They tell me Theo Karamus send them.'

'What about his son?' Marcus asked.

Chen shook his head. 'He know nothing.'

'Well, we're going to make sure that he continues to know nothing. We must also make sure that Theo Karamus does not find out what we now know. I'm sorry, Chen, but we are restricted by the king to add much to what *you* now know.' Marcus drained the last of his tea. 'All right, then, this is what we'll do: I'll leave at once to visit Captain Cavarro to get him to back up our story that the three of us stayed with him for a celebration party last night. We arrived back here an hour ago to be shocked to find that some of my past enemies had seen fit to attack my home and family. Believing us to be inside, the attackers encircled the house with explosives and set them off. Through a serious miscalculation of the quantity of explosives used, the attackers appear to have blown themselves up without a trace. A large number of unfamiliar horses were seen in the area, but we were unable to catch any. We are therefore unable to identify anyone. Are you with me so far?'

Isabella nodded. 'Good story, Grandfather. Even I believe it.'

Marcus continued. 'Let's give the attackers' horses a drink and a feed, and then chase them away before I leave. I'll stay overnight with Linus and swear him to secrecy. He'll be fine – he'll do anything for us. While I'm there I'll pen a letter to the king detailing what I've just said. Early tomorrow morning, Chen, you'll ride into the city, pick up my letter and deliver it for me. We'll let the king circulate the lie for us. It's bound to spread like wildfire, and Theo will believe it because it's coming from the king and not one of his men will have reported back to him. He will be disappointed that the mission was not successful, but relieved that there are no witnesses, and that we know nothing.

'Next time I'm face to face with the king and Dmitri, I'll tell them the truth. They know what the stakes are, so they'll understand the lie. While I'm gone, Chen, perhaps you would make the summer cottage ready for occupation while we consider what to do about a new home. In the meantime, Isabella, I want you to lie on the couch in front of that fire and get some well-earned rest. You won't believe it, Chen, and I don't know how she did it, but Isabella took care of two burly killers before setting off the explosion that finished off twenty more.'

'Ouch. Thanks for the reminder, Grandfather.'

Zhang Chen did not know how Isabella had done it, but he did believe it. She had always been a most competent student. He grinned at her as he gave her a wink and the thumbs up, and pointed to the couch. She kissed both men, pulled a blanket over her head and was asleep by the time the men had left the cottage.

As Marcus had predicted, the news spread quickly. King Ramesses was shocked twice: once when he received Marcus' letter, and then several days later when Marcus told him the truth.

'This is an outrage and a sacrifice,' he said, 'that you and Isabella will not bear alone. I will continue to support the lie you spread – it is a brilliant one, to be honest – and I will let it be known that damage caused by enemies of a former general will be fully compensated by the state. Work will commence immediately to build you and Isabella the most magnificent home you could wish for.'

CHAPTER 41

Spring blossoms had just started to appear when a messenger brought an invitation to Marcus for an audience with the king. The invitation specified that he was to come alone. Isabella accompanied him to the city, where they stayed overnight at the usual guest-house. The next morning Marcus left for his meeting at the palace, while Isabella visited the city's main library to view some detailed maps of specific areas that held her interest.

More than a dozen boys of similar age and some a year or two older were moving quietly about the library as she searched for a table large enough for her purpose. She had known most of them all her life and had played with several at her home, as well as at theirs. She waved to them and they waved back with broad smiles. Bit by bit they managed to find reasons to move to tables surrounding Isabella's.

Eventually she found a map of particular interest, spread it out over the table and leaned forward to study it in detail. Her long blond hair tumbled over her shoulders in soft waves to brush against the surface of the map. After several minutes of deep concentration, some instinct caused her to straighten, lift her head and look around.

The boys had stopped what they were doing and were staring at her with open admiration, as if it were the first time they had noticed her. In many ways it was. She turned a shade of scarlet on seeing that the boys were mesmerized by her. They in turn were embarrassed when they realized they had been caught staring. In an automatic response she grinned and wagged a finger at them. The boys relaxed to see that she had taken their obvious interest as a compliment. Although embarrassed, Isabella was also *excited*. The blossoming she had been waiting for had at last started.

Marcus had already arrived back from the palace when she returned to the guest-house. When she asked how his meeting went, he simply stared at her with glassy eyes and shook his head. Isabella decided to wait until he was in a better frame of mind before she asked again. They had an early dinner and she went to bed while Marcus sat in a chair and stared silently into the unlit fireplace. She tossed and turned restlessly as her mind replayed over and over how the boys in the library had so openly displayed their interest in her.

They arrived back at the plateau the following afternoon. Marcus stepped down from the wagon and helped Isabella as she jumped to the ground. Chen was already there to take the wagon to the barn and care for the horses.

As Marcus watched the wagon move out of sight, he sighed and turned to Isabella. 'We need to talk,' was all he said as he walked towards the cottage. Isabella simply nodded and followed. She knew he would speak when he was ready.

The construction of their new home was already under way. Despite their protestations, the house would be almost four times the size of the previous one, a veritable palace taking full advantage of the magnificent views of the valley. Marble floors would flow throughout, and beautiful granite, terracotta and travertine were already stockpiled for the masons to begin their work in early summer. Isabella had almost fainted when she had first seen the architect's drawings.

Marcus came straight to the point as soon as they were seated in the tiny lounge. 'Isabella, I've been seconded to the army for the campaign. I'll maintain my rank of general, but not in a command capacity. There will be a number of other generals in command, and Karamus will be the supreme commander. The king wants me to go as an adviser, as I'm the only current general with battle experience. I told him I have too many personal responsibilities to take care of, and that I would have to decline his invitation. He insisted; he said it wasn't an *invitation,* and went on about the national interest and how General Karamus did not have his full confidence despite what he and his father have achieved. After recent events, of course, he can never trust them again. I'm afraid I couldn't refuse him.'

'Of course you couldn't, Grandfather. There was never a doubt in my mind that he would need you on the campaign. The men need your experience. You really have no choice. You *must* go, for the sake of the men as well as the nation.'

'But the risks are horrendous. I won't have a command so I will be safer than if I were in the front lines. But I do have to be near the center of things, so if our lines are breached, I'll bear the same risk as the other soldiers.'

Isabella slipped off her chair and came over to sit on the floor in front of Marcus. She leaned an arm on his knee and took his hand in hers. 'I fully understand the risks. It's war, and that is simply the way it is.' She gazed up at him with a look he had not seen before, the look of a tiger immediately before it pounced. 'You need not be concerned. What responsibilities are you referring to?'

'Well, the property, the farm, the animals for a start.'

'Not a problem. Others will take care of them.'

'Chen?'

'No, I have other plans for Chen. Mary's family will take care of the farm, and most of the animals.'

'Most of them?'

'I will be taking care of *Barca*. So, what else?'

'There is the little matter of the one and only love of my life: my beautiful granddaughter.' He squeezed her hand as his eyes watered.

'Well, you need not worry about me, my beautiful Grandfather. I made my plans a long time ago when I knew that you would join the campaign.'

'You knew?'

'Of course. I always knew you would have to join the campaign.'

'So what are these *plans* you've made? Where do you propose to stay while I am away? It could be years.'

'Yes, I know. And my plan is simple: I will be going with you!'

Dumbstruck, Marcus slumped back in his chair. He shook his head and closed his eyes, only to open them and see Isabella calmly studying her fingernails. When she saw she had his attention, she folded her hands together on his knee and placed her chin on top, looking up at him like a green-eyed puppy.

'Impossible! You can't be serious. Anyway, it doesn't matter what *I* think; it simply will not be allowed. In three months you will be only fourteen. *Fourteen!* What are you thinking of?'

'But it does matter what you think, Grandfather. No one will dare refuse you.'

'The king will refuse me.'

'No he won't. He won't refuse you. Oh, and by the way, Chen doesn't know it yet, but he will be coming along as my guardian angel. I can work as a nurse and Chen as a baggage handler as part of the camp followers, so we won't be a burden to anyone. I will, of course, take *Barca* with me. So, Grandfather, when are we leaving?'

'*We* are not leaving. *I* am leaving and *you* are not! You'll be staying with Mary, while Chen works the property.'

'Oh dear. Poor Mary.' Isabella went back to studying her fingernails.

'What do you mean: *poor Mary?*'

She took a long moment to bat her eyelashes a few times and twist her hair around her fingers. She sighed dramatically. '*Poor Mary* won't be quick enough to catch me when I run away and follow you from a distance.'

'You'll do no such thing, young lady!'

'Well, it's the only practical way, if the other part of my plan is denied me.'

'And which part of your plan is that?'

'The part where I intend to die on the battlefield – with you and Uncle Nicho by my side ...,' Isabella turned her head to one side so Marcus would not see the tears, 'and next to Yannis.'

'Ah ... I see.' This time it was Marcus who turned his head to one side. He finally turned back and sighed. 'Very well. I'll talk to the king, but don't set your hopes too high.' He leaned forward and kissed the top of her head.

'Thank you, Grandfather.' Isabella squeezed his knee and batted her eyelashes at him again.

'Will someone *ever* win a debate with you?'

'No.'

Marcus rolled his eyes and groaned.

CHAPTER 42

'*Impossible!*'

'That's exactly what I said, Your Majesty.'

'She is not yet fourteen, for heaven's sake!'

'That's also exactly what I said.'

'And she's … what else *exactly* did you say to her, Marcus?'

'About a hundred things, and none of them made a difference.'

'And what was her reaction to your protestations?'

'She said she volunteered last year to be the first to join the campaign. She wants to fulfil her wish, sir.'

'I seem to remember something about her volunteering. But what's this about a wish?'

'Her wish is to die on the battlefield next to me and Nicholas – and Yannis Christos.' Marcus looked embarrassed as he continued. 'She said that … ah … that she would simply run away and follow me from a distance until she saw the opportunity to join us on the battlefield. Isabella gave me no choice but to argue her case with you.'

'I can scarcely believe what I am hearing. So, her wish is to perish, fighting beside you and the handsome young Lieutenant Christos, eh?' Ramesses glanced out at the terrace, where Isabella sat on the stone steps gazing out at the clear blue waters. He stared at her for a long time before he finally shook his head and turned back to Marcus. 'Marcus, please ask Isabella to come in, and I'll give her the bad news myself.'

Marcus nodded. *I'm sorry, Isabella, I've done all I can.* Isabella turned as she heard him open one of the glass-paneled doors and walk on to the terrace. 'Isabella, the king wishes to speak with you. He indicated he wished to personally give you the bad news.'

A shadow crossed her face, but she merely shrugged, took his hand and they walked into the conference room together to face the king.

Ramesses came straight to the point. 'Do you have anything else to say, young lady, before I give you the bad news?'

'No, Your Majesty. Grandfather knows how I feel, and I know he would have said everything just as well as I could. Whatever your decision is, sir, I will abide by it.'

'Well, you had better sit down, both of you, for the bad news.' As soon as they were seated, he placed both his hands on top of hers and looked into a sea of green.

'I'm afraid that the bad news, Isabella, is that you are going to war!'

Isabella stared at Ramesses for a long moment without speaking. She felt relief and satisfaction flow through her like a raging fire. She rose slowly and wrapped her arms around the king's neck and held him in a long embrace.

'Thank you, thank you, thank you, Ramesses,' she murmured as she finally let go and kissed his cheek. Tears streaming down her face, she turned to embrace Marcus. 'Thank you, Grandfather, I love you so much.'

Turning, she fled the room through the open door to the terrace. She kept running at full speed across the grass and over the flower beds until she reached the water's edge. There she threw out her arms as if to embrace the last rays of the sun as it kissed the horizon.

The two men stared at her outline: a swirling silhouette with arms outstretched against a blazing ball of orange. Her arms descended as slowly as the sun and did not touch her sides until the giant disc had slipped beneath the horizon. It was as if she had held the sun and controlled its descent. *Perhaps she had,* both men thought.

As they watched, a young girl turned away from the water and a young woman walked back to the palace. 'Now that was a sight to behold, Marcus,' Ramesses said as he moved away from the window.

'Indeed it was.' Marcus hesitated, but he had to ask the question. 'What made you decide that Isabella could come with me, sir?'

'If she were not permitted to join the campaign,' Ramesses replied, 'I do believe that she would simply follow you a half day behind. That would leave her alone and exposed to the elements, as well as to a multitude of other dangers. At least this way, she'll be surrounded by thousands.'

Marcus nodded. 'Yes, there is that, sir. She will also have her own bodyguard – possibly the most dangerous man in the nation.'

'Excellent! Besides ...' Ramesses added with a smirk.

'*Besides?*'

'Besides, I have no doubt Isabella will prove to be the most valuable asset of this campaign.'

This time Marcus smiled broadly as he nodded. 'Yes, there is that, too.'

CHAPTER 43

Summer approached, but it was still unusually cool. Ramesses stood with his back to the fireplace, thoroughly enjoying the heat that radiated against his aching back. He faced the four people he liked and trusted more than any others: Dmitri, Marcus, Nicholas and Isabella.

'It's hard to believe it's more than a year since we first heard of the coming war. And here we are, planning an attack. We're doing the very same thing as those northern barbarians.' Ramesses glanced at Isabella, who appeared decidedly impatient. 'Sorry, I'm rambling on a bit. You have the floor, Isabella. You asked for this meeting.'

Isabella walked to the giant map on the wall and picked up the wooden pointer next to, using it to stab at several locations. 'Keep these places in mind, please. They could become very important, depending on how we perform at the first ... *encounter*.'

Ramesses and the others nodded, but no-one spoke.

'Vlado Karamus will, of course, carry out the initial attack. Because he doesn't have our trust, I believe we should hedge our bets with a backup plan.' With her infectious giggle, and eyes flashing wickedly, she added, 'And just for you, Dmitri, I also have a Plan C.'

Dmitri grinned and slapped his thigh in delight. 'I'll have you on my staff the moment you're old enough, Isabella.'

'Tell us about your backup plan.' Ramesses had walked over to study the map while Isabella was speaking.

'It's in two parts. Dmitri will install a *second*, and secret, pigeon network throughout the continent. During the campaign, he and I will communicate only through that network. The potential benefits are priceless, the additional cost negligible.'

'Excellent!' Ramesses seemed pleased.

'The second part will come into play only if the initial attack doesn't have the result that we'd hoped for. It's complex and it's costly, and I will need a huge quantity of something that is almost impossible to get hold of – something that's *extremely* dangerous!'

'What on earth are you talking about?' Nicholas asked. 'What is it that you'll need?'

She told them.

Ramesses took a step back as if struck. The others were too stunned to speak. Smiling broadly, Isabella swung the wooden pointer back and forth between her thumb and forefinger. She loved to shock. 'I did say it was extremely dangerous.'

Marcus was confused. 'How on earth are you going to get hold of forty tons of gunpowder?'

'I just happen to know of someone who can provide it when the time comes, Grandfather.' Deliberately leaving out key parts that she knew they would never agree to, she went on to detail more about her ideas,

Dmitri was the first to speak. 'You do have a gift for being able to think outside the square, Isabella. Your back-up plan would be a very significant undertaking. If implemented, it will require our best engineers, plus thousands of tradesmen and laborers. Now that we've resolved the matter of *communications*, I can see you've turned your mind to *deception*. You would be quite the magician if you were to carry this one off. It's going to take me and my team of analysts a little while to get our heads around it.'

'You've kept your thoughts much to yourself. Is that wise?' Ramesses frowned at Isabella. 'There will be many dangers on the campaign itself, and no-one is immune from the spreading illness. Your plans might be essential to our very survival.'

Isabella looked stricken. 'Oh … I … you're right, Ramesses. I hadn't considered that. I'll provide Dmitri with a detailed report of all of my plans. Dmitri, if something should happen to me, then please implement or discard my ideas as you see fit.'

Dmitri nodded. 'Thank you, my dear.'

Ramesses appeared relieved. 'I guess we can now move on to the next plan?'

'It will involve not only gunpowder, but naphtha – also known as Greek Fire, the most dangerous mixture known to man. I'm afraid the next plan is considerably worse than the previous.'

'Oh dear! I think I'd better sit down, then. Your last one almost knocked me off my feet!'

CHAPTER 44

It was time to take back control from his general, Emperor Kuiper thought. Maurice needed a reminder as to who was the emperor. Aloise's annoyance remained undiminished, with the Russian portion of his treasure already close to exhaustion. Moreover, he had had to send for the portion hidden in Sweden, as well. The remainder would then be retrieved to be close at hand and, somehow, he had to keep knowledge of it from Margarethe. He was not a happy man.

It was late spring and the temperature in the library was pleasant. Aloise remembered that it was more than a year since the general had first shown him the map of the target country and had gone out of his way to highlight the diamond mines. He snorted with annoyance and quickly sat down as he heard footsteps approaching.

'Good afternoon, sir.' General Von Franckel made a polite bow as he entered.

'General,' the emperor said, without enthusiasm.

'You wished to see me, sir?'

'Yes, I did. Sit down, Maurice.' The general sat and quietly waited to be told why he had been summoned.

Aloise leaned back and stared coldly at Von Franckel. 'I've been thinking about the list of men and materiel you presented last month.'

'Yes?'

'You have chosen all the best officers *and* the most experienced troops for the campaign.'

'That is correct, sir.'

'Well, leave the total number unchanged, but you will take only one-*half* of the best officers, and only one-*third* of the best soldiers. I don't care whether you make up the difference from lower-rate career soldiers or from the conscripts. That's it. That's all I wanted to let you know. A new list by the end of May will be fine. Oh, and at the same time, let me know how the cannons are coming along.'

Von Franckel felt as if he had been encased in ice. He sat frozen, barely able to breathe. He was furious, furious at the proposed change and what it could mean to the campaign, furious with the emperor for interfering in army affairs, but above all, furious at what the order meant to his *real* plan.

Aloise studied his fingernails, thoroughly pleased with the general's discomfort. His gaze flitted about the bookshelves as he fought the urge to laugh. He could barely wait for the general's reaction.

'Surely you jest, sir. I trust you're not serious.' Von Franckel finally found his voice.

'Oh yes. Quite serious.'

'This is going to be one of the largest campaigns the world has ever witnessed. To guarantee success, my army has to present as the most professional, well-armed force ever assembled. I can't afford to sweep across Europe with a bunch of amateurs.'

'Ah, thank you for bringing up the matter of weapons. I meant to mention that, too, but I forgot. How remiss of me! You will take only *one* thousand cannons. Leave the remaining thousand with the home army. The same goes for the other new weapons: pikes, longbows, crossbows, slings and so on. You will take half, and leave half.'

'But, sir, with respect, that is unreasonable, especially at this late planning stage.'

Respect indeed, my fine friend! 'On the contrary, my dear Maurice, what is unreasonable is sending all my best officers and soldiers where they are not needed.'

'But they *are* all needed!'

Aloise was pleased. The conversation was headed exactly where he wanted it. Maurice had obviously forgotten that because Aloise had once been a general, he was not totally ignorant of battle strategies. He waved a finger back and forth. 'No, no, no! They are not all needed. You told me so yourself.'

'I did? When did I say that?'

'You told me that when the Southern forces see your two hundred thousand men lined up on their border, and stare down the barrels of your cannons, they will surrender on the spot, knowing themselves outnumbered and outgunned. Didn't you tell me that, Maurice?'

'Why, yes … I, ah …'

'And didn't you say that in all likelihood, you would not incur a single casualty?'

'Ah ...'

'So! There you are, then! If it's all over at first sight – and at a considerable distance – the Southern generals won't know if they are confronted by professional soldiers or straw-filled scarecrows. We would therefore be sending two hundred thousand of our best officers and men to where they won't even be throwing sticks at a bunch of women.'

Although Von Franckel knew that Aloise had been a general during the Spanish campaign, he had not thought he had the experience to spot the flaw in the strategy. He knew he was a dead man if the emperor suspected that the flaw was deliberate, designed to support his real plan. He had underestimated the emperor.

'I, on the other hand,' Aloise continued, 'will have a problem that you won't have.'

'Yes?'

'*England*, my dear chap!' the emperor said in a poor attempt at an aristocratic English accent.

'I don't follow, sir.' Von Franckel followed only too well as he saw his master-plan start to crumble.

'As soon as the English hear that all of our cannons, our best weapons and the cream of our armed forces are six months to a year away from here, they will engage our navy in one area, while they land their army in another. *I* will be the one defending the nation with an army of amateurs.'

'That's only *if* the English should hear about it.'

'I'm not going to pin my future on an *if*, Maurice. Think about it. You would have the very best of everything and, according to you, you will have no risk. I, on the other hand, would be facing the risk of an invasion with mostly conscripts and only a handful of experienced officers to defend the nation. You now know what I wanted to tell you, and why.'

'England is low risk, sir. They are not likely to find out what we're doing, or how we deployed our men and materiel. And even if they did, they would think twice about taking on our navy.'

Aloise did not bother to respond. *The discussion is over, Maurice. It's time for your reminder of who is emperor.* He looked casually around the library. 'By the way, do you remember last year when you showed me your map in this very room?' He spoke softly, menacingly.

'Yes indeed, sir. It was late winter.'

'Do you remember the servant on duty that day?'

'Mm … thin young man, curly hair?' Maurice had only a vague recollection.

'That's him. Francesco, a mute. Well, the next day I went back to the library to get a coat I had left on my chair. And there he was! Francesco. He didn't see me so I watched him for a minute or two. He was fussing about the room so much it was hard to know whether he was cleaning it up or searching for something, something from our meeting the day before, perhaps. I have to be on the lookout for spies all the time, you know. I was very annoyed. I didn't know what he was up to, and I obviously couldn't afford to take any chances.'

'What happened?'

'I made an *appointment* for him, at *the block*. He was dispatched within the hour.'

Von Franckel was appalled. 'Didn't you have him explain what he was doing?'

'Oh, don't be silly, Maurice, the man was mute. If anyone annoys me, I make an immediate *appointment* for them.' He paused. 'Now then, was there anything else you wanted to say before we finish up?'

'No, sir.'

'I look forward to seeing your new list next month.'

CHAPTER 45

Zhang Chen was getting the beating of his life. The powerful kicks came at him, fast and furious. Next came the fists, then the elbows; the feet and knees, and finally the shins. Without a pause, it started all over again. Teeth clenched and features grim with concentration, he was forced backwards in a slow circle. From the relentless hits, he was protected only by the two huge pads strapped to his hands and the mask that covered his head and face. His only other option would have been to retaliate which, of course, he could not.

Constant shouts from the two sweating combatants in the graveled arena echoed across the plateau. Four soldiers resting between their bouts with Marcus watched the two with great interest. Especially interesting to them was Isabella's sharply muscled midriff. They shouted with approval when her kicks were executed with both feet off the ground.

Training sessions had doubled to four hours every day since Chen had upgraded the structure of his teachings to Master status more than a year earlier. In between their morning and afternoon sessions, Isabella continued her sword-fighting training with Marcus. The rest of her days were taken up with study and research. Her competitiveness and fitness were legendary. No-one could match her strength or speed on the track.

Thanks to Isabella's dedication, Chen had reached a level of fitness that had eluded him even in his youth, and later, as Zen Master. Life was perfect and he wanted nothing to ever change it. He had no inkling that within minutes his life, and his very soul, would be crushed in a collision between his past and his future.

The session finally drew to a close. He smiled and raised the pads in surrender before tossing them to the ground. After he removed his head gear, Isabella moved back and stood at attention, facing her mentor.

Chen gave her an almost imperceptible nod and they both dropped their arms and bent their knees. Then, in unison, their knees straightened and their arms flew up as they executed a full backward somersault. Landing gracefully on their feet, they faced each other and bowed, completing the session.

The Zen Master relaxed and wiped his brow, watching with amazement as Isabella raised her arms above her head and, in a blur of speed, hurled her body backwards until her hands touched the ground behind her in a full somersault. Repeating the maneuver rapidly several times, she finished with a backward somersault, without her hands touching the ground.

The young soldiers jumped to their feet with enthusiastic applause. Having been drawn to the barn window overlooking the arena by the earlier cheers, Marcus smiled and shook his head. He had never seen anyone perform such a feat, but he understood only too well why she had done it.

Isabella bowed and grinned at the soldiers, a young girl showing off in front of a group of handsome, appreciative young men. Marcus smiled and stepped outside.

'Isabella,' he called, 'time for lunch. Chen, please join us.' To the soldiers he said, 'Mary will bring you some lunch in a few minutes, lads.'

Seated in the cottage lounge, Marcus waited until Mary had left to tend to the young men before he spoke quietly to no-one in particular. 'It's time to talk.' He buttered some bread, took a bite and sat back in his chair, looking at the other two while he chewed.

Isabella and Chen gazed at him for a few moments before Isabella asked, 'Do you want to tell him, Grandfather, or shall I.'

'You, darling. Better if it comes from you.'

'Very well.' She turned to Chen and placed a hand on his. 'Chen, our dearest friend, we have to tell you that we will be leaving here soon, very soon, probably next month. We could be gone for years.' Placing her other hand over his, she added, 'We might never be back.'

Chen was visibly shocked. The blood drained from his face and his body shook uncontrollably. 'No,' he whispered, 'you cannot! You cannot go and never come back. You are my family now, both of you. Isabella, you are the child I never have, the daughter I never have. I not exist without you. You cannot go!'

'We must, Chen. We have no choice. You'll understand why we must go after you hear what I'm about to tell you.'

'Then I go with you.'

'*Yes!* We want you to come with us, Chen. We need you – *I* need you.

But it's dangerous, *very* dangerous.'

'*Dangerous! Hah!*' Chen snorted. 'Nothing dangerous for Zen Master, Isabella. You know that better than anyone! One day, when I retire, you become Zen Master. If you need me, you say no more. I come with you.'

'*Zen Master?*' Marcus looked puzzled. At the same time he was relieved. He had already told Ramesses that Isabella would have a bodyguard in tow.

Isabella glanced at Marcus and smiled. 'Later, Grandfather. I'll tell you all about it later.' She looked back at Chen. 'Let me tell you what I mean by *dangerous*, Chen. I won't ask you to keep this secret because I know that you will.'

Chen never spoke a word for the next hour while Isabella related what had transpired over the last year and a half. Marcus left to put the young soldiers through another training session. They did not know how soon they would be putting their new knowledge to good use.

When Isabella had finished, Chen rose, went to the window and stared out over the peaceful fields in the valley below, thinking that the future might not be peaceful for much longer. He was elated. His new family would remain intact, and *he was going to war*. What more could a born warrior wish for? His life had finally reached its pinnacle.

Isabella walked over to stand by his side. He turned to her with a broad smile.

'You quite right, Isabella, my chosen daughter. It dangerous, *very* dangerous. But it not *war* that is dangerous.' Laughing, he stabbed a finger at Isabella and then at himself. 'It you and I who are dangerous! I not scared when I have you to keep me safe!'

Isabella giggled happily and wrapped her arms around him in a tight embrace. 'Thank you, thank you, Chen, for coming with us. I know I will be so much safer having you with me.' She reached up and stroked his face with her hand. 'And thank you for calling me your *chosen* daughter. That is the most beautiful thing anyone has ever said to me. A daughter is usually *born* to a man, not chosen, and often is not loved. To be chosen, or adopted, is so, so special. I know that you have chosen me above all others because you love me.' She wiped tears from his face and kissed his cheek. 'And I love you, Zhang Chen. I am now your daughter and I choose you to be my father.'

Isabella's very last word had shocked him, and he felt himself crumble within as he wondered how she would really feel about him if she knew that, when he was fourteen years old, he had decided to murder his own father.

CHAPTER 46

Marcus was seated with the soldiers at the small amphitheater when he saw Isabella appear across the arena and hesitate for several moments before walking over to him. On the way she wiped her face several times with the back of her hand. When she reached him she sat down and rested her head on his shoulder, without a word. The soldiers exchanged glances, sensed a family moment, and quietly moved to the far side of the oval for some friendly combat.

Feeling her tension, Marcus put his arm around her. Neither spoke for several minutes. She finally looked up at him, her enormous eyes brilliant aqua in contrast to her pale, serious face.

'What's wrong? Did Chen decide not to come after all?'

'No, Grandfather. He's coming with us. A thousand horses could not keep him away.'

'But there is something else.'

'Yes.'

'Tell me.'

Isabella hesitated for several moments before she told him what had transpired inside. 'As much as I love you, Grandfather, and loved Daddy, I have missed not having a father figure in my life, and I don't have a mother who can choose another for me. I think it's time for me to have a new father, and there will never be one better than Zhang Chen. I've already told him so. Do you mind terribly?'

'I approve completely,' Marcus responded without hesitation. 'Zhang Chen has loved you like a daughter for many years and will be the perfect father for you.'

'I'm so happy, Grandfather.' She threw her arms around him.

'You know he would die for you without hesitation.'

'Yes, I know.'

'And I'll tell you something else, just between you and me. By the time you have wrapped a certain someone around your little finger over the next few years, I suspect there is a young man who will also be happy to die for you, mark my words.'

'Oh … you!' She punched his chest and wiped her eyes.

After giving Marcus a kiss on the cheek, she rose. 'I'm going to spend a bit of time with *Barca*. We'll do some more practice of arm signals and whistles. I can get my beautiful horse to do almost anything now. Believe it or not, I can even make him laugh!' She chuckled happily as she headed towards the outer paddock.

Near the stone fence, she let out three short piercing whistles. Moments later her beloved stallion raced toward her, mane flying in the slip-stream.

Marcus watched until she disappeared. Then he made winding-up motions to the soldiers on the other side of the oval. They would stay overnight in comfortable surroundings, purpose-built in one of the barns.

Heading to the cottage, he looked forward to sharing a glass of wine with his new son.

CHAPTER 47

Final preparations to mobilize were made as summer approached. Admiral Georgeonous had reported that the uptake of conscripts from the navy was substantial. The possibility of glory and death on the battlefield, instead of death by drowning in the stinking bilges of a navy vessel, had proven irresistible.

No-one seemed to notice that the cavalry, army troops and camp followers who regularly headed in a northerly direction rarely returned, and then only in small numbers. The pigeon stations were intensively tested with two-way traffic, posting information relating to the spreading illness as a cover.

Isabella had provided Ramesses and Dmitri with her lists of men and materials required to implement her back-up plans. Dmitri would make sure that nothing would be ordered or transported until after the last of the campaign participants had departed. He had raised his eyebrows at a particular category of specialist on Isabella's list. Those specialists were a rare commodity.

After Alphonso had served breakfast at the modest table on the lawn overlooking the ocean, and had moved away to his usual spot, Dmitri pointed to the puzzling entry on Isabella's list.

'You will of course have noticed this category, Ramesses. It's the most intriguing one of all.'

'Yes, I did wonder about that one. There are not many men in the world with that kind of expertise. I think my contacts in Egypt might be able to assist, however, I have actually already sent an emissary to make enquiries. We need to know urgently who is available and at what cost. A king's ransom, I should think.' He laughed at his own joke. 'What on earth do you think she has in mind?'

'Well, I placed a half-dozen of such specialists in a large bowl, poured forty tons of gunpowder over the top of them and stirred the ingredients gently with a wooden spoon. When I saw what the recipe produced, I decided not to ask any questions.'

Ramesses chuckled. 'It's difficult for a grown man to concede that a girl of fourteen has an intellect of such magnitude. There have been such people in the past; they are rare but one does come along every few generations. Isabella is one of those destined to be a giant of our time. I accept who she is and what she is – she is so far ahead of any of us, it would be futile to attempt to second-guess her. She has been the inspiration and energy for this war effort, and as far as I'm concerned, whatever Isabella wants, Isabella gets!'

'I agree entirely.' Dmitri remained silent for a long moment before he placed his cutlery on the table, looked directly into Ramesses' eyes and spoke softly but with passion. 'We have about a year left to put everything in place to secure Isabella's fall-back positions. Things have gone so well recently that a year is more than enough to provide for the remaining supplies. Our main focus can therefore be on planning for the specialists and manpower needed. I believe we are now ready for war, so it's time has come to make our move. Good luck, Ramesses.' He extended his hand.

The king nodded and looked at Dmitri somberly as they shook hands.

'Good luck to you too, Dmitri, my friend. Send word to Marcus and Isabella at once. I will give the order to mobilize for war within the hour!'

PART II - THE MAGICIAN

CHAPTER 48

'I have a little gift for you, my dear.' Dmitri slid open a desk drawer in his private office and removed a small, exquisitely carved wooden box. It had been given many coats of oil to bring out the magnificent grain of the hazelwood. As Dmitri slid it across his desk, Isabella could see a plaque of pure gold inlaid on its surface. She stared at the plaque, then up at Dmitri, eyes wide. In relief on the gold was a large *I* as the center part of a large *M*. The combined letters – *IM* – were formed by a cleverly crafted serpent with its neck and smiling face forming the *I*. The scales of the serpent's body were tiny jewels of different colors that glittered in the light. Its eyes were represented by two large green emeralds. Beneath the initials was a name deeply embossed in the gold: ISABELLA MONDEO.

'Oh, Dmitri, it's the most beautiful, exquisite thing I have ever seen!' A small giggle escaped. 'But I have no idea what it is.'

'The box and its contents were made by the nation's most prominent jeweler. It is beautiful, isn't it? The jeweler will never make a similar one and will report anyone asking to have a copy made. Go on, open it.'

Inside was a security seal – a reverse mold of the initials carved on the plaque – set in a pure gold ring that fit snugly into a recess, held in place with a small silver clasp. To one side a square gold lid opened to reveal a supply of wax, a small candle, shallow spoon and a gold chain. The owner could wear the seal as a ring or a necklace whenever it was out of the box.

'I'll show you how it works.' Wax was heated within a minute and a seal secured to an envelope. Isabella inspected the final result with awe and pride. The seal was almost as magnificent as its bejeweled twin on the plaque.

Dmitri held up the envelope. 'I'll keep this in a safe place for future comparisons, and I'll provide you with a copy of my seal. I have also attached your seal to these ten small cards to be used only when I will need to provide someone with authentication. Apart from Ramesses, only you and I will know about these cards and their true purpose. The jeweler has made the structure of the serpent's scales so complex it will be impossible to forge. This way, our most secret communications will be safe. Now then, we need to get down to business for the last time. After tomorrow you'll be gone and our communications will be by pigeon, or by messenger this way.' He waved the envelope again before placing it into the drawer.

'You are truly amazing, Dmitri. I only hope I can live up to the trust you must have in me to give me such a thoughtful gift. Thank you so much.'

He simply nodded and looked nervous and emotional as Isabella handed him her final list. She waited quietly while he quickly scanned it, nodding frequently as he turned the pages. When he got to the end he folded it and slipped it into his coat pocket. 'Are there any copies of this report?'

'Only in here.' She tapped her head.

'Marcus, does he know the details of your plans?'

'No, only you know the full details – and Ramesses, of course.'

Dmitri nodded. 'Good. Everything on your lists, all of it, will be supplied on time, and in the places you want them. I'm going to start straight away to arrange the things you said you might not need until the result of the first battle is known. Why take chances? If we later find we don't need them, we can simply have them brought back. But if they should be needed, then I would rather be ahead of the game instead of trying to make up time while you're in full retreat.'

'I was actually hoping you would say something like that.'

Dmitri nodded his head slowly, lowering his voice to little more than a whisper. 'In regard to your last plan, however, Ramesses was quite upset when he got to that part. I can only hope it will never be required.'

'Hopefully, it won't. But if it *is*, it's the only way. It would be the last stand and will define our people. You do see that, don't you?'

'Yes, I'm sad to say that I do. The soldiers will be prepared to die for their nation, but I am astonished that you feel you must do the same.'

'I have to. I can't expect such a sacrifice unless the soldiers know I will be at their side to join them in their journey to paradise.'

'Paradise? I thought I remember you saying *hell*.'

Isabella grinned. 'No, Dmitri, *we* will go to paradise. It is the enemy who will roast in the fires of hell!'

•

It was still dark when they rose the next day. Marcus, Isabella and Zhang Chen breakfasted with Ramesses and Sophia. Dmitri arrived just as the food was placed on the table in a small private dining area off the kitchen.

After breakfast everyone rose in unison and headed towards the front of the palace, where their wagons had been made ready for departure. Ramesses embraced Isabella, shook hands with Marcus and Chen, and then turned and walked quickly inside with his wife, before his emotions got the better of him. He did not expect to ever see any of them again.

CHAPTER 49

They arrived with their two wagons at the designated meeting place on the outskirts of the city an hour later. Dmitri had watched them leave from the door to his office after a tearful farewell. He and Isabella had promised to be in touch on a regular basis through their private communication network.

Marcus and Isabella were in the first wagon, Chen close behind in the other. Each wagon was drawn by two horses, with an additional four loosely tethered to the back. Marcus and Chen had brought their favorite war horses. Isabella, of course, had brought *Barca*. The others were pack horses to pull the wagons.

The arranged meeting place consisted of little more than a small grove of olive trees, some large rock outcrops and a narrow dirt road winding its way towards the distant hills. There were no farmhouses in sight, and no signs of life other than the group awaiting them.

There were about twenty men and women, most on horseback. A few sat in four wagons, each drawn by four horses. Eight men, unshaven and dressed like peasants, sat quietly on horses separate from the others. Soldiers.

The others remained close to the four wagons piled high with supplies tied down with oilcloth and ropes. Camp followers.

One of the soldiers nudged his horse forward. A powerfully built man nearing forty, with a thickening waist, intelligent eyes and a friendly face, he smiled at Marcus as he gave a smart salute. 'General Mondeo, my pleasure and my compliments, sir. I am Sergeant-at-arms Emile DaSilva, liaison officer between the army and the camp followers.' His smile broadened. 'I am not the only liaison officer, sir. There will be several other sergeants assigned to that task, so I'm not as important as my title suggests, I'm afraid.'

'Keeping everyone happy and organized is a very important task indeed, Sergeant. No army can run smoothly without men like you.' Marcus returned the salute with a smile. 'Let me introduce my granddaughter, Isabella, and Zhang Chen, who will accompany us throughout our travels.'

DaSilva smiled and nodded to Isabella and Zhang Chen. 'Please excuse our appearance, Miss Isabella. We were ordered to dress like the local peasants and to look our worst. Had we known we were to meet a lovely young lady, we would have shaved and worn our smartest uniform. You would not believe it right now, but we are all really very, very handsome.'

Isabella laughed. 'I'm sure you are, Sergeant, and I'm sure I'll see you all in uniform one day. In the meantime, please call me *Isabella*.'

'Of course. Thank you, Isabella. You can call me *Sergeant*.' He paused a moment before he chortled. 'Just joking. Please just call me Emile, Isabella. That goes for all of you. Let's keep it informal among ourselves while we travel.' DaSilva turned and roared at his men. 'That does not apply to you, you scurvy bunch of peasants. You will continue to call me *sir*. Yes, *sir*, and absolutely anything you say, *sir*. Understood?'

The soldiers straightened to attention in their saddles and saluted their senior officer, shouting at the top of their voices: '*Yes*, Emile, sir. Yes, sir, and absolutely anything you say, Emile.'

DaSilva laughed. 'No meals for three months for insubordination! All right, everyone, let's get going. We'll stop every hour or two to rest and water the horses. We might even take the time to have some refreshments and look after any other personal needs.'

They were all in a jovial mood as they started the first leg of their long and dangerous journey.

By the end of each day they were aching from the hard seats of the bouncing wagons. Isabella would frequently ride *Barca* to give her back a rest and to give her stallion some welcome exercise. Young and spirited, *Barca* loved to run. Isabella had brought several bags of treats so that they could continue to practice their special tricks. Occasionally she and Chen were able to wander away from prying eyes to get in some practice. The sessions were necessarily short but conducted at the maximum exertion level and helped to ease their aches and pains.

During the first week, the nights were spent in tents placed in two separated semi-circles close to a central campfire. Soldiers and camp followers took turns with night guard-duty; no-one considered it strictly necessary in friendly territory, but Emile insisted that discipline never be relaxed.

The women were allocated tents separate from the men. Isabella shared a tent with two women cooks who took great delight in imparting their culinary secrets with her. She was pleased to learn, and in return, helped them on a regular basis.

'Your man will love you all the more, Isabella, if you present him with a beautiful meal every evening,' one of the women had told her with a broad smile during food preparations on the first night.

Isabella laughed. 'Well, I won't have to worry about cooking for a man for a very long time.'

The woman glanced at the other cook with a knowing smile before looking back at Isabella. 'Perhaps not as long as you think. You haven't noticed how some of the soldiers look at you, have you?'

'If I had, I would have fastened their hands to the table with my fork!' Isabella hissed.

It was early afternoon at the end of the first week when they reached a large farm with several cottages and barns scattered over the surrounding hills. General Karamus had spent the previous two nights there and had resumed his journey that morning, leaving behind a few of his soldiers to follow the next day. The day was warm, and the horses automatically headed for the shade of a grove of tall trees.

A prosperous-looking man appeared at the front door of the main house and walked over to greet the new arrivals. After introductions they were invited into his home for lunch. They would be billeted in the various cottages and barns and, as she headed for the house, Isabella thought dreamily of a night's sleep in a comfortable bed. When some camp followers automatically proceeded to the kitchen to assist with lunch preparations, she followed them without a second thought.

At the door to the kitchen, Isabella saw three men wearing long aprons and a young woman in a white cotton dress gathered around a rectangular food-preparation table. As the new arrivals entered the room, the men looked up, while the young woman turned to face them, then flinched and dropped her chopping-knife. She made no attempt to pick it up, staring wide-eyed at Isabella. Isabella stopped in her tracks and caught her breath, astonished.

The girl appeared to be in her mid-to-late teens, tall and full-figured. Her cotton dress had a matching cotton belt, tied around an impossibly tiny waist. Wavy auburn hair with a brilliant copper sheen framed an exquisite face with enormous hazel eyes. Her cherry-red lips parted when she smiled, revealing perfect teeth. It was the loveliest face Isabella had ever seen. She had never thought it possible that a girl could be so beautiful.

After quick introductions the group set to work, and lunch was prepared and placed on the dining-room table in less than ten minutes. The auburn-haired girl seemed sullen and never left the kitchen. Marcus had kept a spare seat next to him at the table and pointed to it as soon as he was able to make eye contact with Isabella. She smiled her thanks, but shook her head and pointed to the kitchen. *I will eat with the staff, thanks, Grandfather.*

At the kitchen table, Isabella enjoyed the meal while she listened to the small talk. Each time she glanced in the direction of the girl, who had earlier introduced herself as Melissa Petrova, she found those beautiful hazel eyes unwaveringly focused on her.

They finished their meal and rose to clear the table, while a few headed for the dining room to do the same. Isabella was about to tip scraps into a bucket for the farm animals when she felt a nudge on her arm. Melissa leaned lightly against her until her lips were just inches from her ear.

'Don't worry, Isabella,' she whispered, 'I'm not interested in you in that way. I was just reflecting on what a pity it is that we won't be friends. I don't think I'm going to like you very much.'

'Why, what have I –' Isabella hissed and noisily scraped another plate to cover the sound of their whispering.

Melissa interrupted with another whisper. 'You haven't done anything. I just don't like *competition*. I've never had to worry about competition before.'

Isabella grabbed another plate. '*Competition?* What on earth are you talking about?'

'Come with me. Let's help clear the dining room table and you'll see what I mean.' Melissa took her gently by the arm and propelled her through the door and into the dining room. The buzz of conversation died away to a murmur as heads swiveled to stare at the two girls moving about the room. Melissa deliberately took her time to stack plates and motioned for Isabella to do the same. Conversations had slowed to mumbles by the time Melissa picked up a stack of plates, nodded to Isabella and headed for the kitchen.

'Soldiers!' she sighed. 'They're all the same. I'm afraid they're alone for too long. Now do you see what I was talking about?'

'Well, yes, of course. Most of them stopped talking to stare at you. That was pretty obvious and not surprising. You're very beautiful, you know. I'm old enough to understand that, but what's your point?'

Melissa sighed again. 'No, you don't quite get it. You were too busy focusing on cleaning up. Most of the men were staring at me, which, of course, is only to be expected as I'm older, but several were looking your way as well. If you were plain, or even just pretty, they would *all* be staring at *me* just as they have for years. Look at me. I just happen to look the way I do. I can't help it. I was simply born this way. It's going to be the same with you. I'm so used to being looked at I've just assumed I would never have any competition. I swear I nearly fainted when I saw you walk into the kitchen. Now come with me before there's nothing left to clean up, and this time glance at the soldiers, not just the plates.' She took a deep breath, held her head up and walked through the door like the goddess she was, motioning for Isabella to do the same.

As soon as they returned to the kitchen, Melissa pointed to the buckets. 'I think these should be taken to the pigs.' Once outside, she turned towards Isabella. 'Well?'

Isabella simply nodded, red-faced. This time she had noticed the men's eyes following her around the room.

With their keen sense of smell, the pigs detected the food heading their way and squealed with excitement. As soon as the girls reached the enclosure, they emptied the buckets over the low wooden fence and laughed as they watched the pigs go into a feeding frenzy. Melissa tipped her empty bucket upside-down on the ground and sat on it while Isabella continued to lean on the fence to watch the pigs. 'It's exciting at first, Isabella, but then it gets a bit boring when it happens all the time. Are you bored with it yet?'

'That's only the second time I've noticed being looked at that way. The first time was just some young kids, like me.'

'What? You can't be serious. How old are you, anyway?'

'Fourteen.'

'*Fourteen!* Oh, I thought you were at least sixteen. You're so tall and very strong-looking, like an athlete. *Fourteen.* You seem so mature.' Melissa suddenly laughed. 'Oh, I'm so relieved!'

'Relieved? Why relieved?'

'Well, you're only fourteen. I'm eighteen, nearly nineteen so you're hardly competition, after all. By the time you're old enough to be competition, I will have married my rich, handsome nobleman and have six children.' Melissa jumped up and gave Isabella a crushing hug. 'We can be friends after all,' she cried as she let go.

Isabella laughed. 'That's very nice, Melissa, but we won't have much time to become friends, I'm afraid. We're off in the morning.'

'Uh-uh. Guess what? So am I, my beautiful no-longer-competition new friend.'

'Oh, stop it, Melissa! You'll turn me into a conceited snob. Seriously, I thought you lived here. How long have you been here?'

'Two days.'

'Two days? Why are you here, then?'

'I arrived here with a group of fifty to meet up with General Karamus and his soldiers to be one of their camp followers. The creepy general took one look at me and thought he would make me his. I heard from my camp friends that he told his officers and soldiers I was off-limits. I was to be his and no-one else's. I had to duck and weave for two days to keep his grubby hands off me. I even had to disappear into the woods with a blanket during the nights. I have never been anyone's, and he would not even qualify to be last on my list. I will be no-one's until I meet my husband. So there!'

'So why are you not with the general and his men? They left this morning.'

Melissa smiled brightly before resorting to a pained expression and a voice to match. 'Oh, *oh*, I was so ill this morning, I was surely going to die. I said to tell the general I was so ill I must have caught the illness that's sweeping the continent. He and his men left so quickly he didn't even take the time to say goodbye to me – and after he so desperately wanted me! Oh, how rude and inconsiderate of him! The funny thing was, though, I felt perfectly well within seconds of seeing the rear end of their horses. A truly amazing recovery.' She doubled up with laughter.

Isabella laughed with her. 'So where will you go now?'

'Why, with you, of course. That handsome General Mondeo has already invited me to join his group of camp followers.'

Isabella was shocked, her knees so weak she crumbled onto Melissa's still upturned bucket to hide her dismay.

'I'm just so excited! We'll be such great friends. Isn't that wonderful, Isabella?'

Isabella had no idea where Yannis was, but she knew that sooner or later they would meet up, and now Melissa would be there, too. Yannis could not fail to notice her – everyone noticed Melissa. It was Isabella's turn to not want competition from someone so lovely. Fear of competition had done a full circle in an instant.

'Yes, wonderful,' Isabella mumbled without enthusiasm, suddenly feeling as ill as Melissa had pretended to be that very morning.

CHAPTER 50

Dmitri was true to his word. He watched as the Mondeos' wagons turned the corner before he quickly walked up the steps to his office. Immediately dividing Isabella's lists into ten, he placed them in separate envelopes closed with his personal seal.

It was mid-afternoon when he called for his wagon. He told no-one where he was going, but anyone watching would have seen him heading north. As soon as he reached the outskirts of the city, he turned and went west for a while, then turned south again and traveled some of the city's backstreets before finally pointing the horses towards the Summer Palace.

The envelopes would have the king's seal alongside Dmitri's, and would then be handed to a select few of the King's Guard. None of them would have any idea of what the others were to do.

The people, the special weapons and equipment, the food and special provisions, the gunpowder and naphtha would soon be on their way.

Captain Yannis Christos was a long way from home. Spain. His planning for the needed men and materials had exposed an unexpected weakness: quality horses. The horses he had been able to muster had been of reasonable quality, both as pack horses and for general use with mounted troops, but few were suitable for the cavalry.

War horses needed to be strong, fast, intelligent and not prone to panic. Spain was not the only place to procure such mounts, but it was renowned for quantity, with a huge breeding industry. During the years of Muslim occupation, the Arabian horses had been cross-bred with the best of the local horses, producing stock in high demand by any nation contemplating hostile actions against its neighbors. It took a special horse to carry the weight of a strong man with weapons and armor.

Yannis was dressed to kill and threw money around as if there were no tomorrow. As soon as they heard what he was looking for, many of Spain's top breeders and their merchant colleagues met with him, bringing their most beautiful daughters along, in case the mysterious buyer turned out to be not only wealthy, but an eligible bachelor.

By the time Yannis left with several thousand of Spain's finest horses, he had left enormous sums of the king's money behind, as well as a large number of broken hearts – not to mention disappointed fathers, who had seen great promise in this most charming and rich young man.

Navy ships had been converted to carry the animals so that no-one would know their ultimate destination. From several different docking locations, the horses were herded inland in batches of five hundred. Trainers were assigned from the very first day.

Yannis sent a message to Nicho that his task had been completed and he was headed home for further orders. He knew he would soon be ordered to join the main campaign.

It was slow going. Hills followed valleys, mountains followed hills before it started all over again. In many places there were no roads, simply faint tracks from previous riders and wagons. The days passed too slowly, the nights too quickly. Five days after Marcus' caravan had left the farm, it rained heavily for three days without respite. They had no choice but to make camp and wait it out. The ground had become too soft for the wagons and horses to traverse safely. Only small fires were possible, and hot food and drinks were passed around sparingly. Water penetrated the leather tents from the top and from the ground beneath. There was little to do except doze day and night on damp bedding, and wait. Even the normally irrepressible Melissa was grumpy.

On the morning of their departure from the farm, Melissa had waved excitedly to Isabella from one of the wagons. Isabella had sighed heavily and waved back without enthusiasm, still reeling from the unwelcome surprise that had presented itself the day before.

Marcus and Isabella were seated in their wagon on the second day when Melissa ran over to jump up next to them. She wrapped her arm around Isabella's, pushed her hard against Marcus and wriggled about until she was comfortable.

'I'm coming with you today,' she announced brightly. 'Oh, I do love travelling! It's so exciting and the countryside is so beautiful.'

I'm afraid you're in for a shock when you find out what awaits you at the final destination, Isabella thought sadly. 'Yes, it is nice.' She tried with only moderate success to sound enthusiastic. As soon as the wagons got moving, Melissa started to talk. And talk. Two hours later Isabella glanced up at her grandfather, crossed her eyes and yawned. Marcus took refuge behind a fit of coughing to hide his reaction.

Melissa joined their wagon every day, and despite Isabella's initial irritation, she soon took a strong liking to her. By the time the rains started, they were firm friends and shared the same tent, chatting late into the night. Melissa came from a wealthy family and was well educated. Isabella was pleased to find that she was as bright as she was beautiful.

'I never thought travelling could be so horrible. It's miserable, miserable, *miserable*,' Melissa moaned glumly as they sat on their damp bedding and listened to the rain beating against the roof of the tent. 'What I wouldn't give for a hot bath right now!'

'Very hot and lots of bubbles,' Isabella added.

'And lots of rose water. I love to smell nice.'

'I have soap. I'm sure we can find a muddy puddle out there somewhere.'

'Oh dear, there went the fantasy, swallowed up in a muddy puddle.' Melissa turned serious again. 'We're going to be here for several days after the rain stops so the ground can dry out for the wagons, aren't we?'

'I'm afraid so.'

Melissa cheered up. 'Well, in that case you might as well sit back and I'll tell you my life's story!'

'Oh, I thought you already had!'

CHAPTER 51

Brigadier Nicholas Manassis looked up as someone entered his office. He jumped up when he recognized Yannis and the two men shook hands and embraced. Manassis did a poor imitation of a flamenco tap-dance while Yannis rolled his eyes. 'So, how were the senoritas, Yannis?'

'Hungry, Nicho, hungry. Not enough men to go around – too many wars. If the men are not on a crusade of their own, they're fighting off a woman! As soon as I had bought all the horses we needed, I had to make a run for it.'

'Are you still single, or I am I speaking to the latest cattle baron?'

'Definitely single, and staying that way.' He grinned, sat down, and put his feet on Nicholas' desk. He had been riding for more than a month since leaving Spain, and he was tired.

Nicholas smiled and walked back to his chair. 'You must be tired, Yannis. Why don't you sit down and put your weary feet up on my desk like any other insolent, insubordinate officer about to be demoted to private?'

Yannis raised his heels from the desk and brought them back down with a crash. 'Oh, you're so commanding when you need to be, Brigadier, sir! Very impressive. You're one of the few real men I know who can put his wife in her rightful place whenever he wants to. Just like that.' He snapped his fingers.

'That reminds me, dinner is at our place this evening.'

'Thanks, Nicho.'

Nicholas picked up a file with Yannis' name on the cover. 'I have a new assignment for you.'

Yannis raised his eyebrows but remained silent.

'Much of our army's body armor is already in transit, but your assignment will be to check that everything that's been ordered is delivered within the contracted times and that every piece is transported to the designated areas. The same applies to much of the weaponry, and especially to the composite longbows.'

'What's special about the longbows?'

'Composite longbows are a complicated animal. Your assignment will be to make sure that they have not only been assembled, but assembled correctly. The only way to do that is to test them. Good training for you.'

'Done!'

'That will take you a couple of months. Then I will have a few more tasks for you during the winter months. After that, we'll be off – you and I, that is. It will be time to join the others to get ready for battle. Marcus and the others left many weeks ago.'

Yannis nodded. 'How is she?'

'Who?' Nicholas asked innocently.

'You know very well who I mean. The crazy one. Isabella. The one who got us all into this mess, bless her little soul. Did she go along or did she stay at home?'

'Speaking of home, there isn't one. I have a little story to tell you about their home later. But yes, she's fine, and both her grandfather and the king were unable to stop her from going along. She's done some truly amazing things while you've been away. By the time we catch up with her, you'll have a hard time recognizing her.'

'How so?'

'She's much taller, filled out some, and really strong. She's developed into one of our top athletes. She's grown her hair long, and the color is different.'

'Different?'

'Wait until you catch up with her and you'll see what I mean. She looks amazing.'

Yannis laughed. 'I'll make sure to view her from a distance, or she's sure to kick me again.'

'You can count on it, Yannis.'

At the same time that Yannis and Nicholas walked out of The Barracks building, General Maurice Von Franckel walked into the Northern Region emperor's sumptuous office on the third floor of the palace. He had cautiously waited for his informants to tell him that the last of the emperor's treasure had been received and secreted deep in the bowels of the palace cellars before advising the emperor of *the good news*.

Aloise stood with his back to the door and stared out the window overlooking the river slowly moving through the eastern part of the city. He turned to greet his visitor and gestured to a chair. 'You wished to see me, General? Our next meeting wasn't scheduled until next week.' Beautifully woven tapestries, depicting famous battles of the past, hung on two walls, muting their voices.

'Quite so, sir, but there are a couple of things that won't wait. The first is to let you know how the cannons are coming along. The second involves an apology I owe you.'

Aloise lowered himself into his chair. 'An apology? From you? I can hardly wait. Tell me about the cannons first so I can then enjoy your apology.'

'The cannon manufacture is going extremely well, sir. New dies are in the making for even bigger and better cannons cast in bronze, rather than in brass and other materials used in the past. I can confirm that our target date for the number ordered will be met.'

'Excellent.' Aloise was not particularly enthusiastic. The general's report did little more than meet his expectations. He was more interested in the apology.

'I'm sure you'll find the next item of more interest. You'll remember my dismay at our meeting some weeks ago when you instructed me to change the structure of the troops for the campaign, as well as the weaponry. Over the last few weeks, while making the necessary changes, I've come to realize that you were correct in your assessment and I was wrong. I was too focused on the big picture. I admit I underestimated the input you're able to provide and the benefits that can now be achieved by those instructions. I sincerely apologize to you, sir.'

'Well, you *are* a surprise, Maurice. You have my full attention.'

'There's more, much more. When you hear what I have to say, you'll realize why I owe you the apology.' Von Franckel leaned across the desk, glanced around as if he expected to discover listeners, before he lowered his voice to a more intimate man-to-man level. 'At a meeting three months ago, you made a reference that, from a distance, the enemy would not know if they were confronted by professional soldiers, or straw-filled scarecrows. It was your reference to *scarecrows* that made the difference. Everything you said makes sense if you tie it to that single comment. If, metaphorically speaking, *scarecrows* would serve our purpose, they certainly would not need our best officers to tell them what to do, as you so correctly said.' Von Franckel paused. 'There's something else that *scarecrows* don't need.'

'And that is?'

'Armor, sir, body armor.'

Aloise went quiet while he thought about the comment. He nodded as a smile formed. 'I think I'm starting to see where you're coming from.'

'A modest portion of our army will consist of knights provided by many of the towns and villages throughout the Northern Region. Under their contracts they will supply their own body armor as well as their own war horses, many of which also wear armor during battle. As for the remainder: the crossbowmen and archers, spear divisions, most of the cavalry and about half of the foot-soldiers would normally be provided with body armor by the state.'

Aloise's eyes shone with interest. He was already guessing where the conversation was going.

'Naturally, I reviewed the detailed budget as I was preparing to order the armor. The list is enormous, and includes body armor plating, helmets and shields, chain-mail jackets, leg-wear and so on. I estimate roughly 1,500 tons would need to be molded and made. Not only to be made and fitted, but to be transported. It would take thousands of additional wagons and animals, food and water, just to haul that weight from one end of Europe to the other over a year or two. For *what*, sir?'

'Yes, indeed – for *what*?'

'Why put armor on *scarecrows*? We simply don't need armor, sir. You were absolutely correct. With a thousand cannons pointed across the enemy's borders, and a million arrows ready to rain down on them – who needs armor? My recommendation is that we simply dispense with ordering the armor. The saving will be enormous. In addition, there will be less visible evidence of us being on a war footing until the very last moment.'

'What sort of saving are we talking about, Maurice?' Aloise spoke softly to mask his growing excitement.

'I estimate a minimum of twenty-five – perhaps up to thirty-five percent of the entire cost of the campaign.'

Aloise made some quick calculations, concluding that he would need to expend barely half of the Swedish funds, without further need to access his remaining nest egg. Maurice had not only saved the remainder of his treasure, he had unknowingly saved his own neck in the process.

'You have my authority to remove additional armor from your list of requirements.'

Von Franckel nodded his appreciation.

'Oh, and another thing: you can send 250 cannons with each of army divisions one and two, and you'll take a full thousand. I think my commander-in-chief should have a nice round number to work with. *One thousand* – that has a nice ring to it, don't you think?'

'They will be a welcome addition. Thank you, sir.'

Aloise nodded. 'That thing about the *scarecrows*: that was good thinking, Maurice. I didn't see that one in the whole scheme of things. Perhaps I owe you an apology, too. How about we call it even?' He rose and put his hand out.

They shook hands. 'Now, just one last thing,' Aloise said softly as he made his way around the desk.

Von Franckel stiffened with sudden alarm.

Aloise noticed and smiled as he patted Von Franckel on the arm. '*I*,' he said, 'am going to pour *you* a glass of wine, my friend!'

CHAPTER 52

Preparations were made to leave three days after the rain stopped. The soldiers and some of the camp followers were hitching the last of the horses to the wagons when Melissa grabbed Isabella by the arm. 'Come,' she said, 'there's someone I want you to meet before we leave.' She pulled her to the far side of the field before letting go of her arm.

'Her name is Xu Yan. She was a servant in my father's house for many years. I've known her since I was a little girl. I just love her so much! She came with me when I decided to run away from home. I left that bit out of my life story the other day. I felt a bit embarrassed to talk about that until I knew you better. You're still so very young.'

'Ran away? What do you mean?'

'My father wanted to marry me off as soon as I turned twelve. *Twelve!* Can you believe it?' Both girls grimaced. 'That's younger than you, Isabella. Twelve is the legal age for girls to marry where I come from. I know it's fourteen where you come from, and even that's too young. Because of my looks, Father had lots of offers, big offers, mostly from rich middle-aged men. That's just the way it is. Back home there is hardly a girl over the age of thirteen who's not married unless she's really ugly. Well, I wasn't having any of it, so I ran away. Xu Yan had a similar experience in her country, so she didn't hesitate to come with me. We are two of a kind. And now,' she said happily as she threw her arm around Isabella's waist, 'we are *three* of a kind. There she is!'

A slender figure swathed in cloth from head to toe was about to climb into one of the wagons when Melissa called out to her. 'Yan, Yan, wait! There's someone I want you to meet before we go.' Melissa and the woman hugged each other. 'I've missed you so much, Yan. It was so muddy I couldn't come to visit. Yan, this is my new very best friend, *Isabella*.'

Isabella felt embarrassed as she held her hand out. The woman smiled and bowed formally. Isabella knew Chinese custom well and returned the bow in the correct manner. The woman's smile broadened as she spoke softly. 'Very happy to meet you, Isabella. Very happy Melissa has found new friend. It is very lonely to travel in wagon.'

Isabella was unable to form much of an opinion of Xu Yan. Silk scarves covered most of her face. Only her full lips, fine nose and large almond-shaped eyes were visible. Her gaze was intelligent and wise beyond her years; her smooth skin indicated someone in their late twenties to early thirties. It was an attractive face. They chatted for several minutes until the trumpet sounded for the caravan to get underway.

The two girls ran across the field towards Marcus' wagon, which Melissa had made her permanent transport. Isabella peeled away to Chen's wagon and jumped up to give him a hug. 'Good morning, Father,' she murmured as she leaned against him. 'It's good to be on the move again after so many miserable days. And we've had no practice. We have much catching up to do. Can't have you getting to be a fat and lazy Zen Master.' She laughed as she tried unsuccessfully to link both hands around his massive bicep. To make matters worse he laughingly flexed the muscle. Isabella punched his chest and jumped to the ground.

'We'll meet up when we stop for refreshments. Oh, and by the way, there's someone I want you to meet when we get there.'

'And who that, precious daughter?'

'Oh … someone. Wait and see.'

'It is a *she?*' he asked, worried now.

'Could be.'

'What she look like?' Now he was suspicious as well as worried.

'I'll be honest with you. I have absolutely no idea.'

'I turn around now. Go home.'

Isabella pouted and wagged a finger at him. 'You will follow me and be on your best behavior!'

When she got back to her wagon, she asked Melissa, 'Why is Xu Yan dressed the way she is? Is it a religious thing, like a Nun or Muslim or something like that? Is she married?'

'Nun? Religion? Married? My, my, so many *questions*. No, she's just extremely shy, and no, she's not married, never has been. She always covers herself like that. She's really modest. *Definitely* not like me.' Melissa laughed, put her beautiful nose in the air and fluttered her long eye-lashes. Even Marcus chuckled.

'Why, is there something wrong with the way she looks?' It was

Isabella's turn to be curious.

Melissa's answer was to look at her with a smirk.

Three hours passed before they stopped to rest. The two girls helped with the preparation of food and drinks. The soldiers tended to the horses.

Melissa beckoned for Isabella to join her as she headed towards the other side of the camp where Xu Yan was handing out plates of food to the soldiers. Walking over to where Chen sat on a waist-high rock eating a hunk of bread, Isabella grabbed him by the hand. 'Come with me,' she said sharply. Tossing the bread away, he followed her like a lamb to slaughter.

She was still holding his hand when she came to a stop in front of Melissa and Xu Yan. Chen was staring at his feet. Isabella placed her hand gently under his chin and slowly brought his face up.

'Melissa you already know, of course. I would like you to meet her friend Xu Yan. Yan, I would like you to meet my father, Zhang Chen.'

'Your *father?*' they both responded in unison.

Isabella wrapped her arms around Chen's waist. 'Yes, my father. My adopted father. I am his adopted daughter. Zhang Chen is the most wonderful father in the whole world. There is no-one more handsome than he. Don't you think he is handsome, Yan?'

Surprisingly, Yan did not blush or shrink from Isabella's blatant matchmaking. 'Yes,' she said as she bowed, 'he is.'

It was Zhang Chen who flushed as he bowed in return. He attempted to say something but was lost for words.

Melissa caught on quickly. 'Yan, Isabella asked a favor of you earlier,' she lied. 'Will you allow her favor?'

'Of course. What is it?

'Isabella wanted to know what she would look like if she covered her face the same as you. She would like you to do it to her.'

'Of course. I have many scarves in the …'

'No, no! She wants those you're wearing. Here, I'll help you take them off.' Giving Xu Yan no opportunity to protest, Melissa immediately unclipped some of the finely jeweled pins that held the scarves in place. Yan turned away and stood quietly while Melissa removed them. Slowly her head and hair were uncovered, then her neck and shoulders. Xu Yan flicked her head and her hair tumbled down over the almost translucent skin of her shoulders.

'You can turn around now, Yan, while I tend to Isabella.' Melissa gently gripped Yan's shoulders and slowly turned her to face Isabella and Chen. Xu Yan did not even glance at Isabella but stood looking directly at

Chen without any sign of her earlier shyness. The two held each other's gaze for several moments without saying a word. Finally Xu Yan raised her eyebrows in a silent question: *well?*

Zhang Chen got the message loud and clear. He bowed to her again and found his voice. 'May I visit you, Xu Yan?

'Yes, Zhang Chen.'

'I see you then, Xu Yan.'

'I see you, Zhang Chen.' They bowed to each other and Chen turned and left, almost stumbling.

Melissa held up the scarves. 'I'll help you put these back on, Yan.'

Yan shook her head. 'Not necessary. I go rest now until we leave.' Yan hugged them both and headed for a patch of grass.

'I think I'll go sit with her, Isabella. I'll come over when I hear the departure trumpet. I love you so much. You're an absolute genius.'

'You didn't do so badly yourself. I'll go see how Father is doing.'

Looking confused, Chen was already in the wagon, ready to go.

'Are you all right, Father?'

He nodded distractedly. 'Yes, yes, I all right.'

The yearning for a loving wife remained, but as is common with men, the willingness to make a commitment had diminished over time. He had reached the age where fear had started to outweigh the yearning. For the first time in his life, Zhang Chen was terrified.

CHAPTER 53

The travelers caught their breath as the caravan descended on the dirt track into the main valley. It was stunning, beautiful. A fast-flowing river snaked its way through the center valley on its way into the next. A backdrop of a series of black and grey mountains already crowned with an early dusting of snow, and a few touches of fall leaves mixed with the last signs of wildflowers completed a palette of colors to present a magnificent scene as far as the eye could see. Isabella felt a pain tighten around her heart as she thought about how she intended to destroy every inch of it.

Their journey to reach the valley had included weeks to wind their way through near impossible mountain ranges with lakes so vast it took days to circle their shores. Abundant quantities of pink-fleshed fish, caught with baited nets, brought a welcome change to their diet. Isabella made copious notes and sketches of every lake and its surrounds as they slowly made their way. To the north could be seen the scores of mountains they would later cross into enemy territory to meet their fate.

It was late afternoon before they reached the village close to the fast-flowing river. Two huge bridges led over to a smaller village on the opposite side. The bridges were wide enough to cope with the tripling of the water flow from the melting snow in spring and the wet season rain from farther north. The bridges were one-way in opposite directions to facilitate the sometimes chaotic movement of livestock.

After Emile spoke to the village mayor, who had approached on foot to meet the visitors, he returned and gave instructions as to where each of the groups should camp: the men, the women, the soldiers. Many established camps could be seen alongside the river in both directions and in the vast expanse of the valley. The majority were known to be soldiers, even though there was not a uniform in sight.

Marcus was able to point out General Karamus' camp on the other side of the river. 'I think we'll stick to this side for the time being,' he said with a smile to the small group sitting around the camp fire enjoying a simple buffet supper. Melissa had wrapped herself in Yan's strips of cloth and was ready to become seriously ill at a moment's notice.

When a messenger arrived the following morning to enquire about her condition, he was told to thank the general for his interest, and to inform him that Melissa was moderately better, but still feeling poorly, with alternating fevers and chills. There were no further enquiries, and the general never ventured across the river.

The women were clearing up after breakfast the following morning when a tall, bearded middle-aged man entered their camp. He introduced himself and handed Isabella a sealed envelope. She recognized the seal immediately. Dmitri's. 'My team and I have already been here for more than a month. Our camp is well out of sight several valleys up from where the river splits in two.' The man spoke quietly as Isabella opened the envelope and started to read the two pages. The letter introduced the man and his team and described their assignment.

She finished reading, examined some maps and then addressed Marcus. 'I must go with Jacques, Grandfather. I will be back in three days. Chen will come with me for protection.' She knew it was far too dangerous for a young girl to enter unknown wilderness unprotected.

Marcus nodded without comment or objection.

When Isabella let out a short sharp whistle, *Barca* immediately trotted over for a treat. Within the hour the two were following the tall stranger into the higher valleys.

Jacques showed them around his camp; which was more like a township, considerably larger than the village in the main valley. Most of the accommodation consisted of sturdily built timber cottages, each having a large single room with windows and timber shutters, as well as a beautifully crafted stone fireplace. A few tents were intermingled between the cottages, but they appeared to be for provisions rather than people. There were several hundred men milling about and the women were busy with pots and pans. A bell hung from a small tripod structure in the village center, and when Jacques rang it three times, a group of men of all ages assembled. Isabella told Chen he could have some time to himself. He nodded once and drifted away.

As she watched him go, Isabella's mind drifted to Yannis, wondering where he was and what he was doing. *Will you ever hold me and tell me that you –?*

'We'll go straight to the meeting hall.' Jacques interrupted her thoughts just as Melissa's beautiful face drifted into her mental picture of Yannis. She groaned and followed Jacques to the barn-like building. There were more than thirty men inside and Jacques asked them to settle into groups according to their particular expertise before he introduced them to Isabella. She made sure to speak to each man and shake their hands.

'These are the team leaders, Isabella. They represent carpenters, architects, engineers, artists, map-makers, miners, stonemasons, brick-makers, agriculture specialists and more. As for myself, I'm the secret weapon you asked for.' Jacques smiled at the group with pride. 'I will be immodest and claim that we are the best of the best. The town you just walked through was built from the ground up within a week of our arrival. We even have segregated bath houses and amenities just beyond the ridge. You can have a hot soapy bath before you retire this evening. But only if you wish to, of course,' he added with a grin. He knew of no girl who could resist a hot bath.

Isabella wrapped her arms around herself and gave an exaggerated swoon. Everyone laughed, and the ice was broken.

'Tell us what you want us to do, Isabella,' said Giovanni, the Italian master-carpenter. *Very handsome, actually*, Isabella thought. *Why did I just think that? I've never noticed such things before.* Her mind drifted to Yannis again. She had wandered the camps on their side of the river in search of him without any luck. It had taken willpower to resist the temptation to ask her grandfather if he had any information.

Isabella decided to tackle Giovanni and the others head on. There was no point in skirting the issue. 'Giovanni, and all of you other gentlemen who are almost, but not quite, as handsome as Giovanni –' Her comments were interrupted by a roar of approval from the room, especially from Giovanni, who actually blushed at being flattered in the presence of so many of his colleagues.

Jacques grinned and looked about. 'You never said a truer word, Isabella. We are actually all handsome, aren't we?'

'Absolutely. Now, I need to get something out into the open, and you all need to be quite honest as to how you feel about it. You can see that I'm very young. To make quite sure there will be no misunderstanding between us, I am letting you know that I am fourteen years old, and I fully understand if you have a problem with that. I need to know that you are all willing to allow me to tell you what you must do.'

Jacques spoke on behalf of the others. 'Well, that was very brave of you, Isabella, but let me tell you, we have already been warned that you fear no-one. Everyone in this room attended a private group meeting with the king and Dmitri Talavares. We weren't told what you plan to do, but we were told that it is you alone who will instruct us. We will follow your instructions without question. No-one, especially General Karamus, will ever know of our meetings, or discussions.'

Isabella curled her arm around his and held tight. 'Thank you, Jacques, and thank you, every one of you. That will make it so much easier for us to work together comfortably. We have much to do and not much time to do it. The future of our nation may well depend on what we can achieve as a team. Make no mistake, this will be a team effort, and each team will be equally important.' She let go of Jacques arm and stepped forward to address the men. 'Now I will tell you what we are going to do!'

When she had finished, the men sat in silence, too stunned to speak. Isabella smiled, turned her head to one side, leaned forward and cupped her hand around one ear. 'Yes,' she said, 'I can hear your thoughts loud and clear: *impossible*, she's crazy, can't be done, impossible, impossible, impossible. Am I correct? Well, now I will tell you *how* we are going to do it!'

The mood had changed by the time she was half-way through her explanation. At the conclusion, the excitement in the room was palpable. Isabella was herself caught up in it as she gave each man his instructions. 'Giovanni, I want you to take … Zenos, you and your men will … Alexander, your artists will spread throughout every valley and … Piotr, as soon as we have picked the spot, you and your miners will … Jacques, you know what you need to design. You and Piotr will be working together very closely.' She paused. 'There's something else to which I'll need you all to contribute in different ways.'

Isabella continued until every man had received his instructions. They were astonished that she remembered every name after just a single introduction.

When she finished, she gave each man a hug. 'Thank you so much, gentlemen. We will attempt something that has never been done before. Over the next couple of days, as you drift in and out of camp, we will have ongoing meetings.' She did her exaggerated swoon again. 'Isabella is now about to leave her group of handsome men to go and have that hot soapy bath.' The men gave her an enthusiastic round of applause as she left the room. Once outside, she whistled for *Barca* and went looking for Zhang Chen.

In the following two days, Isabella poured over sketches, maps and engineering plans. When she pointed out specific areas of interest, men were sent to review their earlier observations and bring back updated information. Now that the team leaders knew what her plan was, they knew what to look for. On the third day she approached Alexander with some of the sketches his team of artists had produced. Every detail of the countryside was meticulously recorded.

'Alexander, are these what I think they are? Aqueducts?'

'Yes, there are nine of them near this ridge and three further along down here. The locals use them to divert water in the wet season to their little dams so they'll have water in the dry season.'

Isabella placed three sketches, all drawn precisely to the same scale side by side on the ground. She leafed through several other sketches and selected one. 'And the main river splits here into two large streams that then join up again in the one larger river, yes?'

'Correct.'

'I want to see those aqueducts right now. Bring all the sketches and maps and anything that shows levels of all the valleys under review. Get your horse. Let's go!'

They were back by sundown. Isabella jumped down from *Barca* and ran towards Jacques' cottage. *'Jacques! Jacques!* Are you there? Come out. Hurry! I've found it. I've found the key!'

The door was flung opened, and Jacques appeared on the tiny veranda, his eyes shining with excitement.

'It's time for you to go to work, Jacques. I've found the place for you to start your masterpiece!'

Marcus listened quietly as Isabella recounted selected parts of her adventure in the upper valleys. He was horrified when it dawned on him what the dominant part of her plan included. 'So that's why you need forty tons of gunpowder.' It was a statement of fact, not a question, and spoken with quiet resignation.

'Jacques nearly fainted when I told him what it's for.'

'That's hardly surprising.' Marcus got up and slowly walked away. He was appalled. It was more than he could bear to think about. Isabella rose and followed him to where he was standing quietly at the edge of their campsite. She put her arms around him and leaned her head against his shoulder. He embraced her, and they stood quietly staring into the flickering campfire.

'You've provided Dmitri with more plans like that one, haven't you?'

'Yes, Grandfather. Several, in fact.'

'And are they just as diabolical as this one?'

'M-m-m ... possibly worse, if anything.'

'I don't want to know what they are. Not until I need to know.'

She gave Marcus a squeeze. 'Good, because I didn't want to tell you.'

Zhang Chen and Isabella continued to slip away for their daily training. Xu Yan had been told what their training consisted of, but Chen insisted that she was not to accompany them. He wanted no distractions. She kept asking to be permitted to watch and swore she would remain unseen and unheard. One day Chen relented and Yan accompanied them to their secret training ground.

Yan sat cross-legged on the ground well away from the two combatants and watched the skill and power they exhibited as they fought on a well-worn patch of grass. During the second hour, Chen became hot and unthinkingly stripped off his shirt with a flourish. A loud gasp brought the two combatants to a halt. Yan clutched her throat, staring wide-eyed. She was seeing Chen's massive layers of muscles for the first time. After a moment, she lowered her gaze.

Isabella grinned. 'I take it you two haven't reached the hand-holding stage, have you, Father?'

'*No!* Chinese very reserved and show respect from great distance. Everything must remain proper.'

Isabella lowered her voice. 'Well, now that she has seen some of you, it's only fair that I share a secret with you.' She leaned forward and whispered, 'I have seen her in the bath-house, and she is truly *magnificent*, Father.'

Zhang Chen bowed and smiled broadly. 'Ah ... good to know. Thank you, precious daughter.'

CHAPTER 54

Isabella made frequent visits to her team leaders over the following weeks. Chen accompanied her on every occasion. Jacques was satisfied that all was going to plan and they were well ahead of schedule.

'What about the locals, Jacques – will they agree to what we want?'

'Absolutely. Dmitri provided us with such generous compensation funds to throw around that the locals will agree to anything. In due course they will each be paid more than they would ever get in a lifetime and will be gone before they see what we're doing. No-one will ever know what's going on here. Everything we're doing now is just planning and preparation. The key valley is far away and hard to get to, but if any of Karamus' gang should wander up for a spot of fishing, there will be little to arouse their suspicions.'

'Excellent. Here's my next list. I won't have the gunpowder for quite some time, so you'll just have to place a temporary seal on the chambers. I don't want any animals making their home in them.'

'How are you going to get the gunpowder to us? Forty tons is an awful lot of powder.'

'That's for me to know and you to find out.' Isabella grinned and reached up to kiss him on the cheek and give him a hug to dispel any thoughts he might have about being chastised. 'I'll see you soon, Jacques, my friend.'

Malak and Zahrah stayed in the swimming-pool-sized soapy bath as they watched the beautiful Ayesha glide up the steps and take a towel from the top of a stack. There were no handmaidens in their quarters to assist them with any of their personal chores. No-one was permitted to see the three young women without their burqas, or even to hear their voices.

Every room, and their inclusions, had been perfectly reproduced from portraits displaying interiors of Persian palaces. No expense had been spared in making the young women feel right at home.

Ayesha put on her inner garments, gloves and sandals, before slipping her burqa over the top. It was not until she had opened the cupboard to select one of the veils that Zahrah spoke softly from the bath. She and Malak were no less beautiful than Ayesha. 'I must have forgotten which day it is. Are you going out?'

It was Ayesha's choice of a purple veil that had prompted the question. The only time those veils were worn was when they left the palace. The emperor's family and his mistresses were the only ones permitted to wear purple cloth.

'I'm going for a walk to the city and do some shopping. I am so bored I think I will buy something very expensive just to irritate Empress Margarethe when she has to pay for it. I think I'll make a visit to that gold dealer that you often visit. I know it is one of your favorite places, too, Malak.' She laughed brightly. 'He must think he has such a wonderful customer, when he has no idea that it could be any one of the three of us.'

'I wish we could surprise him one day by all of us going together.' Malak laughed at the thought. They all knew that would never happen. The three Muslim women could go anywhere at any time and spend without restriction, as long as it was only one of them at the time. Simple insurance: if one should decide not to return, the other two would be put to death.

Ayesha nodded and smiled. 'You went last week, so today it's my turn.' She fastened the magnificent silk veil to her head-scarf and allowed it to fall to her shoulders. Her eyes were concealed beneath a tiny visor cap covered by a net. Emperor Kuiper's crest had been beautifully hand-stitched onto the cloth just above the net, with Arabic symbols embroidered in gold thread below it. In public, the conspicuous veils carried the authority of the emperor himself.

Ayesha blew her two friends a kiss and headed for the door to find an escort. Malak and Zahrah waved before returning to the enjoyment of their bath.

Purity and cleanliness of both body and mind were an important part of the Zen Master's teachings. Isabella had found a small rivulet branching off the river to a grove, where it formed a crystal-clear shallow pool well away from the river itself. Though wide enough for a short swim, the pool was well hidden by rocks and overhanging branches of old, water-logged trees.

Melissa was the only person shown its location and was sworn to secrecy. Isabella insisted that the pool was to be their sanctuary for bathing and relaxation away from the young men, who seemed to be taking an ever-increasing interest in the girls. Their privacy was secure because no-one could approach the pool without being seen. They preferred early morning when there were fewer men about to wonder where they were going on such a regular basis.

Isabella whispered to Melissa. 'Time to go. Are you ready?'

A muffled response came from under the coverings. 'I'm too tired this morning, and it's getting a bit cold. I'll go this afternoon when it's warmer. Is that all right? We can both go this afternoon.'

'No, it's fine. I'll still go now. I'm a morning person – it's so refreshing. Go back to sleep and I'll see you at breakfast.'

At the pool she undressed and slipped into the clear water. She used soap sparingly to minimize clouding the water for the creatures that had made the pool their permanent home. The fish had become used to the girls and came out every morning to take a look at them.

Isabella swam the short length of the pool to rinse the last of the soap from her skin, then rose from the water, toweled dry and dressed. She looked around to make sure she had left nothing behind before heading for the narrow path back to the camp and a welcome hot breakfast.

She was unaware that it was not just the fish that had come out to observe her that morning. A pair of eyes, belonging to someone who had made themselves comfortable in the brush many hours earlier, watched as Isabella enjoyed her bathing. The eyes liked what they saw.

After breakfast Isabella wrote a lengthy letter to Dmitri, providing him with a full update. She placed the letter in one of the envelopes he had given her and was about to heat the wax when Marcus poked his head through the entry.

He went to speak, but instead took a second look at the open box, envelope and wax. 'What on earth is that?' He walked into the tent and picked up the box to have a closer look. 'What a magnificent box! Where did you get it?'

'Dmitri.'

'Ah …' He watched as Isabella carefully pressed the seal against the wax and held it there for several moments. 'I might write a book entitled *Isabella and the Spymaster.*'

His granddaughter removed the seal and glared up at him feigning insult. 'And why, may I ask, would you not call it *Dmitri and the Spymaster?*'

Marcus laughed. 'How will you deliver it? It's too big for a pigeon.'

'Several of the soldiers with Emile are from the Royal Guard and have been assigned to me. No-one knows about them, not even Emile.'

'Assigned to you! My goodness! I have no-one assigned to me. It seems I'm just a *nobody.*' Marcus sounded grouchy, but continued to smile.

Isabella put one arm around him while she held the envelope up so he could view the seal. 'I'm just a *thinker*, Grandfather; you are a *doer*. When the battles start, you will be the *doer* and I will be the *nobody.*'

'Ah … As always, Isabella, you are absolutely right!'

It was mid-morning weeks later when the weather was getting cold. Even Isabella preferred to bathe later, after breakfast.

After their wash and swim, Melissa was about to get out of the water when she suddenly turned towards Isabella. 'Isabella, darling, could you please reach out and pass me the robe hanging from the branch behind you?'

Isabella did so and Melissa wrapped the robe around herself in a smooth motion as she rose from the water, revealing nothing. She turned to Isabella, who was still submerged to her neck. 'Wait, stay there, please.' She toweled dry and dressed with the robe still wrapped around her shoulders. 'All right; your turn.' She held out the robe for Isabella to slip into as she rose.

'What's wrong, Melissa?' She toweled dry and dressed with Melissa still holding the robe in front of her. 'Why are we hiding ourselves? You don't need to feel embarrassed in front of me. You have nothing that I haven't seen before, and you are a picture of perfection from head to toe. You are the most beautiful girl ever.'

Melissa's giggle echoed softly around their secret cove as she gave Isabella a quick hug of appreciation. 'Yeah, right, I thought I was, too. Except for you, my pretty. It's about time I lent you my mirror so you can take a look at yourself. I can't believe how you've changed in just the few months I've known you. I thought you weren't going to be competition because of your age, but you're developing so fast you're turning out to be my worst nightmare. I'm afraid you've already tossed me into second place. Oh dear, I'm simply going to have to drown you to get my crown back and give me first choice of the boys.' She paused, a worried look spreading across her face. Lowering her voice to a whisper, she said seriously, 'I have a feeling that we're being watched. Do you feel it?'

'No, I haven't felt a thing.' Still blushing from the flattering remarks, Isabella looked around, trying not to be too obvious.

'I felt it yesterday, too, but I didn't say anything. Today I feel it even stronger. I could be wrong.'

'You probably are, but we had better not take any chances. We'll keep some clothing on in future and I'll tell Grandfather where we are going, and when. I'll also ask Emile if he's seen anyone hanging around the area. Anyway, it's going to be much too cold soon to come here. Let's go.'

Buried deep beneath bushes and leaves, the eyes that had been watching blinked in disappointment.

Marcus promised he would stand watch near the path leading to the cove and went in search of Emile. He returned in less than thirty minutes.

'His men said Emile had to organize a new group of camp followers who arrived yesterday, so he spent the night in Karamus' camp on the other side of the river. He'll be back before dark. One of his men said he'll ride over there to ask him to drop in on the way back.'

That evening Emile shook his head and told them he had not seen anyone suspicious, but would tell his men and camp followers to keep their eyes open for anyone regularly heading towards the southern bluff area.

CHAPTER 55

General Vlado Karamus spent his days visiting the valleys to encourage the workers, and assigned much of his army to help with the manual labor as soon as they arrived in small platoons from all directions. The general was pleased with progress and took full credit for the results. Armies on the march lived off the land, and the larger the army, the larger the need. Karamus knew only too well that the massive Northern army would need every bit of the available produce when it eventually reached the valleys, and he knew that he would be well rewarded for it.

What Karamus did not know was that the logistics and planning for the work and planting were directed by the agriculturists following Isabella's sketches and written instructions. Particular crops were planted in particular places throughout the valleys; grazing land for horses, cattle and other animals was very specifically selected. Huge barns were built near the grazing areas for the storage of hay and other produce to carry them through the winter months. Shelters and pens were built to accommodate the livestock needed to feed an ever-growing army of troops, camp followers and immigrant workers.

Jacques studied Isabella's sketches, meticulously re-drawn to scale by Alexander and his fellow artists, and knew he could never have thought of such a complex and detailed layout. He had to admit that the design work and careful use of levels for the placement of crops and grazing lands were brilliantly conceived, and knew that Isabella was gifted with a commander's eye for terrain. No army would camp on top of crops, while the preservation of grazing land for the tens of thousands of animals was even more important. Section by section, valley by valley, Isabella had pre-planned exactly how and where the enemy would, by default, choose their camp-sites. The sheer size of the enemy forces would require them to string these sites over many miles. The lush crops and grazing lands would encourage them to do exactly that.

Winter was cold beyond imagination, and it did not take Isabella much effort to convince Marcus that their little group should join the team leaders several valleys upstream. They informed Emile that they would take turns to visit weekly for news.

There were several spare cabins and Isabella shared one with Melissa and Yan. Marcus and Chen shared another.

'Ooh … this is so beautiful,' Melissa cooed one day as she shared a hot bath with Isabella. 'Looking out the window at all that snow while we're laying here in a hot bath. I never thought life could be such bliss in winter.' She slapped the surface of the water several times with her palms to make soap suds spray in all directions. Suddenly she became serious.

'Isabella?' she asked softly.

'Yes?' Melissa's voice had a tone Isabella had not heard before.

'Why are we here?'

'Because there are no hot baths in the main valley, silly.'

Melissa pulled Isabella's slippery foot out of the water and grabbed her big toe. 'You know very well that's not what I meant. Tell me or I shall twist this toe in a full circle. Why are we all really here? You've been coming up to this valley on a regular basis for months, and now that we're staying here, you're always in meetings with the leaders. I've seen you through the hall window, and I don't understand what I see. You don't sit with the men as a group. You're always at the front facing them, so you must be their leader. What's going on? Out with it! *Or else off it goes!* The grip on the toe tightened meaningfully.

The two girls stared silently at each other for a long time, Melissa with the hunger for information, Isabella with the knowledge she could not take her best friend into her confidence. Even Marcus knew only a small part of her plans, and he would be shocked if he knew them all. Melissa let go of the foot when she saw tears streaming down Isabella's face. 'Oh, Isabella, what's wrong? What have I said? What have I done?'

It had happened too suddenly and without warning. Isabella's pent-up stress turned into full panic mode, and she was no longer able to control the emotions she had kept hidden for so long. She covered her face with both hands and wept quietly.

Melissa thrust herself forward through the water and grabbed Isabella in a tight embrace. 'Isabella, Isabella! I'm so sorry. I shouldn't have asked. I take it all back. Forget I ever asked. Please don't cry. I didn't mean to make you cry.' Within seconds they were both sobbing on each other's shoulder.

Isabella finally regained control and wiped the tears from her face. Then she wiped Melissa's.

'Do you love me, Melissa? I mean, really, really love me as your best friend?'

'Of course I do, Isabella. I will only ever love my husband more. I swear it.' She wiped her nose and managed a giggle. 'Even though I do *hate* you for being more beautiful than I am.'

'Oh ... you!' Isabella splashed suds over her friend. 'And I will only ever love my husband more than you. Do you trust me just as much?'

'Yes, of course I do. I trust you with my life.'

'Then I can tell you that you're right, there is something going on, but you must trust me that I can't tell you what it is. Only the king and one other have knowledge of it. Not even Grandfather knows what it's all about. Our lives depend on total secrecy – yours, mine, and everyone in the valleys. Melissa, listen to me: it is imperative that no-one, absolutely no-one, ever knows that I even *have* secrets.'

'Don't worry. I understand. You must not breach the king's confidence. I'm sorry to have asked. Please forgive me.' Melissa grabbed both of Isabella's hands.

'No, no, I'm glad now that you did.' Isabella's laugh rang out in the tiny bath-house. 'My shameless display of emotions has actually made me feel much better. I no longer have to hide the fact from you that I do have secrets. It's such a relief I feel refreshed. Thank you for trusting me.'

They finished their bath and dressed in appropriate heavy clothing to withstand the intense cold on the other side of the door. As Melissa grabbed the door handle, she turned to Isabella with smirk. 'Well, let's hope your little war goes well, my pretty,' she said cheerily as she flung the door wide open.

'*What* ...?' Isabella stammered as she leaned past Melissa to slam the door shut again. 'What do you mean – war?'

Melissa counted off her fingers, one by one. 'Secrets, King involved, a team of experts, soldiers, camp followers. Oh dear, I've run out of fingers already, but I don't need any more. Five fingers equals –' She paused while she dramatically waved her arms about. '*War!* Besides, there's something else that proves I'm right.'

'What's that?' asked Isabella weakly.

'That crestfallen look on your face!' exclaimed Melissa triumphantly. Then she grew serious. 'Your secret is safe with me, I promise.'

Isabella realized that one of her earlier opinions of Melissa was correct. There was an intelligent young woman behind that beautiful face. She reached over to open the door. 'Melissa, darling, be aware that the lives of every person in the valleys below now depend on your silence.'

Jacques could hardly contain himself at their meeting that afternoon. 'I'm afraid I haven't been able to wait until you head north next summer. I've decided to make a start with my project. Don't worry, no-one will notice. We've already started on the tunneling, and it's going very well. It's only the surface ground that's frozen. We're off and running!'

CHAPTER 56

General Von Franckel's fellow generals and senior officers had been
bitterly disappointed when told that two-thirds were to be left out of
the campaign, and the undoubted glory that they would have shared. Over
time, however, they had come to realize that the emperor's command was
a fact of army life and that nothing could be done about it.

Each division commander was supplied with maps that detailed every
lake, river and stream along their designated route. Apart from food, not
a single animal could travel far without a constant supply of water, and
without the animals the three armies would go nowhere. The preservation
and well-being of the animals ranked above that of the soldiers. That was
another fact of army life.

General Von Franckel arrived at the palace to keep his pre-arranged
appointment. It was not yet spring but the weather was unseasonably
warm. The meeting had been arranged so he could present his latest report,
which included the plans for mobilization. In the meantime, he had taken
the time to restructure his own plan. Not as perfect as his original one, but
it would have to do.

A uniformed guardsman greeted him at the entrance and led the way
to the emperor's study. He stopped just outside the double door so the
general could go in alone.

Von Franckel felt ill the moment he entered the study. Aloise Kuiper
was standing by the window overlooking the exquisite courtyard below and
talking animatedly to a handsome, expensively dressed man in his thirties. A
dark blue velvet cape was draped elegantly over the man's shoulders, falling
to just above his knees. Heavy gold embroidery had been painstakingly
added to the cape's edges, except the bottom edge, which had short gold
tassels. High at the front on each side of the cloth was an embroidered
crest: the royal insignia. They both turned to face the general when he

entered the room. Von Franckel heard the doors close behind him and had the distinct feeling of dungeon doors shutting him away for eternity.

'Ah, there you are, Maurice, my friend.' Von Franckel's stomach churned. Too friendly. Bad omen. 'I dare say you are already acquainted with my guest.' Aloise was smiling broadly.

Von Franckel was indeed acquainted with the emperor's guest: Carlos Bucher, nephew of the recently departed King Harald VI, former Earl of Missignon, former junior general in the king's crusade to Spain. He was also better known to his former troops as the *"take no prisoners General"*, as well as *"Bucher, the Butcher of Missignon."*

'And Carlos, you of course know Maurice.'

The earl smiled and extended his hand to the general, who had no choice but to take the hand of the *former* everything – except for still being his generation's most cold-blooded killer.

'Why don't we sit down, Maurice? You seem a little pale. I expect it's the change of weather. A little wine will do wonders for us all.' Aloise pointed to Von Franckel and then to the side table to make it clear that the general was to play waiter during the meeting.

Von Franckel poured the wine and handed each their glass before taking his seat. He took a generous sip from his own and had to admit that it did make him feel better, but it did nothing for his apprehension. He looked around the study and waited for someone to speak. There was nothing he could say until he was told why the *former* earl was present. He knew he had been outmaneuvered, yet had no idea what it meant.

Aloise emptied half his glass in a single swallow, leaned back in his oversized chair and raised his glass to Von Franckel. '*Saluté*, Maurice. I have good news for you.'

The general felt no better and said nothing. Carlos Bucher was present for good reason and he knew it was not something that would please him. He waited for the bomb to land in his lap.

'I understand you'll be ready to mobilize soon. Early spring, is that right, Maurice?'

'Yes, sir. The animals can't travel without access to vast supplies of water, so yes, I expect we'll be off early spring, give or take a week or two, depending on weather conditions.'

'Ah, well, there you are. That's the good news, Maurice. It will be the *Earl* who will be off, actually, not you. He will be the one to lead our campaign.'

The general could not move or speak. Only his mind was in motion and it was spinning rapidly out of control.

Taking the general's silence as tacit agreement, Aloise pressed on. 'I've appointed Carlos to the most senior rank of general, Maurice – oh, sorry, *second*-most senior rank. You will, of course, outrank him, and you will remain my overall commander-in-chief. In return for his services to the nation, I have reinstated his former status of Earl of Missignon. He will, therefore, in future be addressed as *Your Grace*. Carlos has provided me with a written oath that he and his family will never lay claim to the throne. However, Carlos will be given the protection, rights and privileges of his former royal status. He will be the only one to regain royal status, by the way.'

'And what will I do?' The general's voice was little more than a whisper. He was deeply worried. Had the emperor also made an *appointment* for him?

'You will remain here to take control of all communications to and from the earl. You will coordinate any needs he might request: supplies, weapons and the like. Naturally, troop reinforcements will be out of the question. That's where you come in, Maurice. I need you and your men here.' What Aloise did not say was that he also wanted Von Franckel where he could keep an eye on him.

Von Franckel felt slightly better: if he was *needed,* he was not about to be given an *appointment.* He immediately discarded his second plan and started to outline a third. It was pointless to object so he simply nodded for Aloise to continue.

'Many months ago I mentioned that I had concerns about the English. Well, I hear they are winning the battle against this disease that's cursing us all, so that makes me more nervous. Here, you'll have most of your best officers and soldiers. The naval vessels are being fitted out, so we'll soon let those island barbarians know we also have five hundred highly polished cannons to wake them up for early breakfast. This will virtually guarantee success both in the south as well as at home.'

Von Franckel had to admit Aloise made good sense. By the time the emperor had finished, Von Franckel had a new plan. It was in fact better than his initial one, and the treasure would be within smelling distance. *Perfect!* He was ecstatic and had to fight hard not to show it.

'When you first mentioned the change of commanders, sir, I'm sure you'll understand my shock and disappointment at not leading the campaign. But now that I see the full picture, I must say I like it. It's a good plan; it has my full support and so does His Grace. I'll do everything in my power to assist his campaign.' He nodded to the earl who acknowledged the formal address and the reference to the campaign as now the earl's.

'One little thing before we finish up, Maurice. If any of your generals object to His Grace suddenly being in charge of the campaign, just give them a friendly reminder that they can call in at any time to make an *appointment*. Or, better still, tell them I can arrange for someone to pick them up if they prefer.'

The general smiled warmly, his emotions back under control. 'Don't worry, sir, I don't expect any objections. But if there are …' Von Franckel slid his sword part-way out of its scabbard before savagely slamming it back in with a clatter of metal. The inference was clear.

'Excellent, excellent!' Aloise rose. The meeting was finished. 'We'll continue our meetings on a weekly basis, Maurice. Nothing's changed except there will be the three of us in future.'

'I look forward to it, gentlemen.' This time he was the first to extend his hand.

'Well, that went better than I thought it would go. I expected him to squeal like a pig on the way to slaughter.' Aloise sat down and pointed to the bottle and his empty glass. It was time to make sure Carlos Bucher understood that an emperor would always outrank an earl. The earl smiled and poured the wine. He understood exactly what Aloise was conveying by the gesture and he didn't mind, not in the least. His part of their bargain made it well worthwhile.

'Do you trust him, Aloise?' It was the earl's turn to remind Kuiper that their secret agreement would ultimately elevate Carlos Bucher to be Aloise's equal, and that they would therefore be on first name terms in private. Aloise smiled warmly at the earl; he also didn't mind. In fact, he found it pleasant to have someone call him by his first name.

'Up to a point, Carlos. He's always been loyal, but there seems to be something lurking behind that urbane façade. He probably resents me because although he was a better general than I during the Spanish crusade, I am emperor. Maurice is without doubt our best soldier, a brilliant military tactician. I recommend you not discard any suggestions he might throw your way.' Aloise was unaware there was something dangerous lurking beneath the earl's urbane façade, too.

'Point taken, Aloise.' The earl handed Aloise his glass and turned towards his own seat. 'The reasons you just gave him have a substantial basis of truth, which made them eminently believable.' With the earl's back momentarily towards him, Aloise did not notice his neck and shoulders twitching, his eyes narrow or his fists clenching almost to the point of snapping the stem of his glass.

Aloise waited for the earl to be seated before responding. 'Maurice, of course, must have no inkling of the *real* reason for the change of leader. He simply would never do what I want *you* to do.' Aloise leaned forward and lowered his voice to speak to the psychopath who, unknown to him, had just traded places with the elegant earl. 'There must be no misunderstanding as to what your task will entail.'

Bucher, the *Butcher of Missignon,* raised his glass to Aloise and then took a long sip. 'First, I will accept the enemy's unconditional surrender and take control of their nation. I will then follow the blood-lines of their royal family to the bitter end and eliminate every one of its members. I will eliminate every officer of the army and navy, and every member of parliament, together with their extended families; I will also eliminate any industrialist at the first sign of refusal to cooperate, and lastly, I will eliminate anyone who dares to even raise his hand to object to anything. I believe that about covers it, Aloise?'

'I do believe that about covers it.'

'Oh, there was just one more thing, Aloise. It almost slipped my mind – how remiss of me! After completing those tasks, I will issue threats against the remaining nations in the South. They will capitulate, and you will then declare me emperor of the Southern Region and all will live happy and rich for ever. Well, at least you and I will.' The handsome Bucher winked at Aloise and produced his most charming smile of the evening. It was the mesmerizing smile of the cobra.

Aloise laughed and enthusiastically toasted Bucher, spilling some wine in the process. Neither of the two had any inkling of yet another alter ego buried deeper still beneath Bucher's smiling façade, one far more dangerous than even the murderous psychopath.

The woman stepped into the lane behind the Persian gold-dealer's shop and walked unhurriedly for several minutes. She looked around briefly when she reached the familiar archway and iron gate. Satisfied, she moved through and silently closed the gate behind her. A zigzag path through an exquisite garden of brilliant flowers and palms led her to a slated patio and into a huge lounge-room, where a man was waiting for her. The room had numerous large windows cut into the white-washed walls, but no glass, to allow its occupants to enjoy the gardens that completely screened the property from the streets, and from prying eyes.

The woman removed the black veil and carefully placed it, together with the purple veil and headscarf, on a side table. She gave a small bow to her host and pointed to a heavily cushioned lounge chair. 'Come and sit with your back to me, so I can rub your neck and shoulders. While you relax, you can tell me all about your meeting with our esteemed leader last night.'

The man loved the way she bowed to him, despite her influential position within the palace walls. He poured himself a glass of wine on his way to the chair, but knew not to offer her one. 'The campaign will get underway in a couple of weeks ...' he began as he felt her gentle hands massaging the base of his neck.

The woman waited until he had finished before her hands moved from his shoulders to his face. She traced her fingers gently over his forehead, nose and lips before she leaned forward to speak softly into the ear of the handsome Earl Carlos Bucher. 'When this is over,' she said, 'he is in for a big surprise, my darling.'

Twenty minutes later, the shopkeeper lifted a cushion and removed an envelope left behind by his visitor. As always, it was sealed and addressed to the Caliph.

Von Franckel was out of uniform when he appeared at the palace a week after his previous visit. His message to Aloise had requested a meeting between the two of them only, and in the strictest of confidence.

The general was ushered into Aloise's office, where he saluted the already seated emperor. Aloise smiled at him. 'Sit, sit, Maurice. I can hardly call you *General* dressed like that, can I? You specifically asked that His Grace not know of our meeting today, so I surmise it must be about him. Is he plotting a royal comeback? What is it?'

'No, no, sir. Nothing like that, I assure you. I have no problem with His Grace at all. I'll come straight to the point.'

'Good idea!'

'It's about the armor, sir.'

'Armor? What about the armor?'

'Well, the lack of it, to be more precise. I've been wondering whether you mentioned to His Grace the fact that we dispensed with ordering armor.'

'Hm … no, I haven't, actually. I hadn't given it any thought at all, to be honest. You've obviously given it some thought or you wouldn't be here.' Aloise sat back, suddenly worried.

Von Franckel crossed his legs and folded his arms across his chest. 'It's more of a *potential* problem than an actual one. It will require a judgment call by you, sir. I was, of course, unaware of the change of leadership until last week, so there has been no manufacture of armor for the campaign. You now need to consider whether to tell him, or not.' Von Franckel raised his eyebrows.

Aloise nodded his understanding.

'If you *don't* tell him, he probably won't find out until he's at the border of the target nation, and lining up the cannons. In all probability he won't need them anyway, as we discussed, so it won't matter. On the other hand, he most likely will be furious that he wasn't informed.'

Aloise nodded again and smiled. 'Yes, that would be a reasonable assumption. And if I *do* tell him?'

'Well, that's the tricky part. There are two problems. The first, as mentioned, is that he's likely to be furious he wasn't told that armor had not been ordered in the first place. He would not even consider the cost factor.'

'And the second problem?'

'He could insist on re-instating the ordering of armor.'

'What are the implications? You've left this one to last, so this is the one you've been thinking about, isn't it? This is the one that has made you come to me in secret.'

'Yes, it is, sir. It would take a year to manufacture the huge volume of armor required. That would obviously force the campaign to be delayed for a year. It would not simply be a matter of reversing the cost saving of twenty or thirty percent. A double-sized army for the additional year would have to be supported while sitting around with nothing to do. And of course hundreds of thousands of animals that are now ready for departure would have to be fed, and man-power would be needed to look after them for another year. In addition, the risk of discovery of our plans would increase tenfold, putting the entire campaign itself in jeopardy.'

Aloise's face had turned deathly white, and a cold sweat had broken out. 'Good heavens, I hadn't considered any of that. I decided to put the earl in charge of the campaign so that I could retain your services here to look after the national interest. Oh, dear God, what have I done?'

Without comment, Von Franckel let the emperor stew.

'What sort of extra cost are we talking about?'

'Probably double the entire cost of the campaign, possibly more. Now that we are about to mobilize, costs are running at their peak. I know this is the most difficult decision you've ever had to make, sir.'

It had taken Aloise less than a second to make his decision. If he informed the earl, he risked having to provide armor, which would mean financial ruin for both himself and the nation. If, instead, he cancelled the campaign, all the local problems would resurface and he would still face financial ruin – or worse.

He rose and walked to the window. He then proceeded to pace the office from side to side. The delay was no more than pretense. 'The likelihood is that the armor won't be needed anyway, so it won't matter, and he'll get over his anger soon enough. No, too many risks if I tell him now. He might just decide to quit. I will then have to send you and I'll have no one here I can rely on if the English, or worse, those dreadful Stavanger Vikings, decide to come for a bit of local shopping – or chopping, depending on your sense of humor.' He laughed mirthlessly. 'No, no, far too dangerous. The answer is to say nothing. Once he's on his way, he can't turn back. What do you think?'

Von Franckel nodded, keeping a straight face. He was ecstatic. 'I believe that's a good decision.'

Aloise walked towards him and put out his hand. Von Franckel rose to take it.

'I will take it as a personal favor if our conversation goes no further. Ever.'

'Of course. That's why I came in the strictest confidence.'

'I think it's time you called me *Aloise*, Maurice. I really don't know what I would do without you to watch my back!'

Von Franckel almost choked.

Von Franckel departed the palace the same way he had arrived – by a secure and little-known side entrance. Deep in thought, he quickly melted into the nearby crowded streets. He failed to notice several street vendors watching his every move. He smiled at the thought that Aloise had not realized that he had been led into a trap by agreeing to remain silent.

CHAPTER 57

An army of laborers moved in for the re-tilling and plantings at the first sign of the spring thaw. Nature's fertilizer stocks had been built up both before and during winter, and were abundantly available. Within weeks, the valleys were bursting with crops reaching for the sun. There was little doubt that two full crops would be achieved before the Southern army needed to vacate the valleys.

The first sign of spring also brought movement of great significance in the Northern Region. Each day thousands of troops departed in different directions. Pomp and music entertained the public every morning.

The men and equipment that made up the three armies had already departed when the earl visited the palace for his final orders and a farewell to Aloise. Those formalities dispensed with, he took his leave. He made sure to wear his most spectacular royal uniform and cape for his departure, and paraded himself through the entire city for all to see and remember on the day he returned in triumph.

Conspicuous among the more traditional uniforms were the brightly colored turbans and flowing white robes of the brigade of Arab mercenaries.

Von Franckel hurried up the palace steps early the following morning. He had wanted to be sure that the earl was well out of town before he visited Aloise.

'Good heavens, Maurice. You are so early. What's the panic?'

'I was wondering whether anything came up regarding armor?'

Aloise smiled. He knew exactly why Maurice was there and why he had waited for the earl to leave. 'No, he never said a word, and no-one else ever mentioned it in front of him. So everything is up and running as scheduled.'

Von Franckel sighed. 'Well, to be honest, Aloise, I have to admit to being relieved. I fear, though, that he's going to be beside himself with rage when he does find out.'

Aloise reached out and patted him on the shoulder. 'Well, the silly man should have asked, shouldn't he, my dear Maurice?' They both smiled and Von Franckel was invited to join Aloise for breakfast.

The spring plants sprouted as the weeks passed, and so did Isabella. She was closing in on her fifteenth birthday, filling out and growing at a blistering pace. The soldiers no longer tried to hide their admiring stares and, as Melissa had intimated the previous year, Isabella was getting so used to it she barely noticed. Her mind remained focused on one man only, and she searched the camps on both sides of the river for him every day.

It was mid-morning and Isabella looked quickly around her tent for any forgotten items while she made final preparations to meet Chen for their daily training session. He had already gone on ahead to do his warm-up exercises. Melissa and Yan had decided to stay at the pool a little longer, while Isabella returned to prepare for training. Marcus remained on guard duty at the entrance to the path leading to the cove.

The sun was already warm and Isabella realized it could be a hot session. She changed into a brief leather halter top and short leather-tasseled skirt that reached half-way to her knees, leaving bare her midriff and most of her legs. Light ankle-boots completed her training outfit. From her bag she pulled out a beautifully crafted soft leather cap she had designed and made herself. She had personally hand-stitched the band to fit securely around her head, allowing abundant room to accommodate her long, golden hair.

Just as she grabbed the tent-flap to leave, she glanced down at herself and had a change of mind. Too revealing, she decided, and not appropriate with a valley full of young soldiers. The halter top was replaced by a cotton shirt and a light leather sleeveless jacket. The skirt was replaced by one slightly longer.

Isabella decided to secure her hair after she had met up with Chen at the clearing, and placed the cap back in the bag, checked the strap and tied the bag around her waist. She spent a few moments with *Barca* to give him his usual quiet hug while she hummed and stroked his beautiful neck. *Barca* made strange grunting – almost chuckling – noises deep in his throat as he enjoyed the stroking and waited patiently for her to leap onto his back. As soon as she was ready she leapt up on his slippery back, dug her heels in and *Barca* sprang into action.

To reach the sparring ground she had to pass close to the cove's entrance where Marcus stood guard. She saw her grandfather and Emile sitting on a rotted log, deep in conversation. Isabella waved and was about to continue when, without warning, she was suddenly overwhelmed with rage. *What's happening to me?* she thought desperately. Her rage increased to hot fury and she felt her head spin and throat tighten. *I'm out of control. I've lost my sanity.* I've gone from sobbing with Melissa to being angry with Grandfather. She tried to vent her fury by screaming, but no sound came out. Instead, her rage increased. Two years of frustration over Yannis had caught up with her.

She pointed *Barca* towards the two men at full gallop and did not stop until she was only paces away. Her voice returned in those few seconds.

'*Grandfather, where is he?* Why isn't he here? *Tell me!*' she yelled at him. Marcus was shocked. Isabella had never previously raised her voice to him. 'I've searched every camp for him, every day, and *nothing*. You've seen me searching and you've never said a word. It's been two years. I swear if he is not here soon, I'll forsake him! I hate him! Is he dead? Is that why he's not here? Is he dead? If he knows what's good for him, he'd better be dead!'

Marcus had jumped up and scrambled to the other side of the log. Emile did the same. 'No, no, darling! He's not dead. I haven't spoken of him because I thought it would just bring you more pain. I hoped you'd get over him in time. You know it would be better if you did, but I can see that you haven't. I'm sorry, Isabella.'

'So now you know I haven't, and I never will. Never! So tell me. Where is he?' Isabella calmed down rapidly now that things were out in the open between them.

'I had a message from Dmitri that he had already left with Uncle Nicho early spring. They're due here any time soon. In fact, they have to be here soon, don't they?' Marcus sent her a warning sign with his eyes that she should not respond directly to that message in front of Emile.

'Any time soon? You mean like any day?'

'Yes, absolutely. Any day now.'

Isabella jumped down from *Barca* and rushed to Marcus. 'I'm so sorry I raged at you, Grandfather. I don't know what came over me. I just lost control in an instant. You know I love you, don't you? Nothing's changed.' She kissed him on both cheeks.

'I know, darling, I know. You'll meet up with him soon enough, and then you can tell him yourself just how much you hate him. Now be off with you. And don't ride over the top of the new camp.' He pointed to a camp that had sprung up overnight, directly in her path. He just hoped Yannis was not already married.

Isabella leapt back on *Barca* and resumed her ride to the training ground. Her excitement built up so much she drew her sword and swung it in circles above her head as she rode. Changing direction slightly to skirt the new camp, she pointed *Barca* towards a rise that overlooked the valley, less than fifty paces from the new camp. A number of soldiers were milling about, many having a late breakfast, and they gaped open-mouthed at a female warrior, sword glinting in the sun, flashing past them at full gallop on a long-maned white stallion. Isabella shouted her excitement to the entire valley and brought *Barca* to a shuddering halt at the peak, pulling the mane hard to make him perform a well-practiced maneuver.

Barca reared his enormous muscular body up at full stretch, almost perpendicular to the ground, his pure white coat and mane spectacular in the brilliant morning sun. He whinnied loudly and continuously as he made a full turn on his hind legs, his forelegs beating the air while Isabella clung to his long mane, still swinging her sword.

The sun turned her hair into a golden halo that swirled wildly around her head as the stallion continued his spin. Her finely muscled legs held on to *Barca* in a vice-like grip.

'Go *Thunderbolt!*' she yelled. *Barca* dropped to the ground and leapt forward like an arrow from its bowstring, streaking off towards the secret sparring ground. *Barca* was at full pace as they thundered past the tents of the new camp. So focused was Isabella that she failed to see the soldiers watching, awestruck.

'That was the most magnificent sight I have ever seen,' Marcus said to Emile, who nodded his agreement.

'That was the most magnificent sight I have ever seen,' Major Yannis Christos said to the soldier next to him, who nodded, the hand holding his breakfast frozen in mid-air and his mouth open in amazement. Yannis had been standing outside his tent buttoning up his shirt when he first saw the rider appear, then veer away to head for the rise. His fingers had stopped all movement as he watched the entire performance mesmerized.

'I wonder who on earth that was?' he said to the soldier as the rider disappeared into a cloud of dust. He slowly returned to his buttons.

His mate groaned and went back to his breakfast. 'I don't know, Major, but I'm in love and I'm going to find and marry her before someone else does.'

'You might be too late, Telly. She could be married already.'

'No way, Major. No wife could ever look that good, and she seemed a bit young, barely marriage age. And no wife would ever be allowed to ride around like that. No, take it from me, she's not married. But her single days will come to an end as soon as she meets me.' Telly grinned wickedly, but good-naturedly, and chewed noisily on his chicken bone.

Yannis nodded and made preparations to look up old friends and comrades.

Emile looked at Marcus after Isabella was out of sight. 'What was all that about, Marcus? Who were you talking about? Why such a fuss?'

'Well, between you and me, Isabella has been infatuated with someone for quite some time. It would have been better for everyone if she weren't but, unfortunately, she still is.'

'So what's the problem? She's a beautiful girl. Who's the lucky man?'

'That's just the problem. He's a *man* and although she might look like a young woman from a distance, she's still little more than a kid.'

Emile nodded, deep in thought. 'So who is he?'

Marcus grinned. 'Next to me, he's the handsomest man I have ever seen.'

CHAPTER 58

Xu Yan was sitting by the campfire doing some early dinner preparations when Isabella returned from her training session. Marcus was nowhere in sight and Yan informed her that Melissa had gone for a stroll to the river in search for him.

There was a slight chill in the air and Isabella changed into cotton trousers, a long sleeved shirt and slip-on sandals. She doubled over to gather her hair into a roll and stuffed it carefully into the leather cap that she then adjusted at a sharp angle to one side of her head before she left the tent in search of Melissa. 'I'll be back before long, Yan. If Grandfather gets back first, please tell him I've gone to meet up with Melissa.' She waved to Yan and headed towards the nearest bridge.

Half-way to the bridge she saw Marcus walking rapidly towards her. When he reached her he held her by the shoulder with one hand while he pointed towards the bridge with the other. 'Isabella, he's here – Yannis! He's by the bridge but he's – ' He got no further as Isabella tore away from his grip and headed towards the bridge at a rapid pace.

'He's – ' Marcus started again, but Isabella was gone. 'Oh, dear.'

Isabella was approaching the bridge through grass and gravel terrain when she saw the tall, powerful-looking soldier with his back to her. He was wearing a senior officer's uniform and his hair was shorter, but she recognized him instantly: *Yannis!* He appeared to be alone.

Her mind raced as she got closer. *Should I just kick him, or should I find something smart, funny or clever to say?* She opened her mouth to call out to him, but her heart was beating so hard she could only hear the blood roaring in her ears, and nothing escaped from her throat. Two years of agony and now she was mute!

She slowed down to give herself time to regain control, and was about a dozen paces away when she stopped in her tracks. As Yannis shifted from one leg to the other, it became clear he was speaking to someone. Only part of her was visible, but it was enough. Isabella felt her legs turn to jelly, and a pain stabbed her heart and stomach. She recognized the woman's dress instantly. Her greatest fear had turned into reality: *Melissa.*

Yannis had realized that the soft footsteps behind him had suddenly stopped. As he started to turn, his shoulder moved enough to reveal Melissa's face. She had not seen Isabella approach. As the girls' eyes met, Isabella was astonished to see Melissa's widen with surprise. A look of panic and dismay spread across her lovely face. Yannis completed his turn.

Isabella walked slowly towards Yannis, and at the same time reached up to remove her cap. Her golden hair cascaded across her shoulders and almost down to her waist. She flicked her head to settle the thick mass and then turned to gaze directly at him.

'Hello,' she managed lamely. 'Remember me?'

Behind him Melissa covered her face with her hands and groaned.

Yannis flicked his eyes at the new arrival with bemused appraisal. He could see that the girl was very young, already a budding beauty and surprisingly tall. But when he caught sight of the huge, almond-shaped, emerald-green eyes, recognition dawned. 'Well, well! Hello. How could I ever forget you?' Yannis smiled broadly. Isabella had never seen anyone more handsome.

'Oh, ah … , Yannis, this is my best … friend,' Melissa stammered. The panic had subsided, but the look of dismay remained.

'It's all right, Melissa; Yannis and I are already acquainted.'

Yannis took in her mass of golden hair and nodded slowly as realization dawned on him. 'That was you this morning, wasn't it? On the hill, on the white stallion?'

'Yes, did I wake you?'

'No, not at all, but you had my whole camp in uproar with that performance. You were quite spectacular. Many of my men are busy writing letters to you.'

Melissa looked bewildered. *This morning? Performance? What performance?*

Isabella cocked her head to one side. 'I'm often thought to be a little older than I really am, but to save some embarrassment, you had better remind your men that I am only barely of age.'

Yannis smiled and nodded. 'I'll do that. Yet in their defense, I will add that from a distance it's easy to think you're a little older. It's partly because you've become so tall, Isabella, and so quickly.'

'Grandfather. He's possibly the tallest man in the army. My father was almost as tall. I hope I've just about stopped growing.'

'And what have you done to your hair?'

'What do you mean? I haven't done a thing to my hair.'

'It used to be short and silvery, almost white. Now it's thick, long, and golden.'

'It darkened with old age,' she smiled, 'and I just let it grow. I see yours is much shorter. And your beard is also shorter.'

'Regulations. Senior officer rank requires it.'

'Yes, I noticed your uniform. You look very young to be a general, Yannis.' Isabella deliberately smirked.

Yannis put his hands up and took a couple of steps back. 'You're not going to kick me again, are you?'

'Of course I am, but not at this very moment.'

'*General?* You're a *general?*' Melissa's voice was little more than a squeak as she tried to wrest back control of the conversation.

Yannis turned and smiled at her. 'She's kidding, Melissa. Kids have a tendency to do that. No, Isabella can see that I'm a major now. For some strange reason there seems to be a shortage of officers, and promotions have been more rapid than usual. Last time we met I told her I was a second lieutenant, so she kicked me; she almost broke my leg. In fact, you could say she kick-started my career.' He laughed. 'But now that I know what to expect, she'll never be able to kick me again.'

In a speedy blur, Isabella slipped out of her sandals, moved forward, twisted and, with a high kick, struck Yannis gently on his shoulder with her bare foot. Instantly reversing the moves, she gave him a considerably firmer tap on his other shoulder. Yannis had not even had the time to raise his hands in defense. Moving back, she folded her arms. 'Sorry, Yannis,' she said with a grin, as she slipped her feet back into the sandals, 'but that was an invitation not to be missed.'

Melissa stood wide-eyed, mouth open in shock. She had no idea that Isabella had such fighting skills. Neither did Yannis. He shook his head in disbelief. With that speed and skill, Isabella had just sent him another message: she could strike him at will any time she wished. He was lost for words and they just stared at each other for a long moment.

Isabella looked past Yannis at the crestfallen face of her best friend. She knew she was still a child in Yannis' eyes and was careful not to appear to lay claim to him. If she could not have him, she would make sure her best friend would. Walking past him, she stepped behind Melissa to wrap her arms around her. In a tight hug she kissed her friend's cheek and presented her to Yannis.

'So, I see you have already met my very best friend. I was going to introduce her to you when you got here. Melissa is absolutely the most wonderful friend I have ever had, and the most wonderful girl you will ever meet. And is she not also the most beautiful girl you have ever seen, Yannis?'

Yannis looked at them both and opened his mouth to speak. Melissa instantly pointed a finger straight at him, her eyes blazing. 'You had better not answer that, Yannis!' she hissed. 'Don't you *dare* answer that! Isabella and I will be best friends until death. Neither of us could ever forgive you, whatever your answer.' She turned to Isabella. 'Thank you for the compliment, Isabella, but now you've embarrassed him, you naughty thing!'

'I'm sorry, Melissa, I just wanted to make sure Yannis noticed how beautiful you are.'

Yannis looked at them both with a smile. 'Thank you, Isabella, but I had already noticed.' *Good one, Isabella. If you had been born two thousand years ago, you would have been the first person to throw yourself into the lions' pit just to find out what it's like to be eaten alive. Well, now you know.*

Yannis had to get back to his men, so he gave the girls a lazy salute and went for his horse, which was tethered to a tree closer to the bridge. Marcus had invited him to their camp for dinner, and he had promised to come.

The two girls walked back to their camp arm-in-arm. Melissa was moaning. 'Oh, Isabella, I can hardly breathe. I was just strolling along the river-bank with Marcus when Yannis rode by and recognized him. I've never seen anyone so gorgeous. *Oh*, and when he smiles … I feel ill. Do you think he likes me?'

'Of course he likes you. You're so beautiful, he would be mad not to like you, and Yannis is certainly not mad.'

Melissa moaned again. 'I thought I had a good chance until you came along. I nearly fainted when you pulled your cap off and your gorgeous hair tumbled out all over you. I would have simply died if he said that *you* were the most beautiful girl he had ever seen.'

'Don't be silly. I'm barely of age. He would not allow himself to have any interest in me. He is a grown man, and you heard him say I'm only a kid. I would have kicked him into the next valley if he'd shown any interest in me.'

'Oh, I hope he's interested in me, I really hope so. I think I'm in love with him already.'

Isn't everyone? Isabella thought bitterly.

CHAPTER 59

Marcus watched with foreboding as a messenger rode across the northern bridge at full gallop and headed directly towards their camp. He felt his stomach tighten. It did not take a genius to work out what was coming. The others came out of their tents at the sound of the thundering hooves.

'My respects, General Mondeo.' The soldier gave Marcus a salute. 'General Karamus requests your presence urgently. Miss Mondeo also, if you would be so good. He is waiting for you in the conference tent, sir.' The soldier saluted again and dug his heels into the side of the horse.

Marcus headed to his horse and nodded to Isabella, who let out a shrill whistle to summon *Barca*. Melissa stared at Isabella with curiosity. 'Did I hear him correctly? General Karamus asked for you to be there as well?' She shook her head in bewilderment.

'Well, someone has to pour the tea, my dear,' Isabella quipped as she leapt onto the back of *Barca* and headed at full gallop for the bridge, with Marcus in close pursuit.

There were about forty officers in the tent, including a number of generals, Major-General Manassis, a number of captains and Major Yannis Christos.

Isabella hugged her uncle and nodded at Yannis, who smiled grimly and nodded back. Isabella had been surprised at Yannis' recent behavior. He and Melissa were constant companions, but her friend had expressed her frustration to Isabella that he had not yet kissed her, nor made any advances. One evening, when Yannis had joined them for dinner, Melissa wandered off to the women's amenities. While the others were cleaning up the remnants of dinner, Isabella found a quiet moment with Yannis.

'Yannis, do you like Melissa?'

'Yes, of course I do. She's a lovely girl.'

'She likes you very much. She's very, very fond of you, you know. And she is so amazingly beautiful. There's not a soldier in the whole army who would not want to marry her. But you don't seem to be paying her the attention she deserves.'

Yannis had fidgeted and looked around to make sure no-one was within hearing. 'Well, I'm fond of her, too, but you and I both know what's coming – and soon. It might last one day, or perhaps years. We'll be fighting for our lives, and everyone else's. I can't afford to be distracted at any cost. *You* don't get distracted by anyone or anything, so I know you understand. It's too easy for a man to be distracted by someone as beautiful as Melissa. But life creates its own priorities, doesn't it?'

Isabella had nodded without comment.

'But you can help me, Isabella. Help take some pressure off me. She's a lovely, lovely girl, as you know, and I don't want to hurt her feelings, but the time is just not right for Melissa and me.'

'How on earth can *I* help, Yannis?'

'You could throw a bucket of cold water over her.'

Isabella had burst out laughing, joined by Yannis.

Her mind returned to the present as General Karamus rose to address the meeting. 'Our scouts have made visual contact with the enemy.' He pointed at a map stretched out on the table in front of the men. 'They're spread out over a vast area and moving extremely slowly. It will be June in a couple of weeks and the scouts have estimated they will then be here.' The general pointed to another location. 'They're really struggling because of their cannons, as Isabella predicted. The scouts estimate their division numbers at somewhere between 70,000 and 90,000. They are so spread out that there's no way they can all line up against us. You were quite right in your overall predictions, Isabella.'

Many of the senior officers seemed bewildered at the general's references to Isabella, but said nothing. They would question their commander after the meeting.

'Based on the scouts' reports, we have nothing to worry about from their divisions to the east and west; they are simply too far away to be of concern. That will change later, of course, but for now, we only have the one army to contend with. I trust you will forgive my use of the word *only.*' A chuckle circled the room. 'Based on best estimates we'll face battle conditions late July, so we have some two months to get our act together.' He turned and smiled at Isabella. 'I think it's time you tickled your pigeon army into action and work with Dmitri to commence the distribution of the mobilization messages.'

'Consider it done, General.' Isabella nodded at Karamus.

'I believe that concludes our meeting. Thank you all.'

'Isabella!' Yannis ran to her side on the way out of the tent. 'I'll ride back with you and the general. I have to speak to Melissa about something.' Isabella's stomach tightened as she nodded without speaking. The three rode back to the camp side by side. No-one spoke. They all knew that the moment had finally arrived.

Back at the camp, Chen, Yan and Melissa waited anxiously. They knew something important had happened. Yannis slid off his horse like the dancer Isabella remembered.

He wasted no time and took Melissa by the hand. 'Honey Bee,' he said softly, 'something is about to happen, and I'm afraid my time is going to be fully taken up with my new orders and the command of my men. I'm not permitted to discuss the matter with anyone, but Isabella can probably confide in you some of the details from time to time. I simply won't be able to see you very much for quite some time. I'm so sorry, but I won't even be able to stay for dinner this evening. I'm going to have to give my men their new orders, and make preparations to leave the valley.' Yannis held her by the shoulders and kissed her on the cheek. He looked around and nodded to the others, inserted a foot into the stirrup and was gone within seconds.

Melissa stood riveted to the spot, utter despair on her face as she watched Yannis disappear. 'He only kissed me on the cheek,' she wailed. She stared wide-eyed at Isabella. 'You know what's happening, and when. It's what I guessed, isn't it? Tell me. When will I see him again?' Without waiting for an answer she ran to her tent and threw herself on her bed.

Honey Bee? Isabella snorted. *Honey Bee!* An intimate term accompanied by a kiss on the cheek. A contradiction in terms, she thought. *Honey Bee, indeed!* She snorted again.

Watching Yannis disappear into the distance, Marcus thought about what was to come. As a general, he had planned, directed and fought on front lines beside his men in many battles. His nation had too regularly been at war with more than a few of its neighbors, sometimes attacking, sometimes being attacked. Fortunately, most of those neighbors were now allies within the Southern Region. Marcus had been his nation's most successful general and had never failed to achieve a victory, but he knew the next battle was going to be different. The Southern army was vastly outnumbered and it would take place in enemy territory. On this occasion he would be no more than an observer and adviser.

In that role, Marcus worried about new weaponry being introduced at an alarming rate into every nation's armory. New metals, technology and methods of manufacture were changing the face of warfare, resulting in horrific and ever-increasing casualties on both sides of a conflict. The increasing power and range built into the crossbow alone dictated new battle strategies in both offense and defense, and now he had to face cannons for the first time. Marcus feared that Ramesses had placed his faith in him based on his past record rather than what he was now able to contribute as a long-retired former warrior. He knew he was out of his depth.

Crops were harvested at an increased rate and transported both north and south, together with a vast amount of livestock. Some of the land already harvested was allowed to lie fallow, while other sections were immediately prepared and replanted to produce an fall crop. The valley would be their sanctuary after the battle – if they survived.

Over the following week, thousands of pigeons flew in all directions, and to countless destinations, as soldiers and their camp followers were directed to their new points of assembly.

Sergeant-at-arms Emile DaSilva was one of the few who had been informed of the true purpose of the unfolding events. He meticulously planned the string of camps where food and rest would be provided to the retreating survivors of the battle as they headed back across the mountains to the valley.

Time and again, Isabella rode over the area surrounding the chosen battleground to familiarize herself with every aspect of the terrain, accompanied at all times by Chen. It simply seemed a practical thing to do: never plan an action without an exit strategy.

Their army was to cross the mountains and hide in the hills above the grasslands where the confrontation would take place. On closer inspection she found these grasslands to be vast, flat and tinder dry, the dust rising in a cloud behind them as they rode. Every day at about noon, a breeze came in from the east and rapidly accelerated over the flat terrain. On the return journeys in the afternoons, the dust raised by their horses turned into mini-tornadoes that in turn sucked up more dust. Isabella looked at this swirling phenomenon with apprehension. It was an unforeseen element and she always worried about unknowns.

She had no inkling of the significance the wind would have on the battle, just days away.

CHAPTER 60

The Earl of Missignon was enjoying himself immensely. When all the royal families had been disenfranchised, he had immediately become unimportant and he had sunk into a depth of fury and despair. The families had been permitted to retain their wealth, but wealth was of no interest to the earl. Power was what mattered in his life.

He had been an earl and a general, a man to respect and fear. Life or death had been dispensed as he saw fit. He took whatever and whoever he wanted. Objectors were instantly eliminated. Then, suddenly, after the death of his Uncle, King Harald, it had all been taken away.

Now he had it all back. He rode out in the finest royal outfits, a different color for each day, and was always flanked by his personal entourage of 250 black-uniformed knights. The inhabitants of cities, towns and villages came out to view and cheer his army as it passed, taking the opportunity to trade goods and services to the soldiers and their camp followers.

The earl consulted his maps and saw that within days his army would reach vast grasslands ahead of the hills that led to the alpine passes. He knew they had to hurry in order to reach the southern side of the mountains before winter set in. Progress had been slower than anticipated and the cannons were at the end of line, unable to keep up. If caught in the mountains when the first snow fell, they would be trapped there until spring. The cannons, therefore, would have to enter the fearsome terrain first. He decided to assemble a major camp on the grasslands to allow the cannons to catch up, and then give them priority passage through the mountains.

General Karamus called a meeting of officers in his conference tent, including Marcus and Isabella in the invitation. His scouts reported their observations several times each day, and the latest was that the Northern forces had reached the grasslands several days earlier. They were now busy setting up an ever-expanding camp as troops and their baggage train arrived.

'Very well, thank you for your reports, gentlemen. Issue orders and prepare your men to take their place, as detailed in your sealed envelopes. Some of you will also find your new rank in those envelopes. We will present the declaration of war and issue our challenge at sunrise on Saturday. Have your men assembled, armed and ready to march at four that morning. Good luck and God bless.'

Marcus and Isabella rode back to their camp in silence. As they tethered their horses, Marcus reached out and squeezed her hand. He watched her as she walked to her tent, where Melissa and Xu Yan waited for news. Marcus left to find Chen.

Eyes wide with apprehension, Melissa jumped to her feet as soon as Isabella entered the tent. Her friend doubled over, gasping for breath.

'What's wrong? Are you ill? Come and sit down, for heaven's sake!' Melissa grabbed Isabella by the shoulders and tried to steer her towards her bed.

Isabella gently pushed her away, her face drained of color. 'Saturday ... Saturday!' she gasped. 'The death and carnage starts on Saturday.' She sank to the mattress with her arms wrapped around herself. 'Oh, what have I done? What have I done? Oh, God, please forgive me!'

Melissa knelt down and hugged her friend. 'What on earth are you talking about? You haven't done anything!'

Isabella looked up through tear-streaked eyes. 'Oh yes, I'm afraid I have. I'm the cause of all this, Melissa. I'm to blame for all the death and injury that is about to happen. That's why I've been at all the meetings. I'm the one who started this war!'

Melissa's eyes widened with shock as she slumped down on the mattress next to Isabella.

General Karamus arranged for one of his trusted officers to release a pigeon bearing a carefully encrypted message to his father. *Everything is going to plan, Father.* Next, he entered his tent to finalize and date the communication that was shortly to be delivered to the enemy commander-in–chief.

Melissa recovered quickly and sat on her bed with the mug of water handed to her by Isabella. She sipped quietly as she watched Isabella's hands move like lightning to produce a short note that was then folded into the tiniest envelope she had ever seen, and sealed with wax. Melissa had never seen a wax-sealed message before. She shook her head, unable to comprehend just who her friend really was.

Isabella glanced up at her. She knew she would have some explaining to do. She smiled as she held up the tiny envelope. 'Pigeon post,' she said as she ducked out of the tent. 'I'll be back in a minute.'

When she returned, she knelt down next to Melissa and opened her arms. 'Come here,' she said softly. 'Let me tell you a story.'

With that she gave the outline of her story but left out a number of specifics, and all reference to Yannis. Some things were private. She was not going to interfere with fate, wherever it might lead.

Dmitri received Isabella's message the following day and put in motion some of the actions he and Isabella had agreed to before she had left the previous year. He had both a spring in his step and a worried look on his face as he hurried to meet with the king.

CHAPTER 61

Theo Karamus received the message from his son a few hours later. He was excited when he sent messengers to his *Inner Sanctum* business associates asking to meet that afternoon. As soon as they arrived and were seated, he got down to business.

'The confrontation will take place in the next few days,' he informed them. 'You already know what Vlado will do. He will confirm his actions and we will have that information before anyone else. I and my squad will then immediately execute the king and his family and secure the City Palace. You each have instructions for your designated tasks. Every member of parliament is to be liquidated, including Trellinis. That idiot has become a patriot and will pay the price. Dmitri and his senior officers are to meet the same fate, as will the others on your lists. The coup is to be completed within four hours of my receiving the message from Vlado. Any questions?'

There were none. His visitors were as excited as Theo.

It was two in the morning and Marcus was about to mount his horse when Isabella and Chen suddenly appeared out of the darkness, both fully dressed and ready to go. Terrified, Melissa had embraced Isabella before she left the tent, begging her not to go.

Marcus ordered both Isabella and Chen to remain in the camp, but quickly found he was wasting his breath. Isabella simply ignored him and leapt on to *Barca*. She flicked her head for Chen to follow and allowed *Barca* to trot quietly out of the camp. She knew exactly where she needed to be to overlook the events that would unfold as soon as the sun rose. Marcus shook his head, sighed heavily and fell in behind Chen. An hour later they were in place and silently shared a cold breakfast that Isabella had packed the night before. As they ate they could hear faint metallic sounds in the distance – the soldiers were getting into their armor.

At four precisely, they were given the signal to move into place. First came the cavalry, next the archers in full armor and accompanied by the shield-bearers. They were followed by several divisions of crossbowmen. All headed for predetermined locations on the hills that led to the grasslands. Spearmen were in regimental rows eight deep, followed by heavily armored swordsmen; then came more cavalry and, lastly, the reserves.

By six they were in place. One thousand paces separated their front line from the edge of the Northern Region camp. General Karamus sat quietly on his horse in his most flamboyant attire, flanked by senior officers and a messenger, and waited for the sun to rise.

Alexander duPonti, the Royal Scribe, and several of his colleagues, together with dozens of artists, lined the ridges of the surrounding hills high above the battleground. Their task was to record and sketch events as they unfolded.

The sun cast its first rays of light, and long shadows crept like ghosts across the dry ground. A few soldiers were already up and dressed, ready for an early breakfast and the heat of the midsummer day. One of them stretched, glanced at the rising sun with pleasure and stared towards the hills and mountains that he knew would look as magnificent as they had the day before.

It was early, so he was still tired, and surely the hallucination would vanish after he'd looked away and taken a few moments to clear his mind. He sighed heavily and turned back towards the hills. It was not an illusion – it was a nightmare.

'Oh God!' he whispered. 'Oh my God! I must be mad.' The early light had at first revealed just a small portion of the hills, but, second by second, it revealed more. It was not a dream. He opened his mouth to scream a warning, but no sound escaped. Panic-stricken, he ran towards the tent of the man he feared more than any other: *Carlos Bucher.*

As she watched from the top of the hill, Isabella saw the running man and realized that two years of planning had come down to the next few seconds. She nudged *Barca* gently, and he slowly moved forward. Marcus and Chen followed.

The soldier stumbled into the unsuspecting men guarding the earl's tent, knocking them over in the process, before hurling himself onto the floor. The earl jumped to his feet, enraged at the intrusion, and at his men for not stopping this madman.

Before he could act on his rage, the soldier was on his knees, babbling and stabbing his finger towards the hills.

'What are you going on ...' was as far as he got before the soldier interrupted him.

'Sir, look at the hills! Look at the hills!'

The earl sighed, strode out of the tent and looked towards the hills.

General Karamus had moved forward two hundred paces with his small entourage and, strangely enough, he was enjoying the moment. He knew exactly what was going to happen. From this moment on, all events would be under his control. He had never felt more relaxed as he sat patiently on his horse and waited for the panic that was about erupt throughout the camp in front of him.

The earl walked slowly to the perimeter of the camp to take in the impossible vision. His mind worked rapidly but still he could not quite comprehend what he was seeing.

Karamus watched bemused as the man snapped his fingers for his clothing to be brought to him, while two soldiers raised the royal standard. 'Our intelligence was correct,' Karamus said to no-one in particular. 'It is indeed the earl. Time for a little music.' He nodded to one of his men who raised a yellow flag. Within seconds a slow rhythm from a hundred drums could be heard around the perimeter of his army. Each fourth beat was louder than the others, a signal for the 6,000 swordsmen to smack their swords against their steel breastplates. The sound was deafening, relentless. Karamus grinned. 'That should put a spring in the earl's step, yes?'

The earl felt the vibrations from the clash of metal against metal through his whole body. The hillsides leading to the mountains, as well as large parts of the tinder-dry grasslands, were covered by a massive army: cavalry and uniformed troops, in full combat gear and ready to strike at the drop of their leader's hand. Most of the earl's own army remained spread out over twenty miles of roads leading to the camp. Many of his troops had scrambled from their tents in terror at the intense sound reverberating across the terrain. They had literally been caught with their pants down.

He knew at once that they did not stand a chance; they were about to be annihilated. He felt his heart sink. Defeated before he had even drawn his sword, he simply stood quietly and waited for the inevitable attack.

•

'Do you think he's seen enough, Corporal?' Karamus asked.

'I do believe he has, sir,' the corporal replied smilingly.

'Off you go then.'

The corporal set off towards the man, who had by then dressed to show he was the commander-in-chief. When he was within twenty paces of him, he dismounted, dropped his weapons on the ground and walked forward, still holding the reins of his horse. Six paces from the commander, he saluted and held out an envelope given to him by General Karamus.

'Compliments of General Karamus, Commander-in-Chief of our Armed Forces, sir. He has asked me to request that you read the enclosed letter in the strictest privacy – that is, no-one other than you is to be privy to its content, sir. I will retire two hundred paces and await your answer. It is requested that you answer within one hour. Thank you, sir.' The corporal saluted the earl and returned to a point half-way between the camp and General Karamus. On the way he retrieved his weapons.

The earl walked rapidly to his tent. By that time, his most senior officers had gathered around him, and the entire camp was on full alert.

'Shall I prepare the men for combat, sir?'

The earl glared at the man with contempt. 'Don't be stupid, General. Look at them! They are ready for us! The moment they see a single man pull a sword, they will be over us like a swarm of ants. We'll all be dead in twenty minutes, you fool. They've given me a letter, which means they are not going to attack just yet. It means there will be terms to consider and, best of all, it means we won't all be dead in twenty minutes. Now order me some breakfast, and leave me in peace. I must have an answer back to them within the hour.'

He waited for breakfast to be delivered before he broke the seal and pulled out the letter, gagging immediately when he read the first line: *Declaration of War*. He felt no better as he continued to read. The declaration was signed by King Ramesses of the target nation in the Southern Region, countersigned and dated that morning by a General Vlado Karamus, Commander-in-Chief of their armed forces. *So, that wily old fox, King Ramesses, had got wind of our plans.* The demand was that they stand down immediately and surrender or suffer the consequences. By the time he had reached the bottom of the page, he was shaking. He had been caught completely unprepared. The southern nation had taken the initiative, and the war was already as good as over. There was absolutely nothing he could do.

The earl held the declaration in one hand and the envelope in the other. It suddenly struck him that the envelope felt thicker than it should be. He opened it fully and looked inside. Another letter. Two pages. *Interesting.* Within seconds he realized the reason for complete privacy. A relieved grin spread across his face as he slumped into his chair. He was astounded at the content of the letter: the details, the sharing of the spoils, the names of those to control the nation's commerce. *So, King Ramesses is not the only wily old fox in the South.*

He paced the tent while he thought about this sudden, unexpected turn of events. Could he turn disaster into triumph, certain death into certain victory? Von Franckel's early promise to Aloise of few, if any, casualties could be kept after all. A reprieve had been handed to him; it was a gift not to be ignored. He would agree, and the demands would be honored. By law, the terms of surrender between commanders-in-chief on the battlefield had to be honored.

The earl opened his box of writing material and quickly wrote his response, exactly following the instructions stipulated in the second letter. He then added details of a proposed strategy and a timetable to comply with Karamus' demands. Several minutes later he was at the perimeter of the camp holding up the sealed envelope for the messenger to see. This time the soldier did not bother to remove his weapons as he approached to take possession of the letter.

General Karamus rode a hundred paces away from his officers before he opened the response. *Excellent! Exactly what I demanded.* Within days, his father would implement their plan and he, Vlado, would be the leader of his nation.

He rode back to his men and, on the way, allowed a sad expression to settle on his face. He saluted his officers. 'I'm sorry to say that their commander has not accepted the terms and conditions put forward by the king. The Declaration of War is, therefore, enforceable, and we are now in a state of war.'

One of his generals looked toward the enemy camp. There were no visible signs of the soldiers preparing to arm themselves. 'I'll give the order to attack at once, General.'

'No, you won't, General. You will give the order to stand down the men.'

'Did I hear you correctly? Did you say *stand down the men*, sir?'

'You heard correctly. Stand down the men. Tell them to return to their camps for a good meal and a good night's sleep. We will attack at first light tomorrow.'

'Attack in the morning? We have them dead to right. We should attack immediately, sir.'

'You have your orders, General.' Karamus dug his heels into his horse and headed up into the hills, leaving his officers in a state of bewilderment. They had no choice but to ride to their respective divisions to issue new orders.

Flanked by Marcus and Chen, Isabella had moved down the hill and past the reserves. She was well within sight of the action below and frowned as she saw the soldiers turn their backs to the enemy.

'What's going on, Grandfather? I don't understand what I'm seeing.'

Lost for words, Marcus simply shook his head. Major General Manassis and Lieutenant Colonel Christos headed towards them at a gallop. Yannis arrived first and came to a halt in a cloud of dust next to Isabella.

'Isabella, what are you doing here? You shouldn't be here! It's far too dangerous.'

Isabella untied the strap holding her jacket together and opened it to reveal her sword on one side and the shorter dagger-sword on the other. 'I told you from the very start that I would be on the battlefield with you and the men. Besides, it's hardly dangerous with your men running away like a bunch of frightened rabbits before the fox. So what's going on?'

Yannis shook his head and gave up his futile attempt to caution Isabella. He knew that no-one would ever tell Isabella what to do. 'Karamus' orders. Everyone's been ordered back to camp. I guess we'll find out when we get there.'

Isabella glared at Yannis, then at Nicho and Marcus. They all shrugged and shook their heads. She stared furiously at the disappearing back of General Karamus, now well ahead of his soldiers drifting slowly back to their camps.

The officers were waiting in the conference tent two hours later when General Karamus entered to address them. He came straight to the point.

'Assemble your men at six in the morning, not four. Every man is to be in battle position at eight precisely. I will then assess conditions and issue orders, depending on what I believe the enemy might have in mind. They may still decide to stand down and surrender. Thank you all.' The general turned and made to leave the tent when one of his junior generals spoke.

'General! Excuse me, sir.'

Karamus stopped and turned from the exit. 'Yes?'

'Why didn't we attack this morning, sir?'

Karamus stared at his questioner with unconcealed contempt. 'For God's sake, man, their soldiers were in their tents, half asleep. It would have been a massacre. That would hardly be the gentlemanly thing to do, now would it, General? We're not barbarians! Have you no mind for politics? Think how that would go down in our history. I gave the enemy the choice to stand down permanently, or be subjected to an attack in twenty-four hours.'

'Well, we could have given them an hour or two instead of twenty-four, surely. Our chances of success were excellent, sir.'

'Our chances will still be excellent. The difference is that tomorrow we will fight with *honor*.' Karamus glared at his general. 'Those are your new orders. Follow them, or resign and leave the army in disgrace! That goes for anyone else who lacks the courage to fight with honor.' He turned to the exit.

'General …' Marcus spoke up. Every officer turned towards him, including Karamus, who stopped in his tracks.

'Yes, General?' Karamus gave his most friendly smile, yet his eyes glittered, cold as diamonds.

'Tomorrow is Sunday, sir. I think you might find that too many soldiers on both sides will refuse to fight on a Sunday for religious reasons.'

General Karamus looked surprised, but Isabella sensed a degree of pretense. 'Oh, yes. You are quite right, of course. That simply hadn't occurred to me in all the excitement. Thank you, Marcus.' He turned back to his men. 'New orders, gentlemen. All times will remain the same, except that the day of attack will be Monday, not tomorrow. I'll arrange for a message to be sent to that effect to the earl.' Karamus turned and left without another word.

The junior general who had voiced his opinion shook his head as he left the tent. 'I don't believe this,' he muttered. The other officers drifted from the tent without a word.

Isabella stopped Marcus outside by gently taking his arm. 'As commander-in-chief, Karamus should surely have known that many soldiers will not fight on a Sunday.' She already knew the answer.

'Yes, he certainly should have. It's hard to believe he would have forgotten the religious aspects of battle strategies.' Marcus shook his head in disgust and amazement.

Isabella kept her thoughts to herself. *He didn't forget about Sunday,*

Grandfather. That's the very reason he chose a Saturday to confront the enemy, and then stand down: he had always intended to give the enemy the additional day. He had simply waited for someone to bring up the subject of Sunday before he had to do it himself.

Xu Yan was in a rush of nervous energy as she placed platters of food on the table, buffet-style. The group was all there, including Nicholas and Yannis.

Isabella was too angry to eat. 'This changes everything. *Everything!* We had them within our grasp and Karamus has let them off the hook. Catching the enemy napping is the classic way to win not only battles, but wars!' She pulled at her hair in frustration. 'On Monday they'll have their cannons lined up and we'll be slaughtered!'

Yannis stared at Isabella. 'You were right, Isabella. A surprise attack was your plan from the very start, and it would have succeeded beyond expectations. We had them at our mercy. Your strategy would have won us not just the battle today, but possibly the war. It took our esteemed leader just minutes to put at risk all your good work and planning.'

Melissa stared wide-eyed, unable to believe what Yannis had just said about Isabella.

'Thank you for saying that, Yannis.' She looked at her family and friends seated around the table. 'There are a couple of things that worry me terribly. The first is that only we few here, plus Karamus and his senior officers, know of the cannons. Most of the foot-soldiers certainly don't. When the sun rises on Monday, they'll be staring down the barrels of a thousand cannons. If they don't mutiny and run – and I wouldn't blame them if they did – they'll be obliterated within minutes, blown to pieces, every one of them. I'm afraid for all of us now.'

Her shoulders slumped before she continued. 'There's not much time, but we could send a message to King Ramesses, asking that he consider, with the senators, relieving Karamus of his position. Either way, I can see no way out of this mess other than to submit on Monday, but I promise I will not rest until I find out why Karamus sold us out!' *I knew it*, she thought, *you've been up to something from the very beginning, Karamus. You have just turned certain victory into certain defeat, and I'm going to find out why.*

'What's the second thing that's worrying you,' asked Marcus.

'I need to do a little bit of work on that.'

Later that evening she wrote a short encrypted note to Dmitri, informing him of the day's events and her suspicions. She also included special requests to be urgently conveyed to the king for consideration.

CHAPTER 62

Sunday was quiet. Soldiers sat around listlessly while they contemplated their fate on the morrow. The camp followers worried about the soldiers, many of whom had become their friends over the months. They also wondered whether they would have anyone to cook for the following evening.

During the afternoon, Isabella took Zhang Chen for a long stroll through several camps. They called in to Major General Manassis' compound, where they found him busy discussing battle tactics with his men. When he saw Isabella and Chen, he broke off for a short chat. Their conversation finished with a long embrace between Isabella and her uncle. Nicho promised to be careful and, yes, he would look after himself. He returned to his men while Isabella and Chen continued their walk.

Hundreds of soldiers throughout the camps were working with the camp followers to prepare wagons for the next day. Few spoke and the soldiers' faces were grim. During their walk, Isabella peered into one of the wagons and knew instantly the reason for the soldiers' grim expressions. The wagons were being prepared for themselves.

Securely tied in the bottom of each wagon were rolls of rough-cut bandages, clean cloth for wrappings, sharpened knives and axes for cutting limbs, and jugs of raw spirit to sterilize wounds and stumps. Isabella shuddered as she recognized the heat equipment and compounds used to cauterize wounds.

Isabella grasped Chen's arm. 'Oh, Chen – Father – it tears me apart to see this. These poor men are preparing for their own death or terrible injury. It's all so unnecessary. This should never have been allowed to happen. To my dying day, I swear that Karamus will pay for what he's done.'

Chen put his arm around her shoulder. 'He will pay for sins, precious daughter. When this is over, the Zen Master will punish him for lack of respect for his men. He will not return to his nation alive.'

Isabella stopped and turned to face him. '*No*, Father! That's not punishment; that will only allow him to escape his sins. I don't know what he's up to, but I have no doubt that it's treason. And it must be *publicly* punished and shamed, not hidden behind an obscure death.'

Chen bowed to her. 'You have wisdom beyond your years, beyond mine, precious daughter. You are correct. That is how it shall be.'

Isabella took his arm again and they continued their walk. At the next camp she noticed something different when she happened to glance into one of the wagons. She looked into several others and saw the same. Intrigued, she approached one of the soldiers loading the wagons. He turned towards her and smiled.

The man was enormous, the biggest man she had ever seen. He was bare-chested, his huge muscles gleaming with perspiration. Isabella had to bend her neck back as she looked up at him with a smile.

'I feel sorry for the enemy that will have to face *you* tomorrow, soldier.'

The soldier grinned broadly. He loved to be admired and his size acknowledged. 'I am Johan, Miss. Yes, tomorrow I will find out if my heart will measure up to the rest of me.'

'That was a beautiful and honest thing to say, Johan. Your family would be proud to hear that. I know that I'm proud to have you on our side.'

'Thank you, Miss. I know you. You're Miss Isabella, granddaughter of General Mondeo.' It was not a question.

Isabella was surprised. She was far from home and had never been near this camp. 'How do you know me?'

Johan grinned. 'Everyone knows of you. You and your magnificent horse are seen often, and talked about. The soldiers love to look at you.'

That could be taken two ways, she thought, and decided she had better leave it there.

'Tell me, Johan, those large coils of rope I saw the wagons – why so much?'

Johan shrugged. 'That's just us. This camp is made up of mariners who enlisted in the army. Sailors never go anywhere without rope, lots of rope. We use it for everything: sails, berthing, towing, securing, boarding enemy ships. The list never ends, Miss Isabella. Here, we will use it for repairs, towing the wagons or tying down the dead and wounded tomorrow. We are sure to find many uses for it; rope always comes in handy, I guarantee it.'

Isabella nodded. 'Interesting,' she said softly. She reached out and squeezed his arm. 'I will seek you out tomorrow night, Johan, to make sure you and your men made it safely back.'

Johan simply nodded and looked away as his eyes watered. He felt sure she would be viewing his corpse.

That evening, Dmitri's message was quietly circulated among the small group. No-one spoke. Isabella was disappointed, but not surprised. The government's position was that if General Karamus were dismissed, his father and the other industrialist would at once withdraw their support. Without an efficient infrastructure to support their campaign, their only option would therefore be to surrender immediately.

Monday's confrontation therefore had to proceed in the hope that the day would not result in defeat, or surrender. There was a chance, albeit a small one, that surrender could somehow be avoided. However, Marcus had been provided additional powers, to be used only in extreme circumstances. If, in his opinion, it appeared that the Southern army was about to be annihilated by the earl's cannons, Marcus was given the authority to arrest General Karamus, and to then offer surrender.

Melissa clung to Yannis' arm when he returned from his men later that night for a short visit and to say goodbye. He did not look confident that he would survive the battle. He embraced Melissa, gave her a kiss on each cheek and wished her well. She covered her face with both hands and ran sobbing to her tent. Yannis next hugged Xu Yan briefly and shook hands with Chen. He nodded to Marcus. 'I'll see you in the morning, sir,' he said as they shook hands. Marcus nodded goodnight to Isabella and retired to his tent to leave the two alone. He thought Isabella might wish to say a few last words, but doubted she would reveal much. He knew she was far too careful.

Isabella had no idea what to say, so she turned and walked with Yannis to the ridge where his horse was tethered. She looked up at him in the fading light. 'You're a brave soldier, Yannis, and I know you'll do your duty to the bitter end. I'll be watching from the hill, and if I see you fall, I promise you that *Barca* will have me by your side in seconds, no matter where you are. I started this mess, and I intend to fight and die by your side, just as I told you long ago.'

'There's no need for you to risk your life out there tomorrow, Isabella.'

'It's not about risk; it's about destiny.'

'Are you going to tell me now why you kicked me years ago?'

'No, but it was a message, and here's the next one I promised you. Sorry,' she murmured as she kicked his leg, though not too hard.

'Ouch! Can you at least tell me what that message is?'

'Yes, I can tell you about that one. That one's for good luck tomorrow.'

'Thank you. I'm going to need every bit of it.' Yannis gently touched her shoulder and disappeared into the night without another word. Isabella stared into the darkness long after he had vanished from sight.

CHAPTER 63

The Southern army was in place at the nominated time, and the scribes and artists back in position. Isabella was half-way down one of the hills, flanked closely by Marcus and Chen. The two men had given up all attempts to persuade her to stay behind the line of reserves.

It promised to be a hot day and Isabella has chosen to wear the brief halter-top with the short skirt, but in a concession to modesty, she had slipped a knee-length light sleeveless leather jacket over the top. Her weapons were carefully secured around her waist beneath the jacket. She had bunched her hair tightly inside the leather cap.

Isabella insisted on being close enough to study the order of battle for both sides and keep a visual on Yannis, who was in command of the light cavalry and stationed at the very front. Karamus and his officers were further back, in the wide gap between the archers and the crossbowmen. The general had split his most senior officers into two groups: one on the slope leading down onto the grasslands, the other on the grasslands itself, just behind the cavalry. The two groups contained every officer of the rank of major and above, with the exception of Lieutenant Colonel Christos. It was law that the commander of the cavalry strike force at the front line be at his post and ready to respond instantly to a trumpet call to attack.

Karamus looked resplendent in his most colorful uniform, complemented by a brilliant deep blue and red cape tied around his shoulders. It was of paramount importance that he appear as grand a sight as his opposing commander-in-chief, the Earl of Missignon. His horse had been positioned close to his standard-bearer, who would hold his personally designed crest and colors. He was proud of the fact that it was about to be viewed by more than 60,000 soldiers ready for battle.

Major General Nicholas Manassis, as one of the most senior officers, was also in the group positioned on the hill, but he remained at the fringe at the back of the group to stay as far away as possible from the general. Karamus disgusted him. Good soldiers, and his closest friends, were about to die because of him.

At the first sign of light, the drums sounded their beat and the swordsmen's thunderous clash of metals rang across the plain. Within minutes, the light revealed two armies: 20,000 on one side facing 40,000 on the other.

Isabella caught her breath when she saw what the enemy had achieved in two days, thanks to General Karamus. The main camp had been moved several miles away. Cavalry, archers, crossbowmen, spearmen and regiments of swordsmen were lined up and stretched back as far as the eye could see. As the sun rapidly crept across the grasslands, the earl could be seen on his horse at the very front of his army, and he appeared as relaxed as General Karamus had been two days earlier. She spurred her horse down the slope at a slow trot. Marcus and Chen immediately followed in near panic.

'Isabella. *Isabella!* Where are you going? Stop! What are you doing?' Marcus was frantic.

Isabella did not stop until she reached the edge of the gap where the group of officers were stationed between the archers and crossbowmen. *Barca* pranced back and forth while Isabella stared intently at the enemy lines. Chen pulled up alongside.

'What are you doing?' Marcus hissed. 'We're not allowed down here, and that includes me!'

Isabella ignored his questions. 'Look at them, Grandfather! Look at them. What do you see?'

Marcus's horse was as agitated as *Barca*. The horses could sense something in the air.

Marcus looked over the massive army facing them. 'I see a million too many troops, that's what I see. Other than that, nothing. What is it you see that I don't?'

'That's just it. *Nothing.* Something is very, very wrong. I don't know how it's been done, but this is a set-up.'

'What are you talking about?'

'Look at them. That is not how a battle order is set up, even if you outnumber your enemy two-to-one. You must take every advantage. Where are the cannons? *There are no cannons!*'

Marcus shook his head in astonishment. Indeed there were none. In the heat of the moment and with the breathtaking sight of the two armies, he had not yet taken it all in.

'And where is their armor? Except for the knights behind the earl, no one is wearing armor. That's nothing short of suicide. They saw our armor on Saturday.'

'Perhaps they think their number is so superior they don't need to waste their time putting on armor.'

'Look at their longbow archers! They have been placed out of range of our troops, where they can do us no damage. We are within range of their crossbowmen, yes, but a salvo from them will result in only light casualties for us because we're fully shielded, while they are not. A few quick salvos from our crossbowmen would leave their cavalry and archers in shambles. They've placed themselves at our mercy. If I had my way I'd attack immediately. We can win this battle, Grandfather, even though we're heavily outnumbered!'

Marcus saw the logic in her analysis, and thought of additional ways to take advantage of the earl's mistake.

'You're right. We can!'

'We *can*, but I'm afraid we *won't*, Grandfather,' she said in a softer tone.

'Why? What do you mean?'

'Remember, the earl is a battle-seasoned general. He's not so silly as to set up his army in such a way that even a fifteen-year-old can recognize his mistakes. No, he has not bothered to be careful because he knows he doesn't need to be. Just look at him sitting there; we can kill them by the thousands, and he's laughing at us because he knows it's not going to happen. This is all a sham. If I'm wrong you can put me to the sword. I don't know what it is, but something is going to happen, and it won't be pretty. Just wait, and watch.'

Marcus looked at Isabella's intense face as she studied the scene below, and knew that her logic was accurate as always. A natural tactician, she had the ability to analyze a situation in seconds. He knew he was seeing the birth of a future general, a general far superior to himself. Reaching out to her, he held her hand while they sat on their horses and waited for the inevitable nightmare to begin.

The scratching of charcoal pencils was drowned out by the drums as the artist sketched every detail of the scene below. Alexander duPonti and his fellow scribes were busy writing. Each had been given designated tasks so they would not all write the same thing. Their writings would later be collated into a single manuscript, in chronological order.

Time seemed to stand still as the two armies stared at each other. The drum beat had ceased and the plains were bathed in an unnerving silence. The only movement was an occasional swirl of dust kicked up by a light breeze from the east.

Two mounted regiments of Earl Carlos Bucher's most trusted knights stood quietly behind him, seventy-five on each side. He turned to their commanding officer.

'What's happening, Captain? How are they progressing back there?'

'It will be a while yet, sir. They seem to have struck a problem with securing the bolts.'

'Very well.' The earl chuckled as he observed the army facing him. 'Let them sweat in their armor over there. They could do well to lose a bit of weight. Soldiers are getting far too lazy these days.'

Hours passed slowly while the men on both sides stared impassively at each other. The soldiers were not overly anxious to see the situation change. As long as they continued to stare at each other, they remained alive.

Isabella watched as cavalry horses from both armies were led in batches to water troughs. The swordsmen were forced to remove their helmets because the sun was heating the metal enough to cause serious damage. Soldiers fainted at regular intervals, and many had to remove their armor. The responsibility for her past actions weighed heavily on Isabella's mind.

Marcus spoke softly in the stillness. 'I've known armies to stare at each other for days before someone made a move. Each side waits for the other to move first, in the hope that it will be a wrong one and open up opportunities for defending or mounting a counter-attack. Speaking of which, I'm going to have to talk to Yannis about something I see that I think might create a problem.'

'Well, Karamus should make the first move, Grandfather. He should attack. The longer we sit here, the more chance there is that the earl will bring the cannons to the front. I still can't quite figure out why the earl has not done so already. If he does, it would definitely be the end of us, so you would have to exercise your power. There is another potential problem.'

'More problems? How can we possibly have more?'

'It's almost midday. I've noticed that every day at this time the wind starts up, slowly at first, but and by mid-afternoon it kicks up dust like you would not believe. Because I have no idea of what's about to happen,

I don't know how that will affect us. All I know is that in a few hours, visibility could be difficult.'

Marcus could think of nothing to say to that.

The captain returned and whispered to the earl, who listened carefully and nodded with rising excitement. Without looking directly at his captain, he murmured just loud enough to be heard, 'Are you ready, then, Captain?'

'Yes, sir. We're ready.'

'Give your first signal now.'

The captain drew his sword half-way out of its scabbard and immediately pushed it back into place. A knight in the regiment raised a small flag. The signal was passed back to where a soldier raised another flag. Thus the signal to make ready traveled two miles in less than ten seconds.

Karamus addressed his group of officers. 'Men, I am about to give you orders to – *Julius*, drop the standard over on an angle to the left, would you, please? It's blocking my view of the enemy commander.'

Julius was flustered. 'Oh, sorry, sir. I'll move at once.'

'No, I don't want you to move. That will spook the horses. Just drop the standard to the left a bit. Ah, yes, that's better. I can see him clearly now. Thank you.'

'There's the signal that everything is ready over there. Signal your men again, Captain,' the earl said quietly.

The captain repeated the action with his sword, and this time the flags raised were of a different color.

'As I was going to say, men,' Karamus continued, 'I am about to give the order to attack. I have delayed taking any action for quite some time while I've studied the enemy forces and considered what our tactics will be. You will have noticed that the fools have neglected to set up their cannons. They must think their numbers are overwhelming enough not to bother. That gives us an edge.'

One of the junior generals interrupted. 'They have also neglected to wear their armor, General.'

Karamus was astonished. He had been so unconcerned about the enemy's strengths and weaknesses, he had not noticed their lack of armor. 'Yes, that was the first thing I noticed,' he lied, 'and it is, in fact, the main focus of my tactics.' He kept a close eye on the horizon while he spoke. *At last, there it is!* Two tiny trails of dust rose in the air to the northwest.

Yannis was not far away from the three observers and prodded his horse gently through a gap between rows of longbow archers. He was pale and unsmiling when he reached them. 'You should not be here! You're much too close and could be caught in the middle. You must move back at once. It's getting late and the order to attack is bound to be given by either side at any moment. General, please take Isabella away from here, somewhere safe.'

Marcus nodded. 'We will move, but first there is something you might not have noticed at ground level.' He filled Yannis in on Isabella's observations and opinions.

Yannis looked grim. 'I had noticed the lack of cannons, of course. They were the first thing I looked for. But we're so low to the ground down there I must admit I had not noticed their lack of armor. Their archers are pretty well covered by their shields at that level. And their swordsmen further back – well we can't see them at all.'

'Something else, Lieutenant Colonel.'

'Yes, General?' Battle conditions required formalities.

'I noticed a slight crescent shape forming in the enemy lines at the northern end. They could be preparing to move a line of soldiers around our right flank. Keep an eye on it. If you get a chance, get up there and set the crossbows loose on them. Not even their cavalry is wearing armor.'

'Yes, sir.'

'Good man.'

'You must not fail me, Captain. You must not fail your nation in the most important moment in its history.' The earl's voice was low, menacing. 'You know what you must do: ensure only the general survives. The most essential part of your mission is to allow no-one else to survive. You and your men are to take special note of what the general is wearing. He has made himself unmistakable. As soon as your mission has been completed, he will call for surrender.'

'Yes, sir.'

'You will not make any attempt to return from behind enemy lines until you have fully completed your mission. Any attempt to do so will result in the immediate death of you and your men on your return. Your men do understand that, yes?'

'Yes, they do, sir. We will succeed or die, sir.' The captain stared at the enemy facing them. 'Sir, do you think there is any chance that they will launch an attack while we carry out our mission?'

The earl glanced at the horizon to his left. 'No chance. They will have no-one to give the order while you're doing your work, and no-one afterwards. Besides, they can see they are outnumbered more than two to one. No, there is absolutely no chance that they will launch an attack. Better get back to your men. Good luck, Captain.'

'Here is how we are going to do it,' Karamus said slowly. He had to time his words and actions precisely. 'First I will give you your orders to attack, and then I'll repeat them to the other group while you instruct your men ...' Manassis was at the back of the group listening carefully to the general. He was facing the same direction as Karamus and saw the approaching cloud of dust. As he scanned the horizon in other directions, he turned his head to look to the side and was shocked by what he saw. *Isabella,* his beloved niece and only living relative, was two hundred paces away in the center of the battlefield, just as the general was about to give the order to attack. She had to leave immediately! Without a moment's hesitation, he gradually pulled the reins tight until his mount backed away. He pointed it towards Isabella at a slow trot. No-one noticed him leave.

Yannis also glanced at the horizon and frowned. A twin cloud of dust was expanding and getting closer. He turned back to the three. 'Something's happening, and fast. I must get back to my men. Please go now.' Marcus and Chen turned to leave. Yannis leaned down from his saddle and rubbed his lower leg while he looked at Isabella. She got his message and smiled.

Yannis smiled, too. 'My leg tells me I will survive the day. But just in case I'm wrong – stay safe, Isabella, and have a good life.'

'I won't be far away.' She pointed to a small hill nearby. 'I'll be watching from there and I'll come to you if I need to.' He gave a small wave and headed towards the center of the gap between archers. On the way he had to pass Nicholas.

They pulled up alongside each other, their horses facing opposite directions. 'What's happening, Nicho? I can see something is going on, but I can't work out what it is.'

'Karamus is about to give his order to attack, so I have to get back to my group as quick as I can. But I caught sight of Isabella right in the midst of it all and came to tell her to get away at once. There are probably only minutes left now.'

'Don't worry, Nicho. I've already spoken to her. She's promised to move to the hillside with Marcus and Chen.' He turned automatically towards the hill to confirm his statement. To his dismay, Isabella was sitting quietly on her stallion exactly where he had left her. She saw them look her way and gave them a small wave.

'Oh, God,' Yannis groaned as the two men were forced to return the wave. 'She's not going to move at all, is she?'

'Yannis, promise me something. If something should happen to me and not to you, promise me that you will look out for her until she is an adult. She might seem all grown up, but the reality is that she is still little more than a kid. I can promise you she will always do anything you say.'

'I promise, Nicho. I'll protect her with my life until she's an adult.' They shared a soldier's handshake and were to move when Yannis held up his hand.

'Hold on a minute. That cloud of dust is changing shape rapidly.'

'At my signal the crossbowmen are to ...' Karamus had a look of puzzlement on his face as he stared at the cloud of dust that had split into two distinct trails, with dark centers forming near ground level of each. He pointed and shouted dramatically. 'There won't be time to give my orders separately. The enemy is up to something so I'll give my orders to both groups at the same time. Quickly now! Follow me!' He turned his mount towards the officers on the grasslands.

One of his generals cried out in panic, 'But sir, that's too dangerous. We will all be together in the one spot. That is against all regulations, sir.'

Karamus snarled at him. 'Well, those regulations were not written in the heat of battle, were they? Now follow me, you fool, or you'll have no orders to give your men!'

Karamus was a happy man. *Everything is going precisely to plan*, he thought as he rode away, leaving his group no option but to follow. With such overwhelming odds and soon no officers to direct his men in attack or defense, he would be regarded as a national hero for surrendering and thus sparing thousands of the nation's brave soldiers from certain death.

The earl turned in his saddle to face his knights, now lined up two by two. 'Get ready to move as practiced,' he screamed. The captain raised his arm in acknowledgement.

•

Yannis stared across the void between the two armies. 'Nicho, the earl's knights have altered their line-up. I must get back to my post at once.' He was about to spur his mount into action when another movement caught his attention. He pointed past Nicholas' shoulder. 'Nicho, what's going on *over there?*'

Nicholas turned his horse and was dumbstruck by what he saw. General Karamus and his group had almost reached the second group of officers, the standard-bearer leading the way.

'That's impossible. He can't do that! We are about to be attacked. He must spread his officers, not concentrate them. We will be vulnerable. I have to warn them! Good luck, Yannis, my friend.'

The two men punched each other's shoulder, embraced quickly and left in opposite directions. Manassis dug his heels into his mount to catch up with his fellow officers. He was too late. Events moved too rapidly.

Marcus and Chen had turned in their saddles to see that Isabella was not behind them. They brought their horses back down the hill at a gallop to pull up alongside her a few seconds later. Marcus roared, 'Isabella, we have to get out of here now!'

Isabella did not bother to answer. She simply pointed towards where Yannis and Manassis were staring in horror at the two groups of officers merging into one. Marcus, a former general, knew only too well the dangerous implications of having all officers in one place. His mind was in turmoil when he heard Isabella gasp, 'Oh, Grandfather, I said it would not be pretty but I never dreamt it would be anywhere near as ugly as this!'

The knights trotted in formation to meet up with the sound getting nearer by the second. The earl looked towards his adversary's standard-bearer and saw that the two groups would merge into one in about ten seconds. *Perfect timing, General.* The earl knew that victory would be his without a single casualty other than a few of his knights. Mere mercenaries, expendable, he could not care less about them. He was about to become the nation's greatest military leader, and he roared elatedly in anticipation of the carnage he would soon witness.

The earl's body vibrated as hundreds of hooves, carrying massive weights, thundered past on either side of him. With his hands clenched to the point of pain, and neck and shoulders starting to spasm uncontrollably, his laughter became a long bloodthirsty howl of bloodlust as the psychopath – Bucher, *the Butcher of Missignon* – seized control of his mind.

CHAPTER 64

Isabella held one hand to her mouth and gripped *Barca's* mane with the other as she watched the worst of all horrors unfold before her eyes. Marcus was shocked into complete silence. Zhang Chen's handsome features were as inscrutable as only an oriental face can be.

'Oh Yannis, don't get in front of that, I beg you,' Isabella whispered. The three could do little more than watch.

Two formations, each of twenty horses, with their powerfully-built riders, thundered through two gaps that suddenly opened in their own front line as rehearsed. One gap was a hundred paces to the north of the spot where the two groups of Karamus' officers had just merged. The other gap was a hundred paces to the south. Each group consisted of two rows of ten horses. Between the horses were heavy ropes carefully crafted into a sling and tied to the pommels of the mounts. Each sling contained a huge log with spikes attached in such a way that the log would not slide backward in the sling when it struck its target.

The logs projected ten feet in front of the leading horses. Narrow slots had been cut into the tips, and razor-sharp, six-foot-wide metal blades had been bolted into each side. The highly polished blades were angled slightly backward and curved to slice like the reverse side of a scythe. The undersides of the deadly battering rams were three feet from the ground. Anyone who did not get out of their way, or under them, was doomed.

As they thundered across the void at full gallop, seventy-five knights fell into formation directly behind each ram. It took just seconds to cross the gap and strike at the Southern army's front line. Yannis' cavalry had no choice. Their mounts acted on instinct and fled to the side to avoid the charge hurtling towards them, irrespective of what their riders might have intended to do. There was little doubt, however, that the riders would have done exactly the same. The longbow archers were next. They had no choice, and little time. They ran; they jumped; they fell or threw themselves prone to the ground to avoid the blades. Those who did not move quickly enough felt little as they were torn apart, their armor of no use against the speed and power of the deadly blades.

Once through the lines of archers, the two groups turned to the right and left respectively along the gap between the archers and crossbowmen. The latter were unable to fire at the attackers because their longbow comrades were in their direct line of fire. The earl had cleverly thought of that. The two groups then turned back towards the archers to cut a new path for their escape. This time the soldiers knew what to expect and had already hurled themselves to the ground. The two groups made their escape without further casualties.

At full gallop, the knights entered the gaps created by the battering rams. Once through, the two groups turned towards each other and headed directly to their target, cutting off any avenue of escape. Swords drawn, they had the group of officers encircled within seconds. One hundred knights surrounded and faced their targets while fifty faced outwards to fight off any interference, and to protect the backs of their fellow knights. They had to hold their positions just long enough to complete their mission. The slashing commenced immediately.

Isabella's hold on Marcus was like a death grip. 'They're all going to die, Grandfather. Except one, Karamus. Just you wait and see.' She gasped and pointed. 'Oh God, no! Look! Uncle Nicho is pushing his way into the circle of slaughter.'

Bucher had calmed down and dispassionately watched the event occurring at the center of the enemy ranks. He had correctly assessed that the longbow and crossbow archers would take no action against the knights for fear of striking their own officers, or soldiers. The officers' only defenders were the spearmen and swordsmen, and Bucher was confident that fifty of his best knights could fight them off long enough for the other one hundred to complete their mission. He did not care whether his knights made it back or not. It was a small price to pay for a good day's work. His ram-brigades had got back without casualties, as expected, and it was time to consider what he might have for lunch.

Nicholas pushed his way through his own men to reach the circle of knights facing outwards. Several knights were already lying mortally wounded on the ground. His own men had fared worse. The knights held the advantage because they slashed downwards. The spearmen had to contend with the knights' armor and shields. To make matters worse, they were shoved out of the way by their own swordsmen, who swarmed in like a pack of wolves, but their swords were even less effective than the spears. They had difficulty reaching up to stab at the knights, having first to get past the horses' heads and shoulders. The knights cleverly kept their mounts moving back and forth, allowing the knights to inflict terrible wounds on the swordsmen by slashing from above with full power.

Nicholas pulled out a long cord and flicked it at the foreleg of one of the nearest horses. Like a whip, the cord wrapped itself around the leg, and Nicholas pulled with all his strength. He was a powerful man and the horse stumbled forward and onto its knees, throwing the rider over its shoulder and directly on to Nicholas' sword.

'Good one, Nicho,' roared one of his soldiers. 'Let's do that again and I'll take him as he comes down.' It worked perfectly. Another one down. Permanently. But it was too slow. He had to get to his officers, so he tossed the cord to the soldier.

'Here, take it. It works. You do it with someone else. Find others to do the same. I'm going in there.'

'No! You're crazy, Nicho. You'll die in there. They have no chance. These knights are not yielding an inch. They are clearly on a suicide mission. There is no way we can get to our officers in time to save them. Stay out here, Nicho.'

Nicholas shook his head. 'I'm the only senior officer not in there. My place is with them. I know how to get in there.' He took a firm grip on his sword, dropped to the ground and started to scramble between the legs of the horses.

'He's disappeared.' Isabella was frantic.

'Try to calm down. Uncle Nicho is a soldier and he is doing his duty. There was every chance this was going to happen to him, anyway. Everybody down there is at mortal risk.'

'Yes, I know, I know. But not this way. Not for a total sham!'

'I know, darling, but you're not supposed to be here to see any of this. I'm not supposed to be this close myself. Come on, let's go. We should go back up to the top of the hill, where we were supposed to be from the start.'

Isabella snorted and ignored him.

•

Yannis left his subordinate officer in charge of his cavalry unit and rushed to join the swordsmen. He saw what they were doing with the cords and combined with another soldier to do the same. The knights were tiring and Yannis, being tall and powerful, had little trouble sending six knights to their doom within minutes. Suddenly he felt a sword enter his shoulder before a comrade took care of the assailant. It was slow going after he resumed his attack.

'You're right, Isabella.' Marcus' voice was quiet and without emotion, resigned to the coming defeat. 'Our officers have no chance. The knights have been very, very clever. Most of our men are expert fighters, but those near the center can do nothing, being blocked by their own men. They can only sit on their mounts and wait their turn to be slaughtered.'

Isabella groaned in frustration. Marcus heard another groan and thought little of it until the groan became louder. He looked at Isabella in alarm. She was also alarmed and staring wide-eyed at Zhang Chen. His groans turned into a raging roar. Throwing his head back, he roared to his gods and to those he had served as Zen Master.

Zhang Chen then ripped off his light leather jacket, followed by his shirt, to expose his massive shoulders. His muscles stood out like cords. A long curved sword hung on each side of his narrow waist. He quickly untied his pony-tail, allowing his glossy black hair to cascade over his shoulders. Slipping his fingers into a pocket, they came out covered in a black, waxy substance. Wild-eyed, he expertly streaked his face and pectorals in a well-practiced, but rarely used oriental pattern, a pattern that transformed him into the beast known only to his peers as *the Dark Warrior*. The whites of his eyes were bloodshot with rage and burned bright red as he turned to glare at Isabella and Marcus. With a flick of his hand, his sheathed dagger – the sacred Zen Master's dagger – spun in the air towards Isabella.

'Keep safe, please. Karamus not get away with this. Fear not for me, precious daughter. No-one can defeat *the Dark Warrior*, the Zen Master!'

Before either Isabella or Marcus could respond, Zhang Chen drew both swords, threw his head back and roared in fury again. He spurred his horse and howled his way into the melee like the fearsome warrior he was trained to be.

Isabella could do little more than sit on *Barca* and weep silently. She knew only too well what Zhang Chen was capable of, but had no idea of *the Dark Warrior's* powers.

Nicholas felt a tooth fly out of his mouth when a hoof came up unexpectedly; he then heard a rib crack from another kick. He continued to push and shove his way through the horses' legs and fallen bodies. Several times he used his sword to guarantee fallen knights would do no further damage. The next body that fell near him was one of his own men. The officer's glazed eyes moved in and out of focus as he looked at Nicholas with slow recognition.

'Nicho, get out,' he wheezed. 'We're all done for. It's a *trap*.' His last words were slurred as blood bubbled slowly out of his mouth. 'Karamus … Go tell …' His words faded as his body relaxed and his eyes lost focus.

Nicholas continued to crawl through the forest of legs. The screams from the dying and shouts from the swordsmen trying to fight their way into the circle, were deafening.

More bodies fell from their mounts. A few were knights, but most were his comrades. Dozens fell within minutes. Those who did not die immediately were soon trampled to death by the frantic horses.

He heard a voice shouting orders. A voice he knew well. 'Make sure they're all dead!' Karamus was screaming 'Every one of them! When you've finished, make sure all those on the ground are dead. Some might play dead. Stab them all through the heart to make sure!'

Nicholas half rose to get a better view of the center of the melee. Karamus had two enemy knights between himself and his own officers to protect him from attack from that quarter and he watched without emotion as his former fellow officers fought valiantly to their death.

Nicholas was giddy with shock. It was so tightly packed at the center that no-one had noticed him. Everyone was intent on killing their foe at rider level. He spat out another tooth while he planned his next move. He knew what he had to do; he just had to work out how to do it in the tight surrounds.

He was shocked again by the most terrifying sound he had ever heard. Sweat was pouring off his body, but he still felt a cold chill move down his spine. It was the roar of a hungry lion paralyzing its prey with fear. He turned his mind back to focus on his mission, which was to do exactly what the suicide squad was doing: destroy his target at the exclusion of any attempt to protect himself.

•

As his horse came to a halt near the edge of the dwindling circle of death, *the Dark Warrior* leapt on to its shoulders and launched himself on top of the swordsmen with both his swords drawn. Four quick steps on the shoulders and heads of his comrades brought him to one of several riderless horses being pulled away as the defending knights succumbed to their attackers.

The Zen Master had mentally choreographed his attack during the seconds before he launched himself onto one of the knight's mounts. He purposely commenced with the blood-curdling howl of *the Dark Warrior*. Friend and foe alike froze momentarily in shock and terror. That was all he needed. The knights' body armor protected the bulk of their torso and the helmet protected the head, but their arms and legs were free to use their swords and control their mounts. Fully occupied to protect themselves from below, the knights were defenseless against a new and terrifying attack from above. A war-painted and near-naked, red-eyed, muscle-bound howling giant was upon them like a thrashing machine. It was the knights' turn to be trapped.

The Dark Warrior jumped from horse to horse as the two sharp swords flashed in the sun – moves practiced for decades and backed by the strength of ten men. He knew where to strike. Arms and hands with swords still attached, quickly parted company with their host. Legs suffered wounds designed to maximize blood loss. Some knights were left to bleed out, while those who instinctively tried to stem the blood died even faster from a second slash. Almost thirty of the outer circle of knights were fatally wounded in the first minute. Soon there were no more, and *the Dark Warrior* turned his attention to those attacking the officers. There were still about seventy of them, and they had their backs to him. They stood no chance.

The swordsmen quickly pulled away the riderless horses and gained access to the remaining knights desperately trying to turn their mounts. But it was too late. *The Dark Warrior* jumped from horse to horse while his blades slashed like two bolts of lightning. The swordsmen swarmed the perimeter and pulled the dead and injured knights off their mounts. The tide had turned.

Isabella watched wide-eyed as Chen launched himself from his horse and flew across the backs of the swordsmen to reach the knights' mounts. She saw him stretch out, raise his swords towards the sky and throw his head back. By the time the sound of his howl reached her ears, she had already turned *Barca* to face the other way. She had seen his sword routine many times and had no wish to witness the bloodbath she knew would follow. Even Marcus had to turn away.

'Grandfather,' she said softly, anxious to take her mind off the carnage behind her.

'Yes?'

'The attack on our officers is going to be over in a matter of minutes. When it is, our forces will either be forced to surrender or fight an all-out battle. If we go to battle conditions, I believe Yannis could be the most senior officer left.' She paused and felt her body shake uncontrollably. 'He's going to need a lot of help.'

'I'm way ahead of you for once. I've been considering the options under the power given me by the king, but I believe the best outcome could be achieved if we attack. I've just taken a quick look, and since you turned away a couple of minutes ago, Chen has taken care of more than half the knights. I saw Yannis battling them a short time ago, and I'm ready to go to him in the next minute or two. Much will depend on whether I'll be able to stop Karamus before he and the earl make their next move.'

'As much as you know how I fear for your safety, I see no other option. You have to take command of the army! The men are going to need a real general.'

Someone had brought a wine-barrel for Bucher to stand on to get a better view. 'What's happening over there?' he cried out to the two soldiers holding the barrel steady. 'I can't quite see what is happening, but it looks like some maniac is going berserk. The ranks of my knights have thinned by half in just the last couple of minutes.' He stared for a few more moments. 'They had better do their job if they know what's good for them.' He slid his sword noisily up and down in its scabbard as if to threaten them.

Major General Manassis continued to fight his way between the horses' legs to reach his target. On the way he was forced to climb over the rapidly mounting heap of bodies. He knew the direction to go, and he knew he would recognize the general's horse when he reached his destination. The blood-curdling screams continued, but now they came from a dozen pair of lungs at the same time. He looked through the forest of legs and saw that it was not as dense as it had been minutes earlier. The knights were losing rapidly.

The moment was close. He was within two horses of his target and straightened slightly to get a final bearing on the general and his protectors. Only six or eight of Nicholas' officers remained alive, fighting hard for survival.

He gasped at the horrific sight that confronted him. Zhang Chen was moving from horse to horse, slashing his way through the knights, with the swordsmen close behind him pulling bodies and horses away. The remaining knights were panic-stricken, in a frenzy to complete their mission before the madman reached them. Karamus' eyes bulged with fear.

Everyone was distracted. The knights were focused on killing the remaining officers or trying to find a way to fend off Zhang Chen. Karamus' eyes were riveted on Zhang Chen.

Perfect! Thank you, Zhang Chen. You have saved the day more than you will ever know. Nicholas managed to push his way between the last two horses that separated him from Karamus. He gripped the mouth-guard of the general's horse as he thrust his sword through one of the protectors. The man had been focused on the rampaging *Dark Warrior*, and was taken completely by surprise. Karamus spun in his saddle to see a smiling Manassis holding his horse and a sword pointing directly at his chest.

'Good day to you, General Traitor, sir. My mission is to execute you for your treason, and the crime against your nation and your loyal men. And now, farewell to you, General Traitor!' Nicholas thrust his sword as he spoke. But Karamus was quicker than he had expected. He managed to knock the weapon to the side of his chest, causing only a superficial wound.

'Kill him, kill him – he's after me! If he gets to me, you are all dead. All of you! Dead, dead, dead! Do you hear me? Kill him! Now!' Karamus pulled at his own sword as he screamed at the knights. Some of them spun around to find the source of the new threat. One was the captain, who knew the general was right. The knights had no hope of survival if he were killed. Thousands more would die in the battle that would surely follow. He desperately kicked his mount to force it past the horses that separated them.

Karamus managed to get his sword out and parried Nicholas' second thrust. Nicholas was powerfully built and an expect swordsman, and the general would normally be no match for him, but in those close confines, it was impossible to conduct a normal fight. He saw the knights' captain forcing his way towards them and realized his mistake in giving himself the pleasure of announcing Karamus' impending death. There would be a price to pay for that. His focus shifted momentarily to see Yannis fighting his way towards the center, only a few horse lengths from him. Nicholas made ready to complete his mission.

He looked up, smiled at Karamus and, in a seeming lapse of concentration, allowed his sword to swing to one side. Karamus saw the opportunity, and with a triumphant roar, thrust his sword deep into Nicholas' upper chest. It penetrated his body completely. With only seconds remaining before the knight captain reached him, Nicholas had deliberately made himself an easy target. He was ready. As soon as he felt the sword slice into him, his own weapon flashed up with his full power behind it. It pierced Karamus' chest and protruded from his back.

'*Oh,*' Karamus groaned, 'this is not how it … *ahh,* this can't be … *Father!*' He shook his head in bewilderment as his eyes glazed. Suddenly he lurched forward, blood seeping from his mouth. As he hit the ground, the force thrust the sword all the way into his body to the hilt. His blood seeped into his standard, mixing with the colors he himself had chosen.

'Yannis, where are you? Yannis? Can you hear me?'

'I'm here, Nicho, to your left. I'm coming to get you.'

'I see you. Yannis, listen to me. Karamus is dead. With him gone, there will be no-one to offer surrender, and the enemy might decide that their only option is to attack. We must therefore strike first, and strike hard. Do you understand? Get going, get away. For the sake of our army, our nation, you must get away right now! That is a direct order from your commanding officer. Attack or all is lost. It's up to you now, Yannis. You are the most senior officer left. You're in command of the army now. Do you understand?'

'Yes, yes, but … '

'Go, Yannis. You have your orders, Lieutenant Colonel. Your orders are to attack …' Nicholas felt hot, then numb, and stared down with surprise at the shiny object protruding from his chest. As he sank to his knees, he failed to recognize it as a sword. He looked desperately for Yannis, but the younger man had already left. *A good man,* he thought, *the perfect man for Isa* … The light faded to darkness as he slumped forward.

The knight pulled his sword out of the Major General as he fell and looked at his captain. 'Captain,' he yelled, 'mission completed. They're all dead. Let's get out of here! I think there are only about twenty of us left.'

The captain glanced around frantically to assess their situation. 'No,' he yelled, loud enough for his men to hear. 'If we go back, *The Butcher* will have us beheaded for failing our mission, for not protecting General Karamus, and causing the battle and deaths that is now likely to follow. We would die in disgrace. No, we must stay and fight to die as heroes.'

A moment later, the captain felt a hand grip his helmet and yank his head back. He looked up to see two red eyes, and sunlight sparkling off a blur of steel.

CHAPTER 65

'*Back to your posts, men!*' Yannis yelled to the swordsmen as they finished off the last of the knights. 'On the way, spread out and yell to everyone to get ready to attack. There are no other senior officers left, so all corporals to captains are to take charge. Some of my cavalry will come to you with instructions in a few minutes. The signal to attack will be when you see me lead the cavalry charge.' He beckoned for his subordinate to bring his mount.

'Yannis, wait!' It was Marcus who had just arrived and heard the last words. He slid off his horse and handed the reins to a soldier as he ran to Yannis.

'Marcus, I'm sorry, but Nicholas didn't make it out of there. The last words he gave me were orders to attack immediately.'

Marcus nodded sadly. 'I saw him enter the circle and no-one came out, so I guessed as much. He was the bravest of the brave.' He looked at Yannis and the surrounding soldiers. 'To attack is the correct decision, but it must be done the right way. Yannis, do you mind? You're the senior officer now. You don't have to listen to a word I say.'

'I don't mind at all, sir. The men deserve every chance they can get. Right now you're our best chance. Consider yourself in charge, General.' He glanced at the soldiers gathered around them. 'General Mondeo is in charge, agreed?' The men nodded as one.

'Thank you, Yannis. Men, gather around. Quickly now! This is how we are going to do it.' He pointed to one of the soldiers. 'You – get the trumpeters down here at once, I'll tell them what to do. *You* – get ten crossbowmen and ten longbowmen here. Some of you take off and call out that we will attack in five minutes. Yannis, tell your man here to warn your cavalry, and then move one quarter of them towards the right flank.'

Yannis took hold of his mount and waved his man away to carry out the instructions. He then turned back to listen intently to Marcus, knowing that he needed all the help he could get. Besides, history had shown that the man leading the first cavalry charge did not have an enviable survival rate. Yannis knew only too well it was simply not practical for him to retain overall command.

The trumpeters and archers arrived first and gathered around Marcus. 'Men, the first thirty seconds will be decisive. At my call the cavalry will charge and the crossbowmen will simultaneously open fire above their heads. Half will fire a salvo into the enemy cavalry, followed a few seconds later by the other half.' Marcus gave each group precise instructions quickly but clearly. 'Longbowmen, you will then move forward into the space vacated by the cavalry, and spearmen, you'll move forward in phalanx formation. Yannis, remember to use each cavalry withdrawal to water the horses. Everyone remember that the enemy is without armor and will be too busy holding their shields to fire back.' He turned towards the swordsmen.

'Yes, what about us? I thought we'd miss out, General,' one of them called out with a grin.

'Sorry, you don't get to go home for supper just yet. You will work together with the spearmen and will protect each other. First you will fall in behind them.' He explained what they had to do. 'Now don't worry about trying to remember everything, men. I'll control the trumpeters, and you all know your own sounds and signals. It seems a lot, but rest assured, what I have just said will take place in less than ten minutes. What happens after that will depend on how the enemy reacts. Go now, men. Good luck, and may God be merciful.'

The men saluted and rushed off to relay instructions.

'Good luck to you too, Yannis.' Marcus shook his hand.

'Marcus, I promised Nicholas that I would help watch out for Isabella until she's an adult, so I simply have to come back. Did you manage to get her to a safe place?'

Marcus shook his head. 'I gave up trying. She's just over there on the rise, behind you.'

Yannis turned and groaned when he saw how close she was, sitting on *Barca* in the gap between the archers. He waved and gave her a soldier's salute. In response she raised her foot and kicked the air before waving back.

He pointed to the gap behind the crossbowmen and waited for her response. She nodded and immediately moved *Barca* to the space indicated.

'Good girl! She'll be safe there.' Yannis turned back to Marcus. 'She finally did something she was told.'

'Why am I not surprised that you'd be the one she'd listen to?' Marcus replied with a chuckle. 'Let's go!' The two men slapped each other's shoulders and left to lead the attack.

Yannis was a shimmering figure through her tears as Isabella waved back to him. She saw him point and understood what he wanted her to do. Knowing it might be the only time she would ever be able to obey him, she did not hesitate. The two men she loved more than any other were about to die, while she could do little more than sit and watch.

'What do you see?' Bucher asked the soldier now standing on the barrel.

'I can't see any of our men, sir. It seems likely they've all been killed.'

'Incompetent fools! They could not even perform a simple task for their nation. What else?'

'It's all quiet and lots of men are milling about.'

'Can you see General Karamus? Is he one of the men standing around?'

'No, sir. No sign of him.'

Bucher paced back and forth. 'Well, it might not matter if Karamus has been killed by mistake. They will simply select someone else to offer their surrender.'

One of the generals surrounding Bucher turned to him and asked, 'Are you sure they will surrender, sir?'

'Of course. What else can they do?'

The officer appeared nervous as he was forced to provide the obvious answer. 'Well, sir, if they don't surrender, their only choice is to attack.'

'Don't be stupid, man! They can't attack. They are outnumbered, outgunned and have no one left to say the word *attack*. They are lost! They will surrender. Mark my words, General.'

'Yes, sir.'

Another general pointed to the enemy front line. 'What are they up to? A section of their cavalry is moving towards our left flank. What do you think, sir?'

Bucher snorted. 'Who cares? Just keep an eye open for whoever will be riding over to offer their surrender!'

'*Fire!*' Marcus shouted to one of the trumpeters who had the instrument at the ready. Marcus had moved near to the back line where he and the twenty trumpeters would be out of range of the enemy's powerful crossbows.

'What's that?' Bucher frowned as he watched a cloud of grey rise into the clear sky. Within seconds his front line was in chaos as thousands of long steel arrows and metal bolts rained down on his cavalry. 'What are they doing? Are they insane? The idiots are attacking us!'

The cavalry were felled by the hundreds, the horses colliding with each other in their attempt to escape the unknown. Seconds later they were struck again as a second salvo landed.

The generals did not wait for Bucher to issue orders. General Alvarez screamed out as he ran, 'To your posts, men. Prepare to counter-attack!' A third and fourth salvo struck as he ran, now into the lines of the bowmen. Another general was running just a few paces ahead of Alvarez when he suddenly changed direction to head for a gap leading to the rear. A second later, a bolt entered his back and flew out of his chest.

Alvarez raged in fury. *You moron, Bucher. So arrogant you didn't plan for the unexpected. Now it's your own men being butchered. You should have made sure our men had body armor. Idiot! I'll make you pay for this!*

A bolt struck his thigh before he had time to realize that crossbow ammunition would easily penetrate body armor. Another struck his neck. He stumbled to the ground and moved no more.

You were right, Marcus, Yannis thought when he heard his call to action. Thirty seconds exactly. He and his men had intently watched the carnage just a few hundred paces away and were ready for the signal.

'*Charge!*' he roared, spearheading his men into the chaotic lines of the enemy cavalry, half of which had already been lost. The opposing numbers were now approximately even. The enemy's mounts were still in panic as the last of the bolts smashed into their lines. Yannis knew that his men had to make full use of their advantage. It would last only minutes.

The longbowmen rushed forward the moment Yannis and his men advanced. Just as he crashed into the first of the enemy cavalry, he heard the hiss of thousands of arrows above his head heading towards the lines of enemy longbowmen. They were followed by wave after wave of missiles fired by the crossbowmen. The enemy's screams of pain and terror spread over the grassland as they automatically fell into a pattern of retreat. They had no defense against such an unexpected and powerful onslaught from a highly trained and well-armed force.

•

Isabella had calmed down by the time she heard the trumpet call and saw Yannis raise his sword. Her tears had ceased, but her heart was pounding as she watched him quickly close the gap between the two armed forces at the head of his men. He was the first man to crash into the enemy lines.

She watched intently every move orchestrated by her grandfather, as well as the movements in the enemy lines. Her mind worked out each action as she would have implemented it, and she took great satisfaction when the trumpets confirmed her calculations within seconds.

From her position of height she was able to see the terrible toll inflicted on the enemy. Thousands were already on the ground. The sea of men around them was moving away rather than forward. A state of panic? An ordered retreat? Isabella was not sure, but it seemed a positive sign. So far, their own casualties were modest. A few enemy archers had found the time – or the courage – to return fire. Being able to penetrate body armor, their crossbows had inflicted the most damage. Some hundreds appeared to be dead or injured among the Southern troops. On the grasslands, the Southern army was moving forward at a steady pace, enabling them to fire farther into the mass of enemy ranks. The spearmen were preparing to charge, seemingly anxious to enter the fray. Isabella found it hard to believe their attack had commenced just minutes earlier.

Yannis attacked again and again, slashing to his left and to his right, before moving forward to the next target. Within minutes his men had accounted for almost half of the remaining enemy cavalry. He looked around to see their commanding officer screaming at his men to retreat rather than attempt to re-group. The officer had correctly calculated that his men were already outnumbered two to one and were unable to withstand the speed and momentum of the attackers. *A smart officer*, Yannis thought. *That is exactly what I would do under the circumstances.*

Bucher threw himself behind the barrel as soon as he realized what was happening. He looked desperately for a safer sanctuary, where he could assess the situation and issue orders. There was none. Within seconds he saw one of his generals stumble before being struck by more missiles. A few seconds later, a second general hit the ground and lay still.

Looking behind him he was horrified to see his archers being decimated and the lines in disarray. Suddenly a new sound penetrated the screams of his men: an unmistakable thundering shaking the ground. *A cavalry charge!*

Being directly behind his own cavalry, Bucher knew he was in a vulnerable spot. Much too close for comfort. If the enemy should get through, and he was captured … he had no choice. He ran.

He ran through the lines of longbow archers, past the crossbowmen and into the rear lines of spearmen and regiments. He hardly breathed as he ran, expecting at any moment to feel an arrow or a steel bolt pierce his body. Bodies of his men were trampled underfoot as he ran. Several time he felt tugs at his clothes.

Suddenly he found himself out of range. To make certain, he ran a little further before stopping to catch his breath. He closed his eyes, slowly turned around and willed his mind to give him a vision he could cope with. After a few moments, when he opened his eyes to take in the scene, the sight was devastating.

Most of his cavalry had been annihilated. The archers had succumbed by the thousands. He quickly estimated casualties of dead and injured at well above 10,000, and more were falling by the second. He looked to the enemy lines and estimated their casualties to be no more than a few hundred.

The Butcher was furious. He would make his men pay for their incompetence. To allow an inferior enemy to inflict such casualties was unforgivable.

'*Counter-attack!*' he screamed at his men from the backline. The command had no effect. His army continued to flee the onslaught.

Isabella watched the spearmen quick-march across the gap before they closed ranks as they reached their cavalry comrades. A trumpet rang out and she saw Yannis raise his sword and wave to his men. Seconds later the cavalry rode through gaps in the phalanx formations to head back to their own lines. Yannis was the last to leave. Her heart skipped a beat as she watched him suddenly turn and ride back towards the enemy lines. *Oh, what are you doing, Yannis? You have survived so far. Please don't go back!* She made ready to ride to his side.

With mounting panic, she watched as Yannis reached one of the phalanx formations, leaned down and grabbed the arm of a man kneeling on the ground. With one mighty heave he swung the man up onto the back of his mount. The horse turned in a cloud of dust and headed to safety at full gallop.

Isabella almost fainted with relief.

•

Bucher was not a happy man. He watched as enemy spearmen thrust their way into his front lines, while missiles continued to fly in waves above their heads and into his soldiers. The Southern swordsmen came next, darting back and forth between the phalanxes and creating havoc without remaining in one spot long enough to be confronted. Their archers continued their forward march at a steady pace, and he could see their range getting closer to his own position. He moved further back.

So did everyone else. His army was in retreat without being ordered to do so. The attack was relentless, giving his men no time to regroup or plan an effective counter-attack. His troops were falling in such numbers that their only thought was to escape the rain of death.

How can they be so effective without leadership? Bucher wondered. *There was no one left. Or was there? There had to be! The enemy could not strike so decisively without effective leadership. The order of battle reeked of someone with considerable battle experience.* Bucher nodded slowly, deep in thought. *Yes, that must be it. It had to be a general, a very experienced general from the past. Whoever he is,* he thought, *he is a brilliant tactician.*

That left him with only one option. It would take some time, but it was guaranteed to stop the attack and win the battle.

'*The cannons!*' he roared. 'Bring the cannons to the front! Now, or I'll have your heads sent back to your families!'

Marcus moved forward with his army, watching every move that might point to a counter-attack. *So far, so good,* he thought. His fate, and that of his men, depended on how he acted and reacted to every move. He was so intent on the actual progress of the battle that he did not see what Isabella saw.

Isabella had moved up the slope to get a better view of the scene below. She judged that the earl had to take drastic action within the next minute or two, or order a full retreat. With an enemy upon its back like a pack of wolves, he would be aware that full retreat was more dangerous than a counter-attack. That knowledge caused Isabella to look away from the actual battlefield to search for any unusual activity. That was when she saw what Marcus was unable to see.

Six men were riding at full gallop towards the northern flank. *They were obviously carrying new, important orders,* Isabella thought. *What could they be?* It took less than a second for her to find the answer. The enemy had one weapon that the Southern army did not, a weapon they had failed to deploy in the first place, and that would win the battle for them.

The cannons!

Thousands of men swarmed around the cannons. They hitched horses and oxen to the carriages, and loaded kegs of gunpowder into wagons that already contained the round, smooth cannon-shot. They could see what was happening to their men at the front and worked at a furious pace to complete their task. The cannons were dispatched to the front the moment they were ready.

Isabella sat alone near the top of the hill and surveyed the rapidly developing scene below. Her mind raced with calculations of times and distance, and a series of *what ifs* and counter-moves to each. With a casualty rate of up to fifty for every cannon-ball fired into soldiers in tight formation, there was little doubt the Southern army would be annihilated five minutes after the opening fire. The earl knew that. Isabella knew that.

She was surprised at the sudden icy calm that swept over her like a cloud, as her mind considered each scenario. Her heart slowed and she felt a power surge through her body, a power she had felt before and was comfortable with: the power to control events when she was needed. Their army had to escape the cannons, and she had to find the way to do it.

As the afternoon had worn on, she had noticed the wind strengthening as expected. Her eyes whipped from the cannons to the raging battle, to the grasslands, to the wind, to the hills, back to the cannons, to the wind getting stronger, to the battle and, finally, back to the wind. The wind. That was the answer. *The wind!*

She took a deep breath and pointed *Barca* downhill at full gallop. Half-way down the slope, she brought him to a halt so rapidly he reared on his hind legs to regain his balance.

'Find Johan!' she screamed at the men. 'Find Johan and send him to General Mondeo.'

'What? What do you – ?' one of the men called out in confusion.

'I said, find Johan. He is a former sailor. You can't miss him. He's the biggest man in the army. Send him and twenty of his men to meet up with the General. Do it now!' Without another word she spurred *Barca* and continued down the hill at full gallop.

•

The first cannon neared the northern flank. Bucher watched from a safe distance behind his troops. Orders had been issued that anyone leaving their post would be severely dealt with after the battle. With a choice of die now or die later, the men had no option but to stand their ground. The casualties were horrendous. Bucher could not care less who died; he never did. As soon as the cannons were set up, the tide would turn rapidly and permanently.

'Thank God you're alive, Yannis! I nearly came to you a couple of times!' Isabella gripped Yannis' hand so hard she almost pulled him from his mount.

'It's not over yet, but so far my luck is holding out. He is a genius, your grandfather.' He was about to admonish her for being at the front line when she cut him off.

'Yes, he is. But things have changed. Come with me. Quickly!' She let go of his hand and kicked *Barca* into action, giving him no option but to follow.

They reached Marcus in less than a minute. He had already moved the major part of the Southern troops forward, past where the enemy's front line had been before the attack.

'Grandfather! Yannis! Listen to me. You are too low here to see what's happening at the northern flank.' They listened in stony silence, their faces losing color as she filled them in on her observations from the hill.

'What will we do, sir?' Looking desperate, Yannis directed his question to his new commanding officer.

'I, ahh ...' Marcus was lost for words as his mind struggled with tactics to counter the new threat. Fighting cannons was simply impossible.

Isabella saw a blood-smeared giant jog across the field from the front line, followed closely by twenty men in similar condition.

'Never mind,' she shouted at Marcus and Yannis. 'I'll tell you what we need to do, and here are the men who are going to help us do it.' The two men simply nodded, having learned not to ignore Isabella's logic.

She addressed the new arrivals immediately. 'Johan. Men. The enemy is about to bring forward hundreds of cannons. Once they start firing, our army will perish within minutes. You are going to help save them.'

'What are we going to do?' Yannis asked.

'We are going to prepare for an orderly withdrawal.'

'What?' Yannis was shocked. 'As soon as we withdraw, they'll turn on us. They will wipe us out even before the cannons open fire. Our men will die like cowards on the run. Isabella, the men will prefer to die fighting. Our attack has been going well. We might still be able to stop them before they get their cannons lined up.'

'Yannis, look behind you. The enemy has stopped moving back. The earl has obviously given orders to hold their ground. He is sacrificing his men while he lines up his cannons to destroy us. Our momentum has slowed and will soon stop altogether.'

'She's right, Yannis.' Marcus agreed. 'I have noticed there's been very little forward momentum in the last couple of minutes. So what are you saying, Isabella?'

'Yannis, listen. Your men will never be seen as cowards. Look at them! Every one of them – they're in there fighting to the death. We have nothing to lose by withdrawing and re-assessing our battle plans to fight on another day. But we have little time. My assessment is that we have less than one hour before their cannons annihilate us.'

Yannis nodded. 'You're right. General?' He looked at Marcus, who just nodded. Yannis brought his mount next to *Barca*. 'So how do we withdraw without the enemy carving holes in our backs?'

Isabella smiled for the first time in hours. 'That's the easy part. The earl must get his own men *behind* his cannons before he can open fire. He will therefore sound a full withdrawal within fifteen minutes to give him the room he needs to place the cannons. We'll sound our withdrawal immediately after he does. He won't care, knowing we won't have enough time to escape the range of his cannons. It will take more than an hour for our men to climb back up that hill.'

Yannis reached out to take Isabella's hand in his. 'Our future is literally in your hands. So tell us: how do we escape the cannons?'

She smiled at Yannis and looked down at the surrounding soldiers. 'We will do what illusionists do best: we'll use smoke and mirrors and let the audience see what they expect to see. Now listen, this is how we'll do it ...'

When she had finished, Johan could not resist giving Isabella a formal salute. 'Let's go, boys, we have work to do. We have an army to rescue.' Yannis pointed to her spot on the hill and raised his eyebrows.

'Yes, of course, Yannis, anything you say,' she grinned as they all headed in different directions. *Barca* only got a few strides when she heard Yannis call out.

'Isabella, wait!'

She brought *Barca* about, slowed, and trotted towards Yannis. 'Yes, Yannis?' Her heart was pounding.

'I'm still breathing, so you must have brought me luck. We're in for a torrid afternoon, which means I could do with another kick.'

'Happy to oblige, Yannis.' Isabella kicked his leg. Hard.

'*Oh!*' Yannis gasped in genuine pain, taking a few moments to catch his breath. 'That ought to see me safely through the day.' They both laughed as they parted company. Marcus had already disappeared, and Yannis was soon working his way through his front lines.

Isabella headed for the hillside and had almost reached safety when suddenly everything changed drastically.

CHAPTER 66

Earl Carlos Bucher intended to extract a terrible revenge for the devastating losses to his army. One by one, the cannons were lined up, starting from the northern end. The braziers – sturdy coal buckets – were already being lit as kegs of gunpowder were placed beside the cannons. Soldiers removed lids from kegs while others carried and stacked the smooth stone shot. Each cannon-ball required two men to carry it in a strong sling.

As soon as he received word that three cannons had been lined up and others were rapidly being put into place, Bucher nodded to the colonel standing at his side. 'Sound the withdrawal, Colonel.'

The colonel raised a flag, a movement repeated by soldiers in both directions. Within seconds, trumpets signaled the troops to disengage. Needing no further encouragement, they literally ran from their attackers. Seconds later, the withdrawal signal was heard from enemy positions.

'They are going to withdraw, sir.' The colonel was alarmed.

'Well, of course they are,' Bucher snapped. 'They are hardly going to pursue us now that they know we have dug our heels in.'

'They might escape, sir. Should we give chase?'

'No need. With their armor, it will take them an hour or more to get up that hill. We'll be ready to fire in twenty minutes. Just aim all the cannons at different points on the hill and we will blow them to kingdom come before they get half-way up. Fools! They should never have attacked us. They should have surrendered as soon as they knew their officers had all been killed. Thousands of good men have died for nothing. Now I'm not going to give them the opportunity to even consider surrender. They will pay the price for their folly. I'll kill every last one of them.' He sucked his breath in angrily. 'How are the cannons coming along?'

'Should be five lined up by now, sir. All are aimed at the hills as instructed.'

At the far northern end of the line, a man holding one end of a sling carrying a cannon-ball slipped in blood that had pooled from his dead and dying comrades. As he fell, the soldier on the other end was pulled off balance. The cannon-ball rolled out of the sling and struck a hot brazier with tremendous force. White hot coals sprayed into the air.

The two men looked at each other in horror. Both knew instantly what was about to happen and ran for their lives. They did not run fast enough.

A few of the coals fell into the opened kegs, where they hissed momentarily as white smoke flashed into the air. With a deafening roar the kegs exploded, causing an entire wagonload to go off a moment later. Three cannons disintegrated from the shockwaves, as did hundreds of personnel standing within a hundred paces.

The blast was felt by Bucher and the colonel, who both stumbled to their knees. Then Bucher jumped to his feet to survey the damage beneath the huge cloud forming in the distance. He glared at the colonel. 'They were lucky they were all killed, or I would have had their heads for their incompetence.'

The shockwaves were felt all the way to the foothills. Isabella felt them. *Barca* felt them and was immediately overwhelmed by fear of the unknown. The magnificent stallion reared up and spun a full circle. As soon as his forelegs hit the ground, he bolted at full gallop. There was little Isabella could do other than desperately hang on to his mane.

Barca took the easiest and quickest course to escape his fear. Downhill. He galloped away from safety, directly toward enemy lines. Isabella screamed but it made no impression on *Barca*. Within seconds he was racing along the perimeter of the front line. Near the northern end his bulging eyes suddenly focused on a massive black-and-white mushroom rising into the sky. To escape this new threat, he did what any animal would do: he stopped abruptly, spun and bolted in the opposite direction.

Isabella had, as always, been riding without a saddle. She had no chance. The sudden change in direction hurled her off as if her mount had been greased. She hit the ground, tumbled several times and came to rest on her hands and knees, only to see *Barca* disappear between the cannons, behind enemy lines.

That was not all she saw. She had been dumped directly on the enemy front line, where soldiers in their thousands were lined up to her left and right, many staring at her, open-mouthed. She quickly looked around. No help in sight. She was on her own.

Reaching inside her jacket, she pulled out her sword and Zhang Chen's dagger and held them up to face her enemy, just ten paces away.

Yannis spun in a panic. The sound was unmistakable. A girl's scream! There was only one girl on the battlefield. He watched with growing dismay as *Barca* ran directly at the enemy lines, only to spin around and send Isabella tumbling end over end.

He groaned as he saw her jump to her feet, draw her weapons and face the enemy mere paces away. Thousands of soldiers surrounding Yannis had also seen Isabella's misfortune, but could do little more than look helplessly at each other.

'*Marcus*!' Yannis yelled desperately.

CHAPTER 67

Isabella ran south along the front before enemy soldiers had time to react. It was pointless to run away from the line; a rider could easily pick her up, no matter how fast she ran. Her eyes searched for *Barca*, her only means of escape. There was no sign of her beloved stallion. Whistles had no effect. It was a hopeless situation, so stopped running and turned to face the soldiers. Slipping the dagger back into its scabbard under the jacket, she checked that her cap was still in place –to her surprise, it was – and lowered her sword.

Isabella resigned herself to be taken prisoner. She had heard of the earl's *take no prisoners* directive, and knew that her life was in peril.

Most of the soldiers were busy preparing the powder, braziers and cannon balls, and paid scant attention to a lone enemy. But not all of them. One, sword drawn, leapt from the line with a roar of anger, accompanied by shouts of encouragement from his comrades.

He was young, strongly built, and ugly. Blessed with a protruding forehead above deep-set eyes, and a mouth fixed in a hateful grimace, he reflected the crazed courage that only battle fury can produce.

Isabella was flooded with relief. From the very beginning she had been prepared to die on the first day of battle and she would now fulfil that part of her declaration. She would have preferred Yannis by her side, but knew that not all wishes come true. *Better dead,* she thought, *than what awaits me as a prisoner.*

She considered her attacker as he commenced his charge. It was more a stumble than a run, and his knees were unsteady. The man was mentally and physically exhausted from constant fighting. Isabella was young, lithe, fresh, healthy, extremely fit – and skilled. She knew she could take him. *After that, a mere thirty thousand to go...*

Parrying the first thrust, Isabella easily struck one of her own, more of a test of her adversary than a serious attempt to injure or kill. She brought out the dagger for protection from strikes to her left side. The man was big. His bulk, more than his skill, forced her backwards. She managed to get to his other side so that her backward movement continued in the direction where she had last seen *Barca*. Her sharp whistles continued at regular intervals, but there were no sign of her only means of escape.

'Lay them out in straight lines, face down, six to the row, twenty rows. Quickly now, boys!' Johan stood back and spoke calmly while his men laid out the shields as instructed. The former sailors were on the grasslands, well behind their own frontline. The troops on the lower parts of the hills were streaming downhill to join the main body of the army already marching towards the center of the flatlands. Heavy footsteps kicked up a mass of dust as they moved away from where they could see the cannons being aimed.

Cavalry officers had already collected masses of rope from the wagons beyond the crest of the hill, where the artists were still drawing at a frantic pace. Half the seamen threaded ropes through the hand-grips inside the shields while the others used sturdy twine to secure the shields to the ropes at regular intervals.

'Now tie the ropes to your pommels. No one moves until the dust is thick enough to completely obscure us. When you move, make sure that you stay behind our troops at all times. The wind will do the rest. Get ready, men. A few more minutes should do it.'

'Marcus, you'll have to do the rest on your own. I'm going over there to be with Isabella. She'll be killed or captured any second! I can see her fighting a swordsman.'

'You can't go! You'll be killed. They will swarm all over you, thousands of them. You won't stand a chance.'

'I know that, but it doesn't matter. What matters is that I'm at Isabella's side, as she promised in front of the king to be at mine. I have to go.'

'Yannis, listen to me. I want to go to her as much as you do, but first we must carry out her instructions. You heard what she said: to save our nation we must save the army. We must, therefore, save the army first, no matter what happens to Isabella. If either of us went to her now, we would have no chance to save her, but even if we did, do you think she would ever forgive us? Her life in exchange for our army and our nation? I don't think so!'

Yannis nodded, despite his frustration. 'You're right. She would rather die, wouldn't she?'

'You're starting to understand and respect her as much as I do, Yannis. Now, let's focus on our tasks. When everything's in place, we'll both go for her. In the meantime, Isabella will take care of herself, I know. She's a better fighter than you and I put together. If she's captured, we can possibly get her back with a king's ransom, and I know just the king who will be happy to provide the money. Let's go.'

As the soldiers quick-marched across the plains, their eyes were glued to the spectacle of Isabella's weapons glinting in the sun like cascading diamonds.

In his eagerness to impress his colleagues, the young soldier thrashed his sword like a windmill in a storm. Isabella parried every strike so easily she could hear murmurs of admiration from the watching soldiers. The man tired rapidly. At the same time Isabella grew stronger as her body warmed to the action, which seemed little more than a light sparring session with Chen. Within a minute it was the man who was moving backwards. Isabella quickly switched to his other side and moved forward, left hand on hip like a competition swordsman. A sharp, angled slash by the soldier brought his sword close to the ground, where exhaustion made him unable to commence the upward movement for a full second, leaving him fatally exposed and providing Isabella with ample time to have sliced off his hands as well as his head. The man knew it, and Isabella saw the sudden realization in his eyes. He knew he should be dead, but wasn't. Moreover, his adversary was giving him time to regain his composure and his stance. A murmur of disbelief came from the soldiers who occasionally glanced their way.

The young soldier had been more intent on watching sword movements, rather than the person opposite. Now he narrowed his eyes to look more closely at his adversary as he continued his attack, more slowly this time. *Who is this person? Why didn't he kill me when he had the chance?*

He looked into green, almond-shaped eyes, flawless skin and a face that had been perfectly constructed by nature. A striking face. Isabella saw hesitation in his eyes and in his body language. She looked back at him, a half smile on her face as she pursed her lips to emit two more sharp whistles.

The whistles focused the soldier's attention on her lips. They were not the lips of a man. A man could not have a face so perfect and smooth, lips so full and naturally red. It dawned on him that his opponent was not a man. He had been fighting a girl, a very young girl, who had beaten him convincingly! His pulse raced as his anger was replaced by humiliation.

Exhaustion finally got the better of him when he slipped in pool of blood. He staggered and fell on his back among the bodies, arms wide, sword still in his hand. Without the strength to move, he would have been at the mercy of even a child.

Isabella also stumbled in her forward momentum and came to a stop above him, her sword directly over his heart. She just needed to lean forward and it was over. The man knew his life was hers for the taking. His comrades could not save him in the split second it would take to push the sword into him. The soldier looked up into the green eyes of the most extraordinary face he had ever seen, the face of an angel. He had never envisaged that his life would be claimed by *the Angel of Death*.

On the realization of imminent death, his features relaxed. Bitterness and fury faded, leaving behind a face that was plain, ordinary, but no longer ugly.

Isabella moved the sword from the man's chest and gave him a couple of gentle taps against his cheek. Then she lifted the blade carefully away from his face, smiled and blew him a kiss with her left hand, after quickly reversing the direction of the dagger away from him.

Now she needed a few seconds to plan her next move – *escape!* She spun to dart away without any idea where she would run. She didn't get far. Four soldiers had rushed towards them, swords drawn, when they saw their comrade's predicament.

'Sir, the enemy is streaming *downhill*! They must be mad. Safety for them is over the ridge. They must have their orders mixed up.'

'On the contrary, General.' Bucher spoke calmly and with great satisfaction. This was shaping up even better than he had hoped. 'They are doing exactly what I would do under the circumstances. Their general has seen where we have aimed our cannons. He also knows we will be ready to commence fire with some of our cannons within ten minutes. It would take his troops on the lower part of the hills an hour to reach the ridge, and much more for those already on the flatlands. All that armor has now turned into a handicap for them. No, their only hope of escape is downhill and as quickly as possible onto the plains, out of the range of the cannons.'

'Any chance of them escaping, sir?'

'None. What their general does not know, bless his soul, is the range of our cannons. It's three times greater than any other cannon ever built. He has made a terrible mistake simply through lack of knowledge. Their army can run for an hour and we will still get every one of them.'

'Should we not re-aim the cannons to the plains, then, sir?'

'Yes, it's time. Most of the enemy has already disappeared from sight, so they're unlikely to see us move the cannons.' Bucher laughed. 'The wind is our ally, General. That is something they did not count on. They won't even know what's happening inside that dust-storm. Every shot will kill at least fifty of their men. They will be smashed so hard they won't utter a sound. And in that dust the other soldiers won't even see what's happening next to them. They'll just keep plodding along like good little soldier-boys. All right, give the order to change the aim, but hold your fire until I give the word. I want to make sure they have all had time to reach the plains and are in the direct line of fire.'

Yannis groaned in frustration when he saw Isabella facing four men with swords drawn. His own men were long gone except for twenty of his closest friends and colleagues. The small group was on foot and moving slowly forward as the dust became heavier. He wanted to get just within vision of Isabella, yet be almost invisible to the enemy, who were either focused on her or preparing their cannons. Yannis felt a cold chill move down his spine when he saw the aim of the cannons being moved from the hills to the plains, where his army had been heading.

Isabella could easily be mistaken for a young man by the way she's dressed, he thought. *She also fights like a man. That means her adversaries are more likely to try to kill her than capture her. Isabella, reveal yourself. If they see you're a young girl they will prefer to capture you. Why, oh why, don't you do it to save yourself?*

Moments later he felt ill when it came to him why she had not revealed herself. Death was preferred to capture. He turned away; it was not something he could bear to see. 'Let's go, men. Someone please bring me the army's best mount.'

'What are you going to do, sir?'

'I'm going for Isabella, Corporal.'

'You'll be killed, sir.'

'So be it.'

'What do you want me to tell General Mondeo?'

'Tell him I'm sorry to go without him as we agreed, but he is the one who must lead our army. He's too important to our nation right now. Tell him that Isabella would never forgive him if he came for her. I'm the only one Isabella will accept to be by her side right now. Rest assured he'll understand exactly what I mean.'

Corporal Luis Valdez nodded and addressed the men. 'You heard what he said, men. You have your orders. Twelve men are to stay with me here for a few more minutes, and spread out just inside the edge of the dust.' He turned to Yannis and saluted. 'I'll bring you my personal mount. Except perhaps for *Barca*, I assure you there is none better on the continent. Good luck to you, Yannis!'

Yannis returned the salute and faded into the dust with the rest of the men.

Isabella could hear officers running along the front, shouting instructions. Horses and heavy ropes were attached to the gun muzzles to drag their aim away from the hills and instead towards the grasslands where the entire Southern army had been heading.

The four soldiers thought they were about to deal with a man but hesitated, confused, when they saw the kiss blown to their comrade at the moment they had expected to witness his death. They were amazed that the combatant had spared his life.

Isabella's heart sank when she realized she had another fight on her hands before she could put her mind to a means of escape. She had no option and, without a moment's hesitation, she attacked the four soldiers.

The four men had been busy lifting cannon-balls and kegs, and were already as exhausted as the young soldier still lying on the ground. Isabella slashed and parried, ducked and weaved between the four to make sure none was given the chance to get behind her. She also kept an eye out in case other soldiers joined the fray. None did. Over the shoulders of the soldiers, she could see that the surrounding hills had been completely blanketed by the dust storm. The grasslands had disappeared from view as the dust continued to sweep towards the line of cannons. Another series of whistles. No result. *Where are you, Barca?* She was desperate, out of ideas. It was time to mix the teachings of her grandfather with the teachings of the Zen Master.

The four men in front of her tired rapidly and appeared worried, never having fought someone so quick and as skilful. None could have suspected that she had spent the greater part of her short life being trained daily by the chief trainer of her nation's most elite soldiers.

A trumpet call sounded and within seconds cannon-fire at the northern end of the front boomed across the plain. It was the sound of the most destructive weapon the world had ever known. One after the other, the cannons fired in the order of placement, slowly working their way south.

Two of the four men had pulled back from sheer exhaustion and were the butt of jokes from the sidelines for their inability to subdue a lone soldier. One of the remaining two lunged with his sword. Isabella parried in a swirling motion and forced the sword upwards. She then bent to the side and her leg flashed up to strike the man's hand above his head. His sword spun away and into the air. She instantly changed direction to get a leg behind his hip, while she reversed her own sword and pushed the grip into his chest. He fell flat on his back and out of harm's way of his spinning sword. They all watched as it hit the ground, point first, and swayed back and forth like ripe corn in a breeze. The fallen soldier had first-hand knowledge of her speed and knew that he was at her mercy; she was only a pace away.

Isabella's strength had reached a new peak; she felt superb, and in control. But she was getting hot and the leather jacket restricted her movements. With four adversaries to contend with, there was no choice. She could no longer hide who she was – the jacket had to go.

In one smooth motion she flicked the strap holding the jacket-front together, and swept it off her shoulders. It flew through the air and landed several paces away. The cap remained in place, but it felt loose and slippery from her perspiration.

Isabella smiled and bowed to the fallen man, pointed to his still swaying sword with her own, and took several steps back. It was a clear invitation to rise, unchallenged, and pick up his sword.

None of the men moved as they took in the unexpected sight before them. Long bare legs, a wide expanse of bare midriff and slim waist left them in no doubt. A young girl, a girl who had the fighting skills equal to the best their own army had to offer! The observers fell silent. The only sound was the ear-shattering boom of the cannons as the firing crept closer. Isabella smiled at the four men and took up an exaggerated dueling stance.

The fallen soldier got to his feet and pulled his sword from the ground. As he looked at her, his face softened, and he gently shook his head and moved back. Isabella pouted and gave him a look of disappointment. The soldier could not resist a smile and flicked his head towards the man behind him. She nodded in acknowledgement and turned slightly to face the other man. Their two comrades who had moved aside earlier leaned on their swords and watched with interest.

Isabella's new adversary stepped forward and swung his sword. She parried easily – too easily. There was little strength behind the strike. Young and strong as he was, Isabella knew he was capable of much more. He had given her the message that his heart was not in it. He had no wish to kill a young girl. She locked her gaze on him and gave him her most brilliant smile. Then, with lightning speed, her sword flashed once, twice. She twisted around and her leg came up to knock the sword from his hand. Her sword flashed again, at full strength, towards his right knee. A hairs-breadth away, it stopped, accompanied by a loud shout of *hai!* The man stared at her in wide-eyed disbelief. Immediately, they understood one another: neither would harm the other. Stepping back, she gave the soldier a small bow and another brilliant smile. Cheers and applause rang out from the sidelines. None of those soldiers had expected entertainment in the midst of battle.

Slowly Isabella moved several paces back and looked at the four men. She had no idea where she would go, or what she would do next, so she simply smiled and shrugged at them. They glanced at each other with no idea either of what to do, and shrugged in return. Isabella was unable to restrain herself and let out one of her distinctive half-child, half-woman giggles, which caused the men to break out in laughter. Only the boom of the cannons confined the sound of laughter to their immediate surrounds.

One of the soldiers pursed his lips into a silent whistle. The message was clear: get your horse back here and get away before someone else steps in. Her options had been reduced to two: *escape or capture.*

Isabella nodded her thanks and immediately emitted several whistles, which were mostly drowned out by the thunderous roar of the cannons. None brought the response she prayed for. She had no idea what she should do next.

Fate intervened.

CHAPTER 68

As Isabella moved away from the men it brought her closer to the thundering cannons behind her. Her first adversary had regained his strength and was up on one knee no more than six paces away, leaning on his sword for support. He gazed at her with unashamed adoration.

Suddenly there was a yell from close behind. Unable to make out what the man was shouting because of the roar of the cannons, Isabella flicked her gaze to the five men in front of her for a clue. She was shocked to see their eyes widen in horror as they pointed and cried out to her – a warning. Something horrendous was about to happen directly behind her. The four men dove to the ground as the younger man started to rise.

Isabella instinctively knew that she was the one in mortal danger and spun to face her doom. Her brain raced so fast that the scene in front of her seemed to unfold in slow motion. Already loosened, her leather cap flew off as she spun. Her carefully rolled hair was released and flew upward in a wide arc around her head, forming a golden halo. The weight of her dagger and sword swung her arms high and wide, the blades glinting like diamonds under bright light. The power behind her spin fully flexed the muscles of her arms and legs; the exceptional definition of her abdominal muscles was thrown into relief by the sun on her bare midriff.

It was a vision – frozen in a moment of time – of a golden-haired gladiator about to slay the dragon. None of the hundreds of soldiers watching would ever forget that sight. It was a moment that would be spoken about for decades. It was a vision that would be immortalized.

In that same moment, Isabella's own gaze was on six soldiers behind their cannon, wide-eyed in the knowledge of the horror they were about to witness. There was no time to react or evade the threat she faced.

She was staring directly into the massive barrel of a gun, less than two paces away and pointed at the center of her chest. She could clearly see the stone cannon-ball and part of the wadding behind it that held the gunpowder tightly into place. The gunner had already touched the wick with the red hot metal touché and was unable to undo his action. Isabella saw the wick sizzle and smoke as it disappeared into the touch-hole and ignited the powder.

A huge flash of light and smoke shot up and out as the gunpowder ignited to propel the cannon-ball out of the muzzle. Still frozen in that split second, Isabella knew instantly that her life was over.

She felt her chest explode. Her last vision was of her arms bouncing on the ground as her legs flew up into the clear blue sky.

Then there was darkness.

'*Oh, God, no!*' Corporal Valdez cried out at the top of his voice. He could hear the other soldiers shouting in dismay. They had watched Isabella spin in front of the cannon, cap flying off and hair whirling around her head like spun gold. Next they saw a massive cloud of white smoke pour from the cannon's muzzle to partly obscure a tangle of arms and legs, followed by a thunder roll that reached them a second later.

Valdez hid his face in his hands and fought hard to control his emotions. He knew how much the soldiers loved and respected Isabella. She was their mascot; she was the beacon on the hill, the untouchable golden-haired goddess they loved from afar. Yannis was not the only one who would risk his life for her – there were thousands, including Luis Valdez. He was thankful that Yannis had not been there to witness her demise.

CHAPTER 69

Darkness. Silence. Utter silence. So this was death. Isabella had thought that heaven would be quiet, but that there would be vision and light, not darkness. Perhaps she was in hell. She *had* expected hell to be dark. That seemed reasonable enough. And the pain! *Oh, the pain! Her chest!* Why was there such pain after death? And the sensation of spinning. Her entire body was spinning, arms and legs in all directions. *Ah, so that's why the pain. It's still happening. I'm not dead yet – I'm still dying!*

Suddenly there was light. Bright, blinding light.

Her eyes flew open.

She was still spinning, tumbling head over heel. Finally she stopped rolling, finishing up on her hands and knees. The pain in her chest and back was intense. Her face almost touched the ground as she coughed several times – smelling gunpowder, tasting gunpowder. It seemed odd that she could not hear herself cough. She could hear nothing. Her head came up at the same time that she straightened to a sitting position to look around. Mere seconds had passed.

Directly in front of her was the young soldier whose life she had spared. He was on his knees and as stunned as Isabella. She knew instantly what had happened. He had tackled her from behind at full speed and strength to knock her out of the way just as the cannonball exited the muzzle. She had felt the searing heat and blast of the gunpowder as it discharged.

Another smell entered her senses. She looked around, and then down. They both saw it at the same time as pain suddenly swept across the young man's face. The leg of his uniform was smoldering fiercely from the gunpowder blast.

Isabella felt around desperately until she found what she was looking for: Chen's dagger. She motioned for the soldier to lie still while she swiftly cut away the cloth from the knee down and tossed it aside. Only a couple of superficial burns were visible on his calf. Gently she placed her cool hand on them and kept it there.

The two looked at each other as an understanding passed between them. She had spared his life and, in return, he had risked his life to save hers. On impulse she moved forward, still on her knees, and hugged him briefly. He did not touch her, but she saw his lips move as he pointed over her shoulder. She raised her eyebrows and his lips moved again, but still no sounds came. The muzzle blast had completely deafened her. She shook her head. The soldier suddenly realized she could not hear because neither could he.

He pointed again with increased animation. Isabella let go of him and turned to see what he was pointing at. *Barca!*

Drawn closer by the most recent whistles, *Barca* had recognized her golden hair and trotted towards her. He had finally become used to the noises and smells. The closest cannons had already fired and the men were busy reloading the powder, pads and shot; it would be relatively quiet for a short time. The stallion was about two hundred paces away. *Perfect, Barca, my darling!*

She turned back quickly to kiss her savior on his cheek. He looked as if he were about to faint. Because of his unfortunate appearance, he had never been kissed by a girl, and he knew he would never again be kissed by one who looked like an angel.

Isabella squeezed his hand, picked up her cap and weapons, and ran. She raised her arm, brought it down in a slow arc and pointed. A series of staccato whistles followed and *Barca* knew what to do. The stallion swung away from the front line at an increased speed for several seconds before he turned back in a large semi-circle to head directly for the cannon that she had pointed at. Isabella started to jog and gradually increased her pace as her mind maintained precise calculations of speed and direction. Another arm signal and more whistles. Her speed suddenly exploded into that of the competitive athlete she was, just as *Barca*'s speed increased to a fast canter.

The nearby cannons had recommenced their fire, but the soldiers seemed more intent on watching the spectacle unfold. Some lit the fuse of their cannon, some did not. The gunner on the cannon Isabella had chosen for her launch-point, did.

Her strides became longer and more structured as she closed in on the cannon. Just as her powerful legs launched her to the top of a powder-keg, she was horrified to see the wick disappear into the touch-hole in a shower of sparks. *Not again!* she thought. Too late. She was fully committed. From the keg she flew on to the hot muzzle just as the cannon exploded and the shot thundered out. Her momentum carried her up onto the carriage wheel and high into the air through the mushrooming cloud of discharge.

Barca's smooth back suddenly appeared directly beneath her as she emerged out of the cloud of smoke. Exactly as they had practiced a hundred times, she landed on his back near the shoulders and grabbed a handful of his mane. She had just synchronized her rhythm with *Barca*'s stride when she realized she had a new problem: she was behind enemy lines.

There were already more than 200 cannons lined up and firing. Hundreds of soldiers busied themselves loading and firing, loading and firing. Thousands of others stood further back to watch the spectacular sight through the smoke and constantly thickening dust cloud. To escape, Isabella knew she must break through the front lines at the southern end. Breaking out sooner would place her directly in front of the muzzles, and she had no desire to tempt fate again. There was also no point in trying to race to the southern end. It was too far; the soldiers had merely to close ranks and she would be their captive within seconds. She would have to brazen her way through the crowd.

She quickly flicked the dagger and sword to grasp them by the blade and held them up high to face the enemy yet again. A couple of whistles and gentle kicks in the right place and *Barca* changed his trot to that of an Arabian show horse, prancing and hopping forward while she swung the reversed weapons above her head.

The soldiers had seen her spare the lives of their comrades; they knew she was little more than a child and meant them no harm. As one, they parted to leave a path. After a hundred paces she decided to take a chance to ensure her escape. Soldiers love daring, and they love a hero. They would love a young heroine even more. A gentle kick turned *Barca* around to gallop back to where they had started. She brought him up on his hind legs and did a full turn near where the young soldier was still standing, watching her. Bringing out the cap she had tucked into her waistband, with a flick of her wrist, she spun it across the cannon and into his hands. She blew him a kiss and with a wave of her hand, pointed *Barca* back to the south. The soldier flushed with pleasure and knew he would be the toast of his regiment.

'*Go, Thunderbolt!*' Horse and rider headed towards the southern end, this time at a full gallop, as she waved her reversed weapons.

Although still partially deafened, she could hear a faint chorus of cheers, together with admiring whistles, and she noticed with a smile that the soldiers had parted like a tide. The men had seen the performance of a lifetime in the thunderous roar of the greatest firepower that had ever been unleashed. At the end of the line she slipped her weapons back into their scabbards, gave a brief wave and headed into the dust storm. She had made good her escape!

Sounds faded as soon as she was enveloped by the dust, where visibility was down to less than twenty paces. Agitated by the lack of vision, *Barca* began to twist and turn. Unable to hear the cannons clearly, Isabella soon lost her bearings. If she forced *Barca* to move in the wrong direction, they could find themselves back in front of the muzzles. She had no choice. She had to remain where she was until her hearing returned, or the dust lifted.

She slid off his back and gently stroked his neck to keep him calm in the raging dust storm. She was lost.

CHAPTER 70

Bucher had noticed unusual activity to the south and, occasionally, some cheering floated above the sound of cannon-fire. It was not until he leapt onto a horse that he saw long golden hair flowing behind a rider heading south. A woman! On the front line? Impossible! 'Find out what's going on, Colonel!'

The colonel was back in five minutes. He looked as if he had been laughing. 'Just a kid, sir. She must have been watching from the hills when her horse panicked. It kindly dumped her right on top of our front-line troops, and she spent the last half hour fighting her way out.'

'Fighting? Didn't you say she was just a kid?'

'She was. But, apparently, she really knew how to fight. At one stage she was dueling four soldiers at once, and no-one could get near her. Not only that, on several occasions she had some of the men at her mercy, but stood back and allowed them to retrieve their weapons to continue the fight. Not once did she draw blood when she could have done so on a dozen occasions. She ended up there by pure accident, and apparently never intended to harm anyone.'

'And they let her get away? I have tens of thousands of soldiers down there and they couldn't catch a kid! I'll have their heads on a platter to keep me company at dinner!'

'From what I understand, sir, she was a bit more than just a kid. More like a young woman and, by all accounts, quite a beauty.'

Bucher snorted. 'Any soldier who ends up at the mercy of a young woman should be put to the sword, Colonel. Perhaps you would like the pleasure. Or do I have to perform that tedious task myself?'

'With respect, sir, we've lost thousands today, and you would expect morale to be at its lowest point. I have been witness to rebellion and desertion at times like these. Instead, the morale of the troops down there is at a high. All their talk is about the girl, her fighting skills, her beauty and spectacular escape. They say her green eyes were so bright they lit up the battlefield.' The colonel laughed. 'I think they've all fallen in love with her, Your Grace. After seeing her spare their comrades they didn't really want to capture her and possibly see her mistreated, or worse. Every soldier loves a hero, no matter which side they're on. It would be counterproductive to mete out punishment, sir. I believe the girl has unintentionally done us a favor by lifting the spirits of our troops right now.'

'Well, perhaps you're ...'

'Besides, sir,' – the colonel pressed home his advantage to protect his men – 'a young girl like that is of no threat to us. As a prisoner she would cause us more trouble than it's worth, when we must now focus on other matters at hand.'

Bucher capitulated. He sighed. 'Very well. Perhaps you're right. A young girl can obviously do us no harm.'

Fifteen minutes later sight remained limited, but sound had started to return. Isabella moved her head from side to side to try to locate individual sounds and get her bearings. Thunder from the cannons rolled across the grasslands to mix with the echoes that bounced back from the surrounding hills. It was still too soon to establish direction accurately enough to make a move. If the dust cleared suddenly, she could again face capture.

Barca stood quietly with his eyes closed while Isabella squinted into the swirling dust. A dark outline seemed to suddenly appear to one side, only to disappear the next moment. She rubbed her eyes and squinted again. Nothing.

Despite the heat, an ice-cold shiver ran up her spine when the tall outline reappeared. It seemed to shimmer in the heat, and then faded as the wind whipped up another thick layer of dust. Suddenly this dark shape reappeared and became even taller as it moved towards her, picking up speed as it approached.

Isabella felt her heart pound to the point of pain, and fully understood *Barca*'s fear of the unknown. *Please God, don't forsake me now. Don't let me be taken prisoner after what I've just been through.*

The tall shape was upon her in a final rush. It was a man on horseback, his head swathed in cloth for protection against the dust. He came to a sudden halt directly next to her and leaned down, extending a powerful arm for her to grab. Isabella looked up to where the rider's face would be. Only his eyes were visible as they peered out of a tiny gap between the wrappings. Recognizing the dark brown eyes immediately, she almost fainted with relief.

Yannis!

Holding tightly onto *Barca*'s reins, she wrapped her arm around his and, lithe as a cat, leapt up behind him. 'Hang on tight,' he called as he maneuvered his mount to turn. Isabella needed no further encouragement and tightened her arms around him. 'But not that tight!' he yelled as they started to move forward.

'What did you say, Yannis?' she murmured in his ear. 'A cannon fired right in my face and it's deafened me. I didn't hear a thing you said. You'll have to say it again. A bit louder, please.' She had heard him perfectly well, but stretched forward so that he could press his face against hers.

Instead, he chose to yell. 'I just said to hang on tight, but – '

Isabella cut him off in an instant. 'Oh, thank you, Yannis. I'm so weak and tired. I don't want to fall off so I promise to hang on real tight.' *All is fair in love and war,* she thought, an expression she had heard often, and she had just been through the war part. There might never be an opportunity to get so close to him again, and she felt no guilt whatsoever.

Yannis maintained a moderate pace for the sake of the mount. The hill was steep in places and the horse, although strong, was carrying a double load. It was slow going, but Isabella did not care how long it took. They finally reached the ridge, where the wind was howling, the dust at its thickest. Isabella kept her face pressed against his back, her eyes tightly closed against the dust.

'How many cannons are up and running, Colonel?'

'Almost three hundred, sir.'

'That's enough. Send a message.'

'Yes, sir.' The colonel flicked his head at a nearby captain, who left immediately.

'Tell the men to keep firing, but slow down the rate a bit. It will only take a few rounds from each cannon to finish them off. Those not killed by a direct hit will be crushed by the rolling balls. I just love hearing the sound of those cannons, don't you?'

'Well, there is something else, sir.'

'Yes?'

'I'm told by the gunners that each cannon is capable of a maximum of five shots before they heat to dangerous levels. They take about a day or so to cool down, depending on weather conditions.'

'Very well, take them to four shots each, then. That's more than enough to finish off the enemy army, and ten more like it.' He laughed. It felt wonderful to be back in control after such a disastrous start to the day. He was already thinking about how to explain the horrendous loss of life to Emperor Aloise Kuiper.

The colonel flicked his head at another junior officer.

Suddenly, they were on the other side of the ridge, and the wind decreased immediately. Isabella opened her eyes to see visibility improve to a hundred paces. Within minutes the dust had almost disappeared, and they were back in a normal world. Yannis pulled up and half turned in his saddle to look at Isabella. He leaned closer to her face. 'You should be all right to ride *Barca* the rest of the way. Can you hear me all right? Is your hearing getting better?'

'Yes, much better now, thank you. Is it far to go?'

'About two hours. We had to find a narrow pass where we could hold off anyone chasing us while we escaped.'

She had just escaped hell to reach paradise, and she intended to stay there until the last possible moment. This time she did feel some guilt. 'Two hours!' Isabella put on her most pitiful face. 'My legs are so tired,' she lied. 'I don't think I could grip *Barca*'s slippery back for that long. Would you mind very much if I stay where I am?'

'No, no, that's fine. Let's go. There's some water just up ahead for the horses.' He tapped the mount and they started to move.

Isabella held on to his shirt and leaned close to his ear, but was careful not to touch it. 'Yannis?' she said softly.

'Yes?'

'You came back for me, through the blinding dust and within a hundred paces of the enemy lines. If you hadn't stumbled across me when you did, you would have ended up directly in front of the cannons. You risked your life for me, Yannis.'

'Oh, well …'

'You should not have risked your life for me. Except for Grandfather and Zhang Chen, I didn't think anyone would risk their life for me.'

'You promised you'd come to my side if I should fall. I feel the same about you, Isabella. I would have come for you sooner, but Marcus stopped me. He insisted that your plan must come first, and I'm sorry to have to admit he was right.'

She squeezed him hard. 'Lucky for you, Yannis! I would never have forgiven you if you had done otherwise. My life would simply not have been worth living.'

He winced. 'Marcus knows you well. That's exactly what he said.'

'Well, thank you for coming for me.' She rested her face against his shoulder.

He winced again. 'I think you might be right when you said we're fated to die together on the battlefield.'

'Why do you say that?'

'I just can't keep you from the center of battle, can I?'

'Not a chance. I was born for this.'

'Then I guess we're fated to be by each other's side. I guess that's just the way it is.' The horses were trotting at a comfortable pace.

'Except when you're at *Honey Bee's* side.'

'What? Honey Bee? Melissa's side? Why would I be at Melissa's side?'

'Well, we won't always be on the battlefield and then you and Melissa ...'

'There is no *me and Melissa*, Isabella.' He sounded cross.

'Oh, I thought ... well ... you know ... *Honey Bee, my darling*.' She finished the last words in a deep, husky voice, squeezing him again.

A wince brought Yannis' laughter to a sudden stop. 'You're actually hilarious sometimes. Well, you thought wrong. Most names have a particular meaning and Melissa told me her name means *the honeybee*. In fact, she was the one who asked me to call her by that name. It wasn't something clever or romantic that I came up with.'

'Oh.'

'You're right, though. Melissa is very beautiful and she's a lovely young woman but, amazing as it might seem to most, I'm not in love with her. Not yet, anyway. This is not the time to fall in love.'

Isabella remained silent for several moments. 'Do you think you'll ever fall in love, Yannis?'

'I would like to think so, but all in good time. There's no hurry. First, there will be years of battles to fight.'

'Years? You really think we can win?'

'With you on our side, Isabella, we can't lose.'

She squeezed him once more. He winced again.

Several rough-cut timber water troughs could be seen ahead. The horses recognized them instantly and increased their pace to a canter. Only the sounds of birds and the slurping of the horses penetrated the quiet of the wilderness as Isabella enjoyed a few minutes of tranquility. She had slipped to the ground to stretch her legs while she watched the horses drink. As soon as they had finished, she walked over to Yannis' mount and reached her arm up to him.

'Other side, please,' he said. He seemed tired, she thought, as she walked to the other side and reached up again. He reached down for her and Isabella slipped easily behind him a moment later. She slid her arms around him, gently this time, as he tapped the horse.

'Yannis?'

'Yes?'

'I've heard you groan a few times. Is something wrong? Are you hurt?'

'Mm … well, I had a little argument with one of the knights. Very hostile he was too, the blighter.'

Isabella gasped in fright and removed her arms. 'What happened? Where are you hurt?'

'It was just a sword. In the shoulder. A soldier's war wounds have to start with a first one.' He chuckled and winced at the same time.

'Has it been dressed?'

'No, it will be all – '

'I've got some dressings in *Barca's* saddlebag. Stop right now and I'll clean and dress it for you.'

'It's fine, I'll be – '

'You get off this horse right now, Yannis Christos, or my next kick will see you land head first in the next province!'

'All right! All right!'

Yannis said he felt better after she finished dressing the wound, but he actually looked worse. He was ashen-faced and had to be helped to his feet. Isabella was frantic with concern about blood loss, and the most feared curse of the battlefield: infection.

'You're not at all well. Would you prefer I sit in front so you can hold on to me for support?' Isabella had spoken with genuine concern, but immediately regretted her unintentional choice of words. Long ago she had promised herself she would not play the temptress, although the pain of restraint was excruciating.

'*What*? You must be joking! *Me*, hold on to *you*? Dressed like that?' He snorted. 'I would rather arrive at camp dead than turn up holding onto a little kid. I'd never live it down.' He gripped the saddle. 'Now, could you give me a bit of a leg up, please?'

Isabella put her hands on her hips, eyes blazing into his. '*Little kid!* How dare you call me a little kid, Yannis Christos? I might have been when you first met me, but I'm not that much shorter than you are now. And … ' She paused as she thrust her face forward. 'I am of age now, you know. I'm legally old enough to marry! So if I'm old enough to be someone's wife, I'm hardly a little kid!'

'Being *of age* as you call it means nothing to me. The legal age of fourteen is ridiculous, even if some stupid old men have declared that to be the age that girls can marry. Sixteen or more is acceptable, barely, but at fifteen you are still far too young. I'm sorry if it offends you, but to me you're still a little kid.' He smiled weakly as he added, 'I have to admit, though, that you don't look like a little kid any more. Now, give me a hand up, please, *big* kid.'

'Hmph!' Isabella snorted as she provided a lift. When he was settled, she slipped up behind him and slid her arms around his waist. She rested her face gently against his good shoulder as he nudged the mount forward.

After a few minutes Isabella put on her best whining voice. 'It's only because you rescued me and saved my wretched, worthless, miserable little life that I forgive you for such a terrible, terrible insult. I really should kick you again, you know. *Oh Yannis*, I'm absolutely devastated. Shattered. I'm so broken-hearted.'

'Oh, for God's sake, Isabella, shut up, will you?'

Isabella could feel Yannis' body shake with suppressed laughter. A full-strength giggle burst out of her and quickly changed to uncontrolled laughter as Yannis, too, chuckled. He cried out with pain at that, which made him laugh even louder. The sounds of hilarity rolled across the valley as they released the day's pent-up emotions and tensions.

'I'm getting a headache, Colonel,' Bucher complained. 'Tell them to cease fire, pack up and go home. Except the cavalry. I have a very special job for the cavalry.'

'Yes, sir,'

'Now we'll just wait for the dust to settle. The wind is dropping already. Time for a drink while we wait, don't you think? Get all the generals together and bring some of my best wine, would you?'

'Yes, sir!' The colonel grinned.

An hour later Yannis and Isabella entered the safety of the overnight camp. They were greeted with wild cheers as soldiers, camp followers, and their friends jostled for space around them. Unable to get close, Marcus, Chen and Yan watched and waved teary-eyed from the edge of the crowd. Melissa watched with concern when she saw Yannis slumped on his mount as it entered the crowd. Her eyes widened with more than concern when she saw Isabella, bare legs and midriff, on the back of his mount with her arms around him.

Isabella beckoned her over. 'Melissa, get a couple of the men next to you to help Yannis down. He's taken a sword right through his shoulder. I've had to hold him all the way to stop him falling off his horse. I'm afraid the poor man's completely helpless.' Isabella saw Melissa almost faint with relief.

Yannis turned in his saddle to stare at Isabella and opened his mouth to protest. Unseen, she stabbed her index finger into his lower back so hard he winced in pain.

'You see? He's in agony, poor man. Isn't that right, Yannis? Quickly, help get him down. Keep your distance from him, Melissa. He's in pain from head to toe. If he tries to speak, place your hand over his mouth.'

Several bystanders helped Yannis slide to the ground while others brought a stretcher. As they lowered him onto the stretcher, he looked up and rolled his eyes at Isabella while trying hard not to laugh. She settled her green eyes on his with a half-smile, raised her eyebrows and cocked her head to one side as she used to do years earlier.

Isabella slid down from the mount and handed the reins to a soldier without comment. He knew what the horses needed without being told. She pushed her way through the crowd and threw herself into the arms of Marcus, Chen and Yan.

'I never thought I'd make it back,' she said through tears. 'I don't know how I made it. I got away, then I got lost and then, all of a sudden, there was Yannis. He found me in the middle of that sandstorm, almost directly in front of the cannons, and brought me back to safety.'

Marcus was too emotional to speak and just nodded happily. Chen and Yan were too busy hugging her to say anything. Yan finally found her voice. 'Come, Chen, we will make Isabella and Yannis most beautiful dinner they ever have. We will have big party.'

Isabella embraced her grandfather. 'You were right, Grandfather,' she whispered into his ear. 'You told me once that Yannis would one day risk his life for me, only I never expected it to be so soon. You have no idea how close he came to be blown to pieces when he came to search for me.'

'You shouldn't read too much into that, Isabella. I hate to see you hurt, but Yannis is very taken with Melissa, you know. She is just so amazingly beautiful. And you must realize that Yannis only views you as a child.' He patted her shoulder as if to provide some comfort.

Isabella almost snorted but managed to keep a straight face. 'Oh, yes, *Melissa*. Yes, of course, he would be so in love with Melissa, wouldn't he? Who wouldn't be?' She looked up at her grandfather. 'And yes, you're quite right. I can tell you for a fact that he does not react to me in any way other than as to a … little kid.' *Lucky for you, Yannis*, she added to herself.

She moved back and lowered her arms. 'And I will tell you another fact, Grandfather.' She looked down at herself meaningfully before looking up again. 'I'm not going to be a little kid for much longer!'

The way you're developing, the end of the week should see you out, Marcus thought.

'Isabella.' Marcus' tone had changed.

Isabella turned away. She knew that tone and knew what was coming. 'Yes, I know. Uncle Nicho. I saw what happened. I know he's not coming back.' Marcus saw her tears and pulled her to him.

'I saw him enter the melee, Grandfather, and he never came out. He joined his fellow officers, knowing that there was no chance of survival. He could have stayed away and survived. But he didn't. Such courage. A true soldier. I'm so proud of him. Mother would be so proud of him. I wonder if I'll ever have such courage. I will miss him so much.'

Marcus nodded, unable to speak. Only after he had composed himself did he say, 'As for courage, Isabella, I saw you, all alone, pull your weapons and confront an army. You are every bit the soldier he was. I'm going to miss him, too. He will be remembered as a true hero.'

He had no idea how wrong his pronouncement would prove to be.

CHAPTER 71

The commanding officer saluted. 'We are ready, sir.' His cavalry was lined up in formation behind the major, swords drawn as ordered.

A heavy breathing Bucher sidled up next to the major on his own mount. With eyes fluttering and shoulders twitching, he had never felt so excited; his blood-lust was near boiling point as he shouted to the troops. 'Men, you are about to witness the result of the total annihilation of a nation's army in a single battle. Today will be a victory our nation will remember forever and you will remember that you played a part in it.' He paused for effect. 'And you will also remember that this victory, and your glory, was achieved under my command. There are bound to be a handful of survivors, and it will be your duty to make sure there is no-one one to dispute our resounding victory over such a cowardly surprise attack upon our army. Let us proceed – and remember, *no prisoners!'*

'*No prisoners, sir!'* they roared back.

Bucher turned and smiled icily at his faithful officer. 'Get the wine ready, Colonel, and plenty of glasses to pass around. I want us all to enjoy the nectar of the gods as we dispatch the last of the enemy to join their twenty thousand comrades in the kingdom of eternal pain. Quickly now! The dust is disappearing by the second.'

Bucher's entourage moved past the mound of dead officers and knights that had not been fully obscured by the dust, and continued towards the center of the grasslands. There were no sounds, no cries of pain. Nothing. Utter silence. Bucher held up his hand and grinned triumphantly at his men. His cannons had pulverized every soldier. The psychopath was having his greatest moment.

They sat quietly on their mounts while the grassland slowly revealed itself. Visibility improved gradually as the minutes passed. One hundred paces, two hundred, four hundred, a thousand paces.

Bucher stared in horror at the sight before him. The officers and soldiers turned to him as he scanned the killing field.

Not one soldier, living or dead. Not one horse. No discarded weapons. No armor. *Nothing!* Earl Carlos Bucher saw absolutely nothing but tufts of wild grass, rocks, dust and empty hills.

'Impossible,' he whispered. His eyes narrowed to slits. '*Impossible!*' he roared. 'Tell me what I am seeing is impossible! Tell me!'

No-one spoke. The first to speak would surely lose his head.

Bucher closed his eyes for several moments. *I'm dreaming. Get a grip on reality. All right, time to get on with it, men, while I have some wine to celebrate.* He relaxed and opened his eyes again and saw – nothing. He fought to keep from throwing up.

Looking at the nearest general, he asked softly, 'What happened here, General?' Then he roared, 'Did you forget to shove cannon-balls into the muzzles?'

The general was furious at the insinuation. *You dare pull your sword on me, Bucher, and I'll skewer you quicker than you can blink.* He placed his hand over his sword on the side facing away from his detested commander.

'No, sir,' he replied calmly. 'If you look closer, you will see thousands of shattered cannon-ball remnants strewn all over the grasslands as far as the eye can see.'

Bucher focused into the distance. The general was right. He could see whole as well as smashed remnants of cannon-balls strewn everywhere. 'So what happened, General? What are we looking at?'

The general was secretly delighted at the earl's predicament. 'Sir, I believe we have just witnessed a performance by the greatest magician the world has ever known! At the peak of a raging battle, the magician has gathered a 20,000 strong army directly in front of our cannons, and then made it vanish into thin air! Nothing less than sheer genius.'

CHAPTER 72

Dinner was early to allow time later for Marcus and Yannis to meet with junior officers to discuss future strategies. Heavily bandaged, Yannis had recovered surprisingly well and joined in the festivities, with Melissa clinging to his arm like a cub to its mother. Ale and wine flowed freely, and there were endless toasts, with most of the words drowned out by cheering and background noises.

Several toasts were directed towards Zhang Chen, who was looked at with a mixture of awe and fear for his exploits earlier that day. However, most seemed to be directed at Isabella, who sat quietly throughout.

The party atmosphere eventually eased and many drifted away for a well-earned rest, leaving about one hundred when Yannis rose, letting out a few exaggerated groans for Melissa's benefit.

He held up his watered-down ale and addressed the gathering, 'A meeting of officers will commence within the hour, so I now propose a final toast before some of us have to leave.' He raised his glass higher. 'Isabella, you will be remembered as one of our nation's most remarkable young women, and we're all so proud of you. Here's to you and your achievements today.' There were rousing cheers as the revelers up-ended their glasses and mugs.

Still standing, Yannis continued, 'Before we leave, I would like to add that Isabella and I earlier discussed the amazing events of the day, and we'd like to share some of the information with you. Isabella will go first. Isabella?'

In a soft voice, Isabella related how she had unexpectedly found herself on the front lines, her dueling with several soldier, and how her life had been saved by one of her combatants because she had shown him mercy. The audience gasped as she recounted how the soldiers, in recognition of her swordsmanship and gallantry shown to her combatants, had opened a path for *Barca* to aid her escape. Loud applause followed after completing the story with her dramatic rescue by Yannis.

After Isabella indicated that she had finished, Yannis shook his head in amazement, grinned and held up his hand. 'With just one miserable little rescue, I'm hardly worthy of mention! Gather around, everyone, while I tell you the story about how Isabella rescued an entire *army!*'

Corporal Luis Valdez called out. 'Yannis, ah, I mean *sir*, after you finish, I can add a few thing as I would have been among the last to see anything before the dust totally blanketed the front line. I actually witnessed the cannon explode in Isabella's face!'

Another voice called out from the back of the crowd: Alexander duPonti. 'And we have something very special to show Isabella, but it will take some time to complete. One of our artists will need to spend a little time with you, Isabella, but I promise you it will be worth waiting for.'

Yannis gave both men the thumbs up, lowered his voice, and started to tell the story to his spellbound audience:

> Marcus had heard the enemy trumpets sound the withdrawal. He immediately held up his hand in front of his trumpeter, counted slowly to ten and brought his arm down in a slashing motion. Others had been told what to look out for, and immediately swung into action.
>
> Cavalry reserves near the ridge had already swept over the top to arrange for every available wagon to be emptied and brought to the ridge, just out of sight. The troops on the grasslands trudged directly along its center, deliberately kicking into the surface as they went. The wind did the rest. Fine sand and dust was sucked into the air in whirlpools and carried towards the enemy lines. Ahead of them, Johan and his men were busy preparing rows of shields tied to lengths of rope. By the time the troops reached and passed them, Johan's men were almost obscured from the enemy's view by the dust. The troops continued their march into relatively clean air.
>
> 'Remove all armor!' Marcus shouted the order and Yannis rode along the lines of soldiers on the hill, giving instructions. 'Place them in neat stacks and start marching downhill. I repeat, *downhill*. The enemy will change the aim of the cannons away from the hills, and onto the grasslands where they can still see everyone is heading.'

Minutes later, Yannis pulled up next to Johan. The giant barely had to look up at Yannis. 'We're completely blanketed by dust, Skipper. The enemy is blinded, they can't see us now. Give us the word and we're off.'

'Skipper?'

'Sorry, boss.' Johan chuckled. 'We're used to calling the boss *skipper*. You're the boss, so you're the skipper. Do you mind?'

'Johan, you have my permission to call me anything you want for the rest of your life.'

Johan grinned and winked. 'Right you are, Skipper.'

'All right, let's move it.'

The ropes had been tied to the saddles of the men's horses. Ten riders slowly moved away from the enemy lines at a forty-five degree angle; the other ten moved at the same angle but in the other direction. The dragged shields ploughed the ground to expose the dry sub-surface to the wind. The result was astonishing. Johan's mounts did not have to move faster than a walk to raise enough dust to obliterate the entire grasslands from the enemy's view within minutes. Like an explosion, the wind then drove the dust over the hills and up to the ridge.

Yannis raised his arm, and a bugle sounded for the men already on the grasslands to make a right turn and quick-march towards the hills. The men heading downhill paused, fully turned, and marched back up the hills towards the ridge. Masked behind the screen of dust, these sudden changes in direction away from the plains went unseen by the enemy.

Yannis had 3,000 cavalry mounts at his disposal and made good use of them. Every rider brought ten horses tied together to pick up the soldiers on the grasslands, who had the greatest distance to walk. Two to a horse, 1,500 horses carried 3,000 soldiers to the crest, where the soldiers dismounted and the horses proceeded to water troughs to refresh and rest. The remaining 1,500 horses stopped half-way up the hill, where another 3,000 soldiers dismounted and marched the rest of the way, while those horses returned to the grasslands for a second load to take all the way to the crest. The two groups of horses rotated so that they were watered and rested after every second load.

'Time to bring the wagons,' Marcus shouted to Yannis, who acknowledged with a salute, and raised a flag to a man watching from the ridge. Screened from the enemy by the dust, the wagons flooded down the slope to pick up the weapons and armor, which were then unloaded beyond the ridge. Wounded were attended to on the field, and those unable to walk or ride were transported in the wagons. As the marching soldiers passed the ridge they picked up the unloaded weapons and armor before continuing. Ownership would be sorted out later. The last to leave the slopes in the wagons were the dead.

By the time the first cannon-ball blasted across the grassland, the last of the Southern army was more than half-way up the hill and invisible to the enemy. Marcus was at the rear, determined to be the last man to safety.

Yannis caught up with him. 'We're almost there, General. The last man should be over the ridge in about ten minutes. By the time the enemy finds out what's happened, it will be too late in the day for them to do anything, but I've set up defensive positions just in case. Besides, they've lost so many soldiers I don't think our beloved earl will want to lose more. He already has a lot of explaining to do. Quite frankly, I wouldn't like to be in his shoes right now.'

Marcus nodded in agreement. 'What's your estimate of their casualties?'

Yannis grimaced. 'It was horrendous down there. They were piled waist high in places, poor souls. I would have to say at least 10,000, perhaps as many as 15,000 dead, plus untold numbers injured.'

'Ours?'

'Approximately 600 dead; less than 2,000 wounded. That's 600 more dead than I would like, but from a battle point of view, and considering what we were up against, I would have to say we've done well. Nicho's last order was surely the most effective military order ever given, sir.'

'Indeed it was. We would not be standing here if the earl had moved first. Every one of us would be dead by nightfall. He's a *take no prisoners* commander, that one. It's time to revert to first names, by the way.'

Yannis nodded and looked up the hill as the last of the men disappeared over the ridge. 'Are you satisfied that the army is safe now, Marcus?'

'Yes, I'm satisfied.'

'Then I say it's time to get Isabella out of trouble.'

'Absolutely.' Marcus hesitated. 'Any ideas?'

'None. I'm just going to ride straight at them and keep slashing to give her a chance to get away.'

'That's certain death. There are thousands of them.'

'It might be enough of a diversion for her to escape. She might be able to scramble onto my mount. Right now, she is the most important person we have. Besides, you'll be with me, so it will turn out fine. I left some men on the fringe of the dust to keep an eye on her. I'll head down there for a quick update while you check progress up top. I'll come for you in five minutes.'

'I'll be waiting.' The two men saluted and rode off in opposite directions.

There had not been a sound from his audience while Yannis told the story. No one had even refilled their glass.

'You deceived me, Yannis. You never intended to come for me at all, did you?' Marcus smiled as he wagged an admonishing finger at him.

Luis Valdez waited for glasses and mugs to be replenished before he stood and faced the audience. Delighted to be the center of attention, he knew his exciting eye-witness account would be retold many times. He related every detail of Isabella's dueling, and was not disappointed with the reaction.

'Oh, Isabella, how can you do all these things?' Melissa cried out. 'You are out of your mind!'

With a grin and a shrug, Isabella responded, 'It seemed like a good idea at the time. I could hardly ask them to make me a sandwich to go, could I?'

Yannis was sitting directly in front of Isabella while he listened to Luis. He was realizing just how capable a young woman she had become.

He looked into her eyes as they sparkled and flickered from the firelight and saw a different person to the one he had seen that very morning. He knew then that the *little kid* had left for good. The memory of their shared laughter echoing across the valley flooded over him like a wave.

Yannis rose abruptly. 'It's time for the meeting. Sorry, Isabella, no rest for the wicked, I'm afraid. We need you to be there as well.' He leaned down to kiss Melissa's cheek. 'I'll see you tomorrow, Melissa.'

Luis Valdez watched wistfully as Yannis kissed Melissa, sighed heavily and walked into the darkening night.

CHAPTER 73

The junior officers crowded into the meeting tent around Marcus and Yannis. Isabella sat cross-legged on the ground at the far edge of the crowd, fighting hard against falling asleep.

'Men,' Marcus addressed the crowd, 'we're all tired so I'll get straight to the point. Yannis and I have made up a list of promotions, interim only, until confirmed at home base. The list, together with a report regarding today's events, has already been dispatched. Although I expect all recommendations to be approved it is, of course, possible that some senior officers will be sent to us, but it would take weeks for them to reach us. I'll pass the list around now, so you can see who will take which position while I continue.'

Marcus waited for the hum of excitement to die down. 'There is another interim promotion to consider. Many already know about Isabella fighting alone on the front lines while we made good our escape. Yannis and I agreed to join forces for a rescue attempt. However, he first ensured the escape of the army before going to her rescue. He then deceived me by going alone. I was furious when I first found out, but quickly calmed down when I realized his reasoning. Yannis is a soldier who put his army, his men and his nation before any one person, including my granddaughter. He also deliberately left me behind so that the army would have at least one senior officer to lead in the event of his demise. That shows that Yannis is able to rationalize, prioritize and make crucial decisions under battle conditions. As lead in the first cavalry charge, his courage proved to be without equal. I therefore included him in the list, to be promoted to general. Not only that, my recommendation is that he be appointed commander-in-chief of the campaign itself.

'Yannis might seem young for that responsibility, but there have been many younger, and he has now proven his credentials.' Marcus glanced around the room for several moments. 'It's common for the soldiers in the field in battle conditions to choose or approve of their commanding officer. So, I ask you: are there any objections to my recommendation?'

A murmur and nods swept the crowded tent. Finally a voice spoke. 'General, there appear to be no dissenters. I would like to add that Yannis was seemingly everywhere on the battlefield to organize our escape. The timing, planning and organisation were amazing. Our escape from being blasted to pieces is something we'll treasure forever. Without that plan we would now be dead – every one of us. Simply brilliant! Yannis is to be congratulated, and he should certainly be our commander-in-chief. I believe a round of applause is in order.'

Yannis jumped to his feet and raised both arms. 'Wait, wait, wait! Quiet, please.' A hush fell over the crowd. 'Thank you for your kind words, Yancko. Ah, I mean *Captain Geraldis*. There is much truth in what you said, but I must make something clear to all. Those of you who remained at the end of the party now know how we escaped, but for those of you who were not there: yes, the plan was brilliant, and it did save our lives, but the thing is, it wasn't my plan.'

Marcus and Yannis turned their heads towards Isabella. 'Your savior is sitting over there, half asleep,' Marcus said softly. 'Isabella gave us the plan just minutes before she attacked the enemy single-handed. We simply carried it out.'

Those still unaware of Isabella's role in their escape, turned to stare at her. She looked up at them, grimaced and shrugged. 'Just one of those spur-of-the-moment things,' she said with a yawn.

Yancko walked toward Isabella. 'I hardly know what to say. To say surprised is an understatement.' He looked around the tent. 'I will take the liberty, however, to speak on behalf of everyone here. Without your plan, there would have been no escape. Thank you for our lives, Isabella.' He reached down, picked up her hand, and kissed the back of it. 'I do believe a round of applause, then – for Isabella – is in order.' Isabella nodded her appreciation through the applause.

Marcus returned to business at hand. 'We must now plan our next moves. It's an open floor. Let's hear your thoughts and ideas. We'll then use the best of them to come up with a strategy.'

An hour later the general thrust was to attack the enemy at regular intervals, and to inflict maximum damage before fleeing. From the sidelines, Isabella shook her head slowly, but did not speak. One of the newly promoted officers said, 'We did extremely well today before the enemy brought out the cannons. Up to that point I estimate the success rate at between ten and twenty-to-one in our favor. If we can continue to fight better than the enemy, we might be in with a chance.'

There was a murmur of agreement from the crowd, but a soft voice cut across the hum. 'Folly, folly, folly.'

The tent went quiet instantly. 'What was that, Isabella?' Marcus asked.

'Folly, folly, folly,' Isabella repeated, a little louder.

No longer was there a General Karamus to scoff when Isabella spoke. The men knew that Isabella had paid her dues and had earned their respect, so they stared at her with interest.

Isabella rose and walked over to the man who had just spoken. She knelt beside him and put her arm around his shoulder. 'You are all of similar mind so please don't think that I'm criticizing you, Major Llandro. I, too, thought the same not so long ago.' Isabella evidently remembered every man's name and new rank. 'It's all in the numbers.'

The major feigned a swoon. 'For your arm around my shoulder, Isabella, please feel free to criticize me for a week. I don't often get young beauties draped around me these days.' That brought laughter and a cheer of agreement.

Isabella smiled and left her arm where it was. She knew she had just won another ally when the going got tough. 'Fighting *better* might win us some battles, but it won't win the war. Think about the numbers today. We were up against more than 40,000. Next time, they'll have their cannons at the ready, and we'll be up against more than 60,000. When the Second division arrives we'll be up against double that, and you can triple the number and double the cannons when all three divisions have met up. We can't possibly achieve the same attrition rate as today, but even if we did, the ultimate result would be the same: their numbers will continue to increase as rapidly as ours decline. That would put us on the road of no hope. Agreed, Major?'

Major Llandro nodded. 'I guess you're right. As you say, it's all in the numbers.'

Isabella gave his shoulder a squeeze, rose, and walked over to Yannis, her shoulder brushing against his as she sat down and faced the crowd. Marcus leaned forward slightly to give Isabella a silent message: *you're sitting a little too close to Yannis!* She thrust her face forward a fraction, eyes flashing, to give him a message of her own: *mind your business!*

'So what are you thinking, Isabella?' Yannis asked, completely oblivious to what was going on under his nose.

'Well, as a matter of fact, I do have a plan.'

'We're back in business.' Captain Geraldis looked pleased. 'Brains as well as beauty! Let it be known to one and all present that when you decide to open your queue for a suitor, you can count me in!'

Isabella laughed. 'Why, thank you, Captain. It will be some time before I open any line, but when I do, I'll place you near the front.'

Yancko pursed his lips and frowned. 'Hm-m-m. *Near* the front. That sounds a little like you already have someone in mind to be *at* the front.'

Isabella flushed as she wagged a finger at Yancko. 'Now you behave yourself, Captain. I'm too young to have anyone in mind.'

'Isabella?' Yannis sounded impatient.

'Yes, General Christos.' Isabella dug her elbow gently into Yannis' waist on his good side as she addressed the men. 'It won't be a matter of fighting *better*, it will be a matter of fighting *smarter*. If we attack now, they will be waiting, and they have the numbers to trap us. We must make the enemy move against *us* so we can trap *them*. A war strategy must accurately surmise what the enemy is likely to do, and then make them pay for *their* folly. This is how I see events unfolding. You had better make yourselves comfortable, gentlemen.' Isabella was fully awake and in her element.

'The earl suffered horrendous casualties today, and he has a lot of explaining to do, both to his own men, and to his government. One more day of casualties like that will see his head served up to his emperor on a platter. Therefore, he won't pursue us. He'll wait for his Second division, which won't arrive for eight to ten weeks. The Third division is so far to the east they won't join him until next summer. So I believe we can disregard them for the time being. By the time the first and Second divisions prepare for the trek through the mountains, winter will be upon them, and it will be too late to start.'

Isabella paused to take a sip of water while the men digested these facts. 'They will, however, spend time leading up to winter to move the cannons, powder and other heavy equipment deep into the mountains to save time when winter finally breaks. I'm counting on that. It means we have fall to next spring to regroup. You can relax. We are not in imminent danger. You can start to make plans to return to our sanctuary in the valley. Time and the coming winter, gentlemen, are our friends.'

Marcus asked, 'What do you think, Yannis? You're the commander-in-chief now.'

Yannis looked at Marcus, and then at Isabella. 'Isabella makes good sense. Let's do it. Decision made.' That brought a cheer from the crowd.

The men were only too happy to look forward to a few months of peace – and life.

Isabella twisted her mouth. 'There is just one more item, if I may?' The crowd quietened immediately. 'I'm afraid you won't like what I want.'

Yannis felt a knot of concern form in his stomach. He had seen first-hand how Isabella seemed to seek out and thrive on danger. 'What is it that you want, Isabella?'

Isabella folded her arms across her chest, appearing almost aggressive. 'Twenty brave soldiers, 190 riding horses, plus ten wagons with enough horses to haul them. The men must be ready to leave by five in the morning.'

'And this is for …?'

'There are almost two hundred missing soldiers, and they can only be close to, or behind, where the cannons were placed. Most are probably dead, but there may be some injured. All of them have been on the battlefield the whole afternoon and evening. If there are any survivors, they won't last beyond midday tomorrow when the heat sets in. They must be rescued first thing in the morning.'

'The enemy will probably take revenge upon anyone who turns up. The men you want to send are likely to be killed.' Yannis sounded skeptical.

'Perhaps. That's why I stipulated *brave* soldiers. That's also why I said there's something I want that you won't like.'

'What is it we won't like?'

'Included in the 190 horses, I want the 150 horses that belonged to the knights.'

'*What?* Those are the most magnificent horses I have ever seen. Their worth is beyond imagination.' Yannis was horrified. 'We can put those horses to good work with our best men.'

'See? I told you that you wouldn't like it, but I want them, and I won't take no for an answer!'

Yannis calmed down. 'Why those particular horses?'

'What's more important? Our men on the battlefield, dead or injured – or the horses? I propose that we present those horses as a peace-offering in exchange for our fallen soldiers. The gift will also make it safer for the twenty men who will go to get them. It's a good trade, Yannis.'

Major Llandro spoke directly to Yannis. 'As far as I'm concerned, General, whatever Isabella wants, Isabella gets.' That brought several shouts of agreement.

Yancko Geraldis raised his hand. 'Isabella, you'll only need to find another nineteen men, because I'll go. You're right; we must do everything we can to get our men back.' Several others called out that they would join Yancko.

Yannis held his hands up. 'All right. All right. You'll get what you want, Isabella. And Yancko, you can go, but I can't afford to send too many officers for obvious reasons. I'll leave it to you to find some good men.' He turned to Isabella. 'I hope you're not planning on going. The enemy will snatch you if they see you again. I don't want to risk losing you a second time.'

'Madame Rosa Tissone will accompany the men,' Isabella replied.

Yannis looked puzzled. 'Madam Rosa? She's in charge of the theatre productions for entertaining the troops. Why Madame Rosa?'

Isabella stood up. 'Madam Rosa has many talents, but there is one in particular that makes her perfect to assist in this mission. I'm going to see her right now. I'll be back in a little while.'

Yannis looked worried. 'It will be a very dangerous mission. Are you sure Rosa will agree to assist?'

'Oh, I can absolutely guarantee that Rosa Tissone will accompany the men.'

'Very well. I'll see you in a little while then?'

'No, as soon as I return I'll retire for the night. I'm exhausted. Don't expect to see me until tomorrow afternoon. Goodnight, Grandfather.' She leaned down to give Marcus a quick hug and a kiss on his cheek. Still leaning over, she moved slightly towards Yannis but did not make contact as she whispered into his ear, 'Thank you so much for rescuing me today. You were wonderful. Oh, and by the way, you look very *young* to be a general, Yannis. Congratulations!'

Yannis' chuckle was cut short when Isabella straightened and kicked his leg. His eyes opened wide with pain and surprise. The watching men were stunned into silence. '*Isabella*, what the – !' He rubbed his leg. 'What did I do to deserve that?'

'You deserved that for risking your life to rescue ...' Here she paused, placed her hands on her hips and glared at him, '... a *little kid* like me. Good night, General Christos.' She flicked her thick hair over her shoulders and stalked from the tent to a round of applause.

Yancko groaned with disappointment as he instinctively knew whom Isabella had placed at the front of her queue.

An hour later, as she lay on her straw mattress, Isabella's most vivid recollection of the evening was that Yannis had referred to her in a public forum as a young woman. *At last! It's been almost three years. Will I have enough time?* His words echoed in her mind a hundred times before she finally drifted off to sleep. Her last thought was of staring down the barrel of an exploding gun.

CHAPTER 74

A lone figure, hooded and wrapped in a soft shroud that reached the ground, slowly materialized like a ghost out of the early morning mist. Seconds later the figure was followed by a number of men dressed in loose shirts and baggy pants. Less visible against the background of mist were the horses, led by ropes bunched in ties. The group paused and looked across the battlefield at the sad remnants of the carnage that had taken place the previous day. A small number of officers could be seen overseeing about 50 men undertaking a salvage operation.

Led by the shrouded figure, the group slowly made their way in the direction of the officers, their left hands holding the ropes out wide, their right hands held high to signal that they were unarmed. The officers and the men stopped their work, straightened, and stared at the ghostly apparition with a mix of disbelief and suspicion.

When the twenty men came closer, they paused while the hooded figure continued to move slowly towards the officers, appearing to glide rather than walk. The men were speechless, mesmerized by the unexpected event.

The shrouded figure finally stopped in front of a particular officer and bowed graciously before making eye contact. The officer moved his head slightly to better hear the soft, lilting voice that floated towards him. A young woman's voice.

'I wish to speak to the officer in charge of the salvage operation. Your bearing suggests that you are he.'

The officer was a tall, broad-shouldered man around thirty; intelligent hazel eyes and the customary military mustache featured prominently in a handsome face. He looked directly at the young woman, then at the horses, then back at the woman. Seemingly pleased to have stood out among his peers, he spoke slowly and distinctly. 'I am Captain Andreas

Fransz, and you are correct: I am in command. Who are you and what is it that you want?'

'I am Madam Rosa Tissone, Captain Fransz. The men you see behind me belong to the enemy forces you fought so bravely here yesterday. I am one of their camp assistants.'

The officers glanced at each other, dumbfounded by the blunt confession. A few of the troops instinctively placed their hands on their swords.

'We come unarmed, Captain. We come not to wage battle, nor to interfere with what you are doing, but to ask a concession of you.'

'Concession! You dare come here demanding concessions?'

'On the contrary, Captain Fransz, we are not in a position to demand anything, merely to ask.'

'And what is it that you ask?'

'My husband is among the missing. He is not likely to have survived, but I asked permission to come and search for him, and to take him with us if we find him. We also wish to take our officers and men so that we may give their souls the respect they deserve. If we find any of our men wounded we would like to also take them with us. They should not be left on the field to die, alone and in pain. Should we find any of your troops alive during our search, we will bring them to your attention.'

The Captain remained silent for several seconds. 'Come closer,' he said. 'I feel uncomfortable speaking to someone I cannot see. Please remove your hood. Show yourself.'

Madame Tissone took a step forward. She held Captain Franz's eyes with a steady gaze, reached up with both hands and pushed the hood back, allowing it to fall to her shoulders. Black hair, partly covered by a pale brown scarf, fell in soft waves over her neck and shoulders. Some of the hair had escaped under the front of the scarf to form a short fringe across her forehead.

The men behind the officers shuffled closer. No-one spoke until Captain Franz finally found his voice. 'You seem a little young to have a husband, Madam Tissone. What is his name?'

'His name is Franciscus, sir, and yes, I am a little young, as you say.'

'How so?'

Madam Tissone lowered her gaze, brought it back up and looked directly into his. 'I was of age, but it was not a matter of choice. I was with child, and my parents were not very understanding. Perhaps, if you grant our request, our son might still have a father if we find him wounded rather than … not.'

Captain Fransz turned, walked several paces, turned around and walked back. 'You are brave, all of you, bordering on the insane, actually, to simply walk up here expecting to just wander at will. I suspect that you have something to offer us in return? A little peace offering, perhaps?'

Madam Tissone allowed a warm smile to slowly spread over her face. Her eyes sparkled. The eyes of Captain Fransz and those flanking him never left her face.

Madam Tissone gave a small bow. 'Indeed we have, Captain Fransz. One hundred and fifty, to be exact. Are they not *beautiful*? These horses belong to your brave soldiers who yesterday attacked and killed our entire command. Despite the damage they caused, our troops recognize your knights as heroes. They say they have never seen such courage and say the horses belong to the knight in death, as in life. We are here to hand them to you, irrespective of the outcome of our request.'

'I see, I see.' As he gazed into Rosa's eyes, a sudden feeling of foreboding swept over Fransz like a dark, icy cloud. Something was not right. What was it? This young woman was too beautiful, too composed, too much in control, too … *something*. The captain's right hand suddenly swept across his body and drew out his sword in one swift, smooth motion.

Startled, his fellow officers also gripped their swords. Fransz raised his left hand towards them, stopping further action. He brought his sword down until it pointed directly at Madame Tissone's sternum.

'*Miss Isabella Mondeo!*' he snapped.

CHAPTER 75

Madam Rosa Tissone forced her breathing to slow as her heart hammered to the point of pain. There was no outward change in her appearance as she gazed steadily into the captain's eyes. Fransz raised his sword up to her throat and moved it slowly back and forth, but kept its point a respectful pace away. 'So, tell me about her.'

'What do you wish to know, Captain?'

'Anything, everything. Everyone is intrigued by her. Her bravery would easily see her brazenly turn up here, and at first I was sure it was you, but I was wrong. I am told she has the most amazing green eyes, but you do not, beautiful though yours are.' He lowered the sword until it pointed to the ground, lifted it slightly and plunged it hard into the sand. His deliberate attempt to shake her demeanor was met without a blink.

'She is pleasant enough. Somewhat impetuous, perhaps. She was not supposed to be at, or view, the battle, but flouted her instructions. She is in her teens, and an orphan.'

'Orphan? Tell me about that.'

'Her father was killed in an accident, and her mother died a few months later from a broken heart. She joined the camp followers to be close to one of her few remaining relatives, an uncle, one of the senior officers.'

'Did she lose that relative yesterday?'

'Yes, she did. Just about every officer was lost, Captain Fransz. Her uncle will be one of those we wish to search for; we wish to give him an honorable burial.'

'How was it that Miss Mondeo ended up at the front-lines?'

Madam Rosa smiled. 'There has been much talk about that. It was an accident. Her horse took fright and bolted, and she was thrown off in the midst of your soldiers. No-one fully understands how she managed to get away.'

'Her horse came back for her, Madam Tissone. I saw it myself. Even from a distance I could see what a magnificent specimen it was.'

'Her horse, *Barca*, means the world to her. It was fitting, then, that she be rescued by her horse.'

'M-m-m ... *Barca*. That means *Thunderbolt*.'

'Oh, is that what it means?'

'It might surprise you to learn that she outfought five of our skilled swordsmen before her escape. She had several at her mercy, but spared their lives.'

'It is not in Isabella's nature to put anyone to the sword, especially if they were at her mercy. She would rather allow herself to be put to the sword.'

'When the men realized she was not there to harm them, it became a contest to see who could knock the sword from her hand. No one managed it; it was just the opposite, in fact. The men found it very entertaining. I have never known anyone, man or woman, with such skills, such speed – like lightning.' Fransz put his head back and laughed. '*Thunderbolt and lightning!* What a wonderful combination!' The captain kept his smile, but went quiet as he replayed the scenes in his mind.

'May I ask how you know her name, Captain?'

'The prisoners.'

'You have prisoners? How many, Captain?'

'It would be better that you not know how many, in case our supreme commander decides that their fate is to be a short one. He has a nickname and I'm afraid it is not *the merciful one*. Now that we are on that subject, tell me, Madame Tissone: why would we not simply dispose ... of your soldiers and toss them on top of the others?' He indicated the field with a sweep of his arm. 'Then we could take all of the horses and carry on our merry way?'

'Of course, Captain, you could do so. Quite easily, in fact, as we come unarmed. If you *fear* the unarmed men who have brought you your horses, you should put them to the sword at once. I know you do not fear me, an unarmed woman, but I must of course also be put to the sword immediately. You can have no witnesses to the slaughter of unarmed men who wish to assist the wounded.'

She smiled before continuing, her soft, melodic voice floating towards him like a whisper on the breeze. 'We await your decision. We are anxious to proceed to learn the fate of Franciscus and any injured, if your generosity permits. Our fate is now in your hands, Captain Fransz.'

Fransz turned towards his men as if to seek their counsel, but turned back to Madame Tissone without speaking to them, this time with a smile. He took a deep breath and exhaled heavily. 'I must be feeling lazy. I seem to have lost interest in adding more bodies to the sad sight behind me. Thank you for returning our horses. You have all shown courage to bring them to us in good faith, and we accept them in the same spirit. You may search the field and take your injured – if you find any.'

He looked around at the carnage behind him that seemed to stretch to the horizon. 'I will see what I can do about the prisoners. Perhaps a ransom can be arranged. If so, I will send a messenger to you. I imagine a piece of silver for each will suffice. I hope you find your husband, Madame Tissone.'

'We thank you, Captain.'

The young woman was followed into the field of death by the twenty men. The stench was appalling, but they made no attempt to cover their faces. They split into groups of two and began a systematic search. Searching was relatively easy due to the colors of uniforms.

During the first half hour they found seven enemy soldiers alive, but none of their own. Spears were pushed into the ground and pieces of bright colored clothing tied to the ends as markers.

A short time later, low groans brought them to one of their own soldiers, badly wounded but alive. He was young, barely twenty, and delirious. A dead horse had fallen across the lower half of his body, making it impossible for him to escape without help. It took four men to lift the horse's neck and shoulders to enable another two to drag the man clear.

Rosa caught her breath when she saw the man's injury: his left leg was missing from above the knee. It was such a clean cut it could only have been caused by a powerful blow from a sword. Ironically, the weight of the horse on his thigh had kept him from bleeding out, and had saved his life – so far.

One of the men cradled the injured man against his chest and trickled water into his mouth. His eyes fluttered, and then opened slowly. He looked up, seemingly without focus, before closing his eyes again. A sudden cough splattered water over the young woman kneeling in from of him, but she seemed not to notice. His eyes opened again, this time widening as he looked into the eyes of Rosa Tissone and felt her cool hands on his face. 'Paradise,' he whispered hoarsely, 'at last.' He smiled weakly and lost consciousness.

A cry in the distance signaled that another man had been found alive. Rosa motioned for two men to tie a pressure cloth around the injured man's leg and carry him to the departure point. Several more were found alive during the following hour. When they were certain they had scoured every area where their men had fallen, the group came together for their final grisly task.

'It's time to check on the officers. They are all in the one spot, over there. Then we must hurry back with the injured,' a huge bearded man murmured softly.

Rosa nodded. 'Let's go.'

The bearded giant immediately stepped in front of her. He looked down with compassion. 'There will be no one alive. Every man has been cut to pieces. There is no need for you to go there. It is not something you should see.'

A look of fury passed across Rosa's face before fading rapidly. She reached out to squeeze the giant's wrist and nodded. 'Go then,' she said simply. 'I will go back and tend to the injured and signal the men on the ridge to bring the wagons down.'

Minutes later the twenty men surveyed the scene before them in silence. Every senior officer of their army lay before them, dead, their devastating injuries a testament to the orders given the knights that none was to survive.

Major General Nicholas Manassis lay face down where he had fallen near some of the knights he had taken with him on his final journey. Directly beneath him lay the body of General Vlado Karamus, face down, with a cavalry sword reaching up through his spine, the blade glinting in the morning sunlight. One of the men gently lifted Manassis' body to the side while another put out his foot and pushed the general's body onto its side, exposing the gold-braided handle pressed hard up against his chest. The man reached down, wrapped his hand around the grip and slowly pulled the sword from the body. He held it out for the others to see.

Every officer's sword was embroidered and inlaid differently from others. There was no mistake as to whose sword had been buried in the general's chest.

It belonged to Major General Nicholas Manassis.

'We will take our leave, Captain Fransz. We have loaded our dead in the wagons and we found eleven wounded, including my husband. He is alive, but badly wounded, and unconscious. He has lost his leg, so his chances are not good, but I will move heaven and earth to save him, so we must go quickly. We did also find some of your injured troops and, as promised, have placed marker spears at their sides – not *through* their sides,' she smiled.

'I'm glad you found your husband, Madam Tissone. It somehow seems appropriate after the risk you and your men have taken to come here.'

'I put my trust in finding a gentleman – and well as a soldier – and I did. Again, thank you. And mark my words, Captain Fransz, your God will reward you well for you kindness and generosity. I know it.'

The captain chuckled. 'What? Gold will pour from the heavens and fill my pockets?'

'No, no, not gold or trinkets, Captain. A mountain of gold cannot match the reward that will be yours on or before your dying day. When it arrives, you will feel it in your heart. You will recognize it, and I promise you that you will not be disappointed. Perhaps we will meet again, Captain Fransz. I bid you and your men good day.'

Captain Fransz stared silently at the small party of his enemy as they slowly vanished back into the remnants of the morning mist with their wagons of dead and injured. His face was brooding, his eyes narrowed.

'Sir?' Sergeant-at-arms Mehudi stood a few paces away, leaning on his shield. 'You seem somewhat disturbed.'

'Yes, you are right in your observation, Mehudi. I *am* disturbed, more than disturbed. I can't for the life of me think of the word that accurately describes how I feel.'

Fransz took a deep breath. 'Madam Tissone – she was very brave to come here, Mehudi. Perhaps too brave?' Now that he thought about it, she seemed to have had a calm confidence about the outcome of her approach. Such confidence normally came from experience, or a position of strength, but Madam Rosa was far too young for either.

Mehudi shifted from one leg to the other, nodded sagely and added, 'She did have strong motivation though, Captain: to search for her husband.'

'True, true,' Fransz murmured, still deep in thought, 'but still … there was something that earlier gave me a feeling of foreboding, and I still feel it.'

Mehudi picked up his shield and started walking towards the tethered horses for the return journey to camp. 'Still, I suppose it had a satisfactory result. Madam Tissone found her husband. Somewhat carved up, but still alive. Quite remarkable! By the way,' he added, 'have you thought of a word that describes how you felt earlier?'

Fransz was in his saddle and signaled for his men to move. 'Madame Tissone seemed to read my mind. More, she seemed to *meet* my mind. Somehow, she was able to make me do whatever she wanted me to do, Mehudi. The best I can come up with is that I feel I've been manipulated.'

'Maneuvered, perhaps?' Mehudi offered with a smile.

'*Yes!* That's the word,' snorted Franz, 'but *out*-maneuvered is even more accurate. Somehow, I have been *out-maneuvered.*'

'Well,' said Mehudi, settling into his saddle, 'at least everyone got something from today's events. Madame Tissone found her husband – and other wounded. You secured 150 of our best horses at no cost to us, and you did that without turning us into savages by slaughtering unarmed men and a beautiful young woman.'

Fransz' face brightened. He was pleased that Mehudi had attached the credit of securing the 150 horses solely to Fransz. Those horses were priceless. They would be well received by senior command on their return to camp.

'True, Mehudi, true.' He was quiet for a few moments before he added quietly, 'That was no ordinary young woman, Mehudi. I have a feeling we will cross paths with her sometime in the future.'

'I hope so, Captain,' Mehudi mumbled dreamily. His heart had been swept away the moment she had dropped the hood to her shoulders. He did not think he would ever get that first sight of her out of his mind.

The mist had long gone by the time Rosa and her companions vanished over the crest of the hill. It was early afternoon by the time they reached the water troughs, where the injured were transferred to other waiting wagons, comfortably fitted out with thick furs and leather. Several women tended to their wounds and provided light snacks.

A number of waiting soldiers took over the task of transporting the wagons back to the main camp. Rosa waved her hand to gather the twenty men around her. 'We'll ride on ahead to convey the news of our success. I dare say we will be treated to a nice lunch. But before we go, I want to say how proud I am to know such brave men. That was a very, very risky mission, men. Were you worried?'

The bearded man spoke for the others, who were all beaming with pride. 'Not for one moment, Rosa. You were brilliant. It was like watching a master magician at work.'

She laughed at his compliment. 'You are much too kind, sir. I'm getting hot in here, so I'll get you to help me out of this cloak, please. Then we'll be off.' She held up her arms as two men moved forward and gently lifted the cloak over her head and tossed it into a wagon.

Rosa smiled her thanks as she smoothed down her leather jacket and skirt. The men crowded around, staring at her with mounting excitement as she reached up and untied the scarf to toss it into the wagon next to the cloak. She then placed her hand on top of her head and grinned as she slowly lifted off the beautifully crafted wig to a roar of approval. Golden hair shone in the sun, tumbling in thick waves past Isabella's shoulders. The aqua eyes of earlier that morning now shone green in the afternoon sun.

Captain Yancko Geraldis handed *Barca's* reins to her. 'Would you please face your troops as we present arms?' he asked. 'On your mounts, men,' he barked to the soldiers. He waited a few moments until they were mounted in precise double-formation. '*Present arms!*' he bellowed.

To a man they presented the young woman with a formal stiff-armed salute. 'We are proud to be the very first to serve under your command, Isabella!' Captain Geraldis' voice boomed across the valley. 'Let's go, at full gallop – you take the lead.'

'*Go Thunderbolt!*' Sensing something special from the raised voices, *Barca* spun around at Isabella's command and leapt into action. The troops followed. As soon as they reached full gallop, the men roared continuously from the excitement of the day. Isabella could not resist joining in and shouting at the top of her voice until she was hoarse.

The thunderous echo of two formations of hooves at full gallop, spearheaded by a golden-haired rider on a white stallion, followed a cloud of dust moving from one valley to the next at blinding speed.

CHAPTER 76

Yancko and his men spread the word as soon as they reached the main camp. Within minutes soldiers and camp followers streamed in from all directions. By the time lunch was served, several hundred had crowded around to listen. *Isabella has secured the release of all the dead and injured in a secret mission* were the words on everyone's lips. Her twenty men were treated like celebrities as they sat in a protective semi-circle around her.

Marcus and Yannis, however, were furious. Chen was philosophical and not surprised. Only a woman with the heart of a true Zen Master would risk her life for the dead.

Yancko hushed the crowd as he reported to Yannis, his commanding officer, who was seated on a chair on the outskirts. Melissa was sitting next to him with her hand on his knee. 'Sir, I swear we did not know that Rosa was Isabella until she told us on the way to the battlefield. We were surprised, but I have to admit we were all relieved at the same time. The moment we knew it was Isabella, we knew we'd be safe.' He turned to her. 'We'll follow you anywhere, anytime, Isabella.' Isabella reached out to squeeze his hand, too emotional to speak. Yancko then related the day's events in detail.

'You said prisoners were taken. Did the captain say how many?' Marcus asked when he had finished.

'No, sir. Captain Fransz told Isabella she would be better off not to know.'

'Sorry to interrupt, Yancko, but, in fact, they have thirty prisoners, Grandfather. We'll have to do everything we can to get them back.'

'I never heard him say *thirty*, or any other number,' Yancko put in, frowning.

'Actually, he did,' Isabella smiled. 'He obviously did not want it reported back by his own soldiers that he had divulged confidential information, so he told me in code.'

'I didn't hear any code.' Yancko looked puzzled.

'It was very subtle, Yancko. For ransom, he said we might need a piece of silver for each prisoner. It's an odd phrase, isn't it – *a piece of silver?* Gold is the more common currency for ransom. Attach those words to the most infamous phrase in Christendom and you get *thirty pieces of silver.* They have thirty prisoners, or a number close to that.'

Yancko sighed heavily and shook his head. 'That was clever. I missed that.'

Isabella patted his hand. 'You were supposed to miss it, as were his men.'

Yannis took the following pause to signify the end of the report. 'I guess that's about it. Thank you, Captain. It's time for us to prepare urgent reports for dispatch.'

Yancko looked uncomfortable. 'Well, sir, there is one other item, but it is of a confidential nature. Perhaps a little later ...'

Yannis nodded his thanks and waited for the crowd to drift away. As they departed, Isabella hugged each of the twenty men who had risked their lives with her that day. Soon only the usual half-dozen were left, and Yancko.

'So, what is it, Yancko?' Yannis asked.

'It would be best if no-one else were present, especially Isabella, sir.'

'It's first names when we're in private, Yancko.' Yannis glanced around at the faces of his closest friends. 'And our little group here is as private as you will ever get.'

'But sir, ah, Yannis ... it's about Nicholas. I don't think Isabella should hear this.'

Yannis looked at Isabella. 'Isabella has proven herself to be a soldier of the highest caliber these last couple of days and I believe she is up to hearing anything, even if it's about Nicholas.'

Isabella could have kissed him there and then, but restrained herself.

'Very well.' Yancko looked at Isabella with discomfort. 'Sorry, Isabella. No offense, but this is not a pleasant subject for anyone.' He turned back to Yannis and Marcus. 'We retrieved all the bodies of our officers. We had to pull the knights to one side to make sure we got all of ... ah ... the parts of our men. They had been hacked to pieces, poor souls. Every man was missing limbs, except for two: General Karamus and Nicholas. The general had a single wound, the weapon still in his body.' He hesitated and looked around at the faces staring at him, each knowing that there was something unpleasant to come.

Yannis nodded, indicating Yancko should continue.

'A sword buried to the hilt in General Karamus' chest was his only wound.'

'So?'

'The sword was very distinctive, Yannis. We recognized it.'

'Yes? Whose sword was it?'

'It belonged to Major General Manassis. Nicholas killed his commanding officer!'

Marcus felt sick as he realized the implications of an officer killing not only his superior officer, but the commander-in-chief of the nation's armed forces.

Isabella sat like an ice statue, with an expression to match.

Yannis remained silent for several moments. 'Thank you, Yancko. You and your men have done yourself proud today. It's time for you to get some rest.' Yancko saluted and turned to go.

'Don't forget, Isabella,' Yancko said as he left, 'anywhere, anytime.'

'As for you, young lady,' Yannis said, settling his gaze on Isabella, 'what do we do with you? Tie you up? What you did was amazing, but far too dangerous. You are going to worry me to death. Marcus, she's *your* granddaughter. You talk to her!'

Marcus leaned forward and took her hands in his. 'Isabella, we are all obviously very happy with today's outcome. We're also very proud of you, of course, but for goodness sake, that's twice in two days you have put yourself behind enemy lines. That's pretty much the same as placing your head in the lion's mouth.'

'Grandfather, only the calming presence of a young woman could have prevented the twenty men from being slaughtered in frenzy of revenge. There must have been some fifteen thousand bodies on that killing field. It was hard to tell exactly because they were piled up so high in places.'

'So many!' Marcus shook his head sadly. 'Fair enough. But we were under the impression that it was Madam Rosa Tissone who was going.'

'It *was* Madam Tissone, as far as the enemy is concerned. Rosa is a brilliant wig-maker, but not one to send into an enemy camp.'

'You must stop doing these things. Isabella. I really don't understand why you keep getting yourself into these dangerous escapades.'

Isabella rolled her eyes and sighed in exasperation. 'And I really don't know why you both keep wasting your breath trying to stop me!'

At that they gave up.

CHAPTER 77

Theo and Nina Karamus sat opposite King Ramesses and Dmitri Talavares while the king gave them the news of their son's death. Nina sat impassively, as if she had just listened to the announcement of her own death. Theo's face was a mask of fury as Ramesses recounted how Vlado had died.

Theo had received the summons to the palace less than two hours earlier. He had been ecstatic, fully expecting to be informed that the nation had surrendered to the Northern Region commander. The first thing he did was to send word to his colleagues to be ready to carry out their designated tasks within hours. His only niggling concern was that the king had requested his wife accompany him. That had not been anticipated.

Now he knew. He also knew he was in trouble. Big trouble. His colleagues had to be stopped from becoming impatient and acting prematurely. He had to get out of the palace immediately. It would take only one colleague to make a wrong move, and they would all hang. He had to get the upper hand, and fast.

'My son did not die *by the hand of a fellow officer!*' he roared. 'He was *murdered!* My son has been *murdered* by one of his own officers! This nation has never suffered such an outrage! Never!'

Ramesses jumped out of his chair and stood by Theo's side in an instant. 'There, there, calm yourself, Mr Kara … Theo.' He placed a hand gently on the man's shoulder. 'Theo, Nina, I cannot express how sorry and shocked I am to have to give you this most dreadful news. I know it's of little comfort to tell you that all except one or two of our most senior officers were killed in Monday's battle. I simply cannot imagine how it was that Vlado died by the sword of one of our most senior and trusted officers. Perhaps it was an accident. All I can offer you at this stage is that I have asked for – no, demanded – a full report of all the circumstances, from all witnesses, as to how this happened.'

Theo Karamus rose from his seat and stormed to the glass-paneled doors so that he could remove himself from the king's hand without being offensive. He needed no report; he knew exactly what had happened, and why. Before being killed, Manassis must have realized what was going on and had somehow managed a single strike at Vlado.

He slammed his palm down hard on the side table. 'That is simply not good enough, Your Majesty,' he yelled. 'A report will take weeks, months, and it will never reveal the truth. The witnesses are dead. Dead! Forget the report. I will tell you what the truth is …'

'But we don't yet know what the – ' the king tried to interject.

'I will tell you what the truth is, sir, and the nation is to be told the truth. At once! Today! The truth is that my son died a hero. In the heat of battle against a far superior force, one of his trusted officers, in an act of cowardice and treason, chose to murder. To save his own miserable skin, he wanted to avoid further battle. My dear wife, Nina, Vlado's heartbroken mother, and I demand that our son be publicly declared a national hero who died for his nation, and that Manassis be declared a coward and a traitor.'

Karamus stopped yelling and walked back to the desk to face Ramesses and Dmitri. He continued in a voice of icy calm.

'That statement of the truth is to be included in your public announcement, so that no-one will receive one piece of information without the other. If I should hear of any misunderstanding by the public that might stain my family's reputation, I will immediately withdraw my support for the on-going war effort. I will instruct all of my colleagues later today to do exactly the same. I assure you that the war effort will collapse without our economic and organizational support. Any attempt to protect the reputation of a coward and traitor who has murdered the nation's commander-in-chief will serve only to undermine the very fabric of the monarchy itself. You will therefore call a halt to any further investigation into our son's murder. It is irrelevant. Any report that even hints at staining the reputation of our son will see our nation fall into the hands of the Northern Region within days.'

'Come, Nina, we must leave and inform our family and friends of the untimely death of our heroic son and that a public funeral in his honor will be announced by His Majesty later today. Good day, sir, and thank you for personally informing us of this tragedy.' The two left without another word.

Dmitri sat back and rubbed his face. 'He doesn't hold back does he? There were a lot of threats there, even to the monarchy.'

'Theo's a tough businessman. It's the nature of the beast.'

'So what are you going to do?'

'That's easy. I'm going to do exactly what Theo has demanded. If I don't, the war is as good as lost right now. I'm afraid our good friend Nicholas Manassis will have to pay a hefty price for what he did.'

Dmitri nodded his agreement.

Theo Karamus' colleagues were more than shocked at the news. They were dismayed and frightened.

'Don't worry,' Theo said, trying to calm himself as much as them. 'Nothing will change, other than the time-frame. The North will soon merge their three armies, line up their cannons and that will be that. It might take a few months, but the end result will be the same.'

'What do we do in the meantime, Theo?' Maximus Pannini was shaking with fear.

'Any withdrawal of support right now will look suspicious, so you will all continue as before. Ramesses will scrap any further investigation into Vlado's death …' Theo caught his breath for several seconds. 'So we are quite safe. The king has no choice; he's been told in no uncertain terms that he's finished if he comes up with any report of adverse findings.'

Leno Cavarris remained doubtful. 'Vlado must have intimated to the earl that he was going to surrender. How exactly was that done, and how can we re-instate our position in a later surrender? By then the earl will be dealing with another general.'

Theo felt ill. He had hoped no-one would ask that question. 'Good question, Leno; I'm glad you asked.' He forced himself to smile for the first time that day. 'Vlado secretly included a short note – just a few lines – in the envelope with the declaration of war. It simply said that he was prepared to offer surrender on the condition that the Northern Region would conduct major business in the south exclusively through him and his father. As instructed, the earl then gave a secret signal that he was in agreement. That's it. Simple.'

'That's it? Nothing else? No risk of us being exposed?'

'There is absolutely no risk of something coming back to haunt any of us, Leno,' he lied. 'Now that the Northern Region is on full war footing with a thousand cannons at the pointy end, I can assure you there is nothing that can go wrong. Our army will have no choice but to surrender the moment they stare down the barrels of those guns.' He picked up a cotton napkin to wipe his damp brow. 'I think we might call it a day, gentlemen. I must see how Nina is doing.'

By mid-afternoon several copies of King Ramesses' announcement were dispatched to parliament, public places of assembly and outlying country areas. It was a statement carefully crafted by Ramesses, and edited by Dmitri. Ramesses did exactly what he had been told to do, but he had no intention of allowing the late General Vlado Karamus to take center stage.

The general public was informed that their nation had declared war on the Northern Region in consequence of intelligence received that the most powerful army ever assembled was on a secret march against them. A brief mention was made that their own commander-in-chief had been killed during battle in a cowardly attack by a fellow officer, and that the general would be honored with a public funeral after his remains had been retrieved. Both General Vlado Karamus and Major General Nicholas Manassis were named, but only once.

Ramesses' statement went on to say that he, parliament, and the leaders of the armed forces had unanimously been persuaded by a single person to be the first to make a formal declaration of war, and to be the first to initiate an attack, which, ultimately, resulted in an overwhelming number of enemy casualties. That same person had personally interceded at the center of the battlefield at the point where the enemy was about to counter-attack with the most intensive cannon-fire the world had ever witnessed and she had engineered the escape of the nation's 20,000 strong army without incurring a single further casualty. A day later that same person had successfully negotiated the release of the remaining dead and injured.

The announcement stated that the king, and all members of parliament declared that person a national hero, one who had placed national pride above all else and had then gone on to prove her courage by engaging in hand-to-hand combat on the front lines. It concluded by naming its national hero as one Miss Isabella Mondeo. By sunset, the announcement had swept the nation like a hot wind. One name was on everyone's lips: *Isabella Mondeo*. Everyone loved a hero, especially a woman who was prepared to fight alongside the men on the front lines. The names of the commander-in-chief, and his assassin, were all but forgotten, relegated to the confines of history.

Ramesses had been clever; he deliberately did not disclose Isabella's age. He had given his nation what it required in its hour of need: a genuine and exciting hero. To discover her tender age later would serve to enhance her aura further after she had first been publicly embraced.

And so was born the legend of Isabella.

CHAPTER 78

They were alone. Just the two of them. They were in the spacious meeting tent, with the entry securely tied for complete privacy. It was their third time together. Each time she wore her brief halter-top and the short skirt with the split up each side. At times she heard him breathe, just inches away, as he studied her face and stared long and deep into her eyes. Then he would scrutinize the rest of her, every inch. Occasionally he would touch her clothing, moving the belt or the skirt. But not once did he touch any part of her person.

Isabella did exactly as she was told, turning her face and limbs this way and that, and flexing each muscle when instructed. He was a young man, in his twenties, and handsome – extremely handsome – and he studied her with unrestrained admiration. She would normally have felt uncomfortable at having a man staring at her so long and so intensely. But she did not. She was completely relaxed as she put herself on display.

Bertillini da Napoli was considered a genius of his craft, a master portrait artist. He flitted back and forth between Isabella and a long table that contained dozens of sheets of paper, bowls of charcoal pieces and a large platter of colored powders and pastes. She could see that some of the sketches contained no more than her nose; others featured her lips, eyes or hair. Some individual pages contained numerous parts of her face, including cheekbones, chin, ears and neck. Her eyes featured prominently in several sketches. Clothing and weapons were drawn in intricate detail on separate pages. Every sketch included precise measurements.

Da Napoli's fingers would dart into one swirl of paste after another until he grunted with satisfaction and rubbed the final color on the applicable sketch. Next to it he would write a code for the color combination.

At the end of each session, he stood back to look her slowly up and down before he rolled his eyes with pretended desire and blew kisses to her from his fingertips. Bertillini da Napoli was as feminine as Isabella.

It was exhilarating for Isabella to be so openly admired by a handsome young man, without the presence of danger. She would soon learn that there was always an element of danger in being admired.

An emissary had delivered a short letter from the earl that said he would accept ransom of one gold coin for each of the thirty-one prisoners. There was one non-negotiable condition: the gold had to be handed to him at a specified time and place, and in person, by Miss Isabella Mondeo.

Isabella was furious. Not at the earl, but at Marcus and Yannis for even considering not paying the ransom. 'What are you thinking, you stupid men!' she hissed. 'You know what will happen if we don't pay. The earl will take great pleasure in sending our men back to us: thirty-one heads, minus their bodies.'

Marcus was worried. 'But this would be the third time in just days that you've placed yourself behind enemy lines.'

'Grandfather, think clearly, please! How can I possibly live with myself after seeing thirty-one heads dumped at my feet because I did not personally hand over a small bag of gold? The earl will not dare to harm me. Now stop messing about and go for the gold! I only have four hours to get there.'

Yannis sighed in defeat. 'I'll organize a platoon to escort you.'

'The platoon will remain on the ridge. I want only two escorts by my side.'

'That's too dangerous, Isab – ' He held his hands up. 'All right, all right. I'll get Zhang Chen. Who else?'

'No, not Chen. He will be too recognizable. They will know at once who he is and what he did. They'd be over him like a pack of wolves.'

'Who, then?'

'Johan.'

'The man-mountain? I'm feeling better already. All right, I'll get him. Who else do you want?'

'I want *you*, Yannis.' Isabella had always wanted to say that, but managed to keep a straight face. 'I want you at my side.'

'Well, that's all right, then. Good choice, Miss Mondeo. We shall perish together as expected.' He smiled as he slipped into the saddle. 'I'll be back shortly.'

Isabella stroked her hair as she looked up at her grandfather. 'I'd better go and make myself presentable for His Royal Highness.'

CHAPTER 79

Earl Carlos Bucher was already waiting on the grasslands as the three rode down the slope, Isabella in the lead and riding bareback as usual. The earl had an officer on either side, with the prisoners standing directly behind them. Several hundred cavalry watched quietly from farther back.

Yannis' men remained visible on the ridge, but did not proceed beyond it. When the three were within four hundred paces, the earl put up his hand, palm forward. *Halt.* He raised his hand again to point at himself, before pointing at Isabella. *You and me only.* He nudged his horse forward, approaching alone.

Isabella had changed into pure white cotton trousers with a long-sleeved red blouse and short boots. A slim multi-colored band was wrapped around her forehead, and tied in a bow at the back. Her hair had been brushed to enhance its golden sheen. It was a carefully chosen wardrobe, because Isabella had staked her life on the belief that no-one would forgive an attack on a prettily dressed teen-age girl.

'I am to meet him in the middle, Yannis. Alone.'

'If he tries anything, I'll kill him.'

'I know you will, Yannis.' She nudged *Barca* forward.

The earl and Isabella stopped their mounts side by side, facing opposite directions, and within touching distance. Isabella was astonished at the earl's good looks; she had thought it impossible that anyone could be as handsome as Yannis, but the earl was. Curly dark hair framed a square forehead above brilliant blue eyes. His mouth was sensual, perfectly set above a square jaw with a cleft chin. His dimpled smile completed the perfect face.

Carlos Bucher had never known that buried even deeper beneath the handsome, urbane exterior than the efficiently concealed psychopath, lay yet another alter ego – *Carlos* – a desperate man prepared to risk his own life and the lives of anyone who got in his way for even the slightest show of genuine affection. The earl had never been loved, not even by his mother, and his own father had barely acknowledged his existence. As a child, he had reciprocated by performing unspeakable torture upon pet animals of all descriptions before killing them in a frenzy of stabbing. Later, he had frequently meted out such pleasures upon people. He had longed for a wife, someone to love him. Instead, because his reputation always preceded him, every eligible young woman he met feared him, despised him, and recoiled from him, despite his good looks. It was at last time, Carlos felt, to step forward and seize the moment.

As she spoke, the earl twitched in his saddle before a round-eyed Carlos presented Isabella with his most disarming smile. 'I am Isabella Mondeo and I am here as you requested, Your Grace.' She gave him the courtesy of a small bow.

Carlos nodded and smiled his appreciation at her graceful manners. He looked flushed as he drank in the vision before him. Isabella had by then seen the look often enough to recognize it, and felt herself flush. Finally he found his voice. 'You are courageous to come here, Miss Mondeo, and to meet me alone. It might have been a trick to harm or capture you. Now that I have seen you in person, I know I could easily sell you back to your nation for ten times a king's ransom. And you don't seem to be the least bit frightened.'

'Your nation would never forgive you for doing harm to an unarmed girl of fifteen, Your Grace. You would never live it down. It would be deemed cowardly and unbecoming for a man of royal blood. I am not in the least frightened, simply because I am in no danger.'

'Well-reasoned and quite true.' He smiled and nodded. 'And thank you for so thoughtfully informing me of your age. You were also courageous on the battlefield last week. I'm told you have extraordinary fighting skills and could have harmed some of my men, but chose not to do so.'

'That would have been cowardly and unbecoming for a girl of fifteen, Your Grace.'

Carlos threw his head back and roared. He wiped away the tears of laughter with the back of his hand, and looked at *Barca*. 'A magnificent animal, Miss Mondeo. The most magnificent specimen I have ever seen, in fact, but not as magnificent as its rider.' He paused for a moment. 'I wish to officially thank you for coming today. I particularly wanted to meet you in person.'

'Oh?'

'You have many admirers among my soldiers. You made quite a sensation, and I wished to see for myself if it is possible for anyone to be as enchanting as they say. The price to meet you to find out is this unfortunate lot.' Carlos flicked his head to indicate the prisoners behind him. 'I'm happy to say that, despite your tender age, my soldiers are indeed correct. My private viewing of you has been worth the release of every one of the prisoners – and more, if I had them.'

'Plus this bag of gold, Your Grace.' Isabella's face was on fire, and she was unable to hide the flush spreading to her neck as she untied the bag from her belt and held it out to the earl.

'Permit me to call you *Isabella* and you may take the prisoners … and keep the gold.'

Isabella continued to hold out the bag. 'I'm afraid circumstances preclude that degree of familiarity, Your Grace. The gold stays with you and the prisoners leave with me. However, I will allow you to continue to address me as Miss Mondeo.'

Carlos chuckled. 'You are really something, Miss Mondeo. It is most unfortunate that you are domiciled in the wrong camp, but who knows what destiny will bring?' He paused while he looked appraisingly into Isabella's brilliant green eyes. 'At only fifteen you are still too young to consider marriage, but there is no doubt that your destiny is to marry an emperor.' *And I know just who that emperor will be,* he thought.

'Oh, how sad for me that there are no emperors where I come from.'

Carlos was ecstatic. *She's completely relaxed, and toying with me. She obviously fancies me!* 'Not now, perhaps, but who knows? Destiny holds many surprises, including perhaps a newly installed emperor of the South, who will love you and want you for his empress when the time is right.' He held her gaze for several moments before continuing. 'You will do well to avoid all suitors until you reach an acceptable age to marry – eighteen or so sounds perfect to me. Another of destiny's surprises will surely be that we will meet again, and under friendlier circumstances.

'You may take the prisoners; they have been well fed and they each carry a water-bag. Oh, and you may keep the gold, anyway. I'm sure you will find a charity that can put it to good use. I have no interest in it; its purpose was no more than a cheap and sadly unsuccessful attempt to buy the right to call you by your given name. The prisoners are a personal gift from me to you.

'I bid you farewell and thank you again for meeting with me. Until we meet again, Miss Mondeo.'

Carlos smiled, gave her a formal salute and rode back to his men. On the way he gave a signal and the prisoners quick-marched towards Isabella.

As soon as the men reached *Barca*, she slipped off his back, hugged them all and walked back to where Yannis and Johan waited. Her legs were like jelly and she was unable to meet Yannis' eyes.

Celebrations started early evening and continued late into the night, spreading from one camp into the next. Minstrels and musicians mingled with soldiers and camp followers as they drifted in and out of the main camp.

Johan sidled up to Isabella with a charred meaty bone in one hand and a mug of ale in the other. 'Thank you for choosing me to go with you today, Isabella. The mere fact that you asked for me has elevated me to near god-like status among my men.' He grinned with pleasure.

Isabella laughed. 'You make me feel safe, Johan. No one would dare touch me with you by my side.'

Johan nodded. 'One of the released prisoners said something odd to me on the way back to camp. He said they all owe their lives to you, that they were kept alive because the earl knew they were the only means to draw you into a meeting with him. I wonder what that was all about.'

Isabella giggled. 'Oh, I do know what that was all about, Johan. That's also why the earl wanted me alone. Keep it to yourself, please, but he flirted outrageously with me most of the time we were together.'

'He *what?*' Johan was genuinely shocked.

Isabella giggled again and doubled up with laughter. 'He tried to be subtle at first, but within a minute he seemed to change, and dropped all pretense.' She chuckled again as she straightened. 'The prisoners were his personal gift to me. Thirty-one lives, a peace-offering to start the courting process. The earl told me to avoid all suitors until I'm eighteen, when he wants to marry me and share his throne as emperor and empress of the South!'

Johan's ale splattered in all directions as his mug hit the ground.

CHAPTER 80

Marcus frowned throughout his entire breakfast the following morning. Afterwards, while the women cleaned up, he and Yannis huddled in serious discussion. Marcus sighed heavily when everyone finally sat down and waited for the news. Isabella wore a plain white cotton dress that highlighted her golden hair, which now almost reached her waist.

'We need to talk,' Marcus said. 'We've had a number of messages from home over the last few days. I didn't say anything earlier because they were received out of order, and some were missing. Early this morning we received the last of them, so they now make sense. Over to you, Yannis.'

Yannis leaned forward, elbows on knees, and started to provide information.

The recommended promotions had been approved and authorized by parliament, he said. A complement of junior officers would be sent to replace those just promoted, but they would not arrive for several weeks.

Hugs and kisses were showered on Yannis in congratulation for his permanent promotion to general and commander-in-chief of the campaign.

Here Yannis paused. 'There are two other major items. First, the bad news: Isabella, I will ask that you prepare yourself for bad news about Nicholas.' He waited a few moments before continuing. 'We have been ordered to cease further investigation into the death of Karamus.' Yannis looked pointedly at Isabella as he spoke the name. She was pleased and grateful that Yannis had the foresight not to use the term *General* in her presence. 'Karamus has been named a national hero and – I hate to say this – Nicholas has been named as his assassin, a coward and traitor. Are you all right, Isabella?'

Tears streamed down her face. 'Yes, I'm fine,' she mumbled. 'Just get on with it, please.'

'The order to stop further investigation into the affair has been signed by both the king and Dmitri. Perhaps we can come up with enough evidence to convince them otherwise. We could even – '

'No,' Isabella interjected, steel in her voice.

'But we could …'

'No, Yannis. Do you believe that Uncle Nicho was a coward and a traitor?'

Yannis was shocked. 'No! Of course not! How could you even ask such a question?'

'But that's the point, Yannis. I know you don't believe it. Neither do the king or Dmitri. I don't have to ask anyone here that question because no-one believes it. To collect and send evidence to those who already believe is therefore a waste of time. His Majesty and Dmitri have ordered the investigation to cease because they simply cannot use such evidence. Don't you see?'

'Well, yes, I suppose I do … Well, no, I don't think I do, to be honest.'

'Apply logic, and it's simple. They undoubtedly can't use adverse evidence because it would be counter-productive. Why? It can only be because they have been threatened. Who could possibly threaten a king? Theo Karamus. What could he threaten? It must be a matter of national security. There can be only one answer. If Karamus *junior*,' Isabella sniggered, 'should be exposed for what he was, then Karamus *senior* and his colleagues would pull out of the war effort. We would then be in a very precarious position, which we have already touched on before. I can see the king's predicament. He has put the nation first, God bless him. It is a proper decision and I concur with it. No adverse reports can be transmitted. Do you see now?'

Yannis shook his head in wonderment and nodded. 'Absolutely! Somehow you see what others don't. What do we do? We can't just abandon Nicholas.'

Isabella smiled. 'First we win the war, and then we'll clear his name!'

Yannis looked around at the small group. They all nodded vigorously. 'Done!' he said with satisfaction.

'You said there were two major items?' Isabella's emotions were back under control.

'Ah, yes.' Yannis rubbed his hands with excitement. 'This is going to shock you, Isabella.'

'I doubt it. It takes a lot to shock this *little girl*.' This last was said with notable sarcasm.

A puzzled expression came over Melissa. Yannis barely managed to suppress a groan. *Isabella is never going to let me forget my momentary lapse of discretion.* He was right; she never did.

'The reason for so many messages,' he continued, 'is that the king sent us a public announcement in its entirety. The scribes have matched up the portions and reproduced it as a single document. As we speak, soldiers have been instructed to assemble. I am to make an announcement as soon as practicable – which is actually right now. Follow me, everyone.'

Isabella had fleetingly noticed soldiers and camp followers streaming into the main camp from all directions, but had paid it scant attention. Since Yannis had said she was about to be shocked, she was feeling a knot of apprehension.

Several packing cases had been stacked in layers on a rise to make steps leading to a makeshift platform. 'Isabella, stand next to the cases, please.' Yannis said. 'At the end of the announcement I will reach down for you to come up and stand next to me.'

'*What?*' Her apprehension turned rapidly to nausea and panic.

Yannis patted her arm and climbed to the platform. He raised his hands to subdue the crowd. 'Ladies, gentlemen and fellow soldiers,' he shouted, 'not all can be present at the one time, so I ask that you pass on what I have to say. This is a public announcement that has already been made to parliament and at public forums across our nation a few days ago.'

He took a deep breath and held up a two-page document. 'The first paragraph of this document announced to our citizens that a state of war now exists between our nation and the Northern Region. The second paragraph refers to our former commander-in-chief and the circumstances surrounding his demise. The remainder refers to one person and to one person only. You are privileged that this person stands before you today and will be presented to you shortly. I will now read to you the king's announcement, but I will not read the second paragraph. The document will immediately be put on display for those who wish to read it – at least for those of you who *can* read,' he shouted to loud laughter.

The crowd remained silent throughout as Yannis read the announcement. It described the person who had planned the escape of the nation's army from a full-scale cannon assault, the recovery of the dead and injured, and the release of all prisoners. It concluded by stating that Parliament had decreed that person a national hero, and named that person as Isabella Mondeo.

Yannis lowered the document to cheers and applause. The noise continued as he came down two steps, bent down and extended his arm for Isabella. She looked up at him, eyes wide with shock, and shook her head. Tears trickled down her face.

Yannis waved his arm and beckoned again for her to grab hold. She shook her head once more and doubled over as the moment overwhelmed her. Yannis stepped to the ground, placed one arm around her back, the other around her knees and gently swept her up in his arms. Seconds later he stood on the platform facing the crowd with her, as the applause rose to new heights.

'Oh, Yannis,' she sniffled against his face, 'if you weren't holding me like your bride, I'd kick you again.' She smiled weakly and sniffled again, longer and louder. 'Oh God, I'm sorry! That must have sounded disgusting! Put me down, please, before I make a mess on your uniform.'

Yannis grinned and put her down gently to stand next to him. He held her by the hand while he raised his right hand to quieten the crowd. After a few moments he shouted, 'I have one other announcement from His Majesty the King. Until this moment, only I know of it. Isabella has other contributions to make to the future war effort that few are aware of. To fully authorize her to do so, Parliament has unanimously passed a bill that she be formally and legally inducted into the army at officer rank. Ladies and gentlemen, I give you our national hero, and our newest soldier: *Major Isabella Mondeo!*' He raised their joined hands above their heads.

Yannis let go of her hand and stood back to join the crowd in their applause. When the noise abated, he took her gently by the arm to lead her towards the steps. As she reached the first step he leaned forward, seemingly to assist her. No-one noticed that he deliberately used the opportunity to whisper in her ear: 'You look very young to be a *Major*, Miss Mondeo.'

Isabella turned her face away from the audience as she squeezed his arm. No-one saw or heard her whispered response: 'Touché, General Christos.'

CHAPTER 81

Alexander duPonti climbed onto the first packing case and quickly made his way to the top, where he waved his arms like a windmill. 'Your attention, please! Could officers proceed to the meeting tent? We have a showing of our artists' impressions of the battle, and then we will have a very special unveiling by one of Europe's foremost young masters, Senor Bertillini Da Napoli. After the officers' viewing, the tent will be open to everyone for the rest of the day.'

DuPonti almost fell down the steps in his excitement to reach the ground, where Isabella was still coming to terms with the public announcements. Yannis had been right: she had been shocked to the core.

'Come, come!' DuPonti fussed. 'You must be the first to see it. Come quickly.' He waved at Isabella and her group and headed towards the meeting-tent at a run. Isabella held on to Marcus for support while Melissa kept a firm hold on Yannis. Chen and Xu Yan made up the remainder of their small entourage.

They joined a number of officers filing through the entry, made double-width for the occasion. The four walls were covered with sketches, secured in temporary frames hanging from thin wires on a latticework of light timber. There were hundreds of them. At the far wall, the outline of a massive framed canvas could be seen, carefully concealed beneath heavy cotton cloth. Six feet high by nine feet wide, the canvas was supported at knee height by a solid timber frame. Da Napoli stood next to it, looking like an expectant father.

Isabella circled the room, taking her time to absorb the raw power of the images. Most were in various shades of grey to black, while a few were colored, or only partly colored. The sketches had been sorted into type: cavalry and horse scenes, pikemen and phalanxes, archers and swordsmen. Some sketches were from the perspective of the Southern army's positions; others were drawn as if seen from enemy positions. The detail was astounding. Horses with fear engraved into their bulging eyes, soldiers with expressions of pain and despair. There were scenes of frenetic pace, others of serene tranquility, and some of imminent death.

Isabella closed her eyes and allowed the images to come to life in her mind, superimposed over the noises and smells of the actual events she had experienced. She opened her eyes and the sounds in the room faded as the hanging sketches appeared to challenge her. Several seemed to move towards her, calling out: *Look at me, look at me, Isabella! Save us! Can't you see what's happening?* The more she looked, the more the images cried out to her, begging her to look more closely. A trail of chills ran up her spine. She walked outside the tent to catch her breath. *The images are speaking to me. They have something to say!*

'Isabella,' Alexander called to her, 'come back inside and to the front, please. We're about to enjoy the highlight of the exhibition.' He turned to the audience. 'Ladies and gentlemen, you will have noticed that most of the sketches have not been finished. It will take months of painstaking labor to complete the fine detail that will bring those images to life. The same applies to the portrait about to be unveiled by Senor da Napoli. It will take him a year or more to complete his masterpiece, but he feels he has done enough to provide an idea of what he intends to create.'

DuPonti led Isabella in front of the canvas and placed his arm around her shoulder. 'I will also mention that Bertillini has taken a unique perspective for this portrait. Artists are sacrosanct to both sides of a conflict and can move about unmolested by either side as they record history. Bertillini witnessed the scene that you are about to see from less than one hundred paces, just before he and a few other artists retreated as ordered, into the dust-storm, to join our army's escape. With additional information and images provided by other artists, he has been able to place the viewer directly in front of the main subject, looking out from behind the enemy's front line. You will now have the rare privilege of seeing a masterpiece under construction. Bertillini, if you please!'

Da Napoli reached up and gently pulled a ribbon that allowed the cotton shroud to slide slowly to the ground.

There was a collective gasp and a muffled cry from Melissa. Isabella felt her knees buckle and was grateful for Alexander duPonti's firm hold on her shoulder. She leaned against him, scarcely able to breathe. In fact, no-one seemed to breathe, except da Napoli, who beamed like a proud father holding up his child – his unique creation – for the world to see.

CHAPTER 82

Isabella's heart pounded as she stared directly into an exact image of herself. It was a sensation that few people would ever experience. Even a mirror image is not exact; it is reversed. She understood then why Bertillini has so painstakingly measured every part of her face and form. She had been perfectly reproduced life-size.

Oh God, is that what I look like? There were no sounds from the viewers in the huge tent. No applause, no remarks, nothing.

Da Napoli had recorded only a moment in time, but had captured the juxtaposed powers that exist within the cosmos: life and death, light and darkness, violence and compassion, fear and courage, hope and despair, the present and the future, love and hate, and the most powerful forces of all: good and evil.

The artist's genius had placed the viewer as if in front of a huge picture-window for a glimpse into the seething milieu of apocalypse. The viewer's emotions were intended to be ripped apart by the despair that spread to every corner of the canvas, and to then be offered salvation and hope by the serenity of the main subject and how she touched, and affected, every part of the image.

A section of coat-sleeve and tiny portion of a hand at the bottom right of center showed that the gunner had just used his heated touché to light the fuse burning its way into the touch-hole of his cannon. Another hand at the bottom left of center could be seen with a just-discernible brazier of hot coals. The viewer became the gunner standing ready to mete out death and destruction from the very edge of the window.

The battles and events that had taken place were represented by cavalry, spearmen, bowmen, knights and swordsmen. Scenes of death, triumph and defeat allowed the viewer to comprehend the agony a soldier must endure to conduct war. Many characters had been completed and colored, their uniforms and weapons reproduced so accurately they, paradoxically, brought to life even the dead. Outlines of others would be completed over time.

Isabella was at the exact center, directly in front of the muzzle of the cannon about to fire. Standing behind her were four enemy soldiers, two on either side. Their shoulders were slumped, their swords on the ground. Two had their heads lowered, defeated. The other two turned to look up at Isabella with expressions of wonder and gratitude that she'd had the compassion to give them the gift of life.

To the right, and a little closer, was a fifth soldier, a young man with a protruding forehead and deep-set eyes. He was on one knee with a hand on the ground, seemingly about to spring into action. His sword was also on the ground, but his expression was different from the others. He was staring directly at Isabella's face with unrequited love, prepared to face death for the triumph of good over evil.

Further back on the battlefield was the splendidly uniformed commander of the Southern army's cavalry, his mount up on its hind legs. *Yannis.* The officer's sword was raised high above his head, seeming to hesitate above an enemy soldier kneeling before him, hands raised, begging for his life.

But the most striking feature was Isabella herself. She stood tall, facing the gunner. Her left arm was held high, the magnificent jewel-encrusted serpent-embossed Zen Master's dagger flashing in the sunlight. The other hand held the sword that was descending towards the gunner. Bertillini had cleverly slightly smudged the outside edge of the sword, so that it appeared to be travelling at tremendous speed. Isabella's torso was spectacular. Streaks of sunlight had thrown tiny shadows to subtly bring the muscle tone of her arms and thighs into relief. The knot in the belt of her skirt had been carefully looped to entirely cover her navel. One bare leg was raised higher than the other, the muscles flexed for maximum power. It was a representation of the beauty of the female form – a gleaming Viking-like warrior about to dispose of the gunner and leap out of the evil apocalypse of the present and into the future, to continue her fight for good.

Isabella's face communicated with the viewer without words. Her huge green eyes, perfectly reproduced with mesmerizing effect, were focused directly on the viewers wherever they stood. A half-smile played on her delicate lips. Her hair was the controlling influence over the entire canvas and, ultimately, the key to the masterpiece. Da Napoli had made it flow upwards, leaving her neck, face and ears uncovered to reveal her serene beauty. The hair then floated along the top of the canvas in soft golden cloud-like formations to each corner, and then descended part of the way down each side. Here and there, it parted like natural clouds, allowing rays of sunlight to gently highlight particular scenes: the four soldiers; the young man about to spring into action; the cavalry commander; the knights about to slaughter the officers; Isabella herself. The artist had created a separate planet, a world where the most powerful opposing forces raged in a single moment, a world confined under the cloak of Isabella's golden hair.

Da Napoli had deliberately structured the portrait so that the viewer would finally turn away, not with a lasting impression of death and despair, but with the fleeting image of Isabella. He had named his masterpiece: *Isabella's World.*

When sound finally returned, it swept the room like an explosion. Applause was mixed with shouts of wonder and disbelief. Conversations flowed in a buzz of excitement. Melissa threw her arms around Isabella, almost pulling her to the ground.

'Oh God, Isabella, you are so beautiful, so amazing, so ... so ... Oh, how did I ever get to meet someone like you?'

'Cut it out, for heaven's sake. It's only a painting.'

'*Only a painting?* It's only the most amazing painting of all time. Everyone loves it. Look at them! They can't take their eyes from it. You're so gorgeous.'

'But ... it is a bit revealing, isn't it?'

'No, it's just right. It's meant to contrast your beauty with all the ugliness surrounding you. That's the whole point, my pretty. Bertillini was lucky to find you because you are the only one he could have used to create such a contrasting image. I hate to admit it, but not even my looks would have been enough to counterbalance all that horror.'

'You're embarrassing me with such rubbish. I'm getting out of here.' She gave Melissa a hug and headed for the exit. On the way, she passed Marcus and Yannis, who simply looked at her with dazed eyes, both unable to utter a word.

Outside, she had barely caught her breath when Bertillini bounced up to her. He looked excited and happy. 'I think everybody like. Most exciting painting I ever do. Once in a lifetime. Not finished. Maybe one year, perhaps two.' He shrugged. 'You like?'

'I love it, Bertillini. It has so much emotion I felt I wanted to cry. It's beautiful. I have never seen anything so beautiful. It has so much to say.'

He rocked his head from side to side. 'I hear little *but* in voice. Something you not like? I cut it up and start again! For you, only perfection is good enough!'

'No! Heavens, no, Bertillini. The portrait is truly gorgeous. But yes, I guess there are couple of things.'

'Not one? *Two* things! What, what, *what?*' Eyes wide, Bertillini was bobbing up and down in his anxiety to please her.

Isabella hesitated, unsure how to phrase it. 'Well, it's because I was looking at myself, so I can't be sure, but I seem a little older in the portrait. Not old, just older.' She gazed at Bertillini with raised eyebrows.

'Ah-h ... Isabella, Isabella, Isabella.' He took her hands in his and lightly kissed each one several times, making as much noise as possible. 'Of *course* I make you a little older, but just a little, little, little. It is deliberate. You have been in battle; you are soldier now. I have myself seen you.' He let go of her hands, stepped back and pantomimed a swordfight. 'And now you are officer in army. *A major! So exciting!* I not paint *girl* in my picture. You not *girl* now. Mamma mia! Look at you, Isabella. You beautiful young woman now! That how you must be in my *masterpiece*. Beautiful *woman*. Sorry, sorry, sorry, I *not* cut up painting for that. Now, what the other thing? What? What? What?'

This time she smiled broadly at him. 'My bosom.'

His eyes widened, as did his smile. 'Ah, si, your bosom. I spend much time on your bosom. Such a lovely bosom.' He gave a wicked laugh. 'I not show enough bosom?'

Isabella giggled. It felt strangely liberating to be able to openly discuss her blossoming self with a man for the first time. She knew she held no interest for him in the physical sense, and it felt comfortable to be able to say anything to him.

'Just the opposite. It just seems that my bosom is a little overdone. I would not want anyone to think I was being provocative in my choice of dress on the day. I was dressed for the heat and later dumped in front of the cannons by pure accident.'

Bertillini looked relieved. 'Isabella, Isabella, Isabella, I tell you truth. I *understate* your bosom for that very reason. That is why I spend much time to get just right. I had to *understate*. I thought you about to complain for making bosom *smaller* than your measurement say to me. I must show only celestial perfection of your form to contrast with the surrounding ugly destructiveness that one human can inflict upon another. I must not make you entice. That ruin masterpiece. So I make bosom smaller. So sorry. You understand?'

'I understand, Bertillini, but I really thought … What do you mean by the *celestial perfection of my* …?'

Bertillini was relieved and let his breath out in a silent whistle. 'Your perfection is expressed as if you are from another world come to save the apocalypse of this world. You not use mirror much, no? You must use more and see what others see.'

'I don't own a mirror. I have borrowed Melissa's a few times when I need to fix my hair for special occasions.'

'Ah, si. Melissa. She is so beautiful. Just like me. And she is so vain. Just like me. We are so alike.'

Isabella reached out and took his hand. 'That's actually true, Bertillini. You are truly beautiful.'

It was Bertillini's turn to giggle as he sighed. 'I know, I know, I know. But alas, there is only one that is more beautiful, more *perfect*, than me, and God has cursed me by placing you out of my reach and desire.' He kissed her hand several times before letting it go. 'I shall re-join my adoring public, and it is time for you to go and be close to the one you love, the stupid one who is too blind to see it.'

'*What?* What are you saying? What are you talking about?'

'Isabella, Isabella, Isabella. Bertillini is an artiste; he is sensitive to everyone and everything. You are in love. It is in your face, your eyes, your every breath – and in your heart. You say nothing and keep your distance because it is too soon for you. That is good. You wait. You smart. I see all, I feel all, I say nothing, but we both know who it is you love.' He grinned and took her hands again. 'I was clever. Did you not notice? Go see. I place the man you love where he will always be close to your heart. You and he will be together for eternity. Go see. Go see. Go see.'

Isabella gave him a long hug before he disappeared into the tent. After a few moments to compose herself, she turned, took a deep breath and entered the tent. The room went quiet as she moved past Marcus, Yannis and Melissa, and towards the canvas for a closer look. Heads turned to stare at her in wonder and admiration, a live viewing of the young woman now immortalized on canvas. Bertillini had correctly picked the man she loved. Yannis could be seen in the distance, but his actual form had been carefully placed below her raised arm, next to her heart. She started to worry. If Bertillini had read the signs, who else had? Melissa?

With a small shock she noticed another figure for the first time. Bertillini had placed him at the far left, standing alone between the two warring fronts and gazing directly at Isabella amid the pandemonium. The man stood in a shaded portion of the battlefield, a dark, secretive figure, yet his identity was unmistakable. A red-and-blue royal robe complemented the magnificent uniform setting him apart from his fighting men. His left arm was across his lower chest, his right elbow resting on it while his hand caressed his chin. This was a man deep in concentration, a man contemplating his next move. There was no mistaking the man who wanted Isabella for his empress. How far would he go to possess her?

She turned away slowly and walked over to where Marcus, Yannis and Melissa were waiting for her. After she gave each a gentle hug, they all left the tent arm in arm. Emile DaSilva saluted them as he entered the tent. The handsome Luis Valdez smiled at them as he entered the tent directly behind Emile.

Emotions from the day's events had taken their toll and Isabella was exhausted. She decided to bid everyone good night shortly after dinner. Her last thought as she fell into a deep sleep was the image of herself about to leap the cannon.

Da Napoli's extraordinary portrait was to have a profound effect on Isabella's life. The powers of love, triumph, violence and evil that raged within the portrait were already seeping from the canvas into the real world and destined to envelop her like the tentacles of an octopus – but not necessarily in that order.

The embodiment of *evil* was the first tentacle to stalk her.

CHAPTER 83

It started suddenly. The storm. She could hear the wooden ship groan and creak as it rose and fell with the raging swell. She saw wave after wave rise above the prow to crash onto the deck where she stood lashed to the mast. Breathing became difficult as the waves swirled into her mouth and nose, yet she thought it strange that the water was neither cold nor warm. She could move her legs, but unable to get traction on the deck. Her head ached. It suddenly became clear why. She was lashed upside-down to the mast, staring down at the deck. It was a strange deck, made up of stones, grass, shrubs and dirt. The raging storm faded rapidly to sound more like a gentle breeze rustling through trees and bushes.

Isabella awoke in an instant, and the dream evaporated as quickly as reality flooded her mind. She was bouncing, belly-down, over a man's shoulder. One of his hands was around her waist, the other over her mouth. His shoulder pressed into her chest, making it difficult for her to breathe. He was walking rapidly, groaning, his breath rasping. It was the sound of a man who was determined, but not fit.

Shadows danced as the man made his way under a full moon. Occasionally she saw a flitting shadow that seemed to move in the opposite direction. A wild animal interested to see if prey would present itself? Not once did the man hesitate, obviously knowing exactly where he was going: a carefully selected, and isolated, site. Isabella instinctively knew his intentions.

She considered her options. He was a big man, so it was futile to resist while she was being carried. Instead, she relaxed and pretended to be asleep. *Know thy enemy, Isabella.* Who is he? Definitely someone she knew.

It had to be someone who could move around the camps without challenge – a stranger would surely be challenged. It had to be someone who knew where she slept and knew also to carefully sneak past Zhang

Chen, her bodyguard, whose tent was always placed directly next to hers.

She quickly ran through her mind everyone she knew, focusing on anyone who had looked at her a moment longer than they should have. It came as a shock to suddenly realize just how many soldiers had stared at her too long. One man had already proposed to her. At first she felt offended but her heart softened as she accepted for the first time that she was of age, and men had every right to make their admiration known in the hope of obtaining her favor. That was fine, she decided, as long as it was restricted to looking, not touching. She quickly narrowed the list down to three who had consistently looked at her with more than passing interest. Then she compared the physical attributes of each, and eliminated two. That left just one man.

She knew her attacker. She also knew that some things were more precious to her than life itself, and made a startling decision. Isabella would force her abductor to kill her.

Worried, Melissa crawled on her hands and knees to the tent entry to peer into the dark wilderness. Nothing. Half asleep, she had earlier heard rustling from the direction of Isabella's mattress, but thought little of it. It was not uncommon for one of them to get up in the night to visit the women's amenities. When she had awakened again, Isabella had not returned. It was cool, so she crawled back to her mattress and decided if Isabella had not returned in five minutes, she would start a search. Four minutes later she drifted off to sleep.

The hunter with his prey finally reached a small clearing where he stopped, gently slipped Isabella off his shoulder onto her feet and shook her to wake her. She pretended to awaken slowly and looked up into the face of her abductor. She had been right. Emile DaSilva!

'Emile? What are you doing? What are we doing here?'

'You're old enough to know why we are here, Isabella. We are far from everywhere, so there's no use in yelling. Just do as I say, and everything will be all right.' To make his point, he pulled out his knife and swung it back and forth in the moonlight.

'What are you thinking, Emile? Have you gone mad? Have you lost your senses?' Isabella could see his face clearly in the moonlight and he did look a bit out of his mind. She also sensed, more than saw, a presence in the bushes listening and watching their every move, waiting to pounce on the weakest.

'Yes, Yes! I lost my senses as soon as I saw that portrait. I already knew how beautiful you are, but that portrait …'

'*Already knew.* It was *you.* Back at our bathing cove in the valley. Watching Melissa and me. That was you, wasn't it?'

'Melissa! Beautiful, yes, but she pales in comparison to you. Yes, it was me. Now, let's get on with it. You know what to do.' He waved the knife at her again.

Moving back, Isabella leaned down to remove one night-sock, then the other, and tossed them on the ground to her left.

'That's it. That's it. Toss everything over there. There's a good girl.' DaSilva sounded relieved. This was going better than he had dared hope.

Isabella, however, had no intention of undressing. She was simply preparing her weapons – her feet. 'It's a shame, Emile, that your senseless folly will now cost both our lives,' she said quietly.

'What? What do you mean?'

'I will die in the next few minutes; you will die tomorrow.'

'But I don't intend to kill you, Isabella. You need not die and neither do I.'

'You don't really expect me to say nothing and let you simply walk away unpunished, do you?'

'Yes, of course I do. I know you're in love with someone. I don't know who he is, but he would not want you if he found out, so you will say nothing. Your silence is my protection. I have no reason to kill you. I won't even hurt you.'

'*Hurt me!* You will more than hurt me, Emile. You will destroy me.' Isabella felt her voice break as she thought of Yannis. 'What I have is a gift I will freely give to the man I love when I marry him, and to no one-else. It is my gift to give, Emile, not a trophy to be stolen from me. The only way you will have it is to take it from my lifeless carcass.'

'No! Don't say that. That's not how – '

Isabella cut him off. 'Emile, let me tell you what is going to happen next. Prepare yourself to kill me.' Emile stared at her, wide-eyed with shock. 'In a few moments I will attack you. My nails are sharper than a dagger; my teeth are stronger than a wolf's. I will not attempt to defend myself – I will focus only on my attack. When you stab me, I will not die for at least a minute. In that time I will strip your face to the bone. Melissa will report me missing within the hour, if she has not done so already. Yannis will have 20,000 soldiers searching for me within an hour after that. My body will be found – and quickly. If you run, they will know who killed me. If you don't run, one look at your face will give them their answer. So whether you run or not, they will find you and they will hand you to Zhang Chen. Everyone now knows what he is capable of.' Isabella paused for effect.

'I will be the lucky one. I will die only once, Emile, but *you* – Zhang Chen will make you die a thousand times.'

'Are you ready? I will attack on the count of five.' She crouched into an attacking stance.

Two humans frozen in the moonlight. The larger looked shocked and helpless; the smaller looked confident and ready to pounce. The only movement was a shadow on the perimeter of the clearing.

Emile did not know that Isabella has no intention of attacking him; she had too many options available to her. Emile was large, slow and unaware of her speed and fighting skills. She could kick him unconscious within seconds. She could take his knife and turn it back on him in an instant. Or she could simply turn and run. Her speed among the trees and rocks would make it impossible for him to catch her. *You stupid man,* she thought, *you don't stand a chance. Now let's see what you'll do.*

'One ... two ... three ...'

Emile threw his knife on the ground. 'No!' he shouted. 'No! Don't. Don't attack me.' He backed away, holding his hands up. 'Please, don't attack. I didn't mean for things to turn out like this. The knife was just for show. I could never kill you, Isabella. Oh God, what have I done? I'm going to be sick.' He staggered to the edge of the clearing and threw up near where Isabella had last seen a shadow move.

When Emile came back to the center of the clearing, he sank to his knees, sobbing. 'I'm sorry, Isabella. I don't know what came over me, or what possessed me. When I saw you in that portrait – as a grown woman, so beautiful ... I just went completely mad.'

Isabella picked up her socks and stuffed them in a pocket. 'It's over now, Emile. Let's get back to camp before we're missed. I'll enter camp first, in case anyone is searching. We must not be seen together, understand?'

Emile nodded. 'I understand,' he whispered and staggered to his feet. 'I won't ask your forgiveness because what I did is unforgivable. But I am sorry.'

Isabella nodded and started to walk in the direction of the camp. She had correctly assessed that his resolve would collapse as soon as he was forced to face the reality of his actions. Her gamble to directly challenge him had succeeded. A few minutes later, she heard him speak softly behind her.

'Isabella?'

She stopped and turned.

'I won't be going back, Isabella. I can't face you again, or my men. I can't face anyone. I am too ashamed.'

She nodded. 'I understand. If you wish to go, I won't say anything. I will seem as surprised as anyone that you've deserted.'

'That's not what I mean, Isabella. I can't go anywhere.' He sank to his knees and pulled out his knife. 'I am a disgrace to myself and my family, and worse, I attempted to place shame upon you. Somehow, evil has possessed me, and I must pay the price for my crime. I know what must be done, but I am also a coward.' He handed her the knife, handle first. 'It can only be you to take my life. It is the only way to redemption, and to release my soul from evil.' He raised his chin to expose the base of his throat. 'I know your heart is one of compassion and that you will be merciful and quick, even to me. May the Gods bless you, Isabella. I'm ready now.'

'Are you sure about this, Emile? It really is not necessary.'

'I am sure. I cannot live with the shame I have brought upon myself. Do it now.' He stared straight ahead, eyes unblinking.

'Very well, Emile. I will do it quickly.' Isabella drew the knife back before thrusting it towards the base of his throat with her full strength.

Something was wrong. It was too quiet. Melissa was used to the sound of Isabella's soft, regular breathing next to her, but could hear nothing as she emerged from her slumber. Isabella had not returned, and the position of the moon told her that it must have been at least a half-hour since she was last awake. This time she was really worried. She dressed quickly and headed straight for the amenities area to start her search.

Emile did not blink as the knife flashed towards his throat at lightning speed. His only expression was one of sadness and humiliation. Death would give him the eternal peace and salvation he craved.

Years of practice enabled Isabella to freeze the knife a hair's breadth from his throat.

'Please,' he whispered, 'don't make me suffer.'

'You've suffered enough, Emile. You have apologized. You have recognized your evil and you offered me your life as the ultimate sacrifice for the sin you intended to commit. Your soul has been cleansed, Emile. Your apology is sincere; I accept it and I give you back your life. There is no longer a need for you to feel humiliated.' She put her hand out to help him to his feet.

Emile kissed her hand before he let it go. 'My life belongs to you now, Isabella. You may call upon it any time.'

Isabella put her arms around him and held him for a moment, before she stood back and looked up at him. 'You now have my full trust, Emile, and this matter will never be raised again.'

They resumed their walk back to camp, all fear and apprehension gone from both. This time Isabella did not notice a shadow as it slowly moved away.

Melissa widened her search outside the camp perimeter after searching the amenities area without success. By then she was extremely alarmed and was about to return to camp to wake Zhang Chen and Marcus when she saw a lonely figure appear out of the swirling morning mist. *Isabella!*

Melissa almost fainted and ran to her, sobbing with relief. She had begun to fear the worst. 'Are you all right? I've been searching everywhere for you. Where have you been? I was about to wake Chen and your grandfather.' Melissa held her in a near-death grip.

'No! Don't wake them. Don't say anything to them about this. Ever! I'm all right, Melissa. Everything is all right now. Let's get back to the tent, but please be quiet. I just want to get back to bed. I need sleep.'

'Oh God, something did happen, didn't it? Someone got to you, didn't they? Oh, Isabella, did someone get to you?' Melissa was almost hysterical.

Isabella placed her hand gently over Melissa's mouth. 'Sh-h! Keep it quiet. Calm down. I don't want the whole world to know about this. Yes, someone did try to get to me, but they didn't succeed. Not even close.'

Back in the tent Melissa lit a small candle and got back into bed. It was only then that she noticed Isabella was wearing her bed clothing. 'Oh, I just realized what you're wearing. He snatched you from your bed, didn't he? He snatched you right under my nose!'

Isabella sniggered. 'Little did he know that he would have been safer if he'd snatched Genghis Khan from his bed. No-one messes with Isabella Mondeo. No-one!' She removed the socks from her pocket, sat down and placed them on her feet before crawling over to tie the entry more securely than she had ever done.

'I'm not expecting any more unwelcome callers. I just don't want anyone peeking inside in the morning to get the wrong idea,' she said softly. Then, to Melissa's surprise and delight, Isabella crawled past her own bed to slip into Melissa's and wrap her arms around her. 'Don't ask questions, Melissa. Just hold me. I need my best friend to hold me for a while.'

Within seconds Melissa felt Isabella start to shake, then sob quietly. She did not ask questions, just held her friend tightly against her. It was a full ten minutes before she felt Isabella's shaking subside, followed shortly after by her reassuring slow breathing. A relieved Melissa followed her into a deep sleep within a minute.

CHAPTER 84

Zhang Chen was waiting when she arrived at the secret training ground just before midday. So was Yan. Chen looked smug; Yan looked excited.

Chen bowed formally to Isabella as Yan pulled a blue silk-covered cushion from a small bag and held it against her chest. 'Precious daughter, we have much to discuss before we practice.' He smiled at Isabella's apprehensive expression and patted her hand. 'Better still, perhaps we have rest-day today. You will not focus after we talk.'

Not surprisingly, Isabella welcomed the thought. She was exhausted from the events of the night. She nodded and, as usual, waited silently for Chen to continue.

'Last night, I was there, in darkness. Never more than seconds away.'

'I saw a shadow. It could have been an animal, but I sensed your presence, Father. Not once was I frightened or feel in danger.'

'I know. That is why we talk now and do what must be done.' He nodded to Yan, who moved out of hearing range before he took Isabella's hands in his. 'Only Zen Masters can hear what I tell you. Not wife, not husband. No-one. It is the one secret only for China's ten Zen Master. To become Zen Master you must first learn and master all that Zen Master can teach. I can teach you nothing more. Your skills equal to mine, sometimes better. Only my physical strength separates us. A new Zen Master can only take title if one die or step down. *But,* new Master must first earn the right. New Master must pass special trial. It is something that cannot be taught, cannot be planned. Every candidate strong, and has fighting skill, so trial cannot include fighting. Candidate cannot be told that trial exist until after trial has been passed. That way, no-one can plan trial, no-one can cheat. Very tricky, you see?'

'To pass trial, candidate must prove that power of mind is greater than power of body. Remember always, precious daughter, it is power of mind, not body, which separate man from beast. That why I stay close last night, but not interfere. Such opportunity to show power is rare and might never have happened again. A Zen Master witness is accepted without question. I am now permitted to tell you that such trial exists because you have already passed it.'

Isabella seemed slightly confused. 'I think I understand what you mean, but I don't quite follow where this is going.'

'You have proven yourself to be extraordinary by resolving deadly circumstance by defeating much bigger, stronger foe and turn him into loyal ally. You use your confidence and power of mind, without use of force, or even revealing your fighting skills. You also allow man to redeem himself, cleanse his soul, and give him back his pride. Pride cannot be bought with gold. You also spare his life when he offer you take it. He arrive as your enemy; he leave as your friend, one who will give his life for you. You make your own decision how you deal with crisis. Such things cannot be taught. You did not run. You could have done that easily; you run faster than rabbit. You pass trial better than any Zen Master before you. You have earned final credentials to be Zen Master.'

Chen let go of her hands and waved for Yan to re-join them. She reached into the small bag and pulled out Chen's dagger, still in its scabbard, and placed it on the cushion, which she then held out with both hands, palms up. Chen faced Isabella, picked up the weapon, and removed the dagger from its sheath. 'Only ten such daggers in China, one for each Master. I now stand down and present you with dagger. You have earned your place as one of China's ten Zen Masters.' He carefully placed the dagger, handle forward, in Isabella's hands. The jewels sparkled in the sun while the interwoven gold and silver serpents seemed to writhe their way up the handle and into her palm. 'I very proud, precious daughter. One day we will journey to China where I will introduce you to my mother, and to your fellow Zen Masters.'

'And will you also introduce me to your father?'

Chen froze for several moments 'Not possible,' he murmured and hid his grimace by bowing formally to her, a bit deeper and longer than usual. 'You now *Serpent Warrior*. That all I have to say, Zen Master.'

Isabella bowed in return and felt the intoxicating power of the serpents surge within her as she embraced Zhang Chen, the former Zen Master.

CHAPTER 85

Aloise Kuiper was ice cold with rage. Ice cold with fear. His anger was directed at both himself and Earl Carlos Bucher. His fear was for his now tenuous position as emperor, even for his very life. *I am the emperor! How dare that pompous, psychopathic resurrected Earl threaten me?* It had been subtle and carefully worded, but very real. He picked up the letter and read it for the third time. Yes, the threat was still there, it simply would not go away.

Word had been received a week earlier that the Southern army had surprised the Earl, issued a declaration of war and challenged him to battle. Aloise had kept the information to himself in the hope that after he received the next communication, he could make a public announcement that the Southern army had been defeated, and that the target nation would shortly be under his control. This letter was not what he had hoped for, or expected – far from it. What had occurred was a resounding disaster and he had no idea how to deal with it. He had earlier sent a messenger demanding General Von Franckel's urgent attendance.

Von Franckel sat quietly in Aloise's sumptuous study, sipping his tea as he read the letter. The first question was why had the earl delayed for several days before sending his message? The only answer he came up with was that the earl had needed time to develop plausible excuses for his disastrous performance on the battlefield. How does one rationalize the loss of almost fifteen thousand troops when they possessed the fire power of a thousand cannons? How does one turn disaster into triumph? The answer, he thought, was as obvious as it was simple: *lies, lies and more lies.* Von Franckel decided to assume that every word in the earl's letter was a lie.

Aloise watched the frown on Von Franckel's face deepen as he read. The general appeared crestfallen when he gently placed it on the low table between them. 'This is shocking news, Aloise. Shocking! I have never been so devastated.' Von Franckel had, in fact, never been so delighted.

'What do you think, Maurice? It seems impossible! Can it be true?'

'Oh, absolutely. His Grace would not dare lie to you. I believe we have to accept that every word in the earl's letter is true. I agree with you that he has been subtle in his choice of words regarding the lack of armor, but I believe it is for no reason other than to afford him some protection in the event you should blame him for the tragic loss of life. It's obviously not his fault, nor is any of it yours.'

Aloise felt better and breathed just a little easier. Perhaps he had read too much into the letter. 'We simply can't hide that number of casualties. There are just too many families to inform. Margarethe is so upset she refuses to leave her quarters in case her friends question her. This will be a public relations disaster that could easily get out of control.'

'H-m-m … perhaps not. In fact, I believe I can turn this into a public relations triumph.'

'What? How? What are you thinking, Maurice?'

Von Franckel picked up the letter and pretended to study it carefully. He had already rehearsed his response. 'Well, let's have a look at what he says. Ah, yes, here it is. He says that his initial shock of finding no armor in the supply train was tempered by the knowledge that there was actually no need for it, as no battles had been intended. He goes on to say that the public might see it otherwise, however, and unfairly blame you, or government cost-saving policies, for the thousands of lives lost. To prevent a public outcry or uprising, he proposes that knowledge of the lack of armor remain between ourselves and that we, and the public, focus on the *real* reasons for the loss of lives.' Von Franckel looked up.

Aloise nodded. 'Yes, I believe he has a good point there. Let's keep that information between ourselves. Go on.'

'The earl's army was strung out over many miles, and 40,000 soldiers from the South made a cowardly attack without warning on a mere 20,000 of the earl's forces. He goes on to say that the dreaded disease had already taken a toll of almost 10,000 of his best troops, but he was still able to fight off the superior enemy numbers by using the devastating fire power of our cannons. By the time the cowards fled the cannons, the enemy was down to barely 20,000, with comparatively modest battlefield losses of our own troops. The earl says he will allow his men to rest and regroup while he waits for the Second army to arrive. He will then advance on the enemy, and wipe them out to a man.'

'What does his reference to a *coalition force* really mean, Maurice?'

'He intends to gather an additional force made up of nationals from a number of other nations in the Southern Region, put them in the front lines and actually use them as cannon fodder against the enemy. The coalition army will therefore suffer the casualties before we lose any more of our own.'

'Excellent! Good idea!'

'I'll draft a public notice. Rest assured you'll have nothing to worry about. I'll also let the public know that those truly to blame can be found in the public sector, and that we have already started a search to root them out. They are none other than those well-known agitators who have now committed treason by revealing state secrets and have goaded the Southern nation into this unprovoked attack on our peaceful nation. I can guarantee that all known agitators will disappear like rats into the drains, Aloise. They won't pop their heads up for years.'

By the time Von Franckel departed, Aloise was a relieved and happy man.

So was General Von Franckel. The earl had been humiliated and had been desperate enough to commit information in writing. He had been very clever in his letter, but not clever enough. Aloise had not noticed Von Franckel casually pick up the letter, fold it slowly, and smoothly slip it into his jacket pocket.

As soon as he had received the first communication of the Southern nation's challenge to battle, Von Franckel had sent his best scouts and spies to gather more information. He had learned that 20,000 enemy soldiers had entered the battlefield, and that these 20,000 had dramatically escaped the cannon-fire, vanishing without a trace, and with few casualties. Although the plague was rife in city areas, it had not touched the Earl's army.

His informants had revealed that the enemy's entire officer command had been wiped out, including their commander-in-chief, leaving only junior, inexperienced, men to continue the fight. Therefore, Von Franckel had no doubt that the Northern Region army would prevail. Carlos Bucher had been thoroughly humiliated, had lied, and could be exposed at any time.

Yes, General Maurice Von Franckel was pleased with the day's events as he headed to his city apartment to make himself ready for the relaxing rendezvous to come.

CHAPTER 86

'What's going on?' It was mid-morning and Isabella was both apprehensive and suspicious. Marcus and Yannis were walking on either side of her as she was escorted to the meeting tent. She had been told only that a group of officers had asked Yannis to convene a special meeting.

Marcus looked at her and smiled. 'The meeting will start in a couple of minutes, darling, so you might as well wait and get it first-hand.' Isabella nodded once. Made sense.

The three entered the huge tent, where almost one hundred officers were already seated on benches. They rose as one and saluted the three as they made their way to the opposite end, where three chairs had been placed facing the gathering. Yannis pointed to the center chair for Isabella, and the two men sat on either side.

Yannis rubbed his hands. 'All right, let's get on with it. No formalities or rank for the rest of the meeting. Everyone has an equal say throughout *and* in the decision-making process at the end of the meeting. Isabella, the men have something to say to you, and something to put to you.'

Isabella leaned forward and placed her elbows on her knees, feeling sick. *Now what?*

A colonel near the front was the first to speak. 'Isabella, we are now well aware that you had the foresight to scout the battlefield for days before the event, got to know the terrain, found out about the wind and how to use it. That's the only reason we're all sitting here today.'

Another officer spoke up. 'After your escape from an impossible situation, you had the courage to place your life at risk to get back our dead and wounded. You did it again by meeting their supreme commander to get back the prisoners. You're evidently prepared to put your life at risk for us over and over. We've talked among ourselves, and it's time that some of us did the same for you.' The room went quiet as the men looked for an initial reaction from Isabella.

She leaned back and folded her arms. 'To say I'm overwhelmed would be an understatement, gentlemen. But really, the wind was just a bit of luck.'

'Maybe so,' the colonel said, 'but it's how you used that *bit of luck* that saved our hides. You were able to devise a plan to allow us to escape the cannons. That's why we want to talk to you. Your tender age has proved irrelevant. You're a natural leader, and it's in everyone's interest to take advantage of that. General?' The colonel looked at Yannis.

Yannis turned towards Isabella. 'The officers have suggested that you be given the command of your own brigade. Just a modest one, mind you. Having already seen what you are capable of, they believe that the ideas and strategies that you would employ for your own brigade could be replicated by others, and everyone would benefit. There would be nothing to lose and possibly much to gain. What do you think, Isabella? Would you be interested in something like that?'

Isabella did not respond at first. She was speechless. *My own brigade? My own command?* Excitement built up quickly as possibilities and scenarios flashed through her mind. She kept her arms folded so no-one would see her hands shake. 'Perhaps ... depends ... What do you have in mind?' she asked in her most relaxed tone. It took Yannis mere seconds to bring her back down to earth.

'Well, I thought a few men could be allocated to you. On a non-permanent basis, of course. Later, they would be re-mustered to their original brigades. Maybe, say twenty or thirty men. See how you go. What do you think?'

Isabella rose and walked slowly to the side of the tent while the men watched intently. After several moments she walked back towards her seat. When she reached Yannis, she stopped to face him, her back to the officers. She gave him an icy stare long enough to gain his full attention, lowered her eyes to his shins and looked intently at her right foot, then back to his shins. He got the message and quickly slipped his feet under his chair as far as they would go.

She sat down and faced the officers, smiling sweetly. 'A brilliant plan, General. Let me think. That will give me about six archers, ten swordsmen, and a couple to throw stones at the enemy command post to keep them distracted while my two spearmen threaten their front line. Outstanding! Perhaps you could spare me one horse, so I'll have a cavalry to back them up.' Chuckles spread across the room. Isabella was well known for her sharp wit.

'Oh, *Yannis*, I'm getting really excited now. With an entire one-man cavalry at my disposal, I can develop amazing battle strategies for my brigade. And what about a cook? I'll only need one, of course, to pack two sandwiches for when we surround the Third army, on its arrival.' The chuckles had turned into loud guffaws.

Isabella jumped to her feet and waved the men to silence. 'No, no, wait! I'm serious. I've barely started and already I have big plans. Listen and learn, gentlemen. I can train my twenty men to wear skirts, false bosoms and head- scarves. In full disguise I and my men can attack a small selection of the enemy's women and children and steal their soup cauldron! My cavalry will ensure our escape, and we'll all be able to feast upon my successes!' With that, she sat down.

Yannis' groan was completely drowned out by the officers' roar of approval. He put his hands up to quieten the room. 'All right! All right, Isabella! You have such a … subtle … way of putting your point of view. Maybe I wasn't so smart. So tell us, what do *you* suggest?'

Isabella rose and faced the officers, her face and posture completely changed in an instant. Now it was a face of determination and challenge. She was down to business. Instantly she had the officers' full attention. 'You believe I have something to offer?' The officers nodded. 'You believe you owe me something?' More nods. 'How much you give me will depend on just how much you *really* believe you owe me. So tell me, how much will you give me?' *It was just too easy to lead men by the nose,* she thought.

'We owe you everything, Isabella, so we'll give you whatever you want,' one of the officers called out.

Isabella cupped her hand to her ear. 'Say again? A little louder, please? I don't believe General Christos heard you the first time.'

'Whatever you want, Isabella,' came shouts.

Isabella looked at Yannis with her most innocent face. 'General?'

Yannis nodded, resignation written all over his face. 'Yes, yes! I heard. State your case. Tell us what you want.'

Isabella paced the room for several minutes, finally stopping at one side so that she could address Marcus and Yannis, as well as the officers.

'As some of you may know, I have already started a number of projects with the agreement of the king, to further our cause. This unexpected offer by you, if you agree in full to what I propose, can be of enormous assistance to those plans. But it will only work if you are ready to be shocked as much as you have just shocked me with your kindness. During the last few minutes, I've worked out what I need and what I want.' Isabella let the words hang in the air. *Over to you, gentlemen. Tell me you're ready.*

Marcus spoke for the first time. 'I do believe we are all ready to be thoroughly shocked, Isabella.'

'I want a brigade that I will turn into the best, most feared fighting machine this continent has ever seen. I want a brigade that will have the skills and resources to undertake any task, and in which each man will be the equal of ten enemy soldiers. I want a brigade that would have made Genghis Khan pack his traveling bags and flee. To achieve that, I want one thousand men! Plus something else!'

'What?' Yannis murmured, trying hard not to laugh. The room was stunned. 'And what is the *plus?*'

Isabella held up her left hand and counted the fingers off with her right. 'I want 500 horses: 250 for my cavalry battalion and 250 for reserves, also to carry equipment. I want additional foundry workers to make special weapons and other secret equipment rarely, if ever, seen before. I want the best arrow-and-bow makers. And I will, of course, need enough cooks and camp followers to support one thousand men as an autonomous force. I want to create a force able to fight anywhere, anytime. She paused to allow her audience time to absorb the numbers. Then she added, 'Plus something else!'

Yannis shook his head. *'Plus?'*

She started counting off her fingers a second time. 'I am to have total control over all training. Grandfather will help me, as will Zhang Chen. And last, but not least: I get to choose my men. No more plusses, gentlemen. That's it. That's all I want.'

One of the officers near the back row spoke. 'I suppose you will want to pick the very best of our soldiers from the various brigades? Not that I mind. It's just an observation.'

Isabella was pleased that the question was not on numbers. She wanted to get past that as quickly as possible. 'On the contrary, Iqbal.' Iqbal was delighted that she knew his name. 'I don't want any of you to propose a particular number, or particular men. I will only accept volunteers. That will make it work for everyone, and I will soon let you know the criteria of the men I want.'

'No offense, Isabella,' Yannis said, 'but you might have a problem with men who *volunteer*, as opposed to being ordered, to be under the command of someone such as yourself.'

Yannis was on the receiving end of her icy stare for the second time. 'What exactly do you mean, Yannis – *such as yourself?* Do you mean because of my age? Or do you mean – if you dare – because I'm *female?*' She threw out the challenge to him, but was quietly pleased that Yannis had also not mentioned numbers.

'Oh, oh, I'm in big trouble now, men.' Yannis jumped to his feet, picked up his chair and thrust it out towards Isabella like a lion-tamer. 'I mean, Isabella, both that you are so young – and because you are a young woman.' He waved the chair to a round of applause.

The careful emphasis and twinkle in his eyes told her that he had carefully chosen the last two words for her benefit. Isabella was delighted.

She grinned at his performance. 'Oh, sit down, you clown! I promise not to attack you. Here is my proposition. I will take *only* volunteers, but only up to the maximum of one thousand. If there are only twenty volunteers, then I will take the twenty and not complain. Do we have an agreement, gentlemen?'

The colonel turned his head towards the back of the room. 'We said she'd have whatever she wanted, men. Do we stand by that now that we know what she wants? I stand by it. What say you?' A few heads nodded, and soon they were all nodding.

Yannis crossed his legs and looked up with a smirk at Isabella, who was still standing. 'Well, that settles it. Put your criteria together and I'll arrange for an assembly tomorrow for the selection process. I can promise you won't go away empty-handed. I already know quite a few men who will join you.'

'Thank you, Yannis, for saying that.'

Yannis rose and saluted the men. 'Thank you, men. An excellent result.' The officers rose and filed out of the tent.

'Walk back with me, would you please, Isabella? Do you mind, Marcus?'

'No, no. That's fine. I'll see you both for lunch.' He nodded to them both, gave Isabella a hug, and left.

Yannis sat down. 'Actually, just stay in the tent for a bit, would you? Melissa borders on hysteria whenever she sees you and me within ten paces of each other. She loves you, Isabella, really loves you, but at the same time she reacts like a bee-hive under attack whenever a pretty girl passes within sight. Why don't you sit in Marcus' chair? It's a bit further away, just in case she walks in. She would surely faint if she saw the two of us alone.' He rolled his eyes.

Isabella's heart hammered as she sat down. *Pretty girl?* She liked the sound of that. *At last you've noticed something about my appearance.* 'What is it?' she whispered.

'To be honest, I was more afraid of you kicking my head than my shins. I know only too well now what you're capable of. Just so you know, that first business about 20 men: I deliberately said that to bait you. I wanted to enrage you, to challenge you. I wanted you to take control of the room because I know you can. If I had said two hundred men, you might just have accepted that. I didn't want that. I wanted you to have whatever number that *you* chose, not me. If you had asked for more than a thousand men and the officers agreed, you would have them. Are things all right, then, Isabella, between us? I wouldn't want you angry with me for baiting you. Hey, what's with the tears?'

Isabella wiped her tears with the back of her hand as they both rose and faced each other. 'Yes, we're all right, Yannis. More than all right. And thank you for such confidence in me. Right now I desperately want to hug you, but that's surely when Melissa will walk through the entry, catch me with my arms around you for the second time, and get the wrong idea.'

'Yes, she would certainly get the wrong idea, so we'll dispense with the hug, but thanks for the thought. It might be safer if I go on ahead.' He grinned. 'I'll soon have to think about promoting you now that you'll have your own brigade.' He headed towards the exit, muttering loudly enough for her to hear. '*Colonel? General?* Good heavens, no! She'd soon outrank me! She'd tell me what to do. Can't have *that!* But Yannis, Isabella does that already! Oh, dear, what to do? What to do?' He stooped as he passed through the entry, accompanied by Isabella's infectious giggle.

As his back disappeared from view, she glanced down at herself, this time with a smile instead of a grimace.

CHAPTER 87

Soldiers had gathered in their thousands by the time Isabella climbed the boxes to the platform, high on the hill. It was late morning and she was not one to keep the men from their lunch.

'Men!' She raised her voice and allowed it to float across the crowd. 'You have been informed that your officers have proposed I form a brigade of my own, so I assume you are here because you are interested … Or perhaps you are just looking for a little entertainment. Well, you shall have it.' She paused long enough for the ripple of laughter to fade.

'I will now tell you *what* I want, and *who* I want. First: *I want one thousand men!* I will now tell you *who* I want. I will be at the front of my men, so I want only men who are brave enough to fight beside someone wearing a skirt. Only the brave and foolhardy will volunteer for *that*. I want men who are tall and broad-shouldered. *Tall*, so that the enemy will see *you* before they see your comrades hiding behind you and my skirt.' Laughter broke out among the spectators. They were getting the entertainment Isabella had promised. '*Broad-shouldered*, so the enemy must strike at *you* before they can strike at those behind. I want those who want to be among the first to taste the blood of the enemy. I want those who want to be among the first to join me in the glorious journey to the promised land for our nation!' The crowd was deeply stirred.

'There are many former sailors among you.' These were the men Isabella particularly wanted, and she deliberately singled them out. 'Who among you, brave sailors, would prefer to fight next to me to meet your Maker with a bloodied sword in your hand, rather than drown helplessly clinging to an oar? I will train you into the most dangerous and feared brigade our nation has ever seen. In return, I promise you *three things*. I promise you hard work. I promise you danger, and I promise you adventure. Every day will be the same: hard work, danger and adventure.'

A voice shouted from the crowd. 'Will you have me, Isabella? I can be dangerous if I sharpen the pointy end of my leg.' The man laughed and proudly lifted his wooden leg, waving it back and forth. It was the young soldier who had been found trapped under a horse on the battlefield. 'I have my life only because of you. You risked your life for me, and my life is now yours, if you will have me.'

Isabella was delighted with this interruption. *Every number starts with one, Isabella.* 'What's your name, soldier?'

'I am Stephan, Major.'

'You are brave to be the first to speak, Stephan. That's what I want – only the bravest. On horseback, I will make you equal to 10 enemy knights. You will make a fine cavalry officer. Yes, I will have you, Stephan, and I am proud that you are the first to volunteer. Move towards the front, please. Anyone else with a death-wish, please join Stephan!'

Stephan gave her the thumbs up as he limped towards her. Another voice called out. Johan. 'You have my entire platoon to add to Stephan, Major. We've seen first-hand what you're capable of. Count us in.' As Johan and his men moved forward, others joined them. By the time they reached the platform, they were surrounded by more than two hundred huge former sailors. Isabella's excitement was rising when she was shocked by the next voice.

'Will you consider me, Major?' Sergeant-at-arms, Emile DaSilva, called out from the back of the crowd.

'I will be honored to have you with me, Emile. You will, of course, be one of my leaders.'

'General Christos, being an officer; am I permitted to volunteer?' It was the colonel who had spoken first in the meeting tent the previous day.

Yannis was as surprised as Isabella. 'Of course, Colonel. You will retain your rank, naturally, but bear in mind that Isabella will always outrank anyone in her brigade, irrespective of their actual rank.'

'Understood, sir.' The colonel smiled up at Isabella. 'Adventure! You've got me.' Several other officers, including Captain Yancko Geraldis, joined him as he moved to the front. Recently promoted to sergeant, Luis Valdez gave Isabella the thumbs up as he also moved to join the officers.

Isabella raised her voice again, excited now. 'You had better hurry, men, or you will miss out. Oh, and did I mention that I do love to be surrounded by handsome men? It will be a definite advantage.' There was a roar of approval as the trickle increased to a flood.

'I will provide Emile with a list of the experts and camp followers we will need. Please seek him out if you are interested in being a part of our team. Thank you, one and all, men. It seems I already have my brigade, and I am truly humbled by your response. I promise not to disappoint you.' Isabella jumped down from the platform to rousing applause.

Yannis was the first to move forward and take her hands in his. 'Congratulations, Isabella. If I hadn't been made commander-in-chief, I would join you myself. I have a feeling we're in for some exciting times.'

'Thank you, Yannis. I can't believe they volunteered so quickly. I'll address them again before we go for some lunch.' She took a deep breath and climbed back on the platform.

There was no longer a need to shout. 'Gentlemen, I am so proud to see so many have the courage to join our brigade. Be warned that your training will be completely different from what your comrades get.'

'When will this special training commence, Major?' the colonel asked.

Isabella smiled at her men. 'Today! Meet me in Ascension Valley, one hour after lunch. We'll have a short discussion, followed by a two-hour training session. Thank you, gentlemen. Oh, and please have a substantial lunch. You are going to need every bit of it for energy.'

Ascension Valley was a ten-minute ride from the main camps. It was a small valley, five hundred paces across, flat in parts, rocky and steep on three sides. Even though a brook ran through one side, it was not suitable for camping. Isabella had changed into a lighter outfit with ankle boots. Sliding off *Barca*, she pointed him towards the brook before gently slapping his rump.

Having climbed onto a large rock to be visible to all, with a deliberate motion, Isabella removed her cap to allow her hair to tumble down her back. There was to be no mistake. She was about to address her men for the first time, and she fully intended they knew they were about to take orders from a young woman. That first image was meant never to be forgotten.

'The most effective means of warfare by far is *deception*. *Deception* has the power to win wars. I will not allow you to forget that word. My first task, therefore, is to confess to you that I have already engineered a deception. I deceived every man on the hills yesterday. I deceived senior command, and I deceived every one of you standing before me.' There was a stunned silence from the men.

'I asked for tall, broad-shouldered men who are prepared to be the first to die for their comrades and their country. That was a *deception*. It was intended to entice only the bravest to step forward. You are definitely not to be the first to die. Just the opposite. You and I will fight shoulder to shoulder, and you will be among the *last* to die. I will train you so well that the last man standing will be one of you standing before me. My *deception* has brought me the biggest, the strongest and the bravest, the very men who hand-picked themselves and stand before me right now. I have succeeded beyond my wildest dreams, men. Was that not worth a deception?'

Ascension Valley echoed with cheers and applause. Somehow, the cheers turned into a chant that continued for several minutes; it was a chant that went on to become famed – and feared – as the brigade later was to storm the enemy in battles to come: *Isabella, Isabella, ooo, ooo, ooo! Isabella, Isabella, ooo, ooo, ooo!* The men punched their fists into the air with the rhythm. Isabella was astonished and delighted with the reaction, and felt a shudder of icy excitement spread down her back.

'There are thousands of other important elements of war, two of which are *communication* and *speed. Communication*: this has already been mastered to an extent the enemy cannot match it. *Speed*: much of our training will be based on speed getting into and out of battle, and speed to terrorize our foe. And we are going to start right now! You are about to get two lessons in one. Turn around and face the other side of the valley.'

It's time to start giving orders, Isabella.

Isabella jumped down and walked to the front of the men. She pointed across the valley. 'That tree is about three hundred paces away, and it's slightly uphill. Well, I have an offer for you. It won't be much longer before I will be looking for a husband …' Shouts of approval and proposals drowned out the rest of her words, and she had to start again. 'I will belong to the first man who beats *me* to that tree. Battle conditions, men! Get ready. At the count of three: one … two.' At the count of two, Isabella bolted away like a rabbit. 'Three!' she shouted over her shoulders, as she reached full speed, laughing all the way. The men took off.

By the time the first of her brigade reached the tree, Isabella lay stretched out comfortably on the grass, yawning and buffing her fingers against her leather jacket. As soon as the last man arrived, she sprang to her feet and jumped up on a rock.

'Like I said, men: two lessons in one. *Speed* and *deception* win every time. I deceived you by starting the race before you expected. If the enemy expects one thing, then do something unexpected. I would have beat you anyway, but I promise that your speed will increase over the next weeks and months. I hope you learned something from that lesson. Now then, we are going to race back to where we started. It will be little easier this time, because it's downhill and I'll start from the back line. Same offer applies. I will be betrothed to anyone who beats me to the rock. Battle conditions, men! Get ready. At the count of three: one …' The men bolted as one while Isabella stood back with a satisfied grin on her face. Some of the men stumbled and fell in their haste to beat her to the rock. Isabella trotted slowly behind them, her laughter echoing across the valley like the peal of a church bell. By the time she reached the men, she was doubled up with laughter, as were most of the men.

'Oh, lucky me!' she gasped, 'I'm going to have a thousand husbands. I could almost believe that some of you fancy me. You should be ashamed of yourselves.'

'Not *some* of us – more like *all* of us, Major,' one of the men called out. A sea of heads nodded their agreement.

'Thank you, that's very sweet, but you might change your mind later. I'm not quite sixteen, but I'm afraid I'll be an old hag by the time the last of the thousand weddings comes around.' That brought more laughter. 'But seriously, you took off after the count of *one*. Excellent! That was the whole point of the exercise: you learned quickly and you used it to advantage. I just wasn't sure if the incentive offered was of interest. I'm very flattered that it was. Now I have to work out whom I will marry first. There are so many handsome men among you.' A round of applause followed as she looked intently at the faces surrounding her. 'Actually, that's not correct. On closer inspection I see that you're all handsome. I have an impossible task.' That started the *Isabella chant* in full voice.

The colonel spoke up on behalf of the men. 'Isabella – *Major* – uphill or down, you could easily have beaten us both times, so we know you jest. Therefore no one will hold you to your kind offer. Consider yourself off the hook. But a friendly warning,' he added with a smile. 'Be careful with your promises in future. You have more admirers than you can count, and they all would love to accept.'

Isabella jumped down from the rock to plant a kiss on the colonel's cheek to rousing cheers of envy. She jumped back on the rock with a forlorn look on her face. 'Oh, dear, I've gone from a thousand husbands to none in the matter of seconds. Why am I finding it so difficult to get a husband? Oh, poor me!' She fluttered her eyelashes as the chant sprang up again.

'We will now take a brisk walk up and down the hills. At my signal, we will pause for a single full squat. You will become familiar with that signal. You will see it ten times today. Every day we will add one more. There will be other leg exercises, too. Get used to the agony I will inflict upon your legs. I will be tougher than any officer you have ever served under. And for good reason. Your legs are going to win battles, and your legs are going to save your lives.'

Isabella paused to look at her men. 'I will arrange for baggy clothing to be made for each of you. No-one is to see what we do, or how you develop. When you reveal yourselves on the battlefield, the enemy will feel the first flush of terror. And finally, men, I promised you danger and adventure, so our brigade's first dangerous raid will be inside one of the enemy's camps in January, mid-winter. In our first full-scale battle, we will attack the enemy's headquarters, and that will take place mid-summer. As I said, I will lead from the front on each occasion. You will never be asked to do what I'm not prepared to do. I will be the first in and the last out. Now, let's get to it, men. We have much to do!'

Isabella led them on the brisk walk. The rate was increased to a slow jog on each of the downhill legs. *The poor men have no idea what they are in for*, she thought. *Each day will be more vigorous than the previous.* She could scarcely believe how perfectly her new brigade fitted into her plans. With her own resources, she could train her men to execute her plans without first having to convince army command on each occasion.

It had been a long time since Isabella had been so excited about the future.

CHAPTER 88

It was a week later when Carlos had a rude awakening. He had been half asleep in his tent after lunch and a glass of wine, daydreaming about the pretty *Miss* Isabella Mondeo. *Empress Isabella? That sounded impressive. She was sure to like that. Or perhaps Queen Isabella? Equally impressive.*

When he had heard his men rave about the spectacular emerald-eyed young beauty who had accidentally found herself on their front lines, he had wanted to see for himself. He had quickly realized he had the means to engineer a private meeting: the prisoners. Perhaps his men had exaggerated in describing her? The moment he had seen her, he knew they had not. *Still too young*, he had thought, *but a few years on the shelf would solve that problem.*

Sleepily, he reminisced about his meeting with her and replayed their conversation over and over in his mind. Occasionally he would change his words and hers, to sound better in his fantasy. He had pretended to be subtle, but had been deliberately clumsy in his flirtatious conversation with her.

In return, Isabella had been neither subtle nor clumsy. She had been forthright and strong but, most of all, she had been fearless. Carlos had never known anyone – man or woman – to be fearless in his presence, and here was a mere slip of a girl, a teenager, with thirty-one lives in the balance, telling him how it was going to be. A power radiated from her like the heat of the sun; she burned his skin; she boiled his blood. It had felt exhilarating to at last find someone his equal. Her blushes had told him she fully understood what he was telling her. By the time he had departed, he knew he had made her fully aware of his future station in life and his desire to have her share his future throne.

His reverie was shattered by a voice outside his tent. 'Sir?'

'Enter.'

A colonel slipped past the flap, saluted, and handed Carlos an unsealed envelope. 'This has just been delivered by our men from the south, sir. We now know who *The Magician* is.'

'The Magician, Colonel? What magician?'

'The magician who made an entire army vanish into thin air, sir.'

'Oh, yes. That would be the general who unfortunately escaped our incompetent knights. I don't know how he did it, but he managed it somehow. Whoever he is, I have to admit he was smarter than I gave him credit for. So, what is his name, Colonel?'

'Well, it's not exactly a general, sir, but very close. In fact, a *relative* of a retired general, seconded to their army as an adviser. This is a full copy of a public announcement issued by King Ramesses about two weeks ago. I believe you will find it interesting, sir. In fact, you actually met with *The Magician* shortly before this announcement was made public. Most in our army will also be familiar with *The Magician's* name.' The colonel relished every moment of his recitation and waited for his commanding officer to open the envelope.

'I met with *The Magician?* What are you talking about, man? I have met with no-one for weeks. Let's have a look at who he is, then.' He removed the pages from the envelope and started to read.

He laughed. 'Hah! So it was one of their own officers who skewered General Karamus. Too bad Major-General Manassis is already dead; I would have liked to have skewered him myself – that's the man who caused this whole debacle. Now then, what else does our esteemed King Ramesses have to say? Where does he tell us the name of our magician? It just says here that ... that ... *what?*' Carlos' face turned deathly white as he continued to read. He staggered backwards and slumped into his chair as his knees buckled beneath him. Placing the letter on his lap, he stared up at the colonel with unfocused eyes. *No, it cannot be. I cannot be reading this correctly.* He picked up the letter again and turned to page two. It got worse: *Miss* Isabella Mondeo had convinced her nation's leaders to declare war; Isabella had devised the escape strategy for their army; Isabella had been instrumental in securing the dead and injured from the battlefield, and Isabella Mondeo had been declared a national hero. *No, no, no! This is too much! I had her within my grasp.*

Carlos felt ill. His mind was in turmoil. He had tied his future to this young woman. He broke out in an icy sweat as it dawned on him that he had not, as he thought, finally met *his equal* on the grasslands that day. Far from it. It was he who was not the equal of Isabella Mondeo.

The colonel enjoyed the spectacle: his commander was just sitting and staring with unseeing eyes, the letter having fallen to the ground. The colonel broke the spell by picking it up and placing it on the table.

With a twitching of his neck, Carlos rose and briskly paced the tent until finally stopping to stare out of the open entrance. He placed his left arm across his chest, right elbow leaning on it while he gently stroked his chin. A full minute passed before the ice-cold psychopath turned to face his officer, eyes mere slits.

'Colonel,' Bucher said softly, 'I want you to prepare two thousand mounted soldiers for an excursion across the Southern Region borders. We leave in one week. I have a little errand to … ah … *execute.*'

'Yes, sir. I will see to it at once.' The colonel saluted and left the tent. He rubbed his hands with glee as he headed to the officers' meeting tent. *Wait until you hear what I've just witnessed.*

Bucher returned to pacing his tent to calm down as he read the announcement a second time. He finally tossed the pages onto the table and sat down. He knew he had some serious thinking to do about *Miss* Mondeo. Already turning into a beautiful young woman, he thought, she was obviously highly intelligent and fearless. Yes, Isabella was his perfect future mate and mother of his children. He now knew she could also prove to be an extremely *dangerous* young woman, dangerous to his very existence.

It all boiled down to one thing, he knew. One decision: *he had to decide whether to marry her or kill her.*

CHAPTER 89

Mayor Hector Petroskva knew trouble when he saw it. He had been forewarned that unwelcome visitors were on the way to his town. Men from outer villages had ridden into town in a panic with word that about two thousand mounted soldiers were heading directly to the main township. Friendly shouts by farmers offering food and drinks had been met with stony silence. The soldiers were on a mission and not a friendly one.

Mayor Petroskva stood outside the stone-arched gateway to the town of five hundred as the soldiers approached. He already knew of the war footing between the Northern Region and the nation forming part of the Southern Region. Everyone knew. The news had spread like wildfire. Yet he had deliberately arranged for the heavy timber gate to remain open as a gesture of friendship and welcome. Anyway, there was no point in closing it.

The soldiers spread out and split into columns, officers to the front. A spectacularly dressed man sat nonchalantly on his mount at the very front. A tasseled cape with royal insignia on each breast indicated a man of high status. It was the man's smirk that bothered Petroskva more than the soldiers behind him. Nevertheless, he walked forward and put on his most friendly smile.

'Good afternoon. We are at your service, sir. I am Mayor Hector Petroskva. Our town bids you welcome, and the gate is open for your convenience.' Petroskva had no idea that he had just invited a psychopath into their town.

Bucher nodded for a captain on his right to speak on his behalf. 'We have no desire to enter your village, Mayor Petroskva.'

Relief flooded through the mayor's body. Perhaps this was not the disaster he had initially feared. 'So, how may we be of assistance to you?

Food and wine for your men, perhaps?'

'You will arrange for the town bell to be rung for every citizen to assemble outside the gate. You have exactly one minute to do so before we burn your lovely little timber town to the ground.'

'What? But ... I – '

'You now have exactly fifty-five seconds to ring the bell, you fool.' The captain turned in his saddle to face one of the columns to his right. 'Men, get the torches ready. If the bell is not ringing within fifty seconds, in you go.'

Mayor Hector Petroskva ran like he had never run before. The bell rang just within the allotted time, and minutes later, the townspeople streamed out through the gate. A white-faced Petroskva scurried to the front of the townspeople, where the captain spoke to him again. 'Send some men back with the message that we will shortly send in one hundred soldiers to search the town. Anyone found hiding will be killed instantly.'

Twenty minutes later every citizen had gathered outside the gate. The captain looked at Bucher. 'I have no instructions as to what is to happen next, sir.'

Bucher smiled. 'Of course you haven't, Captain. That's because *I* will determine what will happen next. From now on you will simply follow orders. Understood?'

'Yes, Your Grace.'

Dropping his smirk, Bucher turned his cobra stare on the mayor. 'Separate the people into two halves. Keep families together. I do not wish to separate families. I'm not that heartless. *Really.*' The smirk returned.

Minutes later the citizens had been separated into two groups. Too terrified to open his mouth, Petroskva looked at Bucher for his next instruction. 'Are you standing in front of the group that contains your family, *Mayor* Petroskva?'

'Yes, sir. I am, sir.'

'Now raise one hand above your head. Any one will do.'

Petroskva raised his left hand.

'Ah, you are a very lucky man, *Mister* Mayor.' Bucher could not have cared less which hand came up. He had already made his decision. He turned and spoke briskly to his captain. 'Captain, you will arrange for the group to the mayor's left to be escorted to the village church. Get everyone inside, close the doors and nail them shut so they cannot be opened.'

'Yes, sir.' The captain issued orders and two columns of soldiers nudged their mounts forward to herd the residents through the gate and into the timber-framed church. Bucher did not speak again until he heard the sound of hammers.

He pointed to the town stables. 'Now remove every bale of hay and stack them all against the church walls.'

The captain appeared decidedly nervous. He glanced at his men who seemed just as bewildered. 'Yes, sir.' Not liking where this was going, he nodded to soldiers in the next available column to carry out the task.

Twenty minutes later the men returned to their original positions. Mayor Petroskva was panic-stricken. The threat was obvious. He knew he had to do something, or the church would be set alight. Petroskva was wrong. He was not required to do anything.

'Captain, order your torch-bearers to surround the building and light the bales. Anyone who attempts to escape through the windows is to be executed immediately.'

The captain was appalled. 'But sir, apart from the men, there are hundreds of women and child – ' In one smooth motion Bucher reached his right hand across his body, drew his sword and swung it hard to his right. A second later there was a dull thud as the captain's head bounced once and lay still on the ground. His body slumped forward before sliding out of the saddle.

Bucher crooked his finger at another captain. The soldier nudged his horse towards his commander-in-chief, but had the sense to stop at a safe distance. 'I need a captain who just happens to be looking for a promotion. Now that just happens to be you, young man, unless I am greatly mistaken and instead you are looking to join your comrade.' Bucher raised his voice. 'The same fate awaits any torch-bearer who fails to light his torch.'

The captain nodded. He knew he had no choice. Bucher would simply slice his way through his officers until one obeyed. 'Sir.' With tears in his eyes, he turned and nodded to the column of torch-bearers. After some hesitation and desperate looks among themselves, the torch-bearers moved through the gate. Moments later the bales were ablaze.

Bucher raised his voice to be heard above the screams coming from the church, as well as from the remaining citizens standing behind a white-faced Petroskva. 'Now then, *Mister* Mayor, this is what you will do. You will send messages of today's event to town after town and through one nation to the next. Each town or village is to volunteer half of its male population aged between sixteen and thirty to join my army in its struggle against the cowardly army from the south. The message will continue until I have 25,000 *volunteers*, plus the necessary number of camp followers. I will have my *volunteers* within ninety days, or else fifty thousand soldiers will make a little visit to each of those towns, in which case half their inhabitants will die, and their town will be torched. I was lenient today and spared your town, so consider yourselves lucky.

'I now bid you good day, Mayor Petroskva, so that you may commence your little task. Busy, busy, busy! Off you go, little man.' Bucher gave Petroskva an icy smile and turned his mount to lead his men back to camp.

Beckoning his captain, who broke away from his men to join him, he said. 'Good man, Captain! You did well. I'm proud of you, and a promise is a promise. It has been a most excellent day and I'm feeling particularly generous. I said you could have a promotion, so now choose any rank short of general, effective immediately. Take your pick, Captain.' Bucher chuckled. 'That might just be the last time I call you captain, Captain.'

'I actually like being a captain, so I'll pass on the promotion, if you don't mind. But thank you anyway – sir.' The captain saluted and turned away so the earl would not see the disgust on his face.

Relaxed and with his craving for torture temporarily satisfied, Bucher rode to the front to lead his men back to camp.

Time passed rapidly and weeks turned into months. Each day, Isabella's brigade's training grew more intense, yet the men reveled in their new special fitness and rapidly developing physiques. Even Marcus was astonished at some of the moves and new weaponry that she had devised for the giant swordsmen. He had no doubt that she would be a master tactician for a future generation of soldiers.

Gradually, the Southern army mobilized to head back through the mountains to their previous summer retreat. Isabella and her brigade were the last to leave. She had some special training to supervise deep in the mountain passes, and she wanted neither interference nor witnesses. Dmitri had provided her with the engineers and all the provisions she had requested.

Finally, everything was in place. Bridges had been tested and rehearsals perfected. Isabella decided it was time to return to the secret valley for a well-deserved hot bath before undertaking full rehearsal in snow conditions.

The Magician was ready for her next performance: she would lead two thousand men in one of the continent's most audacious robberies.

PART III - THE VALLEY

CHAPTER 90

It was morning of New Year's Eve, and the Northern soldiers had almost completed their preparations to get thoroughly drunk that night in a futile attempt to escape the bitter cold. Isabella watched with interest from between two snow-covered granite boulders on a nearby ridge as camp followers stoked the bread ovens while dozens of others threw chopped vegetables into stewing pots hooked above glowing embers. Breakfast would soon be served to one thousand of the earl's soldiers banished to the icy mountains to stand watch over cannons, gunpowder and other heavy materiel.

A large circle had been scored into the snow at the center of the camp the previous day. Around the perimeter, oil lamps hung from staffs stuck into the snow every five paces. Barrels of ale and spirits had been placed on cases from where they could be easily decanted and consumed. At the center of the circle was a long pit filled with burning logs and smaller branches collected from the nearby forest. By nightfall the wood would be reduced to the embers that would fuel the evening's roasts.

'We go in tonight.' Isabella whispered to Yannis, who was lying perfectly still on the ground next to her. Head to toe, they were both covered with double layers of fur, but still pressed against each other in search of extra warmth.

'Why are you whispering?' he asked. 'They wouldn't hear you from all the way up here even if you yelled.' His voice was muffled through the scarf that covered his entire face except for his eyes.

'I know. I know. It just seems natural to whisper when I see the enemy.'

Yannis nodded. 'I guess. Better safe than sorry. We will certainly have to play it safe when we go in tonight. We've been watching them for three days, so why tonight? Because most of them will be drunk?'

Isabella had not planned for Yannis to join her on this. When they were alone one November afternoon, he had told her that he was keen to join the mission, and she had responded that, as commander-in chief, his place was with the main army.

'Why should you have all the fun?' he had said with his most disarming smile. 'Nothing's going to happen here until mid-spring.'

Yannis had almost fallen on his back when she thrust her face into his and raged at him. '*Fun!* You think this will be *fun*, Yannis? My men have been training for months for this, and the other thousand men who have volunteered to join us for backup are already going through rigorous fitness training. Every one of them will risk his life. Not only confronting the enemy, but surviving the most inhospitable elements this planet can throw at a human being. They will have to cross mountains through snow, ice and raging rivers. We'll have another full month of agonizing training before I consider the men ready to go. *Fun?*'

'I'm sorry, Isabella. Calm down. It was just a figure of speech. But you're right. I can see that it will be extremely dangerous, and I'm fully prepared to join the training if you'll let me come along.'

'Let you? You mean you're not ordering me to take you with me?' Isabella's voice had returned to normal.

'Absolutely not. It's your mission. I'm asking, and it's your call.'

'You're the general. But let's forget about age and rank for a moment. This is suddenly just about you and me as ordinary people. I've planned every component of this mission for more than two years, and I must be in command at all times, or it simply won't work. I can't jeopardize that for anything or anyone.'

'Yes, yes. Understood. You have to be in command of your own mission.'

'Even if we're forced to confront the enemy or face other crises, it's imperative that I give the orders to resolve the issues. I must decide the priorities at all times.'

'Agreed.'

Isabella had hesitated, nervous. 'Do you fully realize that you're agreeing to allow me to tell you what to do?'

Yannis had grinned down at her. 'And why shouldn't I? You've been telling me what to do since the moment I met you.'

'Oh you!' She had laughed and punched his chest with an open fist, noting that he had looked flushed and excited at the prospect of joining her mission – almost as excited as she was. It had already been decided that it was not practical for Zhang Chen to take part this time.

Now Isabella turned to look at Yannis as he lay pressed up against her on the ridge. 'The probability that they will be drunk and noisy is certainly a factor,' she said. 'They also would not expect anything to happen on New Year's Eve. But the biggest factor is the weather and the moon. We need both moonlight and snow during the night. There are no night-time guards, but a couple of soldiers do the rounds once a day at late morning. My team will obscure our tracks as we leave, but it's impossible to hide them perfectly, and certainly not in the dead of night. A blanket of snow should remove any residual evidence of our presence. The weather can be unpredictable, but based on my observations, we should have both a half-moon and snowfall tonight. Besides …'

'Besides?'

'We have so many barrels to exchange that it will take two nights to complete the mission. Tonight is therefore the ideal time to make a start, and we can only hope for the best tomorrow. We simply can't wait forever.'

Yannis nodded in agreement. 'Hungry?'

'Starving. Let's go. Breakfast should be ready by now.' She held up her hands and gave a series of signals that were quickly passed on to the fifty men lining the ridge. Yannis rolled over and held out a gloved hand to Isabella, who took it in a firm grip, and they slid down the slope together, laughing quietly all the way.

Isabella addressed the group leaders sitting in a semi-circle on the cave floor in front of her. One third of the mission group occupied the cave, while the remainder were hidden away in seven smaller caves within an hour's walk through heavy snow. Group leaders would soon leave to give their men their final instructions.

Smoke from the lanterns and smells from the cooking for 700 men and women unable to properly cleanse themselves in the freezing conditions made for an unpleasant environment. Isabella attempted to breathe through her mouth rather than her nose.

'You've all seen the enemy's layout and where everything is placed. Closest to us and the hill, as I had expected and hoped, are the wagons containing the gunpowder. Then come the long line of cannons, and finally their stores which are next to their camp. The area they chose is the only one between themselves and our valley that is large enough to place all that materiel, so I had no difficulty guessing the location for this mission. I will now provide you with the final summary of what we're going to do, commencing at nine tonight, when the celebrations will be well underway.'

Isabella repeated her explanation of how the two thousand counterfeit barrels would be carried, hand-to-hand in columns, down the slope and exchanged for the gunpowder, which would then be carried back up the slope by the same method. Each team had previously rehearsed their tasks and knew exactly what to do.

'Is there any chance of them recognizing the counterfeit barrels, Isabella?' one of the group leaders asked.

'Good question, Zachary, and the answer is *no*. We arranged purchase of powder, via friendly neighbors, from the same manufacturer in the north: same barrels, same markings. The powder was later replaced by non-explosives with the same weight, re-sealed and brought here last summer. Does that answer your question?'

'Yes. Brilliant!' Zachary nodded and smiled.

'On completion, my team, with their special tools, will come behind and cover our tracks. I will be among the first down and the last to leave. The expected snowfall should obliterate any last trace. Each man will then take one barrel and carry it back to Hertzog's Rock. From there, others will take the barrels to the other side of the first bridge, and then past the rock-fall, to be fully out of sight in case someone should follow us. The bridge will then be destroyed and we'll head for headquarters.

'All right, men, it's time to get some sleep. I want everyone assembled below the ridge, where I've arranged for a hot meal and drinks to be waiting for you. At nine, we go! Too easy. Any questions?' Isabella felt confident and relaxed as she smiled at the soldiers.

One of the group leaders raised his hand. 'Do you have a contingency plan in case we should be discovered?'

'Of course. Run for your lives!' Isabella answered, straight-faced.

There was a stunned silence until the men saw the sparkle in her eyes and a smirk starting to form. Within moments the laughter echoed off the walls of the cave.

'Seriously, though, that's why I brought two hundred crossbowmen with us. They'll be placed out of sight at the ridge, ready for action. I will also have two men standing on a portable scaffold to keep an eye on the party. At the first sign of trouble, I'll give the order to retreat. All right, off to your beds, men.'

'You really do think of everything, Isabella,' Yannis offered as he came up to sit next to her. 'The enemy will party while you'll have two thousand men working like well organized columns of ants. You no longer surprise me, but you never cease to amaze me, if that makes sense.'

'I can only hope I have thought of everything, Yannis.' She leaned her head gently against his shoulder. 'All our lives depend on it.'

'Does that worry you? Does it scare you?'

'No, just the opposite, actually. The fact that the men are relying on me gives me great strength and confidence. Quite frankly, now that we are in the thick of it and about to strike, I can honestly say I have never felt better.' She stood up. The cave became darker as lamps were extinguished. 'It's time to rest, Yannis. We have a very long night ahead of us.'

He nodded as she turned and made her way to her mattress, lying down in the shadow of the flickering lights. Moments later Yannis knelt beside her with his mattress in hand. 'Do you mind if I bunk down next to you?'

Isabella looked up at him. She did not say a word, but raised her eyebrows.

He flicked his eyes towards the men and grimaced. 'The smell is so much worse over there with that crowd, Isabella.'

'You're really not that good with words when it comes to charming the ladies, Yannis. With a bit of thought you would realize that was not a very flattering thing to say to me. I am now considering an act of extreme violence.'

'I'm sorry. I didn't mean that you … ah … God, I've done it again. Me and my big mouth.'

'Never mind. I'm getting used to your insults. All right, you can stay here. No, not *here*! Over there!' Isabella pointed to a spot a body-width away. 'Just make sure you keep your distance. I don't want anyone to think that … you know, that you and I are …'

'Yes, absolutely! Don't worry. I'll keep my distance.'

Hours later his internal army alarm woke him to instant panic mode. He looked around desperately to get his bearing until he was confident that he had remained in his designated spot. Isabella, however, was snuggled up and snoring gently against his side. Slowly, he inched away from her and moved his mattress.

'Isabella,' he whispered, gently stroking her face with the back of his fingers. 'Time to go.'

Her eyes flew open and she sat up. She was fully awake now and also fully aware. Yannis' mattress was a body-width away from her – and so was her own. She knew instantly what had happened. Someone broke the impasse by gently blowing a wake-up call.

•

Isabella was the first down the slope, Yannis was right behind, followed by team one. Four columns, straight and equidistant, ran down to the wagons a short way past the bottom of the hill.

On the flat, the columns spread out to enter between the neat rows of wagons. While the look-outs erected their viewing scaffold, the men got to work. Twenty minutes later, the first of the counterfeit barrels arrived and were carefully placed to ensure they were not mistaken for the genuine article.

Party noises were subdued, due to distance and the noise-absorbing effect of the snow, but increased substantially as midnight approached. A roar across the valley indicated that one year had at last moved into the next. Light brightened and waned as clouds passed over the partial moon. The barrels moved smoothly in both directions and they were ahead of schedule when suddenly one of the look-outs hissed, 'Someone's coming. Several men are heading in our direction.'

'Do you want to stop?' Yannis whispered to Isabella.

'Not yet. It will take them fifteen minutes or more to reach here in the deep snow conditions. We'll give it five. If they continue our way after that, we'll leave. Incidentally, you'll be the first to go.'

'But I – '

'It's not up for discussion, General. The army will need their commander-in-chief if things go awry here.'

'Yes, Major. Understood as agreed.'

'There's a good boy.'

The look-out whispered again. 'It's all right. The men just stopped to – '

Isabella hissed back, cutting him off. 'All right! I get the picture. There's a party and lots of drinking. You don't have to spell it out.'

The look-out sniggered as he nudged his mate with his elbow. The two men sounded like mice squealing over a chunk of cheese.

Isabella sent the signal to stop transporting counterfeit barrels down the slope. 'It's time to get out of here, Yannis.' She quickly gave orders for the men to commence the extraction plan.

'We could get at least another hour in, surely.'

'No. It's too dangerous. It's getting darker. More cloud, less moon. That's exactly what I want – snow. But we have to get out while we still have some light. We have to fill every trench while we can still see them. If we miss just one, there will be a long indent visible no matter how much it snows. Our target number for tonight will have been achieved, so there's everything to gain and nothing to lose by going now. On the other hand, we have much to lose if we leave too late.'

Well practiced with their innovative tools, the clean-up team worked their way smoothly and quickly up the slope just as snow started to fall. Five hundred barrels remained on the ridge for exchange the following night.

Later, they had a subdued party in the cave to celebrate both their success and the arrival of the new year. Exhaustion soon forced the men to drift away to get some sleep. Making moves to do the same, Isabella pointed at Yannis and then at the other side of the cave. 'You're sleeping over there with your friends who, according to you, smell even worse than I do.'

'But it's …'

'No *buts*. I'm not at all worried about you, Yannis. You were the perfect gentleman as always. It's me who can't be trusted.'

'It's quite all right, Isabella. It was bitter cold. I didn't mind.'

She clenched her teeth and looked away. *That's the point, Yannis. Neither did I and that's why you're sleeping over there and I'm sleeping over here.* When she looked back at him, her response had the tone of finality. 'Me here. You there.'

CHAPTER 91

It was after midnight the following night, and deathly quiet. The enemy soldiers no doubt had severe hangovers from the previous night's celebrations.

Even before Isabella had stepped over the row of smooth logs placed along the ridge and begun the descent to the wagons, she had decided that two columns on the slope would be enough to handle the remaining barrels. Within two hours the first of the genuine barrels was moving steadily up the slope. The night was growing colder by the minute. Breathing became not only difficult, but painful. Even with thick cloth wrapped around their faces, the men could not prevent the urge to cough. Yannis seemed relaxed and pleased with progress, while Isabella became more agitated as the night passed.

With no activity within the enemy camp, and nothing to report, the two look-outs became bored and asked to change places with the men switching the barrels. 'We're so cold,' one of them mumbled through several layers of scarves, 'we'll do anything to get warm. There's so much moonlight tonight that two of us aren't really needed to watch the camp, so we can take turns.'

Isabella asked Yannis to make the necessary arrangements. As soon as he left to carry out her instructions, she continued to pace back and forth in the trench, her anxiety increasing to near-panic. She knew she had made a catastrophic mistake. Their well-rehearsed plan would not work a second time. *She had to find a new extraction plan, and she had to win a race with sunrise to execute it!*

Yannis was back in ten minutes. 'I checked the numbers while I was at it. The last barrel is on its way up and the last of the wagons is being re-loaded. We'll be ready to leave in thirty minutes. The extraction team is already spreading snow on top of the wagons. Some of the men can start the back-fill, if you want.'

The team leader shuffled up for instructions just as Yannis finished his report. Isabella grabbed the man's arm in a vice-like grip. 'Manny, after you've finished making the wagons presentable, I want you to back-fill only the trenches between them. After that, make sure you have all your tools and get ready to move out of here. On the way up the slope, I want you to spread out and trample your way up, making as much mess as you can.'

'*What?*' Both Manny and Yannis spoke as one.

'And Yannis, you must leave at once. When you get to the top, tell Johan to get ready for emergency evacuation Plan B; he and his team will know exactly what to do. Tell him the number will be fifty-one. Got it?'

'Got it. Fifty-one. But what – ?'

'Sorry, but there's not much time. Just remember: *Johan. Plan B. Fifty-one.* Then tell Yancko and his team to get down here at once and make sure they're *unarmed*. I have a new mission for them. Oh, and Yannis, tell the leader of the crossbowmen that I won't need their services and that they can help carry the gunpowder. The top priority is now to get those barrels out of sight behind the rock-fall. In case I run late, have men ready to destroy the bridge at a moment's notice even if I'm caught on this side. It's imperative that those barrels are never sighted by the enemy. You need to go now, Yannis. There is much to be done and not much time. Good luck.'

'All right, I'm on my way. But quickly, just a few words, please, Isabella. What's changed? What's the problem?' Yannis sounded frantic.

Isabella pointed to the sky. 'The weather. There's too much light and it's getting colder. That means the weather is clearing. It won't snow, so the risk is that someone will spot something after sunrise no matter how well we clean up. We needed that snow so they couldn't eventually figure out we've stolen gunpowder.'

Yannis quickly sent Manny to start the evacuation. 'How could they know?'

'If they discover an intrusion they'll search to see what's missing. They'll see that the snow is pristine everywhere except around the wagons. They will know that no-one would breach their camp in such atrocious conditions to then leave empty-handed. It won't take them long to figure out what's been taken even though an inventory check will at first indicate that all seems well. If the earl finds out that forty tons of powder is missing, he'll know we intend to use it on them, and he'll do everything in his power to get it back, or stop us – *immediately*. The entire war hangs in the balance, so I simply can't take any chances.'

'But how can you change things with daylight less than two hours away? What will you do?'

The extraction team moved past them and headed for the slope. 'That's why I've been telling you I don't have much time. I need Yancko's men here right now to help me to stage a deception. I have to create another illusion. Yancko and his men are going to commit a second robbery, and then the enemy can focus on that.'

'Where will you steal something else?'

'The main camp, of course. There's nothing else on offer.'

'But they might hear you or see you!'

'If they don't, I intend to wake them up to make sure they do!'

'You will wake …? *You* intend to go into their camp yourself? But Yancko's team consists of fifty men who can – oh, God! – Major Mondeo makes fifty-one. I should have known.' Yannis' shoulders slumped in despair.

'We'll make tracks everywhere, both in and out of camp. That's why I need as much mess as possible. The only place my team won't be leaving any tracks is on the hill, so I need the extraction team to make them for us to complete the illusion. I'll explain that later. How do you hide something in plain sight, Yannis? You toss it on top of a rubbish tip! Now please go! Sunrise won't wait, and every minute you delay puts me and Yancko's men in more danger. I have one last message for you to give to Yancko.'

When she had finished, they stared at each other awkwardly for several moments. Then they reached out and touched ice-covered gloves before Yannis turned to head for the slope. The work had been completed and the remaining men were in the trenches as they made their way to the top. Handled like a barrel, Yannis was propelled to the ridge in five minutes rather than the usual hour.

Yancko and his men slid down the slope within minutes, while Johan bellowed out orders and unfurled his team's precious ropes.

Yancko rubbed his gloved hands with excitement as his men crowded around Isabella for information and instructions. 'We're really going in there, Major? Right into their camp? We're going to rob them? And why no weapons?'

'Settle down, Captain. Questions, questions, questions. Yes, we're about to rob the enemy. This will be very dangerous, so don't get too excited. The reason for no weapons is that there is a real chance we'll be caught in the snow drifts and be overpowered. If we haven't killed or injured anyone, we could hope to be treated as thieves with the potential to negotiate a release. That's also why I stood down the crossbowmen. If we kill a few hundred enemy soldiers and then get caught, it's more than likely that they'll put us to the sword on the spot. They might kill us all anyway, but logic dictates that the odds are slightly better if we haven't harmed anyone. Make no mistake, men: this is a very dangerous mission and this time you are not here as volunteers. We're going in, whether you like it or not!'

'Oh, how I love an assertive woman! We're career soldiers, Major.' Yancko rubbed his hands with delight. 'Danger, excitement and risk! This is what we live for, and that's exactly what you promised us. That's why you're here, too, isn't it? You're the same as us: you're a born soldier and you love it. We're ready for your orders, Major.'

'Thank you, Yancko. It's soldiers like all of you here tonight who win battles. Did you spread out the torches ready for lighting in the way Yannis told you to?' The men nodded. 'All right, men, this is how we're going to rob them. Remember at all times: no names or ranks; from this moment on, we're bandits, not soldiers.'

Snoring could be heard from the enemy asleep in reinforced tents just a few paces from the robbers sliding silently past in the dark. Iron bars made quick work of the clasps holding the doors to the stores' huts. Jackets were removed and placed over the clasps to muffle the sound as they split away from the timber architraves. Any goods that did not make a noise to the touch became fair game for the robbers. Items were hurriedly passed out through the doors before those inside grabbed a last handful as they left. It did not matter what they stole; every item would be dumped on the way out of camp. As instructed, the men made as many tracks as possible on their way back past the tents.

A loud sneeze and cough brought the robbers to an instant stop. No-one moved a muscle. The one thing that Isabella had considered, but could do nothing about, was the risk of an enemy soldier needing to answer the call of nature. Her heart pounded wildly while she waited.

The moonlight was bright, but the man must have been facing another direction. Isabella heard him cough several times before he yawned and shuffled his way back to his tent. She waited another minute before she raised her arm, and the shadows ahead of her started to move towards the cannons. Isabella was behind her men, the last to leave the camp.

Most of Yancko's men were strung out between the cannons and the wagons when a voice roared back at her from slightly in front. *'Oh my God!* Help me! Help me! I've slipped and broken my leg! Oh God, it hurts! Someone help me!'

Yancko was further ahead and yelled back at his man. 'We'll send someone back for you! I can't see you. We'll have to light some torches.'

'Hurry, I can feel the bone sticking out of my leg. I can't move. I'll be caught. Help me!' The man's screams echoed across the valley.

Seconds later, several torches on poles burst into life. 'I said someone will come for you,' Yancko bellowed back. 'And shut up. You'll have the whole camp all over us in minutes, you fool!'

Shouts could now be heard from the enemy camp as Isabella increased her pace. Up ahead she could see more torches being lit, some of them at the base of the slope. A bugle sounded and the camp came alive with men running in all directions. Fires and torches were being lit as men tried to determine what could have created an emergency situation in a snowed-in valley.

'Enemy intruders!' Another bugle sounded. 'To arms, men! They're getting away. Quickly, get after them!'

Ahead, Isabella saw some of her men dart into the rows of wagons, and then back out. 'Get out of there, you fools! You can't hide in there,' Yancko roared. 'They'll find you as soon as the sun comes up.' The men rushed out from between the rows of wagons, discarding the flaming torches on the snow as they headed for the slope. By then, hundreds of soldiers could be seen trudging from the camp through the heavy snow. Occasionally some of them stumbled over pieces of goods deliberately dropped by Yancko's men.

Isabella reached the slope and asked one of Johan's men sent down to assist them up the slope, 'Have you done the head count?'

'Yes, Major. Twice to make sure. Fifty. You make fifty-one. There are five of us to assist, which makes fifty-six. We've got sixty ropes, giving us a few spares, in case someone accidentally disengages from his rope. We'll come up after everyone else is up and safe.'

'Excellent! Let's get going before that pack of wolves is all over us!' She pointed towards the soldiers streaming out of the camp; the nearest was just fifteen minutes away. Yancko's men had followed instructions and had placed several torches in the rows between the wagons, and then a straight row of flaming torches at the base of the slope, between themselves and the approaching soldiers. Isabella hoped that the row of flickering bright lights would be enough to diffuse the enemy's vision of the illusion about to take place.

'How did I go with my broken leg, Major? Did I sound convincing?'

Isabella laughed. 'You certainly fooled me and everyone else in the camp. As a matter of fact, I've just received a message that you also succeeded in waking a village on the east coast of England.'

The men chuckled among themselves. The man who had been chosen to wake the camp was chuffed by the praise.

'We'll start with the ropes from the left,' Johan's man called out. 'Move across from the others to my comrades, one at a time, so you won't get tangled in the other ropes. I'll lower and raise my torch, which will be the signal for you to hold your breath. Move quickly. I want to dispatch each man within five seconds of each other. That will get us out of here in about five minutes. All right, let's go! Watch your head at the top.' Johan's men had already clipped belts around Yancko's men while one of them gently secured a belt around Isabella's waist. A hook at the end of the rope was clipped into a ring on the belt, and everyone was ready.

The man lowered and raised the torch and the first man disappeared into the darkness in an instant. His groan vanished almost as quickly as the man himself. 'Next,' Johan's man whispered.

At the top of the ridge, Johan sliced the air with his arm every time he saw the torch dip and rise. At the signal, four burly former sailors hung on to loops and knots on the long ropes slung over the smooth logs, and hurled themselves down an almost vertical drop on their side of the steep slope. As they rocketed down one side, Yancko's men rocketed up the other. Scores of thick jackets had been placed against the logs so the men would not be killed or seriously injured as they crashed into them.

Hundreds of Johan's men lined the ridge to take their turn on a rope. Their job was done once they had thrown themselves down the slope. From there each group of four headed directly for the first bridge, coiling their rope as they went.

Two minutes later barely half of Yancko's men had disappeared when Isabella spun around to face a new threat.

An officer could be heard yelling to his men. 'Put those torches out. *Now!* Stomp them into the snow. Those idiots have no idea what they were trying to hide behind. If those wagons go, there won't be a hill between here and the coast.'

The voice was loud. Too loud. Too close! No-one should have reached the wagons for at least another five minutes. Isabella's mind worked at crisis speed. How could they possibly have moved so fast? At that speed the enemy would reach them before they could get away. The specter of capture or death in the darkness became a sudden reality as the explanation dawned on her.

'Yancko! Where are you?' Isabella turned and spoke quickly to Johan's man. 'You five: hook up to your ropes at once.' Yancko scrambled forward. 'Yancko, quickly, exchange hooks with Manny. You're up next. They'll follow orders up top without a moment's hesitation if they come from you. When you get there you will order Johan to get his men attached to every rope and jump immediately without waiting for any signals. Never mind the risk of ropes tangling. The risks are much greater if we don't get out of here right now!'

Yancko moved quickly to attach himself to the next rope at the far left. 'Why? What's going on?'

'That voice. It was too close. There's only one way they can have passed the wagons already. Some of the brigade must be experienced mountain soldiers. They have a platoon on skis!'

Yancko groaned. 'I'll stay and fight, Major!'

'No, you won't! And no more mention of rank or names under any circumstances. They will be all over us within a minute or two. They're armed and we're not. We won't stand a chance in the dark. We won't even get the chance to negotiate when they can't see whether or not we're armed.' She nodded to the sailor, who lowered and raised his torch faster than he had ever done. Yancko disappeared in a blur of snow.

'Get ready, men. Here they come!' Isabella could hear the soft swish of skis against the snow as the soldiers headed directly towards the line of torches. They were even closer than she had expected. She could see them clearly and estimated there were around one hundred troops, barely seconds away. Yancko would only just have reached the top, and even though Johan would react quickly to Yancko's orders, many of the men would be stretched in a long line while they waited their turn on the ropes. Isabella knew at once that they would not get away in time. They were about to be captured or killed.

CHAPTER 92

Isabella grabbed her rope and dragged it forward as she moved to place herself between her men and the men on skis. Without realizing the dire consequence of her next action, she pulled at the rope to give herself additional slack to allow her to move freely.

'What are you doing?' Johan's man called out. He, too, had not realized the consequences of slack in her rope.

'First line of defense. I'm the only one who's armed,' she called over her shoulder.

'You're armed?'

'Well, sort of. I don't know whether my weapons will be of much use in these conditions, though. Here, put these under your jackets.' She quickly pulled off her boots and tossed them to the man. She tossed her outer jacket to another.

The ski patrol slowed as soon as they reached the line of torches and drew their swords. They held up their free hands as a screen against the lights and peered into the darkness beyond the flames.

Isabella stood completely still and waited for her moment. Every second would count now, she thought. Every second of hesitation kept the ski patrol and their swords away from her men. Thirty seconds should do it. She focused on the man at center front who appeared to be their senior officer. The power to wage war surged through every cell of her body to transform her into the *Serpent Warrior*. She saw the man's head turn to one side, about to issue the order to attack. His eyes were off her for just that instant. It was enough. Her moment had arrived.

With a battle cry taught her by Zhang Chen, the young Zen Master leapt towards the officer before he could utter a sound, pulling one of the torches out of the snow on the way. The man bellowed as the torch was thrust into his face, followed by crushing blows from a foot to his chest and another to his head an instant later. With his feet fastened to skis, he was unable to counterbalance the forces against his upper body. He toppled sideways into the men alongside. The Zen Master instantly moved in the opposite direction. Her body spun one way and then the other, while her feet connected with heads, shoulders and legs. Within seconds she changed direction again, giving the men no chance to recover from having their commanding officer falling over several of them. Their skis became their handicap. Unable to swing their swords effectively against such a fast-moving target without striking their comrades, the men slipped and fell in all directions. The Zen Master grabbed a second torch and used both as fiery swords to assist her feet as she smashed into one man after the other. A huge cloud of snow sprayed high into the air from the flailing skis, leaving a thick layer of powder on her jacket.

A sudden series of loud grunts and groans behind her told her that Johan's men were at last in action. So were some of the men from the ski patrol. Several of the more quick-thinking at the rear had managed to remove the cumbersome bindings to their skis and push their way to the front.

As they rushed her, the men had no choice but to trample directly over the top of a tangle of skis and other men thrashing helplessly on the ground. The *Serpent Warrior* heard more grunts and groans behind her, followed suddenly by silence. The only sounds now were those of the men in front of her trying to get to their feet. A quick glance behind her told her all she needed to know. She was on her own.

Several soldiers only a few paces away raised their swords to destroy the person who had single-handedly knocked down dozens of their comrades. In the expectation that she was about to face her last moment, the *Serpent Warrior* leaned forward with the two torches and roared into the face of the man who reached her first. He hesitated momentarily before swinging his blade high and striking a powerful blow at her head.

As the man's sword cut cleanly through the two torches, he watched his target literally disappear in a huge explosion of snow. The *Serpent Warrior* had vanished into the darkness.

Isabella gasped with the shock of the sudden backward pull and had to fight to breathe as the man in front of her disappeared. A few seconds later, a solid bump against thick furs told her she had reached the top. Johan grinned at her as he removed the rope and belt, and gave her a brief hug.

'Sorry, Major, I just have to hug you. I'll probably never have an opportunity like this again without being court-martialed.'

'Well, in that case, I'm going to give you a hug right back,' she said and did just that. 'Oh, Johan, what a lucky, lucky day it was when I met you. You are truly my rock. Every time I need someone special, I call for you and you never let me down. And please, when we are on our own, don't ever call me anything other than *Isabella*.' She felt her body shake from a combination of shock and the frigid air. Her feet were dangerously cold. 'My boots, my boots! I need my boots and jacket, please.'

'They're over here.' Johan rushed to grab them from a rock and was back in seconds. 'But first, sit down here.' He pushed her gently onto a rock while he knelt down and untied his jacket, then his inner jacket. He quickly removed her wet socks and thrust her bare feet against his chest, wrapping his jackets around her calves. 'Dry socks!' he roared to no one in particular. Socks were in his hands within seconds and he quickly stuffed them inside his jackets against his skin to remove the frost. He brought out one of her feet to massage it vigorously before he placed it back against his chest to massage the other.

'That was a close call, Johan. Another second and I would have arrived up here in two pieces.'

Johan shuddered at the thought. 'I didn't find out until one of the last men up told us what you were doing down there. No-one, including me, will ever have a heart the size of yours. You must be insane, Isabella, but we love you to death. We could feel the ropes with tension and knew we had a fish on the other end, and up they came. Any rope with slack in it had to be the spares, so we left them until last. I couldn't understand why you had not already arrived until someone mentioned that you had pulled slack in your rope to give you room to attack the ski patrol. You could not have realized the consequences of creating that slack, but as soon as I knew, I told the teams to jump on all of the remaining ropes at the same time.'

Isabella whimpered with pain as the blood flowed back into the muscles and joints of her feet, but overall she felt considerably better.

'I'll keep warming your feet until the others have gone. It will be time well spent, I assure you. The barrels are long gone, so we won't have to carry a thing. We'll catch up in no time. The pulley logs have been kicked into the valley below, and the ropes have been taken away. By the time those barbarians get up here they won't have a clue as to what we did. That was a brilliant back-up plan, Isabella. Not only that, I think it's marvelous the way you always make sure you have another trick up your sleeve. You really are a born magician.'

CHAPTER 93

Only after having removed their skis did the fallen soldiers get back on their feet. In the torch light they all appeared sheepish, except for Colonel Oleg Walenski, who looked absolutely stricken.

'Men, for all of our sakes, we have a few things to consider before we give chase. We were on skis, the thieves were not. General Mendez will know we must have caught up with them by the time we got to the slope, and yet we have nothing to show him. No prisoners and no bodies. As your commanding officer, I will be required to report to the general. What do you want me to tell him? Do you want me to report that we were attacked by one man and that he knocked down more than thirty of us, armed only with a flaming torch, while dozens of thieves that we saw only moments earlier disappeared up that hill in a matter of minutes – when we know it takes more than an hour in deep snow? And Charles, what shall I tell the general about you? You just told me that as you swung your sword to cut the man in half, he simply vanished in a puff of smoke.'

Charles spoke quietly in the dark. 'That's what happened, sir. Only I'm not sure now whether it was a man or a woman. The … the … thing, for a better word, roared in my face when I slashed with my sword. The voice was a bit muffled through cloth, but it seemed high-pitched, much like a woman.'

'Oh, even better! That really helps me a lot, men. A woman!' He stared at his men, more worried than before. 'Would you like me to report that an unarmed *woman* knocked us down before she disappeared in a puff of smoke after the other thieves vanished into thin air?'

'Well, when you put it like that, it does sound a bit … ah …' Charles did not know what the colonel wanted him to say.

'I will tell you what it sounds like, men. It sounds crazy. It will sound like we witnessed a magic show in the middle of a snowfield. Worse, it sounds like a pack of lies. We'll be the laughing stock of the army. If the general doesn't kill us for thinking we ran away from the thieves, the earl will surely have our heads on a platter. You all know of his penchant for doing that deed personally.'

'So what are you going to tell General Mendez, Colonel?'

'I will tell you exactly what happened here tonight. If anyone says otherwise, he will bring shame to himself and everyone else in our platoon. Is that clear?'

'Yes, sir.' A chorus of voices reached Walenski's ears.

'This will be my report. In their panic to hide, the thieves unwittingly left flaming torches among the wagons. Our first priority was the safety of our men in camp and the security of the powder and cannons. It would take only one torch to set off the powder, and without the powder the war effort is as good as over. *General Mendez, sir,* I'm sure that His Grace will be so pleased that his mountain troops made every effort to first secure the powder, even at the risk of their own lives. By the time we reached the slope, the thieves were frantically climbing their way to the top. We terrified the poor wretches so much they scattered their booty all over the place in their panic to escape. By the time we removed our skis to give chase, it was too late to catch them on the slope, but we gave chase and catch them we will.

'Alexis, you will go back and give General Mendez a summary of my report, and tell him that the rest of us have given chase as a matter of honor, even though the intruders are no more than peasant farmers from nearby villages. Tell the general that we intend to teach them a lesson. Tell him that we're well equipped to give chase, and that we'll bring them back with hooks through their noses.

'Take a couple of men with you, Alexis, and take all of these torches and scatter them all over the place between the rows of wagons. Make lots of tracks. A bit of extra *evidence* of our courage won't go astray.'

'Yes, sir.'

'Oh, and Alexis …'

'Yes, sir?'

'Make sure the torches are completely extinguished when you scatter them around.'

'Just as well you mentioned that, Colonel. I was going to set fire to a few wagons to find my way in the dark,' Alexis sniggered.

'Let's get up that hill, men,' Walenski called, feeling considerably better.

•

'They're gaining on us, Johan.' It was mid-morning and Isabella could clearly see the enemy soldiers. 'I really didn't think they would bother to give chase. It's not as if we stole anything of value, and I made sure it was all left behind.'

'Probably more a matter of pride.' Johan barely puffed as he pressed on without looking back. 'Or someone who needs to impress his superiors.'

'I fear it's the latter, which means they won't give up.'

'It will take us about two hours to get to the bridge, so it's going to be touch and go. We have the advantage when we go uphill because of the strength of my legs. It's the same with the men ahead of us. That's why we haven't caught up to them yet. You said some time ago that our legs would save our lives. You were right. You trained us well, Isabella. My legs feel great, even when I carry you up the steepest parts. How are your feet, by the way?'

'A bit painful, but I believe that's a good thing, so all in all, I feel fine. My big worry is the long gentle slope that leads down to the bridge.'

'Yes, I've been thinking about that one myself. Any more magic tricks up your sleeve, Isabella?'

'Yes, as a matter of fact I have. And it's a good one.'

Johan brightened instantly. 'Tell me. What is it?'

'Move faster!'

'Now that's a *good* idea!' Their laughter echoed across the narrow valley.

'We're gaining on them, Colonel. Slowly, but surely. It's a pity it's not all down-hill. Then we'd have them in minutes.'

Walenski was breathing hard as he side-stepped his way up the hill with his snow-encrusted skis and steering pole over his shoulder. The skis were broad, and the timber thick to help counterbalance the sag effect near the midpoint, caused by the body weight. He was tiring rapidly, as were many of his men. Walenski was an experienced skier and practiced his chosen sport at every opportunity during the winter months. But like every ski enthusiast, he always planned ahead to use the ski runs the shortest way up and the longest, most circuitous run to the bottom. Trudging uphill was hard work; skiing down was easy and exhilarating. At that moment, however, he did not feel very exhilarated. 'Big deal, Charles. So we catch up with those two, David and Goliath, up ahead. Then what? I only got a glimpse of others ahead of them and that was some time ago. Those are the ones we really want. David and Goliath will be nothing more than excess baggage.'

Charles nodded. 'I guess you're right, Colonel. We either have to kill them, or we'll have to allocate a few men to guard them.'

'We can't kill them. We might need them for information about the others: who they are, how many, their weapons and so on.'

'You're right,' Charles said sourly. He dearly wanted to have another chance to cut in half the man – or woman – who had so narrowly escaped his blade.

Walenski winced as he stared down the hill at his men. They were all in reasonable physical shape, but the first climb had taken well over an hour and their legs were spent. Some of them now looked up at Walenski with silent pleading in their eyes. He stopped as if merely waiting for them to reach him, but the fact was he desperately needed to catch his own breath without his men noticing.

'Men, when we reach the top, there is a slight downhill run, then a flat to the foot of the next hill. We'll stop there and have a rest and some refreshments, so we'll be fresh for the hill.' Walenski's announcement was greeted with a mixture of groans and muted cheers. 'There's actually no hurry. Even though I haven't been here for a couple of years, I know the area well and, in their hurry to get away, the thieves have stupidly entered a trap. They didn't think we'd give chase, so they simply took off in the easiest direction to get out of sight in a hurry. If it wasn't for catching a glimpse of David and Goliath, we would have had no idea where they went. Up ahead is a gorge and a raging river that never stops or freezes over. The gorge runs for miles in both directions; there are no roads or tracks they can take and there's no way to cross the river. There is only one way out, men – and that is straight into our welcoming arms!'

That brought a long and rousing cheer.

'What was that, sir?' One of the men cupped his hand to his ear.

'What was what? You were making too much noise. I didn't hear a thing.'

'I don't know what it was, sir, but it sounded a bit like laughter.'

Walenski rolled his eyes. 'There you go! I was right in the first place. We *are* nuts!'

'I don't believe what I'm seeing, Johan.' The two had traversed another flat and were climbing a steep hill as a shortcut. To save time, Johan carried

Isabella half slung over his shoulder, facing the rear.

'What do you see?'

'I expected to see the troops not far behind us now that the long slope is just the other side of this hill. Instead they are way back, sitting around a fire. I think I can just make out that they're having food and hot drinks.'

'They're exhausted, Isabella. They don't have our stamina, and they probably also realize they need to conserve enough energy for a fight at the end of the chase.' Johan stopped briefly to turn and take a quick look. 'We've picked up at least half an hour, and with a bit of luck, we might just make it. At least the other men will make it. Oh, oh! They're packing up. Time for us to move. Let's have a snack and a drink while we make our way to the top.' He put Isabella down gently, reached into a bag slung around his waist and brought out sandwiches and two small bladders of water. 'Being a big eater, I grabbed a double helping at breakfast.' They ate in silence as they continued their climb.

Isabella paused at the top to study the terrain and reassess their chances. She could see Yancko's men well over half-way down, and could just make out men on the other side of the gorge carrying the last of the barrels towards the rock-fall. There would not be a barrel to be seen within five minutes. Isabella sighed deeply with relief – the mission itself was safe, but she and Johan were not. Unless …

'I know what you're thinking, Isabella, but don't you *ever* dare say anything like that to me!'

'What am I thinking?'

'It's the way you looked at the ski patrol, then at the bridge and then at me. With my strength and long stride through the tracks made by Yancko's men, you believe I can make it on my own. It's not only in your eyes, Isabella. I know only too well about your heart and your courage. Forget it.'

'All right, I won't offend you by saying it. Let's go, then. Every second counts.' Isabella took off instantly with Johan close behind.

Yannis had deliberately allowed himself to drop back behind Yancko's men, turning constantly to search for a sign of Isabella. He was within minutes of the bridge when he saw her stumbling down the slope with Johan.

Oh, thank God, Isabella, you made it. You're safe. Yannis sighed with relief as he slowly made his way backwards towards the bridge. Suddenly he saw Isabella stumble and fall on her face. He stumbled himself, falling on his back. By the time he managed to scramble to his feet, Johan had already lifted her up and they were back in full flight down the slope.

Johan felt, rather than saw, Isabella's pace decrease. The thick clothing, the boots, the heavy snow, and the energy needed to keep her balance on the slippery track had taken its toll. It had been a grueling, relentless and non-stop few hours in the heaviest conditions known to man, and he was himself almost exhausted. Almost.

'Isabella, I have an idea. Are you up for a bit of fun?'

'This is your lucky day, Johan. You've caught me at exactly the right time for a bit of fun. What do you have in mind?'

'Keep going until I get my jacket off.' Moments later he tossed his huge jacket to her. 'Keep going! Every step counts! Put your arms through the sleeves, back to front. I'll tie it at the back.'

She did as she was told, moving all the time. 'Done, now what?'

'Simply relax. Here we go!' Isabella shrieked as she felt herself suddenly picked up like a bag of feathers and tossed gently, face down, onto the soft snow next to the main trench. Johan had a firm grip of the collar as he doubled his pace, while Isabella slid alongside him on the snow, like a living toboggan.

Johan's stride increased within seconds. His eyes scouted every inch of the trench ahead. He knew he could not afford to fall, or to let go of Isabella. If she slid away from him, it would take minutes to retrieve her – minutes that could make the difference between life and death.

'Johan,' she squealed, unable to keep from laughing, 'this … is … fun, but only … if we … get out … of here … alive!'

Johan merely grunted from the strain, still focused on the trench.

Yannis chuckled when he saw Isabella bouncing her way down the slope next to Johan. *You are a genius, Johan,* he thought as he finally reached the bridge and grabbed one of the ropes for support. The two were three-quarters of the way down when he heard Isabella's magnificent laughter rolling down the slope. He grinned and remembered the laughter they had shared while she clung to him after their escape from the battlefield the previous summer. He was still smiling when he felt the blood in his veins turn to ice. A line of soldiers with skis on their shoulders had appeared at the ridge, their number multiplying by the second. He roared a warning towards the man-mountain before turning back to the bridge. Most of the men were already across, but he could see Yancko at the rear making sure his men reached safety.

'Yancko,' he bellowed and prayed that his voice would carry above the roar of the nearby waterfall and the river raging four hundred feet below. Yancko spun around when he heard the panic in Yannis' voice. His gaze flicked towards the slope and he immediately recognized the crisis. 'Get some swords here, Yancko,' yelled Yannis. 'Quickly!'

Yancko gave him the thumbs up and shouted to the men ahead. The message sped forward and swords were passed back within seconds. Yancko grabbed a handful and staggered back across the swaying bridge to Yannis.

Yannis slapped him on the shoulder. 'Good man! Get ready for the fight of your life. Those skiers are going to be on us in minutes. There is no escape this time!'

CHAPTER 94

Oleg Walenski was full of confidence as he approached the ridge. He knew it was now simply a matter of time before they had the entire band of bandits at their mercy at the bottom of the hill. Instead, he stared in disbelief at what he saw: a well-constructed bridge spanning the gorge.

'They've got a bridge. Those peasants have built a bridge! That's why they came this way. Well, they're not going to escape! We are going over that bridge, and we're going to get that bunch of scoundrels and drag them back by their thieving ears. They cannot outrun our skis. Let's go, men!' He thrust himself forward onto the slopes with his men close behind.

Isabella heard the cries from Yannis and at first thought they were shouts of encouragement. As soon as she saw swords being passed across the bridge, she knew the ski patrol was on its way down the hill. Unable to turn her head to confirm it, she could only clench her teeth. She was no longer laughing. Johan kept going without missing a step.

When they reached the bottom, Yannis grabbed her and pulled her along as she frantically tried to rip off the extra jacket. Johan helped and suddenly she was free. 'Sword!' she screamed. Yancko tossed her one, which she caught with practiced ease. At the entrance to the bridge she turned to face her enemy yet again, Yannis and Yancko on one side of her, the massive Johan on the other.

The troopers stopped fifty paces away to unfasten their skis. Their officer roared at his men, 'Draw your weapons! Force those scurvy bandits to the other side, where we'll make the lot of them surrender.'

Isabella heard him and nodded to Yannis. The ski patrol obviously did not know how many men were actually on the other side. 'Yancko, get to the other side quickly. Make sure no more than twenty men show themselves. And no names or rank. They still believe we're a small band of thieves, and we have to make sure it stays that way.'

Yancko nodded and scurried across the planks like a rabbit, holding the side ropes in an attempt to counter the swing of the bridge. Isabella spoke in a low voice. 'They want us on the other side, Yannis. Never look a gift horse in the mouth, so let's oblige them. They have no idea of the fall-back position regarding the fate of the bridge. Off you go. I'll go last. And no more names for us either.'

Yannis started to object.

'That's an order, Mister, as agreed. Yes?'

'Yes, Miss, as agreed. Get a move on, Jay Jay.'

Johan was no less reluctant than Yannis, but did as ordered and hurried onto the bridge.

The bridge swayed precariously as the ski patrol scrambled onto it. Isabella fell to her knees as she held on to the rope sides with one hand while she gripped the sword in the other. Yannis helped her to her feet, and they continued to stumble one step after the other.

Through gaps in the sturdy planks she could see the dense cloud-like mist swirl up and around the bridge from the massive waterfall three hundred feet upstream. Occasionally the mist would part for the briefest moment to reveal a hazy outline of the jagged rocks below, but mostly the vision extended less than a hundred feet into the two-hundred-foot-wide gorge. She chanced a quick glance over her shoulder and saw that almost the entire ski patrol had crowded onto the bridge, at least eighty men. It was fortunate, she thought, that the bridge had been designed to support big men with heavy barrels.

Twice Isabella felt hands grab at her jacket before she was able to pull away. To make some space behind, she swung the sword back over her head and forced the lead soldier to fall back. That was all she needed. The *Serpent Warrior* whirled and faced the man who had been too preoccupied with holding on to the bridge to properly use his weapon against her back. Stationary, he now thrust his sword towards her. Instead of stepping back, as the man expected, she moved forward to parry the thrust and force his sword above his head. Then, taking a short step back, she twisted around and her foot flashed up to send the man's sword spinning over the side into the swirling mist. Next, she moved back several paces to allow the next soldier to push past the lead man and clumsily attack her.

Having seen her action against his comrade, this soldier adjusted his thrust and increased the downward force of his strike. The *Serpent Warrior* was ready for him. He had no chance against her. She smashed his sword into the planks and immediately thrust her own sword up to lightly touch the man's throat. He froze, his eyes wide with fear.

'Drop it! Drop your sword! Now!' she shouted. The man obeyed. A swift kick from Isabella sent the sword over the side to follow the previous one into the mist. She quickly moved back, only to see their commander push past the man to take the lead. He looked considerably tougher, more determined.

They were six steps from safety when she heard Yancko scream, 'Quickly! Quickly! A few more steps and we'll chop the rope to collapse the bridge.' The engineers had designed the bridge so that the cutting of a single key rope would instantly unravel the entire structure and send it crashing into the gorge.

Colonel Walenski was just two steps from Isabella when he heard Yancko scream. He immediately recognized the danger and knew he had to get to Yancko and his assistant before they could cut the rope. Yancko's man was standing behind him facing the other way to support two solid logs secured into deep holes. *If I can get to the first man, I can get the other before he lets go of the posts to grab a weapon.* 'Come on men, faster!' He made a lunge for Isabella, but his hands slid on the snow on her jacket.

Isabella moved back and screamed at Yancko. 'No! Don't cut that rope!' She spun around as she tore off her scarf to face Walenski.

'Stop!' she screamed at him. 'Truce! Truce! Stop! Listen to me! Please!' She stood her ground and forced Walenski to stop. He took another pace forward that placed him within grabbing distance, but Isabella did not move away. He stared at a young, lovely face, her eyes a blaze of green fury. 'Will you listen to me? Your lives depend on it. Do we have a short truce?'

Walenski nodded while he thought fast. He knew he needed a few more seconds, anyway. If he was quick, he thought, he might just be able to grab the young woman. The thieves were unlikely to cut the rope if he had hold of her. Then again, they might sacrifice the girl to save themselves. He also thought it strange that she had stopped instead of moving even faster when the man had called out to her. She could easily have made it to safety, and that would have been the end of Walenski and his men.

Walenski nodded again. 'What?'

'We don't want to die, or be taken prisoner, for stealing nothing. You've got it all back. Every bit of it. We also don't want to kill you; you're only doing your job. I propose that you all move back to the other side. We'll destroy the bridge when you are off and safe. That way we will all be safe and live for another day. What do you say?'

'How do I know I can trust you? Any of you?' Walenski glanced at Yancko and the other men.

'You saw that I didn't move away from you just now. That means I've put my own life at risk to trust you to make the right decision.'

Walenski quietly considered his options. He could grab the girl and just maybe a few of his men could make it to safety before the two men cut the rope. The odds were slim. It would be a catastrophe for his men, and he would be blamed and shamed forever if he should be unlucky enough to survive.

'Very well. We have an agreement and a truce. I...'

A loud voice cut him off. *Charles*. He had recognized her, and was still furious at not having sliced her in half early that morning. 'No Colonel! You can't trust her, or the men. How can you? We don't know them. They're just a bunch of thieves; they have no honor. I guarantee they will destroy the bridge as soon as we move away. Grab the girl now. They won't cut the rope with her on the bridge. Pass her back to us and we'll storm them.'

The man is actually quite smart, Isabella thought. He had a good point. There was only one way to counter it. Head on.

'Colonel ...?' Isabella raised her brows.

'Walenski. Oleg Walenski.'

'Look at the men, Colonel Walenski. Twenty of the biggest village people you will ever see. If your men rush them, they will be met with a flurry of action. Most of your men will be hacked and pushed off the cliff into the gorge. They might get the upper hand eventually, but you will lose at least two for one, probably more. That means you will lose at least forty men. That's a heavy price to pay to overpower twenty men who just tried to steal a bit of food. Think about it. You will never be promoted beyond your current rank, no matter what you achieve in future.'

'No, Colonel, don't listen to her!' Charles shouted.

Isabella cut him off before he won the day. 'There is an easy way to resolve this. I will walk back to the other side with you. After you are all off and safe, I will return alone. In the meantime, my life will be in your hands, Colonel. There is your guarantee.'

'Colonel!'

'Shut up, Charles. I have the responsibility for the lives of my men, not you. If you're wrong in your opinion, we will all be smashed to pieces on the rocks below. We didn't know that the bridge can be destroyed in an instant. The girl has offered us our lives. About turn, men, and get a move on. That's an order!' Walenski turned back to Isabella. 'Thank you. I don't like to think what might have happened if Charles were in charge. Look, if it were up to me, I would say you don't need to come with us. However, for the sake of appearances in the acceptance of your offer …' His voice trailed off.

'It's all right, Colonel. I'll come with you.' Isabella turned and tossed her sword to a stricken-faced Yannis. She could read his thoughts: *Oh, no, not again!*

Ten minutes later most of the soldiers were already off the bridge and were busy with their skis and baggage making their way back up the long slope. The last to step onto solid ground, Walenski turned to address Isabella. 'You showed a lot of courage to accompany us across the bridge. You know of course that, now we are safe, we could easily take you prisoner, and there is nothing your friends can do about it.'

Isabella had a knot in her stomach. She had been only too well aware of just that. 'I put my trust in meeting both an officer and a gentleman, Colonel. I'm sorry that we have caused you so much grief, but we are not really thieves, as such. We are simply people who have fled the cities to get away from the illness sweeping Europe, and find it difficult to forage for provisions in these appalling conditions.'

'I understand. You may leave, and I thank you again.' Walenski gave her a salute and Isabella had to restrain herself from returning it.

'Good day, Colonel, and good luck to you,' she said, and meant it. The colonel moved several paces away from the bridge. It saved his life.

Charles had not finished. 'Don't let her go, Colonel. Let's take her with us. I recognized her kicks. She's the one who attacked us this morning and knocked us to the ground. That's the woman I was about to carve up when she suddenly disappeared in a puff of smoke. She is a *witch*, Colonel! Only a witch can do such things. There is more to this than meets the eye. We need answers and she can give them to us. Grab her!'

'Shut up, Charles! That girl you're calling a witch had her sword at the throat of one of my men, and spared him. That is not the action of a witch, you fool! She is a savior. This young woman has just saved our lives, including yours, your ungrateful dog! I have given my word and she goes back to her friends and that's that!' Walenski turned and lowered his voice as he addressed Isabella again. 'I'm sorry about this. You had better go now while I deal with it.'

'Thank you, Colonel.' Isabella was about to turn away when her eyes opened wide with shock. '*No!*' she screamed, panic-stricken for the first time in her life. '*You don't know what you're doing!*'

CHAPTER 95

Colonel Walenski spun to see Charles with his sword raised above his head for a powerful blow on the key rope. 'No, don't, you fool! That's an order!'

'You refuse to take her prisoner, so the witch dies. And I'm going to report you for dereliction of duty.' The sword flashed down onto the taut rope.

Isabella knew instantly there was no hope. Within seconds, she would be smashed onto the rocks far below. She was already several steps onto the bridge. Too far and too late to jump to safety. Charles had no idea why Yancko had a man standing behind him next to two large logs embedded in the ground, and it was already too late to warn him.

Back-up safety mechanisms had been deliberately discarded in the bridge design to allow instant destruction in the event of close pursuit. The key rope released a knot in the main tension rope that laced through a fulcrum embedded deep into rock and carrying more than one hundred tons of pressure. When released, it allowed the bridge to instantly collapse under its own weight and tension. The two solid logs were for protection from the main rope as it whipped at blinding speed towards the bridge.

Walenski watched with horror the imminent demise of the young woman who had spared his and his men's lives. A single blow of the sword had been enough to slice through the rope, exactly as designed.

At the explosive snap of the key rope, Charles whooped with undisguised triumph. But not for long. Released as if fired from a cannon, the arm-thick main rope whipped straight at the unprotected Charles and sliced both legs off below the knees. One hundred tons of energy behind the sudden slack in the rope saw it wrap itself around his body like a python. Charles let out a bloodcurdling scream as his legless body was lifted high in the air and then smashed onto the planks of the bridge next to the horrified Isabella.

With a roar that drowned out both the waterfall and the raging waters below, the tension was spent in an instant and the entire structure was snapped towards the opposite side like contracting elastic. Almost halfway across the gorge, the bridge seemed to hang suspended for several moments before it changed direction to tumble slowly into the abyss, dragging its two passengers towards the jagged rocks below the enveloping mist.

Colonel Oleg Walenski could hear them both scream as he quickly turned to avert his eyes from the spectacle, only to see two boots with bloodied leg-stumps standing side by side next to him.

It was with a sense of detached reality that Yannis heard a faint scream over the roar of the waters. Seconds later he saw a blur as a man appeared to be dashed against the bridge. *What's going on*, he thought; *Isabella should have been on her way back.*

An explosive sound reached his ears at almost the same instant that a shock coursed through his body from the rope he was leaning against, throwing him to the ground. On his hands and knees, he watched as Isabella and the bridge moved towards him faster than an arrow. Then it stopped and hung in the air for several moments before tumbling almost gracefully into the gorge. In his last vision of Isabella, she spun to face him before falling upside down. Moments later he heard screams as she disappeared into the swirling mist below. Then nothing more.

Yannis raised his head to look up at Johan. His mouth was open but no sound came out. Johan's face was blank with uncomprehending shock. Yancko fell to his knees, both hands over his face to keep from witnessing the moment of Isabella's death.

No, this can't be happening. Not the brilliant, indispensable, wonderful, cheeky, beautiful Isabella! Yannis forced himself to his feet and staggered towards the now slack ropes of the bridge structure hanging limply over the edge. Just as he reached the edge, he felt Johan's powerful arm slide around his shoulders to prevent him falling – or jumping – to join Isabella on the rocks.

'Oh, Isabella, your courage has finally claimed your life.' Yannis' voice shook from emotion and shock. 'You risked your life to save the lives of the enemy soldiers – and they betrayed you. They will pay for it!' He made no attempt to remove Johan's arm. He felt comforted by the strength in it and knew it prevented him from carrying out his original intention: to step into the void and join the young woman he had sworn to protect.

'Look at the colonel, General.' Johan took the chance that Yannis would not jump and removed his arm. 'He's giving us a signal. His body language says it was not planned, and he is offering us the only apology he can – his despair. I saw someone smash into the bridge as it went. My guess is it was that maniac, Charles. The whiplash effect would have got him as soon as he cut the key rope. I don't believe the colonel is to blame, sir.'

Yannis simply nodded and sank to his knees close to the edge of the abyss without another word. Johan and Yancko closed ranks around him to stare silently into the mist, each with their own thoughts of their favorite soldier and her cruel fate.

CHAPTER 96

Good riddance to you, Charles! You deserved what you got, but that poor girl did not. Walenski knew he would never forget the young woman, or her brilliant green eyes. She had given him life at the expense of her own. He turned away from the ghastly boots and walked to the ledge to face the obviously shocked men on the other side. The top half of the bridge swayed gently back and forth, while the bottom half was invisible, shrouded in mist.

Walenski held his arms forward and wide, palms up, in a sign of helplessness and despair. There was nothing else he could offer her friends by way of apology or regret.

The soldiers were solemn as they made ready to leave, no less shocked than Walenski.

'Gather around, men. Thanks to Charles, we need to add a few things to the earlier report and to provide a logical explanation of what happened to him. No-one will believe what really happened here today, or that we owe our lives to one of the thieves – a young woman, no less – who was then murdered by one of our own in a complete betrayal of honor and chivalry. That would destroy us all. So this is what happened: there was no girl, no bridge. The bandits were cornered exactly as we predicted they would be. They were foolish enough to think they could outfight us, so they chose not to surrender. A fierce battle ensued. The bandits, fifty or more, put up a valiant fight, but our superior fighting skills and number overwhelmed them, and one by one they went over the cliff to their death. Amazingly, we suffered only a single casualty, poor, brave Charles, who took a direct *right-handed* blow – remember that, men – that severed his left leg. Unbalanced, he tumbled over the edge.'

Walenski moved over to the two boots, separated the right one – and leg – with his foot and kicked it towards the cliff. He gave it another solid kick that sent it spinning over the edge with a spray of blood.

He returned to his men. 'We have sadly brought back his severed left leg to have something of him for the memoriam. Stieg, would you please get the … ah … thing and pass it around. I want you all to smear some blood on your uniforms; there should be enough in the boot itself. After dispatching – fifty, wasn't it? – thieves, you need to look the part. Except for poor Charles, the day has been a resounding success. The stump will authenticate our story. We'll go over it once more when we get to the last slope before camp. Any questions?'

There were none. The colonel's men wanted nothing more than a simple life, and were more than happy with the story. It made sense and avoided the lengthy enquiries and reports so common in army life. Only one man had questions, many, in fact. Colonel Oleg Walenski.

In many respects, he thought as he trudged up the slope with his skis on his shoulder, Charles was right. Something was not as it seemed. Although not a witch, that girl had the courage and fighting skills to single-handedly attack his entire platoon and lay almost half of them on the ground, including him. It was she who had ordered that the rope not be cut; it was she who had called for and negotiated the truce; it was she who had made the terms and conditions on the run and then put herself up as collateral to guarantee their safety. Not once did the men behind her speak or interfere. That girl had been the one in charge. *She had been their leader!*

There was something extraordinary indeed about that green-eyed girl. She had to have been someone very special. He had no doubt, however, that if he started asking questions his career would be ruined long before he found answers. *All the more reason to keep your mouth shut, Ollie,* was his last thought on the matter.

CHAPTER 97

As the bridge concertinaed towards the center of the gorge, only the sudden tangle of ropes around her prevented the centrifugal force from throwing Isabella off the structure. It took her breath away and paralyzed her muscles, but not her mind. As soon as the bridge reached the center, she felt herself driven into the planks as if hit from behind by a stampeding horse. Then she was weightless, and her strength was back, if only for a couple of seconds.

In a split second she spun and reached through one of the thousands of loops in the ropes holding the structure together and pulled a slack rope back through the loop. She gave it one twist and slipped her leg into the new loop just as she felt the bridge change direction. Down.

There was no time to do the same for the other leg, so she simply flicked a slack rope around it, held on and hoped for the best. Her plan was simple by necessity: if she were knocked unconscious when the bridge slammed against the rock wall of the gorge, there was a slim chance she might be suspended by her legs rather than thrown onto the rocks below.

As she now hung upside down, Isabella saw Charles' crazed eyes glaring up at her with hatred. Without ropes to secure him to the structure when the bridge spiraled down, the new force pushed him away from it, and into the void. He tumbled slowly, end over end, the last of his blood pumping out through the stumps of his legs and turning the mist into a pink halo around his body. His last breath was used to release a scream of terror and fury. Mere seconds had passed since he had cut the rope.

Isabella gasped at the sight of Charles spinning into the mist, and she was unable to prevent a scream of her own as she wrapped her arm around her head to protect it from what she knew would come within moments.

The structure slammed into the side of the mountain with a thunderous roar, spraying planks in all direction. A rock ledge jutted into the gorge twenty feet above the end of the bridge, which swung underneath it and then traveled upwards to strike the underside of the ledge. Half the energy was spent in the one second of uphill travel before it struck the rock, but the blow was still enough to knock Isabella into instant darkness. By the time the end of the bridge returned to the void she was hanging upside down, her arms outstretched as if to embrace death.

Isabella became aware of being lashed upside down to the mast of a ship, the roar of water deafening as it crashed onto the deck. The ship swayed slowly back and forth, side to side. A feeling of seasickness accompanied a blinding headache when she opened her eyes to stare at the deck. It was a white deck. She was confused and turned her face to each side. White. Up. Down. White everywhere. Her legs ached and she was cold. Freezing cold. There was no visual reference point to get her bearing until she looked up at her aching legs and saw ropes and debris stretching up into nothingness. A memory of the screaming Charles spiraling in a pink mist flashed into her brain, followed quickly by the rest of the day's events.

Her mind raced as she considered her options. Rescue? No, it would have been reasonable for anyone to give her up for dead, and no-one could see her in the mist from the waterfall.

You talked your way into this mess to save those soldiers, Isabella; you're going to have to get yourself out of it. There's only one way out, and that's straight up. She knew there was only one thing she needed to focus on. Up.

Her strength made it easy to twist her upper body up above her legs. After a minute to allow blood to flow back and clear her head, she wound one arm securely around a rope before releasing her legs with the other. Holding tight with one arm at all times, she used her legs and free arm to make small upwards movements. *One million tiny movements should do it,* she told herself, and started to count backwards to keep her mind occupied as the *Serpent Warrior* inched her way up the slowly swaying remnants of the bridge.

CHAPTER 98

Yannis was inconsolable. He had sat near the edge for hours, refusing to budge. Yancko had little choice but to arrange for some of the camp followers to set up a small camp nearby where they would spend the night. Several of Yannis' closest friends and officers sat in a tight group around him while others managed to get a fire going.

'On our return to the valley, Isabella was going to reveal the full details of her next plan, which I know includes the use of the gunpowder. I'll need to contact Dmitri at once to find out exactly what she had in mind. Apparently, Dmitri has the details of all of her plans. God only knows how many she's put together.'

'Don't worry, her plans will be brilliant as always,' Yancko said softly as he stared into the rapidly darkening void.

Manny sat on his bunched-up jacket at one side of the group, slumped forward on crossed legs. 'You should have seen her back at the bottom of the slope just before we got away, Yannis. No-one's had time to talk about it yet. You were already up top, Yancko. It was that girl in the portrait – at it again. She was unbelievable. The enemy camp sent that ski patrol after us, and they were on us before we knew it. There must have been close to a hundred soldiers suddenly jam-packed in front of us, swords drawn. We were unarmed and just standing there waiting to be pulled to safety, and about to be slaughtered. But Isabella jumped in front of us and attacked the entire patrol on her own! Within twenty seconds she had dozens of them thrashing about on the ground in a tangle of skis. I swear her hands and feet were faster than lightning. She actually kicked some of them in the head.

'I had no idea she had such skills. It was total chaos. The last vision that I had as I shot up the slope was of a bunch of troopers storming her with raised swords. It must have been touch and go. She put her life on the line and managed to buy us just enough precious seconds to save us yet again. There was nothing Isabella wouldn't do for us. It's enough to make a grown man cry.'

Yannis nodded, profoundly sad. 'Yes, that sounds exactly like what Isabella would do. She is ... was a lioness in every sense of the word. Her fighting skills are already legendary. There's no doubt she was the backbone and driving force of this campaign from the very start. I believe her total lack of fear inspired courage in everyone, including me. Without her, nothing will ever be the same. Quite frankly, the excitement, the hope I felt, has simply left me. For the sake of our nation, I can only pray I get it back.'

'I know exactly how you feel,' put in Johan. 'I wish it had been me on that bridge instead of Isabella. I would gladly have given my life for her.'

'Speaking of which,' Yannis said reflectively, desperate to reminisce, and desperate to maintain the illusion of her existence just a little longer, 'Isabella had a very odd wish in regard to how she wanted her life to end. That's why I almost stepped off the ledge earlier, Johan. I wanted to make her wish come true.' Yannis paused, not sure whether her wish should be broadcast, or should remain private now that she was gone.

'What was her wish, Yannis?'

Yannis hesitated yet again. 'She said ... ah ... she said her destiny was that she and I die side by side on a raging battlefield somewhere. Amazing! What a destiny to wish for. Can you believe it?'

Johan was quiet for several moments. 'Yes, I can, actually. That's a very deep and private destiny to want. Now that she's gone, I suppose I can also share something she told me in confidence about destiny on the day we picked up the prisoners. I wouldn't repeat it under any other circumstances.'

'Oh? What was that?'

'There's someone who had her destined for something completely different. He's going to be bitterly disappointed when he eventually finds out what's happened to her.'

'He? There's a *he* somewhere? Who on earth are you talking about, Johan?'

'The earl, Carlos Bucher.'

'*What?*' Yannis was utterly confused. 'What on earth has the earl got to do with Isabella?'

It was Johan's turn to hesitate. 'The earl has chosen her as his empress after he conquers the South. At their private meeting on the flats, he told her that she should keep away from other suitors, and he would come for her when he considered her old enough to join him as his wife. Despite her tender age, I have never seen anyone look more beautiful than Isabella did that day. The earl must have taken one look at her and fallen head over heels in love, and he proposed to her on the spot. Isabella was the earl's chosen empress-in-waiting, Yannis!'

Yannis was speechless. He started to speak but only managed to stammer and then closed his mouth. After a moment to calm down, he tried again. 'Well, speaking objectively now that it no longer matters, I suppose I can say that I can't blame the earl for falling in love with her. He might be our sworn enemy, but I have to admit that he has superb taste. Isabella was certainly a most extraordinary and beautiful girl, and absolutely someone worth waiting a few years for.'

'*I heard that!*'

A female voice from nowhere in particular. Yannis looked around to see if one of the female camp followers was nearby. There were none within yelling distance. 'Who said that?' he shouted at the men as some of them rose, just as confused as Yannis.

'*I did!* Now throw me a rope with plenty of knots in it! And be quick about it! I can't make it past the ledge without it!'

Yancko was the first to recover his senses. '*Isabella!* Is that you? Where are you?'

'Over the ledge, Yancko, you beautiful idiot! Where do you think I am? Now get me that rope! Quickly! My hands are numb.'

Yancko was in action within seconds. 'Manny, put on one of those belts with the metal ring. Take another for Isabella. Johan, wind two of the ropes with the hooks around those posts. That's it! Get ready, Manny.'

Manny quickly hooked the rope onto his belt and rushed to the ledge. He finally had his chance to do something for Isabella. Johan had secured the ropes and grabbed a long branch from near the fire and held it over the edge. 'Isabella, tell me where the branch is.'

'Three paces to my right.'

Johan pointed to a spot on the ledge. 'That's where you go, Manny; you'll be right next to her. You know what to do. Over you go!'

Within seconds, Manny was next to Isabella, had clipped a belt around her waist and fastened the second rope that had been tossed over the edge. 'All right. You're safe now, no matter what happens. *Ready up there?* Haul us up together so I can keep Isabella from getting cut on the edge.'

Isabella grabbed his jacket and swung him to her side. She gave him a quick kiss on the cheek before he swung away. Ten seconds later she was over the edge, and no-one seemed surprised to see her dart past the other men to slip into the open arms of Yannis. He seemed to know instinctively that he was the one she would come to. Neither was able to speak for a full minute while the men cheered excitedly. Two of them raced to the main camp to spread the news.

Yannis finally found his voice. 'Quickly, let's get you a little closer to the fire. Not too close, though.' He gently massaged her hands while she allowed the heat from the fire to slowly warm her through the jacket. After several minutes she pulled her hands out of his and leaned against him.

'Just hold me again, please, Yannis. After the fall, and that climb, I need to know I'm still alive.'

Yannis hugged her tightly. 'I can't believe it! I just can't believe it! I thought I'd never see you again. I can't believe I could feel such despair and happiness in the one day. We would never have heard you if we weren't sitting by the ledge.'

Isabella turned her face up to his. 'Yes, I could hear you boys talking about me as I neared the top. Thank goodness you were here or I'd still be hanging down there to rot until summer.'

Yannis looked down at her, suddenly nervous. 'Did you hear much of what we said?'

She stretched to place her mouth against his ear and spoke softly. 'It's not often that a girl gets to hear what people say about her after she's dead. I did hear enough of the lovely things you said to hope that the earl is not the only man who will find me worth waiting a few years for. It's not the earl whom I intend to marry!' She gave him a final squeeze and stepped away to hug some of the other men.

CHAPTER 99

D mitri had known that Isabella would be dismayed when she received his note, and he was partially correct. She was not simply dismayed; she was devastated. A grey-and-white pigeon had arrived minutes earlier and was happily pecking away at a tray of seeds with a seemingly inexhaustible hunger. In stark contrast, Isabella was pacing back and forth, her plans in tatters, her hunger gone.

'Grandfather, are you there?' Marcus was prone to have afternoon naps while things were quiet. Isabella heard him rise and the faint sound of a jacket being slipped on. A few seconds later Marcus poked his head through the flap, reluctant to come all the way out into the bitter cold.

'What's up?'

'Plenty. I'm getting *Barca* and heading out to find Yannis. I'm afraid the time for rest has come to an end. The three of us need to talk as soon as I get back.'

'I'll be ready. Yannis went for a ride downstream with Melissa. It's getting a bit late, so I imagine you'll meet them on their way back. They shouldn't be too much longer, though, if you prefer to wait. It's very cold to be out riding.'

'I'm just too agitated to wait. I'll be back soon.' She wasted no time with preamble when she caught up with Yannis and Melissa.

'Yannis, we have to talk! The meeting tent, as quick as you can, please.' Isabella turned *Barca* and headed back at a gallop along the well-trodden path towards camp. Yannis and Melissa had no choice but to follow at the same speed.

Marcus had already started a small covered fire in the tent by the time they returned. Melissa appeared slightly bewildered as they were about to enter the tent.

'Isabella, what do you want me to do? Shall I go to my tent so you can talk in private, or can I join you?'

Isabella hesitated for barely a moment before she hugged Melissa. 'It will be a very, very private conversation, so of course you can join us. Come to think of it, could you do me a favor, please? Ask Chen and Yan to join us as well. I'm going to need all the help I can get right now.'

Thrilled to be included in the inner circle for once, Melissa vanished without another word to complete her task. Isabella waited until everyone was seated around the small fire before she addressed them.

'By now you know much of what I have in mind for the enemy when they reach the valleys. My plan has been underway for some two years, and is actually ahead of schedule. With the enormous agricultural advances we've made, both to the north and south of where we are now, the valleys have been carefully designed to attract the enemy and to direct them to specific places to make camp.' She paused. 'There's no easy way to say this, but I've just received a message from Dmitri that's thrown my entire plan on its head.'

She paused again to allow her audience to digest the information before she continued. 'Tomorrow I'll take you for a tour with Jacques and his team of specialists. I'll show you how I intend to use the gunpowder against the very people that brought it with them to destroy us.'

Her voice shook as she went on. 'It breaks my heart to have to think up such diabolical plans, but what choice do we have? It's that, or our nation falls. It is a duty to plan to inflict the maximum damage to the men and materiel of the enemy. Is that not so, Grandfather?'

'That's what I had to do, darling, in every battle I led,' Marcus answered. 'Anything less would lead to certain defeat.'

Yannis leaned forward, elbows on his knees. 'What is it that you now say has put your plan in peril?'

Isabella rubbed her face and then stared at her closest friends and family. 'Dmitri has been informed that a number of nations forming part of the Southern Region have been forced, under the threat of the deaths of thousands of families, to bolster the front line of our enemy. The North has also threatened to turn their cannons against dissenters. No-one can defend themselves against such firepower. I agree with Dmitri that there is nothing we can do about it. We are stuck with having to face a coalition army made up of our own allies!'

Marcus groaned and held his head in his hands. Yannis was more pragmatic. 'How many in this army?' he asked.

'Twenty-five thousand,' Isabella answered quietly. It was Yannis' turn to groan. The others were too shocked to utter a sound.

Isabella waited for the group to gather their thoughts. 'That's why we have much to discuss. We'll talk some more after our tour, and then we'll have a major decision to make: whether to give up our campaign or continue, which can only mean targeting our coalition friends for destruction!'

Surprisingly, Melissa was the first to respond. 'When you say *we must decide*, who exactly do you mean?'

'That's a good observation, Melissa. By *we*, I mean our nation. As you will all appreciate, such a decision will be a political one, as well as a military one. Ultimately, it will be made by the king in, I would think, close consultation with Dmitri and the senate.'

Melissa nodded. 'Thank goodness. I would hate to think that you, Yannis or Marcus, would have to make a decision of such magnitude.'

'Unfortunately, you're not far off the mark, to be honest. I didn't want to delve into the second part of Dmitri's message until after our tour, when you will have seen the rest of my plan, but now that you've brought it up, I may as well lay it out. Dmitri has asked for individual recommendations from me, Yannis and Grandfather. Based on what we advise, individually and collectively, they will make a decision, which we will then have to abide by. That means that our recommendations will form a large part of their decision.'

A silence lasted for several moments. Everyone was lost in thoughts of the possible mayhem to come or the consequences of surrender.

Isabella rose and slipped into her jacket. 'Well, that's my joyous news of the day. I suggest an early start in the morning because it will be heavy going through the snow in the untracked areas. We'll stay in the upper valley for a few days, so bring the appropriate essentials.'

'Isabella?' Melissa sounded nervous, pensive.

'Yes, darling.'

'I ... ah ... hate to talk out of turn ... or too soon. You know, not having been on the tour yet and all that.'

Isabella knelt next to her friend and took her hands. 'You know you can say anything. I value anything you have to say. That's why you're here at this meeting, remember?'

Melissa nodded. 'Well, obviously I won't be making any recommendation, but I do have an opinion. Whatever you show us over the next few days won't change that.'

'Oh?' Isabella was surprised at Melissa's sudden willingness to be heard. 'It must be a strong opinion if you feel you can't be swayed by what you will see. Let's hear it, then. I don't know whether I'll like it or not, but I know it will be your honest view.'

Melissa flushed with excitement, happy that she was being listened to. 'Well, as you know, your nation is not my nation, even though it already feels like it is. If it were my nation, I would not allow someone to simply walk in and take over by using crude bully tactics, without having to lift so much as a finger. Your allied nations have been forced into making decisions of their own, and they know they will have to live with the consequences of those decisions. They bowed to threats and have allowed many of their citizens to be put in harm's way. So be it; that's their problem. I say we have to make a stand and show them and the world that we will bow to no-one. I say we fight on and prove that such bully tactics will never work!'

Isabella was dumbfounded, as were the others in the tent. *Melissa, where has the real you been hiding all this time?* She rose slowly to face the others, still holding onto Melissa's hand. 'We have all just witnessed the birth of a soldier, a true fighter, and a patriot.' She turned back to Melissa. 'That was brilliantly said, and it's now my turn to say I'm so proud to know someone like you.'

Melissa squeezed Isabella's hand. 'Thank you for saying that, Isabella.'

Marcus leaned forward and looked up at Isabella. 'To be honest, I feel the same. I don't think anything is going to change my opinion, either. How about you, Yannis? Are you willing to express an opinion at this early stage?'

Yannis was staring at Melissa with open admiration. 'Melissa, you and I are as one with everything you just said. I don't think anyone could have said it better. Chen? Yan?'

'I never consider give up. Never surrender. We find new ways to fight. Yan, what you think?'

'I hear what Melissa say. I like very much. Fight must go on. Isabella will find a way.'

Yannis looked at Isabella with a mixture of surprise and relief. 'I know you won't hesitate to take on an army of millions, Isabella, so I hardly need ask *your* opinion. I guess that makes us unanimous. Now, where do we go from here?'

Isabella paced the room while she thought. 'We'll send our recommendation to proceed, but we'll wait until after our tour. That means we won't need to concern ourselves with *whether* we will use my plan, but *how* to make the best use of it. That will simplify our task, thanks to Melissa for having the courage to put us in this strong position. It will allow us to move forward that much sooner.'

Melissa's eyes went wide with pride at Isabella's words. She wiped away tears with the back of her hand.

'In fact,' Isabella continued, 'now that the major decision is already out of the way, we can actually focus on something else. Instead of worrying about taking the lives of our allies, we can actually think about ways to save some of them.'

Isabella moved around the group, giving each a hug and a kiss on the cheek, including Yannis who, for a change, didn't seem overly concerned at the show of affection in front of Melissa.

CHAPTER 100

Jacques was like a proud father the following morning as he showed his visitors his second-greatest monument. Only in Egypt had he created a greater monolith, one that overshadowed even the pyramids.

Surprisingly, Isabella felt wonderful. Her group had arrived cold and late the previous afternoon, and each had taken turns to enjoy a hot bath. A good night's sleep on a real mattress in the warmth of timber cabins had left them refreshed and enthusiastic for their tour of the upper valley. Jacques' most senior colleagues walked in a group close behind and chatted quietly among themselves.

'We're well ahead of schedule,' Jacques said as he pointed from the hill. 'During the dry season we built new culverts that lead to the aqueducts, which in turn have been upgraded to give us full control over both timing and volume of water being released downstream. The upgraded aqueducts are going to be of immense benefit to the valley's future inhabitants. Later, we'll extend the run-off to some of the other valleys downstream that currently get no benefit from the river. That will be our legacy for the future, Isabella, so it won't be all doom and gloom.'

Isabella wrapped her arm around Jacques. 'That is so heartening to hear, Jacques. You know how terrible I feel about the horror I'm about to unleash.'

Jacques patted her hand. 'I understand. But always remember, my dear: you're only doing what you have to do for our nation.'

Melissa stood next to Isabella, but held on to Yannis. 'Jacques is quite right, my pretty. What you're planning is not of your making. If it wasn't for those maniacs in the North sending huge armies and cannons against us, you'd be sitting at home in front of a fire right now, weaving socks like every other young woman.'

'*Me!* Weaving socks! Yeah, right,' Isabella snorted. 'More likely I would be making plans for a crusade against the Persians, or, even more likely, an invasion of China.' She winked at Chen, who grinned back.

'That sounds more like the Isabella I've learned to know,' Yannis added with a chuckle.

Isabella turned back to Jacques. 'Now for the big one, Jacques. Show us your pièce de résistance.'

'Ah! The powder! The ill-gotten spoils from your raid by your gang of thieves! As their leader, you will surely go down in history as one of the greatest robbers of all time. Let me show you the chambers. There are sixty of them, spread over two layers, each a hundred feet above the other.'

'Sixty chambers!' Isabella was astounded, but also excited. 'Tell me more!'

'We've actually spiced up the powder to make it more combustible. It will now ignite so quickly that the explosive factor has been increased by three. The ultimate force will, therefore, be equal to more than one hundred tons, and will result in the largest explosion the planet has ever known. Each chamber contains thirty barrels of powder, so we have two hundred left over. I'm sure you'll find some interesting use for those later.'

'Well, that's an unexpected bonus. But you're right. I will definitely find something interesting to do with the surplus.'

The visitors, including Isabella, were almost overwhelmed by the sheer scale of what Jacques showed them. At the end of the tour, Isabella turned to Jacques and the group of specialists who had accompanied them.

'Gentlemen, as you know, many things must happen exactly as we've planned before the enemy will take the bait and believe the deception. Even though this might not end the war by itself, it will place us in a very strong position to launch the next plan. The success of each plan will put us that much closer to delivering a final knock-out punch, or at least sending them back home with their tails between their legs.'

Isabella turned to the others. 'I think another fireside chat will be the order of the day when we get back to the village. You've seen what Jacques and his men have been creating; now the time has come for me to tell you how I'm going to destroy it. Tomorrow we'll head back to the main camp.'

Sergeant Valdez was waiting for them with another message from Dmitri when they returned to the main camp the following evening. 'It's addressed to you, Major,' he said as he held out the tiny envelope. He smiled warmly at everyone before he saluted and left.

Isabella broke the seal and read the message before handing it to Yannis. 'It's not quite the way I thought it was going to work out, but it makes no difference in the scheme of things. However, it does confirm the timetable, so that's good to know. Let's get Grandfather and have a talk about it in the meeting tent while the others organize some dinner.'

Marcus wore a deep frown when he read Dmitri's message a short time later. 'So, the coalition army has been instructed to arrive in one of our valleys late May. It seems the earl currently has insufficient provisions available, so he's told them to come directly here.'

Isabella nodded. 'He is getting a few provisions forwarded from home, but can't get enough through for such a massive army. Having heard we have a huge fertile area, he'll be anxious to get here as soon as possible.'

'How does he know that?' Yannis asked. 'No one's been sighted coming through the mountain passes to check us out.'

'Dmitri has made sure that our agricultural achievements are widely broadcast at home. That information soon finds its way to the Northern Region, and from there to the earl. We know exactly what they learn, and when. The earl expects our own reconnaissance to come from the mountain areas to their south, so all their efforts to hide their intentions are screened in that direction. Instead, our spies are located to their north, and their observations are simply dispatched by pigeon, either directly here or to Dmitri, who then collates them with other information before passing it back to us here.'

'You certainly set up a good system with Dmitri, Isabella.' Yannis was impressed.

Isabella laughed. 'Much of it was indeed set up in secret with Dmitri, but the great irony is that the bulk of the system was put in place with enormous assistance from none other than Karamus *junior*, the architect of his own demise. Let's hope that creep of a father of his will manage to do the same one day.'

Marcus seemed a little brighter. 'So we should know when the earl starts to make his move without realizing he's being watched?'

'Exactly. We'll know before they even clean up after their breakfast. They have to wait for the ground to harden after the snow melts before they can move their wagons and cannons. It will then take them at least two to three weeks to reach here. Based on Dmitri's message, they aim to be here mid-May, so we should have an exit target of, say, the end of April. We'll tell the others over dinner. Let's go! I'm starving.'

•

'Gentlemen, don't concern yourselves with details!' Theo Karamus was unable to hide his irritation with his *Inner Sanctum* colleagues. 'You must look at the big picture. Nothing has changed. *Nothing!*'

'But, Theo, there *have* been changes. *Big* changes.' Maximus Pannini was troubled. 'Our negotiator, Vlado, is of course no longer with us to directly represent our interests. And the delays have cost us far more than we've been reimbursed by the king. To make matters worse, the longer the delays, the greater the risk that something – or someone – will expose the position we've taken in this conflict.' He glanced around the table for support. 'Perhaps the time has come to withdraw our support.'

'Maximus, I am informed that the earl's army cannot mobilize until well after winter, when the terrain will have dried out. In the meantime, our army will have little to do, and the ongoing costs will reflect that. The substantial costs for the initial infrastructure for the military action are now well and truly behind us, so relax. I assure you that withdrawing our support at this time will be viewed with great suspicion.'

'But Theo, by the time the North gets moving again, they will be more than a year behind schedule. I don't know if we can hold it all together for much longer.'

Karamus' eyes narrowed. Breaking of ranks would not be permitted. 'Through your own contacts, you all know that several of our southern neighboring nations have been forced to gather a coalition force to bolster the earl's army. By the time all his divisions have merged, his army will be bigger, stronger ... and closer. They will be unstoppable! As for a negotiator, the earl knows he can deal directly with me when the time comes. So, like I said: nothing has changed regarding the end result. *Nothing! End of discussion, gentlemen!*'

The small group listened silently to the news while they ate in the dining tent. When she had finished dinner, Yan murmured quietly, 'So soon? I will be sad to leave valley. Very happy here. Happy valley. So beautiful.'

Not for much longer, Isabella thought as she glanced at the pensive faces around the fire.

'Where will we go?' Melissa asked.

'Yannis has arranged to set up a new main camp in the lakes country as soon as the snow melts. It's high up, a couple of mountain ranges to the south. It's about three weeks travel from here, but we'll also have a hidden smaller camp just a couple of days away to the east so that we can be close enough to ... ah ... take care of *business* when the time comes.'

'Will the main camp be a nice one? Like this?'

'I can't see why not. The lakes country is magnificent. You've already been through some of it when we first traveled north. The lakes are teeming with fish, if you remember. There are a couple that I want to explore further.'

Melissa brightened. 'We'll go early so we can pick the best spot for our camp.'

'Good idea.' Isabella smiled at her friend.

'That's probably why the earl told the coalition army to arrive late May. That gives him the chance to choose the best spots for his own army. He's so selfish, just like me!' Melissa giggled.

'Having the full month of April will provide us with an enormous spring harvest to take with us.' Yannis sounded pleased. 'Together with the harvests that we've already sent south, our army certainly won't go hungry for a year or two. How does all that fit into your plans, Isabella?' There was no response from Isabella. She was staring intently at the ground.

'Isabella?'

She waved her arm absentmindedly at Yannis without looking up. A germ of an idea had started to gnaw at the back of her mind, and she was not to be distracted. She rose and paced the small area, while the others sat staring at her. They all knew when not to interrupt. Finally she stood still and looked up at her friends.

'First thing in the morning,' she said softly, 'I'll get hold of the latest agricultural maps and proposed camp layouts for each of the valleys. We'll meet in the big tent to study them after breakfast. Melissa just said something that's given rise to a very interesting idea. I want my thought process to flow without distractions, so I say goodnight to you all. I will see you at breakfast.' Without another word she disappeared through the exit and headed quickly to her own tent.

Melissa looked bewildered, but ecstatic. 'Did you hear that? I said something. I said something very interesting!' She glanced around at the others, who seemed just as bewildered. 'What on earth did I say?'

CHAPTER 101

Luis Valdez arrived early to light the small fire in the meeting tent, and placed a large kettle on the steel that served as both a safety cover and a heating plate. He was about to leave for his own breakfast when Isabella walked through the entry flap with her arms full of maps.

Never waste a golden opportunity, Isabella. She turned to Luis with her most innocent smile. 'Thanks to you, Luis, it's so lovely and warm I think it might be nice to set up breakfast in here for a change. Would you mind helping to set it up? I could send Melissa over with the food and utensils to give you a hand. I'm sure the two of you working as a team will get it organized in no time.'

'Oh, yes, yes. It would be my pleasure, Major.' Luis tried hard not to appear too eager, but his eyes gave him away.

'It's *Isabella* when we're not in military mode, Luis. I'll make sure Melissa brings enough so that you can join us for breakfast. I know how much she enjoys your company.'

Marcus, Yannis and Isabella remained in the tent after breakfast had been cleared away, each with a steaming mug of tea. Isabella carefully placed the maps in a logical sequence on the long table. Each map was to scale, beautifully drawn and colored, accurately representing the many valleys that had been carefully transformed to not only provide an abundance of food, but to become an irresistible trap.

Isabella was profoundly proud of the artists who had so perfectly captured the scope of work carried out by the agricultural scientists and their army of workers. Moving slowly along the table, she pointed out particular features to Marcus and Yannis. 'You can easily see the layout of the fields of wheat, barley, corn, fruit and vegetables, as opposed to the clear areas for tents and amenities. Each valley is similarly laid out. These different symbols signify stables, barns and stock pens; here we have the villages and various forms of accommodation.

'This particular village,' she said, pointing, 'has been specifically designed so that the earl will automatically choose it as his residence and headquarters. That way we'll know exactly where he is. I've made sure that every area, and each valley, will have a full variety of supplies and storage areas within easy reach, so there will be no need for them to fight for the best positions.'

Yannis caught on quickly. 'This is like reconnaissance in advance. You won't need to send in spies to find out where they will be; you've already designated places for them. This is like having our enemy present us with a map of their entire encampment.'

'Precisely. If you know exactly where the body of the enemy is, you can strike at its very heart.' Isabella put her arms around both Marcus and Yannis as they studied the maps. 'And *that*, gentlemen, is the gift that the bright-eyed and beautiful Melissa presented us with last night.'

Marcus nodded. 'This layout is truly amazing, Isabella, but what exactly was it Melissa said that struck you last night?'

'It was her comment about getting in early to select the best spots. If you take another look at the maps, you'll see by the colors that the grazing areas have been placed on the highest ground in each valley. It's all designed in such a way that the enemy will select their camps without a second thought, including where to place their cannons and wagons. Are you with me so far?'

The two men nodded without comment.

'What if we now downgrade an area so that the main army will avoid it, and allocate it instead to the last arrivals – the *peasants* from the south, the cannon fodder, the coalition army? It will need to be an area vast enough to allow for their camp followers and house approximately 30,000.'

'And what's the great benefit of that?' Marcus asked as his eyes scanned the maps for just such a spot.

'If we can place our friends where we would prefer them to be, we might be in with a chance to save a few lives!'

Yannis nodded. 'In short, what you're saying is: let's see if we can induce their high command to pre-select a campsite for them.'

'There you have it.' Isabella took a few sips of her hot tea to allow time for Marcus and Yannis to digest the information.

'My pick at the moment is up here.' Marcus tapped his finger on one of the maps. 'A general must try to think like his opposite number if he hopes to outmaneuver him, so let's try to think like Bucher for a moment.

He can carve up his own forces into as many parcels as he likes to fit them into the most convenient camping areas. It won't matter who goes where. However, he will think differently when it comes to the coalition army. He'll want them in one spot, where he can keep a close eye on them – and by close, I mean right under his nose.'

'That's good thinking, Grandfather. Keep talking while the mind's racing. That's when it works best.'

'Well, that's one reason I picked the main valley, where Bucher is sure to be. The other reason is that the main valley would be the first to move out as soon as they've restocked their provisions during summer. Also, Bucher will want the coalition to be at the pointy end when they leave, so the main valley will serve his purpose well. My only problem is that the selected area is magnificent grazing land. The only other area is this massive plateau that stretches for miles, but it almost uninhabitable.'

'We've already decided to downgrade something, so why not grazing land? You're right about the plateau: it *is* almost uninhabitable – almost. One of the dangers we face is that Bucher might smell a rat later, if he thinks the position of the coalition camp just a bit too convenient. So we'll have to provide them with a little insurance. What are your thoughts, Yannis?'

Yannis was stroking his short stubble, deep in thought. 'I'm down to just two issues. The first is: if we dispense with that area as grazing land, do we really need to replace it? And, if so, where? The second issue is: how do we go about downgrading the grazing land?'

Isabella grinned broadly. 'This is resolving much sooner than I hoped. Let's get down to business. The grazing land can be downgraded by transferring rocks and rubble from the plateau, which will partially upgrade the plateau at the same time. I have an idea how to make the earl later place the coalition on the plateau. He'll never smell a rat if it is *he* who directs them there.' Isabella giggled. 'Will you listen to us? Here we are, cheekily making his decisions for him! Perhaps I should stay behind to help him out. It will save him some time, and I'm sure he wouldn't mind.'

'No, I'm quite sure he wouldn't mind,' Yannis managed between clenched teeth.

Isabella wrapped one arm around Yannis'. 'Now, now, Yannis, calm down. I've already told you that I hope there will be someone else waiting for me in a few years.'

'Hmph! That's not what he thinks.'

'Well, he might be waiting in vain a long time.'

'So you heard what Johan told us before you called out from the ledge?'

'Yes, but I'm not angry with him. He thought I'd been killed. The poor man is still mortified, even though I told him it's all right.'

'The earl is in love with you, for heaven's sake!'

'It would appear so. He made it pretty plain to me what he wanted. Goodness knows why. Surely I'm too young for a man to find me attractive.

'Well, you might be young, but you're already very … Doesn't it bother you?'

'What?'

'That the man's in love with you, of course.'

'Why, Yannis, I'm surprised that at your age you have so little understanding of women. It's every girl's dream for a man to fall in love with her. The earl is an extremely handsome man and it's very flattering that one so handsome and powerful should be in love with me.'

'But not *him*!'

'Well, preferably not him. My dream is for another man to fall in love with me when I'm a little older.' Isabella was still holding him by his arm and reached her free hand up to touch his lips.

'*Preferably?* You already have half the army standing in line – what are you doing?'

'My hands are clean. I want to feel your teeth. Besides, it's time to change the dreary subject.' Isabella's fingers pushed past his lips as she let go of his arm to bring her other hand up to his jaw. 'Open wide. There's a good boy, General.' She quickly slid her fingers back and forth along his upper and lower teeth while she studied them closely, feeling for anything unusual.

'What are you doing? I'm not a horse!'

'Um, not yet you're not. No teeth are missing, but I'm afraid you're going to need a whole new set anyway. Grandfather, could you please see if you can find the most skilful carver in the army? I have an interesting job for him.'

Marcus simply nodded from his chair where he had gone to sit as soon as Isabella had started to play her little game. *Women!* he thought. *They love to play with their chosen man like a cat with an unfortunate mouse between its paws.*

Yannis remained in a state of confusion. 'Have you gone completely mad, Isabella? There's nothing wrong with my teeth. I look after them very carefully.'

'That's the problem. Your teeth are much too perfect, I'm afraid, but I know just how to fix that. Now then, stand still for me. There's a dear.' Isabella gently traced both hands over Yannis' face: his brow, cheeks, nose, lips and chin. She finished by running her fingers through his hair. He looked panic-stricken, having no idea what was happening, and terrified of the scene that would follow if Melissa poked her head through the flap to announce lunch. 'Oh dear, Yannis, I'm so, so sorry.'

'What … what are you talking about?'

'And such a lovely face, too. What a shame! I'm afraid I'm going to have to ruin it. By the time I'm finished with it, your own mother will disown you. You are about to become well acquainted with Madam Rosa over the next few months. Oh, we're going to have lots of fun! Decisions made! We're done! Let's go and have lunch and give Melissa due credit for our plan.'

CHAPTER 102

Training continued without pause throughout winter for Isabella's brigade, and by early spring, the men were the envy of the whole Southern army. Their fitness became legendary, their fighting sessions so intense they brought crowds who considered them daily entertainment. It did not take long for the spectators to take up the Isabella chant, and it quickly became a sound that regularly echoed across the valley.

Yannis was waiting for her when she arrived back from a training session with Chen. 'We have a message from home base, Isabella. I'm not sure whether it's good news or bad.'

The snow was almost gone and the air cold. She accepted a cup of steaming tea from Yannis and nodded for him to continue.

'It's about the enemy's Third division. It was scheduled to meet up with the earl in May so that they would not be too much of a burden on the remaining provisions. However, over the last couple of months, it's been hit by the spreading disease. The earl sent a message to Emperor Kuiper that if they turned up before the disease had passed, he'd put them all to the sword. The emperor had no choice but to order the division to remain where they are. That means they won't arrive in the valley as planned.'

'Let me think about that for a bit.' Isabella sat down to finish her tea. 'By the way, how are your lovely new teeth coming along?'

Yannis laughed. 'We're about halfway there. The worst part is the taste. It's worse than cow manure.'

'I will defer to your superior experience of the taste of cow manure.' They both laughed. 'All right, back to the Third division. Poor souls! I wouldn't wish that disease on anyone, not even them. We can consider ourselves lucky so far. Initially, it will mean fewer numbers in the valleys, therefore potentially fewer casualties when we attack, which in turn means a higher number to pursue us on the next leg of the war. That's the downside. The upside is that the Third division could be out of action for quite some time. The bottom line is that, for the moment, it doesn't change our plans one bit.'

Yannis nodded. 'Agreed. We proceed as planned.'

Emile DaSilva entered the main tent where Yannis was meeting with officers to discuss final procedures for vacating the valley. 'General, a messenger just delivered a letter from the earl.' Emile handed the letter to Yannis.

Yannis examined the front of the envelope before he turned it over to look at the seal. 'This is addressed to Isabella, Emile.'

'Yes, sir. The messenger's instruction was that it was to be delivered to her, and no-one else.'

'So why give it to me?'

Emile looked flustered. 'Well, sir … ah … I would die for Isabella at the snap of her fingers, but the earl's the chief of his army and you're the chief of ours. So it should be your call who gets the letter, not mine.'

'Thank you, Emile. I appreciate your saying that. My call, therefore, is that you deliver it to *Miss Mondeo*, as the envelope is addressed.'

Isabella looked up from the note she was writing to Dmitri when she saw Emile rushing towards her waving an envelope. 'A letter from the earl, Isabella.'

'Thank you, Emile.' Isabella turned the letter over to inspect the seal and noted with perverse satisfaction that it was not as spectacular as her own. The envelope contained two pages of neat writing:

My Dear Miss Mondeo,

By now you will of course be fully aware of Emperor Aloise Kuiper's plans, and the commission given me to carry them out. My orders are simply to continue south with sufficient forces at my disposal to persuade His Royal Highness, King Ramesses, to submit without further bloodshed, injury or damage.

I therefore now give you advance notice that it is my intention to mobilize my troops on the tenth day of June to commence the crossing of the mountains that currently separate us. I expect the journey will take some two weeks or more for the first of our troops to arrive at our new destination.

Your officers will, of course, already have anticipated this and I am sure they have already made their own arrangements to move further south with sufficient provisions for your immediate needs. I will be quite frank and state that the matter of provisions is one of the reasons this letter is addressed to you as I am sure that your compassion is highly respected and will hold sway with your senior officers. We need provisions, and lots of them, for both the men and the animals. It has come to my attention that the valleys you currently occupy have provided you well over this last year or so. I realize that it is within your capabilities to destroy the vegetation and animals that you are unable to transport, and to leave us with little, if anything. I ask that you consider the following and persuade your army's high command to give it due consideration.

Emperor Kuiper has given me clear and concise instructions. If the valley and surrounding areas are left habitable and fully productive, you have my personal guarantee that all citizens will be protected and well treated, and will receive full compensation for all crops and other valuables consumed by my forces. My soldiers currently lack protein, so if some feed-stock animals were left behind for their well being, I would consider that a personal favor only you can achieve for me.

On the other hand, if the valleys are deliberately denuded of all consumables, instructions have sadly been made very clear to me in regard to the citizens. I need not provide details of what those written orders contain other than to say that I will not be permitted to treat them so kindly.

After a couple of months to replenish our strength and reserves, we will again mobilize and continue the journey south to complete our mission as ordered. It is my most dear wish that no harm come to you or your friends at any time.

My letter to you is written on the same basis of goodwill that I professed to you at our meeting last year. Your personal standing in your national community is now widely acknowledged, and you are also admired within our own nation, including me personally. Rather than have you think that my belief in your destiny has diminished in any way, I hasten to assure you that I strongly believe it will be fulfilled exactly as I proposed the moment I saw you.

With kind regards

Carlos B

Marcus read the letter without comment while Isabella sat quietly. He handed the letter to Yannis and went to sit beside his granddaughter. As he did, he turned his face from Yannis to roll his eyes and grimace at Isabella before turning back with his most innocent expression.

Isabella looked away and coughed to hide her reaction. *This should be interesting*, she thought as she watched Yannis start to read. She was not disappointed.

'The nerve of the man!' he exploded. 'He has a hide thicker than Hannibal's oldest elephant. He wants this, he wants that! He expects us to feed our enemy's troops. What he should do is expect his enemy to leave behind scorched earth and a poisoned chalice.' He took a deep breath in preparation for his next tirade.

Isabella took the opportunity to interject. 'Fortunately, he is only requesting what we want him to have, anyway,' she said softly.

Yannis was not to be placated. 'And ... *and!* ... he goes on to threaten to kill the valleys' inhabitants if we don't submit to his demands, and he's shameless enough to blame it on the emperor's written orders. Written orders, my foot! Those orders are his very own.'

'That's quite possibly so,' Isabella agreed.

'*Quite possibly?* It's not *possibly* so, Isabella! It's *certainly* so!'

'Uh huh.' Isabella glanced at Marcus to hide the smile fighting to take shape.

'*And!* ...' Yannis smacked the letter several times so savagely that a small tear appeared on the top page. 'The man has written you a love letter! That's what this letter is really all about. That's why it's addressed to you, *Miss* Mondeo. It's a love letter!' Yannis started to pace the room to calm down.

'Oh? How so, Yannis?' Isabella's soft voice sounded surprised, perplexed. She was thoroughly delighted.

Yannis stopped directly in front of Isabella. He stabbed his finger several times at the first page. '*Here!* Listen to this. He writes: *one of the reasons.* That is of course to signal to you that there is *another* reason. That other reason is that he is professing his love for you again, and he even has the hide to *propose* to you a second time. This time he's proposed to you in writing! The commander-in-chief of the enemy forces! *The hide of the man!* Yannis waved his arms about as he worked himself into a rage. Isabella's delight increased by the second.

'*No!* Really? He proposed again? I hadn't noticed that,' Isabella exclaimed in her most innocent voice. She had indeed noticed it. It was too blatant to miss.

Yannis held up the second page. 'La de dah de dah,' he sneered while he searched the page. 'Here it is, the cheeky blighter: *rather than have you think that my belief in your destiny has diminished in any way.* Best of all – can you believe it? – are his very last words that just happen to be: *I proposed the moment I saw you.* How could you miss that?'

'Well, you're obviously far more insightful about a man's feelings when it comes to expressing love, Yannis.' Isabella was unsure whether Marcus was coughing or trying not to choke. 'It's a bit overwhelming to think that I'm just days away from sixteen, and already someone is in love with me.'

'And wants to make you an *empress,* no less,' Yannis snorted.

'Oh, *my goodness!* Yes, that too. *Empress* Isabella. Fancy that! Me, an *empress.* It does have a rather nice ring to it, though, don't you think?' Isabella gasped theatrically and held her hand to her mouth. She turned to Marcus and gripped one of his hands in hers. 'Grandfather, I do hope there will be another man who will love me as much as the earl when I'm older.' She turned her face away from Marcus to settle an innocent gaze on Yannis.

Yannis appeared confused and chose to pace the tent while he tried to regather his thoughts.

Marcus squeezed her hand. 'I believe that is a distinct possibility. You'll just have to learn to be patient, my darling.'

It was Isabella's turn to cough. 'I need to pen a response, so let's talk about that instead of all this other nonsense about the earl. My opinion is that his demands and threats play directly into our hands. It enables us to leave the things we wanted to, without making it like we've left a baited trap.'

Yannis seemed unsettled, but he had calmed down. 'I have to agree, it does make it easier. All right, let's get a letter back to that rogue and get on with business.'

•

Marcus shook his head and chuckled as he escorted Isabella back to her tent. 'My goodness, I've never seen Yannis so agitated. That letter certainly had a profound effect on him.'

'Do you think he was angry with me?'

'No, of course he's not angry with you. He's unsettled, confused. His mind is suddenly in turmoil.'

'Not jealous, surely, Grandfather. That would unsettle *me*!'

'No, not jealous. He loves you dearly, but not in the romantic sense, darling, and that's the way it should be. He respects you more than anyone, but he doesn't know how you really fit into his life. When he looks at you, he still sees the child whom he met years ago, but today he saw that you're turning into a beautiful young woman who already has one of Europe's most powerful men in love with her. *No, don't roll your eyes at me, Isabella!* Nature has seen you blossom like a summer rose, yet in Yannis' mind you remain too young to think about in the romantic sense.'

'I don't want him to always think of me like that, Grandfather.' She held his arm as they walked.

'He won't. That letter today threw his life upside down, and he doesn't know how to deal with it. He doesn't even realize that he's fighting within himself. In fact, you should expect him to be a bit distant for a few days, so give him some latitude when you're with him.'

'I will. But why was he so upset?'

'Suddenly he's been forced to see you in the adult world. He now knows you can quickly grow away from him at any time to marry anyone you come into contact with. Unknowingly, the earl has done you a favor by sending that letter. It's made Yannis take notice of you as a grown woman for the first time. He knows that you have my consent to marry the man of your choosing when you turn sixteen, and now that's only a couple of weeks off. As soon as he gets used to that, he'll start looking at you differently, I promise you.'

'It's about time he noticed me, the scoundrel! Half the army already has! He'd better look at me differently if he knows what's good for him.' Isabella giggled as she squeezed her grandfather's arm.

So the Earl intends to mobilize four days after my birthday, Isabella mused. She quickly adjusted the time schedule in her mind and focused on how best to construct her reply. No show of weakness, she decided. Perhaps a little tease thrown in?

She finished the letter an hour later, picked up an envelope and called out to Marcus. 'Do you want to read the letter before I seal the envelope?'

'No, no need. I'm sure it will be fine. I'll arrange for someone to take it to the messenger.'

'What about Yannis?'

'No, it's probably best if he doesn't read what you've written. He'll misconstrue everything you've written simply because he'll want to.'

'You're right, Grandfather.' Isabella decided to glue the envelope without attaching her personal seal.

CHAPTER 103

Just short of beautiful, Madam Rosa Tissone was a slightly plump, vivacious woman in her early forties who loved to dabble in her extra-curricular activities whenever the opportunity presented itself. An enthusiastic camp follower who controlled the distribution of stores to the various camps, Rosa came from a theatrical background. Not particularly convincing on stage, she had, at first reluctantly, drifted into a less exciting role in entertainment: make-up artist and costume designer. Within a short time she came to realize that the appearance of the actors on stage was no less important than the lines they delivered. A born artist, she loved her new vocation more than she could ever have loved being a mere actor. Her wigs, for both men and women, were made from human hair of all lengths, colors and styles. Each wig and costume was a brilliant reproduction of the period represented. Both the actors and the audience loved the illusion she was able to produce on stage, and she soon became as famous as any of her actors.

Her good looks made her highly sought after by men from all walks of life, but she had never accepted an invitation to companionship from any man since the untimely death of the one she had loved like no other. Now, everyone knew her simply as Madam Rosa.

On the third Sunday of every month, Madam Rosa produced three sessions of a theatre play, on occasions a musical, for the enjoyment of the soldiers. A large number of them, as well as camp followers, became proficient actors who regularly rotated in roles suited to their particular talent or appearance.

On this occasion, Madam Rosa shuddered as she examined the creature sitting in front of her. Unkempt, greying hair fell across an ugly, hairy face like a tangled bird's nest. The unfortunate man was blessed with a bulbous, wart-covered nose and ears that pushed prominently away from his head. Fumes from crushed onion weed under his shirt produced eyes that were red-rimmed and rheumy. Several rotted teeth jutted out beneath a protruding upper lip, rendering him unable to control the spittle that trickled towards his chin. The man tried to grin, but it did nothing for his appearance other than to make him even more repulsive.

'You are a beast,' she murmured with disgust as her dainty hands flitted delicately over the man's hideous face giving his warts a light cover of powder. 'An absolute beast, you are, Isabella, for making me do this to such a beautiful man. He was so beautiful before I started, was he not?'

Isabella looked at Yannis and shrugged. 'I suppose he might be passably attractive to a couple of women here and there. He's much too grouchy for my taste, though. His current appearance is definitely more in keeping with his inner self.'

Yannis pulled a face, but it only served to make him look slightly better. It had been two days since he had read Bucher's letter, and Isabella thought he still seemed distant in her presence.

'His upper teeth fit perfectly. The carver is a brilliant craftsman and will have the lower set finished in a couple of days. By then not even a Viking troll will kiss him.' Rosa motioned to Yannis that he could remove the dentures carved from rotted animal-bones. 'Let's get that make-up off. My gypsy costume is ready, and so are the three for Mbiti Ranhui. Yannis' costume will be completed tomorrow. It's such a shame, though, to have to hide most of those lovely muscles.'

Isabella nodded. 'The intense training has certainly improved his physique, but it's done absolutely nothing for his personality. Even without the make-up, he is such a beast to me.' She leaned forward to poke him in the chest. 'Always yelling at me. Always treating me so horribly. I'm sure he hates me, Rosa.' She pouted and put on her saddest face.

'Oh, shut up, Isabella! I don't hate you,' Yannis growled as he dropped his dentures in a bowl of brine, and reached for a rag to wipe his chin.

'See? There you go, snarling at me again. You do so hate me. Put those teeth back in, Yannis. Your face suits you perfectly then. You're beastly, beastly, beastly!' Isabella laughed with delight as she continued to poke him in the chest.

Yannis was handed a message as they made their way back from Madam Rosa's. He had been silent while they walked, but now he was forced to speak.

'It's from the family. They'll be here next week. It's taken longer than planned to get here, so there won't be a lot of time for rehearsals.'

'It won't matter. They only need to make themselves familiar with the general area: how to get in and out, and where to place themselves for their performances. Mbiti has the most wonderful voice, and he'll be able to sing anything your family throws at him.'

'You're right, I've heard him. He is amazing. Don't be surprised if my family take him with them when they leave.'

Isabella had asked Yannis' permission for Dmitri to contact his gypsy family to help her complete a complex deception. It was part of her plan to provide a measure of protection for the coalition army. That effort needed to be so open and so blatant that it could not possibly arouse suspicion.

Yannis' grandfather had passed away but his father, though no longer a travelling gypsy, had insisted on joining the family caravan for the occasion. There would be six families, each with a gaudily painted wagon, to entertain the soldiers. Mbiti Ranhui, a handsome young black East African, would join the families for a special task.

'You must be looking forward to seeing your father again, and your uncles and so many cousins.'

'Yes. Yes, of course.'

'Will you introduce me? To your father, I mean.'

'Of course I will.' Yannis stopped, looked around and saw that no-one was paying them any attention. He turned back to her, but seemed lost for words.

'What is it, Yannis? Tell me what's troubling you. You've known me long enough to tell me anything.'

'You don't really think I hate you, do you?'

'Of course I don't think you hate me, you silly man. You will never hate me.'

'Then why did you …?'

'Oh you!' Isabella punched his chest. 'I was just teasing you. Don't you know enough about girls by now to know how much they love to tease a man?'

'That's a relief. I wouldn't want you to believe I thought of you like that.'

Isabella decided to take the opportunity to test the water. 'So how exactly do you think of me?'

He motioned to start walking again. 'It's hard to put into words, because there's simply no-one in the whole world quite like you, and there's no-one who means more to me than you do. The best I can come up with is that I think of you as my best friend. Is it all right to say that, or have I gone and put my foot in it again?'

'For a change, Yannis, you've told me something I like to hear. That was really lovely.'

'So everything is all right, then, between you and me?'

Isabella glanced up at him and smiled as they strolled. 'You and I will always be all right, Yannis. Always.' She saw the tension fade from his face as they continued their walk, a respectful distance between them. Yannis was back to his old self.

Like Yannis, Earl Carlos Bucher flicked his fingers at the paper in his hand. But unlike Yannis, Carlos did it gently. He was very careful not to damage Isabella's treasured letter in any way. It had been delivered just ten minutes earlier and, alone in his tent, he was reading it for the third time. He wanted to be absolutely certain that he had made no mistake in his interpretation of Isabella's carefully chosen words:

> Your Grace,
>
> Thank you for your letter and thank you for your kind offer regarding the honorable treatment of the valleys' citizens, and their chattels. In exchange for your word, the senior officers have asked me to convey to you that all agricultural lands and harvests will remain intact upon our departure. In addition, as a personal concession requested by me, they have agreed to leave behind several thousand cattle, goats, poultry and the like for your men, as well as substantial stocks of feed for your horses and other animals.
>
> I accept that you will honor your word, because to do otherwise would naturally be forever unforgivable. Under the now more conducive circumstances of our relations, I feel it is no longer inappropriate for you to address me by my first name – if you still wish to, of course.
>
> As you suspected, our officers did indeed expect you to mobilize as soon as the terrain made it possible, and our soldiers are anxious to vacate well before your arrival. They are not keen to submit, but they fear your cannons more than any weapon they have ever faced, and will do everything in their power to keep out of their range as they

withdraw. Ultimately, it will be the king's decision whether our men submit before reaching home, or continue the fight for their homeland.

As for destiny, I can only say that I will allow time to resolve that proposition. At the same time I must admit that I do feel special – but then again, doesn't everyone?

Kind regards

Isabella M

Carlos was jubilant. Isabella had managed to deliver her personal gift to him of a treasure greater than a king's ransom: the ability to feed his army. He knew she would have had to fight hard for that. Her invitation to address her by her first name had delighted him. Best of all was her use of the word *proposition* in the last paragraph. It was coded message to him that she had recognized his use of a similar word in the last sentence of his own letter. A final point that she had made was that she felt special – a hint, perhaps, that she felt special enough to be an empress?

Carlos smiled as he acknowledged that Isabella had been sufficiently clever and courageous to issue a threat of her own. In one succinct sentence she had made it crystal clear that they would have no future together if he mistreated the valleys' citizens. *Now there is a young woman well worth waiting for*, he thought. He was desperate for her attention and prepared to accept her message at face value, no matter the cost.

CHAPTER 104

For once in her life, Isabella was utterly exhausted, and it was all because of the gypsy performances. Yannis' gypsy family attracted crowds from every valley for four shows each day for almost a week. Yannis' father, Hamal Christos, was warm and friendly and treated Isabella and Melissa as if they were his daughters, if not as prospective daughters-in-law for his handsome son. Isabella could see the strong resemblance between father and son, even though Hamal's handsome features were considerably sharper than his son's. She decided that Yannis' softer features must have been inherited from his mother.

The troupe included singers, musicians, jugglers, actors and clowns, and an illusionist with amazing contraptions that seemed to make people disappear into thin air. The highlight of each show was the acrobatic team of two superbly fit young men and a beautiful young woman. They danced and twisted, climbed and spun on ropes, rolled and tumbled to lightning-fast music, and finished with a stunning routine of jumping and spinning.

A substantial part of the gypsies' business plan was to separate the audience from the change in their pockets at the end of each performance. Years of experience had shown that the way to do so was to involve the spectators. If, at the end of the last act, they were left cheering with enthusiasm, the shower of coins could darken the sky. The last act – the acrobats – was the key to their success.

From time to time, audience members were invited to participate on stage in some of the acts, particularly the singing or juggling performances. One such participant was Mbiti Ranhui, who, without the audience being aware of the behind-the-scenes arrangements, went on to become a regular feature and a crowd favorite. He was provided with two brilliant jackets for his performances: one sky blue, the other a brilliant green. A third jacket was carefully hidden away. It would be worn only once for a very special performance.

During the morning session of the second day, the master-of-ceremonies asked the audience if there was anyone with enough courage to join the acrobats on stage. Unfortunately for Isabella, the audience included many from her brigade, who were only too familiar with her physical skills. Within seconds the chant spread throughout the crowd: *Isabella, Isabella, ooo, ooo, ooo!* To make matters worse, the master-of-ceremonies for that day happened to be Hamal. She was left no choice. One of the clowns hurried her to a caravan to change into a suitable costume that would allow her freedom of movement.

The glittering skin-tight costume covered her perfect shape and tiny waist modestly from hip to shoulder, but displayed considerably more of her athletic legs than the appreciative soldiers had previously seen. Isabella's years of martial-arts steps made it easy for her to remember, and master, the acrobats' routines, and by the second show, she had become the star attraction. No-one, including the acrobats, had previously seen complete unsupported forward and backward somersaults, and by the end of the week Isabella was coaching the team to perform moves they had never thought possible. At the end of each performance, the shower of coins was heavier than the summer rains.

A small party was held during the week for Isabella's sixteenth birthday, and Hamal arranged for the troupe to perform a private show. She was thrilled, and sat holding his arm for most of the show. A special bond had formed naturally between the two, one that became stronger each day.

During the performance, Isabella looked up at Hamal and asked, 'Mr Christos, I don't know much about Yannis' background other than a brief mention of gypsies. Has your family always been gypsies? Did Yannis leave the troupe to join the army?'

'No, Yannis was never part of the gypsy life, and I was a part of it only until my late teens, but I did love every minute I had with them.'

'It seems like such a happy life. Why did you leave?'

'I fell in love with the most beautiful girl I had ever seen. Yannis' mother, of course. It was an easy choice to make at the time.'

Isabella tugged at his arm. 'Oh, that is so beautiful. Tell me more! Tell me about your gypsy family.'

'The gypsy side only goes back as far as my parents. The entire background goes back as far as my great-grandparents. My great-grandfather was a soldier in Genghis Khan's army as it swept through Persia. A daughter, my grandmother, was born soon after.'

'Genghis Khan!' Isabella's eyes were wide with excitement.

Hamal smiled, warming to the story he had not related for a long time. 'My grandmother had twins, a boy and a girl, in Persia, but the whole family was by then considered outcasts and fled to the kingdom of Hungary. Unfortunately, Hungary was on Genghis Khan's shopping list, and that part of the story does not have a happy ending. The boy twin, my father, was taken in by an Italian family and given their name, Christos. He later married a local girl, a Corsican, and had four children, one of which you are now sitting next to. So when you look back, Yannis comes from an interesting mix of Mongol, Persian, Corsican and the southern islands.'

'My goodness, that is just so fascinating! And what happened to the girl twin?'

'My auntie was sent to China and never heard from again.'

'Oh.'

'Anyway, my parents had to flee Italy because of the constant wars and crusades, and thought they'd be welcomed back on Persian soil. They were sadly mistaken but were eventually welcomed into a gypsy family. I say *family*, but it's actually made up of about twenty different families from anywhere and everywhere. It was a wonderful life.'

'How exciting! But also so sad. With such a tough history, it's easy to see why Yannis makes such a brave and wonderful soldier.' Isabella leaned her head against Hamal's shoulder and while she watched the rest of the show, she reflected quietly on what she had just heard.

As much as she enjoyed the performances, and thrilled to the rousing cheers at the end of each, Isabella was glad when the time came for the gypsies to hitch their horses to the wagons for the next leg of their journey. They would return to the valley in a few weeks to entertain the Northern army, and Isabella had no intention of performing in a revealing costume in front of her prospective husband, Earl Carlos Bucher.

Except for a few remaining tents, there was little to indicate that Jacques' beautiful village had ever existed. He and the ten remaining engineers wore broad welcoming smiles as Isabella and Yannis rode into their midst.

Jacques reached up to run a hand lovingly over *Barca*'s head and neck. 'The most magnificent beast this world will ever see, Isabella. I've saved some treats for him.' He looked up and smiled sadly as Isabella dismounted. 'I'm afraid I can't offer you the same, though. The bath-house has gone into the ravine with everything else.'

Isabella flicked *Barca*'s reins over the pommel and gave Jacques a hug. 'Believe it or not, but we have duplicated your bath-house design in the new camp a dozen times over so that the men, as well as the women, can enjoy the pleasure of a hot bath. We'll have unlimited water available to us in the lakes country, and heating fuel is everywhere.'

Isabella moved across the small path to give a warm hug to each of the ten delighted engineers, who had thought they would miss out. Only Yannis was left out.

'No one is likely to ever come this way,' Jacques said as they made their way to the meeting tent on the other side of the site. 'There is simply no reason to come here, but just in case, we intend to make sure there is absolutely no trace of anyone ever having been here. It turned out to be the perfect spot to work, as you predicted. It's been easy to get rid of everything. We simply dump everything down the ravine right next to us, and the event on the big day will remove any trace.' He gave Isabella a wicked grin as he mentioned *the big day*.

She nodded. 'It promises to be a big day, doesn't it?'

Jacques held back the tent opening for her. 'We'll be here one more week. We'll then dump the last items into the ravine and move over to the other side of the valley, where we've got a few tents set up. From there we'll be able to see your fire beacon, and we already have our own response beacon built under a large shelter, just in case of sudden rain.' He pointed to a table at one side of the tent. 'Hot tea and snacks are ready for you. Help yourselves, everyone, while I lay the maps out for the final review.'

Yannis was relaxed as he watched Isabella lean over the maps next to Jacques and sip her steaming tea. He felt her power and enthusiasm for life surge through him whenever she was close, leaving him charged and energized. He had long ago admitted unreserved confidence in her, and never questioned her actions or decisions. He found them well-reasoned and always correct. At sixteen, she could now be considered an adult, he knew, perhaps just barely in actual years, but certainly in mind and appearance. He had been speechless when she had first walked on stage in the brightly colored costume. Never before had he seen anyone so beautiful, and with such poise. While he had watched her perform the seemingly impossible, his mind had drifted to the day she would ultimately meet and fall in love with someone. It never occurred to him that she had already done so.

Yannis now stood to one side and watched as Isabella, still leaning over the maps, unconsciously brought her right hand up to push her thick hair off her face. Unexpectedly, she turned her face and saw an expression once on the faces on boys in a library long ago. Except this time it was a young man of twenty-three staring at her. They both turned a shade of red as their eyes met for a moment before they looked away.

'... and each chamber is set to detonate in the exact sequence you planned, but let's go over it once more.' The first part of Jacques' sentence was lost in the sudden roar in Isabella's head, as her heart hammered wildly. Jacques went on to detail every moment from the time he would see the smoke from her fire beacon.

He finished with a summary. 'The first sequence – we'll call that zero hour – will take place nine minutes after seeing your signal. The total time to complete your task is estimated at twenty minutes, but I suggest you get out well within that time, or you could all perish. We have two of the latest mechanical escapement clocks to assist us, one of which will be with your own timekeepers on the day. We'll view the sequences before we disappear faster than a bee in a smokestack. No-one back home has any idea, have they, why you wanted a massive forty tons of powder when two tons would have done the trick?'

Isabella grinned and shook her head. 'No, I kept that one to myself. They wouldn't believe I could possibly get away with anything like this. Speaking of tricks, the whole idea is to create the greatest illusion of all time.'

'Rest assured, it will be!'

'You seem to have thought of everything.'

'I hope so. We can now provide the coalition army with the visual evidence they need to allow them to follow through with that part of your plan.'

'Oh, what would we have done without you, Jacques, and your gorgeous engineers and tradesmen? Thank you all so much. That's all I can say and do now. Your nation will do more for you later. You have created the masterpiece of the century and little old me is going to sneak behind your backs to destroy it!'

'It's been a delight working with you, Isabella, and a thank you is as much a reward as we would ever want. Now, I suggest a quick lunch as I know you'll be anxious to get back. I know you have much to do. Your mounts have been watered and fed and are ready to go.'

CHAPTER 105

Right on time, after an early breakfast for both man and beast, the wheels that carried the cannons, gunpowder and the heaviest materiel started to groan their way through the mountain passes. Due to the massive number of soldiers following, staging camps were placed so close they were almost continuous. Food, fodder and water had already been sent ahead to ensure the beasts of burden would perform their given tasks without undue delay. With its insatiable appetite for consumables, the earl's massive army had already denuded the landscape for hundreds of miles in every direction.

Although Carlos Bucher was anxious to arrive at his next destination, he remained behind for a few days to hone his skills as his nation's foremost archer, and to work on his memoirs. There was no hurry, he thought. He would easily catch up with the slow-moving artillery convoy well before they reached the lush valleys. He himself never went without the very best of provisions, but he looked forward to the adulation he knew he would receive when his soldiers saw the abundant supplies of fresh meat and crops soon to appear on their plates. *Ah, Isabella, what would I have done without your help?* Thirty-one prisoners was a bargain for what you have given me in return.

His memoirs did not mention Isabella once. It could appear treasonable, he reasoned, if his writings were accidentally viewed prematurely by hostile eyes. However, he had left regular gaps and spaces to edit her in when it was safe to do so. He would complete his memoirs immediately after she became his wife – *no*, he corrected himself, his *empress!* In the meantime he regularly enjoyed her company in his upgraded daydreams, especially now that he was permitted to call her *Isabella.*

It had been left to Marcus and Emile to manage the logistics of moving the soldiers out of the many valleys. The great majority headed directly to the lakes country, high in the mountains two nations farther south. Others, including Isabella's brigade, were directed to a smaller, carefully disguised camp two days march from the main valley.

Melissa and Xu Yan had left in tears for the lakes country, where Marcus would join them in a few days. Yannis insisted it was essential that an experienced general always be safeguarded, particularly as Yannis himself would be placed at high risk, both when he penetrated the very heart of the enemy camp and in the battle to follow.

Marcus, Yannis and Isabella toured the main valley for a last inspection before their own departure. Isabella exhibited keen interest as she walked through a small selection of the hundreds of village homes lining both sides of the river. Jacques had joined them at the village entrance for the occasion.

'My engineers had great fun with the design of this village. Our designs, but your ideas, Isabella. I just wish I could be here on the day to see it all happen.'

Isabella patted him on the arm. 'You'll be watching something even more spectacular where you'll be stationed.'

'Yes, perhaps so. Let's have a look at one of these bridges.' Jacques spent five minutes before he gave it the thumbs up. 'Looks good. The timbers are well soaked in pitch and should burn well. My only suggestion would be to place some bales of hay in the cavities beneath the spans. If the logs don't generate heat quickly enough, you could ignite the bales to speed up the process. A bit of insurance never hurts.'

'A great idea. Thank you. I'll arrange for it to be done at once. We're going to ride up and check out the plateau, so we'll catch up with you a little later for lunch.'

The plateau and the former grazing area immediately below it had been completely transformed. The wide expanse of grazing area had been carefully reconstructed to make it undesirable, but not uninhabitable. The plateau itself was even less desirable, but considerably better after much of the rock and debris had been moved down to the grazing areas. To improve the plateau for habitation would be relatively easy with 25,000 coalition soldiers to assist: simply toss offending items into the ravines on the far side.

After a bit of fossicking, Yannis rode away to inspect some of the ravines, while Marcus and Isabella remained to overlook the magnificent valley for the last time. 'Perfect!' Isabella exclaimed with satisfaction. 'Everything looks perfect.'

Marcus nodded as he looked over the vista before he turned to Isabella. 'Yes, perfect! Just like you, darling. You look perfect, stunning in fact.'

'Why, thank you, Grandfather. Girls do love to be flattered.'

'It wasn't flattery. It was simply an observation. We're facing a high-risk battle in just a few weeks, yet you look surprisingly happy. I take it all that business with the earl and Yannis has resolved itself?'

'Yannis does seem to have settled down a bit. The Earl hasn't been mentioned, but I figure a bit of competition won't do me any harm.' She smiled cheekily.

'Ah, yes, a bit of competition to give him something to think about, eh? And that's why you're so happy?'

'Well, only partly. The thing is, I've reached a small milestone in my life. I know I'm still very young in his mind, but the fact is that I have already reached marriage age and Yannis is still single, so I'm in with a chance. I also caught him looking at me very differently the other day. The look was unmistakable, so I know he does find me attractive. I didn't have time on my side when I fell in love with him, but time has moved in my favor. If he doesn't eventually express an interest in me, then so be it, but in the meantime I'm very happy with where I am right now. I'm going into that battle in a few weeks with a smile on my face, no matter what happens.'

'And Melissa? What about her?'

'She is certainly strong competition, but I hope to be up to the challenge when the time comes. Melissa is my best friend, and I'm not going to entice him away from her. I'll only want Yannis if he falls in love with me in his own good time. And that's enough questions, Grandfather – I suggest you quit while you're ahead. Besides, Yannis is on his way back. His poor ears must be burning like campfires.'

It was an exodus of epic proportions as the soldiers streamed out of the valleys that had been their home for almost two years.

Isabella's brigade was to be the last to leave. No-one, other than a few select villagers, would be permitted to view what they would do on the day before departure. Alexander duPonti and a select number of his scribes would remain to record the events of that day and, in particular, record the precise times taken for each exercise.

The evening party for Isabella and her thousand men to celebrate the completion of the last exercises had been planned for several days. Tables were laden with summer berries, fruit and vegetables, together with dozens of spit-roasted cattle, pigs, goats and poultry. Musicians drawn from both the army and the villagers completed the party atmosphere.

It was the largest and most lavish party Isabella had ever attended, and it was almost overwhelming for a girl of sixteen who was also the party's main celebrity. Crowds followed her every step, hung on her every word. The grandmaster of dressmakers, Madam Rosa, had presented her with a magnificent formal evening dress made especially for the occasion. In embroidered red silk, the figure-hugging dress flared at the knee to drop elegantly to just touch the ground. Rosa had been careful to make it modest at the upper front in deference to Isabella's age, but it was bare-shouldered and partly backless. Her golden hair was wound around and upswept, leaving her neck and ears fully revealed. Her pale complexion contrasted perfectly with the red of the shimmering silk. She looked absolutely radiant.

Isabella was initially escorted to the party by a proud Zhang Chen, who was soon mortified to find himself pushed aside by the swirling crowd desperate to get close to their glamorous idol. Every now and again, he grinned as he caught one of her kisses blown above the heads of the crowd.

It was impossible for Isabella not to notice the admiring glances of the soldiers, including Luis Valdez, who just stared when the two came face to face after she was able to mingle more freely with the crowd. She wagged an admonishing finger at him, her eyes glittering from the reflected fires. 'Shame on you, Luis Valdez! It's just as well Melissa isn't here to see you look at me like that.'

Unable to speak, his face turned crimson as he stumbled away and looked around desperately to see if Yannis had seen the encounter. The reference to Melissa was not accidental, and Isabella was pleased with the response. In her peripheral vision she had noticed Yannis looking her way several times, but she had forced herself to glance elsewhere. She did not dare to meet his eyes for even an instant.

Marcus had never been so proud of his granddaughter and spent considerable time by her side. He remembered his daughter-in-law well enough to realize for the first time that Isabella was more than equal to her mother in every way.

At one point the two finally met up with Yannis, who looked relaxed and happy in the party atmosphere. In the social environment of the occasion, he shook hands with both Marcus and Isabella.

'My, how formal, General Christos,' Isabella said, presenting him with a deep curtsy with her hand still in his. She smiled broadly while she held his eyes to indicate that her response was neither a rebuke nor sarcasm.

Yannis was delighted to have been graced with a curtsy for the first time in his life. 'Well, the occasion makes formality seem appropriate, somehow. And ah … you look quite formal yourself, Miss Mondeo. You ah … look very nice. Very nice.' He stammered as he stared at her, as if worried he was about to put his foot in his mouth again.

'Thank you, Yannis. I don't mind the odd compliment here and there, to be honest.'

Yannis seemed relieved and quickly changed the subject while he was on safe ground. His eyes twinkled mischievously in the firelight. 'I thought things went very well at rehearsals today. Everyone knows exactly what to do, and when. It's going to be an absolute piece of cake on the day. All we have to do is somehow get out alive!'

'Now there's a novel idea, Yannis. I'll make a note.' Isabella laughed so loud she doubled up, with both Yannis and Marcus joining in. After they recovered they made some small talk until Yannis said he would speak to some of his men before retiring for the night.

Marcus sneered as soon as Yannis disappeared into the crowd. '*Nice! You look nice*,' he said, mimicking Yannis. 'That was the understatement of the decade. The man is stark raving mad. You don't look *nice*! You look sensational!'

Isabella was a little more circumspect. 'Grandfather, you're just a little biased, so perhaps that's where I'm really at – *nice*. I can only hope that he liked what he saw.'

Marcus rolled his eyes. 'Now *that* was the understatement of the *century*!'

It's about time!

Emperor Aloise Kuiper was furious. Time and again, Aloise had railed against General Maurice Von Franckel about *His Grace's* seeming penchant for doing nothing. First, the earl had spent time licking his wounds after a minor skirmish with a vastly undermanned Southern army. Instead, the man should have given his foe a hiding! Next, he had been waiting for the Second and Third Divisions to join him. Always something! *And all the while the man was enjoying the finest food and wine at Aloise's personal expense!*

He had at last received Maurice's report that the earl was on his way to his new headquarters further south. The report went on to say that the coalition force had been directed to join the earl after he had settled in. When the Third Division reported being free of illness, they would also join him. With an angry flick of his wrist, Aloise tossed the report onto the small table, where it floated across the polished surface and dropped to the floor.

It's about time!

CHAPTER 106

The Southern army had departed a full week before the earl's scouting party entered the valleys. Their job was to select the most suitable site for each division before breaking it down to the smaller group components. Immediately behind them came the camp followers, who set up temporary facilities for the bulk of the army that would enter in the following days.

Carlos Bucher was delighted with his new, albeit temporary, headquarters, both with the magnificent scenery and the abundance of consumables left behind: grain, fruit and vegetables, cattle, goats and sheep, pigs and poultry of every description. Stables, barns, fodder and grazing lands provided shelter and ample provisions for the animals.

The earl moved into the compound specifically built for an army headquarters. It included a large number of smaller cottages nearby for the more senior officers and their adjutants. The camps grew quickly throughout the several valleys as the Second division arrived, and by the end of the month, the Northern army's two divisions were fully ensconced. Two weeks later saw the arrival of the Southern Coalition Army, a reluctant party to the cause.

After the cold and barren lands of his previous surroundings, Colonel Oleg Walenski was more than a little pleased as he inspected the two rooms of his small cottage, just one hundred paces from his supreme commander's. Far superior to a miserable tent, he thought, as he rubbed his hands with unbridled delight.

No less pleased was Captain Andreas Fransz, billeted to a one-room cottage a little further away, but still within easy walking distance of the main compound. A little less pleased was Mehudi, Fransz's adjutant, who was billeted to his usual tent erected immediately next to his captain's cottage. He did not complain, however. No-one ever complained. It was the quickest way to be booted out of the army with a tag that read *deserter* tied around the neck. The shame of that made complaints a thing of the past.

By eight, it was already warm when the earl took his morning stroll to the river while his personal staff prepared breakfast. Rather than salute, he nodded to some of his fellow officers on the way past the cottages. Several soldiers were outside their accommodation tending to their wash and, in some cases, shaving. Although few saluted because of the temporary informal conditions, most greeted him with a *Sir* or *Your Grace*. None were in uniform, including the earl, who intended to practice his archery later that morning.

A sound caused him to suddenly stop and cock his head to one side. At first he thought he had imagined it and was about to continue his walk when his senses told him he had not made a mistake. He glanced at Colonel Walenski, who was standing outside his cottage trying hard not to cut his throat while shaving with his razor-sharp knife. 'Ollie, do you hear something? Listen.'

Walenski stopped all motion while he listened, turning his head slowly from side to side. 'No, Your Grace, I can't … wait! Yes, actually, I can hear something.'

'Find out what it is, Ollie.' Although spoken softly, it was not a request.

'Yes, sir'. Walenski quickly finished shaving, grabbed his shirt and was about to move when the source of the sound became immediately apparent. A number of brilliantly colored wagons appeared over the rise in the distance and made their way down the winding track that led into the main valley. Walking alongside were several men juggling a variety of indiscernible objects, accompanied by other men and women playing rapid-fire music on stringed instruments.

'Gypsies, sir!'

'Better tip out your shave water, Ollie, or they'll steal it. I'll go and get breakfast out of the way, then I'll be back to see what they're up to.' By the time he returned an hour later, the gypsies had just pulled their wagons to a stop close to the southern bridge. A large number of soldiers had followed them to the river to get a closer look at the spectacular wagons, and perhaps a little entertainment.

The crowd parted to allow the earl passage just as the stage producer and former actor, Madam Rosa Tissone, in a spectacularly florid dress, climbed down from the lead wagon. Costumed gypsies followed, pouring from the other wagons to wave at the crowd. As soon as the soldiers caught sight of the young woman acrobat in her skimpy costume, they surged forward to roar their approval. In an instant the girl leapt up onto the shoulders of her two team members, who then held her high above their heads in the palms of their hands. She stood with her arms outstretched and smiled seductively at her adoring audience. With a flip of the men's hands, the girl somersaulted to the ground to deafening applause. Even the earl was impressed and joined in the applause. He had no idea that Isabella was the architect of that dangerous maneuver.

'L-a-a-a-d-i-e-e-s and gentlemen, I am Madam *Tessa*,' Rosa's experienced stage voice rang out across the entire audience. 'I and my h-u-u-u-g-e and talented family are here to *entertain* you. But only if you want us! *Does anybody want us?*' Hamal looked on in awe, wishing that Rosa could be a permanent addition to his relatives' troupe. As she moved closer to her target, she waited for the roar of the crowd to subside before continuing.

'What a *be-ooo-ti-ful* valley; what a *be-ooo-ti-ful* part of the world to entertain in! O*h! ... my! ... goodness! ...* What a *be-ooo-ti-ful, be-ooo-ti-ful man!*' Rosa stared wide-eyed at the startled Earl Carlos Bucher as she placed a hand on the ample proportions that covered her heart. 'You already know, sir, that I am Madam Tessa, but did you know that I am unmarried and so, so lonesome on my travels across this lonely planet. Someone please hold me while I faint!' Laughter echoed across the valley as Rosa performed a theatrical swoon and fanned her face. Even the Earl could not hold back and doubled up with laughter, partly to help cover the flush that Rosa had noticed on his face. Mission accomplished. The Earl would not refuse them now.

She waved her arms to subdue the crowd before she addressed the earl again. 'I know you must be desperate to keep me close to you, but we do need permission from your commanding officer to stay. O*h*, I'm feeling faint again!' Another round of applause swept through the crowd. 'Could I prevail upon you to bring me your commanding officer so that we may make some arrangements with him for a short stay to entertain you all?'

The earl reached out, took Rosa's hand in his and raised it to his lips for a light kiss. 'Of course, Madam Tessa. It will be my pleasure. I will bring him to you at once.' He bowed before he turned, winked at his men and walked away.

Rosa allowed him to move several paces before she called out to him. 'Hey, beautiful soldier-boy!'

The earl turned, startled. Never in his life had he been summoned.

Rosa fanned her face again. 'Forget about bringing your boss, my love. Bring a priest so he can marry us!' She turned and shouted to the crowd. *'My lonely days are about to come to an end!'*

The earl's laughter was even louder than the crowd's as he resumed his walk. Music started up and the jugglers sprang into action. The beautiful acrobat was nowhere to be seen. *Leave the soldiers desperate to see her again and they will easily part with their money,* Yannis' father had said. He was right. The soldiers' eyes could be seen searching the troupe for another glimpse of the girl.

Fifteen minutes later a hush swept the crowd as it parted to allow a rider to approach the wagons. The mount was magnificent, its rider even more so. The man was in full military uniform, heavily decorated with spectacular insignia not seen on even the most senior generals. Around his shoulders was draped a midnight-blue cape with a royal crest. The rider came to a stop directly in front of Rosa.

'I regret to inform you that the priest was unavailable, Madam Tessa; will an Earl do?'

Rosa looked around desperately. 'Oh my God, I'm not about to faint this time – I'm going to *die!'* The crowd roared, completely won over.

It was Carlos who slipped gracefully off his mount to again take her hand. He kissed it as he bowed formally to her. 'I am at your service, Madam. Allow me to introduce myself.' Despite the humor that he knew Madam Tessa had deliberately injected into her repartee for the benefit of the crowd, it pleased him immensely to be so openly flattered in front of his men. It was easy for him to accept that her comments were not a complete fiction; he knew full well that he was handsome.

'And now allow me to introduce you to my lovely family, Your Grace.'

'Please, please, please! *Carlos!* I am *Carlos.' Tessa is no match for Isabella in the beauty stakes,* he thought, *but she is in fact very attractive, almost beautiful, vivacious and fun.* He knew she was older than him, but he was totally enchanted and looked forward to some entertaining times ahead.

Tessa smiled her delight at the privilege offered to her as Carlos gave her his arm. 'This is Hamal, a wonderful musician who also alternates with me as master-of-ceremonies. Here we have ...' Rosa quickly introduced the more prominent members of the troupe.

Carlos raised his eyebrows when she introduced Mbiti Ranhui. 'And how, exactly, does Mbiti fit into your *family,* Tessa?' He glanced around at the other faces, none of whom bore any resemblance to Mbiti.

'You won't believe this, Your ... *Carlos,* but we heard Mbiti sing one day during our travels in East Africa some years ago. We kidnapped him that very night and told him he was now one of us and if he ever attempted to escape, we would kill him.' The group standing around, including Mbiti, enjoyed a laugh. 'Besides,' Tessa added with a twinkle in her eyes and a wicked laugh, 'he's so handsome I would have kidnapped him even if he had the voice of a frog.'

Carlos grinned. 'I believe every word of it, Tessa. Mbiti sounds like he is worth a visit to one of your shows. I presume you put on shows? I hope my men will be able to afford the price of attendance.'

'Absolutely, Carlos. Entry to every performance will be free. Speaking of which … let's go to my humble home and hammer out a deal over a glass of wine. Hamal, would you do the honors please, darling?' She smiled and squeezed his arm. Marcus had arranged delivery of several bottles of the finest wine on offer in the Northern Region for this very occasion.

An arrangement was struck five minutes later. Three weeks, four shows a day, free entry, but the audience would be asked to shower the stage with coin donations if they enjoyed the performance. Madam Tessa proposed that Carlos receive ten percent of the proceeds for generously allowing them to perform for his soldiers. With a broad smile, Carlos demanded fifty percent and they settled for twenty-five a few seconds later. He was assured that the proceeds from 130,000 well-paid soldiers would be substantial, especially when the female acrobat would be the last to appear on stage to work the crowd into a generous mood. The girl had a natural ability to make the soldiers realize that she would remain on stage only as long as the money flowed.

The two touched glasses to complete the deal. 'This is a most exquisite wine, Tessa. It's better, in fact, than anything I have in my own larder. I recognize the maker, though. You certainly do travel in style.'

Tessa winked at him. 'We do all right, Carlos. Just wait and see. You will be surprised at the return you'll receive from your investment in us.' *You will be very surprised indeed, Carlos,* she thought as she leaned forward to pour him some more wine. 'By the way, I hope I didn't offend you with that *beautiful man* bit. I do use that opening on occasions, as you can imagine. It goes down very well to get a crowd going. But I can only use it when there actually is a handsome man to pick on. To do otherwise would humiliate a man if he knows he's not handsome, and it would embarrass the crowd. They would take my comments as sarcasm against one of their own. In your case, I didn't know who you were, yet it's obvious you're very handsome, so I was confident that no one would be humiliated or embarrassed. But with you being an earl and all … goodness, when I said I was going to die, that bit was absolutely true!' She took a gulp of wine and put on a well-practiced worried look.

Carlos laughed with delight as he clicked her glass again with his and then emptied his in a single swallow. 'Don't worry, Tessa, I loved it. I loved every second of it. To be quite frank with you, I haven't had so much fun in years.' He held his glass out for a refill, but almost dropped it in shock when something suddenly crashed into the wagon, and several objects toppled to the floor.

'Oh no!' Rosa groaned.

'What the …?' Carlos flew out of his chair with hand on sword.

Hamal poked his head in the door. 'Sorry, sorry, sorry, sir!' He looked sad-eyed at Rosa. 'It's only Horse. He's dying to get to work after being stuck in his wagon all day.'

'Horse?' Carlos looked bewildered, but relaxed when he realized there was no danger.

'It's a nickname. *Horse* is normally a good-natured man, but when he wants attention he simply does anything he feels like to get it. All he likes to do is to work, so I think it would be best to simply pick the spot to set up our stage and facilities, and let Horse do the rest.' Rosa filled their glasses and beckoned Carlos to follow her outside. 'I'll introduce you, but please prepare yourself for a shock. He's not quite in your league in the looks department, but he is a lovely man underneath. And I do emphasize *underneath*, Carlos.'

They stepped to the ground and came face to face with Horse. Carlos spilled half his priceless wine on the ground as soon as he saw him. Without a doubt he was the ugliest man the earl had ever seen. Almost everything about the poor creature was hideous: his hair, ears, nose and wart-filled face, but even worse was his mouth. Both his upper and lower teeth, brown-streaked and rotted, with several broken, protruded past his swollen jaw-line and lips. The man was badly stooped from a curved spine, yet he showed pride in his physique by wearing a jacket cut off at the shoulders, to show off his powerful biceps.

'Nice to meet you,' Carlos gasped and took a large gulp of wine to steady his nerves.

'I *Horse!*' the man bellowed back at him and thumped his chest with a powerful fist. 'I work!' he bellowed again. 'I good. I strong. I *Horse!*'

'You will indeed be hoarse if you keep yelling like that,' Carlos said good-naturedly as he took another sip of wine to disguise his smirk. He felt Rosa give him a gentle nudge in the ribs.

Rosa spoke gently. 'Horse, darling, you can start unloading and put it all over there for now until we pick the exact spot for you. Hamal will show you. Off you go, my love.'

Horse nodded and attempted with little success to grin at Rosa. He then bobbed his already bent body up and down in a ghastly attempt to bow to Carlos, who stared back in fascinated disgust. Horse managed to hide his own disgust – just. *My, no wonder women turn to jelly. You are a handsome devil, aren't you? But here's a promise to you, Bucher the Butcher Boy: I will kill you before you ever lay so much as a finger on Isabella.* Yannis again acknowledged Isabella's genius and often-used mantra: *the best place to hide is in plain sight.* Here they were: the two opposing commanders-in-chief, on a war footing, standing directly in front of each other, and each laughing at the other. Horse's laughter, heavily muffled through the rotted bones, was mistaken by Carlos for a series of grunting noises as the bent man disappeared toward the equipment wagons at the rear of the caravan.

Carlos watched the creature leave. 'I can see why the poor man's nickname is *Horse*. He certainly does have the teeth of a horse.'

Rosa almost choked. *Little do you know how right you are, Carlos. Those teeth are indeed from the carcass of a horse.* 'No, no, Carlos. That's not the reason for his nickname.'

'He works like a horse?'

'No, his name is Hortensio. Such a beautiful name, but because of his speech impediment, he can't say it. The best he can manage is *horse* – so everyone calls him *Horse*.'

Carlos stared blankly at Rosa for several moments before his face collapsed and his mouth fell open. He doubled over in laughter, gasping for breath before he managed to straighten and inhale. His body bent backwards as the roar of his laughter finally hit the air before he staggered on jellied legs to the steps of the nearest wagon. Looking up wild-eyed at Rosa, he bit down on his wrist to try to regain control as the next explosion erupted.

Rosa wagged a rebuking finger at him while she tried not to laugh, but the twinkle in her eyes only served to make matters worse for Carlos. He came up for air and bit into his wrist again as tears streamed down his face. It was a full minute before he managed to draw enough breath to gasp. 'The man's name is Hortensio. *Hortensio! Horse!* Oh, God, that's so beautiful! It's priceless! I won't be able to stop laughing for days.'

Rosa rested her hand delicately on his shoulder. 'I have to admit that the moment was actually quite funny, Carlos, but also a little sad if you think about Horse this way: you can only *truly* love if you can love not just those who are beautiful, but also those who are not.'

Memories of his unloving mother tore at the very fabric of the vulnerable Carlos' soul as he looked up at Rosa and yearned for her affection. Finally he calmed down and wiped his eyes. 'You know, Tessa, that was a beautiful thing to say and I shall remember it always. Now listen, you've given me the best morning of my life, and I'm going to arrange a welcoming party for you this evening. You're all invited. Even Horse. I promise you a great party. As much as I enjoyed that wine, I'm afraid wine in the morning does make me sleepy, so after I give orders for 10,000 men to organize a little party for you, I intend to have a nap.' He rose and kissed her hand again before snapping his fingers for his horse to be brought forward.

As promised, it was a great party. All of the invited visitors attended. Except one. Horse. Horse was too busy removing the make-up that made his face and scalp itch worse than if he were trapped in an ants' nest.

Privilege of rank enabled officers to be the first to attend the performances. It was not until the third day that Rosa brought Yannis the news in his wagon, where he was hiding, that their next target was in the audience. Horse had ventured outside on a few occasions so that his appearance would be well known and talked about when he eventually wandered up to the former grazing land. Rosa had led him to a vantage point where he could view the target for later identification.

'Excellent,' he said, after they were safely back in the wagon. 'I'll leave very early in the morning so that I can get back while it's still relatively cool. I don't want to take the risk of the make-up melting in the heat.'

Rosa nodded. 'The make-up takes two hours to do, so we'll start at three in the morning. You can leave anytime after five. It will take you an hour each way plus an hour or two for discussions, so you should be back before ten. The make-up will be fine until midday. By the way, your father was saying earlier that his family told him they have never performed in front of such huge audiences days on end, and they have never seen so much money pour in. The soldiers simply can't get enough of Madison when she's prancing around on stage in that gorgeous costume.'

Yannis laughed. 'The sound of those coins hitting the stage is deafening even inside my wagon.'

'She is one beautiful girl, that Madison. All that exercise has given her the figure of a goddess, the lucky little thing. No wonder the soldiers go wild when they see her. Those boys never expected to see someone that gorgeous out here in the wilderness.'

'She's very beautiful, no doubt about it.'

Rosa gathered the bags of make-up and headed for the door. Stopping, she turned back to Yannis. 'But she's not a touch on Isabella, is she?'

Yannis looked up, then away, but remained silent.

'Yannis?'

'I'm inclined to agree with you, Rosa. Isabella is in a league of her own.'

Rosa was pleased as she stepped down to the ground. As a woman, she had quickly recognized the spark in Isabella's eyes whenever she looked at Yannis, but she had not noticed the same spark in Yannis'. *A little reminder now and again will surely not go astray,* she thought. Isabella deserved a man of courage like Yannis when the time was right. Rosa remembered how it had taken years to attract the eye of the man she had loved, but it had eventually happened. Years of joy and happiness had followed, but ended suddenly when she had to watch her beloved husband slip away to illness, on a bitter winter's day. It had been the saddest day of her life.

CHAPTER 107

Being ugly was Horse's greatest asset. No-one wanted to get close to him. As he made his way towards the hills, few soldiers gave him more than a cursory glance before quickly looking away. It was his very ugliness that made him invisible. Rosa's expert handiwork was never subjected to close scrutiny.

Horse chose the path to the top carefully. Those who saw him noticed no particular pattern of direction, but it was slowly, erratically, upwards. He finally reached the vast area below the plateau, where he strolled about, seemingly impressed with the view of the valley below. However, his real interest was elsewhere, and he gradually made his way towards where he knew his target would be enjoying breakfast.

Horse located the table and placed himself behind a number of officers deep in conversation over their plates. He made sure he faced his target seated on the other side of the table. His target knew he was there and tried hard not to look in his direction, but instinct eventually took over, forcing him to take a quick glance. Horse was ready for him.

Holding the man's gaze, he shouted at him. 'I *Horse!* Big walk. I hungry.' He pointed at the long buffet table at the side, laden with food.

The soldiers sitting directly in front of Horse spun around, wide-eyed with alarm. His target smiled at him. 'Of course, Horse. There's plenty there. Help yourself.'

Horse spoke quickly and maintained eye contact. 'Horse not take. You give.' He pointed at the target, then at the table. He saw his target sigh and say something to the man next to him as he rose. He looked at Horse and flicked his head towards the table.

Horse got down to business the moment they reached the table. From his stooped position he looked up at the man in front of him, and spoke low and as clearly as his teeth would allow. 'I'm not the least bit interested in your food, General Manacek. I need to talk to you and your most senior officers in private, and right now. I must be out of here within the hour.'

The general was stunned, but his professional bearing carried the day. 'I'm *Major*-General Manacek, and who exactly are you?'

'I know Bucher demoted you to Major-General, sir, so that you would not outrank any of his own generals, but to me, King Alphonso and your nation, you remain *General* Manacek. Now move closer to me, please, so that you block the view of my face from your men when I remove my teeth.'

Horse waited a moment before he quickly removed both dentures so that Yannis could smile at the general with two rows of pearly white teeth. 'Ah, that's better,' he grinned. 'These things taste like cow manure and please, don't ask me how I know. I've been over that joke already. Now, quickly, before I put them back in, please get your seven co-generals together in the meeting-tent in ten minutes. Just do it casually so no-one notices. I know where it is and I'll slip unnoticed into it and wait for you.' Yannis held up his hand when he saw Manacek about to resist, or protest.

'General, not even your most senior officers know that King Alphonso advised you privately to expect a message from Isabella Mondeo. Well, I now have that message for you. Oh, and don't forget to bring the envelope from the king to authenticate her message,' Yannis slipped his dentures back in and Horse looked up at the general with a sickly grin.

At the mention of Isabella, and the envelope that only he knew about, the general was all business when he stepped back. 'I'll get the men at once, sir. We will meet you in ten precisely.' He smiled, casually picked up a crispy chicken leg and sauntered among some of his officers, placing a gentle hand on a shoulder here and there.

Horse picked up some food and pretended to eat as he slipped away. He found the tent unguarded as expected, and no-one saw him step inside to wait for the meeting that would shape the battle soon to erupt.

General Manacek's fellow officers stared with dismay at the person waiting for them. Horse tied the entry cords securely, grunted, and waved the eight men to the chairs he had already arranged. He waited for them to be seated before he spoke.

'You all know me as Horse,' he began quietly, noting the men's surprise at the way he spoke. He slowly straightened, removed his teeth and pushed his fingers under the wig to gently prise it off. Holding it up like a prized scalp, an almost handsome Yannis smiled at the astonished faces in front of him. 'You will have to excuse the nose and ears, which must remain, so I can get out of this valley alive. Allow me to now re-introduce myself. I am General Yannis Christos, commander-in-chief of the Southern army, the very army that Bucher the Butcher requires you to confront!'

There was a stunned gasp from all the men, including Manacek. 'Gentlemen, please listen carefully. I have to get back before the heat of the day destroys the make-up on this beautiful face. Before embarking on this mission, General Manacek had a secret meeting with King Alphonso. Yes?' Yannis looked at the general, who nodded. 'At that meeting His Majesty informed the general that he had received a personal visit from our nation's spymaster, together with a small token, and a message from King Ramesses. That token, together with certain information, was then handed to the general in an envelope closed with His Majesty's personal seal. No-one has seen the token, not even the general.'

Yannis sat down and glanced at the general. 'General, I now ask that you break the seal of that envelope.' The general brought out an envelope from his jacket and did as asked. Yannis removed an envelope from his own jacket. 'You will find a card in your envelope. The card has nothing other than a seal on it. It was delivered from one king to another, and then directly from your king's hand to you.' Yannis handed him the envelope he had taken from his pocket. 'Now carefully compare the seal on the card with the seal on this envelope, which contains a letter from Miss Mondeo. Please read, and then pass her letter to the others to read. When you are finished, we will burn everything, and I will have just two questions for you before I leave. General?'

General Manacek nodded and opened his envelope. He studied the two seals carefully before he looked up and nodded to Yannis. As he finished reading each page, it was passed from man to man in complete silence. They all appeared stunned, but excited.

Yannis waited a few moments after the last man had finished before he spoke. 'Gentlemen, you are not to discuss this with any of your other officers, no matter how senior. *Ever.* Most likely you will take these secrets to your graves, whether on the battlefield, or otherwise. Now then, the first question. Do you understand every detail that is in that letter?'

After a few moments of silence, Manacek spoke on behalf of his fellow officers. 'Miss Mondeo's instructions are quite clear.' The other men nodded.

'Good. Now for the second question. I will need individual answers. It must be unanimous, or it simply won't work. Are you prepared to follow each and every one of the instructions, exactly, and without question or hesitation? We'll start with you, General, as you are the most senior officer.'

'A most definite *yes* from me, General Christos.' Manacek nodded to the other officers to declare their positions. It was unanimous.

Yannis tossed the paper and envelopes into the small fire and stood to face the men. 'Thank you, gentlemen. On behalf of myself, and Major Isabella Mondeo, I salute you all.' He momentarily held the eyes of each man as he saluted.

'Major? Isabella is a Major? What, a real Major?' Manacek looked startled.

Yannis grinned. 'She's not only a real Major, she is without doubt equal to the best soldier and officer in our army and, as much as it pains me to admit it, that includes me. She's authorized to implement and head any military action, such as the one that is alluded to but not fully detailed in her letter to you. You will see her in action very soon, gentlemen. Isabella will take the lead in the next battle. I must now take my leave.'

One of the younger officers smiled. 'I have a quick question for you, General, before you go. I might not get the chance again, and we'd all be interested in the answer.' He flicked his head towards the other officers.

'Yes, of course. What is it?' Yannis picked up his wig.

'No matter that there is a war going on, information and rumors fly in all directions quicker than a summer wind. Isab – Major Mondeo is a national hero in your nation, and everyone talks about her. Many rumors get a life of their own, but one in particular the soldiers love to talk about is that she is turning into quite a beauty. Is there any truth in that rumor, sir?'

Yannis wanted a few moments to consider the question, and waited until he had finished fixing his wig and had picked up his teeth, before he answered it. 'I believe you can take it that the rumor is true.'

CHAPTER 108

O ver the following two weeks, Jacques had carefully controlled the upstream aqueducts to gradually increase the river flow to the extent that Major-General Manacek knew the time had come to request the planned audience with the earl.

'Your Grace, some of our men are very familiar with this area, and I've been informed that the river system can become extremely dangerous. It can happen quickly if the northern rainy season should suddenly hit. Everything flushes straight down this river. The men camped nearest the river could be in great danger.'

The earl sat comfortably in his small office with his feet crossed on the top of his desk. He stared silently at Manacek and pursed his lips in suspicion. 'And tell me, *Major*-General Manacek, why would you have concerns about my men being in danger? I would have thought you would be more disposed to sit up there and cheer while you watched my men being swept away.'

Manacek was following Isabella's script precisely, simply adding a few words of his own here and there. 'That's rather ingenuous of you, if you don't mind me saying so, sir. We are both only too well aware that we are not here because we want to be. But at the same time we recognize that your soldiers are no different from ours: they are just young men ordered to do a particular task. We would not sit up there and cheer if we saw decent young men being swept to their death. That's simply not who we are. What you *propose* to do about it is of course entirely up to you.' The last sentence, and the loaded word, was exactly as Isabella had written it. She had then predicted what the reply would be. She was correct again.

The earl placed his feet on the floor and sat up straight. 'And what would *you* propose should be done, Gen – Major-General?'

'To move everyone further back in the order that they are now camped would be a horrendous task, sir. The simple way would be for us to move to the plateau, and for those nearest the river to move to where we are now. Everyone else simply stays where they are. Easy.'

'Why not simply move the endangered men directly to the plateau, and leave you where you are?'

Isabella had even anticipated that question. 'The plateau is not far short of hell, sir. Your men would resent being ordered there, and they would resent us even more than they do now for having superior quarters. Worse, they might convince you to stay where they are. Nothing will then have been achieved and they would remain in danger. The river might not overflow, of course, but who can say? We all know what nature is capable of doing without warning. I'm sure you've seen the river rise alarmingly already, sir. The rains are not far away. But if nothing dramatic happens, well, there's no loss. There is potentially much to gain and nothing to lose.'

'And you can clean up the plateau to make it habitable?'

'It won't be that comfortable, but we can make it livable. It's only going to be for a few weeks, anyway.'

The earl rose to his feet. 'Very well. Do it! I'll leave it to you and Ollie to organize it.'

'Yes, sir.' Manacek turned to go.

'And Manacek?'

'Yes, Your Grace?'

'Thank you. I appreciate it. It won't be forgotten.'

'It's for your young men, sir, not for you.'

A flush swept the earl's face. Then he relaxed and laughed. 'I even appreciate your honesty. I know it took much courage to say that to me, so I take no offense.' He slapped Manacek on the shoulder. 'Good man. I'll see you later.'

Major-General Manacek left the Earl's office, moved through an outer office, and walked into the sun. He was thrilled as he hurried back for a quiet meeting with his co-officers. *Isabella, you said: don't make it too easy. Insult him if you have to. He will respect you for it and it will make the proposal that much more believable. Just follow the script, you said. You are one solid-gold genius, Isabella.*

Through the window of his little prison, Yannis watched with interest over the following days as a hive of activity took place on the plateau. Soon, some of the camps nearest the now raging river started to move to the hills to take the place recently vacated by the coalition army.

The gypsies had *reluctantly* agreed to stay an additional week due to public demand. Had the demand not been so great, they would have found another reason to remain: the extra week was an essential part of Isabella's plan.

Yannis was lying on his mattress studying one of Rosa's stage plays when there was a knock on the door and it slowly opened. A hand appeared, enticingly swinging one of the rare bottles of wine back and forth.

'Are you decent, Yannis?'

'Yes, I'm fine.'

'Aarggh! Just my luck! I was hoping to catch you in your bath.'

Yannis grinned. 'Come on in, Miss *Tessa*.'

They soon touched glasses in a toast. 'Tomorrow is the day,' she said, 'and then we're out of here.'

Yannis took a sip. Not much of a drinker, he did, however, enjoy that particular wine. *And so I should, it being Europe's most expensive.* 'I think we've all had enough, Rosa. I think even Madison is getting tired of the men constantly in a frenzy over her. The earl, though, won't be happy to see us go.'

'What do you mean?' Rosa asked suspiciously.

'He fancies you, Rosa. I've seen you duck and weave his verbal advances time and again, so I know he's dying to get his hands on you. He seems a different person whenever he's near you, reminding me of a little puppy desperate for your affection. You're an extremely attractive woman, Rosa, still in your prime. You must surely be tempted. I hate to admit it, but the Earl has to be the most handsome man I've ever seen.'

Rosa's eyes watered as she reached out to cup his face with her hand. 'Oh, you are such a dear, Yannis. Thank you for saying that. When a woman slips into her forties, the flattering comments are unfortunately less frequent than they used to be.' She gave his face a gentle squeeze and removed her hand. 'You are right, though; he is a handsome devil, extremely handsome. But tempted? No, not for a moment. His nickname alone is enough to scare any woman away.'

'Well, you had better find someone else to tempt you, then. You are too good-looking, and too good a woman not to have a good man by your side.'

'It's by choice, Yannis. I've been alone for quite a few years and quite happy to be that way, frankly. But just between you and me there is, in fact, someone who could interest me if he should ever notice me. He's *also* an extremely handsome man, which is always a bonus.' Rosa was unable to suppress a giggle as she took a sip of wine.

Yannis was shocked. He knew of only one other man who was also handsome, and not far away. 'Not Father, Rosa? He's married. My mother – '

'Oh, stop it, darling! Of course it's not Hamal. Yes, he's handsome, but no, it's someone else. Nothing is ever likely to come of it, so I'll keep it to myself. If it should work out, I might just get what I have always wanted and never had: a beautiful family all wrapped up in one. Oh, God, could I ever be so lucky, Yannis?' Rosa leaned forward and Yannis realized that she had begun to weep silently.

He moved over to sit next to her and put his arm around her shoulder. 'Of course you can, Rosa. You deserve to be the luckiest woman in the world.'

He would have been even more shocked than earlier had he known just who she had in mind.

'General, quickly, come and confirm, please. Major Mondeo has given us the signal.' Manacek's officer poked his head into his tent and spoke rapidly but softly. Manacek rose, picked up a piece of fruit and strolled leisurely past a number of tents as he made his way towards a vantage point. He seemed casual and relaxed, but his heart was hammering against his ribs.

'Yes,' he hissed in confirmation. There it was. The signal. Mbiti was wearing a brilliant canary-yellow jacket for a once-only performance, visible much more than his other jackets. 'Very well, they will be off in the morning, and *the big day* will be the fourth day from today! Let's get the other selected officers together right now and tell them what their new orders are.'

Yannis was right: the earl was genuinely upset when he bade Rosa farewell. Carlos suggested she remain as his personal guest, but Rosa was wise enough to know what that could mean, and gently declined. Carlos' eyes watered when she embraced him in farewell. He looked like someone about to lose his best friend.

Horse was at his usual ugly best, and bobbed up and down in front of Carlos in a futile attempt to show respect while the gypsies climbed into the wagons. In a move that surprised everyone, it was Carlos who extended his hand to him. The two men stared into each other's eyes for a brief moment as they shook hands.

Only the Devil would ever know what each thought of the other.

•

The caravan headed north to avert any sign of suspicion. Hamal had enjoyed himself so much he decided to stay with the troupe for a few weeks before heading back to his own family in the south. Not until the following night did Yannis and Rosa bid each other a teary farewell. Rosa would be escorted to the main camp, while Yannis slipped away to follow a circuitous route back towards the disguised camp. There, he and Isabella would prepare the men for a battle, the likes of which the world had never seen, not even in the days of Genghis Khan.

Isabella's brigade would strike in two days.

CHAPTER 109

Everyone looked ready and relaxed when Yannis rode into camp. Clothing, equipment and weapons were neatly laid out in rows, ready to step into at a moment's notice. Most of the camp followers had already departed, taking with them everything except the bare essentials.

Isabella waved excitedly and ran to Yannis as soon as she caught sight of him by the water troughs. 'Oh, Yannis, what a relief to see you! We've all been so worried about you and Rosa. I would love to hug you, but that would only send rumors flying, so I won't.'

Yannis laughed as he reached out and squeezed her arm. 'You're right. This will have to do. There are already so many rumors out there it's best not to add more spice to them.'

Isabella was horrified. '*What?* You don't mean that …?'

'No, no! Settle down. They're not about you and someone else.' He paused briefly for effect. 'They're only about you!'

She grinned and hit his arm. 'Oh you! Now I know you're just pulling my leg. Tell me how it all went! Did everything go to plan? Did you see the earl?' She took him by the arm and led him towards a table stacked with snacks and hot tea..

'Slow down. One thing at a time. Let's sit first. Yes, I did see the earl. In fact, we shook hands.'

'*No!* You shook hands? *Oh*, I only wish Bertillini had been there to paint a picture. Two warring commanders-in-chief shaking hands. What a sight!'

Yannis chuckled. 'Well, actually, one commander-in-chief shaking hands with a twisted beast who wore buck teeth made from the rotted bones of a horse. I don't think even the great Bertillini could do much with that sight.'

Isabella looked blankly at Yannis for a few moments while the image formed in her mind. Then she doubled over and exploded in laughter. Yannis loved hearing her laugh. So did the hundred or so men nearby, who gave her a rousing cheer and a round of applause.

'So, did the two of you get on well, then? Best friends, are you? What did you think of him?' Isabella calmed down and leaned on the table for support.

'Apart from being handsome, not much.'

Isabella brought her eyes back to Yannis. 'You thought him handsome?'

'Pretty obvious. I can see why women would find him irresistible. Rosa thought he was the most handsome man she had ever seen. You probably thought the same when you met him.'

Isabella looked away for several moments before turning back to him. 'Well, yes, I did, to be honest. It's quite natural for women of any age to notice things like that. I've only ever seen one man who can match him.' She jumped to her feet and reached for his arm again. 'Everyone is ready for battle, Yannis. There's absolutely nothing more to do now. Come with me. I want to show you what I'll be wearing on the day. Rosa made it for me when she made your Horse wardrobe. If I die in the valley, I'm going to die in style. No-one will ever forget me. I absolutely love it. You will absolutely hate it!'

Everyone was in place. It was almost time to go. In exactly thirty minutes the 500-man brigade would move to the position where Jacques' response beacon would be in direct line of sight: the signal to attack.

Isabella sat comfortably bareback on *Barca*, occasionally glancing at Yannis, who sat silently next to her on his mount. He appeared so uncomfortable as he tried not to look at her that she had to fight the urge to laugh. Yannis had indeed been shocked when she showed him the battle uniform Rosa had made for her. *'There's hardly anything to it!'* he had cried in horror as she held up the pieces in sequence. Isabella loved to shock and had been thrilled at Yannis' reaction.

On the other hand, her men loved it and had immediately started the *Isabella chant* when they had first seen her ride up to them earlier that morning. Now, as she sat quietly waiting for the moment, the men were already used to her battle attire. Yannis was not.

Isabella wore a colored band around her head to keep her hair over the back of her shoulders, where it fell in golden waves to her bare waist. Tight leather shorts were barely covered by a leather modesty skirt, split to the waist on each side to allow unrestrained kicks. From the waist, she was bare up to the handcrafted leather and wool halter that cleverly covered the front and wrapped over the shoulders with an additional layer of hardened leather for protection. Rosa had stitched Isabella's rank insignia to each shoulderpad. A narrow strip of soft leather tassels across the back covered the straps keeping the top in place. A dark brown woolen cape was attached by studs to each shoulderpad to cover her otherwise bare back. Rosa had somehow managed to design the studs to instantly release if anyone should grasp the cape.

Isabella's legs were bare except for ankle-length boots. Though light, they were specially constructed with tips and outer rims of steel to add power to her already deadly kicks. Light calfskin gloves allowed a firm hold on the magnificent sword designed for her by Zhang Chen. The intricate carving of interwoven serpents around the grip and pommel counterweight had been completed by a master craftsman.

A light smear of olive oil over her bare skin highlighted Isabella's muscular legs and abdominals in the brilliant afternoon sun, completing her new battle persona. Her gladiator-like appearance was in no way overshadowed by the 500 men sitting quietly on their mounts behind her. The men had for the first time collectively removed their baggy clothes to don their new battle gear. Shields, armor breastplates, and leg protection were standard. The rest was not. The massive display of lightly oiled muscles was designed to strike fear into the enemy ranks, which consisted mostly of untrained conscripts straight off the streets of the Northern cities' slums. Yannis looked as fearsome as the men behind.

Isabella nudged *Barca* towards him until their legs pressed together, which forced him to look at her. 'Five minutes to go. Look behind you. What a sight! Don't they look fantastic?' Yannis twisted in his saddle and nodded. 'Everyone has done so well in building themselves up. You too, Yannis, you look fantastic.'

Yannis flushed with pleasure that Isabella had noticed his hard work. He finally took the courage to look her up and down. 'I only wish I could say that you, too, look fantastic rather than … ah … spectacular.'

'So you do like my battle-dress after all?'

'No, I don't. It just shows too much of you. The men are going to have a job concentrating on the challenge at hand when we storm into the camp. And the enemy will most likely remember what you look like more than what's going to happen in the valley.'

'*But don't you see*, Yannis? That's the point. I'm now old enough for even Grandfather to allow me to marry. I'm an adult now in every sense of the word, so there's really nothing inappropriate about showing the same amount of bare skin as you and the men behind us. There must be close to 60,000 soldiers just in the main valley alone, and there's every chance that we'll all be killed. In case I'm killed, I want to make sure that I'm noticed and talked about so that our nation will remember me – and the battle – with pride for a thousand years. No matter that we might be defeated. It's very important that I make my presence known. I have to stand out. Do you understand?'

Yannis seemed more relaxed and smiled. 'I guess. When you put it that way. I'm sorry, Isabella. I keep forgetting you're officially an adult now.'

'So everything is all right between us?'

'Of course. We will always be all right.'

'One minute to go. Are you as ready as I am?'

'Ready as you are, Isabella.'

'Time to go, Yannis.' She gave his arm a quick squeeze and raised her other arm. 'For the first time, I will be at your side in battle, and that's exactly where I want to be. We're about to face our greatest peril, yet I feel exhilarated.'

Not as exhilarated as Sergeant Valdez, who was on his mount watching the two directly in front of him quietly murmuring to each other, legs touching. He drew his sword when he saw Isabella's hand rise and come down in a slashing motion. Luis winked happily at the muscular one-legged Stephan next to him as the brigade moved forward to where Jacques' beacon could be sighted.

Isabella turned *Barca* to face her men. 'Three o'clock.' she shouted. 'Our beacon has just been lit. Just a few more seconds, men, and we will be in the thick of it. Don't forget to regularly check on the twenty timekeepers. We must be in and out in less than twenty minutes from this very moment. Follow the plan exactly as we rehearsed, unless we strike unforeseen problems. In that case make sure you break away from whatever you're doing no later than the fifteen-minute mark, and head out of the valley. It will then be every man for himself. Good luck to each and every one of you.' She presented her men with a formal salute that was returned with a rousing cheer.

'Isabella, I think that's it!' Yannis pointed to the horizon.

'It is.' Her raised sword sparkled in the sun. '*Stephan!*'

Two horse-lengths farther back, Stephan raised his sword. '*Charge!*' he roared and swung his sword in a slow circle. The brigade moved forward at a trot before Stephan swung the sword a second time to signal a canter, and a short time later, a full gallop. In the lead, as usual, was the *Serpent Warrior*.

CHAPTER 110

Thousands of Northern soldiers were enjoying a lazy afternoon in the late summer sun when many of them looked around, puzzled. A faint thunder-like noise could be heard, but there was nothing visible to determine its source. Most shrugged and went back to soaking up the sun, while others stared towards the south, where the noise seemed to increase by the second.

Two riders at full gallop with a cloud of dust rising behind them were suddenly seen streaming towards the center of the camp. Seconds later they were followed by another five riders and then dozens that quickly turned into hundreds. The Northern soldiers were frozen to the spot, bewildered at the sight of hundreds of muscle-bound giants, brandishing swords, spears and flaming missiles, storming along the inner perimeter of their campsites. They simply stood and stared open-mouthed as the riders sent a stream of flaming arrows into the two bridges spanning the fast-flowing river that separated the main body of their army. Other riders stormed along the camps and slashed at anything and anyone that got in their way. Dust kicked up by the hundreds of horses rose like an angry storm cloud to mix with the acrid smoke billowing from the bridges. The noise was appalling. Screams from injured and terrified soldiers could be heard above the bellowing of Isabella's men.

The soldiers, drowsy from the balmy summer sun, could not comprehend what was happening around them. To make matters worse, many were mesmerized by the sight of a spectacular female warrior, her cape and long golden hair streaming behind as she sped through the melee shouting instructions to her fellow gladiators. Isabella had deliberately chosen both the time and her appearance to create confusion and disbelief. She was within the very heart of the enemy and knew every second of delayed reaction was critical.

Moments later, the villagers on both sides of the river fled towards the hills on horseback, or in hastily hitched wagons, adding another layer of dust and noise to the unfolding chaos. They knew that an attack had been planned, but not what was to follow.

Isabella's men sent an uninterrupted stream of flaming arrows into the camps set well back from the river and the cottages that lined the length of it. Crossbowmen instead aimed their fiery missiles at the camps on the other side of the river, the western side. Within minutes flames, smoke and dust blanketed the entire area.

The earl was deep into his afternoon daydream when he first heard the thundering noise. Believing it nothing more than his men training, he rolled over and dozed off again. A minute later the sound of shouts and screams brought him out of his slumber and stumbling to the door. He flung it open to stare in disbelief at the scene before him. Buildings and tents on both sides of the river were ablaze. Dust and smoke made it difficult to discern exactly what was happening, but he was heartened to note that that attacking party amounted to no more than a few hundred.

The earl slammed the door shut in a rage and headed to the bedroom to select the appropriate uniform and weapons to make his presence known. He took his time, deciding there was no hurry. With a massive army at his disposal, he knew this attack would be little more than a bee-sting, a quick in and out by a bunch of disillusioned misfits who thought they could actually make a difference. *Idiots!*

The Northern army was slowly getting its act together, but not efficiently or effectively. Senior officers, particularly generals, were men who had been given their rank simply because of social connections, or had purchased it for prestige, a practice only too common in many armies. The inexperienced officers shouting orders to the conscripts did little more than add to the rapidly growing chaos.

Isabella's secret instructions to General Manacek to entice the earl to move his troops well away from the river was designed to buy the brigade several precious minutes before they were effectively confronted. Because she had planned every detail of the attack, she was the first to see the flaw that could undo that advantage. The northern bridge had not fired up according to plan.

Men streamed towards the attackers from the far-flung camps on both sides of the river, and Isabella felt the first sign of panic when she saw soldiers start to cross the bridge from the western side. The key to success was to cut off the enemy from the west to prevent being outflanked and to be able to escape through the main street of the village, which would provide them some protection from attack from the east.

Isabella screamed at her bowmen. 'The bridge, the bridge! We must stop them crossing!'

Well aware of the significance of being outflanked, Luis Valdez pushed his mount to the bridge entry the moment he saw enemy soldiers reach it on the other side. His mount was magnificent. A huge, fully trained war-horse, its entire body was covered in a skirt of chain mail and light bronze head protection, and plumed in red and yellow, the colors of his true homeland. The horse knew exactly what to do without prompting. It charged the men as they streamed off the bridge, moving rapidly left and right, back and forward again to knock the enemy over like skittles. Luis slashed with his sword at those that managed to get close enough to attack him from the side with swords and spears. He was strong, he was quick, and he worked desperately to keep the soldiers from creating a beachhead from which to launch an attack against Isabella's exposed flank. Dozens of bodies were scattered around him, many injured but most dead.

Several bowmen dismounted and ran to the river's edge to allow a lower trajectory for their arrows. Crossbowmen took aim at the far side, and a flurry of flaming missiles soared under the bridge on both sides of the river. Before they had left the valley, Isabella had instructed her men to liberally lace the straw with gunpowder so it would ignite instantly. It did. Within seconds flames burst across the full width of the center spans on both sides, preventing further entry by the soldiers from the western side. With no other way to cross the raging waters – courtesy of Jacques opening the aqueducts for maximum volume – half the Northern army could do little more than stand and watch the carnage on the eastern side.

General Manacek stared for a long time at the mayhem far below before he finally turned to his senior officers. 'I suppose we'd better go and give the poor earl a bit of a helping hand, don't you think? Or at least look like we're making an effort.'

The officer raised a flag and a bugle sounded for the men to line up for the march down the hill. He grinned and turned back to the general. 'It's a shame we won't get all the way down. I would love to get a closer look at Major Mondeo. Even from a distance she looks magnificent.'

Manacek nodded without smiling. 'That she does. Her letter didn't spell out exactly what was going to happen, but the way she skilfully maneuvered us up here makes me believe that down there is the last place on earth we want to be right now.'

Isabella had glanced towards Luis several times and was amazed at his courage and skill. She had no idea that he could fight like ten men, methodically and efficiently, a natural killing machine. Instinct told her that there was far more to the mild-mannered Luis Valdez than met the eye.

Seeing he was heavily outnumbered, she fought her way to help him. Chen was directly behind her and shouted to Johan and some of his men to reach Luis in time. They were too late. As Luis slashed his sword down on one man, another took the opportunity to thrust his spear deep into his body. Using the spear for leverage, the man pulled Luis to the ground, where another soldier pushed his sword into him before raising it with both hands for a blow to his neck.

The soldier never saw the glitter of steel in the sunlight as Isabella's spinning serpent dagger entered his throat. The man dropped to the ground like a stone. Johan and his men reached Luis seconds later and fanned out to attack the remaining soldiers who had made it across the bridge. The latter did not stand a chance against the size, strength and fighting skills of Zhang Chen, Johan and his men. Twenty seconds later, the flank was secured.

Isabella slid off *Barca* and rushed to Luis' side. Chen jumped off his mount to stand over her, protecting her back. Johan pulled out the spear and quickly packed the wounds to stem the bleeding, but it looked bad. Luis opened unfocused eyes that flickered for several moments before they closed.

'Isabella, Isabella,' he whispered.

She put her mouth to his ear. 'I'm right here, Luis. I'm here. We're going to get you out of here.'

'No, too late.' His voice faded. Isabella put her ear to his mouth to hear his next words. 'Isabella, don't tell Melissa I love her. It will only sadden her.'

'I won't. I promise. Melissa will know you as a hero. Rest now, Luis. We'll get you out of here one way or another.' She could not bring herself to say *dead or alive*. She looked around to take in the scene before running to her men. 'Get Luis and his horse to the village gate. One man stays with him, and we'll take him with us when we leave. Dead or alive, no one gets left behind! That includes me, thank you very much!' She jumped back on *Barca* and was back into the melee within seconds.

Isabella glanced south towards the mounted time-keepers, clearly visible from any angle on their hilly perch. Initially twenty, each stood for one elapsed minute, with every fifth rider sporting a plumed helmet, for easier counting. Each minute one rider turned and rode away. Isabella counted two plumed, plus four: fourteen minutes to escape, five minutes to detonation. That meant her swordsmen were already on the march down the slope beneath the plateau. *That will stir them up some*, she thought grimly.

The earl swung the cottage door open so violently it smashed against the inside wall. He took a quick look to make sure there were no unwelcome surprises awaiting him. Satisfied, he stepped down to survey the scene and was appalled at the sight that met his eyes. His beautiful camp was ablaze from one end of the valley to the other. The two bridges burned fiercely, cutting off reinforcements from the other side of the river.

He pursed his lips. Reinforcements cut off, and one flank permanently protected by the river. *Now that was a clever strategy.* This was not an attack by idiots. This was carefully planned to demoralize his soldiers, and it seemed to be working. Most had actually moved away from their attackers to get weapons. Those that were already armed seemed reluctant to attack until more of their comrades became available to support them.

The earl could see why. Never had he seen such giants. He had heard of gladiators of old, but these were the real thing. Just the mere sight of their huge muscles glistening in the sun was enough to keep his men away. A plan for a counter-attack began to form in his mind as he watched. Only minutes remained to work out how to encircle and trap the insurgents. Their plan would surely be to make their escape in the next five or ten minutes. He shook his head as he realized his plan would not work: the attackers were too smart. Their back-up plan would be to simply abandon the horses, remove their armor and jump into the river. The fast-flowing water would see them safely out of the valley inside sixty seconds.

The earl strode towards the river, hoping to come up with another plan on the way. Suddenly a new sound cut across the cacophony already echoing throughout the valley. He froze in his tracks before spinning towards the plateau to face the new threat.

'Oh, my God!' he murmured. Hundreds of men, even more fierce-looking than those by the river, were marching towards the valley from a ridge below the plateau. *What is that noise?*

•

Even from a distance Yannis recognized the earl, resplendent in his royal regalia, as he stepped out of his cottage to survey the scene. He grinned at a fantasy of rushing up to him, bobbing up and down and grunting, *Me Horse, you donkey!* His grin broadened when he saw the earl spin to face east, the shocked stiffening of his body clearly visible even from that distance.

Two hundred of Isabella's gladiators slow-marched down the slope from the east, well below the plateau and well out of reach of the coalition army, and those that had moved to the former grazing land below the plateau. At every fourth step they struck their swords hard on their shields and kept up a steady chant of *Isabella, Isabella, ooo, ooo, ooo!*

With the exception of Johan, the men were the most physically imposing in Isabella's brigade. Tall, broad-shouldered from years of rowing battleships, and bulked up from a year of special training and nutrition, these were men seemingly from a different era. The crash of their swords on their shields rang out louder than a thousand drums, and their chant made them sound like an army of religious fanatics. According to plan, they would not enter the battle below, but the shock effect on the enemy soldiers was just as devastating.

Yannis turned away to look for Isabella. They were never away from each other's side for more than a few seconds. There she was – off *Barca* and next to her men, whirling as kick after kick sent soldiers crashing into those directly behind. Her men then moved forward to finish some of them off, while others simply ran for their lives. *What a woman!* he thought as he moved next to her.

It felt like the battle had lasted for hours, but Isabella knew the chaos was deceptive – only minutes had actually passed since she had given the order to attack. A quick glance showed that twelve time-keepers remained. Almost time! She felt apprehension and excitement sweep over her like a storm and had to fight the urge to throw up. Years of planning and the work of the world's finest engineers would hopefully come to fruition in the next few minutes.

As always, Chen was next to her, his only task being to protect his precious charge. The mere sight of his awesome body and two flashing swords kept enemy soldiers well away. It was Isabella who kept up a devastating attack on them.

Yannis was suddenly next to her and she pressed herself hard against his side. 'Where have you been, you cad? I've missed you.'

'Oh, here and there, messing about. But I'm back to save your pretty hide.'

'Well, you have about two or three minutes left to do it. It's getting extremely dangerous now. So far it's all going to plan. The enemy soldiers are streaming towards us from the higher ground, but if they reach here a minute or two earlier than planned, it's all over for us.'

'Still willing to die by my side, then?'

'It's my dearest wish to die by your side, Yannis.' *Well, my second-dearest wish.* 'How about you? Are you ready?'

'Absolutely.'

'Either way, we're almost there.' She pressed herself harder against him and took a quick glance at the time-keepers. 'We have two minutes.'

Several hundred Northern soldiers puffed hard as they stormed over the ridge to reach the grazing land at the very top of the western side of the river. Aware of a narrow bridge three miles downstream, they knew that if they could get there in time, they might be able to cut off the intruders making their escape. The attack had come from the south, so it was likely they would escape the same way.

Thousands of horses occupied the grazing area. A few had been allowed to roam, but most were confined to designated areas by demountable fences. Isabella's archers – 250 – also occupied the area, hidden out of sight in a small but dense forest of firs.

'*Attention!*' the master archer called to the Northern soldiers, who froze instantly at the sight of hundreds of muscle-bound giants pointing their weapons directly at them. 'You have exactly sixty seconds to turn around and go back where you came from. We will fire immediately if anyone draws a weapon. You know full well that you will all be dead within twenty seconds. You have a simple choice: leave or die. The count starts now: one, two, three …' The soldiers disappeared well within the sixty seconds.

'*Longbowmen,* secure those thousand horses and depart at once. *Crossbowmen,* to the ridge! Flame your missiles. *Prepare to put the flames to apocalypse!*

CHAPTER 111

Earl Carlos Bucher turned away from the men he saw marching down the hill to a sight even more distressing – *Isabella!* Isabella as he had never seen her: her golden hair flowing all the way to her bare waist, her muscular torso and legs glistening from oil and perspiration. He could scarcely believe how she had matured in just one year, not only physically but in self-assurance. Fury and fear mixed with pride as he realized that Isabella was now a woman in every sense of the word.

A loud groan escaped when he saw her gaze lock onto his. Isabella nodded and smiled at him even as she fought amid a mass of her comrades. He knew that only a true empress would have both the courage to attack the very heart of her enemy and the audacity to smile at their commander-in-chief.

The earl finally found his voice as he ran towards the river. 'Rush them! Kill them all! Capture the girl! But no one touches her. I will personally kill any man who touches the girl!' Even as he ran, his thoughts were focused only on how he could safeguard their new relationship.

Jacques and his men kept a close eye on his clock. Every man was in his place. Yellow flags were at the ready to signal those on the other side of the valley.

'I feel ill,' Jacques said to no-one in particular. 'They've been fighting now for almost ten minutes, and God only knows if any of them are still alive in the center of that ants' nest. I certainly hope things are working out for her as planned – there'll never again be anyone like Isabella.'

He raised the yellow flag high over his head to make it visible to everyone. 'Ready, men. Here we go! Light the fuses!' The flag swooped down.

Seconds later, red flags signaling fuses lit – and danger – were raised on both sides of Europe's biggest dam.

Jacques screamed his very last instruction to the men: '*Run!*'

Isabella had searched for their faces among the enemy from the very beginning of the attack. One would do, but both men would be better. Not even Dmitri or the king knew of her secret mission. A quick glance at her time-keepers told her the fuses were lit. Only seconds remained.

She tapped Yannis' arm and leapt up on *Barca*. That was the signal for her men to jump onto their horses. *Make sure your mount is under control within the last minute, men!* she had ordered. From the additional height she saw the two enemy soldiers she had been searching for: Captain Andreas Fransz and Colonel Oleg Walenski.

Isabella deliberately focused her gaze to lock on theirs. Her dramatic appearance had been designed to capture their attention so that when she found them, they would be looking at her. Neither man was quite sure who she was, only that she was immediately familiar. She smiled and nodded to them, reinforcing their confusion. She also caught sight of Earl Carlos Bucher running towards the river shouting and waving at his men.

'Yannis, do you see any casualties we have to pick up?'

He shook his head. 'No. So far so good.'

'When we leave, I go last. That's a direct order from Major Mondeo to General Christos.'

Yannis grinned and saluted. 'Orders are orders, Major.'

The *Serpent Warrior* raised her sword and swung it in an arc. In the bustle of the melee, that was nothing out of the ordinary, but her men had been watching for the signal within that last minute and knew what it meant. The remaining time-keepers had disappeared.

Isabella took a firm grip of *Barca's* reins just as she heard new instructions shouted from behind the build-up of soldiers facing them: '*Rush them! Kill them all! That's a direct order from His Grace. But no one touches the girl. Anyone who touches the girl is a dead man!*'

Yannis looked at Isabella with raised eyebrows. 'Well, this looks like it, Isabella. But it does seem that at least one of us will get out of here alive.'

'You're not going anywhere without me, Yannis,' she hissed back at him, drawing her dagger and pointing it at her heart. 'My serpent friends will make sure that you and I arrive in paradise together.'

A split second later, they arrived together in an apocalypse.

'*Fire!*' Blazing missiles exited the crossbows on the western ridge to streak across the clear summer sky and slam into scores of barns spread out on the hillsides. Within seconds the bows were reloaded for a second salvo, and another, and another. 'To the horses, men!'

Each barn was occupied by one of Jacques' men, already on horseback and dressed to look like a village farmer. The thump of the flaming missile on the roof was the first signal to get ready to release a latch, open the barn door and escape the burning building. The men held their breath and waited for the second signal, which arrived seconds later.

Half the fuses had been cut at a length to burn for exactly sixty seconds before they reached their targets in the upper chambers; the other half were timed to burn for ninety seconds to reach the chambers below ground.

The first fuses reached their targets right on time.

One-third up the massive wall of the dam, twenty tons of enriched gunpowder ignited in carefully sealed chambers designed to magnify the compression power of each explosion.

As a scientist, Jacques watched in morbid fascination not only the explosion, but its ongoing effect. Would it work as planned? Were their calculations accurate? Would it have the effect Isabella hoped for?

Jacques and his team had their answers a second later. From their viewing point high on a nearby hill, they were instantly knocked to their knees. They watched the ripple effect of the shock-wave as it traveled from the massive dam wall to the hills on each side of the valley, then into the earth that lay before it. The valley floor lifted in a low wave-like motion and spread forward and sideways as it traveled downhill. The hills on the sides shook like jelly as the shock-wave raced over and through them just below the surface. Then things got worse.

Even Jacques gasped as the immeasurable water pressure from the twenty-seven-mile-long lake was suddenly released. It seemed as if the water were suspended for a second in the air, until it thundered out of the massive gap that had suddenly appeared across the full width of the dam. The initial mass of water leaned out like a huge wall before it hit the valley floor, releasing a second shock-wave as great as the first.

Jacques was laughing with excitement. He had never witnessed a spectacle as breathtaking as this that he and his men had created. He felt like a boy who had just committed the ultimate mischief. 'Here it comes, Isabella. You've got exactly what you asked for! Stay on the ground, men. Grab hold of anything you can. The next one is going to be even bigger. Hang on for your lives!'

•

Seconds after hearing a low rumbling roar that seemed to come from nowhere in particular, *Barca* staggered sideways, bumping hard against Chen's mount as the shock-wave traveled up his legs. Yannis' mount reared up to spin on its hind legs and almost threw him out of the saddle. Several of Isabella's big men were thrown to the ground, but as instructed, they had the reins carefully wrapped around their arms and they were back in the saddle in seconds. They had been warned: no horse, no escape.

Soldiers streaming down the hills to join the fray were thrown to the ground, forced to crawl on their hands and knees in confusion. Hundreds of blazing tents, already deliberately destabilized, tumbled to the ground.

A heavy veil of smoke from the camps and bridges hung over the full length of the villages on both sides of the river. No one noticed the men in baggy farmers' clothes moving at a brisk pace down the main street on each side of the river to give a quick tug to ropes trailing out of the open front door of every fifth cottage. When the rope was tugged, a bolt flew out of its latch to release the counter-weighted wall from its axis and allow it to slowly topple forward. As planned, the wall was designed higher than the width of the room to guarantee a strike on the wall opposite, which was secured by a single dowel only. In a slow-motion domino effect, wall crashed into wall, cottage into cottage. Huge quantities of fine ash secreted in the roof cavities swirled high into the sky as the cottages came crashing down.

Higher on the western hill, a similar phenomenon occurred as men on horseback tugged their ropes before escaping through the barn doors to disappear into the smoke-filled landscape. Behind them, toppling barn walls sent thousands of bales of hay tumbling down the slope. Within seconds, mushroom-like clouds erupted into the sky as huge quantities of fine ash and blazing rooftops quickly turned the hay bales into infernos.

Everyone froze. Isabella brought *Barca* under control within seconds. She waved her sword in slow circles above her head as she screamed at the enemy soldiers in front of her: '*Truce! Truce! Truce! Earthquake! Earthquake!*' As if to underscore what she was yelling, another strong tremor made *Barca* stagger to the side again and almost brought him to his knees.

No-one needed convincing as they felt the ground move and witnessed buildings collapsing, while smoke and fire blanketed the valley from one end to the other. '*Withdraw!* Cease hostilities!' she yelled at her men. 'Get out now! Head to high country!'

At full gallop, her men struck out for the northern gate of the village. Isabella told Chen that they should separate for the escape because the confusion would make it too dangerous for either to worry about the other. But that was not the real reason for her instructions.

The giants on the hill had turned at the first tremor to head back up at a jog. As rehearsed, Isabella's hidden reserves stormed over the eastern ridge with 200 horses, thus completing their escape.

The lower chambers were constructed beneath the dam wall, but tunneled deeply below ground. Each chamber had been engineered to seal and recompress the initial explosion to increase its power. The sheer weight of the dam wall then directed the massive explosion and shockwave down into the subsoil.

Jacques bounced on the ground as if on a storm-tossed ship as he watched the remainder of the dam wall vanish into a massive crater of earth turned to liquid by the explosion and water that followed it down. Fully unrestrained, the lake leapt forward like a furious tiger at its prey, with the roar of a thousand storms. The wall of water hurtled into the upper valley, as if desperate to catch up with the initial release just thirty seconds earlier. Jacques' shouts of delight were completely drowned out, as were those of his team.

This time Isabella saw it coming. Her eyes opened in genuine shock at the sight of the ground heaving in front of her. Already half way to the village gates, she jumped off *Barca* and held the reins in a tight grip.

Within seconds the shock-wave hurled her onto her back. She shook her head and spat out a mouthful of dirt. When he had seen Isabella jump off her horse, Yannis had done the same and then ran to her the moment the shock-wave passed.

He reached out to help her to her feet. 'Are you all right to ride?'

Taking his hand she got up and had to spit again before she could speak. 'Sorry, that was not very lady-like, was it? Yes, I'm fine. Let's go. Let's get out of here.' She jumped back on *Barca*. 'We're last. Go! Go! I'll be right behind you,' she lied.

Yannis followed the path of his men, who had already escaped down the dirt roadway through the smoking remnants of the village. The buildings and river on their right side and the smoking buildings on the left of the roadway provided reasonable protection from the enemy.

Feeling exhilarated, Yannis careered down the narrow roadway.

Seeing no-one making an attempt to stop them, he twisted his head to give Isabella a relieved grin. There was no-one behind him! *She must have fallen off Barca!* He stopped in a panic, while his eyes desperately searched the road and the smoking buildings on either side. No-one. He was alone.

He lifted his gaze higher and beheld the impossible. Isabella was riding at full gallop back into the heart of the enemy camp!

CHAPTER 112

Isabella had few concerns about the risk she was taking by riding back into the enemy stronghold alone to fulfil her secret mission. She had carefully crafted her response letter to the earl and knew that, if she were captured, he would not kill her. Anything but! And after she heard his orders that she was not to be touched – on penalty of death – she knew she was safe even from capture. No-one would dare lay a finger on her.

Many of the soldiers were still on their knees, surveying the damage and wondering how best to start the recovery process. Isabella felt an urge to tell them not to bother, as there was worse to come. She instead deliberately pulled *Barca* up on his hind legs close to Fransz and Walenski and shouted at everyone in the vicinity: 'Get up to high country now! Run! There are lakes everywhere upstream. If that earthquake breaches just one of them, it will destroy every valley in its path! Go! Run!'

She swung her focus to Fransz and Walenski and smiled at them both. Long ago, she had decided that one of them would carry the message for her secret mission. Fransz seemed perplexed, confused; Walenski looked shocked. She knew that Fransz was not sure if he was looking at Isabella Mondeo or Madam *Rosa Tissone*. Colonel Walenski, on the other hand, knew exactly who he was looking at, and she could see that he was shocked by the implications. She had counted on that. The olive-skinned man standing beside Fransz simply stared at her with admiration. Mehudi. She remembered him and gave him her most brilliant smile.

'If just one lake is breached, this valley will be flooded within minutes, and we'll all die,' she shouted at them. 'Get your horses and get out! Every second counts. Tell His Grace to flee at once to high land until the danger passes. And make sure you give him a second message from me: the danger from us will not pass. Give him that message at once, or he will have your heads for breakfast!'

The *Serpent Warrior* gave the two men a formal salute, another smile at the obviously love-struck Mehudi, and dug her heels into the side of the rearing *Barca*. '*Go, Thunderbolt!*' she yelled as she headed towards where she knew Yannis would be waiting for her in a rage.

'I don't believe what I'm seeing,' Fransz whispered. *Thunderbolt and lightning!* What a sight!'

Colonel Oleg Walenski was quick to take charge. 'You heard what she said, men. Let's do it. Everyone to the hills! Tell everyone you see. We can't get the message to the other side of the river, but there's nothing we can do about that. Nothing might happen, anyway, but let's get those messages to the Earl, Andreas. I don't like the idea of gazing at His *Disgrace* from a silver platter while he's enjoying his poached eggs in the morning. He's just over there, and in a state of shock, by the look of it.'

Yannis almost fainted with relief when he saw Isabella heading his way at full gallop. *Whatever it was she had to do,* he thought, *it had certainly been quick.* The last thing he saw just before he turned his mount towards the south gate was Earl Carlos Bucher and other officers running to their horses. He only gradually increased speed to allow Isabella to catch up to him, and by the time they reached the southern gate they were both side by side at full gallop.

Isabella had been right about Yannis. He was furious. 'What do you think you're doing, you crazy woman? What have you done?' he shouted at her.

'Ooh, you're so handsome when you're angry,' she shouted back. 'Later. Concentrate on the bridge. We've got just minutes to get out of here alive!'

Bugles sounded the enemy withdrawal, but few soldiers had their horses in the lower section of the valley. Isabella had deliberated designed the grazing land to be at the highest level for the protection of the horses, and to reduce available transportation on the day.

The earl was the first to get away, with the main body of officers not far behind. Soldiers were simply ordered, or dragged, off their mounts by their superiors. Half way up the steepest part of the hill, the earl caught up with the coalition army on their way down. *More alibi*, Isabella had told General Manacek.

'Turn back!' he shouted. 'We could be in danger from the after-effect of the earthquake. Head for the highest ground.' Manacek resisted a grin as he signaled to his bugler to sound a speedy withdrawal.

The officers were cantering up the road when the earl suddenly stopped and turned in his saddle to face Fransz and Walenski. 'What's that?' he asked.

Walenski looked up, startled. 'What's what, sir?'

'That noise. I can't make out what it is, or where it's coming from. It sounds like a far-away storm. What is it?'

Fransz heard it first. 'I don't know, sir, but I don't like the sound of it. Let's keep going.'

Isabella's brigade was strung out in a well-rehearsed spiral, crossing the narrow bridge in single file at maximum safe speed. The spiral diminished rapidly as the riders reached the other side and disappeared straight up the hill.

Near the entry Yannis and Isabella waited patiently to follow the last man in the spiral. Finally it was their turn, and they were half way across the bridge when Isabella heard it.

'Uh-oh!'

'Is that what I think it is?'

'This is not a good time for a discussion, you crazy man! It might just be a better idea to move like you have never moved before, Yannis!'

'What do you think, Mehudi? Do you think Isabella Mondeo and Madam Rosa Tissone are one and the same? The proclamation from the South said it was her, but I thought they could have made it up for a bit of propaganda.' Fransz and Mehudi were not far behind the earl and Walenski, but he knew they could not hear him above the rapidly growing noise.

'Has to be, Cap. There's no way I could fall in love with two different women as beautiful as that. And that warrior outfit! Have you ever seen – '

'Oh, shut up, Mehudi! I suppose a wig would explain the hair. But the eyes, Mehudi, the eyes! Madam Tissone's eyes were bordering on green, though not quite the green we saw a few minutes ago.'

'We could have made a mistake in the early morning light, Cap. On the other hand, I have heard of Nordic people who have pale eyes that change with the light. Only one person can have eyes that size and shape.'

'That would certainly explain the feeling I had about her that day. That girl was brilliant, so relaxed, confident and most of all, fearless. She controlled me like a puppet, Mehudi. She could have made me do whatever she wanted me to.'

'Oh, me too.' Mehudi groaned in ecstasy.

'Shut up and be serious for a minute. Have you ever seen such courage? That girl came back alone to stand directly in front of us, surrounded by our men. I can easily imagine Madam Tissone capable of doing just that. I agree with you – Madam Tissone and Isabella Mondeo are one and the same. She risked her life to warn us of potential danger. If it turns out she's right, she's nothing short of God's messenger. I've said it once and I'll say it again: we haven't heard the last of Isabella Mondeo.'

Oleg Walenski was panic stricken as his mount scrambled up the hill behind his despised commander-in-chief. Walenski had recognized Isabella the instant their eyes connected, despite having been convinced she had been killed when he saw her plunge into the gorge with the hapless, and legless, Charles. Any lingering doubt was dispelled when he saw her deliberately acknowledge him with her eyes and a friendly nod.

The implications were almost too horrendous to contemplate as he sifted through the facts. Isabella was no bandit and neither were her men. Isabella had been the one to call *earthquake* and *truce*; it was Isabella who had screamed at her men to cease the attack and evacuate the camp. Only the commanding officer could issue such orders. She was as obviously in command today as she had been on that winter day when she had saved his life, and the lives of his men.

There were only four things she could have targeted in the desolate winter camp. The soldiers: the *bandits* were leaving the compound when they were discovered, and none of the soldiers had been harmed, so they obviously were not the target. The stores: the entire Southern army was well provisioned and Isabella's brigade had no need for provisions – certainly not at the risk of entering the enemy's camp. The theft of stores was therefore no more than a diversion. The cannons: the South most certainly feared the cannons more than anything, but their sheer weight precluded even one cannon being carried off, much less a thousand. That left just one item, and it was the reason for his state of panic.

Isabella's attack in the mountains had been a commando raid, and they had been after the gun-powder!

He cupped his hands around his mouth and called out to the earl. 'Your Grace, I need to urgently talk to you about Miss Mondeo.'

'Oh, for heaven's sake, you fool,' the earl yelled back over the noise that had become almost deafening. 'Can't you hear that something is about to happen? This is not the time to talk about Miss Mondeo, or anyone else.

Leave it for later. Just keep moving.'

Walenski did not appreciate it then, but his despised commander-in-chief had just saved his life.

The lake was unable to pass through the gorge quickly enough, and the water banked up to near its top with the pressure of billions of tons behind it. By the time it reached the exit point where the two rivers joined, the pressure was enough to strip a man's body to the bone in an instant. Into the first valley the water swept like an angry ocean tsunami, greedily seizing everything in its path: trees, earth, rocks, camps, cottages, barns – and soldiers.

Up the rises of the valley the roaring waters swirled. Eventually they fell back to re-join the surge, exponentially adding to the power of the main body. By the time the water reached the largest valley, it carried almost enough force to push a mountain out of its path.

From his high position, the earl was able to view part of the next valley up-river. What he saw made him grip Walenski's arm so hard the man cried out in pain. No one heard him. The noise of a thousand hurricanes turned everything else into a world of silence. A veritable mountain of dark brown water and mud spewed from the valley further along, stripping everything in its path. It then swirled in a wide arc to attack the main valley below.

'My God,' he whispered, 'I just hope we're high enough.' No-one would have heard him even if he had screamed.

The charred remains of the bridges disappeared in an instant. Then the village went, the lowest camps, the officers' compound, the barns and more camps as the water tore towards the hills on both sides. As it continued its angry path south, it took everything with it, including all evidence of what might have caused the supposed *earthquake*.

Carlos found it difficult to breathe as he watched the torrent of water tear through the valley below. His heart hammered while he thought of his fate had Isabella not risked her life to get the message to him. She was a very clever young woman, he thought. She had sent Ollie and Andreas with *two* messages, the second to tell him that the danger from the enemy would not pass. Of course it would not pass – that was what enemies did. He knew that and Isabella knew it. She had issued the threat of him having the messengers' heads for breakfast for no reason other than to make sure he got the *first* message: *there is danger, so get out until it passes.* Isabella had risked her life to return alone to the place of battle, specifically to save his life. If she were not already in love with him, she was certainly giving it enough consideration to ensure his safety.

What courage it had taken for this young woman to enter the very heart of the enemy camp alone and unprotected! What a woman, and how beautiful she had become in just one year! She had taken his breath away just as she had on the day he had first seen her, and he had not wasted a moment to let her know how much he wanted her. Carlos had come to accept, and embrace the fact that Isabella was his intellectual superior, but he no longer resented it. In fact he reveled in it and loved the very thought of it. Despite the devastation below, his chest swelled thinking of how he would bask in her reflected glory and be the envy of the world for having the affection of a wife so beautiful. The most admired empress the world would know for a thousand years! *Nothing, no-one would be allowed to get in their way!*

Carlos prayed that she had managed to escape.

Hundreds of men lined the ridge to wait for their beloved Isabella to join them for the ride to the overnight evacuation camp. They knew she would be the last to arrive. Now they were nervous. Unable to speak over the roar of the torrent, they could only sit and watch the mass of water, mud and debris sweeping through the main valley. So far, there had been no sign of their idol. Several soldiers jumped from their mounts and ran to an overhang for a better view of the slope below in the hope of catching sight of her and Yannis. One of the men turned back to his comrades moments later and pointed down the hill while he drew a finger across his throat.

Isabella was just behind Yannis as both mounts scrambled towards the ridge. Occasionally they would look at each other and point if one saw an easier path. Every few seconds they would glance over their shoulders in morbid fascination at the tsunami chasing their every step up the hill and rapidly closing on them. Massive volumes raced towards the hills on both sides, creating hundreds of whirlpools as the centrifugal force of water that wanted to recede was instead pushed even further up the hill by the power of the temporary lake behind it.

The whirlpools sucked up everything in their path, including the subsoil, creating muddy new estuaries as the rising water followed the contours of the land.

The last few times Isabella had glanced over her shoulder, she was encouraged to see that although the water was still rising, it had not gained on her. She realized that the higher the water reached, the wider the area to accommodate it, and she gave Yannis the thumbs up the next time she caught his eye. He returned the gesture with a relieved grin, and kept going.

Suddenly *Barca* shuddered when his hind legs kicked twice for purchase instead of the usual once. He regained balance to surge ahead again, only to stumble seconds later as his legs kicked several times with little effect. By then Yannis was well ahead and had reached a safe height.

Isabella knew instinctively that she was in trouble, big trouble, and she knew why. The ground surface had become unstable, and *Barca* was close to panic. His constant kicking and jumping made it impossible for her to hold on despite her strong legs. She knew she would have to get off before she was thrown off. To control the fall she threw herself off at the right moment to avoid landing on her head. A second earlier she had tossed her sword to the opposite side, to prevent being accidentally impaled on it.

Yannis turned in his saddle, expecting to find Isabella directly behind, only to see her hit the ground and cartwheel downhill into the surging mud.

CHAPTER 113

Without the extra weight *Barca* managed to stagger forward and eventually find solid ground. Yannis knew immediately what had happened. The whirlpools had sucked up enough of the subsoil to create an expanding void beneath the hill, the perfect conditions for landslip. In his last image of her, Isabella vanished into the center of a whirlpool. Horrified, he had no idea what to do. It did not help when he looked towards the ridge and saw one of their men pointing down the hill and making a slicing motion across his throat.

The whirlpools were powerful, but shallow, and because of the heavy sludge, relatively slow. Within seconds of being sucked below the surface, Isabella hit firm rock. She allowed herself to sink to a squat and then thrust upwards at full strength at an angle, in the hope of breaching the side of the whirlpool. A slight change in pressure on her face told her she had broken the surface and she chanced a quick breath. She could see nothing until she quickly scraped some mud from around her eyes.

'Oh God, another one!' She managed a quick breath before being drawn into the next whirlpool. This time it was easier because she knew what to do. She repeated the previous action and cleared her eyes before taking a breath. The strong current was pulling her rapidly downstream. Looking around desperately, she could see where the land leveled out slightly, and decided to try to move in that direction, knowing it would become shallower.

As soon as he spotted her, Yannis ripped off his breastplate and other armor, called to the men on the ridge to retrieve it and Isabella's sword, and then ran. It was almost impossible to keep up with the speed of the swirling mud as the main body of water tore at it like a mother demanding its child. His fitness was the only reason he was able to keep running at full pace for almost thirty minutes, following the contours of the land. At last he saw the sludge slowing as it thickened.

Isabella made no attempt to fight the power of the current. She knew that was impossible. All that mattered was remaining on the surface, breathing and retaining some strength in case opportunity presented itself. She was heartened by an occasional glimpse of a bare-chested Yannis desperately trying to catch up. Several times she attempted to wave, but found it impossible to lift her arm from the sludge.

Yannis saw an opportunity when the mud had to travel around a pointed section of land which allowed him to run across a small hill and finally get in front. He waited for the precise moment and jumped in next to her, slipped one arm around her waist and used the other to help keep her face above the surface. Within seconds she had wrapped herself around him like an octopus. Too exhausted to speak, she simply groaned as they were dragged along by the mud.

The water's momentum finally abated after a half hour and slowed the sludge enough for them to strike ground close to a clump of trees. Exhausted, they lay stretched out side by side for several minutes, half buried in the mud and unrecognizable as human beings. Even Isabella's hair was little more than a dark clump of mud wrapped around her head and shoulders. The only visible features were their eyes after they dared to open them. They looked at each other in astonishment.

'My hero!' Isabella groaned, 'always there when I need you, and as handsome as a mud pie.'

'And I've never seen you look more presentable.'

'So, if I look that good, would you like to kiss me?' Isabella puckered her lips, indistinguishable beneath a thick covering of mud. She knew he would not dare to kiss her.

'Very tempting, but I think I'll pass, thank you.'

'Just as well! I wouldn't want my first-ever kiss to taste like a mud pie. Yuk!' She looked around with a touch of concern. 'Seriously, though, Yannis, as lovely as it is to rest, I think we should make a move before the men find us and get the wrong idea. We still have our arms around each other. This is definitely not a good look for a general and a major in His Majesty's army.'

'Good idea.' Yannis slid his arm from under her waist and rose slowly to loud squelching sounds.

'You'll have to help me up,' Isabella groaned. 'I can't lift myself out of this glue.'

Yannis nodded, leaned down and slipped one arm under her knees and the other all the way around her back. Or so he thought.

'*Oi!*' she hissed.

'What?'

'What do you think you're doing?'

'Lifting you up.'

'Not where that hand is, you're not! Move it, and fast, or you die! Mud or no mud … that area is strictly for my husband only!'

'Oh, sorry. It's hard to tell what's what in all this mud.'

'No-one gets an early mark with this *kid!*'

'You can forget about the *kid* bit. I do view you as a woman now.'

'Yes, actually I did notice that. Now get me out of here.'

Isabella slipped her arms around his neck to support the lift. When he was fully upright, she grinned brightly. '*But* … the muddy kiss is still on offer,' she said and puckered her mud-caked lips again.

Suddenly she felt an instant of weightlessness before splattering full length into the squelching mud. Stunned, she managed to roll to one side, then onto her knees, where she spat savagely several times before looking up into the smiling face of a mud statue.

'*Oh* you beast! You horrible, horrible *beast!* I hate you! I hate you!'

'I already told you I'll pass on the kiss.'

Ten minutes later the first of mounted soldiers followed the sound of laughter to find the two sitting face to face, waist deep in the mud, taking turns throwing handfuls of mud over each other. Isabella was the first to notice the men. Her laughter stopped immediately. She twisted in the mud to call out, 'Luis! Tell us about Luis!'

CHAPTER 114

They sat quietly on the edge of the plateau and watched the water rush through the lower valley. The earl knew that the flow would eventually return to normal, and then would come the grim task of damage assessment. It was already obvious that he would be out of action for quite some time.

To Manacek, who sat nearby he said, 'General Manacek, there are probably twenty to thirty thousand survivors sitting on the hillsides right now who owe their lives to you for your suggestion to move to higher ground.'

'It's *Major*-General, Your Grace.' Manacek corrected the earl's slip of the tongue.

The earl shook his head. 'It's *General* from now on, and I thank you.'

'Thank you, Your Grace, but in all sincerity, I can't take much of the credit. My suggestion to move was based on no more than the risk of the river rising substantially. No-one in the world could have envisaged something like this.' *Except one*, he thought happily.

'I understand that, General, but nevertheless, your move to the plateau brought 25,000 of those most at risk to a safer place, and they have all survived. Had they not moved, they too would have perished in what will without doubt be known for eternity as the valley of the damned. So again, General, I thank you.'

'When you put it that way, I suppose it was a fortunate benefit from the decision on the day. Any ideas what we'll do next, sir?'

'Also fortunate is that the cannons and wagons were already situated on high terrain, ready to move, and well away from the path of the water. Our fire power remains intact. We'll just have to take things day by day for a while, but one thing is certain: we will be forced to remain here for at least another year while we regroup and re-supply everything that's been lost.'

Manacek nodded gravely, while inside he was jumping for joy. Isabella had saved every man and woman in his army, as well as the camp followers. Everything had happened exactly as she had predicted in her letter to him. He coughed and turned away as he was struck by a thought: *Isabella, if you ever come face to face with the Devil, he'll make a run for it!*

General Spiro Manacek was not entirely correct. His delight would later turn to shock in the belief that Isabella had instead switched places with the Devil, when he and his entire coalition army became her next target for destruction.

The earl turned his attention to Colonel Walenski. 'Now then, Ollie, what was it that you were so desperate to discuss about Miss Mondeo while the world was collapsing around us?'

Walenski shook as he opened his mouth to speak. A minute after the earl had told him to leave the matter of Isabella until later, he had almost fainted on realizing his near-fatal error of judgment. If he had informed the earl of his suspicions, the entire story would have unraveled, and his head would soon have been rolling down the hill.

His earlier report of the mid-winter raid in the mountains had been clear: there was no girl; the bandits had all been killed; all the stolen goods had been recovered; nothing was missing. His men had backed the story and were considered heroes to a man, except for *poor* Charles who, they said, had lacked the fighting skills of the bandits and had joined them on the rocks at the bottom of the gorge.

If he had blurted out his realization that the bandit leader had really been Isabella, it would have revealed a web of lies and incompetence and would have resulted in immediate death for himself, every man in his platoon, his general and every other officer who had allowed the enemy to infiltrate and then escape their camp. He suddenly had the unenviable task of protecting Isabella's secret raid on the gunpowder with his very life.

Little did Walenski know that Isabella had deliberately gone out of her way to find him, and then make eye contact, to guarantee his recognition of the message hidden in her mesmerizing smile: *reveal anything about me or the gunpowder, Colonel, and we both know that you're a dead man. You are my man on the inside to cover up any inconsistencies, if ever found, regarding the gunpowder.*

'Events have actually answered the reservations I had earlier, Your Grace. I wondered why Miss Mondeo would risk coming back alone into a hornets' nest of enemy soldiers simply to give us a warning. I was suspicious that perhaps her warning was a risky but clever ruse to lead us *towards* danger rather than away from it – straight into the arms of more gladiators, perhaps.'

'That's actually very good thinking, Ollie. I have to admit that I didn't think of that. Although she's on the enemy's side of the fence, I've never seen such courage – in man or woman – she exhibited today, both when she was there with the men, and later, when she returned alone. Quite frankly, she took my breath away.'

Mine too, thought Mehudi as he listened to the conversation.

'Did her courage have anything to do with your order that she was not to be harmed, sir?'

'In part, Ollie, in part.' Carlos Bucher focused on keeping his voice unemotional. 'When you're the man in charge, you have to think fast on your feet. There's more to consider than just what's happening on the battlefield. There are also political issues, the outcomes of which are hard to predict, so you have to err on the side of caution. Everyone loves a hero, Ollie. Think of the potential consequences on both sides of this conflict if Miss Mondeo had been slaughtered today. One doesn't kill a national hero, especially a woman, young and beautiful. It would have been unforgivable. The price for a political mistake of such magnitude could easily be my own life, so I had to be careful. No, Ollie, Miss Mondeo had to be given a free pass today.'

Walenski nodded. Carlos could see he was satisfied with the answer he had made up on the spot, and he was pleased with himself that he had, in fact, been able to think fast on his feet.

'So what do you now think of her coming back to warn us?' continued Carlos, as he stared vacantly into the valley, so magnificent just an hour earlier.

'Well, we know it wasn't a trap, sir, or it would have been sprung by now. Miss Mondeo obviously could not have known of the devastation that was to follow within minutes or she would not have returned. There's no doubt that she saved the lives of most of us who are sitting here now. For all we know, the extra minutes it took to come back might well have caused her death. I will forever be grateful to her, but I still fail to understand why she risked her life to save the lives of her enemy.'

'Perhaps,' the earl said with a touch of smugness, 'she's met one of us before and risked her life to save the man she loves. An affair of the heart! So romantic, Ollie, don't you think?'

Everyone chuckled, except Carlos, who sat back with a satisfied smirk. None of them realized that a disguised Isabella had, in fact, met all of them.

A plain-faced young man with deep-set eyes sat alone on a ridge below surveying the still fast-moving scene in the valley. He'd also had the privilege of meeting Isabella but, unknown to the men above, he was the only one who had been kissed by her after having tackled her out of the way of a firing cannon.

CHAPTER 115

On the way to the medical camp, Yannis and Isabella spent time partly submerged, but fully dressed, in a clear running feeder-stream which removed most of the mud. Isabella lay prone with her feet upstream to allow the current to flow through her hair while she rubbed it vigorously. By the time they returned to their horses, they both felt considerably cleaner and refreshed.

Melissa met them as soon as they entered the camp. With her dress covered in blood, she hugged them both briefly before pulling them towards the field hospital.

'Thank God you're both safe! Some of the men arrived earlier and said you'd both disappeared in the mud, but I knew you'd be all right. You always are, you two. And you, Isabella, if I'd heard you'd been thrown to the lions, well, I'd pity the *lions!* Come with me now and check on the injured. Most of them are not too bad, but I'm afraid Luis is. He's been unconscious since he was injured and I'm really worried about him. I just don't know whether the poor boy is going to make it.'

'At least he's still alive,' Isabella said softly as she held Melissa around her waist. The poor *boy*, she thought, was actually several years older than Yannis. 'To be honest, I thought we would lose him before the men even got him to the village gate. Luckily, Johan was right there when it happened and managed to stem the bleeding. Sailors don't have much access to medical help at sea, so they're all well trained to look out for each other. Johan has at least given him a fighting chance. Tell me about the others.'

'Twenty-seven injured, some with pretty bad wounds, but not life-threatening, thank goodness. We've used raw alcohol and cauterized the wounds, but there is, of course, still the risk of infection. There's nothing more we can do for them, so we'll just worry about infection if and when it happens. There were actually far fewer injured than expected, and everyone's been taken care of already. Luis is the only one we're worried about.'

'Has a body count been taken yet?' Yannis asked.

'Emile finished that more than an hour ago. He's a really good organizer, Yannis – brilliant, in fact. He set the platoons up in grids and had the numbers double-checked within minutes. Besides the twenty-eight injured, everyone else has been accounted for, fit and healthy.'

Isabella was so relived she buckled at the knees and started to hyperventilate. Yannis put his arms around her and held her while he gently rubbed her back. For once, Melissa seemed comfortable watching them quietly from the side until Isabella regained her breath and Yannis let her go.

Melissa smiled at them. 'All right, then, you two, so much for the good news. 'Now I want to take you to see Luis.'

On the way, Isabella decided she should learn to hyperventilate more often. That was the second time in one day that Yannis had held her, which was a vast improvement on the previous few years. All in all, a very good day, she thought with deep satisfaction. Except for Luis' condition.

Yannis and Isabella caught up with Zhang Chen, and spent time among the men to thank and congratulate them for their exceptional courage and performance during the day, particularly those chosen for face-to-face combat. Every injured man received a handshake from Yannis and a hug from Isabella.

Luis' breathing was shallow, his heartbeat irregular and barely audible when Isabella put her ear gently to his chest. The wound from the spear was the worst; it was deep and had caused a splintered rib that had to be picked clean before being reset and heavily strapped. Thankfully, he had been unconscious throughout the entire ordeal. 'He certainly doesn't look good,' she said grimly, 'but as long as he has a pulse, there's hope.'

Melissa held Luis' hand gently throughout the hour they sat and kept a watch over him. Team leaders approached to provide reports to both Isabella and Yannis. Johan informed them that hundreds of items had been deliberately scattered well below the high water mark: shields, swords, armor, clothing and even a number of saddles. The idea was to give the appearance that Isabella's brigade had suffered substantial casualties during their escape.

Yancko reported that a number of well-rehearsed villagers would provide eye-witness confirmation to the Earl that Isabella had managed to escape with a bare handful of survivors. Other villagers had already been strategically placed to assess the enemy's losses of men and materiel. The three families in the two valleys below the main valley had sold their farms to "investors" the previous year at generous prices. They were uninhabited now, which meant that the excess water and mud could disperse over the hundreds of miles of flatlands without further casualties.

Exhausted, Yannis finally rose to find somewhere to sleep. Isabella automatically took it as a signal to do the same. Melissa reached out and squeezed Yannis' arm without getting up. 'It's not cold, so I'm going to stay with Luis. He might wake up during the night and need some attention. I don't want to leave him alone for a moment. Oh, and by the way, you'd better get cleaned up a bit more – you both still look terrible.'

Isabella leaned down and hugged her friend. 'Melissa, darling, just in case he doesn't make it, there's something you should know and share in silence with him while he's still with us. Luis single-handedly prevented us from being outflanked during that critical first five minutes. I've never seen a soldier fight so fiercely. With unbelievable courage, he deliberately placed himself between us and the enemy to give us the time we needed to secure our positions. Without him we might easily have been overwhelmed, and none of us would be here right now. He saved the day for us, Melissa. Luis was by far the outstanding hero of the day.'

Melissa was too emotional to speak and just nodded as she curled up next to her patient.

'There's something about Luis that bothers me,' Yannis said softly as they searched for a place to sleep. Isabella remained silent, knowing that he had more to say. 'There's something about him … His name seems familiar, but I can't place it. And that horse – what a horse! How can anyone so young afford a horse like that? It is literally worth a fortune. And you were quite right in what you told Melissa about his amazing fighting skills. Mark my words: Luis Valdez is not who he seems. He has fought before.' He looked around and pointed to a spot away from the main body of men. 'How about we get our things and bunk down there? We'll be out in the open, but well away from everyone else.'

'Let's take Melissa's suggestion and have another clean-up first.'

An hour later they lay a body-width apart staring silently at the glittering stars and an almost full moon. Yannis finally spoke. 'Are you all right with us being out here like this? I remember the time when you ordered me to the other side of the camp.'

'Of course it's all right, Yannis. Now that you have no interest in kissing me, I know I'm completely safe.'

'Ouch.'

'What you're really dying to do is to ask me a question. That's the real reason for bringing me out here where it's quiet. I already know what the question is, so ask away.'

Yannis sighed heavily. 'You shocked me to the core back there, Isabella. Why did you suddenly decide to go back into the enemy camp alone? I was petrified. You could have been taken prisoner!'

'Do you trust me, Yannis?'

'I trust you with my life.'

'Will you trust me when I say that I can tell you some things, but not everything?'

'Of course. You're a barrel-full of mysteries, so just tell me what you can.'

'Well, it wasn't a sudden decision to return to the enemy camp alone. It's been part of my plan for more than a year. It was never a question of me being captured. I would simply have surrendered if I had to but, as it turned out, when I heard the order given that I was not to be touched, I knew I could re-enter the camp without risk of capture.'

Yannis sat bolt upright. '*What?* What are you saying? You – surrender?'

'Shh, settle down! You'll wake the whole camp. Now listen to me. I couldn't tell the king or Dmitri of my secret mission. Not even Grandfather, or Chen. Not even you.'

'*Secret mission?*'

'It had to be secret, otherwise everyone would have done everything in their power to stop me. My mission would have been forbidden, and I could not disobey an order from the king.'

'But why not tell me? After today I believe you completely when you say we're destined to die together on the battlefield. You showed me that when you were about to use your dagger to die with me as we were about to be rushed in those last few seconds before the explosion. I will die just as readily for you, Isabella, and for no-one else. Surely that must tell you that you can tell me anything.'

'Yannis, that was the most beautiful thing anyone has ever said to me, but despite that, you would have stopped me, too.'

'No, I wouldn't, I promise.'

'Yannis, you are my best and dearest friend, as I am yours, so please forgive me for not telling you this earlier. If I had said to you when we were heading out at full gallop that I was going to turn back, alone, to re-enter the very heart of the enemy camp, not to mention facing a few billion tons of water thundering through the valleys towards us, for no reason other than to save the life of the commander-in-chief of the enemy forces – what would you have done? What would all of the others have done if I had told them that? Now please be completely honest with yourself.'

Yannis was too stunned to utter a sound.

'I rest my case, Yannis.'

He finally found his voice. 'But why would you want to save the life of that miserable butcher? Surely it's not because …?'

'Don't even think it or I'll rip the beard right off your face. I had many reasons to save his life, but they are complex and difficult for anyone to understand without knowing what I have in mind for the future. That's why I need you to trust me and just let it go for now until I'm ready to tell you. I promise I *will* tell you.'

'I have to admit that if you'd told me this earlier, I would have done everything possible to stop you, so I do understand now why you couldn't tell me. I trust you completely, Isabella. Just tell me in your own good time. I won't ask any more questions about it and I'm not angry or upset, I promise. Matter closed.'

She reached out to squeeze his hand. 'Thank you, Yannis. You have no idea how much it means to me that you believe in me. The lovely things you said to me tonight will live with me forever. We'd better get some sleep now. It's been a long and harrowing day and we have a long ride tomorrow. Good night, Yannis.'

'Good night, Isabella.'

Yannis had no idea what time it was when he woke to the feel of pressure against his left side and a faint breathing sound in his ear. The moon had almost disappeared but he was able to make out the faint outline of Isabella pressed against him. He decided to move further away so that she would not find in the morning that she had unintentionally rolled up against him, as she had done once before. His hand was moving to the ground between them to gently lever himself away when he suddenly froze. Her roll-up mattress had been moved up against his; this time Isabella had decided where she wanted to be. He thought about how the two had faced death side by side the entire afternoon, and he understood her need to remain close to him until the dawning of a new day. He felt the same. He had no doubt Isabella would make sure that both she and her mattress were long gone by morning. So instead of moving away, he reached out to pull a light blanket over them both, careful not to touch her. He gazed at the stars seemingly for hours, before finally drifting off to sleep.

Dawn had just broken when he woke to find himself alone as expected. He rolled onto his back and was startled to see a most magnificent sight: a clean-scrubbed, shiny-faced Isabella sitting on a log by his feet, watching him quietly as she slowly brushed luster into her hair. She had changed from her sparse uniform into sturdy riding clothes.

'Good morning,' she said, smiling at him. 'Did you sleep well?'

He stretched out and placed his hands behind his head to get a better view of her. 'Not really.'

'Oh, such a pity. I had the most wonderful night's sleep I've ever had. You are such a gentleman, Yannis. I knew I would be completely safe with you. I must have disturbed you, though, silly, selfish little me. How about I bring you breakfast in bed to make up for it?'

'That would be lovely. I've never had anyone bring me breakfast in bed.'

'Done. Next, I've already checked on Luis. He's no worse this morning, which is a very good sign. As soon as we finish breakfast, we'll be off. All the injured will follow at a slower pace, except for Luis. We'll leave him here to recover for another day or two before we move him. Melissa said she'll stay with him for as long as it takes.'

Yannis nodded slowly but remained silent, seemingly mesmerized by the vision of Isabella brushing her hair in the early morning sun. He visibly relaxed when she held his gaze and smiled to let him know that he need not look away this time. Finally she grinned and tossed her brush onto her mattress which, Yannis had noticed earlier, had been moved back to its original position. 'I'll get our breakfast now.'

CHAPTER 116

It took a week of hard riding to reach the main camp. During their journey, Yannis and Isabella often talked late into the night, but slept in separate tents rather than in the open. On the fourth day they received the heartening news from late arrivals that Luis had regained consciousness.

They were now sitting with Marcus, and staring silently at each other in the meeting tent after reading the dozens of messages that had been waiting for them. Most were from Dmitri; three were from King Ramesses, and several from outlying regions. Isabella was shaking like a leaf, while Marcus and Yannis were too astonished to speak. Much of the information had first been received by Dmitri, who had then summarized the essential before dispatching it to Yannis' new headquarters.

Yannis finally rose and paced the room. 'Unbelievable, but it must be true. Dmitri has received a lot of independent information to come up with this consensus.' He waved a piece of paper. 'You were right, Isabella, with your earlier assessment that the earl will not be able to chase us until next year. Logistically, it's impossible for him to conduct war until his army is fully re-supplied and enlarged by the arrival of the Third division. Can you believe it? Sixty percent of the enemy force destroyed!'

A groan came from a quietly weeping Isabella, who had never before been so devastated by success. Yannis brought his chair over to sit in front of her, reached out to take her hands and rubbed them gently.

'Thank you, Yannis, that feels lovely, but I still feel terrible. I have to pray for their poor souls. I can't help it.'

'I wouldn't expect you to feel any other way right now – that's only natural. But you did what you believed needed to be done to save our nation. It's not finished yet, but your plan has stopped them in their tracks for another year at least.'

'My next plan was to hit them this winter if we had to, but now that we know that the earl can't move, it will give us this winter to do some testing of my ideas instead. The terrain here will be different, solid ice, and the earl will be able to move over it with his equipment mid-winter, so I know he'll time it to be here the following winter. In fact, I'm counting on it.' She drew a deep breath. 'I know I'll feel better once I start to really put my mind to it. Now, if only you'd rub my feet the way you're rubbing my hands, I'd feel even better. *Yannis!* she hissed as he started to move. 'I was only joking!'

The three chuckled quietly as they began to relax after the initial shock from reading Dmitri's reports. Early estimates were that sixty percent, or approximately 80,000, Northern soldiers, had perished when the release of the massive lake had wiped the valleys from the face of the earth. Only those on the highest ground had survived, which included the camp followers, and almost all the horses and other livestock that had been placed on the prime grazing lands closer to the ridges. The crop-growing areas had been almost entirely destroyed, as were the barns and storage sheds. The earl had written to Emperor Kuiper to inform him of the devastating earthquake, and to say that he needed to restock provisions and to be reinforced by the Third army after he was assured it carried no risk of infection.

'Let's look at the rough numbers for the next round.' Marcus stretched his long legs out in front of him. 'After allowing for the 15,000 or so he lost last year, plus last week' losses, he must be down to less than 50,000.' He grinned with a sudden thought. 'Why don't we send you and Yannis down there now to finish them off?'

'Oh you!' She removed her shoes and dropped one bare foot on his knee. 'Just for being cheeky, you can rub my foot.'

Marcus was happy to oblige. 'The reports go on to say that the Third army has lost more than 10,000 to the Black Death, even though the death rate has now slowed. His army, as a whole, then, has been halved to less than 100,000, plus the coalition. Ramesses was certainly smart when he made sure you came along to carry out your plans personally.'

'What? What do you mean *he made sure?* I thought you convinced him, Grandfather.'

'That's what I thought, but that sly old fox made us both think he was against it so that you'd fight to go. The last thing he said to me was that you are our greatest asset, and he was right. You just happen to have been born with an extraordinary mind for thinking strategically. Almost single-handedly you've destroyed half of the enemy forces, saved our own army, and saved our coalition friends from potential destruction – all for the net loss of a few hundred of our own precious soldiers. In fact, I'm so impressed I'll be happy to rub your other foot if you'll pass it up.' Isabella lifted her other foot up with a grin.

After a few moments Marcus yawned. 'Actually, I feel a little tired, so I'll get Yannis to take over.' He turned to Yannis as he placed her feet on his knees. 'Isabella looks like she's really starting to relax, Yannis, so keep it going for a while. I'm going to leave the two of you alone while I go for a nap.'

Isabella looked at Marcus with surprise, and then with delight when she saw him wink at her as he walked behind Yannis on his way to the exit flap. She closed her eyes and put her head back while Yannis continued the gentle massage.

'Is that all right?' he asked after several minutes when he heard her moan.

She brought her head up and opened her eyes. 'You've taken me straight to paradise, Yannis, and we didn't have to die first.'

'By the way, what were all those documents from Ramesses? The declaration of war and stuff. Are you able to tell me? You don't have to if you can't.'

'It's all right. The public announcement only referred in passing to the declaration of war. I needed a copy of the actual declaration to get the precise words. Being a secret document, only Karamus and the earl had been privy to it. Something about it bothered me from the first. There's something else. In the next few months I'm going to arrange for the artists to re-hang their sketches. Between the declaration and those sketches, there's a story waiting to be told. Believe it or not, those sketches talked to me that day and told me to look at them more closely. Do you remember that day?'

'Absolutely. That was the day Bertillini unveiled his fabulous portrait.'

'That's right. I have never seen anything more beautiful than that portrait.'

'And I've never seen anything more beautiful than the young woman in that portrait.' Yannis stopped rubbing her feet, looking as surprised as Isabella.

Isabella gasped and sat upright but left her feet in his hands. 'Why, Yannis Christos! I do believe you just flirted with me!'

He smiled nervously. 'I believe I did. Your words just made that response pop out without thinking. Sorry. I hope you didn't mind too much.'

'Hardly, Yannis. It was lovely. A year ago I might have felt a bit uncomfortable, but I'm going on for seventeen now. At that ripe old age, a girl doesn't at all mind being flirted with. Did you really mean what you said, though?'

'I didn't mean to say it out loud, but yes, I really meant what I said, Isabella.'

Isabella giggled happily, leaned back and wiggled her toes in his hands. 'Keep rubbing please, Yannis. It's definitely brought out the very best in you.'

CHAPTER 117

Zahrah appeared pensive and distracted as she watched Malak and Ayesha play a hand of cards on an exquisite Persian rug laid out on the highly polished marble floor. 'Oh, what I wouldn't give for the dust, sun and blistering heat of the desert for just one day. I'm so weary of the constant rain in this lonely place. A shopping spree would be just the thing to cheer me up. I would just love to go out and buy something really, really expensive.'

Ayesha murmured, 'Me too.' Focused on the card Malak had just placed face up on the rug, Ayesha failed to notice the fleeting expression of dismay on Zahrah's face.

'*Me to!*' Malak cried, triumphantly picking up the card that Ayesha had been forced to play. Placing her next card on top of the stack, Malak pointed to it, and then motioned to Zahrah. 'It seems we'd all like to go shopping, darling, so let's cut the deck. Highest card gets to ask for the next available day.'

Zahrah nodded reluctantly and moved across the room from the couch.

Moments later, the winner smiled happily.

Sitting comfortably on a couch at the other end of the palace, Aloise Kuiper did not appear overly concerned while reading General Von Franckel's report of the devastating earthquake.

Looking up, he said, 'Shocking as the loss of life and materiel is, we must be philosophical about this, Maurice. The consequences caused by a natural disaster are something the people just have to accept. I don't believe there will be any political issues of concern. Therefore, the lengthy delay before the earl can mobilize is the only matter for discussion.' Now fit and energetic from having shed his excess weight, Aloise was brusque, and all business. 'Tell me your thoughts, Maurice.'

'Well, tens of millions across the continent have already succumbed to this disease, so the loss of our men will seem relatively low by comparison. It's also quite likely that many of our men had already lost their families to the illness before they were themselves killed, so, sadly, there may be few to miss them.'

'Quite. Quite.' Aloise dismissed the subject, quickly turning to other matters. 'The army has been almost halved. I expect that the cost of troop payments and provisioning has therefore also been halved. Even allowing for the lengthy delay, the overall cost should remain largely unchanged. Am I correct?'

Maurice nodded sagely. Emperor Kuiper never ceased to amaze him when it came to numbers. 'That seems a reasonable assessment, Aloise.'

'Excellent! Better still: when *His Grace'* – here Aloise rolled his eyes – 'finally gets off his backside, the army should be leaner, meaner, *and* less costly for the remainder of the campaign.' Aloise rose, signaling the end of the meeting. 'So, it's not all bad news, then, is it, Maurice?' On the way to the study door, he slapped him gently on his shoulder.

Walking down the palace steps minutes later, Maurice shook his head in wonderment. Something from the earl must have rubbed off on Aloise, he thought. Emperor Kuiper was rapidly becoming as cold-blooded as Earl Carlos Bucher.

On reaching his quarters, he slipped through the private entrance, changed into civilian clothing and donned a cap to complete his concealing outfit. Back on the street, he proceeded to one of his many residences, hidden away in a non-descript quarter of the city.

For once, the beautiful Muslim woman had already arrived, a glass of wine waiting for him on the sideboard. They embraced briefly before sitting on the luxurious lounge, where Maurice told her about the earthquake, and of his meeting with Aloise. The woman did not tell him that she had already been informed of the damage by her spies in the earl's army.

'I hear what you say, Maurice, but the constant delays and weakening of the military resources are unsettling. You already know I have friends in high places who expect their pound of flesh for their promised support after the transition of power. Ultimate control of the South is a condition of that support. At this late stage, failure is not an option.'

'Don't worry, my dear. Once the earl has taken care of his little task, my men will take care of *him*. We then make our move here, and it's over!'

The woman smiled sweetly, but remained silent while she refilled his glass. *When this is over, you are in for a big surprise, my friend!*

Passing through the back of the gold trader's shop, the woman retrieved a sealed envelope just received from the Caliph. The message was troubling, but not surprising. Alarmed by recent events, he suggested that she and Von Franckel consider a pre-emptive strike.

Not such a bad suggestion in itself, she thought. The Caliph, however, was not aware of the major obstacle that stood in her way.

Her insurance policy: her relationship with Earl Carlos Bucher!

After scanning the message a second time, she tossed it into the small fireplace and waited until it had been fully consumed. There would be a hefty price to pay if she were caught in possession of that letter. *Her head!*

The shop-keeper heard a tinkle of beads and was pleased when the purple-veiled woman paused in front of him. That always meant a purchase. He was right. She pointed to a small, but extremely expensive, item displayed in the window. As always, he would deliver the item in person.

The man continued to bow his thanks for her custom until she had disappeared from view.

'Enter!' Empress Margarethe looked up at the guardsman who had gently knocked on the door to her chambers.

'Your Imperial Majesty, a trader is at the main gate. A purchase was made at his shop yesterday, and he is here with the goods, and his invoice.' The uniformed young man passed a rolled-up scroll of paper to her.

'I will attend to it personally. Tell him I will be there with his money in a few minutes.'

Margarethe was glad to see the back of the gold trader and his tiresome bows. Making sure there was no-one in the corridor leading to her chambers, she tossed the carefully wrapped article into a trash-box. The box, and others placed throughout the palace, would be thoroughly searched by staff before discarding the contents. Later that night, she knew, someone would be delighted to receive an unexpected bonus, courtesy of Emperor Kuiper. *You can pay for it, Aloise, you stupid man, out of that treasure you think I don't know about!*

Maximus Pannini was seated at the table with his colleagues, but as far from Theo Karamus as he could manage. The man was not only nervous, he was frightened.

Theo was also nervous, but could not allow it to show. This time, he permitted his best wine to be consumed without restraint. To make the men swallow what he was about to feed them, he needed them mellow. Particularly Pannini, who, he had noticed, was doing his best to hide from him.

'So, how do you think this latest event will affect us, Theo,' asked one of the men. 'This time, we can't simply pretend nothing has changed.'

'I agree, Philippe. There have been changes, but the important thing to note is that they won't change the end result.'

'How can you say that, Theo?' Pannini was unable to restrain himself, despite having earlier been determined not to speak. 'The Northern army has been decimated! The earl might even decide he's had enough and go home!'

'For a number of reasons, I seriously doubt that, Maximus. But if he does, so what?'

'So *what?*' Pannini's voice was bordering on hysteria. 'They go home, the earl with a letter from Vlado in his pocket – with *your* name in it! – that offered a stage-managed surrender in return for controlling trade throughout the southern half of Europe. He can use the letter for blackmail, or expose you at any time of his choosing. The earl has proof of treason, and in your own handwriting. Theo, you would be defenseless! And everyone knows how closely associated we are. You fall, we all fall!'

Karamus went cold from the truth of Pannini's words. *Not just my name, Maximus,* he thought, *if only you knew that the letter contains the name of every man in this room.* He had to resolve the matter immediately, or consider a drastic alternative.

'Sure, on the face of it, the news *sounds* devastating, but it's less so when you look beneath the surface. The Third army had not arrived at the time of the earthquake, so they will soon be available to reinforce the earl. The coalition force was camped in a different area and was untouched to a man. By good luck, their cannons had been stored out of harm's way, and remain intact. The earl will still outnumber us five or six to one, and he will have the 2,000 cannons, loaded and primed. So, when he gets here, what do you think our chances will be? Zero! Gentlemen, I can assure you that, despite the recent events, our position has not changed.'

Pannini crossed his arms in stubborn defiance. 'The earl has already lost half of his army, which only goes to show that *anything* can happen. And he still might decide to return home. If he does, he can use that letter to his advantage from day one. I'm not taking any chances. I'm going to start transferring some of my assets to other nations, and I intend to disappear to enjoy life in a safer place at the first sign of trouble.'

Karamus presented Pannini with his most disarming smile. 'We'll, you have to do what you think best for you and your family, Maximus, but I repeat to the rest of you that the Northern army will definitely advance and that, ultimately, our position is assured. I believe this is an appropriate time to call the meeting to a close, gentlemen. Thank you all.' Picking up a blank page of paper, he reached for his pen.

The men rose, bade each other farewell, and filed from the room.

'Oh, Maximus?' Theo neatly folded the page twice and held it out. 'Would you be kind enough to give this to one of my men on your way out? I need him to run a little errand for me.'

'Of course. Good night, Theo.'

Outside, Pannini handed Theo's note to one of the four *Disciplinarians*, nodded and walked into the foggy night.

The man unfolded and read the instructions before passing it to his nearest colleague. It contained only two words: *Kill him!*

Pannini did not notice the two men follow him into the darkness as he headed towards the murky river on the way to his wife and family.

CHAPTER 118

Luis' recovery was slow for the first ten days, but then improved rapidly. Isabella's often-told story of his extraordinary courage and crucial role in the battle had made him everyone's hero, and he soon became part of her close-knit circle of family and friends. It had not taken long for Yannis to promote him to captain for his outstanding performance.

Luis now put down his empty dinner plate and wiped his hands on a cloth before he looked across at Isabella. 'I've had little to do these days except lay on my back and think, think, think. I'm probably over-thinking, but one thing that keeps floating in and out of my mind is the question as to why you didn't just blow up the dam and be done with it. Why did we really go to all that trouble to launch that complicated attack, when the end result would have been exactly the same, but without risk to us?'

Isabella was secretly pleased with the question and glanced at Yannis and Melissa. They were sitting together, but Isabella had noticed that they rarely, if ever, touched since Melissa's return from the medical camp with Luis. Madam Rosa Tissone had also grown closer to the group since their exciting times together in the valley where she had performed so brilliantly in front of the earl as *Madam Tessa*. Having gone out of her way to look her most attractive for the man who held her interest, Rosa now sat comfortably on the other side of Yannis.

Isabella knew that her answer would give her the opportunity to indirectly provide Yannis with some answers to the questions he had promised not to ask. Only he had seen her return to the center of the enemy camp that day, and only he knew about her secret mission. The small group sat quietly and watched her intently while she spent a few moments considering how much she could reveal.

'That's a good question, Luis. The reasons are numerous and complex, and will impact on what is yet to happen, so I can only give you a modified version, if that's all right.'

'Yes, of course.'

'I'll go straight to the bottom line, which is *deception*. If we had simply caused the incident without making a personal appearance, survivors would have fanned out upstream to investigate the cause. The earl would not have been able to stop them even if he wanted to. Imagine the political and public fury in the North if the truth became known. Emperor Kuiper would have at first spent a year making enough new cannons to point at England to keep them off their backs while they sent every able-bodied male in the entire Northern Region to teach us a lesson. There's no way we could withstand such an attack. The only way to prevent that was to make them believe something else, and it had to be very convincing. That's why two years of hard work went into just twenty minutes of action.

'Sometimes, *perception* can be enough to create a new reality. With the combination of the collapsing buildings, tremors, fires and the illusion of eruptions – the clouds of fine ash was wonderfully convincing – and with me screaming *earthquake, earthquake* at the very epicenter of danger, I was able to implant a new and different reality into their minds. They truly believed they were witnessing an earthquake and they need look no further for explanation, and they won't.'

'That's brilliant, Isabella, but how can you be so sure they won't start looking upstream anyway?'

'I can categorically guarantee it. By a whisker, the entire plan went perfectly, and thanks to you, Luis, my darling hero, we all got out alive.'

Luis grinned and blew out his cheeks. 'Only *just*, from what I heard later. In fact, if it wasn't for Melissa I would not have made it. I vaguely remember her holding my hand and hearing her talk to me day and night, encouraging me to hang in there. I just focused on her voice and fought my way back. And here I am – *ole!* He turned to Melissa. 'I will be forever in your debt, Melissa. You'll be in my thoughts every day for the rest of my life.'

Melissa's face was on fire as she quickly rose to collect the plates and hide her embarrassment. Yannis stared at Isabella, wide-eyed and deep in thought. Eventually his focus came back to Captain Valdez. 'I now have a question for *you*, Luis.'

'Fire away.'

'That mount of yours – how on earth did you come by such a magnificent horse? It must be worth a king's ransom.' Isabella was astonished to see Luis visibly shrink within himself. It was a question he had not expected, nor welcomed. His mouth twisted this way and that before he answered.

'Ah, the simple truth is I won him in a bet.' Isabella later found out it was the truth, but not the whole truth. Luis Valdez had taken great care to ensure that no-one would know who he really was, especially Melissa Petrova.

Yannis looked at the darkening sky as he rose. 'Isabella, you said you wanted to have another quick look before you turn in, at the maps of that lake you're interested in. We might have a look at them now, if you like.'

'Good idea.' Isabella tried her best not to look astonished at the lie. A few minutes later she walked into her tent, where the maps were laid out neatly on the conference table, and turned to face him with raised eyebrows.

'I'm sorry for the excuse to get you here, but I wanted to bring up the subject that we discussed recently. I promised not to ask questions – and I'm not going to – but after hearing what you said to Luis, I would like to run something past you. Your categorical guarantee that the enemy won't investigate that day's event just about made my jaw drop to the ground. So much fell into place – perhaps not everything – but enough for me to want to bring this up.'

'As Luis said: fire away,' Isabella replied.

'If the earl had been killed, the new commander might investigate the event, and no-one could then control events as they unfolded. With the earl alive, you retain considerable control over the aftermath.' He paused. 'How am I going so far?'

'So far, so good. Keep going.'

'The earl might not be suspicious now, but if he should become suspicious later, he won't investigate, because any adverse finding would see him executed. If there was no earthquake, then he was massacred by our strategic action. Anyone unlucky enough to bring him evidence of that – well, my guess is that the earl would kill the messenger. You saved his life because *he* is your guarantee that the matter will never be investigated or revealed. He's the one who might ultimately have to protect your secret – and the poor sod doesn't even know he's been recruited to do so. You also saved the earl so that you can maintain some control over what the enemy will do next. His interest in you is a baited hook you can use. Alive, he's valuable, whereas his death could have been a potential disaster. If I'm right, then I fully understand your motives on the day, Isabella. That's it, no questions as promised. So, how did I do?'

'You did very well, Yannis. You only missed one thing, but there's no way you could have known about that. There was a second reason for me going back. I also recruited Colonel Oleg Walenski to conceal forever that we stole the gunpowder. He will protect that secret with his life.'

'How on earth did you manage that?'

'It was easy. I just had to make sure I caught his attention. That's another reason I had to look – using your most delicious word, Yannis – *spectacular*. I knew that once he realized the "bandit leader" was me, he was intelligent enough to figure out why we really raided their winter retreat, and intelligent enough to know that if anyone else should figure it out, he'd be a dead man. Other than that, you got everything right, and you didn't break your promise not to ask questions.'

'I hope you didn't mind me bringing it up.'

'No, I'm glad you did. There are no more secrets between us, so I'm very, very happy, Yannis.' She smiled and cocked her head to one side. 'Now you'd better get out of here before anyone thinks you made up that ridiculous story about maps just so you could get me alone and flirt with me outrageously.'

Yannis looked surprised. 'Why would anyone think that?'

'Because that's what I was hoping you wanted to do, you disappointing man.'

CHAPTER 119

Isabella's men continued to train every day under her watchful eye. It was on one of those afternoons in late fall, as her men left the training field, that she saw several captains from other brigades approach Yannis. Occasionally the little group glanced her way. *What are you up to, boys?* As soon as she saw Yannis heading her way, she quickly toweled away light perspiration from her face and arms.

Yannis smiled as he approached. Isabella stared at him with raised eyebrows but remained silent. 'The captains would like a word with us in the meeting tent. Quite frankly, I'm not sure if you'll be pleased or infuriated? Either way, I know it will be handled your way, not mine.' His smile turned into a laugh.

'Humph! I'm not sure I like the sound of this.' She tossed her towel on a bench outside the tent.

The ten captains were already seated when they walked inside. Yannis still wore his armor and weapons from the training session and remained standing. He brought Isabella in front of the seated men and came straight to the point.

'Isabella, the captains are concerned that you might be exhausting yourself with the continued daily responsibilities of commanding and training your men, in addition to the other matters that they know you and I are working on. They've suggested that perhaps now that things are quiet, you might prefer to have the men re-assigned to their original brigades. That will give you more time to allocate to your special projects, and a chance to get a bit of well-deserved rest. What do you think?'

Isabella felt rage build to the point she thought she would explode. It lasted no more than a few seconds before it passed, but it was enough for Yannis to almost back away.

'*My men! My heroes!* The secret formula for our past successes and for my future plans! The men are magnificent, yet I've barely got them warmed up for the glory that lies ahead of them. I shall never give them up without a fight to the death.' Isabella drew her magnificent serpent sword with a flourish and flashed it around her body in a lightning-fast Zen Master's pattern. 'I shall put to the sword any man who dares take my wonderful men from me. And as for you, General Yannis Christos,' – here she slammed the flat side of her sword against his bronze breast-plate with a massive clang that reverberated around the room – 'off with your head, sir! Swish! Swish! Off it goes! Has my answer been too subtle for you, gentlemen, or would you like me to spell it out?'

'No ... subtlety is not your best suit, Isabella, so you have given us a fair idea of what you think of the suggestion.' Yannis staggered backwards as Isabella gave him another whack of the sword. This time the captains cheered at Yannis' look of astonishment.

Isabella walked over in front of the captains and leaned on her sword. 'Seriously, gentlemen, you now know how I feel about my men. You were all wonderful, and more than fair to me when the brigade was formed, so it's now only right that I be fair in return, both to you and to the men.' She turned to Yannis. 'And also to you, Yannis. You know I carry on a bit sometimes, but your word is law to me as much as it is to your men. I have a proposition to put to you, and I'll accept your judgment without a word of objection.'

Yannis took care to keep out of range of her sword. 'What do you propose?'

'My proposal is that you get Stephan to assemble the men immediately and ask them if they wish to return to their previous brigades or regiments, or to remain under my command. Irrespective of what they prefer, I will accept what your captains say, even if it's against the men's wishes. No-one will hear a word of dissent from me. I love each and every one of you for having given me the honor and the trust of placing one thousand fighting men under my command.'

One of the captains stood. 'Can't be fairer than that. I'll get it organized.' Twenty minutes later he was back. 'They're all outside, General.'

Yannis opened the flap and called for Johan and ten men to enter the tent. Their eyes showed their surprise when they were told what to ask the men, but they nodded without a word and hurried from the tent. No-one spoke. The only sound came from Yannis as he removed his armor.

Isabella felt a knot of apprehension while they waited for the messengers to return. *Perhaps I've driven them too hard. Perhaps I've placed them in mortal danger too often, while the other men in the army have not had to place their lives at such risk. Perhaps the men will take this opportunity to return to their former places without the awkwardness of having to ask me to be released.*

Johan poked his head through the flap and addressed Yannis. 'I've been nominated to speak on behalf of the men, sir.'

Yannis waved him inside. 'So, what's the story?'

'Ah, well, sir, every man has been canvassed and the answer is unanimous. The men say they would be very happy to return to their original regiments, and would be proud to die in battle for their former commanders.'

Still standing next to Yannis, Isabella slowly lowered her face in disappointment, but with resigned acceptance of the outcome.

'That's what the men said they would be happy to do, General,' Johan continued as he glanced at Isabella with a smirk. 'However, what they *really* want to do is to remain under Isabella's command, and they all said they would be proud to die in battle a hundred times for her. The men literally love her to death, sir.'

Isabella placed both hands over her face in a futile attempt to hide the tears that were streaming down her face. She felt Yannis' arm start to move around her shoulder in support, but moved gracefully away. She did not want any public display of affection, or comfort, to be misinterpreted and talked about.

The captains gave her a round of applause while Isabella calmed down. She dabbed her face with a cloth handed to her and looked at Johan. 'Thank you so much, Johan. It means so much to me to know how the men really feel about me after I've put them through such torture every day.'

He grinned. 'The men love every minute of it, Isabella.'

She walked over to him and gave him a hug and a kiss on the cheek. 'Thank you so much.' She then turned to the captains. 'As I said earlier, I will accept it without a word of objection if you wish to countermand the men's wishes.'

The captains leaned together for few moments before one spoke for the others. 'You saved us all last year and now you've knocked out about half the earl's army with very few casualties on our side. We would have to be crazy to take your men away from you. And we mean *your men*, Isabella. They're yours now, permanently, for the rest of the campaign, as far as we're concerned. General Christos? Naturally, you have the last say.'

Yannis spoke up without hesitation. 'You now have a permanent brigade, Major, and we'll inform your men shortly. In due course, I'll record it in the official log and inform the king. Thank you all. The matter was conducted with the utmost courtesy and respect by all parties.'

As the men rose to leave, Isabella stepped forward. 'Thank you all so much. I know it's not normal protocol for a major to kiss fellow officers, but I'm going to do it anyway.' She gave each a hug and a kiss on their cheek. When she had finished, she moved back to stand next to Yannis.

'Speaking of *Major*, gentlemen, I believe it's appropriate that I announce to the men when we come outside that Isabella will be promoted. I'll just have to give a bit of thought to what the appropriate rank should be.'

'If I may, General?'

'Yes, Johan?'

'While you're working on that, there's no reason not to call her what we all call her behind her back, sir.'

'*What?*' Isabella was aghast. 'You talk about me behind my back?'

'Why, of course we do, Isabella,' he said without a hint of embarrassment. 'Every man in the army talks about you behind your back.' He finished with a grin and wink that made Isabella blush.

Yannis was delighted at Isabella's discomfort. 'So what do they call her behind her back?'

Johan stepped forward and whispered in his ear. '*What?* You're kidding! Really?' Yannis stared wide-eyed at Isabella in astonishment. 'Well, well, well! How interesting. Very well, so it shall be. Thank you all. I'd appreciate some privacy for a couple of minutes while I discuss the implications of all this with the ... *Major.*' The last man out tied a loose slip-knot to seal the entry.

'Well, that was all very interesting to say the least. I thought you might like a couple of minutes to relax before facing your men. How are you feeling?'

'I feel a bit shaky, so I will take that couple of minutes.'

'Take your time. While you're getting your breath back, you can tell me why I ended up being the only man in the room not to receive a kiss of appreciation. I was mortified.'

'You've had your chances, Yannis Christos. Twice you declined to kiss me, and to make matters worse, you tossed me into a mud bath to humiliate me for my generous offer.'

'Oh, dear. I'm never going to live that down, am I? And my head? I have an image of myself running around without a head. Would you really lop it off?'

'Well, now that represents a huge dilemma. Do I lop it off or leave it where it is? When I eventually open the line for my husband – and that will of course only happen if I survive this war – the man I choose must be gorgeous and he'll need a head so that I'll be on his mind constantly; he'll need eyes that look at me and like what they see; a mouth to say *I love you* every day; and beautiful lips to give me loving kisses. So, all in all, perhaps I'd better leave your head where it is, just in case you're the only gorgeous young man who bothers to turn up.'

Yannis laughed quietly. 'Why, Isabella Mondeo, I suspect you just flirted with me.'

'I suspect I did. I hope you didn't mind.'

'Touché. And no, I didn't mind. In fact, I've been rather hoping you would.'

'Well, now you really owe me big-time. And please don't make me wait until the end of the war before you start paying me back. We might not live that long! All right, let's go, Yannis. I'm dying to find out what my men dare to call me behind my back!'

Yannis reached out to take her hand in his and smiled when he saw her eyes widen and shine with happiness. They held each other for several moments before they walked hand in hand to the entry. As the radiant Isabella paused at the entry, she would have scorned the notion that not only would another man propose marriage sooner than expected, but that she would accept.

Yannis quickly untied the loop, and they stepped outside to face the waiting men. He wasted no time.

'Gentlemen, I declare that from this moment you will remain under the permanent command of Major Mondeo for the rest of the campaign to save our nation.' There was a pause while he waited for the roar of approval to fade. Isabella's face broke into a broad grin of delight when Yannis held up their hands with fingers intertwined and roared to the crowd. 'Isabella will soon be promoted to a more senior rank, but for the men of her brigade, she will forever be proudly known as *The Little General!*'

Read more about Isabella's fight for both her nation and the man she loves in Book 2 and Book 3

Acknowledgements and Thanks

To my good friend Robert Ally, who was the first to point me in the right direction, a road filled with golden nuggets and pearls of wisdom. Your ever-present energetic enthusiasm has inspired me to press on to become a better story-teller. Thank you so much, Rob. And thank you for your friendship.

To my daughter, Kari Isachsen (pronounced Isaksen for the benefit of (hopefully) my legion of Isabella's future fans) for your expertise and insight in psychological profiling used to add energy and power. Please forgive me, Kari, (and any psychologist who might read my novels) for not necessarily sticking strictly to the medical textbook. The joy of writing fiction is that you can massage the truth to make the story more exciting. I have also taken the liberty of using your chameleon eyes for Isabella. Thank you, Kari.

To my editor, Catherine Hammond: I have so often wondered why best-selling authors invariably use the acknowledgment pages to heap praise upon their editor. Aren't they there to simply check the spelling, verbs and tenses? Not so! That road filled with golden nuggets and pearls of wisdom led to Catherine's door. A dedicated and enthusiastic editor assists with a book's structure, its pace and its logic, and advises on strengths or weaknesses of characters and plots – and on the scourge of so many writers: wordiness. Thank you, Catherine, for going to such lengths to help make me a better writer.

About the Author

Rickard Isachsen was born in Wales, UK, but brought up in Stavanger, Norway, until migrating to Australia at age 13 in the 1950s with his parents and a brother.

He has worked in many industries including television, home construction, corporate and financial consulting, and has operated his own restaurant.

A keen wordsmith since his school days, and now in semi-retirement, his hobbies include cooking and writing. With his over-active imagination, and natural inventiveness, he has a number of novels, including modern-day thrillers, in the pipeline after completing the comprehensive Isabella Trilogy.

Rickard lives in Sydney with his daughter, Kari, a High School English teacher, who is also an avid writer.

Website: www.rickardisachsen.com

CPSIA information can be obtained at www.ICGtesting.com
Printed in the USA
BVOW05s1714040515

398496BV00028B/90/P